# ANDRE NORTON

# THE WARDING OF WITCH WORLD

ASPECT®

WARNER BOOKS

A Time Warner Company

Warner Books, Inc., 1271 Avenue of the Americas, New York, NY 10020

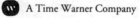 A Time Warner Company

Aspect name and logo are registered trademarks of Warner Books, Inc.
Printed in the United States of America
First Printing: October 1996
10  9  8  7  6  5  4  3  2  1

ISBN 0-446-51991-X

Book design by Georgetta Bell McRee

THE WARDING OF
WITCH WORLD

With special thanks to the household, Ingrid and Mark, who listened and listened and listened very bravely.

And to Juanita Coulson, without whose magnificent index to Witch World the work could not have been done at all.

With gratitude to those who opened gates and dealt with Powers in Witch World

M. E. Allen
Wilanna Schnieder Belden
Clara Bell
Robert Bloch
Elizabeth Boyer
Jaygee Carr
C. J. Cherryh
Juanita Coulson
A. C. Crispin
Ginger Simpson Curry
Charles de Lint
Marylois Dunn
Esther Friesner
Geary Gravel
Sharon Green
Pauline Griffin
Carolyn Inks
S. N. Lewitt
Jacqueline Lichtenburg
Brad and Cynthia Linaweaver
A. R. Major
Ardath Mayhar

Patricia Shaw Mathews
Lyn McConchie
Patricia McKillip
Shirley Meier
Ann Miller and Karen Rigby
Sasha Miller
Diana Paxson
Meredith Ann Pierce
Marta Randall
Elizabeth Ann Scarborough
Mary H. Schaub
Carol Severance
Susan Shwartz
Kiel Stuart
Melinda Snodgrass
Lina Swallow
Judith Tarr
David Wind
Michael Winkle
Rose Wolf
Lisa Woodworth
Patricia Wrede

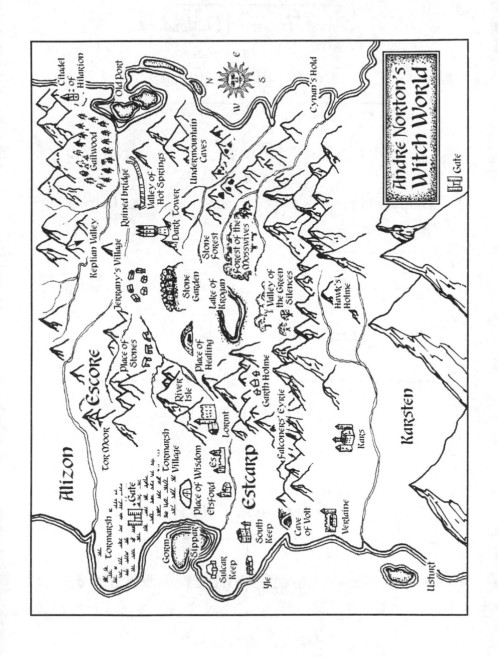

# HOUSE OF TREGARTH

**Simon Tregarth (Outlander)**
m.
**Jaelithe, Witch of Estcarp**

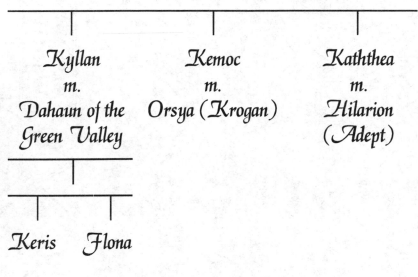

| Kyllan | Kemoc | Kaththea |
| m. | m. | m. |
| Dahaun of the Green Valley | Orsya (Krogan) | Hilarion (Adept) |

**Keris**  **Flona**

---

# HOUSE OF REETH

**Herrel (Were)**
m.
**Gillan (Witch Blood)**

**Kethan (Were)** ............ **Foster Sister**
m.                              **Aylinn (Healer)**
**Uta (Shapechanger)**

# HOUSE OF GRYPHON

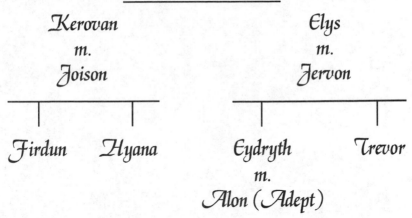

Kerovan     m.     Joison         Elys     m.     Jervon

Firdun    Hyana      Eydryth    Trevor
m.
Alon (Adept)

---

# HOUSE OF GORM

Koris, Marshal of Estcarp
m.
Loyse of Verlaine

Simond
m.
Trusla of the Tor Marsh

# THE WARDING OF WITCH WORLD

# Escore~Alizon Border

Simon Tregarth reined in his Torgian stallion beneath the heavy dull gray of the threatening sky. This was wild country with little in it to attract the eye—rather, one looked from side to side with a rising sense of caution. His own inborn talent of foreseeing, limited as that was compared to the Powers which could be wielded by those about him, had been awake and pricking him since they had broken camp this morning. There was undoubtedly trouble awaiting them ahead—but where did it not wait in this land of ancient sorcery and struggling Powers?

This was not only a gray-beclouded morning; even as far north as they had ridden it was also humid, tempting a man to rid himself of helm and mail, to reach more than was prudent for the saddle flask of water.

"You can always smell it—evil cannot rid itself of its taint!" A younger rider joined him on the hillock, from which they could see the rising land before them. Even time and erosion had not been enough to disguise the fact that the undulating strip of land edging the foothills had once known the control of man—or something else as determined to wring what was wanted from nature.

Simon grinned at his eldest son. Kyllan was a warrior first, but he was also talented to some degree. His helm side veils of mail lay pushed back on his broad shoulders and his head was lifted, his nostrils expanded as if indeed he were following some quarry, hound fashion.

*Some evil lingers—but not born of our time.* The animal Kyllan bestrode also held its head high. A Renthan of the Green Valley, Wegan was no less intelligent than his human companions.

"A trap?" Simon crossed thought patterns with the Renthan.

*No—* Then that thought was broken. *Gray Ones!* Wegan's warning shrilled through the minds of both the men.

Simon did not question in the least that warning, even though his own senses—sight, hearing, scent—caught nothing to betray evil ahead.

The warning had carried also to the rest of their scouting party. They were a mixed lot, but such could be always raised in Escore these days. For in the very ancient home of the Power-born there was a stirring, a sense that the age-long sleep had been broken, perhaps forever. Their party had struck out today because of vague warnings—vague so far. But those keeping the wards were ever alert to the least shift detected by talent.

So in their group rode three of the Green Valley who had held so long only to their own safe refuge: Hatturan, Varse, and Jonka. Beside their Renthans strode the war Torgians of the Old Race who had returned from exile: Yonan and Urik of the Axe, both of whom had known Escore as once it had been; Sentkar, a drifter from the Border wars; Denner out of Lormt; and one who had added himself brazenly to the squad on the second day after they had left their base camp—Keris, Kyllan's son.

Now that youth stirred in his saddle, and his hand jerked a little in the direction of his sword hilt. He reddened and quickly dropped it on the saddle horn, darting a glance at Yonan to see if his overeagerness for a face-off had been detected.

After all, battle skill was all he could bring to bear against the enemy. He carried always the burden of his lack of talent. All *that* fortune had been bestowed upon his twin sister. However, fortune had at least favored him with a natural ability with sword and dart gun.

After it had been realized that he was one of them, Keris had been allowed to continue with them, mainly because this was a land where no sane man rode alone. But that he was steadily ignored by both his father and his grandfather made him very sure that there was going to be a harsh reckoning sooner or later.

Before them, swirls of mist arose from humps on the plain which spoke of former buildings. Keris remembered one of the many legends which were part of the Valley lore of his childhood— that a man oathed to a duty and slain before he had accomplished it continued to exist as a thin shadow of himself until his purpose was accomplished.

Perhaps they stood now on what was once a battlefield. Not for the first time Keris knew the pinch of loss which had been his when he came squalling into the world. Half-blood, yes, but his half of that blood did not carry with it the Power—not as it had with his sister. He had the appearance of his father, but not even the limited gifts Kyllan knew—nothing of his mother's strong talents.

Simon Tregarth straightened in the saddle, brought his mail wreathing about lower face and throat. Perhaps to ride on was rank folly, but his years of battle with the Dark forces had taught him that confrontation was the best of answers. Kyllan's Renthan had swung around and was now facing due north as his rider also made ready for action.

The Gray Ones arose out of the misty mounds silent as those swirls of fog, coming in their hideous fashion, some on two feet, some on feet and hands, their dirty gray coats matted with burrs and dried mud. It was plain that they had come from some distance and with haste. At what summoning?

Simon sent his stallion down from the hillock and directed the rest of the squad to close in a circle with that high ground to their backs. The count of the attacking force was somewhat reassuring. This was not a full pack and Simon was sure that they came to this brush already weary. He shot.

The dart from his weapon caught the leader of the pack in the shoulder and the creature howled

"Yasaaahhhh!" The three of the Valley broke line to use their own most potent arms—the flame whips—and each found its mark.

The Gray Ones wavered. Either these had a caution not usually known to their kind or else they had some order keeping them from moving in. But the fact that they occupied this territory was an added worry. Gray Ones normally fought by haunting the night, patrolling camps, pulling down stragglers, not this openly.

There was no need for one man to give an order to another in such a struggle as this. And those from the Valley were used to handling such threats. Even so, Simon took aim and fired a second dart—not at the leader of the pack this time but at one who skulked behind his fellows for some reason.

The creature leaped into the air, twisted oddly in upon itself, and crashed flat into the mosslike vegetation which carpeted the plain.

That might have been a signal. Yowling threats, the pack drew back, plainly unwilling. And, against their usual custom, two of them picked up the last downed, though they left two other bodies behind them.

The mist appeared to grow thicker. Kyllan unleashed what power he had and linked with the Valley scouts. Together they were able to weave a probe—not that it could do more than just let them know for sure what they already guessed: that there was some Dark Power ahead which was determined to keep its territory inviolate.

It was Urik, his great axe out of his shoulder sling, who swung his Torgian around, but Keris moved with the swifter agility of youth. One of the mounds before them had cracked open as if some planted seed was fiercely inspired to reach the upper world. From the riven soil emerged Sarn Riders, their reptilian steeds' necks stretched to full length so that they could threaten with green-streaked fangs. As did the Valley dwellers, the Sarn Riders carried whips with dark lashes—but the force from those was not marked by flame, rather by shadows. Shadows which could bite and tear and eat away the skin.

Simon shot, though he knew that there was little chance of his bolt dart going home. There was always speculation that the Sarn Riders were not altogether material as this world knew that state of nature.

He was aware that Kyllan, Sentkar, and Yonan were drawing swords. And the swords forged in the Valley had more than just a cutting edge to protect their wielders.

Denner had bent a bow. He was a famous shot, Simon knew, but an arrow against these devils was only a shaft of little power. As had Simon, he coolly picked a target and shot.

A Sarn lash flicked skyward so fast it was a mere trace in the air, to catch that arrow. There was a burst of bluish fire. Then a line of flame ran down the whiplash before its owner could throw it from him, and he doubled in upon his mount. There was no sound to be heard, but Simon swayed a little in his saddle and Keris nearly fell from his. For the cry which had tortured their minds was enough to shake them for that moment. And both rider and mount were now gone.

Stolidly Denner made ready a second arrow. There were, Keris noted, only five of the arrows left and he was sure that in their way they were more precious than many a name-famed sword.

Denner was out of Lormt, that fabled cache of forgotten knowledge. When the Great Turning had kept Estcarp from invasion from Karsten to the south, the force of the magic so deliberately unleashed scored the earth itself and brought down one of Lormt's towers and part of the girding walls. It was revealed that the masonry, thought to be so solid, really covered a veritable warren of sealed rooms and passages, all of which appeared to be crammed with scrolls, books, and chests of strange instruments for which there seemed no use.

The scholars who lived like gray-backed mice within those walls—some for almost the extent of their long lives—had been so overwhelmed by the extent of these finds that they thought of little else than burrowing a way into the next unsealed chamber.

Duratan, once of the Borders and at the time of the Turning marshal and protector of these knowledge-mad delvers, had built up a small force of his own. From second and third sons drafted from the surrounding farms, and from drifting Borderers whose companies had been rent apart during the Turning, and some of *their* sons in turn, he had brought into being a force which had easily reckoned with outlaws and such. It was said openly that while the masters of Lormt sought so avidly for one form of knowledge, Duratan gathered the remnants of another. He sought fabled weapons of the far past—or at least such descriptions that they might be brought into being again. Thus had come Denner's arrows, Keris was sure. But they must be hard to make, since the man from Lormt rode with so few in his quiver.

Now the Gray Ones had slunk back among the mounds while the Sarn Riders were veiled in by thickening mists. Those by the hillock prepared for attack as the riders of the Valley began a low buzzing chant. When that creeping mist reached toward them it was stopped by the Valley magic, plowed up and down, side to side, forming a rolling wall of fog.

Though they expected the Sarn Riders to burst out, there now was no change—save that the clouds overhead were very dark; it might be well into evening rather than midday. It began to rain, huge drops striking at them as if they were blunt-nosed darts.

Simon stirred uneasily. Direct attack he could understand and welcomed—for the pull on him, drawing him forward, grew stronger with every breath he drew. But he had lived many seasons now with magic, enough to be doubly cautious of anything out of nature which his own senses could not explain.

"Jonka?"

The Valley rider's Renthan trotted closer. Under this dull sky, that peculiarity of the Valley race—their ability to change the color of both skin and hair—had now left him gray, and against the wanness of his hair his ivory horns were agleam.

"There is a need," he said, Simon's uncertainty clear to him. "A greater trouble than we thought lies ahead."

Simon waited, hoping the other would enlarge upon that, but it was the Renthan whose thoughts reached him first.

*Those we have faced came at a hurry. Perhaps that which we seek has not Power enough to raise a full range of any Dark fighters against us.* He tossed his head so that the brush of hair between his big ears flopped near his eyes. *They may trail us if we go forward, but such is their nature they cannot hide.*

Simon made his decision. "Loose file, then, and let us ride."

Keris knew a flash of pride. That was indeed Simon Tregarth, legend alive, and in his own veins flowed the same blood. But he must prove it so—and this might well be his chance.

Even as he tightened hand upon the reins, that rolling wall of mist before them swirled higher and then was suddenly gone, as if the drive of the now-steady rain had washed it away. Simon led the way, heading out slowly with the expert ease of one used to many such scoutings, into the humped plain.

There was no sign of any Gray Ones—except the two bodies which had been left by their fellows—and that opening in the ground from which the Sarn had erupted was gone as if it had never been.

The Valley men took the points as they went. Simon appeared to be following as straight a course as he could. Keris, careful not to come under his eye, rode nearly knee to knee with Denner. The Borderer had drawn a flap over his quiver as if those remaining shafts must be protected from the rain.

Keris swallowed and then dared to ask the question he had held since he saw the bow in action.

"Is—is that—your arrows—of the old days?"

Denner was young enough to glance at his questioner with a trace of superiority. "Their making is one of the finds of Lord Duratan. They are very hard to fashion. We do not perhaps know the full process. But—you have seen what they can do."

"Yes—" Keris was answering when the message came, strong enough so even those untalented could understand.

*Ahead*—it was very necessary to get ahead at all possible speed. Simon no longer tried to take a trail which would lead them as far from potential ambushes as possible. Instead he gave the Torgian its will and let it move into an increasing canter. Kyllan dropped behind, surveying the rest of their party. His eyes lit on his son, but there was no recognition in them—Keris might have been any of the force under command.

They were almost across the plain. The mossy vegetation appeared to soak up the rain in a sponge fashion, slowing their pace, but Simon was pushing now.

The first of the foothills lay before them after what seemed an endless flight of time. And ahead, in spite of the storm, flared a orange-red glow. It seemed to be centered in space between two of the hills.

"Alizonderns!" came a warning from Jonka riding to the west. "But they are not on the move. Their hounds are in leash and they watch what lies ahead."

Jonka was joined by Varse. The two Valley warlocks, with Renthans as powerful in their own way, would give adequate warning were those hated westerners to descend to take a hand in this. Alizonderns were enemies to be respected.

With the steady, slowly brightening glow of light ahead, even Keris could pick it up now—that foul emanation which steamed forth from any invoking of the high lore of the Dark. He saw Denner uncover his quiver.

It would seem that whoever or whatever lay ahead had some influence over the weather, for the pelt of rain suddenly ceased as if they had come under an unseen roof, though there was no lightening of the clouds overhead.

Simon slid out of the saddle and Kyllan nodded as he caught the reins of the Torgian his father handed him. This was the old, old game Simon had played now for many more years than he wanted to count. His booted feet sank ankle-deep in the wet moss as he moved forward, using every bit of cover.

The mush of the moss lasted only for a few feet and then Simon felt the rise of more solid footing. He planned to half circle the rise to his right, trusting he could find a point from which he could see. The Valley men and their mounts could pick up any communication he would need to make. But—for one moment only—he held in mind the picture of another, her dark hair, her proud head high: Jaelithe. During the past year, as they had helped to police Escore, he and Jaelithe had often been apart—but never could he feel that something of himself was missing. Now she—

Abruptly he shut off those disturbing thoughts to concentrate on matters at hand. He had indeed reached a kind of lookout, one that Kurnous the Head Lord himself might have arranged.

But what he looked down upon was a puzzle which he strove sharply to bring into proper focus. There were men below, right enough. A number of them were plainly Alizondern slaves born into hopeless labor for all their lives. Only one of the white-haired, arrogant warrior class was visible, apparently sent to oversee the labors of the others.

Equipped with massive chains and wrist-thick ropes, they had apparently drawn into this place—for the ground was deep-rutted behind them—two massive pillars of stone. The red light which gave sight for their labors came not from any true fire but out of a huge kettlelike cauldron around which stood three men of another race.

Simon's lip curled. Both those of good and those of evil had survived not only the Great War of the adepts but all the chaos thereafter. One of those men down there he knew—not from any meeting between them but because he had seen his image summoned up in smoke when Dahaun of the Green Valley had sought danger near and distant.

It was Rarapon, once linked with the traitor Denzil, and as eager as that damned one to regain power. He wore the crimson robe of an adept but kept fussing with its belt and then its collar as if it did not fit.

The slaves were finishing their labor. Deep pits had been dug and now the stones were ready to be raised by pulleys. Simon saw Rarapon make a quick gesture. The Alizondern noble nodded and clicked his fingers. At that signal there were short struggles next to the pits ready to receive the ends of the rocks. At each, two of the slaves turned on a third, one of their fellows, and hurled him down into the dark hole, even as the pillar was allowed to crash into place.

Rarapon moved forward with a strut such as might be assumed by the leader of a great congregation. He raised both hands high and began to weave a pattern back and forth in the air, angry red trails following his fingers.

Now he chanted also, but the sound reached Simon only as singsong noise.

Simon needed no nudging from a talent he lacked—he *knew*! Rarapon was striving to open a gate! Gates were the ancient ways through which the adepts of the Great Age had explored other worlds at their whims—whose secrets, even whose existence in most cases had been forgotten.

The gates had not only taken wanderers and wayfarers out— they had drawn them in. From solitary venturers, such as he had been so many years ago, to whole nations like the Dalesmen of High Hallack, the Sulcars, and various smaller bands and clans.

And they had drawn evil as well. The plague of the Kolders, who had ravaged as much of this world as they could touch. Lately also that invasion overseas made by strange seagoing race of fanatics whom only the skill, blood, and courage of Falconers and Dalesmen together had stopped. The Falconers themselves, the—

None of those who survived that blast of raw magic, uncontrolled, chaotic, could afterward honestly describe the ponderous power which had played with them. Deafened, only half conscious from the terrible pressure against his outward senses and his inward person, Simon dimly saw the pillars bow toward each other and fall, to crush all who had been in that narrow valley. The cauldron glow was extinguished.

Simon rolled over on his back, his arm upheld in a gesture of pleading, to whom or what he could not guess. Then she came. Jaelithe was as visible in his mind as if she stood before him.

"Back, get you back, Simon. Bring with you all those you can add to the force of Light. For there has been such magic wrought as threatens an end to all our world!"

He reached for her now, but she flickered out. Nor did he understand then that the ancient Mage Key had vanished from this plane of existence. It left behind uncontrolled, unwardered other gates against which there would be no defense save the bodies and minds of those doomed to struggle through the days to come.

*

# Arvon, Kar Garudiyn (Castle of the Gryphon)

The day was fair, that Eydryth could not deny. She stroked her harp. Certainly a day to bring music into the world. Yet something kept her from plucking at the silver-blue strings of the instrument. She felt restless and at the same time was disinclined to move out of this warm band of sunlight in the courtyard.

This was not the silent keep her parents had ridden into years ago, felted deeply by dust over the passing years. Instead, for more than her lifetime it had been a dwelling alive with those whose love and camaraderie she cherished the most. Now she was late home from perilous wandering, and she should sink happily into its welcoming peace. But this morning—

Though she had not realized it, Alon had been a second half of her for longer than their actual marriage. Yet in the past few days it was as if a drift of time and space had come between them.

It was surely because of Hilarion—that adept survival of the Old Time who had taken Alon into training, knowing him for what he was, born with the greater talents. She had never seen Hilarion, who lived with the famed sorceress Kaththea Tregarth, half the world away. To her he was but a name, for Alon seldom mentioned those days before their own meeting.

She had seen him weave magic far beyond the control of any

11

that she knew—but that was only in times of great danger, and all that was now safely behind them.

Alon had not gone with the rest—Kerovan, Joison, and their son and daughter; Jervon and Elys her own parents—down to the Herd Marking of the Kioga when the proper colts were chosen for training and the Kioga camp was a swirl of noise and confusion.

No, for the past days Alon had quietly disappeared into the high tower of this ancient pile, and what he sought, or what he wrought, there she had no idea. None save that this was a thing which Alon must choose to tell when and if he would. Still her mind kept pricking her with the thought of Hilarion.

"Eydryth, where is Firdun? He promised—" Her young brother padded barefooted across the pavement of the court with a peevish echo in his question.

They had all gotten over the shock Trevor had provided last year, or at least were no longer overridden by it. On the point of giving birth, his mother Elys had been viciously ensorcelled, hidden away in a state of half-life.

It had been Eydryth herself who had started the breaking of that spell, years long as it had lasted. Her mother had been mercifully freed and within moments had given birth. But it was no baby toddling toward her now. For, having been broken, that power, which had tightly held mother and unborn child released time as well as captives, and in the weeks following his birth Trevor had caught up bodily and mentally with the years he had been denied.

"Firdun?" He stood straight before her now, his thumbs looped into his belt, his lower lip outthrust, taking on the guise of Guret, the Torgian horsemaster, to a comic degree.

Inwardly Eydryth was close to sighing. Firdun, the son of Joison and Kerovan, and recognized by them all as having talent perhaps even past their own way of measuring—was as unlike his sister Hyana as day from night. So far the discipline of his parents had held, but he had refused within the past month to work longer with Alon (of whom Eydryth thought he was jealous).

Perhaps the greatest difficulty of all was the fact he had not been named to the Champions of the Gryphon. Eydryth's own father

Jervon had not been among them, but he was a fighting man without talent and readily accepted that his worth lay in another direction. But Trevor—yes, the newborn—had been named to their chosen circle, though he was but a child. Firdun had not, in spite of his obvious power.

Trevor, however, had fastened upon the older youth as a life model. He dogged Firdun whenever he could and, while Firdun was never harsh with him, he now avoided the child as much as he was able.

"Firdun said," Trevor was continuing, "that we would go to see the horses. The choosing." His large eyes were shining. "Could be one might even choose me and then Father would not say I was too little to ride except with him."

Suddenly Eydryth shivered. She had no farseeing talent, but it was as if a dark troubling had touched her for an instant.

To her surprise, Trevor swung away from her. At the same time she heard the pounding of hastening boots on stairs. A moment later Alon burst into the courtyard and skidded to a sudden stop just before he crashed into the two of them, as if he could not control the force of the necessity which had brought him. One of his hands fell on Trevor's small shoulder and he pulled the small body closer. At the same time he reached also to Eydryth as if he must embrace them both, as he was looking in the same direction as Trevor.

There was nothing to be seen—not for her. But she swept fingers across the harp strings and their answer was much louder than she had sought for—almost nearing the blast of a battle horn.

Alon shook his head at her as he pushed her brother into her arms, taking a position before the two of them. Trevor was wriggling and Eydryth had a hard time holding him under control.

The troubling! It was not just a touch now. From the camp in the valley below, as far as that was from them, they heard a dulled shouting, the screams of fear-maddened horses.

"Garth Howell rides!" Alon spat.

Eydryth shivered. Those of Garth Howell had good reason to hate *her*. Fueled by rage, she had curse-sung one of their great warriors. Yet never before had those shadow ones ventured out of what they considered their own territory. They nested upon their stores of unknown knowledge with far fiercer protection than the scholars of Lormt guarded *their* finds.

Alon was moving toward the vast gate of the castle. Eydryth, one arm about Trevor, her other hand grasping her harp, was quick to follow. But already the others were coming up the castle rise, their horses hard pressed. Kerovan played rearguard and Jervon had drawn sword readily, save that against their foes steel was of little value.

Nevertheless they dismounted, sending the horses into the courtyard with sharp slaps on the rumps. Then, as archers at the forefront of a coming battle, they formed a line.

Kerovan and Alon were shoulder to shoulder, flanked by their wives, then Hyana and Trevor. Eydryth began to hum.

*They ride to the Dragon Crest!*

Eydryth was not surprised by that sudden flashing into her mind. The Lady Sylvya, who was more than half of the Ancient Ones, might share their home, but also she still roamed the hills which had been her joy in youth.

The fairness of the day had dimmed; clouds gathered. From the Kioga camp the din still sounded. Alon gave the command:
"Wall!"

Eydryth's voice swelled. Her fingers were swift on the harp strings. To her voice fit the chant that Alon now uttered, one which was picked up by the others. Only Trevor remained silent, but he moved to stand before the adept, head up and childhood's seeming vanished from his small face. Both hands rose over his head, his fingers clutched as if he grabbed for something hanging here. Then he hurled the invisible.

*They have with them a captive.* Sylvya's mind-words thinned as if between them had arisen a barrier. *Firdun! He is mind-bound!*

Eydryth's voice faltered, Trevor's hands shook, their chanting died away. Alon's features were as set as if graven on the image of one of the High Ancients. He made a slight gesture and they moved a little away from him.

Power—Eydryth could feel it gathering—

Then—

She was hurtled to the pavement, her harp under her bruising her arm, Trevor screaming and clawing at her. The raw chaos which struck at that moment was like no torment she had ever tried to face before. She saw Joison wilt and go down, dragging Kerovan with her.

Alon staggered back, both hands to his head, his features twisted as if he stood in full torture.

Would this continue forever? If so, Eydryth did not believe that any who cowered there could live through it.

However, as suddenly as it had struck, it was gone. They lay still for a long moment, as weak as plague victims who had crawled from their beds.

Sylvya's message shook them back to life.

*There has been such magic wrought as this world has not seen since the final battle of the Great War—a rending and tearing past measuring. Those of Garth Howell lie now as dead and their captive rides to freedom.*

Alon's face was wet with sweat as he rubbed his hands across his cheeks. "That was not aimed at us here, or we who had our minds open would be dead. Hilarion—I must know—"

He swung around as if he would go back at once to the tower where he had been so pent, but Eydryth caught his arm.

"What has Hilarion to do with this? He is an adept of Old, one of the race which brought doom upon us all in that day. Is this some new magic of his devising?"

Alon drew her close. "Not so. I was pupil to him and he is a master of the Light. We strive now to devise a form of communication which can cover great distances. It is my belief that perhaps such raw power unleashed may answer our last problem. But I must know—"

"We all must know." That was Kerovan. "For I think that a very wide door to the ways of the Dark may have been opened, and that all of good need to stand together to preserve the Light."

# PROLOGUE THREE

~

# Shrine of Gunnora, South of Var

Destree n'Regnant strode back from the bathing pool, her wet towel swinging in one hand, the fingers of the other busy with the latches of her jerkin. Destree had never been one to linger over the matter of arising in the morning, with its attendant need for dressing, preparation of food, and the like, but she accepted such as a matter of living.

She had slipped a silver ring over her shoulder-length fall of fair hair, tethering the locks out of the way at the nape of her neck, though some remaining drops of water sprinkled from side to side as she walked.

Already her thoughts were well ahead of her body, busy with the known demands of the day before her. There was the potion to be enflasked for Josephinia, whose joint pain had awakened fiercely during the recent weeks of one storm after another, and she must swing by the Pajan farm to look upon the new colt that was reported a weakling. But there never seemed enough time between sunrise and sunset to do everything.

Also, this morning she had awoken with a faint troubling of mind. It was not a lingering from one of her Lady's outright informative dreams—she would have remembered every detail of such—yet she could not altogether forget it.

The huge black cat, sitting on the steps of the ancient shrine Destree had worked with her own hands and strength to restore, opened his mouth in one of his silent meows. By the Lady, Chief seemed to grow larger every season! He certainly was far more impressive than any of the farm cats of the valley. Cleverer, too, or else the others hid what they thought from the minds of her kind. But Chief was not of this world and so not of the native feline blood at all. With Destree he had survived the ordeals of the Port of Dead Ships, as well as transportation through one of those strange gates. Though this particular gate no longer existed—thanks be to the Lady and her Powers. The cat bonded with her, who was outcast and shunned, in a tie so strong she did not believe even death would break it.

"Ready for breakfast, my lord?" she grinned down at him. "Though I do not doubt your night's hunting has already given you a full belly!"

There was no expression in his large yellow eyes. Instead, he yawned widely, exposing fangs which she knew he could use to good or bad purpose, depending upon the nature of his prey.

Within were two chambers. Destree had restored fallen stones to their places, swept, washed, and then worked patiently to rub down the walls with a mash of scented herb leaves from the garden run wild. The outer room was her own domain for housekeeping tasks, though there was no hint of disorder allowed. A table of the very hard—and precious—varse wood, which held a metallic sheen of the purest gold when it was well rubbed, was accompanied by two benches of the same. There was a corner where a fireplace did not dare to strew any ashes onto the floor, and shelves and a cupboard or two.

Here were no tapestries, no rich carvings, but Gunnora's fancy itself had taken command. For, up from the meeting of wall and flooring around the room had risen a weaving of vines. No matter the season these retained their flowers and their fruits, mingled together, bringing the peace of the outer world in.

The second chamber was the shrine. Destree spread her towel

over the end of the table to dry and surveyed the flowers on the vines.

Not blue—no—that faint shadow which had followed her out of the night forbade that. Then—she made a deliberate choice carefully plucking, by their long curls of stem, a handful of the vine's bounty. The white blossoms which stood so often for a seeker who was not even sure of what he or she sought; the gold for the promise of harvest, which was Gunnora's own high season.

Destree passed into the shrine. Here stood a block of pure white stone such as was to be seen nowhere else in this countryside. Its sides were carved with Gunnora's seal—the shaft of ripe grain bound by fruited vine. She crossed quickly to that, avoiding the long couch placed directly before it, where seekers for wisdom might sleep and learn.

There was a single slender vase on the altar, shaped skillfully as the rare river lilies. Destree took from it the withered flowers of yesterday and replaced them with her handful of gold and white.

She cupped between her hands her amulet, the heritage which served her so well. Its amber felt warm, as if another hand rested within her hold.

"Lady," she said slowly. Of course the Great One could already read what lay within her mind; still, as all her species, she clung to speech. "Lady, if there is trouble, let me serve as you have called me to do."

She was well into her morning tasks when she heard the creaking of farm cart wheels. Stoppering the flask she had been filling, she went to the terrace outside the shrine entrance.

The road up from the village was hardly more than a track and the huge plow beast that pulled the rude cart protested from time to time with a bellow.

Josephinia! But Destree had meant to deliver the potion herself to the farm. Trimble, the woman's husband, tramped beside the work beast, prod ready in hand. But there also swung from his belt an axe, the edge of which gleamed after a fresh sharpening. And coming behind, bows in hand, watching alertly from side to side, were Stanwryk and Foss, the two most expert hunters of the valley.

The small procession took on, as it emerged from the curtaining wood, the appearance of travelers abroad in perilous country.

Destree was already hurrying to meet them.

"What is to do?" Her early morning premonition was now well enforced.

"Woods monster, Voice." Trimble's voice raised to out rumble the cart. There came a whimper, half pain, and half fear, from his wife bundled between rolls of blankets.

"Aye." Stanwryk pushed forward eagerly. "Last night, Labert o' th' Mill—he heard his sheep in a pother an' loosed Tightjaw. There is nothing living in the valley willin' to stand up to that hound, as you well know, Voice. Only then there came such a screeching an' to-do that Labert took to his house an' barred his door. This morning . . ." He paused his spill of words and Foss took up the tale. He was always a man of few words, but today he was freer of speech than Destree had ever heard him.

"First light come and Labert was out—had his bow, he did, an' his grandsire's sword. In th' graze land over th' mill—a dead sheep, more than half eaten—an'—"

Stanwryk demanded his chance again. "Tightjaw—that hound was torn in two—torn in two, I'm sayin' an' I seed th' body for me-self! Just like he was no more than a rabbit under the' wolf's teeth. An' that was not all, Voice. There was tracks, mind you—an' they warn't made by no hill cat nor bear. They was like a man's—but a man with twice the length of foot of Trimble here."

Trimble clumped forward a step or so. "Voice, since we was children, our paps and mams, afore us, we have heard tales of creatures of th' Dark who hunt an' savage all true men. This here shrine of th' Lady, why, 'tis said it was set right here that there be a strong place of Light against the Dark from the north. But this here night thing which has come upon us, truly it be of the Dark, an' we asks you, Voice, call now upon th' Lady that She may hold us under Her cloak."

"Yes," Destree said.

How well she knew that things of evil could wander far. Her body tensed. Had she not fought with one remnant of the Black

Power—that which was set to swallow the crews of ships it captured, even from other worlds than that of Estcarp? Had another
gate gone wild—activated in some fashion so that it had provided a
doorway for a thing from an entirely different world? Or had some
skulking monstrous creature come prowling far south to establish
for itself new hunting grounds? She must somehow discover which
and what they faced. For these people of the valley had no defenses
against any strong manifestation of the Dark.

Did she—? Her hand went to her amulet. She had the Lady, and
promises between them would hold until the world's end.

As Destree worked with Josephinia's poor, pain-twisted body, the
men waited without the shrine. But when she issued forth again
having put her charge under a soothe-sleep, she found only Trimble there, striding distractedly up and down, while the draft animal
sampled the sweet, high-growing grass of the shrine field. Foss and
Stanwryk were gone.

"Voice!" The farmer hurried toward her, his big hands outstretched as if to wring what he wanted out of her. "What can a
man do against th' Dark Ones? Long ago our kinfolk fled 'ere to be
away from such danger. Now—"

Destree laid her hand gently on his shoulder. "The Lady takes
care of Her own, Trimble. She will show us a way."

He stared at her as if he wanted to accept her words as a sworn
oath.

"Foss—Stanwryk—they have gone to raise th' valley that we can
form a hunt. Pacle's hounds—" he shook his head slowly. "Voice,
there has never been a hound whelped in the valley as dangerous as
Tightjaw, nor as sly and clever in th' hunt. Yet this thing took him
with ease."

He smeared the palm of his hand across his face. "Voice, those
who hunt the Dark are many times fools."

Trimble was no coward, that she well knew. He only spoke bare
reason. But how many would listen to it?

"There is another way of hunting." She glanced over her shoulder to the shrine behind. "Be sure that that will be tried."

It was well into midday when the clamor of leashed and impatient hounds and horses' pounding hooves, as well as one man striving to bring them to order, sounded from the cart track. Josephinia had wakened from her sleep and stretched cautiously.

"But there is only a memory of the pain now, Voice," she said excitedly. "I am as new!"

Destree showed her a flask. "Be sure to drink of what this holds night and morn. Also eat sparingly of meat but well of that which grows in the earth through the Lady's bounty."

The ragged body of the assembled hunt came bursting in to shatter the peace of the shrine meadow. Slavering hounds strained at the restraint of collar and the leash. Their handlers were a motley crowd—from lads still to name themselves men to a grandsire or two, they were milling about. Foss pulled off his peaked leather cap and came directly to her.

"Voice—Hubbar's youngest, he was down by th' river an' he saw a thing—a thing of hair an' huge of body, with fangs for tearing. It was by the water laving one arm—for Tightjaw must have left his mark after all. But when Yimmy came with th' news an' we went there it was gone. Now we ask the Lady for arm strength and weapon strength to take it before it kills again!"

"I shall ask," she said, "but this I must say. If this is but some wild beast of a kind new to us, then it can be well hunted. If it is more—then go with caution."

He nodded as he put on his cap again. They were on their way. Trimble and his cart, with his wife now sitting upright clasping the flask to her ample bosom, had a handful to play guard. But the majority struck off northward, into the first thick fringe of the forest. Destree watched them go with concern.

However, what she had to do lay elsewhere. She returned to the outer room of the shrine and quickly stripped off her homespun clothing. Into a large basin she ladled water from the hearth pot and measured into that, drop by careful drop, oils from several different vials.

Then she washed herself from head to foot, even dipping her hair into the basin, smearing the oily liquid over her whole body. Making no effort to dry herself, she then sought the inner room.

Drawing from the couch before the shrine the covering on which the farmer's wife had lain, she substituted another taken from a small chest by the altar. Green it was and brown, gold, and purple, all intermingled so no human eye could follow any pattern, and though it was very old yet it was still intact.

Destree spread it with care over the couch and then stretched herself upon it, folding her hands beneath her full breasts and closing her eyes.

The transition came quicker than it ever had in the few other times she had tried this ritual. Fear—pain—the need to run—run—run—Strange—all the world about was strange, there was nothing to be seen as a guide—yet—fear/pain—the need—the need to escape—

And the world she saw dimly was *strange*.

That strangeness fed fear. The very color of a leaf, the shape of a branch was all wrong. The ferns which beat about her legs as she ran—she shrank from their touch. This was not her world—where had the Lady led her?

She—she had been in the home wood and at peace with herself and the world about. Then there had been the tall stones. One of them had been shiny, and that had attracted her so that she went and laid hand upon it. Then—then she had been whirled away into nothingness and when she could see again she was in this fearsome place where all was alien and wrong.

Destree tried to cut behind the ever-present fear. The Dark? She sought the smell, the feel of evil. But there was none—only confusion and fear, pain—

Gruck! Out of nowhere came that name. She was . . . Gruck! In the same moment that became clear to her, she strove to break the bond. But she realized now where the Lady had sent her. She—she was the hunted monster.

But it was no beast. It thought, it strove wildly to learn what had happened to it. Nor was it anything of evil wandering southward. It now rested under the compassionate hand of the Lady. So somewhere another of those cursed gates had made a capture, and the innocent would be hunted down and slain unless she could prevent it!

Destree's eyes snapped open. She was already pushing herself up from the couch. She paused long enough to return the covering to its time-set folds and then, from a chest in the foreroom, she brought her own woodsrunning clothes. Not the skirts such as she wore for the sake of making the valley people receive her more easily. Instead, she drew on over her still oily body breeches, a shirt, a sleeveless jerkin with oddly fashioned silver latches, boots made for hard service over indifferent trails. There was a belt with knife and small pouch, and at length she pulled from near the bottom of the coffer the backpack she kept ever ready for travel needs, checking to make sure that it held salves and herbs for the treatment of wounds.

There was no question in Destree's mind that she would find Gruck—that this poor refugee from another place was now her charge. Chief leaped out of the shadows and took the fore, entering the woods at a different angle than the hunters had followed. She listened but could hear nothing of their clamor and she wondered how far back into the thickly wooded hills they had gone.

"Gruck?" She sent out a mind-call. But there was nothing to anchor it and so draw her to her quarry. She did not know what Gruck looked like. She knew little more than the creature's emotions at its displacement and perhaps the hunt on its track.

Chief appeared to have no doubts about direction. For want of a better guide, Destree followed the leaping passage of the great cat.

Now—now—she could hear!

The clamor of the hunt suggested that Gruck was at bay. She hastened her pace from trot to run. They must not kill this stranger! It was not of its doing that it had come here. Yes, it had killed a sheep—but that was because it hungered. It had killed a dog which attacked it. Certainly no man there ahead could say that he would have done otherwise in its place.

Destree came into the open. There had been a forest fire, storm-set, here a year ago. The land was all blackened stumps and sprouting green between. And there was a tall rock firmly planted. Around that the battle now raged.

Three dogs lay dead and a fourth crept away, uttering a keening howl. With its back against the rock, the monster half crouched. It was taller than any man Destree had seen, and its entire body was covered with thick curls of wiry black hair. Yet its head was well proportioned by human standards and its green eyes held intelligence. One of its arms had been crudely wrapped in a covering of leaves already torn and half gone.

About its waist, seemingly too small for the width of those heavy shoulders, there was a wide belt, along which ran glitters with every movement of its body.

Why Foss or one of the other bowmen had not already shot it down Destree did not know. Perhaps that was by the grace of the Lady. She raised her voice now. The land about them seemed to amplify her call.

"Hold!"

With Chief running at the same easy pace before her, she cut down into that place of desolation. The hunters had turned their heads at her call, though Foss's attention swung almost instantly away and he had arrow to string now.

"This is not of the Dark." her voice came pantingly. She shoved between two of the men before they knew she was upon them and threw herself into place before the creature at bay.

Foss's face was bleak. "Stand aside, Voice. We owe you much, but we have no place for monsters."

"I tell you"—Destree had her voice under better control now—"the Lady's hand stretches out to this one." She tried to sign the truth of that by reaching behind her to where Gruck leaned weakly against the stone. Her fingertips were fretted by alien fur.

"This thing is a killer. Protect it at your own peril, Voice. If you would have any one in this valley heed you an' th' words of your Lady 'ereafter, you will stand aside."

She could read only a shadow of doubt in a few faces. They were as one on this. Yet her duty had been set upon her. Destree drew a deep breath as she tried to summon words which might break their resolve.

What came was something far different. A huge furred hand shot out and gripped her. She smelled the strange odor of alien flesh sharpened by fear. But there was only an instant for them to cling together so.

The blast which beat down upon them all was none of the La-

24

dy's calling. Destree knew that, before her senses reeled and she clung to her strange companion even as it held to her. This was strange magic, raw, without a check.

Her throat filled with bile as she saw men tossed about like straws in a tempest. The whole world split apart. Not the Lady's doing, no. Nor, she was certain, did Gruck have aught to do with this. Gate— had the gate which had captured this refugee gone as wild as that gate at the Port of Lost Ships when they put an end to it? No, something within her—perhaps the Lady reaching through the torment of assaulting magic—assured her. This was the beginning of something else—something such as no record she knew of listed.

Its mind-blinding attack ended. Dimly Destree saw the men of the hunt helping each other to their feet. One of them took up the injured hound. Then they turned and went away as if both Destree and their quarry had ceased to exist.

# CHAPTER ONE

### ❧ ❧

# The Ingathering at Es City

The city was old, even beyond the imagining of the most fanciful. It was and it had simply always been. No one raised questions concerning the time of its youth; they were too awed by the feeling of leaden age which seemed to breathe from each worn stone. That Power had gone into its erection, from the pentagon citadel which was its core to the smallest of the houses clustering inward toward that promise of protection was known. It was and it would continue to be.

Yet for the first time there was a questioning which grew with each day. For parts of Es which had slumbered dourly through generations were being refurbished. More and more weary travelers arrived along each of the highways feeding into the four great gates.

This was no festival time. Those who had lived quietly, mostly in peace during the passing of one long year to the next, had no part in this ingathering. Tradesmen came to the fore of their booths, their apprentices and children edging out carefully into the streets, while the upper window curtains were looped far back so that the women and elders, usually within, did not miss the sight of such strangers, their mounts, their apparel, their followers.

There was no cheering, as might have arisen to greet the safe return of champions, but rather a muttering, a whispering which sometimes uttered clearly a name or two. Riders were pointed out by senior to junior, who stared in equal awe. For these who came now to Es were part of distant legends—traders' tales, heretofore never completely believed.

They rode or strode in silence also, no small talk, only sometimes the jangle of a piece of equipment, the snort of a war Torgian, or the like.

A tailor grabbed excitedly at the sleeve of his wife, who had come down into the shop.

"'Tis one of the Green Valley, that one! See, he sprouts horns! And the lady with him—she is Dahaun!"

His wife drew a breath which was close to a sigh. "Master Parkin said she was noted fair—but this is a goddess!"

Still they came. From the north, Borderers of those squads which served to hold the passes into Alizon. Out of the river which linked Es with the sea moved others, sleek of body, finned as to feet, who stared about them silently for a moment or so before they began their inward march. There were Sulcar captains, too, their huge, furred cloaks thrown back, their horned or center-ridged helms bright with gold, proving that they were wide-faring, and lucky in that faring.

For three days they came. Only once did the city guard not retreat to give passage. They wavered into an untidy line before two riders from the southland. There was a woman clad in leather and with her plainly a high-born lord of the Old Race. However, it was the steeds which they bestrode that had brought forward the guards.

Men knew of Torgians, famous for their battle readiness. And they had seen, during the past days, those roan-red Renthans which allowed riders from Escore to mount them.

As with the Renthan these new mounts wore no reins, no sign of restraint to any wills save their own. They stood taller than any Torgian and their shining coats were uniformly black.

As they tossed their heads, snorting at the movement of the guards, those close enough could see that their large eyes were of a startling vivid blue—that of the freshest of summer sky. Yet—

"Keplians!" Someone in that crowd had raised the cry. The woman rider leaned a little forward, her hand on the arching neck of the mare she rode.

"We are of the Light!" Her voice had a note of challenge. "Think you we could have passed your defenses else?" She turned a little to wave her hand at the wall behind her.

There was a glow, and then for an instant a flashing blaze of a blue pattern. Those standing there cried out in confusion. Dimly they had known that Es had defenses other than those ready to man her walls with sword and axe, but never in memory had they seen it proved.

The captain of the gate raised his gauntleted hand in salute, his men crowded back, and the two who rode steeds out of ancient nightmares paced on as if they approached their own stable yard. Yet they left witnesses who had seen plenty to talk of, and rumor spread wide and fast. Who the two strangers were and how they had come to make peace with Keplians, monsters of the Dark lands, no one knew. But no one could deny that the woman had summoned the signs of Power to prove they were no peril.

For some six days more the ingathering continued. Supply-filled boats came from west and east along the river. There was such a demand for foodstuffs that farmers as far away as Gottem sent their surplus and made good bargains.

But there was no going forth into the town by the strangers. Squads of the Borders were seen from time to time. One such returned with a group of Falconers who looked very trail-weary. All who came were housed in the citadel and that seemed to be the end of them.

Almost as startling as the coming of the Keplian riders was the arrival of a body of witches escorted by troops wearing the badge of Marshal Koris. Witches had not been seen too much of late years. The strain of the Turning had depleted their ranks. Many of the oldest and most authoritative had either died or been left empty of brain after that effort. The small core left had withdrawn to their own place of training, the Place of Wisdom.

There were six of the gray-robed women and the eldest was certainly no age-worn hag. On the other hand, she had in her company two, robed and even wearing stones of Power, who were scarcely more than children. Those who knew a little guessed that these must be counted high in Power.

The arrival of the witches put an end to the flood of travelers—those gathered in the citadel might well have been waiting for them.

If the city was agog over these visitors, the citadel fairly shimmered with new life. It was as if the stones from which it had been formed drew energy to develop a silvery sheen which was clearly visible at night.

How could it be otherwise, Keris thought as he stood on one of the small balconies near the dome of the building, when within its walls was such a gathering of Power which had certainly not been known since its building—if even then.

That he was here himself rested on the fact that he had been one of that party accompanying his grandfather to the Alizon Border. They had all been questioned extensively, even under the glow of a truth jewel specially sent from Lormt, and surely there was nothing more than they could tell.

Lormt—that seemed to be the kernel of this gathering and yet only its marshal and two of his men were under this roof. There was much talk of a Lady Mereth and—he frowned—of a link with Alizon. All his life long Keris had known that Alizon was the enemy.

But at least that terrible attack of raw magic which had laid them all low had been explained. That, too, Lady Mereth had had a hand in. The Magestone—the Great Key which had controlled the master gate of the ancient adepts—had come to her, and equally to an Alizondern, by right.

There had been a battle of Powers. A black mage who would have seized that control was safely gone—but so was the Key. And the Key had been fashioned to control all the gates. No one knew how many of those there were—or where they all might be. If the Magestone lay now in limbo for all time, then would the gates themselves—those still able to work—go wild and let in upon them such perils as the Kolders? Or would they reach out here in his own world to snatch the innocent and take them ever beyond the reach of home and kin?

He heard the summoning gong which vibrated through the walls of the citadel, and reentered the room he shared with two other Valley born, so cramped were the lodgings by the arrival of such a host. The sound of the gong had died away but not the sound of feet along corridors.

The heart of the citadel, of Es itself, was the great assembly hall four stories high, ringed with balconies for those who were unable to find places on the main floor.

Keris worked his way to a place by the rail and began to pick out from the gathering below those he knew by name as well as those whose deeds were already bard's tales. Ethatur of the Valley and Dahaun, Keris's own mother, with Kyllan overreaching her by but a finger's breath or two. Flanking them on one side his Uncle Kemoc, with his Krogan lady well wrapped in a heavily dampened cloak so that she could withstand a lengthy time beyond the touch of her native water.

On Dahaun's right was a great bear of a man, his heavily mus-cled form made the bulkier by a furred cloak worn as a badge of authority—Anner Osberic of the Sulcars, he who had led the raid on Karsten which would not be early forgotten.

There were so many: dark-haired, pale-skinned lords and ladies of the Old Race, as well as these outlanders. At the far end of the hall was a table set on a dais, chairs along one side of it only, an-cient, tall of back, their once-deep carvings worn nearly smooth. In the center were two raised a little higher than their fellows. And even then one had to have a double set of cushions to bring it high enough for the occupier: Koris of Gorm, Marshal of Estcarp, in re-ality, since the withdrawal of the witches from most active govern-ment, the ruler of a land, which had once deemed him an outcast. His handsome head was high held but his stunted body, in spite of the shoulders of a veteran axeman, could have been dwarfed by most of the company.

To his right the other throne chair gave seating to a woman

whose dull ash-gray gown was in sharp contrast to the brilliant show of color in the garb of those about her. She wore a single jewel—and that, too, as it swung on her breast on a silver chain, was as dull as her gown. Yet it was a far more potent weapon than any other armament within this great hall.

The witches were nameless, as all knew. For a personal name was a potent thing and to surrender it to the knowledge of another was to put one with that other's power. But this one passed by the name of Gull when among others and she was now the chosen link to those remaining within the walls of the Place of Wisdom.

There was Simon to Koris's left, and Jaelithe, his once-witch wife (who held an uneasy truce with her onetime sisters). Then Koris's Lady Loyse, of whom legends had already been woven.

At the end of the table stood a man who had not seated himself in the chair awaiting him. Rather he was leaning forward, handling with obvious care the wrappings of some object which had been placed on the board. Flanking him was Marshall Duratan, chronicler and protector of Lormt, who was watching every movement of that unwrapping as if he expected some outburst of energy to follow.

Keris was well placed to watch that action and he knew the man so engaged, just as he knew well the woman who hovered beside his shoulder as if to offer aid be it needed.

The man was Hilarion, the last (as far as they knew) of the adepts whose playground and experimental laboratory their whole world had been before the Great Change. Though Hilarion looked to be no older than Simon, he had survived years untold as a slave beyond a gate of his own making before being freed by the woman beside him—Kaththea, Simon's sorceress daughter.

There were a handful of others at the other end of the table, but, as Keris's, all eyes were intent on what the adept was doing.

The last of the enfolding covering had been pulled away. What stood there, some six hands high, was a double-pyramid-shaped object, each of the square bottoms being set solid on a length of blue quan iron.

Hilarion moved around the end of the table to the side facing the whole company, where there were no chairs to conceal a full view. And he went slowly, edging his device hardly more than an inch at a time along with him, until they reached the certain point of the board.

For the first time then the adept spoke. "Of old we could look across mountains, under seas, beyond oceans. But like much else, that art was lost with those from whose minds it sprang. You all know of the discoveries at Lormt after the Turning, but before that time I was working with another—Alon, now of Arvon—to bring back a device which would allow such communication.

"Now we face such danger as may equal the Great Disaster. As you well know, the Mage Key, which once controlled all gates, has been discovered. When such power comes, even into worthy hands, it awakens and stirs the Dark. And though that key may be safely lost once more, the Dark is still awake, and old enemies are empowered.

"Those of Alizon have long labored, plotted, to bring us down. They had their compact with the Kolder first, and, when those vermin were driven from our world, they went seeking other aid. Though they profess to fear and hate all Power, there are those among them willing to use any weapon to gain what they would have.

"Therefore, the key when it was found brought out of the Dark an Old One of great power, as well as he who in the beginning first fashioned it. There were those of *his* house still living. And through them the Light arose.

"Through the years we all have known of the gates. There have come through them whole nations seeking refuge—such as those of the Dales—as well as others by chance. And most of these we had reason to welcome. But . . ." the pyramids seemingly having been placed to his satisfaction, he turned more to the company to address them, "the key is gone forever. While it remained in our world—though well hidden—its influences might well have kept a portion of the gates in check, allowing them to work only erratically. Now" —he made a small gesture with one hand—"who knows what has happened? We all felt the terrible unleashed power of the key's passing—we have certain gates we are sure of. . . . However, perhaps I wander from what I hope we can learn."

"This"—he had swung around once more to confront his apparatus—"perhaps will give us word out of Arvon. For Alon has labored there, backed by the Power of the Gryphon, to construct a similar device. If we can communicate, then we need not wait for any ship's voyaging to bring us news which perhaps will arrive too late for us to act effectively."

Kemoc had slipped out of his chair, and Dahaun and Ethatur also, and with them Jaelithe. There was a stir as Gull arose from her seat. With impassive face she followed them, one hand clasping her jewel to her breast.

Kaththea stood now behind her lord, her hands out so that her fingertips reached up to rest upon his shoulders. Behind her Kemoc copied her gesture, linking with his sister, then came Dahaun and Ethatur. Last of all, Gull, after a moment's hesitation, keeping one hand still to cup her jewel, touched the co-ruler of the Green Valley. Keris's hands clasped the edge of the railing so tightly that the edge cut into his palms, but he was not aware of that small pain. He might not carry the talent within him, but no one in that hall could be unaware that such forces were gathering as might well blast the very walls about them were they to be carelessly unleashed.

The tension was like a cloud, one could almost see as well as feel it, and there was utter silence in the whole of that large company.

Hilarion's own hands went out, his arms stretched wide, and each outheld palm seemed to pull with it one of the pyramids, drawing them ever farther apart, enlarging the space between them. He recited no ritual as Keris had expected, but from his outstretched fingers there shot darts of blue flame.

The pyramids caught that force, held it until each of them in turn was afire. Once that was accomplished, from the quan iron slab on which they were rooted came a shaft of light, within its heart a darker core. That grew fast and cleared as it grew, putting on substance, until between the pyramids stood a miniature man—

no figurine, for as the last of the light which had drawn him disappeared, the small figure raised arm in salute.

Keris was too far away to see the mannequin easily, but no one in that company could miss Hilarion's welcome.

"Alon!"

The mannequin bowed his head. "As was hoped, master of learning, so it is wrought." One could have expected the thinnest of piping from such a small body, yet the voice was near equal to Hilarion's.

"There is good reason for summoning—" Hilarion began, when the other interrupted.

"We must be swift—we are seven but we are limited. There was a turmoil of raw magic."

"Yes. The key to the Great Gate was found—and then taken from this world. Now we do not know how the subject gates may be used."

"So." The image of Alon nodded. "Those of Garth Howell ride for the Crest of the Lion—or so they did before the wave struck. There is said to be a gate there—or once was. And Garth Howell is shadowed. They have those among them who can well choose to reach for the Dark."

"We meet in Es in full company, we who are sworn lieges to the Light," Hilarion continued. "We hope to search out which gates still have life in them. Those at Lormt labor to find the way to ward our land, to discover how such gates can be locked forever. We can send a search party to you in the west, but much of your land is unknown and it will take time to cross the seas."

Alon appeared to shimmer for a moment and then stood clear again. "The force is failing. We shall do what we can—the Dale lords and those of Arvon will be warned. Now—"

Again his figure shimmered but this time it did not recover its density, rather was gone. Hilarion himself swayed forward against the table. His hands fell to its surface, plainly holding him upright, and he was breathing as might a man who had won a race for his life.

Nor were those who had backed him in better shape, holding on to each other or the edge of the table as they made their way back to their places. Even Gull's slow pace was close to a totter. And when they half fell into their seats they sat wan-faced.

"This then is our task." Marshal Koris's voice, meant to call a regiment to order, was loud enough to encompass the rising murmur from the throng before him. "Where there is a gate, there is perhaps still an opening through which may come ill. Do not forget the Kolder."

Keris saw Anner Osberic's wide lips shape a snarl.

"There was also but months ago that sweep of ships and men out of nowhere," Koris continued. "Had it not been for the Falconers and brave Dalesmen they might have found foothold here. You of the Sulcars"—now he addressed Anner directly—"have your tale of coming through an ice wall which opened for your ships into our seas."

Osberic nodded. "That is true. We came from the north and there was an ice barrier. What brought us through it we have no legend for, but"—he swung now to address Marshal Duratan—"they say you have found all manner of strange histories recently at Lormt. Perhaps there lies something of our own beginnings here."

Duratan spoke briefly. "If there is any such, Lord Captain, and it is found, be sure you shall know of it speedily."

Simon Tregarth moved forward a little. His hand had been clasping Jaelithe's as if he could in some manner return to her the strength she had loosed for Hilarion.

"There are those of us who came by chance and separately. That spot near the Tor Marsh where I found my way, that I know. And there are others—the Lady Kelsie—"

Among the throng there was a stir as a slight girl moved forward. She did not step up on the dais but she turned to face the company, and it was plain she was straining her voice to reach all their ears. "My gate I know—it lies in Escore."

"And the Lady Eleeri—"

Another stirring of the crowd. This time the woman who advanced was brown of skin, nearly as brown as the skillfully fashioned leather she wore. Her black hair was long and braided, with lengths of blue and gold beads shining within the loops.

"I followed the road of my Old Ones by choice and not by chance," she said. "Yes, I know where I entered into this world now mine."

For the first time Gull now spoke.

"Of the gates, we have always known. In the past . . ." she paused a moment as if she were carefully selecting the words she would speak next, "we held the Power to be a sacred trust given to us alone—that only one female born could know the talent and use it properly, so much was kept our secret knowledge. Now . . ." she paused again to look down on the crowded hall, "we see that, though we in the past wrought mightily to protect our world, yet we were not the only ones chosen by the Light to do so. Now I am empowered by our council to speak directly. This"—her hand caressed her jewel—"can be used as detection for any magic, old or new. If a gate once existed and is no longer in service, that it can tell. If a gate which has lain dormant again gathers Power, or perhaps is the goal of others—that, too, we can tell. But we have no wards for such and at Lormt lies our only hope of finding them.

"Now I believe it is in the minds of those gathered here that there must be those to go forth, parties to seek the gates unknown. For so long we have been at war with our neighbors—Alizon, Karsten—we know nothing of what lies farther south or north except, as Lord Anner has said, what is told in the legendary histories of others.

"In Arvon little is known of the south, or what lies beyond the desolation of the Waste. We do not even guess how much land must be searched or whether we can find all which we seek. The Adept Alon has reported that Garth Howell seems to be taking a hand. There is also news from Lormt and the north that those of Alizon can be once more our bane.

"This much we can offer you: When you send forth your search parties, one of our sisterhood will ride with each. We can communicate over distance—how far, we have never really tried—and our weapons have proven their Power."

Koris and Simon were both staring at her while Jaelithe was nodding.

"This your council has decided . . ." Simon's words were not quite a question but she seemed to take them as such.

"This is decided—we are at your service for this undertaking. For is this world not also ours and what you would do will protect it in time to come?"

"Lady." Koris bowed to her. "We accept, and your bounty is greatly to be cherished. The Light will rise and the Dark be met as it should be. There remains only to choose our parties and ride!" His voice had risen almost to a trumpet's call with that last word.

Keris swallowed, and he loosed his grip on the railing. Ride—ride in the greatest quest any bard could imagine? Had he the slightest chance to be one of those riders into glory?

# CHAPTER TWO

## *Krevanel Hold, Alizon*

Liara, Litter First Lady and Keeper of the Home Hearth of Krevanel, critically regarded her reflection in the long mirror, whose ornate and begemmed frame rather overshadowed its smooth surface. She tongued wet a forefinger and patted one of the forehead curls which stubbornly refused to lie flat.

The stiffness of formal dress was always confining, but from early childhood she had been taught the gliding walk which swung the wide, embroidery-heavy skirts in the proper fashion. One could learn to endure such harnessing of one's body when protocol demanded so.

At least the combination of colors which met her eyes now was not near blinding. By choice and with relief she followed her litter brother Kasarian's taste in selecting dark blues, hunter greens, and shades of rose which melted into silver gray. Her white hair, strained up now with enough jeweled pins that she could actually feel their weight, was perhaps not well displayed by such choices, but the blaze of her tight throat collar and the heavy rings in her ears gave contrast enough. She had never pretended to be a beauty and she knew she was suspect among the high blood because of the freedom of her early upbringing—though she made very sure no one could fault her manners in company.

Today she had chosen to wear the darkling blue of evening sky, the thick vros silks of her clothing webbed and rewebbed by silver stitchery, with here and there a small carved crystal to flash before the eyes. Her collar—a proper hound collar, of course—was fashioned of silver inset with the same crystals, as were the cuffs wrapping wrists which were far less delicate than they looked. Yes, she was readied to oversee the great table in the hall where her littermate feasted.

Liara's slightly slanted eyes narrowed. Why Kasarian shared a guesting cup with such as Lord Sincarian was a question which had troubled her ever since the message of this event been sent to her two days earlier.

They were marked blood, those of the House of Krevanel, and had been, now well into generations. There were those who would joyfully set their hounds on Kasarian—on her—did chance and opportunity arrive.

Their sire had been poisoned at his own table. Her three elder littermates had died in battle overseas—or so it had been reported. Perhaps she and Kasarian only lived now because they had been taken from the keep on the death of their dam and delivered to the care of her mother's litter brother, Volorian.

Volorian's pale shadow of a littermate had ruled there. She had been strict, but she had favored Liara, and somehow the child had also taken the fancy of Volorian himself. He had allowed her more freedom than usual, even taking her with him to visit his breeding kennels and see the fine hounds which were his consuming pride. She knew hounds well, and from Volorian and those who served him, together with her own watchful observation, she had learned something of men.

Alizon was steeped in the debris of blood feuds carried on for generations. The great families had not wiped themselves out in these continued intrigues only because at intervals they turned to attack their neighbors—the infamous Witch Kingdom of Estcarp to the south, and, more recently and with aid from the Kolder strangers, High Hallack overseas.

There were two whelps of her second littermate, but they were mere children as yet. Leaving Kasarian—and her—all which remained of the true line of Kaylania, who had mated with a great mage and so brought a strange and sometimes troubling blood strain into their generations.

Kasarian was always under threat—or so it seemed to Liara. His own sense of self-preservation, the shadow of Volorian (who might or might not move to succor or avenge him), the blood oaths of some of his men had kept him alive. But now—

Liara frowned as she turned away from the mirror, her silver-fretted skirts brushing the carpet. It was almost lately as if Kasarian had taken on a new role in life—that he was making some move which would bring him into open conflict with his worst enemies.

He had begun to disappear at times. However, since questioning the will or actions of the head of any line was simply not to be thought of, Liara had no idea of what occupied him so closely. Kasarian might believe that she was unaware of all which was supposedly the lord's domain.

Liara's lips curved in a small secret smile. He had his tight-mouthed retainers—the tall grim-featured Gannard, his body servant, the castellan Bodrik. What he shared with them in the way of secrets she could only guess.

But—she held out her hands before her to turn the wide-banded ring set with a milky stone on one forefinger. Women had their secrets also. Though her dam had not lived long enough to initiate her into full knowledge, there was Singala, who had been almost a true dam to her. She had opened for Liara, on her return to this hold, the women secrets.

Even as the walls hid passages and spy holes aplenty in the baron's quarters and the main halls and chambers, so did such exist within her own chambers, where, by custom, men could enter only on invitation from the First Lady of the Hearthside. She had soaked up much knowledge during forays along those ways. But what clung the tightest to her mind was the matter of the key.

For the Key of Kaylania was by right the possession of the First Lady. And since Kasarian had no mate, the Key should have been hers. What it meant she had no true knowledge, only that it was a very powerful charm and one for those of the female line alone. She had waited for her littermate to mention it, but his attentions to her were always on the coldly formal level; he was not one to bend to any blandishment from a female. Her lips drew back now to show the tips of her teeth. Better she was one of his prize bitches—he would have been far more open to her then.

But she was deeply concerned now. The House of Krevanel was, by all she could gather, threatened on all sides. Perhaps it was the curse of the ancient mage blood which aroused the easily fired ire of their fellow barons. And if Kasarian became involved in some plot—as she was well assured that he now was—she foresaw a very dark future.

Liara turned her ring again. Welladay, she carried her answer with her. A baron brought down was fed to the hounds; his household could not expect much better. Therefore she carried her way of escape ever with her—a swift-acting potion Singala herself had distilled and swore by.

Liara passed into the corridor, paying no attention to the servitors clad in dark blue livery who bowed and touched house badges as she passed. For this night, she could walk freely through that part of the keep which was usually male territory, since she had been ordered to oversee the feasting table.

Why her littermate wanted her attendance had not been part of his orders. Usually a feasting was for fellow nobles only. Thus she felt a small fluttering which she sternly fought as she went, highheaded and with proper arrogance.

Bodrik himself with two guardsmen kept the great door. And flanking him were three other parties of scarred, gaudily uniformed fighters, the colors of their tunics glaring against the muted hues of the tapestry behind. She knew that these strangers were the personal guards of Lord Sincarian and the other guests.

They all touched house badge to her and Liara allowed herself a very slight nod of acknowledgment. Then Bodrik stepped forward and rapped upon the door. She heard the familiar grating sound of the safe bar being withdrawn and a moment later her way was clear to enter.

The flare of the torches in their holders was doubly bright tonight, as no one liked the thought of shadows when nonpack or nonfriends gathered together.

Liara stood where she was just within the threshold. She touched first her hound collar and then her house badge and inclined her head in Kasarian's direction. He had arisen, as had the three others there, and came to offer his hand to lead her to the top of the board, where stood the tall golden ewer of special blood wine for the guesting cup.

Of the three guests, she knew two. One was Baron Olderic, who gave her an appraising stare. She knew that he held much to her brother's way of thinking, if not openly. But he was old and his influence these days was small. With him was the eldest whelp of the House of Caganian, about whom little could be said save that he was easily swayed to take any stand for the moment.

It was the third man who had the most importance for her: Baron Sincarian. If evil grew itself legs and walked the streets of Alix, then it wore his seeming. Yet no one, not even the Lord Baron Hound himself, could bring him to heel. For all his vile repute he was a well-favored man, perhaps some three or four years older than her littermate.

He had been mated three times and each of his Hearth Ladies had died very suddenly. Whispers of what had caused their demises were only that and repeated with care.

"Lady of the Hearth of the House of Krevanel, Liara."

Kasarian made introduction. Only then did Liara touch collar and house badge, first to Olderic then to Sincarian and lastly the Cagarian First Whelp.

They seated themselves, while she remained standing by the

ewer. Shaking back her sleeve, she poured the first cup for Olderic. But before she poured the second, her littermate spoke again.

"The Baron Sincarian has made an offer to the House of Krevanel. He seeks as his Hearth Lady and mate the Lady Liara."

She hoped they could not read the revulsion in the face she had so carefully schooled to be impassive. Kasarian had this right—and females were playing pieces in the intricate intrigues for power.

"The House of Krevanel," her littermate was continuing, "holds the blood of the Lady Kaylania and therefore possesses a tradition which belongs to that house alone. Any female whelp may state her preference for a mate and none may question it."

Baron Olderic looked shocked and then frowned. The First Whelp's lips twisted as if he wished to laugh at the thought of such nonsense. Lord Sincarian made a small movement as if to arise from his chair but did not complete it.

What was Kasarian's purpose? Liara thought. Did he wish her assent to a future of unbelievable evil, or did he want her heartfelt refusal and so give Sincarian such an insult as would start a feud? If she were to be his piece in some game he should have given her fair warning.

She thought of Kaylania—that legendary lady who had mated with a mage, drawn strange and dangerous blood into their line.

For the first time she spoke, keeping her voice to the monotone expected from a female in male company.

"Does the Lord Sincarian wish to welcome to his hearth one with . . . with mage blood?"

There was a flicker in her littermate's eyes, but she could not tell whether that came from surprise or from satisfaction that she had made some point for him.

Sincarian was staring at her and it was plain that she had suddenly presented a problem.

"This one speaks openly of things most men would keep silent," he said to Kasarian. "Is it that Krevanel now wants all the world to know of its taint? Has dealing with the mages from over the border so set you up in your own estimation? A poorish lot of dabblers they have proved themselves."

Her littermate spread out his hands palm up, no weapon showing. "All here know what has happened lately when mage strove against mage to open once again the great gate. *I am open* in my speech, since it is to the honor of my house to be so."

Baron Olderic nodded as his host paused. "Rightfully so. You are a properly schooled whelp of a line which has long proven its worth to Alix. The Lady"—he deigned to nod at Liara—"also knows her place. You would be a fool, Sincarian, to cross bloodlines with Krevanel. Surely as a breeder of famed hounds you know that. Has not the Baron Kasarian in the years since he ruled in Krevanel made no attempt to take a mate? He is to be honored for his decision. I will so state, even in the high council." His fist pounded the table and Liara feared the cup of wine would be overset.

She risked a glance at her littermate even as she poured the guesting cup for Sincarian. Oddly enough, she had a strong feeling that her bold words had pleased him, in some way fit into a plan of his. But they certainly did not need another feud. As she handed the cup to Sincarian, he stared at her boldly. His look made her feel as if she stood there unclothed while a chamber rat nosed at her.

The First Whelp hesitated before he took the third cup she poured, as if by accepting it he would be in some way besmirched. Yet when Baron Olderic stared at him, he reached for it in a hurry.

Liara set the ewer in place and folded her hands at her waistline, where the length of the wide sleeves hid them. She found herself turning her precious ring about on her finger, knowing her gesture to be unseen. When would Kasarian dismiss her?

She had long ago learned that patience was one of the female's weapon-shields, but it did not come to her naturally. This night it threatened to break bonds. Custom or not, nature or not, she concluded that the time had come when she must speak frankly with this littermate of hers, could she get to him privately.

It was easy, so close a watch did she keep upon him now, to catch that slight shift of his eyes toward the guests. Once more touching collar and house badge, she framed the formal words:

"Be safe within, my lords, even as a whelp lies safe beside its dam in the nursing box. The hearthside is at your service." She inclined her head in their general direction.

They arose as she moved with the proper wide swirl of her skirts toward the door, but she did not look toward even Kasarian again.

Once more she passed swiftly through the halls, and came to the portal of her own domain, where the guards held strict attention and the door bar was drawn at their sergeant's knock.

There were two slave maids in the outer room and Liara spoke to the nearest.

"Go and see if Whelp Nurse Singala sleeps. If she does not, come and let me know. You, Altara," she ordered the second, "aid me off with this stifling weight." She was already plucking at her bodice fastenings.

Liara had managed to rid herself of that cumbersome round of skirts by the time the first maid returned. Altara was carefully pulling out the long, jeweled pins to loose her coils of silver white hair.

"Lady—the whelp nurse wakes. She ate well tonight and is eager to have you come."

Liara swiftly pulled on the short house robe, let Altara tie back her hair with a ribbon, and then waved both maids to the task of putting away the robes of state she had so swiftly shed.

No one could halt the passage of years. Singala, who had once been so much the reigning force in this part of the keep, now had to keep to her bed—her painful, swollen joints making her more often prisoner than not. But no ache or dust of years had slowed her wits, and to Liara she was as Gannard to Kasarian: an ever-present guard, a keeper of secrets, and perhaps the only one within these walls she might trust in full.

The woman, propped against a fluff of pillows, her badly swollen knee supported by a bolster, was gaunt. Her face appeared as if she were veiled by a webbing of tiny wrinkles. Her gray-white skin looked almost part of a mask, but her green eyes were sharp, clear, and took all attention from the rest of her.

"There is trouble?"

Liara laughed and shrugged. "When is there not in this world?

But this trouble . . ." Swiftly she told her nurse of the happenings in the banquet hall.

"My littermate plays some game of his own—courses his hounds on secret trails. I—" She reached forward and took Singala's gnarled fingers into her own, warmer hands and held them close. "You have taught me much, very much. My dam's littermate, the Baron Volorian, by some grace of fate saw something in me which made him treat me almost like one of his own whelps. I have been at his heels in the kennels, and always I listened and learned. Singala, surely it must be true what was said tonight—those of our house have a strange blood strain. There is this also—I want the Key! It is mine to have for it passes by full honor to the First Female of the Krevanel pack, and that I am! I do not know where my other litter brother's mate left it when she died. But I have a strange feeling"—she pressed her nurse's hands even closer—"that in that key there lies something which is mine. And I shall ask Kasarian for it—nor can he by pack oath deny it!"

"Heart Whelp." Singala might have been speaking as she did years ago when Liara came to her for the comfort or warmth of love. "Your litter brother's mate never held the Key—for she was of another bloodline. It was laid away with your own dam's betrothal jewels, which are yours alone."

"Laid away—the treasure room! Did my dam not have a special casket with a double badge upon it? For she was truly of the house blood, being of the litter of Jaransican, who was of the west branch of Krevanel, now gone." Liara's eyes glistened. "So—we have double mage blood, Kasarian and I."

She should feel fear, the proper revulsion of one who had been touched even so lightly by the evil of that magic which she had been brought up to abhor all her life. But she did not—rather she felt a queer excitement, as if she approached some door and would not find it barred, but swinging to her will.

"You have made me free of many secrets of this house, Singala Warm Heart, and so given me what may be greater than any heritage one can hold in two hands. A year ago I found another secret cabinet in the Lady chamber and in it what was left certain records. Time had eaten them, but there were bits left even I could puzzle out. Now you give me this—the knowledge that I may claim the Key.

"I fear for Kasarian. He says little, and never, of course, to me, save on matters to do with the hearth. But he is engaged in some secret dealings, of that I am sure. He disappears for times, some long, some short, when none can see him, and Gannard stays ever close to his chamber as if on guard. Three times has he summoned young Deverian to him, though heretofore he showed no interest in the whelps, save that they mind their tutor and cause no trouble. Tonight he brought Lord Sincarian here and quoted a bride offer— yet Sincarian is such a man as my brother in the past would put fang to the throat. Why does this happen? Why must a female never be told what threatens her hearthhold?"

Singala's bluish lips shaped a tiny quirk of a smile. "Again questions, questions. But to these I have no answers. Nor"—she glanced away from the hold the girl's eyes kept on her, along the length of her twisted, aching body—"am I now one who can search out news for you. And"—her smile was gone—"remember this, Heart's Whelp. Trust is something which can never be sworn to."

Liara nodded. Even if she had a littermate within the female quarters, she would not turn to her for aid—and never to one of the slave maids.

"I must think on this. Now, my dam by choice, get your rest. Gurtha will be stern with me when she brings your sleep drink." She attempted to loosen her hold on Singala's hands, but those crooked fingers now entrapped hers.

"Course with care. You are not of the pack—therefore if they learn this, the pack will pull you down. Oh, Heart Whelp, course with care!"

"As if I would do else. Now rest you, and be sure that I shall do nothing to arouse the pack."

Back in her own chamber she summarily dismissed both maids, seated herself on a bench before her dressing table, and gazed into the mirror. By every sign she was truly of the pack—yet they hunted not by sight but by more subtle means, reacting speedily to such scent as might be given off by fear of even by some faint change of thought. She had watched Volorian's prized breed too long not to know that. Through the centuries that their masters had concentrated on such breeding, perhaps some hound nature had become a part of these masters as well.

She had thought to approach Kasarian directly for an accounting. But one in her position did not do such—it was beyond all proper action and training. Her speech in the banquet hall tonight had been on the verge of lost propriety. He had given no sign of either approval or disapproval that she could now sort out of memory. But she half expected him to seek her out, either for a lashing by tongue or—or what?

Liara slipped a tress of her hair back and forth between her fingers. She had heard traders' tales such as were common in the female quarters. Alizon was not the whole world. There were other lands beyond its borders and the women there had strange ways past all propriety. Others even than the thrice-damned witches went freely about.

There had been slaves brought back from raids on the overseas Dales, though she was too young to remember more than glimpses of the two women who had been part of one of her littermate's loot. They died, and swiftly—one of them taking with her two of the guard before she was cut down, and the other under the lash. For they could not be broken to the ways of proper obedience.

Liara stirred and now her hands flew busily to her hair. She twisted it tightly, bringing out a net to confine it as close to her head as she might. She sped across the room and pressed her thumbs hard, one on the center of a flower carved on the tall head of the bed and one on the two embossed leaves below it.

There was no sound as the panel swung. She kept it well oiled and it had been more often in use these past days than before. There was a small chamber beyond and she felt for the top of the chest there, snapped a make-light to the wick of a lantern. Then she wrenched her house robe over her head and substituted the one-piece garment she had devised with Singala's help and sewn herself in secret. It had a hood which she pulled into place, leaving only a slit for her eyes.

The treasure chamber. She had made that part of her decision. She could have, of course, asked that her dam's jewel case be brought to her, but somehow she wanted the Key in her own hands before anyone else knew it or even guessed that she would want it.

The hidden ways of the hold were a spider web. She kept carefully away from those she thought were known to Gannard or her littermate, as she made her way down and down, sometimes by stretches of ladders formed by finger- and toeholds only, to the lower depths. The lantern swung from a firm grasp on its cord, but its light was limited.

Two years ago during her night wanderings she had found the hidden entrance to the treasure room and now she searched once again for the proper turnings. At the time she had simply explored gingerly, afraid that there might be a hidden alarm which would betray her presence. But now she knew what she must look for. Threading a path between chests, storage boxes, even suits of armor glistening with gems as the lantern light touched them, she came to that table where she had noted a number of smaller coffers.

Swinging the lantern lower, she strove to read the arms engraved on the begemmed lid of each. Dust had settled—except on one! Liara halted. There was the double house badge of her dam. But even as her hand went out to seize upon its lid, her eyes and her sense of caution were keen enough for her to see that this one had been disturbed. She drew a deep breath.

The Key! She hesitated no longer but lifted the lid, the fastening of which showed marks of being forced. There was wealth in plenty to glitter up at the lantern as she swung it closer. With a finger she stirred coils of necklaces, the tumble of two state collars, a sprinkling of rings. No key.

Liara caught her lower lip between her teeth. Kasarian—she was as sure as if she had seen him. He had taken the Hearthkeeper's Key—that which was rightfully hers!

She flipped closed the chest. Females were supposed to hold tight to any strong emotion. You might smile and smile when within you seethed with a storm of anger. She had seen Hearthkeepers accept dire insults with a languid air as if their ears were purposefully deafened to such.

But that did not mean that they could not plan—and act—to

rebalance the scales of justice. Kasarian had her key. Now—now dared she confront him openly?

Liara shook her head at her own thought. No . . . subtle as some new weapon she must be. But first she must learn more, and since she was ready for such searching, she would start now.

It meant venturing into the ways she had always prudently avoided. But a good hound did not turn from the hunt because of a thorn in the foot pad. So Liara began a most cautious journey within the walls of her own home hearth.

The first unknown side turning she took led downward again and she decided to stick with it. Whatever Kasarian was doing, she believed he needed privacy, and he was not going to find that above—even with Gannard and Olderic to screen him.

She thought she must be past the level of even the dungeons now. Then the faint echo of a voice brought her quickly around and into another side opening, which led to so narrow a crack that she must turn sidewise to follow. But the voice was growing louder and now she could distinguish words.

" . . . honor of the house, whelp. You are the son of Regroian, who died to serve Alizon. That your littermate is ill is a pity, but he has done this many times. You will take this into your hand—latching it also to your belt."

Liara's own hand moved along the rough stone, then her nails caught in a crack and there was a jar of sound. She could not turn to go. Her body seemed wedged in and she was helpless, as if she were bound there to await Kasarian's pleasure—for there was no mistaking his voice.

However, whatever lock she had in her folly undone answered that pressure she had unsuspectingly applied. A narrow door, only a little wider than the passage, swung open, gathering speed as it went so that it crashed against the outer surface beyond her reach.

Kasarian, yes, and with him, Nakarian, the younger of the two house whelps.

Her brother whirled. His thrown knife seemed to strike oddly to her left, though she knew that Kasarian was an expert.

He flung out an arm and swept Nakarian back, advancing on

her now with sword out and ready. Liara dropped the lantern. There was torchlight enough in the outer room to reveal her face as she scrabbled with hasty fingers to loose her hood.

Kasarian was already striking. That blade with its custom poison tip should have sliced into her at heart level. Instead the point rebounded with a force which also made him loosen his hold upon the hilt.

He stared at her, at the sword, and then back at her again. Deliberately now he stalked forward and she would not allow herself to try to squeeze away from his weapon. She was of the blood of Krevanel and as a female of that line she would die.

And strike he did, only to once more fail. Now he snarled, showing his teeth like one of the sire hounds.

Liara did not know what protection stood there with her, she only knew that one did. Dimly, very dimly in her mind a faint memory stirred. The Key—the Key was the answer!

"I am First Female of the Line of Krevanel, Guardian of the Hearth. In me doubly, as in you, littermate, runs the mage blood. And I have come for what is mine by pack right!"

His eyes widened, and he dropped his sword point.

"What is yours by pack right, female?" His voice grated dangerously, as it might have had she been an insolent slave.

"The Key of Kaylania, which was of my mother's holding but was not given into my hands."

Kasarian took a step backward. Slowly he shook his head from side to side, not as if he were denying her words, but rather as if he were trying to clear his thoughts.

"Come." He beckoned and then added, "If you can—female who carries mage blood."

Perhaps he meant to cut her down once she was free of this passage. Yet her pride was high and she would not yield to any fear. She stepped down from the level of the passage to the floor and stood facing him.

Those vividly green eyes of his which had widened earlier were now narrowing into slits. Suddenly he plucked something from his belt and tossed it to her with a queer expression of one waiting for some strange action.

Her own trained reflexes answered. Out of the air she caught a key—large, old. And it was warm in her hand, fitting within her fingers as if it were meant to rest there.

But there was something else now—a circle of brilliant light snapped into life and grew. She saw Kasarian suddenly grab the whelp and take from him a packet, which he tossed to Liara.

"Mage blood you claim—mage blood you be!"

The circle of light was turning into an oval, growing taller and taller. She saw Kasarian turn again on Nakarian and strike a blow, knocking the boy to the floor.

"Go, mage! You will find your kennel waiting!"

He gestured to the oval of light, which was now pulsating. It was a door—a door! She took one step forward and then another conscious now only of that opening. Nor did she feel Kasarian's clutch at her wrist twisting the Key from her. At the same time his other hand slammed her between the shoulders, sending her stumbling into the core of that light, into whirling, wringing nothingness.

## CHAPTER THREE

# *Lormt*

Keris pushed the Lady Mereth's wheeled chair with all the care he could summon. She never complained, but he had learned during these past days to watch for that shade of shadow which was the only sign of pain her features ever showed. How he had become in part her feet, and sometimes her hands, he could not rightly have explained, but now it seemed very natural that her wishes were as commands, as those of any Border captain.

The greatest chamber in Lormt, comprising most of the first floor of one of the undamaged wall sections connecting the three still-standing towers, had taken on a new look.

It had been ruthlessly cleared of age-worn desks. Piles of wood-backed books and rolls of manuscript had been stored in coffers along the walls, much to the fretting of that handful of elderly scholars who considered this their complete domain and were being rousted out of it without even a by-your-leave.

Owen and the Mashal Duratan, as well as the Lady Mereth, had attempted to clear the room for action without producing outward mutiny among those accustomed for so long to study there. There had been gusty scenes and in the end desks and materials had simply been moved and their owners told where to find them.

Now the huge chamber was occupied by a long center table, one Keris believed could seat with ease half a Border regiment. It had hurriedly been put together from the scarred refectory tables found here and there, some having been used only for the repository of books. Now it was covered not by a rich banqueting cloth, but by a strip of hide, cut and united again to form a runner from one end to another. And this was the center of present activity.

Men and women gathered up and down its sides and the sound of their voices rose far above a hum. Sometimes there was the sharp rise of argument and then Duratan, or Nolar his Lady, Owen, or the Lady Mereth would straightaway appear to listen and then bring the disputants to some agreement.

Many of those working on that huge map carried trays slung from cords about their necks, trays on which rested small pots of inks, while they held a selection of brushes in one hand or even between their teeth, their jerkins and robes spotted with the signs of their industry.

What was growing before all their eyes now was a strange picture of their world as they knew it. Mountains had been sketched in, rivers ran, forests blotted out portions of the hide.

In addition there were representations of blocky cities and ports, darksome towers. Sulcar charts were much in evidence, those who brought them surveying the new map keenly, often with sharp critical comments, locating ports which had been hardly more than legend to most of those there who were not seafarers.

Already there appeared several of those ominous pentagons which had been chosen for the symbol of the existence of gates.

The searching party for Estcarp and that of Escore were already on the move. Each included one of the witches, and that of Estcarp had located near the head of the River Es indications—very faint but still unmistakable—that a gate had once existed there.

The power needed for communication with Arvon via the adept Hilarion's instrument was too exhausting to those who must use it, and since their first contact they had had news only that those of Gryphon were spreading the news to arouse the Dales. Whether any real searching had begun there no one knew.

Lady Mereth was writing on her slate and Keris read the request over her shoulder.

"Ask the Lady Nolar to find us the Lady Liara."

Keris nodded, positioning the chair broadside so that his present liege lady could see a section of the map which was nearly blank. This was not the territory of Alizon. Why that—that woman of the damned, hound-loving race was needed, he could not understand. As had most of them who had come in contact with her, he tried to ignore Liara entirely. Only the Lady Mereth, Duratan, and Nolar seemed to know how she arrived here in the first place. Though her people were established by very ancient lore to have entered via a gate, they had always been bitter enemies to those native to this land. Had not the Lady Mereth herself, Dales-born in High Hallack, suffered deep sorrow during the vicious invasion of the Alizonderns when they attempted to possess her homeland?

Keris threaded his way through the ever-moving throng about the slowly growing map, trying to catch sight of the Lady Nolar. Instead he nearly stumbled over a small figure robed in such dimming gray that she seemed hardly more than one of the shadows which their many lamps had nearly driven from the hall.

Keris backed away and bowed. "Lady, your pardon."

To his mind witches were mature women, and from his first meeting he had wondered why this diminutive girl, hardly more than a child, had been included in the company sent from the Place of Wisdom.

"She is hiding—the Alizondern." Even her voice still held a childish ring.

Hiding—spying! His revulsion arose swiftly.

The witch shook her head vigorously. "She is not our enemy—though so she has been counted. She watches—not spies. For this is the only way she can learn what we are, what we do. Her people know nothing of trust. Theirs is a hard, dark life and from their birthing they believe fate hangs over them. But this Liara—the older blood is stronger in her than she knows. The Lady Jaelithe perhaps can aid her—for she has also a part to play. Come."

The witch girl led him toward the side of the hall where the discarded desks had been piled as safely as possible. Someone moved there, shrinking back but unable to get beyond his sight.

Keris moistened his lips. He certainly could not speak the devilish language of Liara's kind. But she had picked up a few words—at least names.

"Lady Mereth—she—wants—you—" he spoke a little loudly as he might to one deaf.

Slowly the girl advanced from her hiding place. She was wearing the breeches, skirt, jerkin, and boots which were the garb of many of the women in the room, and her hair, so intensely white that it seemed to shine like a lamp glow, was tightly braided. By such dress she could be any of the Escore women at work on the map. But her heritage was plain in her pale face: that shining hair, and her slanted green eyes, with features narrow and sharp. Alizonderns were half hound according to legend, and Keris thought at that moment that they might indeed be were, able to shape-change and run with their packs.

Liara still felt that she was caught in some foul dream. This place . . . where had Kasarian thrust her in his hate for her—for she was sure only hate had made him send her so? Only that old totterer

Morfew spoke her tongue. But *his* explanation of what had happened was so beyond comprehension that she did not believe it. All this talk of posterns and gates—

She looked at these strangers facing her now. The girl—Liara swallowed and swallowed again—the girl was a *witch*! Centuries of hatred and mistrust lay between them.

The young man—Morfew had told her he was a halfling, part human only, though he looked to be the same as any of the guardsmen passing now and then on errands. He wore a sword and another long holster weapon, which was common, but she wondered for a scornful moment whether all the Green Valley men such as he could stand up against Kasarian, or even of her littermate's guards.

"Lady—Mereth—" he repeated. There was a beginning scowl on his face. She braced herself. Let him try to lay hand on her. These witch people were careless. She had three knives on her, carefully bestowed in hiding but able to be quickly drawn.

However, the name he mentioned was one of the few she really knew, and the witch had already turned and was going away. Liara stepped forward, but kept a careful distance from her guide.

They made their way to the table. There waited Mereth, that strange woman who could not speak but who had written such unbelievable things in proper Alizondern tongue on her slate. She claimed acquaintance with Kasarian, saying even that she had visited Krevanel. She had mentioned things which seemed to prove such a visit, and firmly stated that Kasarian was an ally in what went on here.

Liara came to her side, closer to that upright figure in the chair than she liked, but occupying the only open space. The lady was watching her closely, seeming to try to read with her very eyes any thought Liara might hold.

"I—came." Let this female of the Dales tell her what was wanted, and quickly.

Lady Mereth nodded. Then her fingers moved nimbly over her writing slate and she held that out for Liara to read.

"Do you understand what we do here, Lady Liara? What your brother learned before you?"

"I have heard what has been told me," she answered shortly. "There are gates, such traps as the one my littermate forced me into. These you labor to find and mark so." She pointed to the long map.

Lady Mereth was writing again. "But to you this is a story, yes?"

Liara hesitated for a moment and then shook her head. She had been considering every aspect of the stories told her by Morfew (traitor Alizondern that he was) and this Mereth. Now she had a thought of what really could be behind such meddling. There might be a gate in Alizon, through which an army could be transported into the very heart of her homeland, there to wreak vengeance for what the hound masters had done in the Dales. Long had the witches been their enemies, and there were witches in this very hall here and now.

"I believe that you hunt gates." Again her answer was abrupt.

Once more Mereth's chalk was busy. "We hunt for portals through which the Dark can come to us, not ones to suffer us to travel into the unknown. You believe we threaten Alizon. Not so, but your home may also be threatened by just such a danger as we seek. We labor on two things, Lady Liara. First to find such gates, second to discover that which will lock them against all future opening.

"To do this"—she had wiped away the earlier lines and was writing swiftly again—"we must go into parts of our world of which we know nothing—where even Sulcars and traders have forged no trails. Girl, you have that in your blood which is mine also."

Liara had heard that, too, what Kasarian had been told: that Elsenor, the mage who was their own distant foresire, had come out of time to father this woman, Mereth. All which she had always believed was under threat, and so was she—perhaps.

"I am of the House Line of Krevanel." Her chin went up and she faced this chairbound woman proudly. "I am of Alizon. Anyone within this hall"—she made a gesture with her left hand, keeping her right carefully close to the hiding place of her longest knife—"would gladly see my blood on his or her steel."

Mereth was writing again. "No one denies that your people are hated. But your brother learned that with a common goal even enemies swear battle oaths." Her chalk paused and now her stare at Liara was even more penetrating.

"You are not altogether ignorant. I have enough of the talent to know—this—"

The hand holding the chalk flashed upward, as if, leaving the slate, Mereth would now draw upon the air itself. And draw she did—a complicated design. White it was at first, as white as Liara's hair, then deepening into a blue which drew the girl past understanding to put out her own hand.

The design curled, wavered, flipped, to encircle her wrist. She would have cried out, but it was as if Mereth's own dumbness that moment became hers and she could only stare from the woman to that strange coil which did not quite touch her own flesh but whirled thrice and then was gone.

It was Keris's turn to start and his hand went to sword hilt in unconscious reaction to an act which bore the force of true power. As strange as the truce with the Keplians, now of the Light, who companioned with the Lady Eleeri and her lord, so was such an acceptance of this female from Alizon. Mage blood—yes, he knew that story. It was widespread in Lormt and he knew that it had been passed along deliberately so that Liara might find acceptance among age-old enemies of her kind.

Only . . . there was no misinterpreting what he had just seen. This Liara was not only accepted by the Light; she also was gifted as well. He knew that old twinge of jealousy. To be a halfling and ungifted, while this open enemy was granted such a Power . . .

"What do you want of me?" Sparks of anger in those green eyes made Keris think of a snowcat he had once seen at bay.

The Lady Mereth did not turn to her slate at once. She was regarding Liara now as one must study some pattern in weaving. At length once more her chalk squeaked across her slate.

"Much, perhaps. Look you here." She slid the slate to her other knee and now used the chalk to point to that part of the hide map before her.

Most of this was blank. Keris recognized a fraction of the coastline, but that, also, was cut abruptly short. This was south of Karsten—and he knew well the tale of that single gate symbol on the edge of the sea itself. His own clan, the Tregarths, had helped destroy *that* horror of a portal little more than a year past.

The girl had moved closer, as if her curiosity had drawn her against her will. But Keris was studying the land which was sketched in just above that blankness. Karsten—another ancient enemy. Survivors of his race there had been driven forth as exiles years since.

Pagan, the warlord duke, had taken command after the fall of the Kolder-backed rule. And Pagan had flourished until he was past all caution and had started north to invade Estcarp.

No one would ever be allowed to forget the Turning, when the witches protected their own with the force of such Power as racked the world. Mountains had walked and crumpled into valleys, new peaks had arisen. All the old trails were long gone, though parties of Borderers had been scouting southward ever since they had recovered from the backlash of that swordless battle.

They dared not accept that Karsten lacked gates. In fact there was already a known one near the new border on the southern side, sketched in by the Lady Eleeri. That lay in what had once been Karsten territory—a portion held by the Old Race before they had been hunted down and slain. There she had entered, to travel north and west into the fringe of Escore. And some of the descendants of those who had been driven out were indeed drifting back to restore ruined keeps long held by their clans.

So—the party sent southward would be moving through a land given over to warring nobles and continued chaos. They must go as stealthily as scouts and yet be ready to defend their mission should the need arise.

"... know nothing of that land," Liara was protesting. He must have been so intent on his own thoughts that he had missed some question of Mereth's.

"And it knows nothing of you." The words stood out, boldly scrawled on the slate.

Liara's hand was at her lips and she looked beyond the slate to the nearly empty stretch of hide. "Why?" she said slowly.

"Do you wish a half life among those here, few of whom will give you trust, or a full one you can make for yourself?" Mereth's chalk questioned.

The girl's body was as tense as a boar spear held ready in the hunt. "You yourself say I am not trusted. How then could I be accepted by any of this company who choose to ride into danger?"

"Because," she was answered then by a soft voice rather than the chalk, "you are called Lady of Alizon. The power chooses what tools it will wield."

The small witch had drifted once more to them. That jewel which usually swung on its neck chain now rested on her palm, held out before her. And for a moment, even as Lady Mereth's sending, it blazed blue.

Liara drew a ragged breath and shrank back a step. "I will not be slave to your magics!" Steel glinted in her hand now and Keris moved as quickly, being just able to catch her wrist, though he had difficulty in keeping that hold.

The witch jewel flicked. Another ray of light, and Liara dropped the dagger Keris had not yet been able to wrest from her.

Then the small, gray-robed figure moved closer. "There is no harm in that which is born of the Light," she said. "And whether you see it now or not, that is where you stand, Lady of Alizon, on the side of the Light—even as does your brother. Yes, you will be one of the searchers." She extended the jewel a fraction farther. "I do not select, nor do my sisters; this does. And"—suddenly she half turned toward Keris—"there is also a need for a fighting man."

Keris had not loosened his hold on Liara. "Lady," he said with all respect to this maid who was perhaps ten years or more his junior, "I am no name-won warrior. There will be those in plenty who can better serve than I." The words were bitter. His whole body ached to believe what she had said: that he—the halfling— the ungifted— was a proper weapon for this foray.

She smiled at him almost mischievously. "Keris Tregarth, think what name you bear. Already those of your clan are on such a ride."

"They are," he answered slowly, "what they have always been, sword and shield to wall our world."

"Nor are you any less, Valley guard." Now she was deeply serious. "I have the foresight—which is more of a burden than any blessing. This pathway is also mine and I see you on it. The reason will be made clear in time."

He let Liara's wrist fall quickly, lest he betray the shaking now of his own hand. What he wanted most, and this wisp of a witch child was granting it! The wonder of that made him feel a little dazed.

Then he pushed closer to the table to survey the unfinished trailing lines which disappeared southward into the nothingness of ignorance.

"Var City"—he pointed—"and then the Port of Dead Ships. But inland from there, who knows?"

There came a sound from the witch that was close to laughter.

"Since we are naming names—I am Mouse. And for your question, the answer is, who indeed? Learning that can only come in time."

The days of their labor on the map seemed endless now to Keris. He noted, though, that Liara no longer kept to the shadows but often stood beside Lady Mereth's chair, staring down at that same surface.

He delegated himself to search out the Borderers who had recently scouted south. And then he dared to approach that strange tamer of Keplians, the Lady Eleeri, whose territory lay in the disputed ground.

At his first awkward questions she seemed almost impatient. But as he persisted—though he did not tell her of the witch choosing—she called upon him to go with her, out of the hall, away from the bustle of activity there, pushing through the crowded courtyard where pack ponies and Torgians were being shod and made ready for swift riding.

He still matched strides with her as they came out into the open, away from that half-ruin which was now Lormt. Then they stood together in a wide field—good pasturage at this season.

She neither whistled nor called. But there came two trotting at a flowing gait, hardly seeming to touch hooves to sod. The Keplians: a mare who towered above any horse he had ever seen, and with her a young stallion.

The Lady Eleeri was speaking now—not to him but to the Keplians, as if they were of the same clan blood. And when they surveyed him with those great blue eyes, he knew that, bodily different though they might be, these two had intelligence and power such as was seldom found outside the Green Valley of his homeland. Instinctively he raised his hand palm out in greeting as the Lady spoke:

"This be one who will ride with us. He is of mighty get; those of his blood are those great and noted warriors, the Tregarths."

*This one is a colt only!* The mare tossed her head.

Lady Eleeri looked amused. "We are all foals—until the wisdom-bringing years give us aging."

Keris held himself stiff. He was used to mental communication with the Renthans of the Valley, though he had been overslow in learning to send as well as receive. However, stories of the past still rose from memory to haunt. His father had almost met his death from a Keplian years ago.

The mare's eyes seemed to glare with blue fire now as she looked him up and down.

*We do not company with such.* There was disdain in that verdict. Keris flushed and knew a spark of anger, but he kept silent.

"He will have his own mount," the Lady Eleeri returned. "Keris Tregarth"—now she spoke directly to him—"this is Theelas the great mare who helped bring down the plague of the Black Tower—and her second colt-son, Janner."

Keris gave greeting to the two as he would to any clansman. The mare made a noise which sounded remarkably like a hearty sniff, nodded her head toward the Lady Eleeri, and cantered off, followed by her son.

"They have great pride, these," the Lady said to him. "Prove yourself friend and you will have no better battlemate. But for untold scores of years they were hunted by men and by servants of the Dark and they learn new ways slowly."

"Even perhaps as we," Keris returned boldly. He could not help but admire the beauty of the two seeming horses as they cantered off.

She nodded. "Even as we."

Keris spent more and more time now on his own preparations, for Liara was now fully attendant on the Lady Mereth. There was more strength in her slender body than one might believe, and she had no difficulty with the handling of the chair. Part of his days were spent in the improvised weapons court, where what skills he had already were fiercely polished closer to a master's art. The rest of the time he schooled himself as best he could by studying the reports from those who ventured into Karsten, making the trip each morning to see if anything new had been added to the map—but very little appeared there still.

At last the day did come that it was their turn to ride out. The Sulcars had gone first, since they must travel by wind and wave and not all the year was free of the Great Storms. So had gone Koris's son Simond, his Lady Trusla, and the witch Frost—all jewel-chosen. They headed north, with only the thinnest trace of an old sea log account as a guide.

Hilarion had contacted Arvon once again to learn that two parties were equipped and ready for search—one for the Dales and one to head across the barren Waste itself.

Keris could not will himself to sleep and moved eagerly when the day of their own journey dawned. They were not a large group, hardly more than a scouting party who could make the best use of the hiding places if detected.

The Lady Eleeri and Lord Romar were borne by the Keplians. Keris himself had Jasta, a young Renthan who was truly excited at being part of this adventure. Liara was mounted on a large hill pony—she had had to learn to ride during their time of waiting, since the females of the Alizon keeps never journeyed so. But now she felt at ease in the saddle and had taken on the leading of their pack train of mountain ponies well burdened with supplies.

Mouse rode a Torgian mare well to the fore of their party but not beyond the guards. Those numbered two Falconers, Krispin and Vorick, whose fighting skills were doubled by the aid of the great birds who rode at intervals on the special saddle horns of their mounts but scaled up into the sky at will. Denever, armed with those deadly arrows, a double number now in his quiver, had a place of prominence.

For Denever was of Karsten, a wanderer who had survived the mountain upheaval which wiped out the army of which he was a part and who had cast in his fortunes with those of Lormt. He was flanked by two of the old Borderer guards who had once been his deadly enemies—Farkon and his shield-mate, Vutch the Left-Handed.

So they rode out of Lormt in the early morning, pointed south, where the unknown might wait darkly.

## CHAPTER FOUR

# *Karsten*

The ravaged mountains to the south no longer offered any easy traveling, though there were trails coming into being again. Some were made by those roving Border scouts ever suspicious of some hostile movement from the south, others emerging as game tracks as time passed since the Turning. But the party from Lormt used none of these.

Lord Romar, astride the Keplian Janner, had long been a wanderer, thus now and then he sighted some landmark. On the fifth day after they left the Border behind, Keris was riding point, meshing his mind with that of Jasta, the Renthan he bestrode. It was Jasta who stopped so abruptly that only years of riding experience kept Keris on his back.

The Renthan held his horned head high, drawing in deep breaths of the chill air of the heights, as if he had been on the run. Not for the first time, nor even the hundredth, Keris silently cursed his inability to produce any talent-born ward of warning for himself.

There came a flash in the air over their heads. Farwing, Krispin's falcon, swooped as if to land on a neighboring crag and then soared again. That the bird was on scout Keris knew. And a moment later he heard stones rattle under hooves as Denever's Torgian pushed up beside him.

The stretch before them looked more inviting than that way over which they had just forced a passage. However, that in itself could be a warning. The falcon swooped again, but from among a cluster of rocky spines arose other flyers on the wing. The wind blowing toward the party carried a trace of filthy stench.

"Rus," Denever commented, yet he made no move to use his bow.

The evil birds, their naked, blood-red heads agleam in the sun, were spreading out, speeding toward them. Old lore flashed into Keris's mind—a thrice-circling to immobilize prey for the coming of their masters? He had never heard of birds being used in such bespelling. Again the falcon soared, seemingly unwilling to let near him any of that ghastly flock. For flock it was fast becoming— Keris counted at least a dozen of the creatures now on wing.

"Ssssaaaaa!"

When he heard that sound from behind, Keris drew steel and Jasta half wheeled so that they could now look in both directions. Trotting as if her hooves were on the smoothest of roadways came the Torgian mare which was Mouse's mount, seemingly so attached to her mistress that she even sheltered next to Mouse's camp mat at night.

The young witch held her head at a sharp angle, making no move to watch the trail or control the passage of her mount. Instead her lips were moving, though Keris caught no sound of words.

Above, the seemingly purposeful flight of the rus faltered all at once. Their wings flapped vigorously as if they fought against some storm wind which would carry them away. Yet they continued to struggle.

There was a curdling in the air space between the flyers fighting that battle and the party on the trail. It seemed to Keris that the stones about him appeared to yield up shadows which arose purposefully, thickening into a net—no, a sack—a giant sack as he had seen used as a fishing net.

"Sssaaa!" Again Mouse's voice arose and this time with the snap of a command.

Still the rus fought, but it was clear that they now fought to escape, not to come at any prey. At them, with the power of a full storm gust, came the bag, gathering them in. They were screeching now, their voices echoing and reechoing from the heights about. Keris heard in answer the squeals of the pack ponies downtrail, and trumpet challenges from the Torgians.

Even as the bag closed about the birds, so did it continue to grow thicker, hiding what it held. Then it whirled about in a mad circle, and vanished as might a cloud. The air above was free.

He saw Denever, no longer watching the battle above, move toward Mouse, but already a Keplian strode arrogantly uptrail and the Lady Eleeri was beside the girl, reaching out a hand to steady her. Mouse's eyes were half closed and she drooped.

The Keplian mare tossed her head, glanced from eye corner at the Renthan—for the two breeds seemed in a rivalry of sorts.

*Trap,* Jasta's mind spoke.

"Set by whom?" Keris countered. "What has been loosed here?"

*Well may you ask that,* Jasta replied. *The rus are said to serve the Sarn, but Sarn have never been known to ride this far south.*

Lord Romar had joined them and now slid from the back of the Keplian who was his battle companion. He nodded to Denever.

"There is no other way past this height," he pointed out. "If they have bottled us in . . ."

Keris and the archer joined him afoot. Behind them the Falconer Krispin settled his returned bird on his saddle horn before he, too, dismounted.

However, the four of them advanced with caution, hardly noting that the Keplian and Jasta, both showing ready teeth, followed. What they found as this too-tempting trail rounded an upstanding pinnacle of bare rock—

Keris had seen many horrors of the Dark. He was no green boy who had never yet blood-wet his blade. But this!

Trap it was, and they were not the first to meet with it. There stood a bulk nearly as tall as the roof of a landsman's cottage. It had been fashioned—surely this thing had never really lived?—though of that they could not be sure. It was a monstrous head, something out of the deepest of nightmares. And the worst was that it was somehow a nauseating mingling of human and some reptilian species. Its jaws were well open to show a triple row of great fangs which had the appearance of rusted metal.

Lying on the ground about it were fragments of bodies, most clearly human. Keris swallowed—the stench was terrible, but not as bad as facing what caused it. And here the rus had been feasting.

A skull dislodged by the Keplian lay grinning up at them, plucked bare of all semblance of flesh.

Denever was circling to the left, attempting to avoid touching any of that terrible mass, and Romar was taking the right when they were both struck, as well as Keris, with the powerful mind-send of the two mounts who had followed them, uniting in one message.

*There is no one here.*

"This thing has no life of its own," Romar said with authority. "I guess it is a device once given strong powers to entice prey within reach—as we see by its kills." He stooped and picked up a sword, the blade snapped off close to the hilt but showing no signs of rust or weathering.

He turned the remains of the weapon around. The hilt was

rough with a setting from which jewels must have been pried. Meanwhile Denever was poking gingerly into a noisome mass on the other side of that head. He jerked out, with the point of his lance, a club which rolled until it was stopped by a rack of bones.

"Outlaws, " was his judgment.

It was Jasta who cut in then: *Comrades, this thing is now harmless. Though if it can be activated again, who knows? There is evil here, but it is faded.*

Keris faced the bloodstained snout. "The Port of Dead Ships," he said slowly. "That was also something set by those long gone but kept alive at times. A gate?" But already he knew that that guess was wrong. This was no gate, though it might once have been a defense for some place of evil, even a gate.

*The Witch.* That was the Keplian. *Perhaps it is her doing which broke the pattern. But do we leave this here perhaps to hunger and eat once more?*

There could be only one answer to that. They threaded their way downtrail and reported what they had found. Mouse was seated on one of the cushion mats, her jewel held tight between her hands, while the Lady Eleeri supported her. But as they came, she looked up. There was such a shadow on her small face that Keris was shaken. He could almost believe that she had witnessed that horror with them.

"It is as Jasta has said." Her words came slowly. "The evil is no longer strong, but it may return. We cannot leave such a thing to work its will again."

Farther downslope Liara regarded her heavy boots, a crinkle of pain between her white brows. To anyone who had worn for most of her life soft slippers in a keep, these thick-soled monsters were instruments of torture. Still, the Lady Mereth herself had overseen their making, and the girl had no doubt that the workmanship which passed that pair of falcon-sharp eyes was the best which could be provided.

The reins of her riding pony were looped over a nearby knuckle of rock. Riding, too, left her body sore in places she could not have believed. Whenever she could, she abandoned the saddle and walked beside the line of burden beasts.

To the surprise of all at Lormt, herself included, the wiry, mountain-bred, small beasts were their least troublesome under her control. She knew that most of the party could communicate with the various animals they accompanied. But they considered the pack ponies outside that range of influence.

She had certainly made no attempt at such a talent—it would be witchery. On the other hand, apparently in her presence the creatures could be loaded, herded, used without the vicious attempts at biting and kicking with which they greeted any others. She often caught them watching her as if she in herself were a menace they were afraid to challenge.

There was confusion up ahead. Save for an ever-present rearguard, often Denever (certainly a guard to depend upon if she had need, which she did not), Liara seldom rode closer than shouting distance to the rest of the party, except when they stopped at intervals in their twisting upward climb. When they did come to such halts, she kept with the ponies, suspecting that her presence was of less value than her absence as far as the others were concerned. Certainly she wanted no close contact with that witch whelp, and, though she would never have admitted it aloud, she was distrustful of the Lady Eleeri, who used trail craft like a trained hunter and who was always trailed by her Keplians.

The men, of course, were unapproachable, even though the females of this outer world were as frankly at ease with them as they would be with their own sex. She had first marveled at that openness and then somehow it made her angry inside, as if they had forced her into a kind of invisible prison.

However, she could use her eyes and her ears, and her life in Alizon had trained her to seek out nuances, weigh even the tone of a voice, the flick of an eyelid. Thus she tried to learn all she could without any questioning, making herself a slave laborer for this mixed band.

There came the sound of a scrambling run downtrail and she was on her feet in an instant, grasping for the reins of her pony.

She recognized the newcomer as that halfling Tregarth, enemy born to those of her blood.

"Off pack!" His order came breathlessly and he pushed past her to the foremost of the ponies. The small beast promptly snapped with yellow teeth and Keris barely avoided that vicious nip.

Liara smiled slyly. Then she returned the reins of her mount to the rocky tie and slipped past young Tregarth to the animal, who was prevented only by the length of its lead rope from savaging him as he backed hastily away. There was more sound upslope until one of the Falconers skidded on a mossed stone and fetched up again the rock which had supported her earlier. The hawk mask of his helm was in place and his bird circled overhead.

"Do we camp?" Liara asked. Her hand was now on the pack pony's neck. It did not strike at her, but it began to sweat as if the climb this far had taxed its full strength.

Keris scowled at her. "We need the beasts—to clear our path."

Her hands were busy with the ropes as the men stood watching, for if they ventured any nearer, the ponies rolled eyes and prepared to kick and buck. She was used to this job now, but it was clear that the others were impatient that she did not allow the loads to simply tumble to the ground.

Once the lashings on the ponies were freed, she nodded to the others. "There is need for this. Would you let it lie?" Liara had no thought herself of trying to lift or drag the packs.

However, the men did not protest. Already they pulled the supplies behind a tumble of storm-uprooted trees.

The rearguard was up with them now, short spear out of his shoulder sling, on the alert.

"What's to do?" he demanded.

"There is that beyond which must be destroyed. We need the pack ponies to shift rocks." Keris's answer was immediate.

"Then"—the guard jerked a thumb at Liara—"best get her for the managing of them. No man is going to want to lose a hand or have his feet kicked from under him!"

Keris nodded. Then he spoke to Liara as he always did, aloofly, not meeting her eye to eye. "With your assistance, then, Lady. We need the strength of these beasts and you can best command them."

There was no reason to refuse. In fact she was being sharply prodded by curiosity. Getting into her saddle and settling herself there gingerly, she picked up the lead rope and the three men stepped nimbly aside as she led her procession up toward the ridge top.

The wind was rising and it flowed downslope. Liara made a face. This was like the effluvia from a badly kept kennel—though she had never heard of a kennel neglected to such an appalling state.

The Lady Eleeri and the witch had moved aside from the trail and here was Denever, and the second Falconer. They were squatting, the archer busy with a stick, drawing on a patch of ground brushed clear.

Lord Romar stood there also looking down, and as Liara drew her train to a halt he said:

"Farwing and Swifttalon report that the length of the thing vanishes into the side of the cliff itself. It is like some monster entrapped."

Denever nodded. "Entrapped even as it was set to trap. The evil is sped now, Lady Mouse has said. But it may still return even as fire flickers out of an ember when another stick is laid for its eating. We have here a trace way up—which only the ponies can take. The Torgians and Keplians and Jasta are all too large to attempt it. Even if it were widened, their greater weight and shod hooves would bring them down."

The others were nodding and then the Falconer added: "Farwing reports broken land atop. Even the ponies will have to be surefooted there."

Denever grunted. "Show me a pony that is not that and I shall shout it aloud to all of Karsten. These beasts are bred and born in such country and they are surefooted. So, Lady Liara"—he did not even turn his head to look at her—"if you can get these stubborn animals to climb, perhaps a good third of our job is done."

"Lady Liara." Mouse was standing now, though Eleeri hovered by her as if to offer instant support. "It is true that the Dark has withdrawn from this thing. The trap is very ancient and perhaps, if a will was set to move it once more to slaughter, it has withdrawn. For now your beasts have nothing to fear."

Your beasts—not you and your beasts. Liara nodded but was surprised when Mouse continued:

"Though you see shadows where none walk, there is promise of more—by this." Her hand cupped the jewel. "So do I swear it!"

Witchery! Liara tensed. Was this Mouse girl weaving some net about her, dooming her to everlasting service? But it would not matter, she had already doomed herself when she had taken the hidden ways of Krevanel keep.

"My thanks, Lady." She tried to speak smoothly. "What we can do, these beasts and me, that we shall."

However, when she saw the steep narrow trail up which they had to be urged, she began to doubt her own words. Dismounting, she tested the ropes which fastened the ponies in a chain.

"Here, take you this and test your way." Lord Romar had moved to her side and pushed into her hand a stout shafted spear.

Nodding thanks but concentrating on the trail ahead, Liara looked for the best place to begin that climb. She thought she did not fear heights and certainly in the secret ways of Krevanel she had dared passages purposely made perilous. Slow but sure—that was what was to be kept in mind now.

Liara never afterward tried to guess how long that ascent took her. She kept small spurts of fear under tight control and the ponies did not balk when she tugged at the lead rope. As the climb continued, that stench grew the stronger and she knew what caused it—maggot-infested meat, crust of blood. The field of some battle might lie ahead.

Finally she and her charges reached a leveling off and she was sure they were on the crest. Around them was a tumble of shattered rock—such as might have existed after some stupendous hammer had given blow after blow here.

The ponies were puffing and moved of their own accord away from that near-impossible trail. This was like a shelf against the cliff and she could see no way they might stray. In fact, one moved purposefully to lip at a tuft of coarse gray-green grass.

She had no desire to see what lay below the edge of the drop to her left. The fetid odor was enough to warn off anyone. Yet she made herself go and gasped as she clung to one great rock and looked down.

A serpent—such a serpent as was reported in legend, killed by heroes in their time for the good of all. What showed in the open was the terrifying head, its monstrous jaws open. However, a little more than a hand's-breath behind the backward slope was the cliff wall. Lord Romar had been right: The thing appeared to have been trapped in solid rock.

But—*it* was also rock, showing no sign of life save the grisly remains about its rigid jaws. Witchery past any imagination except in a nightmare.

"Not pretty, my lady!" The men of the party had climbed up now, crowding to the cliff wall for safety.

Her grasp on the rock beside her tightened. "What would you do?" She tried to keep the quaver of her answer to Lord Romar under control.

"We have the assurance of the Lady Mouse that it is now without peril. But the Light does not leave some trap of the Dark undestroyed. We shall use these"—with a sweep of his arm he indicated the sowing of rocks about them—"to bury that thing."

So indeed did they labor, Liara with them, for she must see to the loading of every pony, accompany it to the verge where the men hurled the stones of each burden out and down.

They paused to eat and drink from supplies lifted in a net. Even the Falconers laid aside their proud helms and mail shirts as they worked. There were bruises and small cuts in plenty and Liara once felt the world whirl about her and might have fallen had not Romar's strong hand from behind steadied her.

"Lady, you have done much. It is because of our need that we must ask."

Somehow she shaped her dusty lips into a grin. "My lord, I

would give the full treasure of the Lord High Hound now, that some other of you could deal with these unruly beasts!"

He laughed. "Each of us has a talent."

Her grin turned wry. "And this is mine? Well, we are making the most of it this day."

Now the day was already fading into evening. Looking down, she could see that most of the horror below was hidden by stones. There were dark stains on the walls—where blood must have once splashed high. But the head, except for the tip of the high-held snout, was buried.

However, the sun which had seemed furnace-hot on them at times as they worked was fast disappearing westward. To take the downtrail even in dusk was something Liara knew that she could not attempt. The ponies were nickering, proving more and more difficult to handle. They needed water and forage and if they were forced to further work she doubted if even her "talent" could control them. She announced as much when the next burden of stones arrived.

"It is so," Denever agreed.

The snout was hidden now. She was sure that they might go— but the loss of light trapped them there, unless the men were willing to risk descent. She was not, nor would she demand it of the now head-hanging beasts—one did not course a hound past its endurance.

She heard a call from the head of that trace trail. Two more coming up! First came the Lady Eleeri. She had left behind the bow which was her ever-ready weapon so that she could assist Mouse, though the girl scrambled ahead with a will.

Through the dusk they moved in a glow of light of their own, which emitted from the witch jewel. Lord Romar joined them as quickly as he could wend a way over that uneven surface. They spoke together, but in such low voices that Liara could not make out words.

Then the witchling moved apart from them, on toward the edge of the cliff and that hidden horror below. She held out her jewel and it flamed even higher. Lady Eleeri hurried after her to lay hand on her shoulder as the girl's voice rang out, reaching them all now:

"Earth, air, fire, and water! By the dawn of the east, the moon-white of the south, the sun of the west, the black midnight of the north, by yew, and the hawthorne, Illbane, rowan, all the laws of knowledge—the law of Names, the law of True Falsehood, the law of even balance—may this thing now ever cease to be!" Her voice arose higher and higher, stronger and stronger, until the last words she uttered were like a trumpet call.

From below came a pale gleam which was visible even through the glory of the jewel. Liara edged forward, tightening her rock hold to look down once more into that cut.

The stones they had shifted through most of this day were no longer a ragged heap. The outer ones were palely lit—and under Liara's gaze they appeared to flow together, edge fitting firmly into edge. She was entirely sure that no human hand could shift one of them again.

"Now." Mouse turned her back on that feat of witchery and faced the Alizondern girl. "Rightly you think of the good beasts. They shall have their reward."

She moved slowly over the still-stone-littered ground, swinging her gem from its chain now. Suddenly those links straightened. The stone was held not by her hand any longer, rather floated by itself on the air. And it drew Mouse after it to the rise of the cliff wall.

Liara heard a musical note high and clear as gem struck rock. There was a crumbling one could detect even through the gloom—a darkness—moisture seeking a way out of some hidden bed. The ponies must have scented it, for they started as one toward Mouse. Liara moved swiftly, suddenly afraid for the younger girl, witch though she might be.

The trickle grew thicker, runneled down the rock to curdle between the stones of a rough pool. And the ponies crowded about. Mouse moved between them easily, the gem now swinging from her hand.

As it passed over the ledge of rock they had cleared by their earlier labor, a shadow arose from the surface.

Unbelieving, Liara stooped and felt. Her battered fingers tangled in grass.

"For tonight they will be sustained," said Mouse. "And we may safely take this trail below. This is the night when I must report."

Liara saw them gather at the trail. Still, her body was heavy with fatigue, and she could not face that descent, remembering too well all the perils lying along it. To her surprise, an arm closed about her waist. She did not at first recognize who had joined her. Then when she knew it for young Tregarth, she would have jerked away, but she did not have any strength left to elude him. She could only allow herself to be supported and drawn along.

## CHAPTER FIVE

# Unknown Land South of Var

Those who had come hunting were gone and yet Destree had not tried as yet to free herself from the clasp of this alien out of another world. She could smell the fear emanating from its haired body and did what she could to remain quiet, to use some manner of self-control to ease the other's panic. But her head still spun from that fearsome chaotic blast of magic, and her sight seemed blurred as if she saw not the familiar things about her but their images double-edged.

A black shape came in bounds across the charred ground where the creature had been cornered amid rocks. Chief reared on his hind legs and caught at the edge of her jerkin. His jaws parted as if he howled some war song, but the girl heard nothing.

However, his coming broke the spell. She brought her own hand up to lay upon the wide, heavily muscled arm which had engulfed her when Foss had been about to loose arrow. Slowly she drew fingers through the wiry fur-hair, projecting with all her might that talent which Gunnora had fostered and trained, even as she spoke aloud—though this strayer from nowhere could not hope to understand.

"All is well—there is no fear." *At least not for now*, her thoughts added. "They have gone."

She continued that slow stroking. The grasp on her loosened. Destree looked over her shoulder, tilting her head back to get better sight of the creature's features.

They bore some resemblance to human. There were deep-set eyes now fast upon her, yellow-green, with pupils so large as to occupy all visible space. The nose was broad, with cavities of nostrils which were flushed red within. The jaw jutted forward, wide and heavy. But when one studied the stranger carefully and slowly, the thought of *monster* faded away. Though she who had tasted of its thoughts knew that this was no beast but another sentient species.

Thick lips opened, to be caressed by a thick, purplish tongue. The arm which she touched turned in her grasp and now caught her wrist in a grip Destree tensed herself not to attempt to break.

Her captor for the present drew her hand up to those wide-arching nostrils and sniffed. Out shot the tongue again and touched her sweat-coated skin. But Destree, sure of her Lady's hand in this, did not try to loose herself.

The great head bowed and then her hand was borne still farther upward until the lips nuzzled her flesh as lightly as a floating petal might have drifted on it. Dropping its hold, Gruck stepped back. There was no question now in the girl's mind that this weird stranger believed her a friend.

However, she doubted greatly that anyone else in the valley would see it except as a menace to be destroyed. Gunnora had sent her to ensure its safekeeping; if it meant trouble for her, then she must accept that. Had she not in her time been such an outcast that she had been spat after when she walked port streets, and judged beyond all protests Dark-shadowed?

"Gruck?" she said. It drew back from her a step or so. Against the dark pelt a wide golden belt glistened in the sun now bearing down upon them.

That did service as more than a simple strap, the girl saw. Thrust through attached loops were a medley of artifacts, two at least which bore a very strong resemblance to knives. A plump pouch rode against the middle of the belly.

The workmanship, she believed, even though she could not examine the belt and equipment closely, was certainly not that of any barbaric civilization but fashioned by a people well used to tools.

"Gruck?" If she could awaken some vocal response from the stranger, perhaps she could learn from whence it had come. Destree had never heard of any gate traveler who had returned to its world. However, her knowledge of such was very limited and, without proof, how could she just accept that this poor lost creature might not be sent back to its proper place? But first she must find where it had made its entry.

It held its head cocked a little to one side now, its measuring gaze still centered on her. Chief advanced past her to stand directly before it.

His up-bannered tail moved slowly, but there was no ridging of fur, nor laid-back ears, no hissing or snarling. The stranger suddenly stooped and one of those huge large-fingered hands caught up the cat. Destree started forward—remembering the dead sheep, the slaughtered hounds. Then she saw that Chief was cradled in both hands, being raised to exchange stares on the level with Gruck.

For what seemed a time out of time itself, so caught up was she in that confrontation, Destree watched. Deep in her mind she felt the stirring, not clear as when the Lady would speak, but rather a tantalizing, teasing flutter. She bent what powers she had to touch that communication, to share in what Gruck and Chief had found as a mutual meeting—but it was not within the grasp of her talent.

At length Chief gave a soft mew and the stranger set him carefully down. Now Destree was growing uneasy. Foss and the rest had been scattered by the pummel of that power out of nowhere, but perhaps not so frightened that their fear of this place would last long. They would be the more determined to turn on what they could see and understand, after a fashion: this alien monster. And she remembered Foss's warning. For all her place as healer and Voice, she would not be able to put an end to a second hunting.

"Chief." She summoned the cat and he came to her. Valiantly she began to build a mind-picture. Over the year and months she had been here, this had been a daily exercise, and one in which the cat seemed eager to indulge.

Now she built up, solidified, and sharpened in thought as well as she could the outline of a door, using the portal of the shrine as a pattern. Once she was satisfied with that, she put Gruck on the other side and brought the alien through. Three times she repeated that mental exercise. Chief had watched her unblinkingly, but now Gruck moved. Once more that mighty arm swung out and caught her wrist. Now the great head swung from side to side, the nostrils quivered as if searching for some scent.

It—he—she understood? Destree gave thanks to the Lady in quick thought. Gruck was already moving eastward, drawing her after him, and she did not struggle to free herself.

They kept to the higher reaches which walled the valley, wending a way among the trees which had escaped the fire of the past. At intervals all sense of purpose was taken out of her hands while Gruck and the cat had one of their periods of silent communication. It was as if the stranger depended on some sense of Chief's for general direction.

They rounded the edge of one of the sloping mountain meadows. No sheep grazed here today and she was sure that all flocks were safely pent in paddocks below. Gruck seemed tireless and Destree was glad of the long tramps she had taken in the past to hunt certain herbs and flowers to the Lady's need.

At last they rounded the bole of a huge tree, one of the forest giants which could awe men. Beyond, a thicket had been visibly torn apart, the wilting limbs of lower growth crushed and splintered. It might even have been the site of a scrimmage. Was it here that Gruck had killed the great hound?

But her furred guide now stopped to pull and hurl from their way the debris. And, within a few strides, the stranger stopped short. It turned once more to face her, flinging its arms in a gesture which engulfed the whole of this denuded clearing.

Cautiously Destree advanced. The thick underbrush must have been attacked by Gruck on his arrival here—her thoughts sorted that out. However, there were no standing pillars as she had learned from those of Estcarp and Escore usually marked such a site. Instead there was only a block of dull blue stone, its surface cut with a pattern which was so filled with earth and worn away that only her sight, trained to keenness by herb search, could distinguish it at all.

Gruck took a stride forward, hurling away a last tangle of uprooted brush, to take a firm stand upon that stone. Then those great eyes were filled with entreaty as they turned to Destree.

She pulled loose some of the splintered growth and went to her knees, her hands spread palms-down on the edge of the stone only inches away from those huge pawlike feet.

"Lady!" she made her plea. She was sure that if there was any way this alien could return to whence it had come surely the Lady in Her pity would allow it.

But there was nothing of the feel of Power here—nothing but the grit of soil and stone under her seeking hands. This could be any rock of the mountainside, never put to any other use. Perhaps—perhaps the transportation of Gruck had exhausted all the Power which it had once held. She knew that all the gates known worked erratically. Sometimes they slumbered for years. Sometimes they awoke, to the peril of this world—as when the Kolders marched with death—or to the despair of others from alien worlds who were jerked through and made prisoners, of sorts. Destree felt a piercing memory of one such prisoner and her fate. That one had sealed the gate, that it could harvest no more from the sea—there would be no more dead ships in that port now.

Destree crouched, staring down at the rock, her hands still flat on the lifeless stone. How could she explain to Gruck that there was no return?

Her present problem was one of communication. There was no way she could make clear to this alien what had happened. Such complicated explanations could not be shifted through Chief. She lacked the Power. . . . The Power!

The only hope now was the shrine. If Gunnora chose to break the barrier between them, Destree had no doubt it would go down. But the shrine lay on the border of the valley—it was often visited. And, perhaps because of her interference, Foss and his fellow hunters might already be laying an ambush there. Or could they— where the Lady held Her beneficent rule? She could only hope that the shrine was safe for her purpose, for her need of what she might be able to learn there drew her like a hound's leash about her throat.

There was movement beside her. That massive hairy form had also gone to its knees, facing her across the stone. Now its hands reached out to copy the position of hers, while the large eyes demanded some answer from her.

She found herself speaking, though she was sure the creature could not begin to understand her words.

"The Power is gone." Now she tried to build a mind-picture of a nearly dead fire as the last of its core ashed gray.

The large mouth before her opened and sounds which were so deep that they seemed to come from that barrel of a chest answered her. Though the creature could not comprehend any words she knew, Gruck understood.

Big hands left the stone to hook over the powerful knees; the body rocked slowly back and forth and that deep cry became a kind of desolate keening.

Impulsively Destree raised her own hands to place one on each of those haired fists. "Lady," she prayed silently, "give me now of Thy Power. This is a living creature caught in a dark web of unknowing. May your Will come to its aid!"

And she strove with all her might to summon all of her slowly awakening talent, all she had learned at the shrine, to carry the comfort which had swelled high within her.

Chief pressed against her side, with a small throaty sound. Then

Gruck's massive head arose a little. One paw and then the other rose from those knees, each bearing her hand, and the tip of tongue touched lightly against her skin.

Chief turned, looking up at her, uttering that sound of impatience which meant to follow—even as he had at times led her to some suffering beast.

She and Gruck arose almost together. The cat was already half into the welter of broken branches. Daring, Destree again reached for this stranger, caught the thick wrist, and nodded in the direction the cat was taking.

To her delight that head nodded back. In so little she had managed to establish a very small tie of understanding between them.

Chief had his own ways of forest travel, but today he did not seek out those brush tunnels, rather wove back and forth in directions which offered few obstacles.

Destree was constantly alert for any sound of baying hound. Perhaps the villages had not yet recovered from that giant stroke of Power which was far from any knowledge she herself held. Luckily the shrine was apart from the rest of the settlement. (It was, she had early discovered, far older than the settlement, for the first of the northern refugees who had wandered into this fertile land had found it and left it strictly alone, having no reason to trust any work of an older day.)

However, she signaled Gruck to wait in hiding while she surveyed not only the shrine but its immediate surroundings. Foss was a man of skill and an ambush might well be his first thought now.

But all seemed as it had been when the Lady had first brought her here, wearied and bewildered by doing battle with that evil in the Port of Dead Ships. Now to its peace and safety she beckoned this stranger. For all the size and weight of that massive body, Gruck moved with a kind of fluid ability which in the past she had noted among the Sulcar traders, the Borderers ever alert for trouble. She did not doubt that this creature had many skills—perhaps some she could not dream of.

Gruck showed no fear or wariness after stopping just at the end of the small meadow to sniff the air. Then the paw-feet joined hers on the steps to the portico and she brought her strange visitor into the outer chamber.

Chief went to stand on his hind legs and swing a paw at the pot that stood ready to swing over the smoldering fire. She realized that it was indeed well past noon, and if the cat was hungry so was she, and so, perhaps, their new guest.

Gruck had retreated to one end of the room and stood watching her as she busied herself adding to the portion of last night's stew and bringing out a round of the coarse bread Josephinia had left on her visit. Sawing off a hefty slice of this, she offered it to the guest, and a few moments later saw those powerful jaws chomping away on the offering.

The dark yellow cheese seemed to be relished also and the bowl of the reheated stew was eagerly reached for. Destree had put a spoon into that, wanting to know what utensils might be shared between them. It was promptly put to its proper usage.

Last of all she drew from the small cask under the far cupboard a tankard of herb-infused ale. This could be used, as she had learned long since, to relax the body, open the mind. It worked well with those of her species. Now she was daring to try it—as if it might prove a key to unlock that mind-barrier between them.

Resolutely she nodded to Chief. Well fed and now washing a paw, he withdrew to the outer door, ready to play guard as he had before when she herself had gone mind-roving. With a tankard in one hand, she held out the other to Gruck.

Wide eyes fastened on her. Perhaps it would be refused, but she knew no other way she might hope to accomplish what she knew must be done if this stranger—and maybe she herself—were to survive.

Furry fingers closed about the tankard at last. The alien stood so tall that the massive head nearly brushed the lintel of the inner door as she urged him forward. To Destree's relief and inner joy, the light from the walls glowed brighter—the blue of summer sky, the brown of earth awaiting seed, the green of that which would come of such seeding. She drew a deep breath. Once before she had been welcomed so—on the first day she had found the shrine and dared to enter its sacred heart.

From beside her came a soft hum. Gruck held forth a paw and watched the color play across it. Destree drew her charge yet further in. They reached the lounge bed before the shrine. She motioned to that, seated herself in example.

The huge body settled beside hers. Raising the tankard, she drank three mouthfuls, enough to half-empty it. Then she nodded to the one her companion held. There was no hesitation, Gruck drank, but those strange eyes were now fastened on the altar before them.

More and more the colors spun about them, but there was no sense of vertigo, of being caught up in something which would threaten body or spirit.

Warmth, an out flowing of welcome, of peace.

Then the stirring in her mind—*Goddess* touch? Perhaps, but secondhand. This was not threatening, but it was very different. This time that strange thought-touch came without any fear or pain to distort it.

*No hurt.* Those were not her words, nor any message of Gunnora's. Destree knew too well the aura of those.

Then more slowly, *Go—go back?*

A question. One she could not answer as she wished.

"A gate"—she began to form her own words—"open—shut—not open—Power gone."

There was a feeling of withdrawal, of an empty space.

Then: *Gruck must stay—here!*—The latter part of that was a desolate cry, though it came by thought, not lips.

"Yes . . ." her feeling of peace was gone, torn asunder by what she had to say.

The feeling that she must speed on, break into that despair, struck her forcibly.

"This is the shrine of Gunnora: I am Her Voice." Destree was not really aware that she was speaking her thoughts aloud now. "She sent me to aid you, for all living creatures of the Light are dear to Her. And Her Hand is over you and will hold you so."

Now the mind-touch seemed to twist in his head as if someone fumbled to enter a key into an unknown lock.

*I am Gruck.* The pattern was rough at first and then grew more smooth. A laborer might be learning the way of a new tool. *I am—* there was hesitation and then the exchange continued, *one who walks the woods, and tends the beasts of the Alatar. Second guardsman of the west.*

A paw-hand stirred and went to his belt as if to assure him that that much remained of the past.

*I found a strange stone—light shone from it—when I touched it.* He was making a supreme effort now to control that time of panic that she now experienced with him, in part. *There was first black nothingness and then there was HERE! I hungered for I could find no proper food and—and I killed—but without pain.* The hand on his belt moved to touch a rod looped to it. *There came another beast— one like one red-minded—and that I had to kill with these.* He held out his hands. *For I could not mind-touch it and it was akin to those beasts who are mad with the coming of deep summer.*

"To defend oneself," Destree returned carefully, "is no crime. If you had done evil you would not sit here now at the very heart of Gunnora's place."

*To those who hunted, to you—I am so different of body that you see me as—*

Destree's mind shuddered away from a smudged picture of something indeed so monstrous that she could not believe such lived—save in the very fortress of the Dark itself.

"No!" she was quick to protest. "But, Guardsman Gruck, this I cannot hide from you: There is but one village of people in this valley. They are very simple folk, but long ago their kind were hunted by monsters and so they fled south. They remember the tales of the old days."

His mind-touch was growing ever stronger and clearer. *So I am such a monster returned to harry them? Their hunting will not cease?*

Destree sighed. So had her thoughts already turned. Foss would be out and there would be killing, for she did not expect Gruck to surrender his life without battle. But if there was to be no battle?

She could not stand between the valley and the stranger. Already Foss had warned her that any influence she might have had, had waned. Nor could she expect Gunnora's active aid. What she had now, communication with the refugee, was a mighty gift. But Gunnora was not a warwoman—all her Powers were of peace.

Therefore—there was but one answer. Gruck must go, get as far away from this valley as he could travel. Only . . . where?

To the west lay wasteland and the sea. But to the northeast there was rumored a land in which the Old Ones still lived, and others with them perhaps as strange in their ways as Gruck. Thus he might find welcome there.

But—Destree closed her eyes and felt the drag of great sorrow and loss—he could not go alone. All she had sought to find here, the little she had done in the name of the Light, was that to be extinguished? Death trod many trails in this land; she had skirted such before she reached this haven. Yet it was Gunnora's will which had sent her to Gruck, and therefore she was left no choice.

*I am one who knows the woodland,* he cut into her dreary thoughts. *I can find a place, for where there are forests to guard, then it would be as always.* His head was up and he was staring again at the altar. Then he was silent.

But Destree felt it filling her, also, that outreaching which was all-encroaching. And she had known that urge from old. It had been that which brought her from the desolation of the Port of Dead Ships to this very shrine.

"There is a reason," she said slowly, wanting to deny acceptance and knowing that she could not.

*In my world*—Gruck again touched his belt—*there are certain orders laid upon one. Alatar says, "Go you there, let this be done," and so it is. Nor can one turn aside from duty. I think, you who call yourself Voice, that this Lady Gunnora has already extended a blessing to me, a stranger not of Her following, so that now I am to be sped as if by the Alatar to something which must be done.*

Slowly Destree nodded. She had held fiercely to her strength for many years, standing up to foul usage and facing down strong evil.

For the first time since she was a small girl she felt the smart of tears in her eyes, drops flooding upon her cheeks.

"We go." Again she spoke, with voice as well as mind, and those two words might have been a blood oath offered before one took up shield and sword. "Now—there is much to be done. I do not know how long those of the village will wait before they seek the shrine. We must be gone before they come. I cannot defame the Lady by any struggle in Her own place."

She was wondering whether their communication would fail once they were away from the inner shrine, but it seemed that this gift would last. Gruck first watched her and then helped her make up packs. Herbs for healing, and the ones for clearing the mind should she be allowed to call upon the Lady. There was a thick cloak and two hide packs she had put together to use when exploring.

But save for her belt knife there was no weapon, and for the first time in years she wanted the feel of a sword hilt, the weight of a blade.

Gruck insisted on the larger pack being put together with twice as much in it as his own burden. The girl found herself explaining, as she selected and bagged, the reason for this or that being added to their store. Between times he watched the baking of journey cakes, for which she recklessly used the last of her meal and all the dried berries and nuts of the former season.

It would soon be dusk. She dared not show a light, lest they were already spied upon by Foss and his hunters. But Chief kept trotting out at intervals, slipping as a black shadow through any cover available and always returning with reassurance.

The dark of night would serve them. Her efforts at preparing for their leaving had left her tired, but they must put as much space between them and the village as they could. And Gruck agreed with her. She had treated the wound in his arm, finding it already nearly closed, and he seemed not to feel any stiffness there.

Then came night and for the last time Destree went, this time alone, into the inner shrine:

"Give us fortune, for we shall serve You as best we can," she said slowly. "I know that I am not only Your Voice but now Your hand also and I have a task before me. But—Lady, when all is well again . . . let Your peace be with me."

She stood with bowed head and it was as if a hand touched for a blessed moment the tight braids of her hair.

## CHAPTER SIX

# Karsten Southward

Liara held her eyes stubbornly to the fore and refused to glance backward. After the exhausting struggle through the broken lands, they had gained the holding of the Lady Eleeri, a place which fairly breathed the threat of magic at one, or so Liara held to that thought.

The keep in which they had sheltered to rest and regather supplies was fully as impressive as Krevanel itself—but held none of the grayness of spirit she had so often known in her own suite of chambers there. Light seemed to cling and clothe its walls as the days remained fair and the weather favored them.

Three separate herds grazed in the wide, rich green of the valley. But none of any one herd strayed into territory which was claimed by another. The Keplians were utterly free.

Time and again the stallion Hylan would come into the courtyard and the Lady Eleeri, as if summoned, would be ready to meet him there. That they communicated by mind Liara was well aware, but such talent was not hers, nor did she seek it. It was difficult enough to hold to her belief in herself among those of her own species, for none of her traveling companions awoke in her any desire to know them better.

Having had his conference with Eleeri, the stallion would leave, not only the keep but also the valley. And each time he returned it was not alone. Once he teamed with a mare who bore a crusted slash down her shoulder and nosed ahead of her a foal who stumbled and wavered. Eleeri was already waiting—as if her speech with Hylan could traverse miles. With her was Mouse who ran lightly forward to aid the colt. Hylan's second disappearance was longer and he came back alone. This time there was blood on his own forelegs and one could almost feel the heat of anger which steamed from him.

"Gray Ones," Denever reported that night as they shared out supplies around the great hall table. "They are usually trailers, ready to pull down stragglers. Why do they prowl about now?"

"An excellent question," Lord Romar returned. He had finished his food early and pushed aside his plate. Now he had spread out fanwise on the board before him half a dozen knives, plain as to hilt, but with the blue-green sheen of blade which meant quan iron—that legacy of the Old Ones which was rarer than any gem Liara had heard of.

For this keep was not only the holding of his Lady's claiming, but also held secret stores which delighted the fighters now made free of them. There was a quan mail shirt for most of them—though Liara had refused to take that offered. She was caught in a web of magic; she had no mind to become so entangled that the person who was Liara would cease to be.

"Yes, the Gray Ones nose closely," said Krispin, the Falconer. On his wrist perched Farwing, whom he had been feeding bits from his own place. "Also, their number grows."

"They were the servants of the Black Tower once." Eleeri had taken one of the knives from her mate's collection and was running a finger up and down as if trying so to test its edge. "The tower and he who held it are gone." There was a stillness about her face as if she were remembering only too well something which had struck close to the heart. "Who or what calls them now?"

Mouse sat still, her jewel between her hands. When she looked up, her gaze traveled from face to face about the board. They were clear enough to see in the golden light of the lamps.

"They are drawn . . ." she said.

"By what we plan to do?" Keris demanded, shifting in his seat. He could never doubt the statement of any witch, young or old, but they were far too apt to speak obscurely.

"Perhaps," was the only answer Mouse offered him.

"It is well maybe that we move out soon," Denever said. "If they seek to set a cork to bottle us up here, of what value will a full fight be? Your—your liege—Hylan"—perhaps he, too, found it difficult to accept the Keplian as a full member of their party—"can he say whence these come?"

"Always," Lord Romar answered, "they roam. Not long since, this was their territory. Perhaps they seek to make it so again. But this time they have no Dark lord to give them aid. However, you are right. We have found two gates and mapped them—that through which my dear Lady came, and that water-washed one which Lady Mouse assures us is now and has been a long time inactive. How many lie before us—who can tell?"

Liara felt strangely fatigued, as if somehow the light of the lamps on the quan iron blades had drawn from her some of her energy. She had a full day behind her and, if they marched, a number of aching, burning strides out into the unknown tomorrow.

A hand touched her shoulder and she flinched. Why she had given such a reaction to so light a contact, she could not have told. But it had seemed for an instant that some dangerous shadow slipping by had wafted against her.

The witchling? She still gripped her jewel and Liara could see the power in it was awake or waking, for the light shone between her fingers.

"Sister in the Light." Mouse's voice was hardly more than a whisper, well covered by the sounds of those about them rising and discussing what must be done before they moved. "You have been sadly plundered of what was yours to have. But hold this ever in mind: That which is born to the Light cannot be taken—unless it turns willingly into the darker path. And you will *not*!" Mouse's last word was as emphatic as an order. Then she was gone, leaving Liara, muddle-thoughted, behind her.

She was busied enough the next morning to keep under control questions and the general uneasiness which she was unable to throw off. Though they had now traveled with the party for a goodly length of time, the ponies were as uncontrollable as ever and she must stand by the head of each, keeping it steady, while its load was lashed in place securely enough to stand all tests of a rough trail ahead.

A third Keplian now joined them. Romar told the party, "Hylan is our guard marshal, and this land lies under his protection. Thus he cannot be one of us as he wishes. But the mare Sebra, who is this season barren, joins us at her desire."

They were over the border of Karsten and now they wound toward the southwest. To the east lay the end lands of Escore and there was another party searching there. The Falconers and the Borderers scouted ahead with greater care, for they had entered halfway through their second day afield a countryside which had been mauled and torn by warring. Liara had heard enough to know that after the Turning, when Duke Pagan and all his forces had been swallowed up, this countryside had been ravaged and fought over by outlaws and small lords quarreling for some advantage over their fellows.

For the first time, while she viewed the charred stone of burned out holds, saw unsown fields, with here and there the yellowed bones of a draft animal—or perhaps even a man—Liara realized this is what Alizon might come to with its eternal intrigues and assassinations, its gobbling up of lesser enemies by the greater. She had never before questioned the way of life she had been born into. It was enough to try to see ahead what she could do for her own safety and that of her line. Suddenly she wished that Kasarian rode with her on this trail. She still did not know what ploy her littermate was engaged in, but that he held some touch with Lormt, with the Lady Mereth, there was no denial. Was Kasarian also hunting a gate? The two she had seen so far—a pillar wind-bitten and moss-covered, and then a quiet pond, its waters so clear one could see no sand at the bottom, but rather a stretch of blue-gray rock—were not impressive in themselves.

The travelers were well armed and they rode taking every precaution they could against surprise. She had tried their dart guns but was far from a good shot. Swords were not part of the schooling of a Hearthmistress of Alizon—but knives, now . . . She hugged her right arm against her for a moment and felt the quan iron with its tepid warmth—the blade never appeared to grow as cold as true steel— against her forearm. There were two more in her belt; one rode within the collar of her jerkin between her shoulders, the other in her boot. With these there were few who could match her.

They camped that night in a shatter of ruins that had no cover nearby, so that nothing could steal upon them unawares. Mouse made her report to Gull, though no spoken word was to be heard. Then she informed the others that the sites of four gates had been located within Estcarp but none of them appeared to retain any power. It might well be that the destruction of the Magestone had indeed sealed them all. Yet who could be sure?

Liara shared the rotation of the guard, and by the stars she thought it might be near midnight when she caught that whiff of scent out of the night. Unlike the stench of that thing of the crevice, this had a familiar odor, one which something in her found exciting.

Memory clicked and she was back with Lord Volorian, trotting behind his burly body, trying to keep up as well as listen properly to the stream of knowledge he was half growling at her. Volorian's kennels were famed throughout Alizon. Pups whelped there brought fabulous sums—if they were sold at all. Almost she could feel now the fur on some small, plump, squirming body, hear the rough purr answering to the proper scratching behind the ears.

But—there were no hounds! Liara stiffened; her hand slipped, bringing sleeve knife into her grasp. Perhaps, she tried to assure herself, there were hounds from the destroyed manors and keeps they had seen, gone feral in a pack, interbreeding and managing to live off the land.

She listened with all her might, hearing the scrape of a thick iron-studded boot sole at the next post. Hounds did not hunt silently unless that was brutally enforced by some huntsman. But more and more she believed that somewhere, not too far away, a pack of four-footed danger drew in upon them.

Hound scent? She had as noiselessly as possible shifted her position to face in the direction in which she believed that advance lay. There was a full moon tonight and the open land about the ruin was open to see.

Hound scent? She drew that smell more deeply into her nose and then saw a quiver of shadow advance from a copse of trees well away. Those were no hounds!

Instantly she was alert. She had never seen a live Gray One—and the two bodies she had viewed had been more manlike than dog. But Liara knew what came. And even as she was about to shout an alarm, the enemy struck—with a weapon she had not been expecting—directly at her.

The warning choked off in her throat as she found herself frozen, unable to move hand or foot, and with a weight pressing against her breast as if to forbid her free breath. In the meadow before her, the moonlight seemed to thicken as if some power drew upon it to produce a form.

Liara gasped for breath and gasped again. What stood there? The form of the thing was clearly that of a female, for its silver height was unclothed, but the head—white, sharp-snouted, with red ears, not folded as usual back against the skull, but standing erect as when the hunt was launched.

It was out of a nightmare—but no nightmare she had ever heard of before—a foul mixture which had nothing to do with the will of nature.

Nausea arose within her. Yet somehow her will awoke. There had been no call, no sound which even she could hear. But that—that loathsome character strove to draw her toward it—beckoned her as if in her innermost part there was a likeness, a kinship— NO!

Liara was no longer aware of anything except that thing in the meadow, that which summoned. Around her, fouling her lungs as she breathed, was the thick smell of kennels. The thing's blazing eyes caught hers and held; the form standing there appeared to grow, taller, more solid, more powerful.

*Come—blood to blood—come*, the order continued. While that treacherous part of her own unknown inner self was drawn, it was sharp pain which broke that fast-woven spell. She felt the bite of metal in her flesh.

And straightaway, before the thing could tighten its invisible cords on her again, Liara's own hand moved. She threw her sleeve knife.

She saw the hound-woman raise clawed paws to her throat and then stagger back, then crumple down. Liara whimpered and staggered in turn, until her shoulder thumped forcibly against what had once been the wall of a watch tower. Pain held her in its fist—even as if that knife had entered her own throat.

Through watering eyes she saw the limp white body in the grass. The brilliance of the silver which had made it so visible was fading, just as the smoothness of the flesh vanished. The thing was still female, but the hound head was gone—only a skull thatched with grizzled hair remained.

Liara was able to pull herself straighter—the pain had faded. She could hear shouting and saw a wave of more just such hairy bodies ripple forward.

Nor did the cries of alarm come from one direction only; she was dimly aware that they also sounded from behind. The camp in the ruins must be beset by more than one party.

They were attacked by such a wave of Gray Ones as none in that refuge had ever seen drawn together before. Only the moonlight was their friend; had the sky been clouded, the fierce determination of those without might well have won them a way within.

Of this Liara was barely aware. Since her knife had taken the hound-woman, her arm flopped by her side, so weighted that it might be encased in the stone of the walls. She coughed and coughed again, tasting blood which she spat away.

Keris set a second clip into his dart gun. At least this was one weapon with which he could truly claim expertise. He continually blinked his eyes, trying to ease a smarting which had struck them at the rise of that white pillar of light just before the attack broke. Liara had been fronting that pillar and he was not sure what she had done, but he guessed that she was responsible for its vanishing.

There was another figure up on the wall where Liara had earlier stood and he heard the voice of the Lady Eleeri raised in what could only be a war cry. She was using her bow with the skill he had often seen demonstrated in the arms court, and he was sure that very few of those arrows missed their marks.

Still the waves of Gray Ones came as if maddened past all thought of self-preservation. There followed the high-screamed challenge of a stallion encountering traditional foes, and from the arched entrance below broke the Keplians. One watching them now could well believe in the tales of their devil blood.

Even as a warhorse might be trained to rear and so bring down any footman menacing his rider, so did the mare Theela and the colt stamp death, rip and toss bodies aside.

Then was a breathing space when no new forces came out of the distant woodland. The Keplians made a round of the bodies, once or twice raising a razor-sharp hoof to snap out a flicker of life. However, when they approached that crumpled figure Liara had confronted, they circled it at a distance, their heads down as if they sniffed deeply at what lay there. Then Theela swerved to head for the ruins, her companions behind her.

"Liara?" Though the voice was low, it cut easily through the fog surrounding the girl which had led her to believe she was no longer any part of those who fought here.

Light, brilliant—blue—searing her eyes. She could not lift her deadened arm to shade them. The shine of the hound-head had been almost as strong.

She could not even see who stood behind that mighty lamp, but the voice she knew. The witchling.

At that moment it was as if someone had unveiled a secret for her viewing and she shrank back again against the stone. There was that in her . . . she held a taint which those—those things of the dark could sense, could call—

"They called." The brilliant light still held her fast. "But did you answer?"

Life was returning to her arm, she was able to bring her hand up to her trembling lips.

"I did not then . . . know—"

"Do not hold yourself at fault." Mouse's soft voice was serene. "If you drew them, then also their purpose was betrayed when you brought down their bait. And that very bait alerted our watchers."

"Hound . . ." Liara murmured through stiff lips then. "*We* are the Hounds of Alizon, not merely the packs we raise. And those packs have been used for Dark purposes." She shivered. Though no female had watched an Ordered Feeding, yet the details of such were as known to all as clear as crystal in a collar.. "Your people say I am not of the Dark, but if there is in me that which can draw something searchers want . . ."

Her thoughts were flying very fast now, seeming like a stream of orders shouted in her ears. "If that be so . . . then I have no place with you."

"If you were of the Dark, Lady Liara, then death would have been your portion as you stand here. We are all fashioned by those of our blood gone before, but it is the choices that we ourselves make which can change the weaving patterns."

The light no longer tortured her eyes. Now the Lady Eleeri came to her, still holding her bow.

"This was an attack planned by hate but not by true knowledge. If they believed that they could win through our defenses by the tricks of a half-taught Shaman, then they are the less to be feared. Had they waited—"

But Liara had already caught the logic behind that.

"Waited until we were strung out on the trail, until I was behind with the ponies. Yes, then they would have had their victory."

"Never." The radiance from Mouse's jewel had faded, revealing her as she stood behind the wall of its brilliance. "For I say they believed you to be the way to us and you are not. Nor can you ever be—unless"—she spoke more slowly now—"you allow yourself to doubt, to seek shadow and turn aside from Light."

"How can you be sure," Liara asked, "that I will not?"

They had given her trust, these enemies of old, and she feared trust, feared it because among her own it never held. However, outwardly she accepted for the present Mouse's assurance, though her mind was busy untangling tormenting thoughts.

She did not sleep for the rest of the night, though she lay quiet among her blankets. This quest of theirs—gates upon gates—what had it really to do with her?

That she might ever return to her own place—no. She had been forcibly barred from Krevanel by Kasarian's action. There was no place for her at Lormt, even if she were to turn back, and if she remained among these she had come to accept she might well once more be used against them.

Hound . . . Whenever she closed her eyes now she could see that silver body and the hound-head. She had never heard any tales among her people of such an unnatural creature. But what if that was what Alizonderns were inside? Had they so absorbed the inner natures of their prized, four-footed companions that that was how they would appear to an eye which could truly see—a mixture of human and beast? All those days she had spent with Volorian, her pride that he shared knowledge with her . . . had that time strengthened that taint they did not realize they possessed?

She kept much to herself with the morning and she was busy, for the ponies were unusually unruly. Perhaps the scent of the dead bodies beyond the wall reached them. Secretly she plundered one of the packs, setting aside a packet of journey cakes. Bow and arrows were not her weapon, nor could she help herself to such without it being instantly noted. She still had three of her four throwing knives, and a short sword she had used mainly to hack paths through thorn brush when necessary.

When had she ever had anyone who really cared what became of her? In Alizon she had filled a need and done her duty well enough that those of Krevanel seemed to find her well qualified. Her help with the ponies—that would weigh a little against a second attack of the Gray Ones.

Morning mist became rain and they all turned the hoods of their cloaks up over their heads. But no one suggested that they try to wait out the storm, for Mouse had announced, before the downpour had become too heavy, that there were indications of gate Power somewhere ahead.

Trees gave way to tough grass and clumps of brush, and that in turn to a stretch of gravel in which were upstanding stones set in the general confusion of a forest grove. The ponies had to be prodded into keeping up with the party and then seemed to decide on their own that they were better served by company.

Liara dropped back, as was the usual way if one answered a call of nature and slipped around one of the tree stones, waiting until rear of the Borderers rode by.

Then, shouldering the very small pack which was all she allowed herself, she skulked from outcrop to outcrop away from the plodding party, not knowing or caring now in what direction she headed.

Keris was surprised when one of the pack ponies crowded up beside Jasta. The small beasts usually kept their distance from the mounts of the rest of the party. He glanced back to see that the lead animal closely followed by the rest, yet there was no sign of Liara on her tough mount and she usually kept carefully close to her charges.

*She is gone.*

He started at the Renthan's mind-message. Since the happenings of the night before, his once-vague suspicions of the Alizondern girl had reawakened. Then he had held the next post in line with hers and had seen a strange pillar of light arise facing where she stood. His forehead creased in a frown. It had been as if some fleeting breaths of time had been rift from him and he remembered nothing clearly until the light was overthrown to the ground and he was busied picking off those slavering Dark ones who attacked so oddly without any cover as if they had expected to find the defenders asleep.

He had been with Krispin and the Lord Romar when they had ridden forth, with the addition of the young Keplian stallion, to survey the bodies after the battle. And his ranging had brought him close to where that light pillar had been rooted. Something had shone in the grass and he dismounted.

There was a dead Gray One, of course, a female and larger than any he had ever sighted in all the years they had warred upon such in Escore.

Oddly enough, the bristled face turned up to the light was layered with what appeared to be white paint. And as he stooped to see the closer, he could distinguish flat pieces of stiff red stuff fastened to either side of the skull as if to mimic ears. In the creature's throat was a knife buried near to its hilt, not quite far enough to hide its quan iron blade. And he had seen that knife hurled many times over in the arms court at Lormt, always thudding exactly in the center of the target. That was Liara's. He tugged it loose and rammed the blade several times into the ground to clean it. Odd she did not come to claim it herself; such knives were too valuable to be left lying, even in bodies.

They had been so busied breaking camp that he had forgotten his find and it was only now, when he could not sight the Alizondern girl and Jasta said she was gone, that he remembered.

"Gone—where?" For a moment he felt a sharp flash of fear. Even though the Falconer and one of the Borderers kept guard, this place of many stones offered excellent chance for an ambush.

*To follow her own trail,* the Renthan returned.

"To betray." Keris was not altogether sure he meant that.

*To give us freedom from what she fears the most.* Nor for all Keris's urging would Jasta elaborate on that.

## CHAPTER SEVEN

# Karsten, Southeast of Var

It had been raining, the heavy endless rain which soaked one's garments to the skin, but the land seemed to welcome such a burden of endless drops. Meadow grass gave way to tangles of vines, which appeared to carpet the ground instead of searching for any tree or rock which could bear them aloft. Here and there, sheltered by the larger leaves were huge scarlet flowers which gave forth a cloying perfume and were shaped, Liara thought as she struggled along, not unlike the stripped skulls of shriekers tossed aside after the great day of annual slaughter. But there was nothing else here to remind her of her homeland. She knew that she was entirely lost.

Yet twice fortune had favored her. The first time she had been warned by keen hearing to take cover as a troop trotted by on the remains of a road which had not been kept up for many years. They were huddled in cloaks, those who had them; the rest wore blankets, odds and ends of hides, pulled around their shoulders.

They were not of the Old Race, but a mongrel lot, and from the saddle horn of the leader bobbed the severed head of a woman, anchored so by twisted hair. They were southerners such as she had always heard them described—yet she had certainly seen none of their like in Lormt.

Her next caution that this was not deserted land had come with a heavy rise of smoke. She had hidden out for nearly half a day, her now too slim body pressed to the ground, staring down at a keep which had clearly fallen to attack. She was thankful she was so far away that she could not hear or see clearly what happened there. The troop which seemed to have taken the small stronghold might be better armed and disciplined, but its soldiers, she was sure, were no different from those brutes she had earlier seen.

The keep had fallen, but perhaps there were some who escaped and those mailed riders below might sweep the fields around to make sure of their prey. Liara edged back as well as she could, pulling over and around her the well-leaved branches of a sturdy mat of brush.

At least she could sight no hounds to be set on the trail of fugitives. These southerners apparently never depended on such. She let her head fall wearily back against a tree trunk centering the cover she had chosen.

Her fingers were on her belt. Five days since she had left the party from Lormt. If they had come seeking her . . . But why should they? She had been set among them by necessity, not choice. And time drove them. They would have no time to hunt for her and still cover the ground assigned them—already far too large a stretch for so small a party. Briefly she wondered what kind of a gate Mouse's jewel had found within that strange place of stone pillar-trees. Not that it mattered.

She rummaged in her small pack and brought out the forelegs of a ground-hopping creature she had knocked over with a stone at dusk the night before. Her knives Liara dared not risk, but she had discovered that her wrist skills, honed by practice with the knives, could also hurl stones to advantage. The meat had only been partially seared by the handful of fire she had dared to light and had kept going only for a short time. It smelled rank and tasted worse, but she chewed and swallowed doggedly.

That which she had feared the most, what had in truth driven her apart, was ever to mind. But she had never picked up the odor of the Gray Ones, seen any of their paw prints on overgrown roads or game trails.

Her retreat from overseeing the engagement at the keep had been close to noon. Now it was near twilight when she struck recklessly into the ground-matting vines and saw before her a rise of trees which gave a daunting impression of gloom rather than promise of any shelter. Liara paused once on her steady plodding, which followed a zigzag pattern to allow her the use of any place where the vines thinned somewhat, to send a stone from her carefully selected collection at a commotion among the leaves. To her it seemed that some hidden creature was taking flight and hunger ruled her enough to try to make sure of some catch.

There was a shrill keening and the vine leaves were torn hither and thither as she caught glimpses of a small body and dared to throw again. When the struggle subsided, she advanced to find a bird—large as the fowls at the farmsteads, its fluffed feathers shading into the green of the leaves themselves.

Picking it up by its broad feet, Liara pushed through the remainder of the vines to the first fringe of the wood. Only there, well shadowed by the trees, did the girl stop to examine her kill. Praise be to Uncle Volorian, she nearly said aloud. She had been armored long since to the bloody ways of feeding the hounds and certainly her own needs were as important as theirs. More and more she was breaking through the shell of an Alizondern female.

Now as she grubbed in the leaf mold under the tree, which kept off most of the rain, she looked back at her existence in Krevanel as another life. As she uncovered a stone or two, embedded them in her mold hollow and then searched around for small pieces of brush or half-rotted tree branches, she wondered whether, given the chance (and the assurance of course that her littermate was *not* waiting on the other side to bring her down), she would willingly pass again through that postern gate in the depths of Lormt.

The bird was cleaned and plucked. She had her small fire after several snaps of the lighter, and pieces of meat impaled on some straight sticks over the flames, which sizzled as the fat began to burn into greasy drops and encourage high flames.

Would she keep on ahead through this forest? The fact that she had no real goal was troubling. Remembering the map at Lormt, she made a guess or two and thought she must be close to the southern border of Karsten. There was supposed to be a small nation south of that—mainly of seafarers—called Var. Not of the Old Race, either—would it be wise to strike farther west and try to find refuge there?

The rain had slacked off a little. She fed from the strong, unsalted meat of her catch and wrapped the larger part in leaves for the next day. There was no way she could post any sentry here. As it had been ever since she parted with the company, she must spend a restless night. But she was so tired that she was not sure she could keep alert enough to sense any peril.

Leaning back against the bole of the tree under which she sheltered, Liara blinked and blinked again. She had brought her knives out of hiding and had them under her hand for instant use. The fire she allowed to die, even though she shivered in spite of the thick traveler's cloak about her. Against her will her thoughts kept turning to her fine chambers at Krevanel—to the soft bed, to all the luxury she had taken for granted.

Her skulking away from the party . . . She turned now to consider the decision which had brought her to that act. Alizonderns thought first of their own advantage. She had been tutored from as far back as she could remember to weigh actions in how they would affect herself first, and then others—if there was any advantage in her aiding such.

In spite of the witchling's words, she knew well by all she had been so taught that those who had accepted her only reluctantly at the first would be well rid of her now.

She ached—all toughening learned on the trail from Lormt did not seem to help now. When she swallowed, her throat was sore. Twice she choked and coughed until her eyes watered. Tired . . . so very tired . . .

The dusk of the forest closed in upon her. Her last remembered gesture was to close hand on knife hilt and then, in spite of all her efforts, she slid down into darkness, though there was a part of her which warned that that was dangerous.

So deep was she in exhausted slumber that no spark of warning reached her as they closed in. She aroused, dully aware at first and then with the thrill of pure fear, as she felt hands pawing at her. When she at last gained true consciousness, she found herself staring up into a half-seen bestial face while foul breath puffed down at her as the creature drew taut a rope about her chest and upper arms. She was flopped over roughly and her wrists were lashed together so tightly that the thongs which held her cut cruelly into the flesh.

Then she was rolled back again. She must have fallen prey to these hunters in the early morning, for there was the gray of a well-advanced dawn piercing between these trees to let her see her captors.

One of them pawed at her hair, tangling his wide but blunted nails in the strands enough to jerk her head upward at a painful angle so that when he leaned closely over her they were nearly eye to eye. And his lay within dark pits of his skull, like sparks of fire.

All the dullness of sleep had been swept away from her. She knew that the failure of her own body, her ability to keep on guard, had delivered her to those hunters she had fought to elude. Gray Ones.

They wore no clothing and their haired skins showed patches where scars and running sores were plain to see. The worst was that they were so human in their general stance and bodies. The one who still kept his hold on her was clearly male, but one crowding in beside him, showing sharp-pointed fangs, was a female, though her bared breasts were hardly more than flaps of skin thinly furred.

Two of them were wrestling clumsily with the straps of her small pack, jerking it back and forth as each snarled at the other and tried to win the find for himself.

He who held her head captive spat words at her and Liara had learned enough of the general trade talk which was the common tongue of all who used speech in the north to understand.

"Where others?" He viciously shook her head from side to side and then thumped it against the ground to emphasize obedience to his will by a quick answer.

"Gone." The word rasped in her throat. *Let them put an end to me speedily*, became the one plea she clung to.

He blinked at her and snarled, then mercifully loosed the hold on her hair and hunched away. Liara caught a glimpse of knife blade. There stood her weapon straight in the earth as she had left it when treacherous sleep had overcome her. Why the creature had not already taken it as spoil, she could not guess.

The female pulled at his hunched shoulder, pointing to the two who were now ravishing the backpack. He snorted and spun around.

His companion did not follow him but squatted down in his place by Liara.

She lowered her hairy face and then uttered a sound which was close to cackle. "Dog stink," she observed. "Dog meat good." She ran her tongue over her lips and then her jaws remained a little open, the tip of her dark tongue spattering drops down on the girl.

Liara braced herself against any sign of disgust or fear. So in this much she had been right—those of Alizon did take on some of the nature of their prized four-footed stock. But the female Gray One was busy. She found the latches of Liara's jerkin easy enough to pull apart. And without disturbing the ropes holding her captive, but by the judicious cut of a dull-bladed knife here and there, she slit cloth. She soon had the girl stripped, her rent clothing piled to one side.

Thick fingers gathered up the skin of one of Liara's breasts in a torturous pinch and the girl could not in time smother an answering cry. But she already lay open to the inspection of the majority of the pack.

She fought to close her mind to what they intended to do with her. Would she furnish them with a feast? Or would she be an object for torturous play?

The female gave her another bruising pinch and was ready to deliver a third when there came a low-throated houndlike call, and immediately all those gathered around Liara edged away.

With her head now flat on the ground and little chance to see more than the hairy forms which walled her in, the girl could not view the newcomer. But that these here owed it some form of service was plain. A moment later they all drew back to open a pathway for a much taller form, so enwrapped in a black cloak, so hooded that its features could not be distinguished, coming at a deliberate pace, seeming to lean now and then on a staff which overreached that hooded head in height.

Liara had heard in Lormt and had experienced for herself at least once, when she had fronted that head of stone, that evil had its own odor and so revealed itself for what it was to any of the Light. The Light—how much she could claim to be of that, she did not know. But this thing sickened her until she wanted to spew forth last night's food. A Sarn Rider? Though it was rumored that the Gray Ones were not too often in the company of such.

The staff swung forward and she could not turn her head quickly enough. Its point struck her grimed forehead directly between her white brows.

She felt something like a prick and then . . . nothingness—nothing at all.

Destree had depended so far on Chief as a guide. She was sure they had left the shrine just in time to escape another visit from the villagers and she went strongly believing that what she did was the Lady's will. Gruck seemed to agree to her leadership, but as he went he continually turned his head from side to side, obviously sniffing, now and then putting out a hand to touch a leaf, to point to one of those flying things which were like flowers on the wing.

With constant effort the Voice tried to mind-meet such unspoken queries with a name. Sometimes she was even shaken enough from her desire for haste to attempt to acquaint the stranger with the use of some herb he seemed to locate by instinct. They were powdered by flower petals brought by the rising wind and she knew that a storm was coming. They should find shelter, for these spring storms could turn, without warning, into raging torrents.

They found a mighty windfall, a tree which must have been a giant before some whirlwind ripped its roots free. Then Destree slipped off her pack, pulling grass and brush away from the fungi-spotted wood. Gruck needed no instructions, following her example. But it was he also who dragged up saplings he had harvested with ease and wove them into a roofing. They could not stand erect in their improvised shelter, but they had cover—and just in time.

The storm hit about sunset and they crowded together, Chief tucked between them, chewing on journey cake and looking out into a solid wall of rain.

*Where go?* Gruck's questing thought brought Destree out of a worry about a new patch on the shrine wall which might not perhaps hold against such an assault.

"Escore," she answered aloud, and then realized that meant nothing to her companion. She strove to picture that land as she had heard of it—a strange and eerie countryside filled with the remnants of many alien peoples, of the Light but still with thick pockets of Dark lingering within it.

*From there—go home?*

Destree knew that she could promise nothing. This was no child, nor, for all his appearance, some animal less in intelligence than human. He must have the truth, for only on truth could she build trust.

"There are those there"—she shaped her thoughts slowly, keeping one hand on Chief's soft fur as if that simple link could amplify what she would say—"who know much more than I. If there is a return for you—that they can tell."

He had turned his head a little away; she could only see the rounded shape of it staring out into the rain. His next attempt at communication surprised her, for it no longer dealt with his gate passage.

*This be rich—good land to grow. Its Alatar must love it much.* She more felt than saw his hand go out and run along one of the sapling poles which supported their shelter. *Yet . . .* He hesitated so long that she thought he had closed the path of communication between them. Then he turned to look at her and she could see his eyes like luminous disks in the dark. *There is no guardsman here— none to listen—none to aid—not to fight—*

"Fight!" She was startled. What was this mountainous man-thing beside her used to standing guard against in his own woods?

*That which takes but does not give . . .* He appeared to be struggling for some way to explain. It was as if he could not altogether believe that she did not know what he meant.

"There is never a world without enemies," was the best Destree could answer. "And this I must say in truth—the land toward which we travel has evils in plenty. One must be ever on guard."

*That is my calling,* he returned. *For guard I am, and no place where there is growing things can be totally strange to me.*

She was having difficulty keeping awake and dozed off. When Destree roused in the dim morning light, Gruck was still sitting on his heels at the opening of the shelter, looking out into a world with a stare of such intensity that she believed in some way he was establishing odd ties of familiarity.

The storm had done them one favor. It had certainly delayed the chase after them and cloaked their trail. Even Foss, she hoped, could not pick up any hint of their passing.

One day was like another, except they grew to know more and more about each other. Destree watched with awe when her giant companion confronted a spotted tree cat ready to defend two kits with all the fury of her kind.

He knelt before the cat, which was already poised to spring, and, making a soft sound deep in his throat—not unlike Chief's own purr—he laid down a woodsnark, one of the tree-boring lizards which he had spent some time cutting loose from its inroads on one of the forest giants.

The tree cat snarled, but did not sound any battle cry. Belly against the ground, she crept forward and a paw flashed out with lightning speed to be set on the plump belly of the lizard. Then it and she were gone.

Destree saw him also standing in a brook in the fair light of morning, his golden belt with its heavy dangles of equipment laid aside, until he made the same lightning-swift move she had seen by the long-billed cranes, coming up with a fish for them to break their fast.

Nor did she try to disturb him on the day he discovered a vine withering where it lay upon the ground still half-wreathed about a broken branch and watched him loose the coils of the plant and transfer them with infinite care to another support near at hand.

In turn he was eager to learn from her what she knew of herbs and their uses. However, she harvested few of those that they found, as there was no way to dry them and perhaps no use for them in the future.

The girl kept no count of days and all she was sure of was that they headed northeast. Nor could she be sure if they had passed into Escore.

That they were not away from the ravages of mankind was brought abruptly home to them one day when an anguished scream cut through the air, startling them both to face in another direction.

Destree had no doubt that that was a death cry. She had known the perils of constant struggle too much in the past to escape knowing. Her hand went instantly to her amulet. For that had been a woman's scream.

Gruck was already striding in that direction, and for the first time she saw him free from his belt a rod which was short-sword long but held no cutting edge.

Now her wilderness-trained senses caught the scent of horses and men. She tugged at Gruck's thick arm.

"There may be many."

He made an odd noise and shook free of her grip, his long

strides, which she could not match, leaving her behind. Then she saw him level that rod of his, take aim through a break in foliage.

There was a shrill humming. Cries—death cries also. She clenched the amulet tightly. All knew that the Lady had Her dark side also—that She could deal death when that was demanded. Destree had not moved to stop Gruck.

They pushed through the bushes, Gruck seeming to have no dread of any opposition, to look out into a glade. Three in rusted mail, greasy skins, possessing such features as she did not care to look upon, lay on the ground, and beyond them a twisted white body.

She hurried to the victim—hardly more than a child. Destree straightened out the crumpled form and laid between the bruised and bleeding breasts the amulet.

"Lady, this one has suffered foully. But already You wipe away her tears and she knows no pain. May she go on happy feet through the Last Gate and find beyond all she had most longed for in her life."

They laid the unknown girl in a pit scraped deep by Gruck's great hands. It was he who reached high enough into a newly flowering tree to break blossoms for a blanket with which to cover her before they returned the earth into place.

He went then to the three horses, thin and showing the cruel marks of a whip, and took off their gear, freeing them from all restraint. But to the bodies of the murderers he paid no attention and she did not question him.

Rain began again like tears at what lay behind them as they started on. At last they made one of their camps, but it was clear that Chief was not at ease. He prowled back and forth before their small fire, now and then growling.

And he was still doing so when the amulet became like a lick of fire against Destree's breast. This was the Lady's call and she must answer. Sure of that, she said nothing to Gruck, but started at a steady trot into the rain. Chief, for all his hatred of the water, with her. But Gruck padded not far behind.

Stench—of vile filth—or evil! How far they had come from their camp Destree did not know, but that what lay before them was truly of the Dark she understood. She slowed pace but did not stop. She gestured caution to Gruck, who nodded.

If those gathered there had out sentries, such had neglected their stations in order to watch what was happening. Gray Ones—and a goodly-sized pack of them! They had formed an irregular circle. In the midst of that was a captive. So white was this bare body that it seemed to glow. And over it stood cloaked and hooded one who was not of the pack.

Gruck moved out to where he might be sighted before she could do anything to stop him. He held again that light rod, but this time balanced for throwing, and even as she moved to urge him back, the alien weapon had left his hold. There came a high whistling and the hooded one jerked his head up. He half raised his staff and from its knotted top glowed sullen red light.

But the alien weapon reached its mark first. And the figure collapsed as speedily as if there had never been a form within to hold the cloak upright.

From Gunnora's amulet came a spreading ring of light. Destree heard growls and then screams from the Gray Ones as they lurched back and away from the bundle of clothes and the white body beside it.

# CHAPTER EIGHT

# *Unknown South Karsten*

She's gone!" Keris had back tracked and—with more effort than he thought dealing with any animals could require—herded the pack train. Only the fact that the ponies were linked nose to tail had given him any aid. The slightly larger beast Liara had ridden followed its kind without protest.

"Taken!" The Lady Eleeri started forward, when Mouse's hand came out to stay her.

"Not as you think. She went as her own will drew her, for she feared that which she believes she carries within."

Their party had drawn in about the small, gray-robed figure of the witchling.

"But," for some reason Keris found himself protesting, "was she not tested at Lormt? If there was the touch of the Dark on her—surely she was no adept to be able to conceal such—from you, from your sisters!"

"She is not of the Dark, though through her blood she could be so governed—by a master Power. They call themselves hounds, these of Alizon"—her small face was very sober—"and through countless years of their fostering of such packs, who can say what trait could be absorbed?"

"But"—now it was the Lady Eleeri who spoke—"did you not choose her to this company?"

A shadow of distress was on Mouse's features now. "I did not choose, Lady. This"—she held out her jewel—"drew me to her, even as it did to all of you here, woman, man, Renthan, Keplian. We have a place, each of us, in this venture, and Liara has not yet played out her part. She must go her own way for a space. Now"—she gave a small shrug as if to dismiss the subject—"let us to what this would find." She was already moving, the jewel held out before her.

They had dismounted among this place of stone tree trunks, for the footing was rough and they could move only slowly. Sometimes there were cracks in the surface of the ground in which it would be only too easy to catch a hoof.

The desolation about them, the ever-soaking rain, made Keris feel as if they had been captured by one of those fabled gates and shaken into a world which was no longer that he knew. Jasta was surefooted, yet he dropped a little behind, coming up behind the pack ponies. And his presence seemed to subdue their stubbornness, for they followed Keris's tugging with no great protests.

The pillar trees gave way to a wide-open space. Open to the sky but not to the traveler—for in its center rose such a strange bulk that they halted at the very edge of the pillar land and stood staring at it.

Whereas the other gates the witch jewels had drawn them to were indeed worn away by centuries, this squatting erection made one uneasy to look upon. Keris remembered those strange shapes which abode in the otherworld of that Dark Tower where three of this party had ventured to save a life—and a spirit.

Massive, with no sign about it that it had been in any way pieced together, it was gray-green in color and, like the serpent head which they had buried, fashioned in a form which could only have served the Dark.

Its limbs were pressed tightly to the ground and its back was a warty hump. The face—if that which was at the fore of its ball head could be called face—was plainly close to that of the small, water-dwelling amphibians Keris knew from childhood. Jaws gaped for at least half the length of the head. There was no visible nose, nor any eyes; the warty skin stretched unbroken from jaw to crown of head.

Theela reared on her hind legs and trumpeted a challenge, the fierce blue of her eyes gleaming ever stronger. Those about her were making warding signs. That there was nothing to come from here but evil struck them all.

Although the Lady Eleeri tried to stop her, Mouse moved out of the group now clustered, gathering close as if human and beast sought protection in the presence of each other.

The light of her jewel flickered and Mouse stared ahead. She had taken only a step or so and now she stood still. Her voice, soft as it was, reached them clearly.

"This is—aware. . . ."

Keris's shoulder nudged again Jasta's sleek hide. No dead gate this, but perhaps one which at any moment might suck them in through that great mouth, or spit out at them some new horror hither unknown.

"Theela." To Keris's surprise it was the Keplian mare Mouse summoned. "Eleeri, Romar." She added, then, the names of the other Keplians. Keris was left as Jasta moved forward, though Mouse had not named him. It was a strange company now fronting the lowering thing. Keris knew that the Lady Eleeri possessed Powers, some not even of this world, since she was one who had come through a gate. And the Lord Romar who was her mate had been greatly tried in battle with evil and come forth one of the conquerors.

He could see that even as they stepped forward, the hands of the two humans were moving in gestures, though they drew no weapons. The Keplians—who, until the Lady Eleeri had broken an ancient spell, had served the Dark—went mainly unwillingly. But these Keplians were free, and somehow, even as he stood some distance away, Keris could feel a backwash of Power generated by the three black forms—while Jasta, he was well aware, held within him that talent which was born in all his kind.

"Can it be locked?" The voice of the Lady Eleeri was very steady as she asked that. She had flung one arm over Theela.

"That we have not learned." Mouse cradled her jewel in her two hands to press it against her forehead. "They search at Lormt—but we have not discovered how to seal a gate. If it *were* ever known. We cannot seal, but we can wall."

Lord Romar nodded as if he understood at once what she suggested. He moved to take Eleeri's free hand, though she kept still her touch on Theela.

"Widdershins," Mouse said, and turned. Lord Romar followed, bringing with him his lady and Theela. Behind them abreast came the two other Keplians and Jasta.

They went slowly and Keris saw the lips of the three who were human moving, though he could distinguish no words. However, he was sure that what they uttered were the spells in which they most trusted.

The animals almost appeared to shimmer. In spite of the rain, there was a glistening gleam to all their coats and they kept carefully in line as they went. Three times that strange party made a wide circle about the drop jawed thing.

The power they called touched those who waited. Both falcons suddenly took wing to soar above the bulk, weaving back and forth in graceful flight. And Keris found himself repeating words which held no meaning but had somehow reached into him to be uttered aloud.

There was movement within that gaping mouth, a thick black line, like one of the anchor ropes of the Sulcars thrust out. But in that moment Keris, for a second, caught sight of something else. There was a change in the fall of the rain. It seemed to thicken heavily, to form a wall along the path the dealers in Power traveled.

He was never truly sure, though the memory of it held through the years, if he had indeed witnessed it—that that rope had come within touching distance of the half-illusionary wall and been snapped back.

Those who had spun the web came back to the others.

"We must find a place—away from here," Mouse said hurriedly. "For I must report to those at Lormt. An evil active gate—that must be known. Our walling cannot hold for long—but it may be that my sisters can reinforce warding from afar."

So they trailed once more through the pillar forest and came at last to normal-looking land. It was dusk before they reached soil which bore living green bordering on a river, and beside it they set up their camp. At least with the coming of night the rain ceased and they were able to build a fire and attempt to dry out clothing and eat a larger meal than the last two they had allowed themselves.

Mouse withdrew to a small private place they had made for her by piling the packs together. And Keris went on watch, sharing duties with Vutch and Vorick. Lord Romar was using a rather wan light given off by a ball he carried in his wallet, which he brought out but seldom, to light his additions to the map he carried of their day's passage. They must be close to the south border of Karsten, but this was country Denever did not know. He had led them as best he could through those portions of the rough land which would give them cover. And he had volunteered to scout to the east, which project they were discussing this night.

Keris was glad to be free of his guardianship of the pack train. Even with Jasta's help he found the balky and sullen ponies hard to manage. Yet Liara had never appeared to have much trouble with them.

Liara—and the Gray Ones. For the first time Keris wondered at Mouse's easy acceptance of the girl's disappearance. To be untalented among those with power was to be as one blind or deaf, he thought suddenly. He knew that the Alizondern girl was not accepted cheerfully by the company—the Falconers and Borderers had fought her kind too often. And, considering the age-old hatred the witches had held for them, he wondered that she had been so openly made welcome at Lormt. However, it was also known that those who were struggling there to untangle old knowledge for the good of all did have some odd connection with the hounds.

Where was she tonight? He wondered. She had taken a pack from their stores, but it had only been a small one and he was sure she had no experience in living off the land. Gray Ones—his hand went now to his own belt.

He had forgotten that—the knife with a blade of quan iron which he had found in the curiously withered body after their battle. He knew of Liara's skill and he was certain that the knife was hers—he should have returned it to her. That lapse picked at his mind as he kept sentry.

Denever did head off the next morning, striking farther east and going alone except for his Torgian. Mouse seemed to be at ease; whether she had indeed enlisted some distant Power to hold the gate, she did not say. However, she had another report for them.

In all, nine gates had been located in Escore, where the abundance of talent made the project easier. Five showed signs of life and were under guard. Marshal Koris's searching parties in Estcarp had added three more to the total of those discovered in their own territory. One of these appeared dead but was being watched just the same, and the other two quiescent. Keris was certain that those must have been dealt with temporarily as had that one they themselves had found the day before.

"Was there ever any record," the Lady Eleeri asked when Mouse was done with her report, "how many adepts ventured into this wandering worlds scheme—any list of who they were and their own homes?"

"That is now with Hilarion and Kaththea," Mouse replied. "Hilarion reported two gates of his own and he deactivated them as well as he could. But the adepts were not friendly among themselves. It was their pleasure to make some new find and astonish their fellows, but not explain how they achieved the results they paraded later. However"—her small face was drawn and tired—"most of the Old Ones were of Escore and Arvon—that was the world before the Great Battle broke all apart. Therefore what we may find here in the south are the works of either wanderers, more than usual distrustful of their kind, or of refugees who were scattered after the First Ending."

They did not push on that day. It was plain that the expenditure of talent had been hard on both human and animals. The two Borderers fished to good results and Keris on Jasta, with Falconer Krispin, went hunting. They brought down a good-sized pronghorn and Farwing took four grass hens—such abundance of meat to build up their dwindling stores as they lingered for a second and then a third day to dry it, waiting for Denever's return and some report as to what lay downriver and whether they might expect to run into some of the roving parties which seemed now to provide Karsten's fate.

During a second such hunt on the following day they came across evidence that Karsten still had pockets of life strong enough to hold the chaos at bay. Farwing, on scout, picked out what lay ahead, reporting to Krispin.

"A road"—the Falconer smoothed the head of his feathered companion with a finger—"and apparently one in use. Farwing saw a party traveling it. Perhaps we should take a look for ourselves."

Better know the worst as soon as one could, Keris silently

agreed. If their present camp by the river was not at the edge of an overgrown wilderness, but rather bordered on inhabited holdings, they must be ready to move on.

They dismounted, and Jasta drifted a little ahead as scout. Following him, Keris and the Falconer came through a narrow ravine which provided a path for a small stream with bush growth enough to afford them cover.

There ran the road, rightly enough, and Keris was quick to take the meaning of that space on either side: not quite as wide as an arrow flight, but obviously cleared, so that an ambush would be hard to set.

Whoever ruled this part of the sadly war-torn land had the will and power enough to keep open roads. And roads meant not only quicker movement for armed forces but also for traders. Where went traders there was peace, even if an uneasy one.

The road ran across the stream with no benefit of bridging and Keris guessed there was either a ford or just a shallow flow of water.

The party Farwing had sighted was already close to the fording. There rode a cluster of armed guards and within their circle of protection a litter swung between two sturdy horses, brightly curtained though somewhat tarnished by road dust. A section of this had been looped back that the rider within could view the scene. Keris caught sight of a rich-colored robe which could only be that of a noblewoman, and he saw a silver-banded arm fast-closed about a small, struggling child who was red in the face and screaming as it tried to free itself from restraint.

Behind the litter came three women in more sober garb, their heads nearly hidden by winged caps, mounted on slow-pacing horses. Then more guards. They all held to the plodding speed of the litter horses, though Keris noted that several of the men acted as outriders, seeking the very verge of the cut-back growth for their passage.

"Luscan!" That sharp exclamation from his own companion was startling. Just as the Falconer had spoken, so did the bird on its saddle-horn perch let shrill a carrying cry.

There was instant answer from the wayfarers. The guard split smoothly in two, one half taking their places around the litter and the women riders, the three closest headed toward the ravine while their companions maneuvered to withstand a charge.

Before Keris could move, Krispin sent his mount forward as his bird uttered another screaming call. Then Keris noted that two of the guards wore the equipment of Falconers. Their own birds were mantling and quickly answered Farwing's cries.

One of the three Falconers below pushed up the bird-beaked visor of his falcon helm.

"You ride, Brother of the Eyrie, on oath?" The part of his face Keris could see was that of a much older man, and a seamed scar lifted the corner of his lip to one side.

"I ride on oath," Krispin answered steadily. "I ride in no quarrel against the brotherhood—though the Eyrie no longer exists."

The guardsmen below were taking their cues from the Falconers. There were hands on sword hilts and bows well forward, but they seemed willing that, in this, their own fellow traveler take the lead.

Krispin lifted his own beaked visor and then, as if to make his identity certain to the other, he took off that helm entirely.

"You are Luscan of the Barred Wing Flight," he said. "I was fledgling in the season you took flight command."

"And who was your trainer then?" came quick demand.

"Asshfar—but he took flight long since, even before the rending of the Border."

"Asshfar," the other repeated. "So, boy , what do you now—play blank shield as the rest of us to scrape a living?" His twisted mouth was a sneer.

"I have taken service as my flight commander bade me—"

"With Baron Jerme? You ride boldly enough on his land."

"Cross it only. Those I ride with have a geas set."

Luscan stared at him. "What does witchery and geas have to do with an honest fighting man?"

"Perhaps much. But this I will swear to—by sword and blood, talon and beak—we come not to trouble any dweller on this land." He hesitated and then added in a voice which was a tone sharper, "Be they of the Light."

Luscan grunted, but it was plain that the oath Krispin had offered was binding to him.

"Whose shield badge do you raise?" he asked in a slightly less arrogant tone.

"That of two lands, perhaps even of Karsten, since that which we seek lies also here, as we have already proven twice."

"Riddles!" That rather querulous voice came from the woman in the litter. "Speak plain or be taken for what you are—masterless and eager to profit by such freedom."

The two other Falconers urged their mounts a few steps forward until all three faced Krispin. Keris tensed, knowing that if this turned from speech to sword, he would have a part in it.

"There is threat of the Dark for all men of good spirit." Krispin made no move to resume his helm. "We come out of Estcarp, out of Escore, out of Lormt, to seek the seeds of death."

"Witches!" Again it was the woman who spoke. "Have they not brought enough death upon us? Where lies my dear first lord, servant of ill power? Under the rocks of the mountains, lost forever."

Her voice was nearly lost in a rush of wings. All four of the falcons had, by no order Keris was aware of, taken flight. At the same time Jasta's warning hit him:

*Trouble. An ambush set and now they grow impatient. Their master is not an easy one.*

Down the stretch of road still before the cortege there frothed and bubbled, rising out of the grass of the verge, their natural hiding place, rasti—the great rat things who lived only to kill and eat.

Perhaps the scouts had not sighted this because they had been seeking more normal dangers. The screams of the women rang as high and violent as the neighing of the frightened horses. Though they might grow no longer than a man's forearm, yet rasti in a pack could well bring down a horse and rider.

Keris raised his voice in the Valley battle cry. "Light for sword—Light," and Jasta bore him forward at a run. They met with the tail end of the pack. Jasta's head went down. He caught one of the bloated brown bodies, snapped and flung it into the midst of the others, while he reared on high feet to bring forehooves into smashing play.

Keris fell into the familiar rhythm he had known ever since he had first ridden forth with Kyllan. He had left sword in scabbard. In his hand the fire lash of the Valley guard cut down into the pack and the screaming of those he seared ended as their own fellows turned upon them. For that was the nature of the foul beasts: Often they could be turned from their attack in order to satisfy their ravenous hunger on the bodies of their own kind.

Keris cut a path through the pack before they seemed truly aware of what enemy harassed them. Then Jasta wheeled and back they went, the flame lash sending sparks of light to catch in the fur of those it did not actually touch.

He was no longer alone in the battle, but was aware of war-trained Torgians stamping and rearing—though the steel used by their riders was far less efficient than the weapon from the Valley.

Keris was aware of a falcon in dive, turned to one side, and quickly reversed the swing of his whip to kill the rasti attacking from his left. The smell of scorched flesh and blood was like a mist rising among them.

He saw suddenly a block of the creatures heading for the horses of the litter. Those huge animals went wild, screaming and rearing. The litter came free at one pole, throwing into the dust of the road the child while the woman hurled herself after to protect the little one with her own body.

Now he must use care. The plunging of the litter beasts continued, along with their screaming, as brown bodies leaped out of the dust to sink teeth into their flesh. Hampered as they were by the remains of the litter, they had little chance of defending themselves.

But it was the woman and child which mattered. Jasta needed no word from him. The Renthan took a great leap and landed directly on the first of those razor-toothed creatures. Keris was instantly out of the saddle, before the woman. He shortened the lash, burning his fingers in the process. But now he could stand and beat down the rasti, while the woman had curled herself into a kind of ball, the child unseen in her clutching arms.

They came—three times—and their attacks were such that he could somehow believe the woman and the child were their primary prey. But it was also plain to him that this horde had never before faced the fire lash and they had no defense against its measured swing.

Then . . . he stood faced by a mound of dead beasts. None of those stirred.

*They are dead,* Jasta reported. There was a long streak of blood down one leg of the Renthan and he lowered his horned head to lick at the wound. Save for the pain in his hands where he had shortened the lash in midst of battle, Keris was untouched. But having relooped the lash, he went down on his knees beside the woman, laying a hand gently on her shoulder.

She quivered and cried out, a small, whimpering sound.

"They are all dead, Lady. But did any reach you? Such wounds must be quickly treated."

Her elaborate headdress slid into the dust as she at last raised her head. Then Keris was elbowed aside by one of the other women as they gathered about her. From what he could see, neither she nor the child had been touched.

"You, youngling." Keris swung around with a snarl and found himself looking up into the face of Luscan. The Falconer's mount ran blood in several places and he himself showed a growing spot of crimson on one leg. "You are no fledgling of any flight I have heard of—nor do you fight as any I have seen. Who and what are you?" This harsh demand on the part of the older Falconer sparked Keris's anger.

"I am no birdman." He used the common word for Falconer and did it deliberately. "I am Keris Tregarth out of the Green Valley—but doubtless you have never heard of either my house or my home."

"Tregarth—he was at the taking of Gorm," Luscan said slowly.

"But you are a youth and he was a seasoned fighting man of perhaps three times your years."

"He is my grandfather," Keris replied shortly.

"Yes, your people keep records of their get." The older Falconer nodded. "Also I am not as ignorant as you think, fledgling, for I have heard of the Green Valley and those that kept alive the Light through all the Darkness. What other power have you beside that fire which answers to your will?"

Keris shrugged. "What I have been taught, I know." It was no business of this man that he did not carry the talent which should have been his birthright.

"And to some purpose." Luscan nodded. "It was fortune's favor that your shield man stopped us here. Had we ridden into that . . ." He looked at the mound of rasti bodies.

The train were beginning to sort themselves out into some kind of order again, though they did so after sending scouts, who not only viewed the distance for any movement but also used spears to stir the verge grass—though Keris believed that another attack was not imminent.

That rasti and Gray Ones roamed these southern lands was not good hearing. It had always been thought that both species never ventured far out of Escore. And he had no desire to be trailed by another such pack as this one.

The woman sent for him before he prepared to ride—for this news must be taken quickly to those they had left behind.

She was very pale and when she tried to speak, the words came one by one.

"They—tell—me—you—are of a great house of the north." Now she was growing more eloquent. "That I can believe. Also that you mean us no harm. If any stop you this side of the river, show them this." She jerked impatiently at a coinlike pendant hanging on a bedraggled ribbon around her throat. "Blood debt is owed. I, of the House of Righon, do swear to that."

The old formal words used in ceremony came back to him as if from another life, and he thanked her.

Meanwhile Krispin was gathering from the now-free speech of

the guards much information about the countryside and which lords might welcome and which might hunt them down merely because they rode out of the north.

With the smell of blood still in his nose, Keris started back to the river camp. They might not be bringing meat this time, but he knew that the information would be very welcome to the party.

## CHAPTER NINE

# Lormt, South Karsten

The two women in the small room faced each other. Both were well wrapped in shawls, as the chill given off by the walls could be piercing if one lingered for any length of time.

Lady Mereth strove to settle herself more comfortably on the cushioned seat of her wheeled chair. Her writing slate was in her lap, but she only fingered her chalk, did not put it to use.

The gray-robed woman opposite her displayed features sharp nearly as a hawk's. On her breast rested a dull jewel, but her hands were busy with something else, a ball of pearllike glimmer with glints of color showing for an instant now and then. Gull, leader of the witches in Lormt, stared down at this as if, though it lay within her grasp, she feared its touch. Finally she spoke, her voice a monotone. She might have been trying to stifle in part what she must say:

"Five reports of evil moving—and all from the south borders. Yet our gate hunters surely have not awakened all this. Something else draws our ancient foes."

Lady Mereth's chalk squeaked. "Draws?"

She saw Gull tense, and the witch did not answer directly. "Sarn

Riders, Gray Ones . . . rasti, even, which are usually herded only by their appetites. And certain others, ones who have never actively risen against the patrols of Light, yet did not welcome ever our coming into their territories. Now they sweep south. Are they drawn, you ask? I needs must say yes. Last night Mouse reached us with a tale of a rasti attack near the border of Var—clear across Karsten, even as they met with Gray Ones just a little earlier.

"That gate they found—it was awakening. It takes four of the sisters now to keep steady watch, to hold the cover on it, and our number are limited. Yes." She pressed her hands tightly about the ball. "However, I do not believe it is that gaping evil they seek, these southbound ones."

"A greater one?" Lady Mereth wrote.

Gull nodded. "The fire of magic struck far when the Magestone went from us. Such could awaken the Dark as well as the Light. Now those of Escore sweep their southward borders and report this exodus which has never been known."

"We have found many accounts of the Mage Wars here since we started a distinct hunt for such," Lady Mereth wrote. "Yet there was something else mentioned several times—ask Morfew if you wish a full account. Power is of the land, it courses under the surface like unseen rivers of everlasting fire. Therefore those who deal with that power, or are born of dealings with it, instinctively do not venture too far beyond the sources they feel. Karsten never knew Gray Ones, except perhaps a small band or two on a quick raid, and then just along the Border." As Gull read and nodded, Lady Mereth erased the filled slate and wrote again. "Rasti, the Lady Eleeri knew, but that again was in the Borderlands. These other presences you mention, have they ever stirred far from their native haunts before?"

"None such has been reported in our time."

"The worst that any gate threw upon this world," the chalk moved on, "was the Kolder. And from all accounts their gate was opened from the other side. But what, Learned Sister, if there now waits a gate in the south, perhaps controlled by a force beyond our knowing, which has found some barrier weakened and now summons to aid that to which it is akin?"

Gull's clutch on the ball was now so tight that it would seem her fingers were sinking into it.

"Yes." Her voice was a mere whisper of sound. "And Hilarion can no longer raise Alon in Arvon. Garth Howell"—she spat the name with a cat's hiss—"is not Lormt but it also harbors secrets.

"But do we suggest sending an army south—when we know so little?"

Mereth sighed and squirmed again against her cushions.

"Learned Sister, already time treads fast. Crops must be harvested to the last grain stalk, the smallest apple. There is no way Marshal Koris can call levies to arms without visible cause in Estcarp. While those who police Escore now have all they can do."

"So." Gull's word was almost a verdict. "We wait—let us hope for not too long."

Lady Mereth thought of the small party struggling into the unknown land so far away and sighed. Marshal Duratan could release no more than a squad. Even if they sent out a call for unpledged Falconers they could put no true army in the field. She wondered what happened now in her beloved Dales land. The triune of lords who established a loose rule after the invasion by Alizon might not even be still in existence. As for what might rise in Arvon—one guess was only worth another. That they had lost contact with Alon had sent Hilarion back to his own castle, to labor with the same equipment he had used before.

"Mouse . . . she is very young. . . ." Mereth touched on a subject which had bothered her from the first.

Gull did not turn her eyes away. "Mouse"—her monotone was even softer—"is one such as comes to us perhaps once in a hundred generations. She will be one of the greatest All Mothers we have ever had. But the finest sword must be well tempered before it is readied for battle. Already her sending is such as few can equal. Look you—"

She steadied the pearly ball on her knee, her fingers well to its bottom so as not to hide the sides. Lady Mereth made the effort to lean forward as far as she could.

Gazing balls she knew well, but this was not crystal as the others she had seen. Now the colors on its surface grew sharper, flowed, thickened, until she had an eerie sensation that she was something mighty and beyond human looking down upon a world in space.

Figures moved there, grew sharper, became recognizable. Travel-worn they were, honed to the point that Mereth understood them to be at their most alert. She studied them face by face—but—

"Liara is not with them!" she wrote.

"Liara made a choice— No," Gull was quick to answer as Mereth's protest could be read in her face. "Not one of the Dark—rather more greatly of the Light than she knew. Her part is not yet—nor can we be sure what it shall be." Gull leaned closer to the ball. "Mouse, sisterling," she called.

Then the world Mereth surveyed was blotted out by a small, sun-browned face. But the eyes . . . those did not belong to any child.

Lips moved, but it was in her head not with her ears that Mereth heard the answer.

"The land seems barren of people, but before us once more stand mountains, and our scouts ride to search out some possible path. We have seen no more of the Dark Ones, but there have been traces—things move in the night and only the strength of the Light hides us. There is something astir—though still far away—yet it is not to be denied."

"Heard and understood, sisterling. If you need heart power, call—all we can raise will be yours."

It was only a pearl-colored ball again. Gull leaned back in her own chair, appearing more gaunt. "South—ever south."

"May the Blessing of the Flame be theirs," Mereth wrote the age-old prayer, one she had not used for years, and then added: "But what we can all do we shall, and Lormt's secrets are unending."

The mountains rose before them, clothed for half their heights with heavy growth so dark green as to seem nearly black. The trav-elers had long ago left behind them any sign of man's work, though they knew that to the west lay the wide valley of Var and its city.

Here there were not even game trails, and both birds and animals seemed very few.

When they camped at night they drew close together, human and animal. Even the ponies no longer showed any stubbornness about being picketed close to the campfire.

It was Keris who blurted out on their third night of attempting to find passage south something which he believed they must have all noticed.

"Rasti—Gray Ones—I found a paw print in the mud of a spring this afternoon. Do they accompany us but are not yet ready to attack?"

Krispin, as usual, had settled Farwing on the horn of the saddle he had loosed from his horse. "They come, yes. But that they hunt *us* . . . I wonder."

*They are called.* No one could mistake the snappish mind-voice of the Keplian Theela.

"Called!" Keris's hand instantly went to the butt of his flame lash.

The mare was far enough into the circle of the firelight that they could see her nod her head like a human.

*Something seeks—that which answers it comes.*

Now all their heads swung toward Mouse.

"That which the Dark bred, held as liege in Escore, is moving south. I think we shall find it also. Whether we can deal with it . . ." Her child's face was set as that of a woman facing some dangerous task. "But it is there—it waits."

Though all his life he had called the Green Valley home, known the peace which dwelt there past all troubling, still Keris had always been aware that that was only a small fortification against what might roam beyond. Clans of the Old Ones years earlier, hunted out of Karsten, had been led by his own father to the resettlement of land about the Valley. Scouts rode many ways and there were some portions of Escore in which fury only drowsed and might awake at any time.

That ancient enemies were also journeying south was a hard thought for them all. Though they controlled many talents and

Powers among them, they were but a handful, and who had yet been able to count the enemy?

There was one question which concerned them and it was Jasta's mind-speech which stated it. *A gate—already used by the Dark— a force drawing ready to strike northward?*

"There is this," Mouse answered slowly. "It has long been known that each land holds its own power which nourishes and supports those who are able to draw upon it, knowing or unknowing. The Gray Ones—the rasti—are of Escore. So it is true of the Sarn Riders, though such we have not seen trace of. They are not attuned to what lies here." She put her hand flat down on the ground before her. "This will nourish, even as earth nourishes seed and root, only what is native to it. The farther one strays from one's own place, the less power. . . ."

"Lady Mouse." It was Denever who had moved to face her straightly. "We of Karsten who were not of the Old Race had no earth-born power—that was why the Kolders forced the old duke to put your Old Ones to the horn. I served Duke Pagan because I was liege man to Lord Grisham and my oath was given him. I rode the north part of this country as my lord's man and though there were places, yes, which we avoided because of the Old Ones' honoring, yet never did any witchery arise. If the power of their land could not save the Old Ones at the time of the Horning—and they did have witchery—weak indeed must it be. It may well be true that the evil of Escore flits south now but will this land then turn against those who are of it?"

"No one, living or perhaps among those Gone Beyond," Mouse answered him, "can unriddle the way of power. This much I have learned. My own"—her hand was on her jewel now—"takes longer for its raising, demands a greater price when I use it. And we are far from Estcarp."

*Be not so sure, Witch Maid.* Theela's thought struck deep. *You speak of powers within the earth—well, some be of the Light. Have not your own kind said Light draws light?*

"As Dark draws dark," Keris said flatly. "However, this much I know from scouting in Escore. Gray Ones—and rasti—do not like the cold of heights, nor overmuch the shadowing of any forest. Both face us now."

"Right," Krispin cut in. "And do we have any choice?"

The Lady Eleeri shifted. She had been inspecting a coil of bow strings, testing each as it laid across her knee. "No. It is south. And do you forget Sebra's find today?"

The Keplians took turns running loose, yet one always seemed to be well to the fore of the party when they set out each morning. Sometimes the sleek, beautiful animals disappeared for half a day or more, which never seemed to bother either the Lady Eleeri or her Lord.

*Yes.* The new Keplian mind-voice was less strident than that of the mare, but still well assured. *There is a canyon. The stream in it is low—there is forage in plenty and as one goes—it climbs.*

"With the dawn we send our feathered brothers." Krispen was smoothing the head of his own falcon. "Their sight is keenest of all."

So it was decided. Keris took his share of sentry duty and, when relieved, wrapped himself in his bedroll. They had camped in a half clearing, backed on one side by the rise of a low cliff. The heat of the fire he had just fed before he went to rest was reflected back by the stone, though it was chill and damp even a foot or so away.

It seemed as though he had been asleep for only a moment when—he was elsewhere!

He crouched belly down to the earth, seeking somehow to become a very part of it, not to be identified. His heart was pounding and his mouth was dry. No man lives without feeling the touch of fear, but what Keris suffered now was an all-encompassing terror. Yet something kept him from yielding what remained of his rational self to this assault.

Before him was a clear space in which stood a rough monolith, perhaps worn by ages of wind, so that its true nature could no longer be distinguished. But it gave off light and that deepened, spread. Light that was blue.

The fear which held him planted was as heavy as if a great beast's paw pinned him down. He could only watch helplessly what was happening before him.

At the foot of the time-battered statue stood a woman. And there was about her now the same air of command as he had many times seen—in his mother, in the witches. She was dressed in rough trail clothing; there was a pack at her feet as if she had shifted it to free herself for battle. However, though she wore steel, she had not drawn any blade; instead, much like the witchling Mouse, she held something in her hand which glowed.

She was not the only one who had gone to earth there. Keris could see, only partly behind her as if a body rested behind the discarded pack, the limbs of another, slighter form.

Strangest of all was her second companion. The creature towered well above the natural height of any man the Escorian had ever seen and it was completely covered with frizzled fur. Yet it stood on hind legs and wore about its middle a wide belt, glistening in the light, from which hung a number of artifacts.

"By the Power of the Maid, by the Power of the Woman, by the dire Power of the Hag . . ." the words beat into his brain and it seemed to him that that pressure which held him captive shifted a little. "By the Power of earth from which we come, to which we return in our allotted time, by the Power of the sky where rides Our Lady's Own Token, by the air we breathe, by the fire which serves us—by this very land—show yourself for what you be, shadow of shadows, Dark out of Dark!"

The hairy creature had freed a rod from its belt and held it as a man might hold a familiar weapon.

"Show yourself!" Her words rang again as a battle cry.

That which had held Keris eased. He saw a curl of movement just beyond the edge of the blue radiance. And he wanted nothing more than to drop his head upon his arm, not to see—*that*!

What human could shape words to describe such a thing? Bile rose in his throat to choke him and he swallowed convulsively.

"Face now Her wrath—for you are unclean, not of the Light. Face Her . . . Sardox!"

The shadowy coils wavered. He could feel the menace in them still.

*There shall come a reckoning, earth slut.* No voice—only a thought. *And now this much Sardox lays upon you and those beings you think to shield—for certain laws hold both Dark and Light. You have challenged me, setting yourself up as a champion of that feeble Lady of yours. Therefore from this hour forth you shall travel as MY will takes you, that we shall meet again!*

The woman laughed. "Brave words, Sardox. You have striven to break my ties with the Lady for three days—and even that you cannot do, for this earth answers not to you. Only my Lady can name me champion—and I am but one of the least of her servants. Still this night you have not taken me or those with me. Get you to *your* lord and answer to him for your defeat!"

"Keris! Keris!"

His body was whirling through a vast space—there was nothing to which he could cling; rather, he was a plaything of such winds as his world did not know.

"Keris!"

He could not even move his jaws, his tongue, his thought to answer.

"Keris!"

First it was like a stab of pain, and then it was an end to all fear, freeing him from the place of winds. He became aware he was panting, as worn as if he had raced heedlessly up some mountain slope. Then he opened his eyes and saw first that comforting beam of light and then Mouse's small anxious face behind it. He was no longer wrapped in his bedroll but was lying with his head on the Lady Eleeri's knee, and she was wiping his face with a dampened cloth which smelled wonderfully of herbs so that for a moment he could believe himself back in the Green Valley.

Dawn light gave those gathered about him substance and he could read the concern on all their faces.

"I—" his voice sounded like the croak of some swamp-born thing. "It—it must have been a dream!"

Mouse was shaking her head slowly. "It was a sending, a true

131

sending. Though why it came to you—" there was a shadow of surprise on her face now.

He could only remember for an instant his old pain. "True. I have no talent, halfling though I am."

"We are what the Great Ones make of us," she returned. "But speak now of this sending—for it was meant for us and we must know."

Then Keris launched into a description of his vision, dream, sending, or whatever it might have been, and found that it was easy to remember the smallest details as he continued.

As he described the woman he had seen standing battle-ready against that which flowed in the Dark, Mouse nodded.

"So," she said now, and her jewel glinted the brighter for a second, "now the Oldest Ones stir. Gunnora." She bowed her head as if she were paying homage to some great one of her own craft. "From the world itself comes Her Power—when we evoked the changing of the mountains, so did we deal with Her. Our roads led to the same goal but have ever been apart. Say once more these words Her Voice spoke."

Keris discovered that he could recall them now as easily as if he read them from a written page held before his eyes.

*Sardox!* It was the mind-voice of Jasta which cut through the end of that retelling. They all looked to the Renthan.

Jasta tossed his horned head high. *Each people,* he said, *have their memories. We remember Sardox, for it was he who wrought until he brought forth the Sarn Riders, and worse. It was thought that he was snuffed out in the Great Battle. And now it seems he looks south.*

Keris was aware of a shifting among those who ringed him in. Trusted and tried as they were—yet no man of his time could imagine facing the wrath of those who had moved before the ancient First Breaking of the World.

"So"—the Lady Eleeri drew her herb-scented swab across his forehead for the last time—"we ride. And in the way Sebra has scouted."

Vutch took his place with the pack ponies, though Keris had

hoped that it was not apparent he found so difficult the everyday actions necessary for breaking camp. That he could hold to his seat on Jasta without faltering gave him something of encouragement and he was eager to leave what had become to him an ill-omened place. But Mouse's mare matched pace with Jasta, and for that he was not so happy.

That he had been struck down by the Power of a known source lay deep in his mind, and he feared that memory now. Never would he forget that force which had pressed him, into the ground, held him captive while it reached for its more potent foe.

He tried to fix his mind more on that huge, hairy creature which companied with the priestess. It was totally unlike any he had ever seen in Escore, which was alive with oddities, for it was there that the most unscrupulous of the adepts had wrought that greatest evil of all, dabbling in the very stuff of life to form new species for their profit or pleasure. He knew well the earth-dwelling Fos, the water-needing Krogan, the Flannen. Jasta, good friend and comrade, was also of such begetting.

And there were the Gray Ones, the rasti, the Sarn, and now this last invisible thing which had brought to such a high pitch all the fear his own body could generate.

Perhaps the witch could read his mind, for it was as if she had followed his thoughts.

"This hairy one"—she might have now been speaking aloud her own thoughts—"its like is listed nowhere. Yet it is of the Light or it could not have so stood within the circle of Gunnora's service. It may add much to our own knowledge when we meet with these other travelers." She spoke confidently, as if she expected to come across them at the next curve of the passage.

They had not gone far down it, both falcons aloft, Shama himself playing advance scout, when the Lady Eleeri's Theela stopped short, whether at her own wish or her rider's, Keris could not tell. However, the Lady was leaning forward on the Keplian's back staring at the rise of the canyon wall.

The sun did not strike directly into this cut and, as Sebra had observed, it gradually sloped upward, leaving the running stream an arm's length below. Yet the daylight was clear enough to show that that greenish surface was not featureless stone.

Instead shadows flitted back and forth across it, though there was nothing to throw such patterns. Some were but abstract markings and others quite clearly were those of vegetation, with flying things winging from one curved branch to the next.

To Keris's amazement, Mouse laughed. "A plaything, long since forgotten. Look you to those ledges across the stream. Are they not seats for those who would watch?"

"But for what purpose?" burst out the young man. The more he watched, the more aware he was that there was nothing offensive or evil—no peering forth of demon faces, no outward clutch of taloned paw.

"A play of learning, perhaps. Others may have had their Lormt. These do not threaten and for us they have little meaning, but they have meant much for others once on a time."

What they meant now was an irritation, for one looking up at the play of shadows could pause, form a barrier for the next in line. Jasta and Theela both swore that to them the wall was clear, so that shifting maze was only visible to the human members of their party.

Still, in spite of all his efforts at ignoring the show to which there seemed no end, Keris found his eyes continually drawn back to the figures cavorting there. He was beginning to recognize some forms of birds, also what seemed to be flying lizards with wings which appeared nearly transparent within their ribbing. Then there was a large squatting plant which all the airborne flutterers seemed to widely avoid. And—

The screech of a falcon broke the fascination of his last stare as Swifttalon came to Vorick, settling on the saddle horn perch of the Falconer who was well in the lead.

The rider turned his head to relay the news his bird had brought. "There is an end to the canyon ahead but also a way out."

And what a way it was, they discovered as they squeezed by a massive rock which had three-quarters closed the passage and came up to face what could only be a staircase. Gathering at its foot, they surveyed this new impediment. Humans might make that climb—even the Keplians and Jasta and the well-trained Torgians—but could they ever force the pack train upward? And what lay at its top?

## CHAPTER TEN

# The Mountain Ways South of Var

Gruck seemed to have a natural sense of seeking out the best of trails. Though he had shouldered a pack which was growing steadily smaller, he also carried the girl. Destree, following in his footsteps, wondered at his continuing strength. Since they had turned abruptly south after that momentous meeting with Power such as she had no real words to describe, the Voice tried hard not to depend too heavily on her companion, to carry an extra share of this trek.

There was no map, no wavereader such as the Sulcar ships had to keep them on course—only this pressure to go forward. But of one thing Destree was sure—it was not fully by the order of that thing they had fronted; the Lady had also a hand in this.

Liara was their present problem. Since they had brought her out of the hands of that leader of the Gray Ones, she had been one empty of mind, one whose person lay deep chained within her body. Destree had clothed her as best she could from her own extra gear, but there were no boots to cover those very slender white feet.

Nor, when she was urged to stand, could they lead her more than a step or two over such harsh footing.

She would eat, if Destree would put food in her hand and then bring that hand up to her mouth; she would drink when the water of mountain springs was held to her lips. But her eyes were blank and she appeared to see no more than if she had been struck blind. In fact Destree had begun to wonder if that was really the case.

She had known her at once for what she was—an Alizondern. Though what a woman of that race was doing here—unless she had been dragged for countless leagues by captors—she could not begin to guess. Her thin features appeared sharp, akin to those of the monster hounds which had been the scourge of the Dales as Destree had heard during her days as a sailor on Sulcar ships. Unable to free her hair from the tangles wrought by the thick brush through which they often had to move Destree had shorn off the nearly waist-long locks and the girl had not seemed to notice, certainly made no complaint.

Destree no longer tried to keep any track of the days. Incidents which happened lingered in her mind. Certainly she would never forget the night of the Shadow Being, or the time Gruck had used another of his belt equipment to bring down a leaper, the largest Destree had ever noted.

She had given thanks to the Lady and paid respect to the bones of the creature, which she had carefully returned to the soil, glad for the sustaining meat. Mostly they had existed on a strange diet which Gruck seemed to favor—leaves of some plants, and even insects which she no longer had to struggle with herself to eat.

Once as they worked their way farther up into the higher reaches of the mountains, they had suddenly rounded a crag to confront a snow leopard, its muzzle dyed with the blood of a mountain pronghorn it had brought down.

The giant had halted and then gently laid the girl at his feet. He reached for no weapon, holding out his paw-hand as might a man giving the peace sign to a newly met fellow traveler.

The leopard had snarled. Destree had seen its body tense. Then from Gruck's deep throat there had come a sound not unlike the purr of a well-fed cat. The leopard's head turned a fraction on its shoulders as if striving to catch every nuance of that sound. Destree saw its body relax.

Gruck stooped to pick up the girl again and then turned a little to the west, so that they passed well away from the leopard's feast.

*Such are like the warrior cats of Alatar,* his thought touched her. *Mighty in battle. They hunt cleanly and do not mangle their kill. Nor do they slay save when they must fill their bellies or defend themselves.*

Destree longed to ask him more about his own world. That he apparently followed the ways of the Lady, living close to the earth and its creatures, she already knew. Yet something kept her from questioning. Had she been snatched—say, from the herb garden of the shrine—and plunged into a totally different world, would she want it recalled to her memory?

However, their meeting with the snow leopard had an effect they had not foreseen. For the first time the girl he carried did not lie limp in his big arms. She was staring straight up into his face.

There was first such a flash of terror-fed horror that Destree sprang close to the giant's side, fearing the girl might try to fight her way free. And since they stood on a stone-studded slope that might end in disaster.

The Alizondern cried out in a language Destree did not know, but she picked up easily the fear which nearly maddened the girl. Gruck had moved quickly to put her down, where she went to her hands and knees while he strode back, away, leaving Destree to face her.

The girl flung up her head and that sound coming from her now was not words, rather the howl of an animal driven nearly out of its mind by terror. Destree moved.

Though the girl fought and clawed at her, she got one hand at the thin nape of the other's neck while, not trying to avoid the raking fingernails which tore a path down her cheek, she pressed against the other's forehead, pushing aside the sweat-plastered hair so that her amulet might rest directly against the girl's clammy flesh.

Destree had used this before, twice, when she had had to deal with hysterical patients, and she knew what it would do. At the same time Chief, who had kept himself apart from the girl ever since they had rescued her, came trotting between the stones and sat with his wide yellow stare.

The wildness in the eyes of Liara's face began to fade. Just as the hands, which had torn at Destree and left bloody evidence of their force, straightened and fell to the girl's lap.

Now Destree dared to draw her into an embrace, striving to put into that act all the warmth with which the Lady had gifted her, all the reassurance—all the security. So they crouched together. Now the girl was crying, great tearing sobs which shook her whole nearly wasted body. One of her hands raised, did not quite touch the bloody seam a nail had left on Destree's cheek.

"It is nothing," Destree soothed. "You have been in the hold of the Darkness—now you have broken through. Gruck"—she turned her head a fraction and he moved a little forward—"is our guardsman, warrior, friend. He is of those the Lady holds in Her hand, and none She holds so will bring you harm. I am Destree"—she could not quite keep the small note of happy pride out of her voice—"whom the Lady called to be Her Voice."

The girl drew the shuddering breath of one who has sobbed herself close to exhaustion. Now her arms went out in a hold to equal Destree's earlier one and she looked straight at the giant, then to the cat.

"Me." She used the trade tongue of the northern lands. "I was once Heathmistress and First Whelp guardian to the house of Krevanel. What I am now . . ." her hold on Destree tightened, "I do not know. But—" there was a flare of fear again in her green eyes. "Lady—I must give you warning—I fear there is in me, perhaps in all of us who nurture the hounds—that which draws the Gray Ones."

Destree smiled. "Child, be sure that the Lady would not welcome you if that were so. But how came you south so far from Alizon? Is there then war again in the north?"

"Not war . . ." Then, as if she must tell this healer—for healer she truly was—all she could, she poured out what lay behind her, ending with her capture by the Gray Ones.

Though Destree's hold on her was still comforting, yet Liara sensed that this was indeed such a story as the other must arm herself to accept.

"So—that storm was only the beginning," Destree said, as if she thought aloud. "And we are promised dire trouble in the south—yet that is where the Lady points our steps."

"Let me go." Liara could say that and yet she could not loose her hold on the older woman. "The Gray Ones—"

Slowly Gruck had approached them again and now he squatted on his heels. Chief leaned against a heavy, hairy thigh while the giant smoothed the cat's fur until he purred.

Destree's thought sought the hand of the giant's. "How much did you understand?"

*Gates*, he returned in thought, and also made a harshly guttural sound in his throat. *So was I caught—so may others be entrapped. If these Power workers would seek out gates for their complete closing, then service is like to that given to the Alatar—to be offered gladly by all who follow the Light. Also, we are being drawn south—perhaps through the will of this Sardox, perhaps in service of your Lady. I think that it might be well to seek out these others, perhaps bring them warning, if they do not already know of what may be sniffing along their trail.*

Liara loosed the hold of one hand on Destree and rubbed her grimy forehead. Then suddenly she spoke, her voice scaling upward as if once more she were entering to the clutch of panic.

"Lady—I hear in my head. Those who deal with magic are tainted so. See, now the Darkness shows in me!"

"Not Darkness, Liara—you are now daughter to the Lady. She gives many gifts—the opening of thought to thought is one. Did you not learn that at Lormt?" She smiled.

"Now, these rocks are too hot to perch on with any comfort. Let us move on. Gruck will carry you until we can decide some proper foot coverings, for your flesh would be torn to pieces here. See, even my trail boots have their own tale of gashes."

For a moment Liara's features tightened as if she were about to object to that. The giant held out his hand and her small, dirt-grimed one was swallowed in his grasp. She stared intently into his wide face, and their eyes locked for a moment, and then she said:

"There are dreams which one can be caught in, so deeply that all seems real. Perhaps this is a dream, but if it be so, I accept it."

They moved out of the glare of the sun on the dark rock and came to a cup of welcome shade. Destree shared out food and for the first time Liara ate for herself, though Destree was glad at that moment that it was dried bits of the leaper and not some of Gruck's grubs she had to offer,

*They—these who come from the north—*the giant's thought-speech was not interrupted by the clump of his mighty jaws—*were heading south and west?*

He leaned back a little, his hands braced on his knees, his head turning slowly as if he made some detailed thought record of all he could see here.

Liara nodded. "There was a country called Var by the western seas, but there they did not plan to go."

"This is a wide land," Gruck continued. "Can those of the party who have such Power link minds to guide us?"

Slowly Liara shook her head. "Nor might they wish to. I know that the witch—she must have guessed what pulled the Gray Ones upon us. Why would they want me to draw the attention of the Dark to the path they take?"

*You, Sister in Service—*that head swung now in Destree's direction—*does this seem true to you?*

"Only from one way of thought—" Destree was beginning when suddenly Liara cried out, pointing skyward.

"Falcon—see, it comes to search us out!"

The bird had turned in a wide circle and was indeed heading back toward them. Destree watched it eagerly. She had served on ships where Falconers had been marines. And where there were falcons, surely those who called them brother could not be far away! It was swooping lower; waving or calling to the bird would mean nothing, for it answered only to the signals of its bonder. Yet, when it made two circles about them and then sped westward, she was sure that their presence would be speedily known to those who had launched the bird.

It would seem that they must retrace their way, Keris thought. How far must they rove now? The flight of steps facing them could be climbed perhaps by humans, but the pack train could not attempt such a feat.

They established a temporary camp. As he went about his regular duties Keris wondered how many of his companions were as disheartened as he. There was very little talk among them and most of them were frowning.

He passed by Mouse, who was sitting a little apart, her now well-worn and hem-tattered robe huddled about her as if she needed some shelter against a chill wind. Her hands were folded in her lap, but her attention was all for that forbidding flight of stairs. Was there, Keris wondered fleetingly, some trick of the Power which could waft them to the top? After all, in their time the witches had moved mountains as if those were child's buckets packed with sand. But Mouse was one alone, not a whole council-in-order of her kind—not that he believed that the witches, who had nearly wiped their kind out of the world by such action in the past, would be ready and willing to try such again.

He saw a flash of movement across one of the steps—a flick of brilliant color. The thing fled for a space and then spread nearly transparent wings so that he could see its likeness to one of the lizard flying shadows on the wall now well behind them.

Wings—well, only the falcons possessed those. Even as that thought crossed Keris's mind both of the Falconers sent their birds aloft for scouting.

It was still only midafternoon and there was something about their crowning disappointment which seemed to make them all languid. He fastened the last of the ponies to the picket line and the creature, though it showed its teeth for an instant, did not snap at him as he had expected, preparing to dodge.

The Keplians and Jasta were, of course, never picketed, and for some reason they were walking in single file, like mages intent on some rite, along the foot of the stairs. The Lady Eleeri stopped sipping from her water bottle to watch them, her eyes narrowed as if to intensify her gaze.

Keris dropped down not too far away. Lord Romar and the others were busied with that map, which was Romar's particular charge. But no one was making any suggestions. It was Mouse who spoke, and her voice, soft as it was, carried to rouse them all.

"Lady," she said to Eleeri, "what say these you have won to our aid?"

It was the mare Theela rather than Eleeri who answered.

*We can go—and this one.* She nodded toward Jasta. *The dumb-tongued ones*—she used a sharp sneer Keris had never heard before, as she indicated the Torgians—*if they go free of riders or all else in the way of burdens and are aided. But those—* she snorted in the direction of the ponies, *this is not for them!*

Keris's protest was being framed even as Eleeri answered. Much as he detested the small beasts, what they carried with every day's travel southward grew the more important. Boots must be repaired, shoes for the Torgians replaced; the scaled-down necessities by which they lived could not be just left here.

"There is need, Wind-Swift Sister"—Eleeri used both mind and tongue speech to answer the mare—"for what they carry. Nor can nearly half of it be taken on without them. We have willing backs, but we go into the unknown where there may wait such hunters as would welcome travelers heavy with gear."

Lord Romar rolled up his map. "It would be best to wait until the birds return. If there is a way beyond this trap we have gotten ourselves into, perhaps they can point it out."

All were willing to agree to that. But Keris roused himself and went to the dump of packs, noting by the brand mark on the hide cover of each just what was within. The more he looked, the less he believed that *anything* at all could be discarded and they not suffer from its loss later.

Taking advantage of a halt in a place which could be easily defended, the party began to get to tasks of their own setting. The packs were opened for supplies to repair boots, arrow shafts to be fitted with heads, kits for the stitching up of the worst of tears which the mountain growth had left in their clothing.

The Escorian found again the knife which had been Liara's. It was as clear in the sun as if it had never been blood-clouded, but when he held it in his hand he was nearly startled enough to cry out. For the sense that what he held was by loan only and that the Alizondern would return to claim her own was as clear as if Mouse had proclaimed it.

Swifttalon was back first from the scouting, and after communicating with the bird, Vorick reported that there was nothing to the east but mountains rising ever higher, mostly bare now of any growth.

His fellow scout was delayed so long that Krispin was plainly ill-at-ease and paced back and forth, his helm discarded so that he could stare farther skyward in search.

When at last the falcon came into sight, they all felt a measure of relief. The bird came to rest, panting, its bill open, and Denever, who was nearest, held up a small metal cup he had just filled so that the bird drank.

Krispin smoothed its feathers, using those slurred sounds which were soothing and plainly gave comfort. He waited, the others crowding in about him, for Farwing to deliver his message in his own time, when he felt once more strong enough.

Maybe Mouse could pick up the very high-scaled bird speech, but the rest had not been trained to catch it. And it seemed to Keris that they were never going to learn what lay ahead or why Farwing had been so late returning.

"There are others—above." Krispin indicated the staired cliff. "Among them is the Alizondern female."

"Gray Ones?" Denever demanded.

"Not so. One serves She whom some call the Lady, and the third is like no living thing my brother has seen before." Again Krispin caressed the nearly exhausted bird. "They are well to the west, but now they move toward us."

"The Lady," Mouse said. "Then that one stands in the Light and perhaps these are the ones you saw in the sending, Keris. If so, it is plain that their way is also ours in the end."

Theela pushed forward. Her usual mind-speech carried the bite of irritation. *This way can be climbed—have I not already said so? Though those flat-footed ones you call Torgians will need aiding, mountain-bred though they claim to be.*

One of the Torgians snorted almost as if he had caught the

Keplian mare's insult, though as far as Keris knew his breed lacked the human range of mind-touch.

With the exception of Mouse, they moved back to view the packs, most now open to be rummaged through. Denever went down on his knees beside one which had not yet been loosened and came out after a moment's delving with a coil of rope.

This led to a search in which most of them took a part— Though in the end what they had discovered was, Keris believed, not enough to answer any great need.

The Lady Eleeri had pulled one of the pack bags itself out into the open and was on her knees beside it. It was of well-thickened hide, coated on the outer side with a layer of hardened sap from the umpas—the best moisture protection known in Escore.

Straightening the now-flattened bag out on the ground, she began to measure it with the width of her palm and then nodded.

"Here we have fortune's gift. But it must be carefully prepared. One cuts so—not straight but in a circling toward the center." Chopping past the buckles and ends of straps, she began to follow her own instructions, and her blade was keen enough to pierce both covering and hide so that shortly they could see what lay there was a coil a little more than a finger wide, the loops of which answered sluggishly as she caught the outer end and whirled it up and around. It still showed a tendency to recoil, but the Borderers were ready with stones to pull it as taut as they could and straighten it out.

The confusion of the camp grew the greater as more and more of the bags were emptied and slashed after the pattern the Lady Eleeri had set. Keris, moving boxes of stores to clear more working space, came upon Mouse.

She was standing beside the larger pony, which Liara had ridden, and her hands were cupped about its muzzle. Knowing the temper of the beast, he would have moved to pull away. Then he heard a low crooning and saw that not only this larger mare but all the stubborn-tempered train were standing without any of their usual signs of resentment at the nearness of humans.

Mouse looked over her shoulder at him. "These, in spite of their uncertain tempers, have been faithful servants. Loose their picket ropes now."

"But—" he glanced back at the very busy scene behind him.

"They cannot follow—but this is a land not unlike that of their foalhood. Loosen them to find their own place in the pattern of things as should be." There was not only the crack of a command but a certain solemnity in her words. He found himself indeed loosening the halters from the beasts, which for the first time since he had taken charge of them stood quietly under his hands.

Liara's mare turned and trotted down the canyon and the others fell in behind her as if they were a party of Border Rangers under her command.

"What do you do!" Denever came up as the last pony, with a contemptuous flip of its tail, passed out of reach.

"They can go no farther," Mouse answered. "We must do now as best we can."

Once more they sorted supplies, and this time it was a more momentous thing to say this will be needed, that we can leave. For who knew the country beyond, though the falcons had reported that it seemed thickly wooded with no sign of any keep or building?

So the shoes of the Torgians came under strict examination from Vutch, who had harrier skill, with a replacement here and there. The Keplians and Jasta went bare of hoof as always.

They were another day at such preparations and the falcons were sent out once again in the later afternoon, reporting that the three sighted from aloft were still headed along the crest of the stair cliff. Mouse made her report to Lormt and had a fraction of news in return—there had been a Sulcar ship in from Arvon, the crew of which reported rumors of trouble in the Waste and said that a Border guard enlisted from the Dales lords and those Falconers who had settled in Seakeep were on the move, to set up their own defenses. But of those in the Eyrie there had been no word—nor had any come from Hilarion that he could once more have speech with Alon.

Of the Sulcar ship which had headed north to follow the tradition of their own legended gate there had come no news at all.

Keris had not slept soundly through any night since that during which he had suffered from the sending. Now he lay looking up at the stars, which seemed very bright in their hard glitter tonight, and wondered. Such journeys had seemed to be the best of all measures at the great meeting at Es City, when they had been so busied with preparation at Lormt. But they were no army, merely scouts. What if any group of them discovered more than could be faced with any hope of survival?

By the next morning they were ready to make their attempt on the stairs. The packs, cut down to what a man might shoulder, were lashed together with hide ropes and left at the foot of the climb to be drawn up after human and animals had made their successful journey. That which they could not hope to take with them—both in the way of additional weaponry or other supplies—was stacked and covered with piled rocks.

Theela tossed her head and moved out before any signal had been given. She planted each hoof firmly and mounted the stairs as if she had been accustomed to such travel all her life. Behind her came the Lady Eleeri and the Lord Romar, followed by the two other Keplians and Jasta, with a reassuring calmness (or at least Keris found it so) radiating from him.

The Torgians were not as confident and each had to be led up one at a time, a man at either side, with supporting ropes, though Keris could not believe that any such precaution would really protect against the consequences of a misstep.

Twice he himself made that journey, striving to keep his own nerves under control so that the sweating horse he was helping to guide would not sense his unease.

Somehow they were all at the top at last, standing on a wide plateau which seemed to narrow southward like a finger pointing them on. Then began the hauling up of the packs under the heat of the sun, and the constant sense of what might happen if balance was to waver, which seemed to go on forever.

They all lent a hand as necessary, save that Keris had not seen Mouse since she had made the climb with her hand resting on Jasta's dusty shoulder. Once the last pack was up, they simply collapsed where they were in a ragged line along the cliff top. The Keplians appeared to be herding the Torgians to the east, where there were some signs of greenery. Keris thought longingly of water but could not summon the strength at present to move in search of it.

A falcon's scream brought them back to sudden alertness and they scrambled for the weapons they had dropped when they man-handled the store packs upward. Farwing cruised over them, screamed again, and then headed west.

Keris, swaying a little, had gotten to his feet. His rock-scraped hand went for the butt of the force whip. But there was no wave of rasti bursting out of nowhere to bring them down. Rather, two fig-ures moving at a slow but steady pace, with a third clinging to the back of the black-furred thing of Keris's sending. Was this another attack of that experience?

No, for those about him were all astir, and between the party who had come up the stair and those three, Mouse was running as if in answer to a summons she could never disobey.

## CHAPTER ELEVEN

# Into the Unseen, the Unknown, Southward

The three from the east had halted, almost as if, Keris thought, they awaited some sign that they were welcome. Seen in the day-light, the furred giant did not possess, or at least Keris found it so, that suggestion of menace which had been like a cloak about his wide shoulders when the Escorian had been caught in the sending.

The giant creative supported Liara, and Keris could see that there were wrappings about the girl's slender feet, but surely no coverings as would stand up to walking over the rough rock.

Mouse was well out in front, but now Keris, who stood the closest of the rest of the party, ran after her. That he could defend a witch was thought born of folly. Still she looked so small, kilting up her robe so she could run faster, that involuntarily he followed.

The other girl of the trio, whose scratched and torn trail clothing showed hard travel, held out from her breast a pendant of deep golden color. At the same moment she brought that into view, Mouse halted some paces away from the three and raised her jewel. Both blazed—and to Keris it seemed that circles of fire spread out from each . . . but not in opposition, rather uniting, until his skin tingled and his sweat-damp hair moved on his head from the vibration of that Power meeting Power—in equal greeting.

"Greetings to you, Witch." The girl smiled as one would at a friend long sought. "All good to you from the Lady!"

Mouse's sweet trill of laughter sounded.

"And to you, Voice of the One in Three. Of old we have never clasped hands—but a new day is with us." Now she took another two steps forward, her blazing stone resting on her flattened palm, and the other moved as swiftly to meet her, so that when their hands touched, their signs of Power rested one upon the other.

Then the radiance and its Power aura was gone and they were but girl-child and young woman looking peacefully happy, while around the legs of the girl the large black cat wove back and forth purring.

Mouse reached out to Liara, whom the giant had set partly on the ground, though he still supported her.

"Welcome back to us—for all of us are one. So it has been set."

"I am of the blood of your enemies, and perhaps . . . more!" It was as if Liara were forcing those words out in warning.

Mouse laughed again and gave a small flip of her hand backward to indicate the company who had drawn in there.

"We are many things, and each of us has a strength which is needed. Look upon us—do we wear the battle masks of enemies?"

Keris saw Liara draw a deep breath. Somehow her hands went

out and the giant loosed his hold on her, so that she tottered forward close enough that Mouse embraced her and whispered something which brought the Alizondern girl's head up, banished the shadow of uncertainty from her gaunt face.

Suddenly she shook free of Mouse's hold, retreating to catch once more at the arm of the giant.

"This is—" she began, and there was a shading of defiance in her voice.

"Gruck, Guardsman of Alatar in another place and time." To Keris's surprise, Mouse promptly named the giant. She might have known him as well as the Lord Romar. "There are in all worlds those that serve Light, and with that in their heart they know each other. And this be Chief"—she indicated the cat—"mighty warrior, also from beyond."

She had been approaching the giant, looking very small and frail against the hairy tower of his great body. Now she was looking up into his face and there was no longer any lightness in her words.

"There may not be any return for you, Guardsman. Nowhere have we any record that those who have come to us through a gate have found their way home again." Her small hand stroked the kinky fur of his forearm. Had he been of Liara's size, she might almost have taken him also into her embrace—or so Keris thought at that moment.

Gruck's other hand completely hid hers, and then he lowered his massive head and brought her small finger up to his lips. Those parted and a purple tongue tip protruded long enough to touch her flesh. That the giant was rendering some formal salute was apparent.

As they moved on to where the travelers had piled their packs above the stairs, only Mouse stayed close to the new arrivals. The trip up the stairs had been so exhausting and had taken so long that night was well on its way.

Shouldering the packs, they headed for that bit of green, still visible in the twilight, into which all their four-footed companions had vanished much earlier.

What they found when they came to the edge of a drop—for it

became plain that what they viewed were the tops of growth and that the level of the ground fell here—was a valley which was certainly larger than they had foreseen.

A stream ran through it and two of the Torgians, looking hardly the size of the ponies from this height, were standing hock-deep in the flood, dipping their noses in now and then for a quick gulp. The rest of the animals were spread out, grazing avidly, and the look of the grass from above suggested that here was better fare than they had had for some time.

The slope downward was easy enough after facing the stairs, and the sight of water brought them all down it at a good pace.

Keris doffed his helm and thrust his whole head into the clear waters of that stream. When he sat back on his heels and looked around him, he noted something strange about this oasis of growth and water among the rocks.

In the first place there were no trees, nor any sign of brush except when the slopes in some places gave way to the valley floor. Also it seemed in some manner . . . shaped. Shaking his wet head, he had a sudden impossible vision of a giant spoon being used to scrape out this hollow.

In addition—they had suffered so much from such attacks in the wooded lands below that they were now accepting such as a normal part of life—there were no biting insects. None of the grazing animals flicked a tail or threw up a head to deter the attention of those flies which had been the bane of their existence only three days earlier.

Nor were there any birds. The falcons rode the saddle perches, but there was no other winged life to be seen.

A shape moved out of the dusk to kneel not too far away. It was the giant. Though he had both huge hands in the stream, he was not apparently engaged in washing. Instead he grabbed handfuls of a shoreline plant, thick of leaf, which when disturbed gave forth a pungent though not unpleasant scent.

Heaping his harvest beside him, Gruck selected one clump, swirled it again in the water beyond where his occupation had muddied it, and champed it between his great teeth with apparent satisfaction. He caught Keris in his sight and immediately tossed some of his crop in the Escorian's direction.

Keris knew something of herb lore. No one of the Green Valley could escape schooling in such. And he thought he recognized here a water plant, difficult to find in his own land, but which could be safely eaten by the traveler. Breaking off several of the tough leaves, he washed them as Gruck had done and chewed.

The taste seemed to be a medley of flavors, and was, after living on trail rations, doubly palatable. He nodded his thanks to the giant and hastened to pull free another mouthful.

From eating he turned to harvesting, and with their hands high-piled and dripping, they brought this find back to the camp. Nor were they the only ones who had benefited from exploration of the countryside. The two Borderers, who had gone off to make sure that the Torgians were safely accounted for, came back carrying their helms filled like buckets to the brim with stone-centered fruit, each as big as one of Gruck's thumbs.

As they shared these around, Keris saw the girl Destree, whom Mouse welcomed as an equal, was quietly collecting the discarded stones. Keris had two in his hand and offered them to her instead of pitching them back into the grass, and she smiled and nodded.

"Bounty must be ever returned," she said. Keris recognized another version of his mother Dahaun's Power. If one accepted the fruits of the earth, then one must return something of equal value. No plant was harvested in his home valley that an offering was not placed where its roots held deep. And he could guess that with the coming of light in the morning she would plant again all the stones of the eaten fruit.

There was no way of making a fire here. Oddly enough, dusk seemed to last for long time, so that they were not separated in the dark but could see each other. Nor did there seem any reason here to set a watch, with the animals grazing about to sound any alarm.

"This is," said Lord Romar, working on the mending of his mail, "a place set aside . . ."

"It is like a place of the Old Ones, those who walk now among the stars yet would touch earth to keep green memory," replied the Lady Eleeri.

Even as she spoke, there was a sudden light flash in the heavens toward the south. Instantly Keris felt a troubling. It was as if far off someone touched a thread, quickly, quietly, testing. . . .

Mouse, who had drawn a little apart, after her fashion, to await any message which might come, stood, a shadow among shadows, watching where that falling star had shone.

"We are," she said slowly, "where my Power does not work. For there are two Powers ancient in this world. Mine which is inborn and yet must be sharpened by training and ever added to by learning, and yours, sister"—she turned her head a little and Keris thought she spoke to Destree now—"which is of the earth and all it holds. Is this not a land in which your Lady might happily have her being?"

"Yes," Destree answered. "Therefore, sister, it becomes *my* duty to call."

Was it a call, or a song? Keris could not have answered that. With it arose an ever-increasing purr which somehow he could not decide was Gruck paying tribute to something he, too, well understood, or the cat at ease with life.

They had not yet explored the full of the plateau. The valley had engulfed them, lulled them to the rest they needed. However, one end of that valley pointed to the south and just as they had sighted the falling star, so did now another light arise.

Someone might have lit there a signal fire—in this woodless country! First came a shaft of pearly smoke, very visible in spite of the dark, a column seeking to level with the greater heights around them. Then that smooth shaft appeared to answer to winds they themselves did not feel and it curved to point, not to the sky, but to what lay beyond, ahead of that point of rock.

For a moment out of time it held so, and then it was gone. But all of them knew that they had their answer. Two kinds of Power: one had started them on this journey, now another would send them farther on.

Destree had ceased her call when the plume of smoke first appeared. Now she spoke with authority. "There we are sent, for you are as much caught up in this summoning as are the three of us. We can only obey."

There was no more speech among them. All hauled out their bedrolls, providing what they could for the three least-well prepared. While overhead no star moved.

Keris slipped his weapon belt within a hand's distance. There had been no break in the feeling of peace here, neither was that peace any ploy of the Dark to take them unawares. Yet somehow he was better able to sleep with his hand upon it. There was movement in the dark farther out; the animals seemed to be drawing in toward the camp. Had Jasta, the Keplians, seen those signs? He did not believe that even the Lady Eleeri knew Theela and her kin well enough to answer, and one did not question the Renthans on the subject of Power—for they had their particular share of it also.

The peace of the valley seemed also to be soporific, as the sun was warm when the sleepers began to rouse. They did so slowly, as if some of the urgency which had ruled them in every morning camp before had been allayed.

There was no hurry about moving out, either—no one mentioned any such need. The party split into two, the smaller group consisting of the Lady Eleeri, Liara, Destree, and Mouse, heading westward to a quiet pool near which Gruck had done his harvesting the night before. The men, in the other group, stripped off gear and too-well-worn clothing at a point beyond a stand of the fruit bushes to the east.

Keris had expected the water to be chill this high in the mountains, but it was no more brisk than one of the Valley pools and as freshening to his body. Gruck did not follow them into the stream, but from that many-looped belt of his he brought out a tool which opened into a comb, which he began to use, having dipped it in the water, to curry his thick hair. Keris, emerging from the stream and drying himself as best he could on an undershirt he had discarded, watched this toilet for a moment or two. Then, feeling some wariness, he went to the giant and motioned from the busily stroking comb to the back and shoulders which Gruck, short of a snake's limber contortions, could not reach.

The giant nodded and handed over his comb at once for Keris to set to work. This was rather like grooming one of the Torgians and yet under the strokes of the heavy metal teeth the hair was far closer to a kind of thick fur than unclipped horsehide.

Also, though there was a light musky scent, it was not as heavy as that left behind after thorough work on a mount. As Keris was busied with his voluntary task, the giant reached for a heaped pile of small plants which he had apparently assembled before he had begun the combing. Unhooking an intricate clasp, he laid aside that heavy belt with all its appliances and stretched it carefully out on the grass before he crushed the leaves and began to run them over his body as one might apply soap.

Emboldened, Keris nudged one of those large shoulders and reached for some of the pulp, trying to apply it carefully to the portions he had curried.

*Good to be clean.*

He was used to mind-send, though this was on a new level. But somehow the words startled the Escorian.

"Good," he agreed quickly enough.

"You're making a good job of it, fledgling!" Keris looked at Krispin, who was holding up a much-creased and yet fresh body shirt, trying to shake it free of the worst wrinkles before he put it on. Having dragged it over his head and tucked it into breeches still wet from a vigorous sloshing in the stream, he settled down beside them, his eyes on that belt.

"You bear strange weapons, brother-in-arms," the Falconer said to the giant. "For I must think that some of this you carry is indeed weapons."

Again came that slight off-center mind-send. *I wear guardsman's gear, birdman.* But he offered no further explanation. Krispin hesitated, still staring at the belt, and then shrugged. If this new member of the party wished to keep his own counsel, let him. It was the right of every man to speak or keep silent as he wished.

They gathered back by the open packs again and set around reassembling them. There were no ponies now and Keris was well aware that a war-trained Torgian could not be emburdened. As for the Keplians and Jasta, he could not imagine them submitting to such usage.

He noted that the Voice of Gunnora and Mouse had drawn aside and that they were joined after a moment by not only the Lady Eleeri but Theela, the Keplian, as well as the cat Chief. All were facing toward the point of the wedge-shaped plateau, due south as far as Keris could judge, and though he could not see that they spoke one to the other, they could be thought-joined in some business of the Power.

*It calls.* Destree need not have put that into thought. She knew that those with her realized that drawing which was growing stronger, even as she did.

*And*—Mouse's hands cupped her jewel as if to hide it from the light of day—*time grows short. Our way lies there.*

So they moved out, reluctantly—and rightly. For as they came up out of the depression of that place of peace, they were all seized again by the need for haste, with a foreboding which grew the stronger as they approached the point. The Borderers and the Falconers kept the reins of their mounts, while the Keplians and Jasta trotted free. At the Falconers' signals their birds soared up and out, heading south at far greater speed and with better vision than the party below.

They had managed from what was left of their supplies to cobble a pair of boots for Liara, and she kept close to the giant, insisting on shouldering a pack the doubtful Destree allowed her.

Krispin suddenly shook his head so that his helm's falcon crest took on a tiny vestige of life. "There is land below and a great forest," he reported Farwing's sending.

Only a short time later they came to the point of the wedge. Land below, yes, and by the dense green look of it completely overgrown. But— they stood on the verge of a cliff. There was no stairway waiting here, nothing but sheer rock, and between them and the green of the land below floated wisps which might even be low-lying clouds.

Vorick exploded with an oath. "We do not have wings," he spat out the obvious.

"But there is a road waiting!" The young Keplian stallion Janner suddenly pushed past the Borderer and his horse and trotted out—

On air! Yet he did not fall, but rather moved parallel with the point of the cliff as if he trod a road as well kept as an Estcarpian highway. Vorick's horse tossed his head and neighed, pulling at the reins the startled Falconer still kept tightly held.

"There's nothing there!" Krispin protested, and fought to keep his own horse back from the edge.

Keris shed his pack. Perhaps for someone used to the surprises which could turn up in Escore this was nothing too startling, but he found it very hard to make himself keep his eyes on Janner, the ambling cat, and then Theela and Sebra frisking along with nothing under their feet. Jasta now moved up beside him and Keris flung up an arm to stop his regular comrade in arms.

"What do you see?" he demanded. Around him the others were having trouble with their Torgians, who seemed intent on following the Keplians even though usually the two species kept well apart.

*A road,* Jasta returned without a moment's hesitation.

Keris threw himself belly down and forced himself to crawl to the seeming knife edge of that monstrous cliff. Clinging as best he could to the stone on which he lay, he stretched out his right arm and swept it through the air. His fist struck painfully against a solid object which his sight assured him was not there.

It seemed that he was not alone in his exploration. Though most of the others were trying to herd the horses back, he saw Mouse and Destree follow his own feat of wriggling forward and reaching out. Then both the witch and the Voice apparently were moved by a shared idea, for they swung their Power jewel and amulet out into space.

Keris heard the click of each strike a firm surface, but there was no manifestation of the Power in answer—no lighting up of either jewel.

Mouse slipped back. "There is something there, but it is not for our eyes."

The Lady Eleeri stood up and whistled, a clear, carrying sound. Below, Theela's ears flicked. Whatever footing gave her support manifestly led down. The mare was already past at least two-thirds of the cliff face. But now she wheeled and came trotting back. The rest of her clan and Jasta followed. Chief paid no heed to a summons he apparently believed was not for him.

Lord Romar stooped and picked up a pebble, flipping it out. It hit to bounce and then pitch out into space and fall. Watching it go was not a pleasant suggestion of what might happen to one taking such a path blindly.

In the end, even as they had climbed the stairs at the other end of the plateau, so now they were condemned to a similar way of proceeding—in reverse. For where men had urged the Torgians up those steps sweating out a fear of a misstep, so now they clung again to their horses and tried not to look down at a road that was not to be there.

The Keplians took their superiority in the matter as only a just tribute to their species and the four women became their charges, edging out, with the cliff nearly brushing their shoulders as they took one cautious step after another.

Keris saw the sweat beading Vorick's face below his falcon-masked helm as he stepped from firm rock onto nothingness and then began a slow descent. The others followed one by one. Keris had reshouldered his pack and Jasta was waiting. But—he turned his head in search of the giant. He was not of this world; could some such magic as this defeat him entirely? Jasta might aid, though there was little either of them could do, even together, if that huge body took a misstep.

"Can—can you see?" Keris asked, afraid of what the answer would be—justly. For Gruck shook his head. However, he was fingering a packet on his belt and from that drew forth a coil of what looked like silver spun nearly as fine as thread.

He stood with it in his hand for a full breath or two. Then Keris swallowed twice and found that he *could* say what he must.

"If Jasta wears a leash of that"—he indicated the wire—"and I also hold, then can we move? Jasta sees the road."

Gruck looked to the Renthan. *You offer this, four-footed brother?* His mind-speech was hesitant.

*A loop for the neck.* The Renthan approached him, close enough for such to be set before his saddle. *Then against the cliff face for both of you. If I see any obstruction, you shall know in time.*

Thus the three of them formed the rearguard—most of the others a good space ahead now. Keris wished he could shut his eyes. Yet his sight held determinedly to that surface which was not there. Why such a road had ever been laid out he could not imagine, unless it was meant for a far more efficient barrier than any wall he had ever seen. That the animals were not affected by it was the travelers' only salvation as the humans crawled down that way that was not. This road was such a manifestation of Power as even Keris, who had grown up surrounded by varying degrees of the talent, had never seen. Plainly, as if they looked up to see some curse hung over them, they must deal with this pathway that even a witch could not see. He did not forget how the tools of both Mouse and Destree had proven useless.

When they reached the foot of the cliff, the animals were as fresh as if they had only been ridden for a canter down a pleasant road. But the humans, from Mouse to the giant Gruck, subsided suddenly to the ground as if their legs had been stricken useless, most of them determinedly turning their backs on the way they had come.

Keris was quickly aware of one thing. Even the exertion and stress of that descent did not settle on him as suddenly as a blanket of humid heat did now. It would seem that they had descended from the normal world into one which was totally unknown. He heard a cry and turned his head.

Coming in great bounds which made him shudder was the great black cat Destree called Chief, who had been recently not much in evidence, as he went hunting for more than the fare which satisfied the rest of the party. His last leap took him hurtling through the air into Destree's arms, and she clutched him as if he were a treasure lost and found again.

This second coming of Chief seemed to break their stupor. They began to get to their feet and turn to view the way south. What they faced was the thickest wall of tangled and interwoven growth that Keris had ever seen. From it wafted strange unwholesome odors of vegetation decaying over centuries undisturbed. There was movement among the vines and branches which suggested a concentration of life, though they caught no sight of any body.

Destree felt Gruck move up beside her. He stood, his hands curved near his belt, his head up, his large nostrils stretched to their greatest extent, as if he could foretell through scent alone which might lay in wait there.

## CHAPTER TWELVE

# Jungle Passage, Unknown South

Well"—Vorick stood hands on hips surveying the densely massed green before him—"short of swinging a good forester's axe, there's no hacking a way through that!"

"To say nothing," Denever said, "about what may be mindin' some business thereabouts and will not take kindly to strangers crashin' in."

However, the movements they had noted when they had first come to this narrow open space at the foot of the cliff no longer appeared to trouble the foliage. The heavy humidity made it difficult to draw a deep breath and when one did, the faint smell of rot was something that Keris, at least, had never met with before.

Destree, Chief weaving about her legs once more, moved up to face the same green wall a little apart from the others. The open space which gave them room for movement was cramped, and the Torgians showed openly a nervous distrust for this shrouded land which must shadow everyone entering it.

She fingered her amulet. It remained lifeless. If the Lady had an answer to their problem, She was not yet ready to share it. At present their hopes were pinned upon the falcons, which had taken once more to scouting, west and east, along the top level of the cliff down which they had just made their way.

If there could be any break, any chance of penetrating this thickly grown land, the birds alone might sight it. She stooped, and, for the comfort of feeling him close, she picked up Chief. He speedily draped himself about her shoulders, his prick-eared head brushing the braids of her hair. However, there was no purr to sound reassurance. Liara slipped between two of the mounts and joined her.

"This is a land not meant for us!" she said.

"Yet it is one we must face," Destree returned flatly.

She glanced around. Their packs were in a pile by the cliff wall and there the Lady Eleeri was busy sorting out meager portions of supplies. All which they might need to nourish their bodies might indeed lie ahead in that green gloom but, knowledgeable as the Voice was, she could sight no plant—without venturing closer than she wished—which could be added safely to their rations.

It was Gruck who passed her and the Alizondern girl now, advancing with the slow steps of one scouting enemy territory toward the outer edge of that wall. Still afar from touching distance of the growth, he came to a halt, his feet slightly apart to balance his weight as if he faced some possible battle opponent.

Then his hand flicked up and out, and something Destree could only see as a flash through the air aimed for the thick stem of a thing which could be either an oversized unopened bud or a tightly curled knot of leaves.

The giant's cast caught it fairly and he jerked it toward them. There was a moment when they saw that thin line, nearly invisible as it was, become taut and then the sharp sound of a crack and the giant's catch came sailing back through the air. He avoided it with an agile twist so that it landed on the stone, its arrival drawing the attention of the others to circle the thing.

None of them, even Gruck, made any attempt to touch it. In the first place its size was such that Destree could only compare it to one of the prize melons shown by landworker Wukin last season. In color it was as blandly green as the rest of the walling trees, vines, and bushes.

But as it lay on the stone where it had landed with such force, that green began to change. Like veins there appeared a network of thick, upstanding lines across it. Those were first pinkish and then grew ever darker—like watered blood.

Chief spat and suddenly voiced a howl right in Destree's ear, nearly deafening her for an instant. Vorick sighted upon it with the spear he chanced to be holding.

Destree heard the thump of hooves: the three Keplians and Jasta were now pushing their way into the circle of watchers.

Gruck made a complicated twist of the wrist and the thin line he held was free of the pod. Now there was a shifting in that. One end was splitting open into sections, and those cracked wider and wider apart.

A whiff of musky, sourish odor arose as the two top sections suddenly arose straight up. Again there was movement, as out of the remains of the pod crawled unsteadily what first appeared to be something close to the rock snakes Destree knew well, save this was much thicker in its midbody—a body with seeming scales the same color as the trees ahead.

The thing raised a snakelike head in which were set ovals which perhaps served it for eyes. Then it opened a mouth large enough to nearly split that head in two, displaying fangs, from the two large fore of which dripped reddish liquid.

Having left the remains of the pod, it lay on the rock for a short space. None of those watching made any move toward it. Then that thick hump on its back split in turn, became wings so nearly transparent that only a pattern of webbing might be truly seen. Keris recognized one of the shadows from that place beyond the cliff—this was a flying lizard.

Chief leaped without warning from Destree's shoulder, leaving deep scratches. He crouched now in his fighter's stance, and the thing was certainly not completely blind, as it swung around to face the cat.

"No!" Destree moved, but not as fast as Liara, who stood a fraction closer. The Alizondern girl's hands closed on the cat and he twisted and turned, trying now to vent his rage upon her.

"No!" Destree near shouted now. "Let it be!"

She swung her amulet between the fighting cat and the lizard thing. The latter's head seemed to rise a fraction higher. Then its mouth snapped closed and the wings fanned the air. Moving with a speed which moments before the watchers would not have believed possible, it scuttled in the direction of the jungle. Its wings spread and it took off and out, hidden in a moment by a tangle of vines.

Destree pointed to those reddish drops still glistening on the stone where it had lain. "Poison," she warned.

"So now we have trees which give birth to poisonous flying things," Krispin said. He stopped, picked up a stone, and tossed it to cover the stain before grinding his heel upon it. "How did you know?" he demanded directly of Gruck. "Or was it by chance only that you showed us this new possible disaster?"

*It called.* The giant's thought was simple. *It was time to be free—though that it did not say. Only that it called.*

Lord Romar gave a small, harsh laugh. "We must take it to mind not to answer such appeals again, large friend. Also"—he looked back to the jungle—"who can tell what else may possibly entrap the unwary?"

No one answered him, for out of the air sounded the cries of the falcons, and their bonded brothers were quick to receive them, standing quiet in that communication the rest could not understand. Vorick reported first.

"There is no possible opening for perhaps two days' journey or more to the east."

However, Farwing had better news, perhaps some hours' travel to the west a river issued out of the cliff face—perhaps thus did the lake in the safe valley drain. It straightaway entered the jungle and its waters might well offer a road of sorts. At least the travelers would not have to cut a way in, for the waters had already done that for them. And it pointed due south, in the direction they all knew they must go.

The narrow strip of open rock was rough and they divided some supplies for the Torgians to transport. Not even the Falconers rode—though their birds were on the saddle perches.

In fact, as they sorted once more through supplies the Lady Eleeri and the Keplians gathered together and Jasta sought out Keris.

*Battle brother,* the Renthan hailed him, *it will be share and share alike. You wear a pack—can I do less? For you are a warrior even as I.*

Apparently the Keplians had come to a similar decision, for they allowed Eleeri and Romar, but them alone, to secure packs on their backs.

With Krispin in the lead, harking to Farwing, who picked up landmarks, they started out. They went slowly, for none of them had as yet completely thrown off the effects of that ordeal of walking on air. It might not have strained their bodies, but the demands of nerve control laid upon them had been heavy.

The strip of clear space at the foot of the cliff widened slowly as they went, giving them room to move in a tighter body. But they could see nothing more than the high stone to the right and the waiting menace of green to their left. Nor did they reach the promised river until dusk was well advanced. Keep going, Keris thought, because they *had* to have the promise of it made truth.

In spite of the growing dark, they could see that where the water flowed from the cliff face it was clear and none of them, human or animal, refused to drink. But as the water advanced toward that tunnel in the jungle, it grew murky. Across its surface danced specks of green, as of sparks thrown off from a fire.

They set up their rough camp and shared out supplies thinly. The four-footed members of the party fared better than the humans, as they cropped eagerly that grass spreading up the riverbank.

"Lady." Lord Romar came up to where Mouse stood a little apart, her hands fast clasped about her jewel. "What advice do you have for us?"

She did not look at him as she answered. "Lord Romar, you have also the talent and it has been tried in desperate fires. You have what burden lies upon us all now."

"To go on," he replied in a low voice. "But even a fool would mistrust a march through these waters."

"There will be a way." Mouse sounded utterly confident. "That which would have us will not waste what it would feast upon."

Keris, within a short distance of the two, knew that curl of fear which caught at any before a battle was enjoined. So—if the witch-ling believed their journey would be aided by the enemy, then they dared not allow themselves to be entrapped by any offering. A boat here—its very appearance would make it suspect.

This night they set sentries once again. The dank and debilitating humidity did not vanish with the day and they were immediately aware of a new and vicious attack. The flies and insects which they believed had made their lives a misery during other intervals of their journey were as nothing to the swarms of winged and crawling tormentors which sought them out now.

Destree opened her herb bag and shared out what she could of pungent dried leaves in an effort to keep them off. But when she reached the end of her supplies speedily and those she had shared seemed to do little good, she went to stand by the riverbank. This night a moon arose to ride high, making the water a sheen of flowing silver.

She took the amulet from her neck and held it high. To Keris it seemed that the moon's radiance enveloped it until she held a small lamp. And she sang.

Once again Gruck, moving out of the deeper shadows, crouched behind her, and his deep purring caught on the notes of her wordless song, until all the camp save for those two lay in silence and even the animals, beating tails and tossing heads against the onslaught of the flying things, eased and stood rock-still.

Then—

"OOOOOOWaah—" The cry might have been that of a hound ready for the hunt, but it issued from the slender body of the girl who stood now with one hand on the giant's shoulder. There was nothing soothing in that night-shattering cry—it was no petition, it was a dire warning.

There came a breeze, certainly not from the direction of the jungle, for it held none of that cloying rottenness. Keris realized that the cloud of thirsty bloodsuckers about him was gone.

The song had died, yet the echo of the fierce cry seemed to hold above and around them for a short passage of time. They only knew that that winged and crawling army had vanished and now the sound of the water flow arose again.

Liara swung around to face them. The moon seemed caught in her short crop of silver hair. Her face bore a defiant expression.

"Hound knowledge can count for something," she snapped, "even here. Do you think our packs are allowed to suffer from fleas, or ticks, or the blackflies of the coursing season? By right I have not the knowledge of how to banish them, for I am female, but one learns if one keeps open ears and is silent in company. My uncle Volorian knew the pack cry, and here it is mine!"

"All of good use is of the Light. It is of benefit to living creatures, so it blends when the Power is summoned," Mouse said. "This is not my Power, but that of the earth and the beasts which roam it— yet it protects as effectively as any gem."

Thus they spent the night, and if armies from the jungle sought to bring them down, there was no sign of any such attack. Such a success was heartening—that they had descended the invisible way had been one victory, and now they had been nourished by a second. There was a feeling of new energy and the need to be busy about them all.

Again it was Gruck who dared the first attempt on the jungle. Without any explanation he splashed into the river, keeping close to the bank, the water rising to swirl just below the cincture of his belt. Though Destree sent a frantic mind-call after him, he did not so much as turn his head.

Once within the entrance of that cave of growth they watched him scale the shore, planting one large foot partway up the bank while he bent to lash out at the thick growth. There were squawks and cries and a thrashing of leaves.

Destree, feeling she must follow and yet not knowing what aid she could offer him, saw the muscles beneath his shaggy pelt stiffen. With a mighty heave he brought out of its hiding place a log so thick that his own wide reach could not encompass it. It skidded from his hold luckily near enough to the riverbank to roll down into the water with a mighty splash.

The giant paid no attention to his first catch; now he was bent nearly double, striving to see through the torn vines to where the log must have come from. Again he put his full strength to the test, this time venturing farther up the bank to do so.

He was almost hidden now from their sight, but the wild weaving of leaves and branches let them know that he was once again busy.

Suddenly he appeared taking two strides back toward the rest of the party standing unable to understand what he wished or needed.

*Rope*—

Destree whirled to get the coils Sebra had carried since they had reached the foot of the invisible way. Krispin and Denever were already gathering those up. Oddly enough, the Keplians, who had after their usual way kept apart, now moved forward, Theela deliberately stepping first into the river water, though she delivered at the same time a disgusted snort.

A flick of her head and one of those coils of rope were caught between her teeth. She jerked it from Krispin and now she moved toward where Gruck waited, the water rising about her sleek hide.

For a space of perhaps a breath or two the giant and the Keplian faced each other. Destree believed that they exchanged some messages—but if so, it was on a mind-plane beyond her reach.

Gruck took the rope, swiftly fashioned a loop in one end. Then, even to the amazement of the Lady Eleeri, he tossed that loop over Theela's head while she stood still and allowed such bondage.

Jasta pushed past Keris, snagging on his way another coil of the hide rope. Behind him trotted the two other Keplians.

"So—that is the way it is." Lord Romar did not linger to take off swordbelt or mail, but waded in, the waves of water set up by the other's splashing well up to his shoulders. But even those battering waves of the water did not hinder him from making three neck loops in the stretch of hide and then heading toward where Gruck had disappeared, carrying the loose coils of the rest.

As he passed Theela, who was standing as firmly rooted as a rock, he looked back.

"We'll need even more hands here." He must have picked up some message from the mare.

Keris splashed in, and heard the Falconers and Borderers follow. Then Destree brushed past him and, before he could stop her, was scrambling up the crumbling rock down which the giant had rolled the log.

There was a completed netting of hide ropes, linking men, Keplians, Renthan, and the two best-trained of the Torgians, before Destree showed her sun-browned face on the bank above.

"At the signal," she called, "pull with all your strength!"

Keris could not conceive of the size of any tree log which would so engage all their efforts. But he stood, feet a little apart and ready.

At first it seemed that they were straining to move one of the mountains behind them, something so earth-rooted it could never be freed by such puny efforts.

Then—

The line of humans and animals was nearly thrown full into the flood as the strain suddenly ceased. Yet the lines of hide were still taut, while a second or two later what they fought against seemed as firmly set as ever—but not quite.

Water splashed up against Keris's cheek. Eleeri, her hawk features sharply set, was steering Mouse, supporting the girl who was so much shorter that the river water washed her chin. Behind came Liara, her face set with determination.

Up the bank they pulled themselves, smearing arms and legs with clay. Then they disappeared where Destree had stood only moments earlier.

Meanwhile those in the river held their hide ropes taut and

waited for a second signal. Keris was aware of not only the mutter of the stream but the heavy breathing of both men and animals. But otherwise the jungle before them was quiet.

There were movements he could not see, hidden by the growth on the banks above, twitches and short pulls to which he instinctively adjusted his own hold.

Once more Destree appeared, a scarecrow figure so bedabbed with leaf muck and clay that she was like an ill-made image of herself.

"Pull!"

They threw themselves into the task. There was no answer at first and then, unwillingly, something began again to move in answer to their efforts.

Keris could hear the snapping of vines and branches. Some whipped viciously through the air, while torn leaves rained down into the open, plastering stickily to the men and animals.

Slightly to the left of where Destree had stood there rose what looked like a barrier of sorts, coated with the loose leaves, dangling vines. Again they halted—all of them looking up at that low wall.

Now it was the Lady Eleeri who showed herself to one side, her muddy hand actually resting on the top of that barrier.

"Back! Out!" By mind-speech and word she almost screamed those orders, then leaned forward to slash at the nearest knotting of rope with her sword. They went, some of them backing through the water without taking time to turn.

There was a shudder along that barrier. Eleeri took a quick leap to the side, crashing into a vine-draped growth to which she clung.

Out and out, farther and farther projected what seemed to be no tree trunk but a platform of some kind. It was covered with masses of leaf muck and clay, yet that had scraped away from the bottom in places and Keris could see what seemed to be a smooth surface, certainly no barked wood.

It teetered for a moment on the edge of the bank and then, over balancing, skidded out into the air and down, causing waves and a curling of water from which those below escaped with some difficulty.

All Keris could think of, as he wiped the muddy water from his eyes and somehow made it back to the bank, was that the roof of some fair-sized garth had taken wings to land before them. But a closer look showed him that this jungle find had more of the appearance of a merchants' barge such as he had seen on the Es River.

It rode low in the water, wavelets lapping down and then over the edges, but he could see that it was not shallow. Rather, the interior was filled with ancient debris shed by the jungle. And it certainly could not be of wood, or it would long ago have rotted away.

They approached it tentatively and then once more put their ropes to use to tow it back toward the open space at the cliff foot.

Destree crouched back in the vast hollow where the thing had lain, Liara crowded beside her on one side, Mouse, her sodden robe plastering heavily against her, on the other.

On Destree's knees rested Gruck's head. His deep-pitted eyes were closed and his breath came in uneven gasps. There were bloody tears in the fur on his shoulders and his whole body shook as if he lay unprotected in the snow of high winter.

How he had finally, even with all their help, gotten that find out of the clutch of the earth she would never understand, but that he was near the end of his strength she knew. Now she leaned closer over him, not taking her amulet from about her neck but keeping it linked with her, as she let it lie on his forehead. There was a launch of a fur body nearly as dark as the one she nursed as Chief nestled down, half covering that wide chest.

Hesitantly Liara moved. She stretched her thin body, less than two-thirds the length of the giant's, beside his and clasped as much as she could against her. Her tongue showed between those oversharp teeth and she licked Gruck's chest near where his mighty heart was visibly laboring.

Mouse fell to her knees. She held high her jewel and, though there was no sun here to bring it radiance, it glowed. Eleeri moved behind the witch, laying hands on the girl's slight shoulders, willing into the rising Power all she herself could give. This gentle giant was not of their species. It might be he could not answer in his extremity to what they would do—but what they had to give, they would.

The witch jewel blazed. Now its radiance came in waves, and each succeeding wave stroked farther down that long body until Gruck was enclosed by it. Eleeri felt her talent answer, drawn upon. She strove to summon it from the very depths of her. All the knowledge of her grandfather—shaman knowledge, some of it stretching back to the beginning of mankind—she fought to channel into Mouse.

What happened at the river now meant nothing, only that this stranger who had come to be a deep part of their company must be saved.

Liara raised her head. "His heart—it is beating stronger." Once more she returned to her licking, as a hound mother might fight to restore an injured whelp.

Mouse was sagging; twice she dragged herself more straight. And Eleeri's hands and arms ached as if she had carried some great burden for days.

They were unaware that others moved around them now, hesitant to come closer, knowing that Power worked to the upmost peak these could raise. Then Eleeri felt hands fall also on her shoulders in turn and into her flooded a new wave of strength. Under her own touch in turn, Mouse was straightening again, and the jewel blazed like a fallen star.

On Destree's knee Gruck's head turned a fraction. His eyes were still closed, but he was speaking in grunts she could not understand. On sudden impulse she leaned even closer.

"Guardsman of Alatar, return! The trail still lies waiting ahead."

She tried to strike into the mind which moments before had been closed to her. Gruck opened his eyes.

*I come*— It was as if he answered her summons.

It was on Theela's back that they brought the giant back to the cliffside camp. And there, floating, though still uncleared of debris, was what he had won for them.

Gruck, propped against a backing of packs, looked at it after Destree had gotten down him a strengthening potion.

"It is a boat—of sorts—our transport." Lord Romar had settled down beside him. "But how did you know where it lay?"

Slowly Gruck shook his head and then grinned, sweeping his tongue across his thick lips.

*It—it called to me. This—*he waved a hand toward the waiting jungle—*is like part of my homeland. There we know—when a tree dies—when even the egg of a varch is broken in the nest.* He touched his forehead with his finger.

*I knew that there was something there, not rooted, not part of the proper life where it lay. You have much Power. But Power is not all alike. We guardsmen are one with the forests—what is natural there does not call.*

"You said that lizard thing called." Romar rubbed his hand along his chin. "Yet do these not know naturally themselves how to break their pods?"

Gruck shrugged. "Concerning such life I know nothing. Only that that one needed help."

Whoever had left that barge must have vanished long ago. The more the travelers cleared it, the more work seemed to stretch before them.

It was Destree who sought out Mouse before the witch made contact with Gull. "Does it seem to you that fortune serves us too well?" she asked.

"We know we are summoned," Mouse replied soberly. "But the Light can provide as well as the Dark. Lord Romar says that the current in midstream is strong enough to speed us on our way, and they have cut poles to use. This much I know—we go to meet that which will not be refused, nor can be avoided."

There was little talk among the travelers that night; they were too tired. But Liara looked up at the stars and lay awake for a time. Her actions as part of this company seemed to have opened one of these gates all were mad about. The Hearthkeeper of Krevanel was fast disappearing and perhaps in the end no one would care—even herself.

# CHAPTER THIRTEEN

# The City Lost to Memory, South

Luckily fortune favored them in some ways. Keris wiped his arm across his sweating face and took a firmer hold on the long pole. Though the current of the river flowed in their favor, they needed the poles to fend off floating weed mats and waterlogged trees. This was the third day since they had left the cliffside. Luckily the river was wide enough so that the green gloom did not quite close over their heads.

None of them had been able to identify the material from which their present craft had been originally fashioned. Once freed of the debris of burying years, it seemed to be almost a giant half-shell or pod, sleekly gleaming as they had scrubbed it clean. But it was certainly not of any wood they knew, or time would have eaten it long ago. Nor did it give off any ring of metal. And to suggest it might be the shell of some monster was more than even the most active imagination would agree.

Who had left it there, and why, they would never know, but Gruck continued to insist that it was not native to the land in which it had been found.

Quarters aboard were crowded, the animals stationed at the centermost point, the humans, who were needed in relays at the poles, around the edge. Their supplies depended entirely on the river's bounty itself.

Some of the clusters of floating weeds Gruck fished out eagerly. There were small shelled things there which could be eaten if one was hungry enough—and they certainly were—and some of the not so waterlogged weed was given to the mounts, who sniffed at it disdainfully at first and then were driven to such graze. Once they had passed under a vine swinging barely a little above their heads across the water, dragged down by a number of round melonlike growths.

It was Keris's flame lash, aimed as best he could with the barge bobbing under him, which cut the vine, and Gruck grabbed at its falling line, hauling it swiftly into the boat.

With visions of more poison-spitting flying lizards, the rest of the party gave the giant as much room as they dared. But with his knife he split apart the nearest ball and the fresh scent of the juice which squirted out was enough to overcome their caution.

They ate half their catch, the humans scraping out the crisp inner sections, the mounts falling eagerly on the tougher skins. And the remaining four they wedged in among their packs.

Several times flying lizards swooped above them and always the hawks became nearly frantic, having to be quickly soothed by the Falconers. But none of the creatures came close enough to attack.

The travelers did not seek any tie with the banks, from their entrance in the water on, keeping to the river by common consent both night and day. There was no guessing what might lie in wait within that fastness of entangled growth, and at least over the water there was a faint suggestion of breeze to fight the draining humidity of the stifling heat.

In spite of the caution which had been drilled into them from their earliest years, the Falconers, the Borderers, Keris, and Lord Romar had been driven to discard their helms, their mail, even the leather quilted underskirts, and bent to their service at the poles nearly bare of body.

It was midmorning on the fourth day when they came suddenly on the first break in the jungle wall. Into this cut the sun beat steadily and there was a heavy droning as if some great creature breathed.

At Lord Romar's quick gesture they poled the barge closer to the opposite shore. Already the men were reaching for their discarded armor and weapons.

Liara moved forward first, and deep in her throat sounded that small growl. But Destree and the Lady Eleeri were not far behind. Yes, there was movement across river—and life—a feasting! Liara saw a limp gray arm pulled into the air as two of the flying lizards fought for a better grip on the already rotting flesh.

There were four such humps quivering under the attentions of the lizards or of smaller creatures who were so fast in their attempts to gather some of the torn flesh that they could hardly be seen.

Oddly enough, the remains were spaced in an exact pattern. And the carnage was grounded on what seemed to be pavement. Towering over the scene was a tall shape fashioned in a position which no human could have held for any length of time, its sharp knees half bent, clawed forepaws resting on them, shoulders hunched a little. The ovoid which was its head bent forward so it seemed to be watching the scene below with critical appreciation.

Clearly it had been constructed of the same red-brown material as the barge and probably by the same hands. But about it hung a cruel madness which seemed to lead those it watched to even greater frenzy in their feasting.

"Gray Ones," Liara identified the slain.

"Servant of the Outer Dark!" Mouse's voice arose over hers. Her hand moved as if she would reach for her jewel, and then she shook her head.

"Such shells are sometimes open for those who come," she said. "If it has not life within it still, let no touch of Power bring it awakening."

They were ready to agree with that and poled valiantly, bringing the barge into midstream, where the current ran the swiftest.

"So still the Gray Ones come," the Lady Eleeri said. "But they serve the Dark—why should they then suffer such an end?"

"Because," Destree made answer, "great Evil Ones do not return any loyalty to those who serve them. It may be that what awaits beyond must have pain and blood to build up its power—therefore it takes from those answering its call."

Liara shivered. "The Dark One," she muttered. "What could he get from us if he used us so?"

"That is why we go." Mouse had turned her head so she could no longer see even the edge of that opening in the jungle.

They were very silent as the barge bobbed on and the men swung the poles. None of them was green to warfare. They had battle scars, and memories which sometimes became night dreams of torment, but there was something about that monstrous thing presiding over the feast of the dead which carried the seeds of a new fear.

There were no more such interruptions to their voyage, though at first most of them expected secretly to come across other massacres. However, they needed to come to an end of this depleting journey. Their mounts were suffering from the poor forage and they were ready themselves to sink under the dank heat which beat at them.

As long as the tree canopy seemed to be so close, neither Falconer would send his bird on scout. However, at dawn the second day after they had left the clearing they sighted a break in that roofing and Krispin released Farwing.

The bird flew swiftly, cutting upward into a patch of open sky as they floated on, impatient for its return. Then suddenly Gruck stuck his pole deeply enough in the river that with his great strength he could for a moment or so halt their advance.

*Faster water*— His message was interrupted by one from Theela, who had shouldered her way among the other animals to the fore of their section.

*Open land—but the river—it falls!*

Lord Romar and Eleeri, long trained by their years of roaming, looked from one bank to another. If they faced a falls or rapids of some sort, their barge would be no place of safety. On the right the green of the heavy growth apparently made a firm stand, but to the left some storm of the past had brought down several trees to crush their lesser fellows, opening up a way.

A flash of wings and Farwing was back. Krispin caressed the bird as they communicated, and then he said swiftly:

"It is true. The jungle ends not far ahead. There is another cliff, but not such as we have had to face. However, the river narrows into a falls, descending thus to a lake."

So at last they had to dare the jungle, if only the fringe of it. Once more their mounts accepted the packs, leaving the humans to open the way. Swords were drawn and ran sticky with saps of different hues and they all tried not to touch what whipped back at them.

The heavy growth did not reach the edge of the drop before them, with a very good reason. Here was a shelf, or perhaps once it had been a road, of the same material as their barge.

No seam or crack marred its surface—it might have been laid yesterday. However, Destree knew as she dared to take her first step out upon it that it was incredibly old. But it was what lay below which held them still and silent for a long moment.

An easy slope of ramp led down to rolling stretches of plains thickly carpeted with matted greenery—though no trees. Here and there some of the jungle vines draped mounds which formed squat hillocks.

"A city!" Lady Eleeri cried, even as Swifttalon took to the air, soaring out over what they could see.

Buildings, yes, turned to mounds, where, in spite of the vine netting, could be seen stone.

However, those were only on the outer edge of this metropolis, for such, they saw in awe, it had been. Destree, who had served on Sulcar ships, had seen most of the largest cities of the eastern sea, but she had never viewed any such spread of buildings new or old. Beyond the stone ones where the jungle fought stood high towers, clean of any growth. She thought these must rival Es Citadel itself.

However, these were not castles, nor any type of habitation she had ever viewed before. For, though a tower extended six even seven stories tall, there was no visible break in the walls of any she could view from here—no dark slit of window. Instead it was as if someone had set up rows of children's play blocks—for they could see even from here the dividing of streets. These also had been built of the material which defied time and nature.

There was a glint far in the distance, and when Swifttalon returned, the bird reported that this must have been a port, for there was much open water beyond. Also he had not been able to see any life except birds. Still they hesitated to start down that road and enter into the city. Estcarp, Escore, Arvon, all had their share of strange ruins, and these native-born were used to take care about any strange erection which could possibly have connection with the Dark.

Though the barge which had served them so well had been of this strange new material, none of them were about to forget that image in the jungle and the impression of cold horror which it had left with them.

They decided at last to establish a camp near the small lake into which the river plunged. There they must hunt, for they were all gaunt and had tightened belts to the last notch.

Then they could explore by degrees and with caution. The birds would be invaluable, and Eleeri insisted that the Keplians could easily sense danger. They did not know what new talents Gruck might produce when it was necessary.

Destree was heartened as she stepped off the foot of the ramp to see a tall standing, the largest she had ever found, of illbane, its ivory flowers scenting the breeze.

That was rare in the world she knew, a very costly and hard-come-by herb. Surely if those who had once lived here had cultivated such, they had not served the Dark, for illbane was a mighty tool against evil.

There were other plants, too, which she knew of old, and they seemed to flourish extremely well in this earth. The terrible humid drag of the jungle was behind them and they walked at a swifter pace and were soon at the place Denever, scouting ahead, had picked out for them.

Open fields, grown waist-high with grass and what Destree was sure was a kind of grain now gone wild, welcomed the animals. Free of any burdens now, they rolled luxuriously and then began harvesting nearby. The Falconers delivered four grass hens disturbed by the horses, which had fallen easy prey to their birds, and Chief brought in a half-grown heeper. Keris and Denever, though they kept away from any of the overgrown buildings, went hunting and then had to call upon Jasta to help transport a small beast which might have been ancestored by a farm cow.

The women sought out herbs and Gruck went into the pond, where some quick work on his part brought out ten fine fat fish. Thus after a long time of near-fasting, that night they feasted.

Once more there was a gathering in a side chamber of Lormt. Autumn threatened, especially after sunset, and braziers were giving forth a limited measure of heat as well as some of the incense believed to clear the mind. For clear minds were needed. But this time it was more than Gull and Mereth who held council there. Willow, Gull's second hand, was another half shadow beside her superior.

Here also were Jaelithe and her daughter Kaththea, Nolar and Dahaun of the Green Valley.

Gull's rasping voice broke the silence. "You have heard"—she made a gesture toward a small table a little apart on which were piled sheets of leaf paper showing dark ink writing—"what has been reported. There is interference from the south. Sometimes Mouse gets through clearly, but again there is silence."

"The Dark?" suggested Jaelithe.

"No, that we would sense at once. Three reports have come in turn from the Sulcar expedition: They have truce with the barbarians but are now before even the boundaries of that half-fabled land. Arvon—what chances there to give us any hope?"

Gull leaned forward a little and stared straight at Kaththea, a frown drawing her somewhat bushy brows together.

"Hilarion labors but—so far the connection cannot hold. And that," the younger woman nearly spat back at the witch, as if she were defending her mate, "*is* of the Dark. Therefore we dare not probe too deeply lest we draw to us something of what our kin must now be facing."

"Now we hear of a city," Mereth broke in, her slate chalk busy. "Did not Mouse tell you in detail of that?"

"Not only of a city, but . . ." Gull hesitated, "we know of the in-drawing of the Dark Ones southward. It would seem that it is this city they seek. They are being watched but our scouts are too few to attempt an open meeting with them."

"A city," hazarded Nolar. "Perhaps also—a gate?"

For a long moment Gull made no answer, and then she nodded. "A gate," she said sourly, as one biting down on unripe fruit. "We hold that earlier one found alive, but it takes toll on the sisters. To hold two such—" Then she turned on Mereth, her cheeks flushed a little as if with anger. "For all your delving, you have found nothing concerning a ward. We hold one gate here, perhaps two, if Mouse can give us early proof. How many may lie elsewhere? But I tell you this—even all the power which made mountains walk to our defense in the past cannot hold much more than we already deal with!"

"Sage Morfew uncovered yesterday a packet bearing the seal of the Mage Arscro." Mereth shifted in her chair.

She heard the sound of quickly indrawn breath. For the first time Willow dared speak:

"Arscro is legend." She stated that as if she hoped it was a fact.

"Legends," Kaththea returned, "have a habit lately of coming to life. But who—or what—is Arscro?"

"One of the Old Great Ones—the first openers of the gates." It was Nolar who made answer, to the very obvious surprise of Gull. "When I was student to Sage Ostbor he had one document which made some reference to Arscro but saying nothing more than that—that the first of the gates grew from his experiments."

"Then let us hope," Gull snapped, "that this sage's find, Lady Mereth, will have some answers which we badly need. In the mean-time . . ." She paused, as if she hated to say the words which she spoke now. "We shall guard and sustain our people—those with Mouse as well as who are farther afield—as best we can and hope for time."

Mouse crouched in the half embrace of the sweet-smelling shrub which had drawn her because its perfume seemed soothing to her troubled mind, and looked out upon as much of that grotesque

179

city as she could see from this small hillock. They had guessed that in reality it was one city rooted upon the ruins of another, ruins which the newcomers had made few attempts to clear away. The worn, overgrown stone humps were in such sharp contrast to those towering windowless, doorless spears of buildings that it somehow triggered uneasiness.

The falcons and then the Keplians and Jasta had been the first-in scouts for them, the animals apparently roaming in their grazing closer and closer to the more crowded center of the town.

So far they had reported no signs of any life except birds and animals. It was as if this forgotten country had never been known to man. At dawn and late afternoon scouting parties of three had begun going out, ostensibly hunting but really penetrating deeper into the midst of the clustered buildings.

But—Mouse had her fist at her mouth and was gnawing at her knuckles, unconscious of the pain—but there was . . . She bit deeper. Gull should be here—one of the Elder Sisters. She could not tell for herself what dwelt like shadows just behind her shoulders. There was a . . . waiting!

Because she was so unsure of what might menace them, she could not call too often—try too much to explain. This brooding *something* might well be waiting for her to reveal Power in just some such way.

So far she had not shared her uneasiness with any of the others. But she wondered if Destree was not also troubled at what might be.

The brush which sheltered her now shook, and fragrant petals showered down upon her. Liara was on her knees, her green eyes bright, her lips tight against those sharp white teeth.

"There are Gray Ones," she said with a certainty which could not be disputed. "Riders also—though their mounts are not honest beasts like ours. Gruck trails them."

So, her uneasiness was banished by so much. Mouse knew now, as if Gull had announced it in cloister meeting, that these straying Dark Ones were moving, against their wills, drawn by something greater than they could understand, toward a final meeting.

"We move camp," the Alizondern girl was continuing. "Vorick has found a ruin which is not altogether swallowed up and will give us temporary shelter, and the Lady Eleeri has sent out mind-call to Theela. The mare will bring the other animals in. Only the scouts are out, but today they vowed to strike clear to the sea—if it is a sea. Can you call them, Lady Mouse?"

She remembered seeing them ride out that late afternoon even though she had been more than half buried in her own thoughts: Denever, Krispin, and Keris. Surely the Renthan would pick up the Keplian warning as it came.

But the men . . . She clutched her jewel firmly and summoned up a mind-picture of each—Krispin in his hawk mask helm, Denever, and Keris, of the Valley and yet not of it.

She held them so and summoned strength with the jewel. Then Jasta answered, and she knew that they would be slipping back with more caution than they had gone, out of any trap newly come enemies might be setting.

Gather they did, at the temporary shelter Vorick had discovered. Either the masonry of this particular ruin had been better ordered or the plants attacking it of less hardy rooting. They were able to push aside a screen of vines and enter into a large hall, the roof of which seemed intact under the prodding of their spears.

The space was large enough that they could also bring in the mounts, and the animals made no objection to being urged under cover.

Their two travel lanterns flashed brightly enough to afford half-light for this hall. But anyone could see that wariness grew sharper by the moment in each and every one of them.

Apparently Liara's report had already spread. They were busy at their packs loosing extra arrows, fresh spearheads, sharpeners for the blades of knives. Mouse saw Keris to one side, his flame lash in his hands, examining intently the butt—perhaps the lash's efficiency was threatened, for he frowned as he did so.

"The Dark Ones gather," Destree observed. "They are few, as far as we can tell. Perhaps the jungle took greater toll of them than we can guess. But there are Sarn Riders—and such are not easily faced. Rasti?"

She looked inquiring to Vorick, whose Swifttalon had flown scout that day.

"They have not been seen. And Swifttalon can track a leaper in a hayfield by the wave of stems alone."

Mouse felt that sharp blow, delivered by no hand, coming out of the very air around her. She held her jewel first to her trembling lips and then to her forehead above her eyes.

Distorted pictures, like tapestry crumpled together, shook her. She was dimly aware of hands clasping her tightly, giving her support. With all the talent she could summon, Mouse tried to make some sense of the weaving pictures. It was as if some constantly whirling mist first revealed and then quickly hid them again.

Then—perhaps she had drawn enough support from those hands to control her talent focus—she saw.

There was a city, or at least a large collection of those same tall windowless buildings. However, this city was alive. Along the street she saw most clearly moved humanoid figures: small, emaciated, barely clothed in tattered and filthy rags. They looked as bleached against those buildings as if they had been buried underground for most of their lives, and they were harnessed together in packs by chains. There were men, and women—and children—all blank and hopeless, to her sight.

These might be beasts driven to some slaughter, for others, larger, brutal of face, clad uniformly in dull black, marched on either side of that pitiful company, swinging whips which only too often raised a bleeding welt on bare skin, seemingly at the caprice of the wielder of that lash.

The captives were urged on, emerging now from the city to a wide-open space. There had been built a platform on which were a number of cushioned seats. These were occupied not only by men wearing black (though it was richly overhung with gemmed chains), but by a number of women who were eating bits from boxes being passed around, laughing and talking feverishly.

One man on the platform was on his feet, leaning forward a little to overlook the captives. He made a gesture, and out of the general lines of his followers below came another who bowed to the one who summoned her. For Mouse saw she was a woman dressed in the same uniform, but one lightened by a green collar which extended well down her breast and which was centered with a pendant.

She made a bow to the leader, but it was one which held a hint of mockery, then stood waiting. He gestured again. A vehicle unpulled by any animal, yet running smoothly, came to a halt beside her and she seated herself to be borne forward around the waiting captives, to the open space farther on, where two pillars stood. Her carrier was followed by a number of others, all carrying uniformed women.

The one who led this procession got out and went to the pillars. From one of those vehicles which had followed her there came two women at a fast trot, carrying between them a squat artifact they set down directly facing the space between the pillars.

Behind this the woman took her place, while there moved in from either side other warriors, all armed with tubes.

The woman set hands to two levers on the top of the artifact and there blazed out a thrust of black-gray which became like a mist filling the whole space.

Then out of the mist wavered a pair of Sarn Riders, their ugly monster mounts acting as if blind, and after them scuttled Gray Ones, bumping into one another as they came, their jaws drooling long strings of yellow stuff.

The tubes carried by the waiting warriors spurted fire, and Sarn Riders and Gray Ones went down. But they were still living when the mist was gone and they were dragged forward by great hooks and torn to pieces between the pillars, their blood turning the ground into a noisome mud.

This the woman leader inspected and then came back in her vehicle to stop below the platform and make some report. Whatever she said was not taken kindly by the leader to whom she spoke. His mouth opened as if he were roaring. Firmly his subordinate shook her head.

Then—Mouse was whimpering and crying, her head against

Destree's shoulder. She was sure of what she had seen. Somewhere they were struggling to open a gate—those creatures of evil. And she could only now believe it was here.

## CHAPTER FOURTEEN

# *Blood Magic, Lost City*

Mouse became aware of a soft crooning, of a warmth as if she lay against the breast of some loving spirit. The horrors which had spun through the "seeing in her mind" still abode, but they were softened; she could no longer taste bile in her mouth.

"Sisterling." No abrupt call such as might come from Gull or one of the sisters she had come to know—this was part of the warmth and the caring. Slowly she opened her eyes and looked up at Destree and another who also helped to support her. That support she needed, for she felt no strength from either bones or flesh—only a great weakness.

It was Eleeri who was crooning, and her hand stroked Mouse's cheek, seeming to leave behind its passage more of the feeling of peace, of safety . . .

Safety!

For a wild instant she was snapped back into that other place and watched the foulness in action there.

"Mouse!" A voice from afar. And one she knew. *That* was Gull! She must answer, report, and she tried to pull herself up from out of Destree's hold.

"We have seen, Sister," that remote voice spoke now. "Through your eyes we have seen. Rest safely until the Dark rises."

Gull's voice died away—thinned perhaps by the great distance now lying between them. But Destree, the Lady Eleeri, Liara, Gruck—all the others she sensed now about her—they were not so removed. And if that gate of torment and death opened—and those were drawn into its maw . . . !

"Please." She could feel that her hands still rested on her jewel, but it was cold to her touch, for now the Power was gone out of it. "Listen!"

The need for warning this handful of companions—perhaps the lack of time—gave her energy enough to find the words, though those came haltingly, to tell what she had seen. Though she did not have strength enough to lift herself far up against Destree and could see only part of Eleeri's face, a suggestion of lighter countenance behind her which must be Liara, she was entirely certain that she spoke to all of them and that they heard.

"A blood gate!" Of them all, Keris cried first from those shadows she could not pierce.

She sensed that he guessed more meaning in what she had reported than most of the others. However, he was of Escore, the heartland of the Old Race, where the deepest of memories lingered.

"A blood gate?" That was a question from Krispin.

But he was interrupted by Vorick. "That flash we viewed came from near the sea! Yet it did not open any gate."

"No," Lord Romar said slowly. "For only half the price is paid. Lady Mouse, surely you have knowledge of evil dealings."

His words might have been keys, unlocking some of the old knowledge which had so filled her days with learning until the call had come from Es City.

"A blood gate—" Mouse's voice caught and she had to stop and clear her throat, "is wholly of the Dark and used only by the Dark. Of such was that which loosed the Kolder curse on us. But that was done from their side by some learning of their own which we did not share. This—this—draws from the deepest evil this world has ever known.

"We believed that some loathesome Power was summoning the Dark Ones from Escore to serve them. That it was, but in another way than the riders and the Gray Ones could guess. Called through the gate, they were slain, with all the pain those others could contrive, opening the way to this world. But only has it been done by half. They can enter now, I believe. But the gate will not remain open to their passage unless some of the blood of that world be as cruelly spent on this side—that is why they brought those captives." In spite of herself she began to shiver.

Mouse had faced evil before. She had helped to destroy one of the ancient vile traps, and that by instinct alone, for she had had no true training then. But this was such a danger as only an army armored with the highest talent could withstand. Gull! Then she remembered, Gull already knew. Her own effort had been so great she had interlocked with the Witch Mistress who had seen even as Mouse had seen.

How much time had they before that pitiful crowd of captives would be driven through to slaughter? And these strangers, as had the Kolders, had weapons perhaps beyond the comprehension of her world.

Eleeri spoke first. "We watch. And you, Witch Daughter, when the strength is again yours, ask how goes the research in Lormt. Since the blood gates were known of old, then also there must be records of them—and perhaps even answers. Now . . ." once more she gently stroked Mouse's cheek, "let Destree call upon her Lady's aid to your healing. For it is plain you have suffered a wounding, if not one of flesh."

If Mouse could have protested she would have, but the Voice of Gunnora seemed to seep into her whole body. Her eyelids were so weighted she could not hold them open, and down into the greatest depth of renewing slumber that soft croon carried her now.

They were but a handful. Keris glanced from one to another in that ruined hall. Against them the might of an army—one undoubtedly such as the Kolder. They could muster a collection of talents—but Mouse had the greatest Power to control, and to see her so reduced promised little good for the future.

Flight was possible, but he knew that no one of them, human or beast, would take to that. If the gate was opened, then what they could do must be done here.

"Kolder tricks," Lord Romar was saying slowly. "They kept us at war for years. It was your grandfather"—he looked now to Keris— "and the Lady Jaelithe who put an end to that. Yet I do not believe that this gate opens on the Kolder world. What we face now is a different brand of Power."

Destree had settled Mouse comfortably in her bedroll, but before she moved away she saw Gruck's bulk nearly fill the entrance to the interior of the ruin. Behind him moved swiftly the three Keplians and Jasta.

When the two Borderers and the Falconers, who were nearest, hurried after him, the giant looked around and shook his head. Eleeri, pushing up beside the men, suddenly nodded.

"He would set an alarm," she said, and Theela whinnied as if impatient to be gone. Keris slipped past the others until his shoulder rubbed against Jasta's.

The giant's big head swung around and those deepset eyes studied the young Escorian. Then he gave a brief nod and started down through the meadowland toward the city. Keris swung up on Jasta, as the pace the other set was difficult for an ordinary man to equal without breaking into a run.

Keris had made three previous scouting ventures into the remnants of the ancient city. There had been, as he thought, no possible way of getting into those tightly sealed towers save by blasting. Now they moved among many of these as Gruck led the way, the Keplians trotting behind him down toward the visible patch of the sea.

Mouse's vision had certainly suggested that the evil forces she had witnessed in action must once have known this country. Else why would their towns, set in such perfect precision, be here?

The Escorian expected that Gruck would bring them down to the seaport side itself, where they had not yet explored. However, having paused twice to sniff deeply, Theela close beside him as if the mare shared another range of thought, the giant turned down one of the silent streets, where even the small thud and jangle of their passing seemed to be instantly swallowed up. Their small cavalcade came to a halt on the edge of an open space, pavemented like the streets with the same imperishable material.

Here also stood a pair of pillars. Sighting those, Keris was sure they had reached their goal. This open field, the pillars, were too like those Mouse had described—save that here the field was deserted.

Keris noted that now their speed diminished, the giant cutting his strides, his head going from side to side as if on constant watch. Theela left, breaking into a trot, the two other Keplians following her. They circled about the pillars, though remaining at some distance from the sinister stones.

*They will stand guard.* Jasta's mind-speech touched Keris. *The big one can use our aid.* With Keris still mounted, he cantered on.

The giant's hands were now busy with his belt and he brought out of a pocket there that same silvery wire Keris had seen him use to snap the lizard pod many days earlier. He motioned to Keris, who quickly joined him.

Pressing one end of the wire into Keris's hand, he gestured for the Escorian to strike out for the farther of the two pillars. Though everything within him dreaded such an approach—what if he were to be sucked through?—Keris obeyed the other's unspoken order.

Meanwhile Gruck, with a flourish of arm to unwind the thread, was heading for the other pillar. Twice he paused for a long sniff but then went steadily forward. Now he reached his right hand, the silver thread clasped between thumb and forefinger, and deliberately pressed the slightly crooked end he held against the pillar.

To Keris's surprise the thread now appeared to be rooted. Clasping the loose coil, Gruck came toward him, pulling the cord taut behind as he came, at what might be shoulder height for a human. Reaching Keris, he took the other end and pressed it seemingly into instead of against the stone.

So thin was that thread of metal that only glints of the afternoon sun made it visible. Gruck caught it and gave it a testing jerk. A twanging of sound answered.

Still it seemed he was not finished with what he would do. Once more Theela and her companions trotted up to him, and this time Jasta translated at once.

*Vines, grass are needed.*

The Keplians and Jasta could tear the growth from the walls of the nearest heap of rubble. However, Keris's knife cut cleanly, and he paid no attention to the sticky sap which covered most of him by the time they were through, and brought their harvest back to the giant.

The giant had taken no part in their ruthless stripping of the ancient stones but rather was inching along on his knees from one pillar to the other. In his hand was a rod, which he held steady in a straight line. A red glow showed on the pavement as that passed over it, and it left a groove behind.

Keris could not help a series of uneasy glances at the pillars. His woeful lack of talent would give him no warning if those Mouse had seen broke through. How long would it be before they could expect invasion?

Gruck pulled the mass of fast-withering vegetation apart. Some he discarded with a toss to one side and other pieces he handled carefully. Having sorted what they had brought, he once more went to work. Into that groove in the pavement he fit certain sections of vine, and as each was so planted, he sprinkled small pinches of what looked like dust which he took from a stoppered vial drawn from his pouch. So he worked with the methodical care of a gardener who had all the rest of the day at his service to complete the task.

He rose to his feet at last, hands on hips, looking from right to left and back again. The notch burned into the pavement was filled.

Then he turned and tramped toward the same rubble where they had torn loose the vines. Down on his knees again he scooped at the soil, darker here and moist, gathering up vast handfuls of it. Seeing what was to be done, Keris, too, went digging. He watched Gruck's transference of the mucky stuff to the now-buried vine sections and followed the giant's lead. Then a jerk of Gruck's head sent him back and away. The three Keplians drew together, Jasta a little apart.

Gruck took up position at midpoint of that nearly invisible strand uniting the pillars. He threw back his head and Keris heard a roll as if distant thunder drummed among the peaks behind them. It continued almost as if the giant need take no breath to sustain that call.

There was a darkening along the line of buried vine. Then small stems arose, whipping back and forth higher and higher until their blind search found the thread, and there they anchored. Anchored and grew thicker, and not only that but they developed—with a speed as if shot as arrows from a skilled bow—great thorns. Nor were those the only products of that fantastic growth. Buds appeared, thick and round, growing even larger.

Gruck was silent. But he took two great strides and caught Keris by the shoulder, drawing the young man back and away just as gleams of color showed among those buds and they opened into huge blossoms, from the centers of which arose puffs of yellowish powder.

*Death!* With the giant's warning in his mind, Keris was once more on the move. How practical against off-world weapons the giant's powers might be, none would know until the time came for testing them. They might not have discovered the complete lock for that gate, but he was sure that what had been done here would win them some much-needed time.

They all felt the need for some communication with those who had sent them, but it was plain that Mouse, wan-faced, somehow even shrunken a little so that she looked even more the child, could not be put to the strain of a call upon those in Lormt.

They ate and then snubbed out their small fire. Jasta and the Keplians had drifted out again into the open land—of them all now, perhaps these were the best as scouts and watchers. They could hope that the aliens beyond the gate might very well have no idea that man and animal might communicate.

But this night only Mouse slept, if sleep she did. Perhaps she had been drawn into some trance state for renewing. The rest sat in a circle about the graying ashes of the fire.

It was Lord Romar who broke the silence which had held them as the night drew closer in.

"Gruck"—he nodded toward the giant, a hulk of denser darkness against the wall—"has given what he can of his talent to win time. Whether his barrier can hold against what those others can bring upon us, we do not know. But . . ." now he looked from one to the next of those about him as if he could see their faces plainly, "to ward for all time this gate . . . We are eleven. Perhaps eleven thousand would be a better accounting for such a task.

"Let us now list what we do have. My race has talents, strengths which can be drawn upon, but I do not possess the Power to focus such except in limited battle. My Lady"—he glanced at Eleeri, who had settled beside him—"has power born in another world and of a different learning. That she won freedom for the Keplians was such a feat as no other attempted.

"Denever has been entrusted with the weapon secret found at Lormt."

"That much, my lord. But I am not of the Old Race and I have no talent except that learned in the fighting courts."

"Thus do I say also," Vutch growled. "I fought the dead of Gorm, and kept the Borders clear where I was sent. But all my Power lies in arms skills."

Krispin cleared his throat, a sound not unlike that made by Farwing. "Falconers are born to sword and shield, and to the fellowship with their birds. We do not deal in Power, though we have fought battles where it was used. But not by us."

Keris's mouth seemed suddenly very dry. "As you know, I am halfling, born to the Lady Dahaun and her Lord Kyllan Tregarth. I am of Escore, which is looked upon as the source of Power both Light and Dark. But—I have no talent." He said it clearly, trying to hold his voice firm.

Suddenly he felt odd, as if he were under critical study—a strange insect, perhaps, in the custody of one of the scholars at Lormt who had a liking for such kinds of knowledge. He turned his head and found himself looking straight into the Alizondern girl's eyes, which seemed to shine green even in the absence of very real light.

"No one knows"—her sharply accented trade speech cut through the dark—"what one is until the last lesson is learned. I was Liara Hearthmistress, Whelp Cherisher, of Krevanel. Among us magic—what you call Power—is a thing of evil so great that you cannot conceive of how we feel near it. Yet, I discovered that my brother has accepted certain magic and will make use of it. Then I made a discovery that my species has other tricks and faults—did I not draw the Gray Ones? Now I strive to forget what has been pushed upon me from birth—and I am still finding that Liara is not what I always believed she was. Think not of yourself, pack comrade," now she said to Keris, "as one mutilated. Rather seek new paths not shadowed by the events of the old. You say you are without talent—does he speak the truth?"

Oddly enough now, her attention swung from him to Gruck.

*What he has will come when there is need.* The giant's mind-speech was quick. *Also as a Guardsman I have talents, which may be strange in this other world of yours, but in which I have been long drilled. Since I can no longer serve the Alatar as I gave my oath, I now serve your purposes.*

Destree shifted a little away from Mouse's bedroll. She had been holding the small hand of the sleeping girl and now she laid that gently back on the other's breast. Her fingers then went to her amulet.

"This is the Lady's battle also. There is a thought which might be of service. Tell me"—she spoke directly now to Eleeri—"I know that the witches hold open the lines of communication with Lormt. But is there one there also who is of the Lady's following?"

Eleeri did not answer at once—rather, it was Liara who spoke a name. "The Lady Nolar. She is a healer and I have seen her light the Lady's lamp."

"Picture her in your mind, Liara. Make her features plain, even see her about some daily task!" There was excitement in Destree's voice now.

They sat in silence. Keris found himself also striving to draw into memory she who was the life companion of Marshal Duratan. Anyone who had once seen her would never forget, for nature had cruelly marked her with a discolored cheek—a red shading which could never be banished.

"Yes . . ." Destree's voice was hardly more than a breath. "So—I see her. Now—by the Lady's favor"—she seemed to be addressing them all—"I will do here what should only be tried in a favored shrine. You"—now she spoke to Lord Romar, and then nodded in the direction of Gruck, and lastly to Lady Eleeri—"must be my guards this night, for if the ties are broken, the worst may fall upon us.

"I must lie entranced, and under the Power you can raise to cover me. However, it must be the Power of the earth, of that which the Lady knows—no magic from the learning of men."

Denever had lit one of their very small camp glows in a far corner of the room and Destree was already unrolling her bedroll. Then she brought forth her pack of supplies and made careful choices, sniffing and discarding, adding a drop of one of her selections now and then to a bowl so small she could cup it in her hand.

When she was finished and had put away the package of herbs, she drew upon their supply of water and washed her face and hands. Then she beckoned to the three whom she had selected as guardians and they moved in, Gruck one side of the bedroll, Eleeri at the head, and Romar at the foot.

Holding high the bowl, Destree made her plea:

"Lady, we are in need. I am one of Thy lesser creations, You who have made our world bear life—but I ask not for myself but for that very life You cherish, since the Dark looms high and its shadow lies upon us."

She drank the contents of the small bowl in a single draft, then stretched out even as Mouse so quietly lay, her hands folded on her breast over the amulet, and closed her eyes. In this very dim light she seemed to become one with the mat and stone on which she lay.

There was nothingness and then a blast of wind. But that was not sharp against her body; rather, it held summer's warmth and the scent of flowers. She might be lying on a bed at rest— No! deep in her, something sparked. This was no time for rest. She had not asked for that, but for something so much greater that she feared her talent might not be such as to grant it to her. Find—she must seek and find!

Now the soft wind vanished, and, as if in reproof of her inner demand, she seemed to be swept along so fast that she was rendered breathless. Find! To that she held firmly.

That which served Destree now for eyes saw light, more brilliant than she had known since she had left the Shrine—for on a table stood two lamps, both turned as high as possible, and on shelves others.

She knew at once where her petition had brought her: This was the workroom of an herbalist, a healer. And she who labored here sat by the lit table, a script so ancient it had been engraved on copper beneath one hand while with the fingers of the other she was tracing out the inscription word by word, whispering as she went.

Suddenly she looked up, staring at where Destree might be if she were indeed present in body. Her eyes were wide, and she stared as one who found belief difficult.

"You—you are a messenger," she said, rising quickly from the stool on which she had been seated. "Yet you seek no witch."

"I am of the Lady's chosen," Destree thought in return.

Nolar drew her hand down her stained cheek—perhaps the return of some very old gesture she had once used in an attempt to hide that marking.

"The Three in One, Guardian of all life, be ever with us." she spoke the words of recognition. "How may I serve Her from whom you have come?"

"Our witch is overborne by what she has discovered. Thus I carry what must be known." Swiftly—she had no idea how long her strength of trance could hold—she described to her listener their new discovery by Mouse, and the need laid upon them. "If you have discovered a ward," she concluded, "it is needed at all cost now. We fear that worse than the Kolders may be upon us. I . . ."

She faltered; the trance was fading, she had never tried her talent so deeply before. "Help—aid—" she got out those last two words.

Then once more the darkness and the wind which had carried her closed in.

Nolar stood but for a moment—awe still touched her. Then she went swiftly to a shelf on which stood a small gong. Swiftly she struck the metal and the ringing tone of it not only filled the room but, as she knew it would, reached out into corridors and rooms beyond.

"Nolar!" came a voice she knew well. She knew *he* would be the first to answer. It was always so—when she needed him, he was there. The marshal was not in war gear, but still he went sword-belted, and all knew that with that well-used blade he could give good account of himself. But against an army with strange and overpowering weapons, turned so toward the Dark that they might open a blood gate? He already had his arm around her.

"We gather in council. However, we are stronger: Hilarion has returned. So already all are summoned."

"To the south," she said in a small whisper. "Oh, Duratan—so far away!"

## CHAPTER FIFTEEN

# Lormt, South, the Forgotten City

It was not such a large assemblage as had gathered at Es City months earlier, but what would be decided here might change a world forever.

Simon Tregarth and Jaelithe, Simon just home from a second

sweep search in North Escore, Dahaun and Kyllan, the Sage Morfew, and, curiously flanked by Gull and Willow (as if they drew in now to make common cause), Lady Mereth. While Kaththea sat, she was not at rest, her body tense—she might have been one of the great cats about to bring down a skillfully tracked quarry. And Hilarion paced back and forth, turning swiftly as Nolar and Duratan came in.

"The alarm." Simon Tregarth, rather than Gull, seemed for the moment in command.

Nolar moved forward until she stood behind the nearest empty stool, though she made no move to seat herself. With a cautious glance at the two witches, she launched speedily into her report. Dahaun's long fingers locked before her, and after the manner of her ancient race her fair hair darkened to a somber black, her skin becoming nearly chalk white.

Hilarion's pacing had come to an abrupt stop and he was watching Nolar as if he would shake the words out of her at a faster pace than she could utter them.

"Well?" Gull looked to the adept. "What mastership of Power can be pulled forth now? Kolder darkness lasted for years and nearly wrecked us. Do we await a second coming of such?"

She was fingering her jewel, and her eyes were narrow as she kept them on the adept. Of old there had been no meeting place for the Witches of Estcarp and any man who claimed Power. But Hilarion reached far back—even before the first beginning of their sisterhood.

"I came with certain information," he returned abruptly. "We have sought afar, even before the first stones of this storage house of knowledge was laid. The gates which were our playthings—oh, yes, I played such games also until I was enwebbed by my own recklessness—were born of the curiosity of a single man: Arscro. And any reference to him and his dealings have been hunted, here, by the leave of your sisterhood"—he inclined his head in Gull's direction—"among all the stores of legend and history your hold.

"What may lay elsewhere in this world—in Arvon, in the parts we now know nothing of, we cannot guess. But the gate plan was born from the mind of a single man, seized upon by his fellow adepts with great enthusiasm, dealt with, refined, sharpened as one edges a sword."

"And what has this to do now with what we face?" Gull's voice was sour and sharp.

"What can be born in one mind can be recaptured. We might have searched for a hundred seasons but for that which Sage Morfew brought us. Together with my own knowledge of the opening of gates, we have an answer of sorts. Whether it will be successful . . ." He shrugged. "There is this about the highest magic: Its results cannot be foreseen, only speculated upon—or tried in desperation."

"Now we here face what has been learned by our southern band," Simon's deep tone cut in. Jaelithe's hand lay on her knees, and his wider fist closed over it as one who would hold what he has past all dispute. "Time is against them. She who speaks for Gunnora—Destree n'Regnant—has stood against great evil in the past and we were also a part of that battle. She says that their witch is exhausted. And how many leagues of mountain and hostile land now lie between us? Even if we had before us the solution—the gate lock—how could we give it to those who need it most? And even if they received the spell, would it answer to them, so far removed from the place it was woven?"

Hilarion shook his head slowly. "Do you think that every one of your questions has not already been made plain—though it was not until this hour I knew how desperate the cause might be?"

For some reason Nolar's attention was drawn away from the men confronting one another to Dahaun once more. The Lady of the Green Valley, she who had been one of those who held firm against the Dark for more years than Nolar could count—she was once more changing. The black hair was silvery as if time laced it through, her face was thin and drawn.

Kyllan must have noticed the change also, for he was on his feet, shoving back his stool, standing over her as if with his very presence he could keep some peril away.

She spoke, addressing Hilarion directly. The two of them might have stood alone in that room.

"You know what can be done."

"What I could try."

"And only you?" she asked.

"Only me—now. It might be a long search to find someone with talent enough, and then even longer to teach such."

The withered, aged look seemed stamped upon her now—her usual many changes were lost in the past.

"Then there is only one way!" She stood and seemed not to see Kyllan's hand come out to her, rather advanced within touching distance of Hilarion.

Now the adept's expression changed in turn. There was a wrinkle of pain between his eyes.

"Who? The Witch Child could not mesh in that fashion. Nor do I believe that Gunnora's Voice can be so unloosed from her Mistress. There is Romar of the Old Race . . . he is talented." Hilarion shook his head slowly. "One of the Falconers? Their mind patterns differ. The Borderers—"

She spoke only one word in answer. "Keris."

"Your son!"

"Think closely, Hilarion. He is partly of the Old Race, partly of an off-world blood—and bred in Escore. Also, he is without any talent to rise and perhaps forbid exchange."

"You know what may come of such meddling with life patterns?" Hilarion demanded.

Slowly the aging look was fading away again from Dahaun. "Those of our blood are birth-sworn against the Dark. He has fought evil since he could crack a flame lash, hold a sword."

"The choice—" began Hilarion.

Jaelithe nodded, understanding the point he was beginning to make. "The choice must be his, and he must also know that the price may be heavy."

Kyllan had moved forward and now Simon in turn had arisen, his face set grimly.

"What is this Power you would work?" Kyllan demanded first.

"The knowledge needed for the closing of this blood gate lies here." Hilarion touched his own forehead. "Nor can it now be used by any except me. Later it may be otherwise, but this is a matter of racing time in the south. There is no possible way of my reaching this lost city in my person. Thus . . ." he hesitated and then went on, "I must have a body, a mind, ready for me to enter there. If Keris consents, he will serve even as I would could I stand there."

"And the price?" Kyllan had edged up beside Dahaun. Though he had learned long since to control his emotions in most situations, there was now a frown and a stillness about his face which equaled that of Simon.

"The price is this." To Nolar's surprise it was the witch Gull who cut into this confrontation. "When this adept withdraws his persona from the boy—what may be left is mindless husk, with no hope of restoration. He has no talent to anchor him."

"No!" Nolar could not stifle that cry. Keris—she remembered the boy who had been so excited over the prospects of the scouting trips, so exultant when he knew he would be one of the seekers. Like her ruined face, he had carried an inner scar—of being a halfling with no talent. Yet it had not soured him.

Somehow Simon's face looked as gray as Dahaun's had been a little earlier. Kyllan slammed a clenched fist into the palm of his other hand; his eyes blazed.

They heard through that tense silence the squeak of Lady Mereth's chalk. She turned over her slate and held it high so they could read the large bold letters she had written.

"To each a choice. Do not lessen him by not offering."

But from the corner of her eye flowed a tear.

Simon put out his hand almost as if he sought some support and he received it speedily as Jaelithe moved to him.

"He is a Tregarth. There is that in him which would not thank you for denying him at least the choice," she said.

"How do we do this?" Sage Morfew spoke up in his soft voice for the first time. "If you contact Keris and make clear to him what has to be done, it must be soon."

Dahaun's hair was now the brown of sere autumn leaves and only her eyes seemed alive in her face.

"He is blood of our blood." Without looking, she caught at Kyllan's hand. "We shall seek. Then—it must be done at once!"

* * *

It was of course a dream—yet so real. Keris lay in his own bed with, around him, the flowered vine walls of the Valley house which had always been his true home. Over his head the brilliant thatching of feathers rustled a little under a breeze. He felt utterly content, one with all around him, as had happened only a few times in his life. The feeling had once led him to believe that he was on the very edge of discovering that after all he carried buried talent.

There was movement and he turned his head a little to see his mother and father seated on mats, watching him broodingly. Perhaps he had been ill.

"Keris." His mother's hand did not quite touch his forehead. "Remember."

How had he come here? This was the Valley of Green Silences, not the strange city. But she allowed him no time for questioning.

"You and your comrades need our aid. There is so little time. You must make a choice, my son."

Now Kyllan smiled at him, but there was something awry in that smile, as if it were very forced.

"Hilarion," Dahaun continued, "has found what may be the warding, but only he can use it. There is only one way he can bring it to the blood gate before evil breaks upon us. Since he cannot travel the leagues between, he must have a body for wearing."

Keris knew the chill of fear. "For every use of power so great"— perhaps he was not really speaking, merely thinking that—"there is a price. What one is laid on this?"

"It can be done only by your free choice, my son. If you willingly consent to be the tool for Hilarion's use . . . it may be that—" She bit at her lip.

His father's hands were on his arms belt as if he had heard a signal to battle. "It may be that when Hilarion must withdraw again—"

"I shall die." Keris brought that out quietly.

"That which is you may be gone. Your body—it may remain for a while."

Keris closed his eyes for a long moment. The fear was waging in him now. What his father had said was worse than any sentence of death.

"The choice is yours!" Kyllan's voice hurt like the thrust of steel into flesh.

Keris looked to his father and then to his mother. Halfling of mixed blood, but it would seem that there was some worth in him if . . .

"I am Tregarth." He repeated the three words as he had so often thought them over the years. "I serve where I am best used. If I perish in the service of the Light, what greater end can be mine? Tell Hilarion . . . his body lies in wait. And the time is very short."

There was a flicker, a dancing of color about him. He shivered. What—what had he promised? But perhaps from the first this had been the weaving of his life pattern, that he might have been born talentless for this very choice. He fought his fear fiercely. How long would he remain himself? When would Hilarion come to take that which was particularly his?

He could see light now, pale, coming from that open doorway in the ruined hall. And he heard a piteous moaning—no, not from him, thank the Great Old Ones. There was movement about him, yet he knew that he must remain in just this place—remain and wait.

Now he was a small pale thing fleeing along a stretch of shadow gray road until he crouched against a wall past which he could not drag himself. His pursuer came.

A flash of light was so great that it blinded the travelers for a moment, used as they were to the dusky interior of the ruins. Mouse sat straight up in her bedroll. She did not touch her jewel, but it was flaming as brightly as if she had called up its power. Destree felt the heat of her own amulet. There was such Power here now that one could sense it to the very bones, taste it.

When she managed to see clearly again, Keris stood, looking beyond all of them to the entrance. Keris . . . ? No! When she stared too intently at him, his body seemed to waver, to be doubled in an odd way.

"Hilarion!" Mouse was on her feet.

He who had been Keris looked to her. "There is that to be done and the doing lies . . . now!"

Paying no more attention to any of them, he started straight for the door, but Liara had caught at Mouse, taking such a grip on her worn robe that she held the witch captive.

"What has happened?" the Alizondern girl demanded. And there were rising murmurs from the rest of them, though some had stepped aside to clear the door.

"Hilarion has come! The ward—he must have the ward!"

"Keris?" There was denial in Lord Romar's cry.

Mouse answered him. "It was his choice. Thus he will serve."

They were all on their feet now, following Keris out into the light of a new day, but Liara now appealed to Destree. "I don't understand."

"Keris has opened the gate which is himself, given full entrance to Hilarion." Destree held to her amulet helplessly. This was of her doing. . . .

"That—" Liara pointed, "that is now your great mage? Then where is Keris?"

Destree shook her head slowly. "Perhaps we shall never know."

She heard a stifled protest from Liara, but her attention was all for the one who led them—though he might no longer be aware that he had any company at all. His head was bare of helm and mail hood; his hands swung loosely by his sides but not near any weapons. The morning wind lifted a lock of his dark hair and then fell away as if even the breeze could no longer touch him.

So they went into the city. Those who bore arms had them, and out from among the towers came the Keplians and Jasta, but the Renthan did not as usual seek out Keris.

Destree heard the mutter of voices about her, but she did not try to sort out any words. They went now to such a rising of Power as she could not imagine—though perhaps Mouse had an inkling of what could come.

The ancient streets flowed by them like water. And Keris looked to neither side, but turned this way and that as if he had come this way many times before.

Then they came into that field. Gruck had somehow made his way close behind Keris as a shield mate might stand.

His handiwork still lived; there was no sign that the vines there had withered. The thorns did not droop and the sinister flowers were red and yellow saucers. There had certainly been no break-through from that darker world.

Now Keris's body seemed even more misty, as if there was a struggle to keep it in form and steady. He—it—stood at the midpoint between those pillars, with the others, humans and beasts, in a semicircle behind him. Only Gruck kept his place closer to the adept.

There came sound, a thunder of it. Gruck's paw-hand was on Keris's shoulder and he jerked him farther back. Destree clapped one hand to her nose and she saw Mouse, white and sick, clinging to Liara, with the Lady Eleeri, arrow to bow cord, edging on to protect them. Blood—the stench of blood heightened by evil—

There came a crash from that barrier Gruck had set. Through the mass of vegetation thrust the broad nose of one of those carriers Mouse had seen in her vision. It tore through the vines but then slewed around and headed to the left, apparently out of control.

However, it was only the first of its kind to pierce the barrier. Those waiting had to scatter in a hurry, for it was plain that these metal crawlers no longer possessed any directing hand.

In one Destree saw a body lolling forward, skimming the pavement next to her. Another carrier nosed through the wide hole the first had opened for it. Eleeri's arrow sang a death note and a man half arose within and toppled over the side, to be impaled on one of those thorns not quite broken from its vine.

There was a jerk and the carrier swayed back and forth. It might be striving to return, but the Power of the gate refused retreat.

Keris moved. He reached for no weapon. Instead his voice arose until it seemed echoed back from the very sky over their heads.

"We are of this earth. What is wrought here was born of that earth."

He held out both hands, palms flat, and on those appeared balls of violet flame which flared as high as if they fed greedily upon the flesh which supported them.

"Arscro!" His ringing call made of that ancient name a battle cry. "Because there is always the balance—let now that balance right itself."

Then those behind him cowered away in spite of themselves, for he was summoning—summoning by names the most Ancient of Ones. And with each name the violet fire blasted higher.

The carrier had trundled through the wreckage at the gate and now stopped. But no one emerged from it. Nor did any other threatening blunt nose of metal show in its wake.

"Rammona, Lethe, Neave, Gunnora—Mothers of earth, Creators of all living things." His voice was as high and as steady as when he had begun, but it seemed to Destree that that wavering of body was growing stronger.

"This is no door for us. By the mercy you hold in Power—make it naught!"

That last cry seemed to ring in the air. The fire he held in his hands flamed away from his body, struck full upon the pillars and all which was between them.

Now the pillars in turn became torches and the violet deepened to the purple Mouse at least recognized as the epitome of Power—perhaps its like never unleashed before.

High blazed that fire and there was no heat from it. However, that blood stench was gone. The pillars were dwindling, leaving not even ash behind.

With their passing went the remains of Gruck's barrier and the carrier which had been frozen there in passage. The other machines which had preceded it had smashed into the rubble of ruins, the windowless towers.

There was a great gust of wind. They had to hold to each other not to be taken off their feet. Then—the plain was bare and under them even that seamless pavement was beginning to crack and erode.

Keris's hands no longer held the fire; they hung limply at his side. Gruck moved with that agile speed he could show when he must, and caught the Escorian as he stumbled.

That curious wavering outline of his body ceased. He was solidly himself again. Or . . . was he? Healer's instinct brought Destree running. Gruck had caught up the young man's body as if it were not of any weight and carried it back to one of the stands of meadow grass, settling there as if in a nest waiting for Destree's aid.

He was not dead, that much her quick check of pulse assured her. But that pulse was slow and uncertain. It was evident that Hilarion was gone and they could only hope that the price of power would not be nothingness.

Gruck put his hands on either side of Keris's head and his own eyes closed. Destree sensed he was seeking life, striving to find where it now lay and bring it forth.

However, it was as if Keris slept—no, not exactly slept, but that what made him what he was had withdrawn . . . past return? She refused to accept that.

Mouse knelt at his other side. Tears ran down her thin cheeks as she said: "Sister, long ago those of my kind severed their Power from that which the adepts knew and used. I—I can do nothing." And she was openly sobbing now while her jewel hung dull and lifeless.

Destree remembered those names Hilarion had called upon: Neave, who held always the way of truth; Lethe, who guarded the gate of birth life; Gunnora—her own dear Lady. She need not call upon Them by voice, They knew what lay in her heart.

Fearing nothing any longer—for those who had manned the

carriers were dead and their blood gate was no more—the travelers trailed back out of the lower city, Keris in Gruck's hold.

What had happened here had wrung the strength from all of them. Even the Keplians walked, their heads hanging as if they had run a full day's journey. Destree, Mouse, and the rest left with Keris, moving camp, having little wish to hide among the dank-walled ruins any longer.

Liara crouched at Keris's feet. "I heard Lord Romar say that his body may live—but his spirit is gone."

She twisted her hands together. "All people have their heroes. My House of Krevanel have added to the roll in Alizon. But to risk the spirit . . . I do not understand—there is so much I do not understand. I only know I *must* learn!"

Mouse smiled sadly. "We learn all our lives long. If we do not, then we are not what we were born to be. Keris believed that he was less because he had no talent. Yet a talented one could not have embodied Hilarion. Sister," she said to Destree, "what hope is there?"

"I do not know, for never have I seen this before—though I have heard of it. We can only hope that he will awake."

Yet, though they took turns at his side, he did not. At dusk Mouse drew well apart, so that the effects of the adept's Power discharge would not weaken her call, and reached Gull with her message.

"This Tregarth?" Gull asked last of all.

"We do not know—he seems asleep."

Gull made no comment. The old distrust of male talent still might hold with some of the sisters. But surely the time for such aversion was gone. They had moved mountains to save their country, but here a man might have done even more.

Dawn was paling the sky. Destree set aside the small spouted cup from which she had dribbled her most potent restorant into Keris's mouth just moments earlier. The potion would keep the body living, but it could not recall the spirit which had left it. The dawn wind brought the scent of the not-so-distant sea.

She had heard the message from Lormt: they were to return; their quest was finished. Already the found gates were being closed and warded. Their own had been the worst because of the blood price.

She was aware of movement near her. Jasta came up to stand beside the unconscious man.

*There is still a spark.*

Destree turned upon the Renthan swiftly. "How can such be reached?"

*Who gives life, Voice? Who would save a valiant one who gave to her earth?*

"Then"—her hand was already on her healer's pack—"I shall seek."

This would be a different kind of seeking than when she had found Nolar, for it was not a seeking in place or time, but beyond them both. She spoke to Mouse, and to Eleeri, but she was surprised when the mare Theela joined them, and then Gruck without a word.

There was a potion to be drunk, then she stretched beside Keris's motionless body. Into her began to flow what they could give her—strength.

There was darkness and she knew that she followed someone who had earlier fled this way. Waves of fear beat at her, as might the dashing waves of the sea. She held tightly to the picture of Keris—not as she had seen him last stretched seemingly lifeless on the ground, but in his full vigor of body and mind.

Down that black road she sped, feeling that in her which was eating at her strength. Then she saw that wisp of a grayish thing which clung desperately to an imprisoning wall.

Only a wisp of a thing—no, that she did not believe. Destree set herself to infusing into it to that other—that one in her memory. There—and there—and there! She called for strength—it came—held—while she built that body, made it whole and no wisp of shadow.

"Keris!" she summoned.

Then she opened her eyes upon the sun and those about her, so united in a friendship bond that it could never be broken. Now she turned her head.

His eyelids arose slowly. There was wonder in his face. Not the face of an idiot—by the grace of the Lady, this was again a man.

"Keris!" Her voice was loud in her joy.

He smiled. "You need not deafen a man, Lady—I am right here."

## Interlude: Lormt

The first of the early fall rains had swept through during the night, again making the crumbled section of the vast pile dangerous with falling bits of masonry. Since the Turning had brought down one tower and a portion of two of the connecting walls, the sages had done their best to ensure no more great collapse (there were enough holding spells cast there, stated Owen, to smother a tempest), yet there continued to be a certain amount of deterioration. Even so, the mainly elderly sages and those they managed to lure into helping them were still entirely intent on locating all they could find in the sealed archives which the first damage had revealed.

But now those more in touch with the world at large had other and momentarily more important matters to deal with. The great hall was still their meeting place and the hide map of their world was still fastened to the long refectory table. There were new markings in a goodly number on the eastern continent pictured there, but very few on the western.

This morning, however, it was not the map which engrossed the company gathered there. They had pushed benches, chairs, and a couple of stools into an irregular circle.

The man, leaning back as if bone-weary, spoke first as the lamps began to gutter out.

"It is done."

A sound which merged into a vast sigh answered him from the others. Tension drained from other bodies, leaving them feeling nearly as weary as the speaker.

But there remained a question which held them tightly bound still in that company.

"Keris?"

Dahaun's hand was clasped so tightly in Kyllan's that it would seem their flesh was melded together forever, even as it was in that distant body of their son.

Hilarion had raised both hands to cover his face, and his answer sounded muffled. "I do not know."

There was the scratching of chalk against slate as the old woman in the wheeled chair wrote a terse message and pushed it to her neighbor, the witch Gull.

Gull fingered her jewel, gave a sidelong glance to her companion Willow. Then she spoke, her monotonous voice sounding harsh as the chalk she answered: "They will be fighting with all the talent they can summon; we dare not break into their struggle now. If he can be saved, those with whom he has companied will save him."

"Small comfort you give us, Gull," Jaelithe Tregarth returned. "But the gate is gone, Hilarion."

He nodded, his head still in his hands. Kaththea had arisen and come to stand behind him, her hands massaging the flesh of his upper shoulders and the nape of his neck.

Gull spoke. "So. And you can chain the other also? Or must you travel yourself to each, since we have more time?"

It seemed to most of them there that she had abandoned the problem of Keris—almost as if some of the coldheartedness of the earlier generation of her kind had frosted her emotions.

Now the adept raised his head and faced her squarely. "Those we have found to be quiescent we can close from afar. That which your sisters hold in the spell of Mouse's laying . . ." There was a crooked little smile on his lips now. "There it must be your Power to lead mine to the goal."

Nolar twisted her fingers, stained a little from the potion she had been laboring on when summoned here. The old and deeply embedded distrust of the witches for men of Power—surely it would not hold now! That a witch and an adept would share their very different but formidable learning would be as overturning in its way than the removal of the mountains.

"The All Mother has agreed to any service needed." Gull's thin lips screwed together as if she found that statement bitter. "Willow will wait for any signal from Mouse. Cricket, Moth, and Ash hold the capping now. You must deal through them."

"Best now, then." Hilarion pulled himself up from his chair, levering himself with his arms. Kaththea was at his side and Nolar's healer's instinct brought her to them both.

Lady Mereth made no attempt to use her writing slate, but her hand caught at Dahaun's and she looked straightly up into that ever-changing face of the Lady of Green Shadows.

There was a strange calmness to Dahaun's features and she spoke something which might be a message for them all:

"He is not beyond the Final Gate, for if that were true, we who gave him life would know. Thus there is hope."

She stooped and kissed Mereth's cheek and went out with Kyllan.

So the party broke apart, some going back to the map. It was Duratan who rapped his fist on the border of the painted hide. "Arvon."

With that one word he expressed the second problem which had drawn them together. Hilarion, for all his effort, had been unable to once more contact Alon. He reported at last that it was not their focus which was at fault, but rather that some unknown Power formed a barrier, and for all of them that was hard to accept. Koris had sent a fleet of three of the swiftest Sulcar ships bound to the Dales, but this was the period of storms and what was ordinarily a three-week voyage might become twice that with ships beaten off the regular courses by the winds and waves.

"If there is news—Simon waits, and we shall know." Jaelithe had no doubt that the tie between she and her lord was such that the leagues between them now would be nothing.

"Terlach . . ." Duratan said absently as if voicing a thought aloud.

"Your Falconer comrade." Jaelithe sounded eager. "He has established an Eyrie in the Dales, hasn't he?"

"They use no Power . . ." Duratan began, and then turned suddenly to sit on a bench. From within his jerkin he brought a small pouch and shook out on the bench beside him a palmful of stones. The colors were alive even in this dim light.

Closing his eyes, he held his hand, palm flat, a little above them for a long moment. The stones shifted, colors separated and recombined. Jaelithe could make nothing of what he was doing, but she knew well that the Marshal of Lormt could easily have scraps of old knowledge unknown to others, ones which only answered to him.

Now she could see that the stones in their movements had fashioned the form of an arrowhead, a black stone backed by two gray, and then three blood-red forming the tip, the rest trailing behind.

Duratan's features became a grim mask. "*Evil*—and note it points west. Whatever fares in Arvon is of the Dark!"

Once more he gathered up the stones, shook them well, and threw, then shadowed them with his hand. Jaelithe could see that the color formation was slightly altered. The tip of the arrow was now a gray stone and three more of a bronze cast separated it from the black and dark.

"So far all is well with Terlach and Seakeep, but they are not removed from the fringe of the Dark. Lady"—he turned to Jaelithe—"what of Garth Howell? Are they as powerful as the witches?"

She searched her memory, trying to recall scraps of her early knowledge when she, too, had worn the gray robe and the jewel.

"As the witches held the power in Estcarp, so we knew that there was our balance in Arvon. But between us there was no communication after the Great War. They had adepts among them and they gave more Power to men. Also they were said to experiment in knowledge which was dangerous to others. They maintain their own guards—something on the order of the Sarn Riders—but no one has said they are wholly given to the Dark. For generations now they have been content to stay within their own boundaries and have little to do with any outside those in liege to them. Like the sages here at Lormt they have given the impression that the search of learning is paramount to them."

"But they are not truly of the Light?"

"Shadowed, we called them. It may be that the burst of wild Power has changed the balance. If so, how can we measure or even guess what they may do? Those of the Gryphon stand against them. And our foreseers promise much from them. But already they may be embattled. It would do us no good to try to raise an army against those armed with Power. We can only go on with our searching here and discover all we can of what was once used effectively."

He gathered the stones and repouched them. "It seems that nothing these days is designed to bring us comfort."

"When Power is loosed, Duratan, that is sure."

They separated from the gathering for what seemed to many of them the longest day they could remember. All of them threw themselves into tasks which they hoped were of importance.

But when the great gong sounded, they instantly dropped what they were doing and reassembled. Dahaun greeted them. Her hair was a flaming glory about her; all the color which had been leached out of her was back. She stood by Gull and even the witch looked less forbidding than usual.

"Keris—Keris is ours again!" Dahaun trilled like one of the birds of her beloved valley. "The gate is truly destroyed and our son is himself!" Kyllan took a couple of strides to draw her into a tight embrace. For the others it was as if the very walls of Lormt had disappeared and they stood in the open sunlight of a peaceful land.

Nor was it much later before Jaelithe also had a report. Captain Hilbec had reached Es City with knowledge concerning Arvon:

that the Dales were suddenly seeming invaded by some evil which soured their lords' minds so that there was open warfare between several. There were rumors of dire trouble in the Waste, and all connection with Arvon no longer existed.

Hilarion broke into an oath at that. He had once more brought his communication device to a side table in the conference room and now he scowled at it. They knew that earlier in the day his Power, joined by the restraining hold of the witches, had destroyed the evil toadlike trap the southern searchers had found. But if they could not reach Arvon, how could he share his discovery, which might be of major importance to Alon?

"So this is it," Kyllan said. "We may have cleansed our own portion of the world, but if the other half is engulfed . . ."

He need not finish that sentence. They could do so for themselves very well indeed.

## CHAPTER SIXTEEN

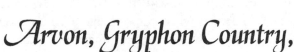

# Arvon, Gryphon Country, Northwest

He must hold to the barriers—thicken them as he could—let those about him feel only fear, pain, exhaustion. That he had been taken riding in Kioga gear and on one of their far-ranging scout horses gave him a small advantage. But those ringing him now must not know him for what he was—Firdun of the Gryphon House.

Had it not been for that wild blow of Power, they would never have taken him at all. But his talent had been wide open and the

Power sweep had rendered him near witless for a space. What chaos stirred now in Arvon he had no possible guess. But that it was mightier than any he had dreamed of, he was certain.

It had been well planned. He still clung to that estimate of the action which had brought him this far from home. Guret of the Kioga had reported an unusual amount of coming and going from Garth Howell. That nest of corpulent vipers had long been used to taking their ease, content with their delving into their store of old spelling and ensorcellment. Men and women both drifted into their holding, drawn by inherent desire for knowledge—but too often it was that of the shadow and it was firmly believed that the major mages there followed the Dark Road.

A sudden vicious jerk brought him up against the horn of his saddle, making breath explode from his lungs, and he did not try to stifle the cry of pain. They had him looped with a long rope, his hands tied behind him, but they had to keep their distance since his Kioga stallion went wild at any close contact with their monstrous scaly imitations of mounts. There were five of them—the well-armed leader and his men (if men those ill-shaped creatures who pounded along behind him truly were).

Firdun knew his own Powers; even now he was not sure of their limits. But he was too linked with those of the Eyrie to call upon them—not until he knew where these would take him and why.

Power worked two ways—a sending might well bring a retaliation unsuspected and unprepared for. Meanwhile, he let himself slump, held tight to his outer defenses of fear and pain, and tried to judge just where they were bound and why.

There was no spoken communication among his captors, and he dared not probe to find if they were using mind-send or merely following some orders given before they picked him up. But his weekly scouting out of the Eyrie had given him landmarks to remember and they were headed as far as he could tell for that high mound known as the Dragon Crest.

He was aware of newcomers swinging in before and behind him, other parties of the strange warriors. Among these were some who wore the rune-sprinkled robes of mages or the drab jerkins of novices. It would seem that Garth Howell, for the first time in centuries, was emptying its wards to the outer world.

The last dizziness which had been part of his undoing at the strike of the great Power was gone. But he still held to his determination to seem no more than he was—in this company the wisest move of all right now.

There was a harsh calling from overhead and swooping over them came a flock of birds, black, huge, red of eyes, cruelly curved as to beak, which suggested that these, too, were not to be easily dealt with.

A sudden side movement of those around him let Firdun see that the other parties headed in the same direction were following their maneuver, leaving an open space for what came. He must continue to keep his head down as might an utterly controlled captive, so he could not turn to see what sped from the southwest.

But he could look from the corner of his eye, and in spite of all his training he was startled. The creature was plainly female and well above any of his captors as to height. It was not running but proceeding in great bounds, during which it spread heavily feathered arms which served to keep it aloft for long spaces.

There were patches of feathers also on the lean body and the head bore an erect crest, while the four digits which might be termed "hands" were long and evily taloned claws.

The flock of black birds continued to circle it aloft and Firdun, daring to raise his head a little, could see that his present companions showed no desire for any close contact with this avian-descended alien.

This clearly was out of the Waste, for its like had never been seen by any of the Eyrie—and they were far traveled, as were the nomadic Kioga, ever in search for new forage for their herds and flocks.

Firdun knew well the old stories which said that the wars of the Great Lords long ago—those which had nearly wiped life from most of this world—had left strange remnants of beings, some holding to the Light, and other warriors for evil. The latter this newcomer certainly was. He did not need his talent to assure him of that, as the whiff of vile odor which blew in his direction when the creature leaped was enough to turn the stomach of any true human.

Their company fell back into line and he could see now the rise of the Dragon Crest. Apparently that was also the goal for the bird woman. Once more their party was urged from its track and this time to humbly give way to a much larger group of riders.

The outer row of these were mainly knights, their faces shadowed past recognition by their weirdly fashioned helms. They surrounded three of the mages. The robes of these were rich with tracings which glinted jewel-fashion under the sun. Two were plainly old, older than any living man Firdun had seen before, as the Old Race did not show signs of age until just before their time to enter the Final Gate. However, he who rode between them and a little ahead, as if he were paramount in rank here, seemed to be hardly more than Firdun himself in age. His smooth face showed no wrinkle, his cheeks even holding a hint of childhood plumpness still.

Unlike his followers, his robe was the color of newly shed blood, and the runes upon it were black. Nor did they appear to have been stitched there but were in motion back and forth. Around his neck was a chain of black metal which supported a globe, dull and lifeless, of about the size to fit into his palm should he wish. His cropped hair was bound the tighter to his head with a band of the same black metal as the chain. However, there was nothing monstrous or mis-shapened about his features. He was comely enough except his eyes seemed very heavily lidded and he rode with them nearly closed.

Just as Firdun had felt the evil of the avian woman, so did he now sense talent. Power rode here, and he was a little shaken. For while Power was of his own heritage and training, and he was kin to those of the Eyrie, this emanation was strong enough to suggest that the young rider was not an adversary to be underjudged.

The party of this leader also drew ahead and Firdun could see movement up the rise of the Dragon Crest. But before his own group started the rise, they were matched by another squad, and these had a prisoner under the same bondage as he himself wore.

It was plain that this man had been very roughly handled, as he was lashed tightly to the saddle of his uneasy horse. His head was turned a little in Firdun's direction and he caught a glimpse of a blood-splotched face.

Hagar! Of all the traders who ventured up from the Dales, or dared the Waste in search of relics of the ancient days, he was the most bold and resourceful. They had been awaiting his arrival at the Eyrie, for he was a good collector of news and usually even the rumors he gathered had a core of truth in them.

They mounted the slope now and it was steep. A lash curled out, striking not only Firdun's horse but leaving a fiery welt on his own skin, slicing through his breeches as if they were no more than a morning's spider web.

The young mage and his party must have already reached the crest. But the two squads with prisoners had fallen behind, since the horses were showing all the signs of going wild with fear. Finally some of their escorts had to dismount, use more ropes, and fight to bring the frantic animals along one stride at a time.

Firdun did not have to exert any will to hold to his outer semblance of fear. He had ridden mounts from the Kioga herds from earliest childhood and he well knew that the one under him was now near the bounds of sanity.

At length they were forced to stop. Two of the squad cut the cords binding him painfully to the saddle, jerked him to the ground, and threw another loop over his neck so that he needed to keep at a near-run behind the knight's horse or be strangled. He could not see Hagar now, but he hoped that the trader would be able to keep up.

The Dragon Crest was one of those monuments left from the days of the Lost Lords. Perhaps it had been a shrine to some personified power. Now it was a pavement of black blocks, seeming to the eye as if to step out upon them one would fall endlessly into some forgotten peril.

The knight was aided in his handling of the captive by two of his men. They whipped circling ropes off Firdun and sent him sprawling out onto that slick black with full-armed pushes so he fell and slid a space, his cheek against the stone.

Then he was rolled over with force as the second prisoner was flung after him. Hagar—would the trader betray him? He could not in this time and place project any illusion to change his features.

The edge of that blood-red robe swung into his limited line of sight. Then from the other side of his body a booted toe thudded home to send him rolling over, face up to a sky where clouds now seemed to be gathering at an unusual rate of speed.

He was also looking straight up into the face of the young mage. The face was handsome, yes, and the lips were curved in a small smile which might have charmed had one not seen the steel-silver eyes above, eyes which appeared to have no discernible pupils.

In Firdun there arose a vile sickness as if something utterly foul had been forced down his throat to be repelled in turn by all his body.

Then the young mage nodded and moved to the left. In spite of his efforts at control, Firdun followed him with his eyes. Now Hagar was the center of the other's scrutiny, but the trader's eyes were closed and he moaned.

There was a skittering sound, a fetid smell. The avian female had taken the mage's place and was eying Firdun, turning her head from one side to another as if she could only view him exactly with one eye at a time.

"Prepare them."

Hands caught in Firdun's armpits and he was pulled up to his feet. He made himself as limp as possible so they dragged him across the black pavement to where a metal grill had been assembled and he was lifted and thrown down on this, fetters snapped to hold him fast.

Sacrifice—

The realization shook him fully awake. He had played his helpless captive game perhaps too long, but he had needed to find out why Garth Howell was on the move. That these gathered here had been responsible for the storm magic he did not believe; some of them seemed to have been completely cowed by it.

Now, he could call upon the Eyrie—but that would also put

218

them in danger. He knew that his talent was great, but he had never been able to meld with the others in spite of all their struggles. They had finally accepted the verdict that he had some other part to play—but not as a sacrifice to the Dark!

They were pushing dried grass and straw under the grill on which he lay, methodically building a fire. He could not shout any spell aloud.

Clouds gathering, darkening, and those black birds of the Waste creature were flying back and forth. No, there were not clouds there—instead there were bags, gray bags beginning to bulge with moisture. In his mind ran the rain spell, but accented now—tending toward raising a cloudburst.

He could hear a stirring about him and firmly shut it out of his mind: clouds—water—water—clouds. There was a flare of flame darting up at his head, singeing his hair, nearly searing his eye. Clouds—and wings—wings were knives to cut those clouds and bring down the full deluge. The birds, screaming, flew hither and thither as if they no longer had any choice in the direction they would go.

Flame struck at his cheek; his clothes were smoldering.

*CUT!*

The birds made strange maneuvers among the clouds and it was indeed as if some great water bag had been slashed and its contents released. Water so thick one could not see through the slanting lines of rain struck full upon the platform. Firdun heard cries, but he concentrated on something else now. Fetters—the metal drew the rainwater; flecks of rust rose on them like seeds forced into growth. He exerted his talent strength and the metal snapped.

He was on his feet in one of the swift fighting movements he had learned from Jervon of the Eyrie. Around him armsmen, mages, were being beaten to the ground, actually pushed over the sides of the platform. For the fury of the rain drew with it now a fury of wind. He could not see the red-robed mage—all were only shapes in this storm from the heavens—but he did see that other bound figure, in fact he nearly fell across him. Pulling Hagar with him, he leaped from the edge of the pavement, allowed the now-slick, clayish sides of the crest to capture and carry them to the bottom.

Though two of the monster mounts of those from Garth Howell blundered past them through the curtain of the storm, Firdun made no attempt to catch at the dangling reins of either. Hagar stirred and somehow his rescuer was able to get the merchant on his feet. He tried feebly to struggle against the younger man's hold but was unable to free himself.

Encased in the mud, which seemed to plaster tighter to their bodies rather than be washed away by the torrent, Firdun staggered in the only direction he could believe would put Dragon Crest behind him now. He could only hope that the fury of the storm was hitting his enemies as hard.

Because he needed some guide, he followed one of the runnels of water from the sides of the crest and hoped that would keep him from the defeat of moving in a circle.

His call upon the storm had drawn heavily on his Power and he wanted nothing more than to flop down in the mud underfoot and sleep. At least Hagar appeared to be recovering from his semiconscious state and kept his feet without so much support.

Though the continued fury of rain and the wind was high, Firdun started when his companion sounded a shrill whistle. He was about to clamp his hand over the trader's mouth when shadows moved through the curtains of falling water and a moment later Sansah, his Kiogan mount, and a dull-coated and smaller dun came whickering toward them.

"Up with you!" Hagar shook himself and to Firdun's amazement the remaining cords which embedded the man's arms fell as if slashed and the trader was already pulling up into his travel-scored saddle. Firdun followed his example, but he did not have time to gather up Sansah's reins before the Kioga stallion was matching, with a steady ground-covering lope, the trader, who now rode straight in the saddle as if his late captivity was only a dream.

They were certainly approaching the edge of the storm now. The punishing wind which had been at their backs since they left the crest, as if to urge them forward, died away and the rain was more that of any seasonal storm. Hagar seemed to know exactly where he was going, and Firdun was content for the time being to allow him leadership.

He was debating within himself whether to try to mind-touch anyone at the Eyrie when the trader brought his mount to a stop and waited for Firdun to join him. The rain was now a mere drizzle.

But Firdun was staring at the man wearing the torn and sodden garments of a Waste trader. As if to induce closer examination, the other threw back his leather-enforced hood.

"You are not Hagar!"

There was no resemblance now to the trader's usual sun-browned and somewhat meager features in the face turned squarely toward him. This was . . . Firdun knew Power as it walked in a human envelope. He shared a home with an adept, and others who were not fully of mankind, save that they all held to a common goal. In his own veins coursed blood which in part had come from no human stock.

Like knows like—except that he was far from being the true match of this former fellow captive. As with all the Old Ones, the stranger did now show human signs of aging any more than might a man in the prime of life, but his eyes . . .

Firdun's clay-fringed fingers arose as he sketched in the air between them a sign he had known since early childhood. The faint traces his gesture left in the air were swallowed up in a blaze of blue for an instant.

The stranger was smiling, a gentle smile such as a teacher might wear in favor of a pupil.

"No, I am not Hagar—though I borrowed his seeming for a space, even as you are going Kioga-clad, that I might ride relatively unnoted through a troubled land. Had it not been for that release of wild magic—" and now he was frowning—"by All the Most Ancient of Powers, what brought that upon us?—I would never have been reduced to be the one whom I seemed and so taken."

"Where did that Power come from?" Firdun pushed. Surely this one who was greater than any he knew would have the answer to that. "Is it of the Dark?"

"Neither Light nor Dark—just Power unleased for a space beyond all dealing with it. As from whence it came—that I do not know. Save it was not summoned within leagues of where we now are. Any of the talent who had their minds open must well have been blasted for a space."

"Garth Howell—"

"Ah, yes, Garth Howell. No, none such could be put to the boil there—though they have some new talent, it would seem, willing to play on the shadowed side, and pay blood price for learning. You are Firdun, son to the Gryphon line. I have been known by several names. Your father will call me Neevor at our meeting—a meeting we must haste to now, for it would seem that events beyond our reckoning stand in the future."

Sorry as the stranger's horse looked, the animal broke into an even canter and then a full gallop at such a speed that the Kioga stallion, for all his vaunted strength, appeared to find hard to equal.

Since such a one as this said they must return to the Eyrie, Firdun could accept that decision. And the first traces of dusk were gathering when they took the ramp which brought them into the first court of Kar Garudiyn—to find themselves awaited. It was Kerovan, the Gryphon lord, himself, who came forward to help Neevor dismount after the fashion of courtly courtesy. Behind him was the Lady Joisan with the guesting cup, while the Lady Eydryth carried a plate on which lay the bread, salt, and a handful of berries for close-kin welcome.

Firdun dismounted under the eyes of Guret, their horse marshal, whose glance at the condition of Sansah brought a frown of reproof.

They were so intent upon Neevor that they asked him no questions, and for that Firdun was content. He sought his own quarters, soaked for a time in a basin pool of herb-enhanced waters, and then dressed. But his thoughts were busier than his fingers.

He had been thankful at first glance to see that the Eyrie had suffered nothing from the wild magic. With such a concentration of talent within its walls, it could well have borne the brunt of a heavy attack. But neither had he told anyone of his own plans to spy on Garth Howell which had been formed a few minutes after he had learned from a Kioga herdsman that several parties had ridden out of that dubious shelter in the general direction of his own home.

Thus, had he come to grief it would have been by his own reckless choice. He stopped combing his hair now and stared into the mirror before him, but what he saw there was not his own reflection, rather another scene years ago, one which had marked him apart from the others and for which he must pay all his life.

He saw very clearly the small boy who was angry with the young girl Eydryth had been, deciding in his impudence to teach her a lesson. There stood the doorway wreathed with rowan and illbane, spell-set to protect a coming birth. It had been his hands which had torn away that protection willfully, thinking only to give Eydryth trouble, but really opening the door for an evil which had lasted for long years and sent Jervon out of his wits, and Eydryth roving even overseas, with even a threat to his father before the end.

Reckless and thoughtless he had been, and perhaps that taint still was set within him—as witness his rash ride forth this day to spy upon an enemy none of them could weigh for Power. It was told that the Gryphon would hold Arvon itself against ill to come, but he was the outsider—he could not meld with them. Any Power he could summon would be his alone. Now there was this matter of wild magic. What if this was only the first of such storms to be set loose and bring chaos to all Light?

They gathered in the great hall, and Kerovan bowed Neevor into the lord's seat at the middle of the table. Firdun looked down the line of faces. There they were—Kerovan and his Lady Joisan, both strong in the talent and Kerovan of stranger heritage. Then Alon, a true-born adept, once apprenticed to the last of the Old Adepts, Hilarion of Escore. Next to him his wife Eydryth, the Song Witch, and beyond her her mother Elys, also of witch blood but later an armswoman who had awoken her own talent, and Jervon the warrior who claimed and won her. Next Hyana, moon-sworn and still in the process of learning how deep was her talent, and last of all

Trevor, only a child, yet those about him were already certain that he was the focus for what the rest could call upon—the point to the spear they held for the Light.

It was Firdun who told the day's story at the lifting of Neevor's hand. And when he spoke of the young mage, Neevor halted him to ask careful questions about what Firdun had noted concerning the man.

"The wheel turns ever," Neevor commented. "You, Alon, are adept-born, though you know not your kin. But, save for Hilarion of the ancient days, you are the only holder of such talent. But if the Light strives now to provide us with warriors, then to even the balance the Dark does also. And should such a one be born on the Dark side and in this land, he would seek out Garth Howell and sharpen his talents there. But that the wind of magic was born of his meddling—that I do not believe. We must check with our own fountain of knowledge—Lormt overseas—and perhaps learn thus what we face.

"This much I know: the vulture woman-thing Firdun saw is of the Waste. She and her winged flock are utterly of the Dark—but the Waste lies well to the south. Tell me, Kerovan, how goes it with the Four Lords? Are their holdings still at peace—Silvermantle, which touches the edges of the Waste, Redmantle, Bluemantle, Gold?"

Kerovan was frowning, turning his goblet around in his hand. "Of clear knowledge I can say nothing. There have been no hunting parties southward for some months, although this is the time of year the young bloods of the lordships take to the hunt. Nor have any traders come our way. The Kioga have remarked on that."

Neevor nodded. "Hints, yes. But sometimes hints have trouble to feed them. The Four Lords have not always been in complete accord. Any more than the Dale lords, who often have an eye for a piece of neighbor's property. You have made a casting?" he spoke now to Hyana.

She looked surprised at being so singled out. "No, Lord, I thought there was no reason—also I do not have strong knowledge of anyone at any of the four courts."

Neevor took a sip from the cup before him. "Tomorrow we shall call upon the Star Tower. Those at Reeth have bindings with the very land and so can often pick up what we may not envision or hear. But I would that there was some way we could speak with those at Lormt, for more than one answer may lie there. The distance is too wide for scrying and also there is the sea between, which wars against any Power."

"There may be a way," Alon spoke up. "This problem of communicating at a distance was one which my Master Lord Hilarion often considered. Together—though we are far apart—we have for a time been working upon some method of mind-send. It lacks but a little adjustment here to use—though I cannot tell how Lord Hilarion fares with his portion."

Neevor's eyes seemed ablaze. "Yes, the adepts had such in the old days—and when a thing has been discovered once, then perhaps it can be discovered again. Also Hilarion has all of Lormt to draw upon. Let us hope you can try it soon."

"There are the Dales," said Jervon, whose earlier days had been given to warfare there, not Dale lord against Dale lord but against the invaders from Alizon. "We were waiting on Hagar for knowledge of what passes there, though we know that one flock of the Falconers have settled at the coast and are building an Eyrie. They fought a mighty battle against invaders from another Dark-damned gate and won."

"I fear you must not expect Hagar this season," Neevor answered. "He lies abed at Norseby Abbey, where the dames try to bring back his wandering wits, for he came staggering out of the Waste two months ago babbling strange words and acting as one caught in a nightmare. Dame Rutha, who has lately become healer mistress, now suspects possession of some sort. And the Great Ones know that land is ridden by enough hungry spirits to seize upon a man who does not take care. Whether he will ever be free again we cannot tell.

"But we can well establish contact with the Dales. While the Daughters of the Flame do not care for us and I think would do little to aid, there were others—those they call wise women, who give homage to Gunnora and are sympathetic to our ways. Yes, there is much to be done. We are like hunters now, facing a web of many trails and not knowing which to be followed for the greatest gain. It is up to us to choose—and very soon.

"We do not know how much Garth Howell's plans suffered when you called down those nature forces upon them, Firdun, but I will not believe that they have been greatly overborne by the loss of a couple of sacrifices. That they are willing to spill blood is a dire warning, and we must set up guards against them."

Neevor looked along the line, though his gaze did not reach Firdun at the end—it could not. "Those of the Gryphon have been foretold. Now I say unto you, make secure all your defenses, and at the same time seek new ways to bend your talents. Those of Reeth will come and others, and in the end you will make a stout stand."

But would it be enough to hold—to reduce Garth Howell to what it had been for years: a place of knowledge? Firdun remembered too well that handsome face turning evil eyes upon him and the thickness of Power which clothed the mage tighter even than his red robe.

## CHAPTER SEVENTEEN

# *Arvon, Reeth, Gryphon's Eyrie*

Broken strings trailed from the hand harp and Aylinn rubbed the cramping fingers of one hand against the other. She was not even sure that she was in the same room, for this one was a mass of debris, smashed bottles, broken jars, and a cough-inducing smell where one of the braziers had fallen and was bringing to sparking flames twisted lines of drying herbs.

Her head ached and she felt as if she had been picked up and tossed aside by some force who had no possible kinship with human life. As she looked around at the wild destruction of months of work, she felt first the heat of anger, then the deadening force of frustration. For there was certainly nothing *she* could blame for this sudden chaos. Unleashed Power of an extent she would not have been able to imagine had it not struck before her. Who? Where?

"Aylinn—Aylinn, are you all right?"

The girl looked now to the doorway. Kethan, her foster brother, seemed to sway a little as he stood there. There was a cut over one of his gold-brown eyes which had begun to dribble blood in a crooked path down his face.

She pressed her hands against the moonsign on her breast from which she was never separated. Somehow she managed to free her wits from that maddening whirl which had struck without warning.

"What? Who?" she asked.

Kethan took a step within the triangular room of the Star Tower to plant his shoulders against the wall as if he still needed some support.

"Wild magic," he answered her hoarsely. "No control!"

"Aylinn! Kethan!" The woman who pushed in to face them both gave one look at what lay before her. Both of her hands flew to her lips as if to stifle some moan of loss.

Aylinn got unsteadily to her feet. "I—I was just trying to harp and then— Who has done this?"

"It had no imprint of our knowing." The man whose hands fell on the woman's shoulders to steady her spoke with a voice which was hardly far above a snarl. "And it was not centered upon us. Were that so, Reeth, I think, would have ceased to be." For a moment the outline of his body wavered in their sight; it might be that a great snow leopard stood hind-legged half embracing their mother. But Herrel of the Weres brought his rage swiftly under control.

Kethan picked up a small bowl which had miraculously survived being pitched halfway across the room. "Wild magic," he said slowly. "Could this"—he made a small gesture to indicate the room—"have been . . . called?"

"Gillan?" Herrel looked to his lady.

The shock of loss was beginning to lighten a little from her face. "It is true that Power attracts Power. But all here is of Green Magic, born of the earth, and such should not draw such destruction."

She stooped and began to gather together the lines of drying herbs, pulling them with a quick jerk away from where some of the brittle leaves had begun to smolder. Aylinn quickly laid aside the ruined harp and began to start the cleanup of that debris-covered floor from her side of the room. Kethan stepped past her to return a now-empty case of shelves to its place against the wall. But Herrel was prowling back and forth, in and out of the door, his soft-footed strides like those of a caged beast.

Each in that room controlled his or her own form of power and was fairly sure of its limits. But as far as Herrel knew they had no enemies. True, he had left the Werebrothers when he had gone with Gillan, whom they deemed "witch" in their foolish ignorance.

But when they had been led to Reeth—for both of them would always be sure that was what had brought them, a purpose which they did not yet understand—his power took another turn, one meant to foster life instead of fanged death. And Gillan seemed to become more and more before his eyes one of the fabled Green Ladies who had once walked the Great Wood of Arvon.

Aylinn, who was daughter and yet not daughter, being foisted unknowingly upon them at her birthing, turned easily to the Moon Magic and had twice gone to shrines apart to study. But the were line held in Kethan—though he had been stolen to be raised as a keep lord—and when the time came he had found his way to his parents through a peril so ancient it might have existed even before the Old Ones walked the land.

But what they held, they held in prudence and for good—to heal, to grow with the Light. Reeth itself had not only welcomed them but held them in a strange kinship of learning as the years had passed. Perhaps they had grown too trusting, believing that the outer world fared as well as they did. Herrel snarled. Once he had been a fighter both with sword and claw. If the Dark arose again, he could bring back memories of those old skills.

It took them three days of labor to clear Gillan's cabinet of lost harvests and reset the shelves. It was too late in the year to replace some that were gone. And it would take several growth seasons to replace what had been lost.

Herrel and Kethan took turns to roam on were nights, always seeking some answer as to what threatened. They made contact with those of the Gray Tower, Hyron, Herrel's sire, himself seeking them out but with no addition to the guesses which they all voiced from time to time.

Doggedly they spent their days wood-seeking with Gillan and Aylinn for what rarities they might find growing. And Gillan combed her garden, only to sort leaves, stems, and flowers with sighs.

However, they were gathered together in the growing gloom of night when the first of their answers came. They had not lit the lamps, for there was a full moon tonight and Aylinn sat in the outer door, her head back, her slim young body nearly bare to its coming rays.

There was a curdling of light on the nearest path of the herb garden. Its appearance brought them all to their feet. Yet none of their many safeguards had reacted to it. Therefore, perhaps, they could safely think of it as a thing of the Light.

Now Kethan could distinguish the outline of a form within it, seeming to draw the light and so solidify. But only the face at last looked out at them.

"Ibycus!" Kethan could never forget the one who had given him his pard belt, made him free to be what he was: a were of weres, and perhaps more after he passed through the ordeal set by his enemies.

The face in the mist smiled, the outline of the head nodded.

"Greetings to the kin of Reeth." The voice was almost as musical as the tones Aylinn had been once able to draw from her ruined harp.

Herrel took a step forward. "I take it, Ancient One, that there is trouble."

Ibycus gave a soft chuckle. "Straight to the point as always, Herrel. Nor is our world ever free of trouble. As yet we know not what we face—save it has set astir much we hoped would continue to sleep. There was magic—in the far east—"

"The Dales?" questioned Gillan. She had spent what had then seemed long dull seasons there, but there were those who had been kind and she wished no ill for them.

"Farther—perhaps Estcarp wars again. Yet this had no touch of witch sending. We strive now to contact the adept Hilarion, since Alon of Gryphon's Eyrie was his 'prentice and they dealt with new learning. Those of the Castle of the Gryphon seek knowledge among the four clans—there is stirring of possible conflict there. And . . ." he hesitated a moment as if to make what he now had to say the more forceful, "Garth Howell has opened its doors to take a hand in some ill game."

"And we of Reeth?" Herrel asked swiftly. "What would you have of us, Ancient One?"

"Them!" A curl of mist broke away and then into two threads indicating Aylinn and Kethan. "The Lady Sylvya—she who suffered under the evil hunt and won free by our aid—has appealed to the Voices in the north hills. As usual they will not answer clearly, speaking in a maze of words through which we must find our way. But this much we have learned. There is to be a mustering at the Eyrie, first to deal with Garth Howell, and then for some even greater task. And the choosing of those for the task is not to be of our making. Aylinn, Moon Daughter and Healer, you have a part in this. Kethan, were and warrior, you also. This is my summons— come to the Castle of the Gryphon, for there is need."

"And for us—what need?" There was a deep angry growl in Herrel's question.

"To hold Reeth, you and my Lady Gillan, as it has never been held before—with all the power you can summon. When we go up against Garth Howell we shall have good need for such founts of strength, and Reeth is now you, as you are Reeth."

Ibycus—or his authoritative shadow—gave them no more time for any questions. The mist swirled and then was gone, leaving the four of them in the moonlight with the scent of herbs about them.

Though there was still the marks of chaos within the tower, here was peace.

Or only the suggestion of it, for all Ibycus had said hung like a warning stormcloud over them. Aylinn held forth her arms, her head turned upward so that the moon encased her fully. Within her the uneasiness was growing ever stronger and it must be battled and put down.

There came a frightening roar from her left and now the moon glistened on sleek white fur as a wide-jawed, fearsomely fanged head raised to once more sound red anger. To her right Gillan had moved into view, her hands and robe stained with the nearly destroyed harvest of herbs, and by her side padded a pard, snarling. Of such was the garrison of Reeth, and so it stood as one.

But how can one defy an unknown enemy, Garth Howell? Aylinn knew the place only secondhand by rumor. Those born with her talents were not welcome there, nor would she ever wish it otherwise. And what part had she and Kethan to play in the action Ibycus had only hinted at?

Together as they had stood ready for battle, so they returned at length to the inner stronghold of the star-shaped tower of Reeth. Those rods along its walls held steady with the bluish haze which meant their usual protection held.

No snowcat now, no pard, the two men pulled forward their usual chairs and Herrel would have seated Gillan also, but she shook her head and tramped back and forth across the wide end of the wedge-shaped room while Aylinn settled by the smoldering hearth and fingered the rod topped with moonflower which was her talent focus.

"Kar Garudiyn is a three-day ride." Herrel broke the short silence. "You will take the were mounts." He did not look straightly at either his son or his foster daughter.

"Then," Aylinn answered, "should we not be prepared?"

Gillan stopped in her pacing. Her mouth was straight set and she wore the face which was hers when some problem raised by the talent confronted her.

"Why Aylinn, Kethan?" she demanded of the room at large. "Ibycus speaks in half riddles as the Old Ones have a way of doing.

231

There is this . . ." She made a small gesture toward the door which gave upon the wreckage of what had once been her particular stronghold. "Power draws Power. This blowout of chaos has already made plain how feeble our defenses may be. Yet Ibycus prates of Reeth as a stronghold. I should have had him look upon what chanced here and then ask what good our defenses were. Now he asks for—" She shook her head. "A force to go up against Garth Howell. Is the Ancient One mad or age-forgetful? And then hints of another task beyond that."

Her eyes were blazing as she came to stand before Herrel, as if he were the one she would rail against.

"We are what we are." Herrel's voice had again fallen close to the growl of his werehood. "And being what we are, what choice have we? If the Dark rises, then must the Light also stir."

Gillan's stained hands wrung together. Then she rounded on Aylinn. "Daughter—though our supplies have already been too well consumed, we shall save what we can for aiding a wayfarer."

Aylinn hastily followed her foster mother back to the devastated storage room, but Kethan heeded his father's gesture in another direction.

"We can war either as men or beasts," Herrel said as he lifted the ponderous lid of a great chest. "You will know which choice is yours when the moment comes. Yet you will ride forth as a man and hold to man's heritage as long as you can, for you will find few that are comfortable with were blood and talent."

He pulled forth a large bag and loosed its cording, bringing out a mail shirt which gleamed blue-green in the sparsely lighted room.

Herrel shook it out and stepped forward, the shirt held out, to measure against his son's shoulders. "Quan iron—a legacy from those who held Reeth before us. Yes, I think it will serve in fit."

Beside the mail there was a helm, bare of any crest, yet with a fore-portion which descended over the face with only eye holes to break its sleek surface. And last of all there was a sword in worn scabbard.

"Your belt."

Kethan freed the buckle, the familiar touch of the large jargoon long since carved into the buckle disturbing him a little. He had been warrior-trained and knew that to depend upon the were form for all battle was more dangerous to him than perhaps the enemy. For always there was an inner battle between beast and man when the talent awoke.

He was oddly relieved when Herrel, having made the weapon fast to the belt, handed it back to him and once more its binding was about him, though the weight of the sword made it strange now.

No normal horse would carry a were—in fact astute fighters among the kin had learned that that hatred of their kind could also serve them as a weapon. But they had their own breed and though Herrel no longer rode with his kin from the Gray Tower, he had two mounts of their shaping for service.

When they rode out of Reeth the next day, they carried well-filled saddle bags—and the blessings of those who cared for them the most.

In Kar Garudiyn there was another gathering at that same hour. The sturdy Kioga scout drank thirstily of the guesting cup, watching over the rim while Lord Kerovan laid out the thin-scraped parchment map and Firdun held down one end firmly. The Lady Joisan had both elbows on the table, supporting her chin as she studied the lines burned into the skin.

"To the east, Horsemaster, there was flattening of one of the tall domes," the scout reported. "Massar rode with us and he had scouted that land well—he has ever a nose for evil and he did not like it that there had been so much astir there lately. We all have our magics, Horsemaster, but can we tell which is the more powerful until we pit one against another?

"The flash signals this morning told us that one party has ridden out of the place. They must intend a journey of length, for they have pack ponies in train. There was a guard of their knights and foot fighters, and at least three robed mages set in the middle as if they were treasure being held against mountain outlaws."

"What color robes, Hassa?"

The Kioga set his emptied cup down. "That was not said."

Kerovan continued to smooth the map with a forefinger. "But they rode southwest?"

"That is so, Horsemaster."

"The bird-thing," asked Firdun, "did that also go with them?"

"No report was made concerning the creature."

Could they hope, Firdun wondered, that that monstrous Waste-bred thing had somehow suffered on the crest? There was that about it which sickened him even to remember.

"Sylvya—" Joisan began, and then shook her head to deny what she was about to say.

"Silvermantle is her goal." Jervon had come to stand beside the table on which lay the map. "They lay farthermost to the west—"

They were interrupted by Elys. Behind her at an easier pace, as if he must protect what he carried from any possible harm, came Alon.

He set his burden carefully on the table and they found themselves looking down at an artifact which none of them could name. There were two pyramids standing with a space between, all connected by a metal base. Alon's face was alight with excitement.

"It works—Hilarion's power and learning. With this we can communicate overseas." Now he stood in front of the strange object and held his hands out. Eydryth had already seized one and Joisan the other; they in turn linked with Hyana and Jervon and in that moment Firdun knew again that sharp thrust of the old inner pain. Even small Trevor came running to form the circle.

Haze curled up from the caps of the pyramids. This settled, and in the centermost part between them it thickened into a wavery figure. The strength of the talent loosed in the room made skin tingle.

There stood in miniature a man Firdun had never seen but whom Alon greeted with exultation as Hilarion.

So they learned—learned of the source of the wild magic which had struck so far—of the loss of the Magestone which might still have kept the gates in check and what was to be done now: the search for gates, and with it the search for that which would safely ward them. So fleeting was that time of communication that there was little chance for questions. Alon did report of the sudden change at Garth Howell and that Firdun had been prisoner for a space.

Hilarion ended with the need for scouting out any such opening as might be used by the Dark, and then he was gone and they were left weak and trembling at the call upon their power. Elys caught Trevor up in her arms and regarded him anxiously, while Firdun steadied his sister and ached within that he could not have helped more.

There was that which he could do—not only enhance the wards of the Eyrie, but lay what protection he could over the wide Valley which the Kioga made their home range. This he proceeded to do as the day wore on and the night came. He ate that night in the tent of Jonka, the chief, with the principle warriors of the clan gathered to listen to what news he brought.

"We shall send out scouts. Tell this to the Lord Kerovan. And we shall continue to watch this place of darkness Garth Howell. There is some coming and going there, but our people have seen none of the high knights since that party rode out to the west."

"Chief Jonka, warn your watchers. Each people has their own power, but that of Garth Howell has been gathered through a series of seasons too great to be counted. There will be snares." He paused to drink the berry wine in his cup.

"Our wisewoman drums, young lord. She is already showing far greater skills than old Nidu ever had. Also she is one who can scent evil," Jonka said with some pride. "We have not had one like her for several lifetimes—perhaps she is the great Sheeta born again. For it was Sheeta who brought us into this land."

Kethan tensed. "Then the Kioga also came through a gate?"

Jonka nodded. "So our lore singers say. We were supposed to have fled a great danger, and the chieftains called upon the Lord Horsemaster of the far stars. He put into the mind of Sheeta what must be done and thus we came here. But that was long and long ago and Sheeta, knowing well the duty laid upon her, then closed that gate under the Horse Star seal. We can show its place to those of the Eyrie if they have the need."

One gate, supposedly sealed, out of how many? Firdun wondered wearily. It was well known that the Dalesmen also had come through a gate. Had this been once an empty world—except for the adepts who had perhaps amused themselves with entrapping strangers to be studied and perhaps unwittingly used in their own dubious plans?

"So now there must be a search for other gates," Jonka was continuing. "Who goes to search, and where?"

Firdun shook his head slowly. "Of that you know as much as I, Horsemaster. Perhaps only your Great Mare will show us a trail."

Jonka nodded approvingly. "Be sure we shall be ready when the need arises. But what of the northern lords? They stand aloof from us and always have. Surely they are not all darkened by the shadows."

"That we must also discover. There have been rumors of quarrels once more close to feuding. The Dark can weaken any tribe or house by subtle meddling—with minds."

Jonka frowned and spat ritually twice into the fire beside him. "Such tricks—yes. We shall call upon our dawn drummer and learn what we can. Bide with us this night, young lord?"

Firdun got to his feet slowly, wanting nothing as much as to take advantage of that offer. "Not so—my thanks for your guesting offer, Horsemaster. But it is best that I return once more to the Eyrie. Remember I have set the three-times-three spells. If you send a messenger, let him give horn call from the road beginning."

He had heard that man could sleep in the saddle if worn enough, and as the night drew on he began to believe that perhaps he could prove that. There were clouds and the darkness closed except for here and there where grew those night-blooming plants whose noxious flowers gleamed brightly to summon the insects which provided them with food. This strip of land had not yet been cleared, but then, the Kioga herds grazed well down valley and the horses themselves avoided such growth.

However, he and his mount were not alone. He had begun to sense that other just after he had ridden out of the camp. Not danger, but a feeling of ease which he had known from earliest childhood. Now he reined in and after a moment gave the familiar summons of a birdlike whistle.

If the female creature out of the Waste had been the personification of all evil, she who came running lightly, the faint haze enclosing her, was the Light embodied. Firdun was out of the saddle and watching her eagerly.

"Lady Sylvya—but why do you run the night?"

Her feather-crowned head arose a little and she trilled her words, which were always half song: "I run at my own will, Firdun, since I am no longer captive to Darkness and the Hunter. Yet there is a stirring and in all of us the old blood warns. But this night I have come for you to urge haste. Neevor, the Elder One, has that which must engage us all."

Firdun bit his lip. "I am not of the meld—"

She flitted closer to him, her moonflower perfume cleansing the air as she moved. "But this day you have wrought very well, Firdun. Not even Neevor—though I would not wish to point it out unless there was dire need—could have set the guards stronger nor with greater authority. All of us in a way stand apart. Am I not the last of my kind?" Her smile faded. "Yet here with you of the Eyrie I have found my place. Never look back and hunt guilt in the past, Firdun, it is not worthy of you. Because of a child's act of destroying the wards and leaving Elys free to the Dark, must you think you must prove yourself always? I fell into the evil and I am free. You, a small boy, saw no harm in the mischief.

"We are all set in patterns. Had your thoughtless act not yielded Elys and her unborn son into the Dark's hold, would Eydryth have gone seeking and thus won us Alon and freedom from that madwoman who would have brought us all down?"

"We cannot lay on destiny our faults," he said quietly. "I do not ask for any judgment save that which I deserve."

Her light touch was soft on his cheek and then he felt a feather-soft kiss.

"Firdun, do not think of the past. What lies in the future will show you yourself far better than we can now guess. Now let us not keep Neevor waiting. It seems he has another task for all of you—for me. I must still go roving, for there are those to be led in to swell our forces."

And with that she was off into the night again, while Firdun wearily remounted and rode. Was she right? Did he cling to his guilt and let it conquer him in spirit? Had his childhood act indeed ended in gain instead of loss? No, a man must stand by his acts and not attribute them to the patterning of forces beyond his true knowing.

There was this left: He did not know even yet the boundaries of his own talent. All which galled him was that he was set apart from the others. However, he could learn how, when, and where he might serve best, and it would seem that Neevor had now some duty he was able to do.

Setting his mount to a faster canter, he looked up into the dark sky. Already he could see the very faint glow of the tallest tower of Kar Garudiyn and sent forth his testing probes. Yes, his wards were all well placed and ready.

## CHAPTER EIGHTEEN

# Arvon, Gryphon's Eyrie, Silvermantle Holdings

Firdun lay stretched on the stone bench of the inner court where the spray from the ever-playing fountain reached him now and then. He was engrossed in the drawing of his will and senses inward, to hold such sentry duty against the Dark until his guardship was over. To help hold the wards with all the power Ibycus was summoning was a road he must travel not in body, but with his inner energy, reaching out to touch each point of ward in turn, making sure the drawing together of forces of the Light would not in turn attract the Dark.

Perhaps in the far-off past when Kar Garudiyn had been the Great Landsil's own dwelling such forces had been drawn, marshaled, and sent forth. No—he must not let his mind stray from the rounds he had set it to go sentry.

This hour all the strengths of the Eyrie, plus the age-old authority of Neevor himself were bent to a single task. The Mantle Lands gave heed to the Voices—but the Voices had never answered directly. Now, with the warning from overseas, they might just be swayed to the guardianship at least of those who had always paid them homage in the Mantle Lands. At least every seeker in any of the holdings would also get the message concerning the danger of the gates and would report his or her true dreaming to the lordships there.

He did not make his mind rounds in sequence; it was unwise to establish any pattern which might be sensed by a prowling talent who would take advantage of the smallest slip. Sharply he saw within the heights near the Dragon's Crest where he had placed one of his more powerful sentinels. Then he switched swiftly to the valley of the Kioga camp. There he did touch Power—but that came according to Jonka's promise. Their spirit drummer was at work.

Southward: a faint fragrance—could the mind *scent*? But that was Sylvya and with her two others, talented strangers who walked in the Light. Firdun had a wavering glance of a prowling pard on guard.

East to the Dales. There were three sites of old trouble, its power now so weakened that it was like a faint sniff of a bad spell. What or who had ruled there once was long gone; only the vile aura of what had been done still lingered—but that was nothing, even if such united strong enough to trouble the barrier he had set.

North lay a wide strip of wild land before the borders of the Mantle Lands, but it had long ago been cleansed of any perils save those directly to the body from strong beast or desperate outlaw.

Now—Firdun put all he had into this outward thrust—Garth Howell. All of the Eyrie had tried at intervals in the past to mind see behind those walls but had never put their full talent to the testing—and it would be perilous action on the part of the full meld to—

Firdun's body suddenly stiffened as he lay. There was a hint of opening—a trap to entice him in? They surely had their own wardens and defenses. But the temptation was great. He scouted that passage, then advanced by the smallest fraction of which he could control his talent. He saw shadows which were certainly indwellers, but also he saw ruins, the fall of an inner wall, a dome roof which had buckled to flatten at least a floor or more. And the shadows busied themselves about these evidences of disaster.

The wild power had certainly wrought mightily here. That half-crushed dome might have roofed some workroom of mages—if those same had been at labor when it struck.

Then—

That vulture face flashed between him and what he tried so hard to see and Firdun instantly shut off the mind-path. He had recognized at once the creature from the Waste. Had she in turn sensed him, or even identified him? Once again his recklessness might well have endangered—

Swiftly his mind-pattern whirled from one barrier point to another. All were holding steady. No more such ventures on his own; he must keep to the duty set him here and now.

Within the great hall Neevor sat straighter in his chair. His two hands lay palm-flat on the table before him and between them rested a ring. The metal loop was of silver darkened by age, and the large stone set to the fore was a dull, clouded gray, as dusky as the metal which supported it.

Eydryth's fingers swept across the strings of the harp resting on her knees. This was not any song to buttress words—rather, it seemed to rouse full attention from those others sitting there.

Kerovan spoke as the last note faded and was gone. "Trouble."

"Yes, those of the Mantles will care for their own." Neevor was trying the ring on one finger after another of his right hand. It was firmly in place at last on the forefinger, covering his flesh and bone nearly from knuckle to joint. "They remember too well the Road of Sorrow, and they want no more such journeying. Though their aid will be limited, they will police their own lands, and should the news from Lormt come that complete warding is available, they will use it. Do not judge them, Kerovan. Remember the night when you camped by that road and what you heard—and felt."

Yes, he could remember very well that night in the wilderness when he had dared with Raill, who then seemed his only friend, and had awakened to feel a great burden of despair he could not understand.

Joisan pointed to the ring. "What is the meaning of that?"

Neevor held out his hand and surveyed the ring there with satisfaction in his voice as he answered.

"A guide. This will give warning of the presence of a gate, one active or not. It will lead where we must go. It is also a weapon. No"—he glanced quickly at all of them—"the Eyrie is a stronghold which must be held. Like it or not, the Mantle Lands are also your duty. Here is the true heart of your power and it must not be weakened by your going forth. There will be those to take up the task, never fear. But we march no army into the Waste and the west beyond; we send only those who have certain talents, each of which fits another piece into the pattern. Of the Eyrie, Firdun—"

He named had just come into the room, aroused by that trail of music, and now he stood staring at the mage. Was it that he might be the weak link in the chain here?

Neevor's eyes flashed and the ringed finger pointed directly at the youth. As he did so, the stone came to life in a burst of violet light, gone almost as soon as it had first shone.

"Thus speaks that which the Voices have decreed shall be our guide. What talent you have will be at need—more than it will serve here. And now"—he pushed back his chair and stood— "hither come two others of our party to be. Sylvya has seen them through the wards."

They could hear the stamp of a horse hoof through the window giving onto the outer courtyard. Firdun was the first through the door he had just entered and the rest were close behind him.

Sylvya had dropped on the edge of the fountain and was dabbling her fingers in the water, her sweet smile bringing peace with its very presence. But the other two were strangers.

There was a man hardly out of his late youth and with him a

girl, whose dark hair was crowned with a circlet bearing a silver moon. The man was tawny-haired and wearing such mail as only the greatest of lords might hope to possess: a shirt of quan iron rings and a helm. His only weapon appeared to be a sword swinging from a belt of tawny fur the same color as his hair, its fastening a graven gem in the form of a pard's snarling head.

She with the moon crest was dressed in stout riding clothes of a dull green, and that color seemed to shift in shade with every movement she made. A second silver moon lay pendant on her breast. Across her knees as she sat in the saddle was a short staff, hardly longer than a wand, and around its upper portion was wound a cluster of moonflowers, supposed only to bloom at night but here spilling out their fragrance in the day.

The mounts that they rode were different from any Firdun, for one, had ever seen—slightly larger than the cherished Kiogan breed, both dappled in shades of gray. The eyes of the one which turned its head to view him were a vivid green and seemed to lack pupils.

"Ibycus!" The man greeted Neevor gladly. "As you see, we are good and obedient children."

The mage laughed. "Of Aylinn I will believe that, but of you, Kethan, perhaps there may sometimes be question. Let me make known to you"—he half turned to those of the Eyrie—"our two new comrades. This is Aylinn, Moonmaiden and Healer, and her foster brother, Kethan, were and warrior."

Were! Firdun was startled. All knew of those of the Gray Tower, the fighters who had held against the Dark, but somehow in his mind he had always pictured them in their animal guise. This Kethan was like any other man save for his coloring—his coloring and that belt to which Firdun's eyes kept turning.

"Our mounts," Kethan was saying as he swung out of the saddle, "do not herd with other horses. They will not cause trouble, but it is better that they be stabled apart."

In spite of the powers Neevor (whom they addressed as Ibycus) had professed for them, those of the Eyrie discovered these new recruits to their company to be no different from other travelers the hold had housed over the years. They were not like the Kioga, but Kethan, at least, might have passed for the son of some Mantle lord.

To Joisan, Eydryth, Elys, and Hyana, it seemed within minutes of their greeting that Aylinn had been known to them all their lives. There was about her something of the Lady Sylvya—a feeling of peace and comfort in her presence.

Trevor had gone at once to the two shadow-dappled horses which loomed so tall over him, and reached up his hands. Each bent head to nuzzle his fingers.

Kethan came up behind the child. "This is Trussant. And the other is Morna. They are the were breed."

The child turned his head a little to view the tall warrior. "Do they then become . . . people?"

Kethan laughed. "No, they are not shifters—only they company with us who are and are willing to share our lives. The horses that men generally know would not do so."

"Will—would Trussant let me ride him?" Trevor had always been horse-mad, Eydryth thought as she came quickly up to where they stood.

Kethan smiled at her. "No harm, Lady, for this little one. If he wishes, let him ride and show us where we may stable them. They have come long at a fair pace and need care as any tired travelers."

Kethan had shrugged off his mail and helm, and even the tawny belt which supported his sword lay across a stall barrier as he worked rubbing down the two horses, answering Trevor's questions.

There was fresh hay which the small boy insisted on putting in the mangers and he watched with intent interest as Kethan sprinkled over each portion of that double handfuls of what looked like brown beans.

"What are you doing here, Lordling?" Guret stood now, scowling, just inside the door of the stable.

"Guret—see the were horses—come." Trevor beckoned. Kethan had turned to regard the young Kioga, who entered with the authority of one who was in his proper place and about to question the presence of others.

"You are Mount Master?" Kethan smiled and made the palm-up friendship gesture of a warrior meeting a friend. "It is not that I do not trust your boys to stable our mounts, but these are of another breed and will learn quickly who is friend and foe. Until then it is better that I care for them."

Guret's scowl did not lighten and he paid little attention to Trevor, who now held his hand and urged him forward.

"Were mounts," he said stiffly. "I have heard of such from the traders."

"They are not to be found save at the Gray Tower and Reeth," Kethan answered civilly. "They are battle chargers and trained fighters."

He did not seek to break through the other's very apparent antagonism. Weres knew only too well how they were accepted by those who looked upon shapeshifting as a thing well within the Dark's shadow.

"This"—he touched with his booted toe one of the close-woven bags which he had unhooked from the saddles—"we add to their forage when they are stabled. It is made from herbs of the Lady Gillan's own growing and serves as grain." He set about reassuming his mail and belt while Guret continued to watch him with narrowed eyes, saying nothing.

Then he stooped and slung over his shoulder first one set of matched saddlebags and then another. They were a fair load, pressing his mail shirt near bruisingly against his flesh, but Guret made no attempt to offer aid.

However, he turned abruptly, brushing past Trevor and heading for the outer courtyard. Nor was he in sight by the time Kethan had reached the stable door. He sighed. It was plain that this stable master was important here. Would Kethan now meet members of a garrison who looked with the same suspicion upon his kind?

It was Firdun who came to meet him now and with an exclamation insisted on taking half of his burden. So he came into the great hall where the others were gathered close to Ibycus, and a guesting cup was pushed into his hand by the maiden they called Hyana, the other set of saddlebags taken.

He soon discovered that there was no prejudice here, but then he could sense that talent was strong within these walls. And those with Powers, if they followed the Light, were always well met together.

Both of those from Reeth found that the hospitality of the Eyrie was indeed to be enjoyed. And they had two days for exchanging stories, those from Reeth learning of the news from overseas and of all that could be learned concerning Garth Howell. Ibycus-Neevor spent much time with the enchanting woman who had led them here. She was plainly not of human heritage, but that she was considered close kin by the others within these walls was easy to be seen.

What they conferred about was not made public, but the others were engrossed enough in preparing for what must come to have little time to wonder.

The decision had been made that a scouting party strike west and south through Silvermantle country to the Waste. That a party from Garth Howell had now been traced as taking nearly the same path seemed to Ibycus-Neevor (who now went by the first of his names) to urge that they follow.

Firdun twice related his sighting of the strange mage, and each time Kethan felt that this stranger he had never seen might well be an opponent to be rightfully feared.

Kethan himself worked with his mounts and the horses the Kioga brought up from the valley—some for extra mounts, others pack beasts. At first Guret and the other handlers were loath to let the were and his pair near their own cherished beasts. It was Aylinn who showed up the second morning they led the horses down into the valley where those selected by the Kioga were herded together. Chief Jonka was there with a number of his older warriors, and also a tall woman wearing a robe painted with strange designs, carrying on her hips a small drum.

Aylinn had taken Morna's reins, the mare nudging her with her head from time to time, while Kethan led the dappled stallion.

There were whinnies and calls and signs of uneasiness among the Kioga beasts, and men moved in to try to quiet them. Then Aylinn's moon staff was lifted into the air. As the uneasy beasts of the valley watched, she passed the garlanded rod carefully over both Morna and Trussant.

The scent of the moonflowers was strong, rising above the smell of dust and the sweat of the Kioga horses. The two standing quietly under the passage of the rod suddenly neighed—the sound louder than was usual to the Kioga.

Then the Kiogas' own beasts quieted. They still stood with all their heads facing toward the were mounts, but there were no rolling eyes and tossing heads now.

Aylinn nodded to Jonka and smiled. "Horsemaster of the Herds, there will be no trouble for your good mounts. Know that there is no evil in Trussant and Morna but that they will all be trail comrades together."

On the fifth morning after the arrival of those from Reeth, all were up at dawn and ready to set out on whatever track Ibycus chose for them. Firdun had made a last testing of wards, and they had news that Garth Howell seemed to have again walled itself in from any touch of the world.

Alon had tried again to contact Hilarion—to no avail. At length they decided that they had only their own knowledge and skills to depend on. Quert and two other of the young Kioga—Obred and Lero—had volunteered, and, when they faced the test of the mage's ring, it accepted them.

They were a very small party, Firdun thought as he straightened his helm and saw the pink of the dawn band the sky. His kin and Sylvya remained to hold firm in the Eyrie, and Ibycus had promised that the ring had other aspects beside those of selection and guidance. He could communicate through its dull stone setting at intervals with Alon. Thus they would keep a slight tie with those who stood firm in the same struggle.

The mage had hinted that they might pick up other allies along the way, but so far no one else came into Eyrie territory. What was happening in the Dales, or in the Mantle holdings, they had no knowledge. But at least the alarm had been given.

Their first day's journey went at a steady pace and through territory well known to Firdun and the Kioga. They saw no trace of any except Kioga herders, yet they set up regular watches at night. When the moon started to wax again, Aylinn planted her staff in the center of their camp and made the proper call for aid in their quest.

On the fifth day after setting out, Firdun felt restless from the moment he awoke, driven to make careful rounds of the camp. It was as if something was pricking him, like a thorn from a wayside bush. So he met face-to-face with Kethan.

"There is a shadow rise," the were said. "Not yet strong enough to trace. Unless you can do so, Lord Firdun."

"But would such a trace be prudent? If there was a searching . . ." He did not know why he thought of that, nor why he spoke of his indecision aloud.

Kethan nodded. "I think it lies stronger ahead in that direction." He nodded toward the west, where the dimness of predawn still held.

"The Mantle Lands stretch north. We must cross the holdings of Silvermantle to reach the Waste. If we are near enough to the Border now . . . But that is for Ibycus to decide." Firdun turned swiftly into the heart of the camp to find the mage.

Though he kept an open mind channel as they went on, he could detect nothing but a trace of power. Certainly nothing which carried the taint of evil. It must be the Border wards, which were set to warn but not to oppose unless what came was of the Dark.

They had been moving through wild country where there were no settlements and certainly no holds. The only life they sighted other than their own party were small family herds of pronghorns, grass hens, and once something which withdrew hurriedly within a pile of rocks but let forth a snarl as they passed some distance away. Firdun saw Kethan's head turn quickly and, his own mind being open for any message, he caught some of the slurred wording of that one.

"Peace, brother-in-fur, we take not your hunting land."

Firdun had a vision of the spotted furred grass cat who had sought hiding but fully resented their invasion of its territory.

Ibycus called the noon halt that day by a spring, where they ate cold rations of journey cake and drank water. Aylinn sifted into the large common container some small red seeds which gave flavor and seemingly higher refreshment as they shared it.

"Beyond the hill"—the mage pointed to the rise from the foot of which their spring sprung—"lies Silvermantle. Firdun, as you ward so you can also pierce—when it is necessary. Vision it for me." He came behind the young man sitting on the ground, and placed one hand on each of Firdun's shoulders.

Obediently Firdun closed his eyes and envisioned a ward wall. But also he sent streaming at it, like a well-thrown spear, a thrust of violet fire. That touched the wall, entered. There was a moment of waiting and then—

Ibycus threw up his head so he was facing directly into the sky. "By the will of the Voices—we come in peace and about their business. Read our hearts and take you the truth."

The wall was gone. Firdun opened his eyes. Ibycus came to where Guret was holding his mount. "Well enough, we are granted passage."

There seemed to be little difference in the land about them as they mounted the hill and found a game trail leading down its other side. If there was some hold or ward tower nearby, there was no indication of any road, or even path which was in use.

They were still in empty land when they camped that night, but had altered their course farther south. Firdun went to lay the night wards—but he never completed that circle he had set himself.

Passing beyond a copse of trees he suddenly stood as if struck by one of the hold spells. And spell it was, he recognized a moment later. Though he strove to draw upon his talent to counter what held him, the familiar counters failed. Now he was striding, in spite of himself, directly away from the camp. Nor could he, he discovered, communicate by mind-send any warning or appeal.

This was broken ground and he slid down into a cut, scratched by the brush which resisted his passage, and then, came out into a wider section. This was open country, bared of anything but the tall grass—

No, not bare! There was a shimmering in the night. Above him where silver-touched clouds gathered, thickened, towers grew plainer, and the castle from which they arose took substance. Now the whole building, huge as it looked, glowed green with ripples of silver, as if it were fashioned from some unknown stone.

Also—as it grew solid, so did it no longer hang above him. Glamorie, strong glamorie: He recognized it for what it was and yet even with that knowledge he could not banish what he was seeing. Now once more he was drawn forward, toward that tall foregate between two towers. He had a sharp thought of a web with a spider within, but in spite of his struggles he could not break the ensorcellment which held him.

The castle gate was open. What waited within? Oddly enough he felt no evil here—no touch of the Dark—yet why was he then entrapped?

"Up to your old games, Elysha?" It was like a shout in his very ear. Past him strode Ibycus, his face twisted in anger.

"Games you taught me. Remember those fine days, my lord mage?" A voice as silver as the lines across the castle walls answered with a tinkle of amusement in that thought-send.

"Elysha—" the wrath in Ibycus's voice was growing hotter.

"Elysha," she interrupted him like an echo. "Always Elysha do this, Elysha do that. But in spite of you I learned, though you would never grant me mageship. Now, I think I will just play a game after all—with this youth. He has possibilities."

In the open dooryard stood a woman. Her hair was night-black and fell about her like a cloud. In her oval face her eyes were huge and deeply violet, and violet also were the thigh-length jerkin, the breeches, and the boots she wore. There were gleaming purple gems to fasten that jerkin, and more braceleted her wrists as she slowly raised her hands in a beckoning gesture to Firdun.

But Ibycus's left arm came across the younger man's body like an unmovable bar. The mage's other hand, with the ring on the forefinger, pointed straight toward the woman.

There was a flash of light so brilliant that Firdun could not see for a moment or two. When he looked again . . .

The castle was gone. And the woman stood wearing a sly smile, her attention on the ring, which was blazing as violet as her eyes.

"You see, my dear and never forgotten lord, you have need for me and must bid me proper welcome, for it has been long. Now your own Power ties me, and you cannot deny it."

Ibycus stood staring from the still-brilliant stone of the ring to her and then back again. She laughed as gayly as one of the maids at a harvest feasting.

# CHAPTER NINETEEN

# Southwest into the Waste

It can't—I won't—"

Firdun had never heard that note in Ibycus's voice before, as if the ever controlled mage were being shaken out of his eternal calm.

"But it does, my dearest of friends," her silver voice continued. "Your own tool now assures you of the fact that you cannot leave me this time. The Dark stirs and toward the end of containing it again we shall once more march together. Now, since you have set me roofless and homeless, let us go to whatever shelter you propose for this night."

That bond which had drawn Firdun snapped. The woman out of the now-vanished castle turned her smile in his direction. It was now not sly and taunting, but quite open.

"One of the Gryphon breed. A good omen—you are Firdun of Landsil's line. Ah, now, there was one who was always most courteous even when he denied you what you wished. So much lost, but then there is always more to be found, and some of it interesting. Since my dear master here"—she nodded toward Ibycus—"has not seen fit to introduce us properly . . . I am one of the secrets out of his past, Elysha, who fetched and carried and craved such crumbs of wisdom as he let fall for my taking. We parted somewhat stormily, I remember. However, I have made very good use of the days since, Ibycus, as you will come to see."

She seemed to carry them along with her flow of words, marching forward as if she knew exactly where her goal lay, and somehow Firdun and the mage fell in behind her. Yet Firdun could actually feel the red rage which still cracked the elder's ever-present armor.

It seemed to the young man that even the fire they had set at the heart of their camp blazed the higher as Elysha came into the circle of its light. Those about it halted in whatever they were doing to stare as they might at some night running thing from the outer dark. Still there was, he would swear, no taint in her in spite of Ibycus's very apparent dislike for her company.

It was she who spoke first. "Since we are to be trail comrades in this matter, let us follow guesting custom. I cannot bless your roof, for you have none save the sky, but for those who stand here I wish all good fortune."

Aylinn moved first. She had been holding a cup in her hands; now she came forward and offered it to the woman.

"Welcome you are . . ." she hesitated, as if trying to find words to fit this new form of formal greeting.

"I am Elysha, Moonmaid." The purple gems about her wrists glistened as she accepted the cup and took the required first drink. "As to what I am—well, opinions on that differ. But you would not find that any barrier of Reeth's truth would stand against me."

Kethan had moved quickly up beside his foster sister. Elysha nodded to him.

"I have known your breed of old, and we were not unfriends. You are Kethan, and in you two bloods flow so that you are both more and less. But the skills you have are never to be thought the less."

The three Kioga had drawn together and Firdun saw Guret's hand was near the hilt of his sword.

"Kioga." Elysha nodded. "Warriors and horsemasters. Not of this world in the beginning but bringing with them into it strong arms and shields for the Light. I remember Chief Ranfar. Now, there was a fighter! He went up against the Quagan and survived— though the Quagan did not."

Firdun saw Guret's amazement and the near openmouthed expression of the other two of his tribesmen.

But it would seem that Elysha now considered they were sufficiently well introduced, for the tone in her voice changed and there was a much sharper note in it.

"I have read the bowl, Ibycus. And I know what drives you and these stout hearts now. Yes, there were gates in plenty in this world. And if some be thrown open now, we shall be perhaps driven like a herd of sheep to slaughter. Also—some days ago another hunter came before you and he has a true guide. Ibycus, Ibycus, how could you of the first power allow Garth Howell to go its own foul way so long unchecked?"

Oddly enough, it was Kethan who caught her up with that statement. "One before us, Lady? Do you mean the mage from Garth Howell?"

"Who else? Well, he has perhaps two days' journey time on you, but we shall use him in turn. For he knows, I believe, just where he is going and his trail will in turn become our guide."

As encased as she had been in glamorie of her spells, that disappeared as she stood among them. Except for the richness of her clothing she seemed to be no different from Gillan or Eydryth— certainly less alien than Sylvya, who had always been a part of Firdun's life. And it appeared that she expected to be accepted in that fashion even though Ibycus settled himself as far as he could from her as they shared out their evening rations.

At the moment their main concern, once their amazement at her coming subsided, was the next day's trail. For one of the Kioga, scouting ahead, now asserted that half a day at their usual pacing would bring them over the Border and into the grasp of the rightly dreaded wildness of the Waste.

Though traders had reported that there were oases to be found, the sere, yellow land immediately facing them offered nothing that they knew of in the way of water or forage for their beasts. Two of the pack train carried as heavy burdens of food for their mounts as was possible.

However, they must find other sustenance as an aid. All of them had heard the rumors that the Waste had once been a rich and fair country until the wars of the mages had struck—in the latter days wantonly, for there were masters gone brain-sick who no longer tried to control their Powers.

Life did survive there. Not only the traders who brought back strange artifacts from time to time, but also weird forms, perhaps born of the very disaster as had riven the land.

Silence had fallen upon the circle about the fire. Kethan broke that.

"Lady," he addressed Elysha, "you have told us that those of Garth Howell have already ridden this way. Are you sure of their path?"

She was inelegantly licking crumbs from her fingers as her great violet eyes turned in his direction.

"I can lead you where they seemed to be heading when they passed my own hold. Do you try your other senses on the trail, then, wereling?"

"Pards do have senses beyond those of men," he answered evenly. "I can at least try. And this much is true: We can usually find water in lands men would consider bone-dry."

Ibycus appeared to have thrown off his sulky frustration and rage, for he nodded. "A good thought. One to be tried."

They rode in their usual pattern when they left in the morning. Elysha had been provided with one of the spare Kioga mounts and took the lead, Ibycus not pushing forward to accompany her. But Kethan urged his shadow-marked mount even with the woman after they passed the valley ahead.

They had carefully filled every water bag or container. Now as they rode, the Kioga brought down with their stone-weighted sling cords two brace of grass hens. But even this much hospitality of the countryside was lost as they approached the end of the valley to face some low mounds which seemed far too regularly set to be of nature's keeping. Seeing some weathered rocks protruding here and there, Kethan guessed that this might have once been a keep, or even a village. But it had now long returned to the grip of the earth.

Elysha reined in when they won to the other side of this jumble out of the past, and pointed ahead. "In that direction."

It was more west than south, but she seemed very sure. Now Aylinn brought her mount forward as her foster brother left his saddle. He doffed his mail and his helm, unhooked his sword from the skin belt. Swiftly he bundled these in the cloak which had been rolled behind his saddle. Then, light-footed, he ran out onto the mounded land.

He was gone for only a few moments and then Firdun drew a deep breath as a light tawny-furred body slipped over the last of the rises, keeping well away from the horses, which were already registering uneasiness, heading in the direction which Elysha had indicated. That form was large for a pard, but certainly there was nothing else to suggest that it was other than the animal it looked to be.

Kethan drew in the multitude of scents which his human nose never seemed able to separate, one from the other. The ground cover here was closer to a brownish fringe and it held a dry, dusty smell. He caught a trace of a hen's passing and crossed a fresh leaper trail which his present body urged him to follow. But the man was in charge of the beast and he went on.

Crossing another low rise, he looked out over a flat land which was floored with baked yellow clay, riddled with cracks. There were stubs of rocks here and there to break the vast monotony of that emptiness. But it seemed to reach on and on toward the horizon. Under the sun the yellow of the earth gave back a haze which narrowed Kethan's eyes to slits.

He did not emerge directly into that emptiness but rather cast along the foot of the last ridge. While a feline hunts by sight and not in most cases by scent, it seemed to him that in this desolation he could pick up the traces of the other party, even if they *were* a couple of days in advance.

Yet as the heat waves from the land before him beat down, he could find no trace of any promising lead. He had neared the end of the mound when he picked up a rush of foul odor, intermingled with several other scents, all highly irritating to both his nose and the spirit which inhabitated his now-furred body.

The trail certainly led out into the Waste and he began to believe, after he had followed it for a number of paces, that he had indeed found what his party sought. Turning back, he leaped to the top of that mound.

Not too far away the others waited. He did not want to send their mounts into a frenzy with a full-throated roar, but he pitched a snarl as loudly as it could and caught the wave of Aylinn's arm in return.

For the time being there was no reason to resume human shape. His pard senses should be far more practical. Aylinn was turning in his direction, leading Trussant. If necessary the stallion would carry him even in this present guise as it was bred and trained to do, but he would keep to the trail on foot as long as necessary.

He could guess that the Kioga and their animals would find this new country pure desolation, and he could only hope that his pard talent could lead them to better.

They rode on under the bake of the sun. The hooves of the horses stirred up miniature dust devils of yellow haze. Kethan still caught that faint foul stench of the party he followed and they were striking in a straight line as if they knew exactly where they were going.

He avoided a rack of fragile bones, the mark of some traveler here who had not been fortunate. Twice he saw rock serpents, but the vibration of the approaching hooves sent them weaving away. Of any other life which might shelter here there was no sign at all. Even the sky overhead was bare of any sweep of bird wing.

Ibycus called a halt at noon, where they sheltered in the only possible alleviation from the sun, a rocky spire. Aylinn came to Kethan who was carefully keeping his distance, to bring him a portion of rations and some sips of water.

"The trail holds?"

*So far,* he told her by mind-send. *Though I cannot truly be sure we travel behind those we would watch.*

They had only gone a short distance forward, that spire of rock which had sheltered them still tall in view, when Ibycus's command rang in Kethan's mind.

*To the east—with care.*

Obediently the pard swung away from the way he had been following. As he did so he saw that the mage had held up his hand and that the ring there flamed.

Now it was that tool of Power which led them. And to something they did not expect, for it could not be seen from the level of the endless plain.

Though there were many cracks in the clay, this was no crack but a deep cut in the ground. Kethan stopped, his ears flattened against his skull, and he snarled as he half crouched, moving forward only a fraction at a time.

The walls of the cut were ragged, still of the yellow clay, as if that form of earth extended far beneath the surface here. Yet this was not a place unknown—though it might lie now in total desolation.

Kethan had seen some of the artifacts brought back by traders—those taking wild chances at collecting things when sometimes a single touch meant death. Here were likenesses to one Gillan kept in Reeth, a strange fashioning of a series of four small pyramids, pressing together, seemingly of metal in which were embedded colors as brilliant as gems.

But these showing in the cut were larger than that curiosity at Reeth. Some were more than the size of his furred skull, and the colors played back and forth among them as if they exchanged rainbows in some strange game of their own.

Though pockets of these studded the walls, those were nothing compared to what floored the crack itself. Here were masses of the same kinds of blocks with triangular caps far larger, forming so rugged a surface as to suggest that no one could find footing there.

Completely bemused by their find, they lined up along the edge of that great cut, staring down. Ibycus's hand had dropped from its level point as if it had been pulled and that ringed finger pointed straight down into the mass of broken bits of brilliant color.

Now by closer examination they could see that the floor of the crack, beneath its burden of weird fragments, arose in the middle, sloping off at each end.

"Vastar . . ." Elysha stooped to pick up one of the bits which lay on the very lip of the crack. "Or do you say that is wrong, Lord Mage?" She glanced with that usual shadow of a sly smile at Ibycus.

To the others the word she uttered had no meaning until suddenly Aylinn gave a little cry and moved back.

"Were those who wrought with the star metal to build?"

Elysha nodded. "And it would also seem that they dabbled in the matter of gates, if your guide shines true, Ibycus."

He did not look at any of them but stood staring down at the bristling flooring of the crack. It was plain by the continued glow of his ring that some source of Power was there.

"Ropes!" he burst forth suddenly. "Will your horses," he demanded of the Kioga, "stand and take the weight of a man descending by saddle rope?"

Guret edged closer to the lip of the crack. "If we can find a place where the ropes do not rub against those." He jabbed a finger at the outcroppings of metal.

"Then let us find such." Since Elysha had joined them, Ibycus's temper was no longer even. And he seemed to have set himself a little apart from the rest of them.

Firdun was moving slowly along the edge, measuring the sharp drop below each stride of earth he covered. "Here!"

There was indeed a limited stretch of the thick-backed clay which had only a small sprinkling of encrustation. Anyone descending there would land not at the highest point of the metal pile beneath but at the opposite end from where they now stood.

Kethan pulled himself away from the company and then walked two-legged once more to join them. As a pard he could not help; this was a man's job.

Then they discovered that Ibycus was set that he and he alone might make that descent. And his icy-voiced orders underlined that, for this, the others would be of little use.

Four of the Kioga mounts were in place and a coil from the packs had been made fast with the skill the nomad horsemen knew well.

Ibycus set a loop of the rope about his middle and edged over the cliff, facing inward toward the clay wall. It would seem that the ruggedness of the side, steep and straight as it was, was an aid rather than a hindrance. Firdun continued to eye narrowly the mass below. In his mind it bore too close a resemblance to a pit trap with sharpened poles at its bottom.

The mage moved quickly as if he had indulged in this form of exercise many times before. However, as his boots crushed down on the uneven flooring, he staggered and caught at the rope, holding fast in order to retain his balance. Slowly he turned toward the mound of metal pieces, several taller than himself. Their colors appeared to grow brighter as he turned. The beam from his ring had shifted and was playing over that rugged mass.

Firdun tensed under the spurt of invisible Power which shot upward. Aylinn swung her moonflower rod, Kethan snarled, while the Kioga uttered cries of astonishment in their own tongue.

For the uneven crown of that metal mound was shifting. Chunks broke off and rolled. While several seemed to aim straight for Ibycus, he did not move and at the last minute they tumbled either right or left to avoid him.

One of the watchers moved swiftly. Elysha held out her two arms, the color of her wide amethyst bracelets nearly as ablaze as the colors rising below.

"We take no treasure, you of Vastar, forgers of stars and dealers with the deep veins of the earth. Your day is past; the long sleep is upon you. Know that for the truth!" she cried aloud.

And she was answered. Not by the mage below nor any of the others, but seemingly from those ruins upon ruins heaped by ancient disaster. It came as a moaning, like the wind of a rising storm, though over their heads no clouds gathered.

The shuddering of the mound of scrap continued. Pieces appeared to raise from their long-held beds to whirl and fall outward.

So far none had struck directly at Ibycus, but such chance might not continue. Firdun half turned to Guret to give the order to draw the mage up out of range.

"You are gone—into the ashes of time," Elysha's voice continued to ring out. "Each age has its proper lives—and then those fade."

From the top of the mass arose now a single piece. Like the bits which formed it, it was a stepped pyramid, but this unjoined to any other, standing alone, and the color of yellow tinting sharply into red played across it.

Nor did it stop in its expansion. Now they could see that it was supported on square pillars, growing ever taller until it was like a roof set on four supports.

"Ibycus," Elysha shouted to the mage. "By the Power of the Great Lords, the Forgotten Kings, and That Which Once Walked the Far Mountains—do what you must do!"

He had not needed that arousal to action. The ringed hand swung high and was brought down from right to left, and then from left to right, leaving visible in the air a plain-cut cross of shimmering blue—a blue which approached the violet of high and purest power.

The cross tilted in the air, spinning around, its speed ever increasing, until those waiting could not distinguish its separate arms. Sidewise so it flew at the columns supporting the pyramid.

Over their heads the sky darkened, and that wailing moan grew loud enough to force them to hold their hands over their tormented ears. But the wheel of light held steady and it cut as easily as the sharpest-edged knife through a mass of clay.

The upheld pyramid— Firdun caught at his sword hilt. He heard the snarl of Kethan now at his side. Had there been, in that last instant before the thing crashed back into the mass of metal from which it had arose, a pair of *eyes*—blistering fiery eyes? Or perhaps that was only some quirk of his own imagining.

What was happening below was quick to erase that from memory. Ibycus no longer stood firm. His body was sprawled among the sharp-edged pieces of rock, and those were still shifting. Nor did they any longer avoid him. Rather they struck hard enough to make his still form quiver.

"Up—up—!" both Guret and Firdun cried at the same time. Kethan reached out to grab the taut rope where it lay across the edge and Firdun joined him as the Kioga urged their horses back from the crack.

"Wait!" Aylinn was beside her foster brother. "You will rip him to shreds against those rocks he cannot avoid."

She reached out with her moonstaff and shook it vigorously. There was a white, sparkling dust from the hearts of the flowers, which sank close about Ibycus. The mage might now lie in the cocoon of some great insect. Yet the dust did not yield to any projection as they carefully raised him from the floor of the crack.

Though the mound had moved, it had not disappeared, only seemed to settle more deeply into the clay. Its colors were fading, dulling. Then they had the mage over and with them again.

He still lay limp, his eyes closed, and on his outflung hand the ring was dull and dead. But Aylinn brought out her healer's bag, and Elysha moved to take the injured man's head on her lap.

Aylinn, with Kethan's aid, managed to get a potion from a flask down his throat. "His Power is drained," said the moonmaid. "He needs to rest until strength comes to him."

Firdun looked around at the sere wilderness. "Where can he recover here?" He knew from his own uses of the talent the draining of strength it demanded. And, from all he had seen, Ibycus had just faced something which was so encased in some ancient sorcery as to threaten life itself.

Aylinn was speaking now to Guret. "Can we sling some way for carrying him between two of the horses? They are well trained and perhaps, coming from a wandering people, you have seen used so before."

"Yes, Lady, this can be done," he confidently assured her.

"Then where do we go?" one of his companions spoke up.

What they needed was water, shelter, forage. Kethan could only guess that that trail he had been following might lead to such. It was a small chance, but it was a chance.

"Good enough," Elysha answered his thought. "Not all the Waste is bare as you see it here. And those we follow will not go off wandering with no true goal in sight. Lead on, were. Of us all you have the best chance to find what we need."

They would have to travel slowly. Luckily it was now nearing night and soon the heat of the sun would cease to beat on them. Once more pard Kethan padded back to where Ibycus had summoned him from the trail. It was fainter now—perhaps the explosion of power back in the crack had some effect on his talented senses. But still he was certain enough that he was right to keep on.

Dusk was gathering when he noted a change in the land around him. The harsh yellow of the baked clay was taking on a slightly different shade. There was a hint of rose about it now. Not only that, but he saw small, red-leafed plants here and there which grew thicker until his paws found a softer carpet.

Then, his head up, he sniffed and sniffed again. To his pard knowledge there was no mistake. Somewhere—not too far ahead—lay water! The mind sent that back to Aylinn as he increased his pacing to a trot.

Among the small mosslike plants now arose bushes. They were hung heavily with rose red flowers, the petals strikingly marked in vivid black. There was a faint scent, not altogether pleasant, and there were swarms of small winged things hovering about each. Luckily those showed no interest in him.

He came to another descent from the level of the yellow plain and waited there once more to contact Aylinn. She was riding to the fore, leading Trussant with his gear. Somewhat to his surprise Elysha had joined her, though her mount gave signs of being none too comfortable with the company of the were steeds.

*Down—but the slope is easy,* Kethan reported.

*We must find a place soon,* his foster sister replied. *Ibycus has not yet recovered. Tonight I must moon sing.*

He glanced up into the dusty sky. What Aylinn would do would also exhaust her, but if she had decided it must be done, then it would be so.

Down the slope he went, the moss continuing as a carpet, the flowered bushes rising around him. Ahead, to draw him on, the scent of water. But he must exercise caution. Those whom they followed might also have seen fit to camp hereabouts, and he flashed another warning back to Aylinn.

## CHAPTER TWENTY

# By Moon Power, in the Waste

The smell of the vegetation, the bushes against which he had to push, the mosslike growth underfoot, began to make him feel queasy. Certainly, though he could readily now pick up the scent of water not far ahead, this strange vegetation might not provide suitable forage for their horses, and the scant store of grain they had been able to carry was not more than enough to share out in a handful or two.

Then his pads felt more solid footing and he paused. Feline night sight was better than that of humans—he had no difficulty making out the fact that he had come upon a road, one which had been smoothly paved. Yet under the limited light its surface was dark in color.

At the same time the water scent was overpowered by a whiff of something else. He smelled a fire—and beasts—and men! He sent a sharp warning back to Aylinn but she already had a message for him also.

*Firdun says there are wards. . . .*

Kethan was swiftly off the road. There was a massed thicket of some kind to his right and he made a quick detour, concealing himself behind it. Once there, he dropped until his belly fur nearly scraped the moss and advanced with the same caution he would have used in stalking a very wary pronghorn watch bull.

His hunter's skills brought him to a second thicket. Now the water scent was very sharp, drawing him until animal will and man will nearly locked.

However, there was a further warning ahead: the glow of fire. A moment later he crouched behind a screen of flower-laden plants which edged a pool—and a screen which was no work of nature.

It was stone-walled, with intervals where that wall was cut away as if to give better access to the water. The fire he could sight lay to his right and was undoubtedly the core of a camp.

Beast senses could give him one report, but Kethan was well aware that in some cases human knowledge and reaction was the better. Lying where he was, he made the change.

His vision was lessened and also his ability to scent, but to his sight now those by the fire were sharply individuals and not just members of a species.

Some of the party, early as it was, were already enwrapped in their sleep padding. He could sight none of the ungainly mounts those of Garth Howell favored. They might well be tethered some distance away. At least as he now was, no pard scent would arouse them—if they could be aroused by such.

By the fire itself sat two as tightly encased in armor as if they meant at any moment to attack, and he suspected that these were the knights he had heard reference to. Across from them were three others. Two wore brown traveling robes such as mages favored and the hoods of those were so drawn forward over their heads that he could not see their faces.

The third made no such attempt to disguise his identity. Kethan, remembering well Firdun's repeated tale of his captivity on the Dragon Crest, was sure that this was the leader of that foul crew. Yet his face was serenely handsome—also the firelight appeared to center upon him now and then as if to make clear that such a one sat there.

He looked young—but with the Old Race (if he were of that blood) there were very few signs of aging. Certainly he had the air of one whose smallest wish had never gone ungranted. Though he was not speaking now, rather sitting looking at the fire—or in some strange way below it—he slipped back and forth between his fingers a wand, shorter than most sages carried, but suggesting it had been fashioned of much richer material.

Suddenly, with the speed of a hawk's swoop, he struck out with that rod against the fire. The flames seemed to huddle together for an instant and Kethan saw those others gathered there edge hastily back.

Kethan could only guess what the stranger intended, but caution made him reach in search of Aylinn. *Ward also!*

The flames had begun to circle, spiral, at the same time drawing more tightly into a column. Now Kethan could catch the rhythm of a chant, so low it was not more than a murmur (though it awakened uneasiness) and he could not distinguish any words.

Now the flames stiffened and held; Power must have melded them so. Then that column split open. But to Kethan's despair he could not see to the other side. He had no idea what the mage now faced. Nor dared he move to better his view for the few very long moments that held so.

But the serene arrogance was gone from the young mage's face as if it had been wiped with a rough hand. His eyes were redly murderous as the fire became once more only leaping flames.

Now he was on his feet in one light movement and apparently giving orders. Those asleep were roused. They were apparently about to break camp. Had they learned of their followers and were going for an attack?

Kethan fed to Aylinn in as few words as possible what he saw. They were bringing those noisome lizard-horse mounts out of the Dark, seeing to the packs which burdened a couple of them. The young mage busied himself drawing patterns in the air with the point of his wand.

Where that sudden warning came from Kethan never knew, unless it was part of his ancient heritage. But as speedily as he could, he shifted. Pard lay where man had crouched.

Those patterns in the air whirled the wilder and started shooting off sparks which flitted out into the gloom of the now-descended night as if they were winged. Three shot over the end of that large pool in his direction. But they did not pause as they passed over him and at last puffed into nothingness some distance behind. If the mage had thought to uncover a spy so, his Power was not aimed at weres.

However, he was the last to get to saddle and he looked back with a careful survey of the pool and its surroundings from the north end where their camp had been.

Kethan continued to lie where he was, but his report went to Aylinn.

*They went north. Circle and come in from the south. Let Firdun test—I cannot pick up any wards.*

They had left the fire burning, but now it was flickering. Kethan longed to cast in that direction, but against a mage—a mage from Garth Howell—he might not have defenses.

He did edge toward one of those openings left in the rim of the pool to sniff at the flood below. To his pard sense it was no more nor less than water and fairly fresh, not stagnant as one might expect in these circumstances.

But he would await Aylinn's decision, for no healer could be mistaken about such things. Now he could hear movement from the dark behind. Best make his change before the Kioga horses would scent him. He arose from the matted moss and slipped into the bushes.

The moon was up now and there were silver flashes moving toward him. Aylinn must have tried to cover up her Power ornaments, but the motion of riding let them gleam through now and then. He was quickly at her side.

"Ibycus?"

"He has not roused. I must speedily call up the Power to awaken him."

"But those from Garth Howell—the mage—Power calls to Power and they will know."

"Firdun will ward and so will Elysha. She is more perhaps than we think her, Kethan. For a long time she was Ibycus's apprentice and I think perhaps his near equal."

The south end of the clearing was a surprise. For here was not only the pool which had been fashioned to service, but columns of slender pillars, each deeply engraven. Aylinn held her moon wand high as the rest of the party joined them, the inert body of the mage still slung between two horses most carefully led by the Kioga.

There was no reaction to Aylinn's gesture. Kethan himself could sense no power. Whatever this place had been in the past, it was no fane to any strength that was greater than its builders.

They had no intention of building a fire. Ibycus was settled on a deep mat between two of the columns. Aylinn having declared the water fit, the Kioga led the animals one by one down, seeing that they did not overdrink. But the rest of them gathered around Ibycus, save for Firdun and Elysha, who disappeared quickly into the night, intent on their warding.

It was not until they returned that Aylinn dropped her cloak and stood in her kilt of silver moons, strung so that with every movement of her slender body they gave off a faint chiming. The crescent moon in her hair, the full disk which lay between her breasts appeared to draw an aura of cold clean light about her. She beckoned to Elysha.

"Of us all, Lady, you have known him the longest and he may so answer to you sooner."

With only a nod, Elysha slipped down beside the mage and placed her hands carefully, one on his brow and one on his breast heart high.

Aylinn's chant was half song. The moon was well across the sky, yet its gleams were still centering on her. From the flowers on her staff came the perfume of their night blooming. Her petition must be very old, delivered in the nearly forgotten word lore she had learned in Linark, for Kethan could not understand; perhaps only Elysha among them did.

The Kioga and Firdun had withdrawn to the edge of that columned run and Kethan followed. This was women's Power and it was best that they be left to it. Meanwhile, Kethan described those he had seen by the fire and the mage's weird confrontation with the rise of its flame.

He knew that perhaps it was his duty to once more go hunting the trail to the north of the pool, but he was near to the end of both strengths, pard and human, and it would do him no good to waver when he should be at his most alert.

In the end they decided that Obred and Lero would circle

around on foot, not venturing too far away from the pool, to seek any traces of that swift withdrawal.

"I do not believe, somehow," Firdun said, "that that warning from the fire, if warning it was, concerns us. This mage is certainly of high rank, and with this talk we have heard of gates set free, he must be going to search for such."

The slow, soft chant ceased, for the moon was now too low to fire Aylinn's power. But Elysha raised her head and there was a look of triumph in her face.

"Ibycus—Neevor." She called by both the names he had carried through the years. "Awake—the battle is done."

The light had grayed enough so that Firdun could see the eyes in that pale set face open, gaze straight up at the woman bending over him.

"Elysha?" Ibycus's voice was frail, as if all the years which must lie behind him had drained the full timber from it.

"The same, Lord Mage. You are safely back with us again, since this moon daughter has sung you home."

His eyes shifted from her to Aylinn, and now he smiled. "Strong is your Power, Daughter of Reeth Tower. For indeed I was far away before you recalled me."

It was light enough for them to see that the pavement under them, the columns, were of a rose shade, against which the growth about looked darker still, yet in the same hue.

Elysha helped him sit up and now he pulled away from her, as one determined to care for himself. Gazing around at the pool, the columned stretch beside it, he held out his hand and stared intently at his ring. But the stone was lifeless again.

Yet his head went up and he drew a deep breath as he now faced the northern end of the pool.

"The Shadow servers!"

"Be quiet and rest." Elysha's hand closed tightly on Ibycus's shoulder, striving to push him back upon his mat.

"Do not play the fool, Elysha, when you are not. Evil has drawn a slime trail here—even though it be gone. And of what kind was it?" With every word he spoke, his voice became deeper and more assured, and it was very plain that the Ibycus they knew was truly returned to them. It was Kethan who came forward and gave him the full story, the mage's set gaze boring into him as if making sure no scrap of memory was overlooked.

"Fire . . ." he said slowly when Kethan was done. "Fire can cleanse, fire can kill, it can answer both to Light and Dark. Whatever that one summoned, he is more than we thought he might be. Garth Howell has troubled strange waters to bring forth such knowledge, nor will they be the better for it in the end."

"It might be well not to push so close on the heels of those," Firdun cut in.

Ibycus scratched his short-trimmed beard. "There speaks your father's son. The Gryphon breed were ever warriors and more conquering than conquered. Yes, we shall give them a day, perhaps two. I think that they are still afar from what they seek. This . . ." He looked about him.

"Ah, where are you, Gweytha, now, I wonder? Your court stands well against time, even though you no longer reign here. There is no shadow remaining—we may eat and drink of the bounty of one long since withdrawn."

Kethan slept, though he had not intended any long rest, and he knew that Aylinn was curled in the same surrender among the folds of travel cloak to which Elysha had drawn her after they had eaten.

To their near-tasteless ration cakes they added berries, deep red and luscious, bursting with juice, which both Aylinn and Ibycus had assured them held nothing noxious, while the horses cropped eagerly of the moss sod.

With the coming of the sun there also appeared birds, strange in color, fearless as they hopped about the travelers in their resting places among the columns.

Firdun awoke at a touch on his shoulder and looked up at Guret.

"The scouts have returned, Lord. Those who left did not try to hide their trail but have gone swiftly, as if to reach their goal was more important than to beware of followers."

"Which may mean they feel they have no reason to fear us." Firdun yawned away the rest of his desire for sleep. Or else, he thought more glumly, they expected such a welcome where they went as would effectively dispose of any trackers.

He saw Ibycus now, standing by the pool curbing. Gathered around the mage were a flock of mixed birds. There were tall, stilt-legged waders, certainly meant to spend their days walking through pools, contrasting in size with small puffs of feather well able to fit in the palm of his own hand.

For the most part their coloring was in shades of rose, but there were a few pure white. And he saw one a startling and vivid blue green. That one perched boldly on the peak of Ibycus's cap as if in charge of the company. Oddly enough, under the sun the pavement, the curbing of the pool, and the columns beside where Firdun had bedded down seemed to emit a rosy haze, almost if a setting sun had altered the blue of the sky. He wondered at the use of this place even as he donned his mail. Though he was aware of a very faint whisper of Power here, he was sure nothing could summon it again. What had given it energy was long since gone.

Then he started and a moment later laughed at himself. That he had seen a pard loop away between columns was not strange. Kethan must have also awakened and assumed his were shape. But he was padding steadily away from the company, and *not* turning north as if about to verify the trail of those others; it was as if he had another goal in view.

Thus Firdun also looked southward. They had faced two of the strange places of the Waste. By report and rumor there were infinitely more. Was Kethan under orders from Ibycus or now drawn to some discovery on his own?

No one mentioned his going as they gathered for their meal and Firdun was oddly disinclined to ask. Aylinn awakened late and did not join them, still gathering her talent strength, though the coming of the night should restore her.

He knew generally of moon power, of course, though none of the four women of the Gryphon followed that path. It was one of the oldest of the talents, but it was growing thin—he had heard that fewer and fewer were born with that trait.

It was true though the Mantle holds were each settled by those of the Old Race and there were healers and wise women, and even female sages and mages to be found, such Powers were not avidly sought and those who held them became in time estranged from their clans and after a fashion kinless, living only for the Power.

Yet in this girl out of Reeth he had sensed none of that withdrawal and certainly her ties, from what he had heard during their journeying, were as tightly kin bound to those of the Green Tower as he was to the Gryphon.

Elysha was more his idea of one of the Greater Talent; still, in some ways she in turn was bonded with Ibycus, whether that mage wished it or not.

On impulse he picked up one of the big leaves they had put to basket use and which still held a good number of berries, carrying it over to Aylinn.

She looked up, seemed a little startled, and then smiled.

"Greetings to you, my lord, and thanks for your thoughtfulness. It is true that one wakes always with hunger when the Power is evoked."

"My name is Firdun." Suddenly it was important to him that titles or honors be forgotten. After all, in this company they stood equal, each with his or her own duties.

Now she laughed, a giggle such as Hyana would give before accusing him of being pompous. She had crammed a goodly handful of berries into her mouth as if indeed her hunger had overridden all daintiness of manners. A small trickle of juice showed at the corner of her mouth and she licked that in.

"Firdun it shall be—even as with Aylinn. Are we all not kin in the Light?"

She made a small gesture and he squatted on his heels, Kioga style, to bring them closer together.

"I do not know your way of Power," he began hesitatingly, not quite sure even yet why he had approached her so.

Again she laughed. "Strange would it be if you did. It is woman Power—like unto the teaching of Gunnora. Is not your sister Hyana one of the healing faith?"

"A healer, yes, but she learned much from the Lady Sylvya and she is—"

"Not of our blood or breed." Aylinn nodded. "My mother heals and she is of witch blood from overseas. My father is were. Or so we believed for many years until Kethan came to us and we learned that evil had wrought at our united birthing—I being truly daughter to a hold lord and he son of those who had always fostered me. Now we are truly brother and sister. Still the talent arose in me when I was very young and my mother fostered it—sending me to Linard of the healers for learning. But their First Lady found that I was Moon-touched also and thus—" she had dropped the berry-stained leaf Elysha had shared with her and now made a small gesture, "I am what I am—and I am well content."

Her eyes were full upon him, gray he had thought them in the daylight, yet with some of the moon glimmer in them. And they saw!

He wanted to twist away—not to face that weighing.

"You see yourself flawed." She spoke plainly. "Flaws can be turned from ill to well if they are examined closely."

He wanted to break that eye bondage, but he could not—and not because she held him in any ensorcellment as Elysha had done.

"I ward," he said slowly, "because I threw away my chance to meld. There are those of the Gryphon and there is . . . me. Though I was but a child, I let in evil, and from that came great grief and my loss."

"You are—" she was beginning, when suddenly her eyes went wide and no longer kept him captive. But her hand groped to catch his arm in a bruising hold. "Kethan!"

Though she spoke that name as hardly more than a whisper, it sounded like a shout. Firdun gained his feet, alert as he would have been to a Kioga battle horn, bringing her with him. For a moment or two she clung to him.

"Kethan!" she cried again.

If there had been some mind-send, Firdun had not caught it. But now Aylinn loosed her hold on him and, paying no attention to the gear scattered about, whistled. There came a clatter of hooves between the columns as the were mounts answered.

"What—" but he had no time to frame a question. Those about

them were astir, but none close enough to catch her before she mounted the bare back of the mare and the beast whirled, the stallion keeping equal pace out and away to the south.

Ibycus pounded his staff on the pavement. "The young fool," he snapped. "No, we cannot put that name to him, for what he follows is born of nature even if it be used by another."

"Do we ride?" Guret could have been speaking either to Firdun or the mage. Behind him the camp was completely astir, packing with speed.

"There is no choice, even though it draws us farther from our trail," was the mage's answer.

But Firdun had already run to saddle his own mount. He took the time to arm himself, resenting each lost moment. Also he beckoned to Obred and ordered that the Kioga move out.

He had scouted enough with the tribesmen to be able to follow the trail which Aylinn had certainly made no attempt to conceal. Now already the columns were behind and he was watching those prints ground into the moss which were his guide.

That some danger had struck at the were, he had no doubt. He had no idea what talent the other could call upon in defense past his shapechanging. As a pard he could be prey for any hunter—even though this land seemed bare of any but the smallest game.

There was a copse of trees and then beyond, the open. Once more the odd reddish tint of the ground was changing until it ended abruptly in a band of the same baked clay over which they had earlier traveled. Save this was not open ground but a maze of rocky outcrops, slimed by the droppings of a huge flock of black birds, their naked raw red heads outstretched to the full as they cried out in a rising din.

Riding back and forth before this broken barrier was Aylinn, Kethan's stallion faithfully at Morna's heels. It was as if the girl were trying to force her way past a wall. . . .

A warding!

Firdun's mind-probe met a will-barrier so tight that the recoil actually caused him a small measure of pain. He had never struck against such before—though he had never really tried to pierce clear to the heart of Garth Howell's defenses.

Now he rode to catch up with the girl, turning his mount so that she was forced to pull in her mare.

"There is a warding—"

"As if that is not plain!" She almost snarled at him as if some of the were blood was also hers. "Yet look—"

She pointed down to the yellow soil and Firdun caught plain sight of the tracks. Cat—pard—Kethan must have come this way.

The birds which had continued to circle and scream above the rocks now began to venture out toward them and the party which had ridden on their trail.

"Rus!" Elysha spat out. "This is their nesting place. But why?" She was leaning forward in the saddle and had caught sight of the pard tracks. Then under her guidance her horse sidled back a fraction, the rest of them withdrawing to give her room.

She dropped her reins and her mount stood statue-still. Raising both hands, with the gemmed wrists purple fire in the sun, she began to move them back and forth, gesturing as one might to draw a curtain.

There was a haze over those rock pinnacles now. The birds withdrew in frenzied flight, probably alighting somewhere beyond, since they were no longer on the wing.

Elysha's groping gestures grew wider until with them her arms moved apart to their farthest extent. If she strove to sweep away that growing haze, her efforts worked in exactly the opposite fashion—it was thickening.

Before their eyes now there were no feces-stained rock spires, not even the yellow ground underneath. Elysha spoke a single word Firdun had never heard. They were looking at an entirely different stretch of country as if the sere desert land had never existed.

Here was the welcome green of newly growing grass, gem-studded with flowers of yellow and red wide open under the sun. And there was also a path of gravel as silver white as a moonbeam.

The path wove back and forth and around but eventually it reached not the forbidding walls of a keep, but rather the timber and plaster side of what might have been a Dales inn of the best sort. Around and over the door of the inn was an arch, vine-covered and boasting blood-red flowers.

All the while there seemed to flow toward them from that green and gracious land a welcome which grew stronger with every breath they drew until Firdun came alive to the danger.

"Glamorie!" Not a word—but a trap, even as Elysha's castle had drawn him. Firdun wheeled his mount between that lure and his companions, even crowding against Aylinn's mare to force the animal back.

Elysha let her arms fall. The fair country they looked upon was once more the filthy roosting place of the rus and those birds were rising again to circle and scream.

# CHAPTER TWENTY-ONE

# The Hold of Sassfang, the Waste, South

The pard lifted his head higher, brushing impatiently through the flowering bushes, petals clinging to his fur, since they seemed to be yet heavy with the dew of early morning. The scent was faint but not so faded that it did not hold true as he went. And this drew him as nothing had done before in his life. The man was buried deeper and deeper within him as he went, while the beast ruled on this trail.

It promised—he was not quite sure of *what* it did promise—but it was such a lure as he could not ignore. Then he came out of the moss-carpeted land and faced—

The pard blinked and blinked again, eyeing what lay before him. His astonishment was such that not even the scent which had pulled him here could hold. Man arose, beast disappeared, and Kethan stood at the beginning of a finely kept graveled path which led by a series of odd curves to such a building as certainly no one would expect to find in this stretch of country.

He had heard from traders that the Dales which attracted yearly fairs had such accommodation for those who traveled to them. Not holds in which any peaceful wayfarer could claim shelter for the night, but what they called inns, which were erected only for the comfort of travelers.

There were no walls here, no signs of any need for defense for those about. Even the wide door was open. Smoke curled up from chimneys at either end of the building and the breeze brought him a suggestion of freshly baked bread—the soft loaves of good living, not the hard journey cakes. Such as he had eaten at Reeth when Old Wife Zentha still ruled in the kitchen quarters there before she had left to take care of her motherless grandchildren.

But—there *was* Zentha! She stood in the doorway with her usual wide smile, even bearing the usual small smudge of flour on one apple-round cheek.

Deep in Kethan something strove to awaken, but when Zentha beckoned to him his man shape impatiently suppressed that prick.

"Zentha!" He might have returned to childhood—except that in his bleak childhood Zentha had played no role. Now he ran, following the odd curve of the path without any heed.

"Laws, now," he heard her well-remembered voice. "Now, didn't them as rides the breeze tell me as how I'd have a hungry man coming to put his legs under the table and hold out his hand for the nearest dish?"

Again that prick far inside, this time more insistent. But Kethan went on. Zentha was backing into the open door of the inn, still facing him.

He set his foot on the wide step, ready to follow. Her hand—no, no hand—rather a set of knife-sharp claws struck out. Before Kethan roused from the ensorcellment he had not known held him, those claws caught at the carved pard buckle of his belt as if they knew the exact trick of its fastening. The force with which it was torn from him sent him nearly whirling like a top.

Gone was the inn, Zentha— He reeled back against a befouled rock, fighting to protect his face and eyes from the rus screaming down in attack. All about him was the yellow of the outer Waste. In his flight from the birds, blood already streaming from his hands from a deep score on one cheek, he brought up bruisingly against a rocky pillar and rebounded to another.

The rus clustered and swooped, claws and beaks tearing at his clothing where they could not reach his flesh, though already they had wounded him well. Somehow he floundered into a kind of crevice between two of the pillars and did all he could think of in his confusion and bewilderment, cramming his body back into that hole.

At least he had defeated the birds for a breath or two. But he had no weapons and he had seen twice what such flying monsters could do at their will, picked bones and tatters of cloth left only to mark their feasting.

He heard a harsh crackle of laughter and peered out of his small shelter. There was no Zentha, of course. In the place of her wholesome self stood a creature he had heard described by Firdun: the bird-female which had been at Garth Howell, or at least one of the same species.

It seemed that she could not view him straight on, that her large eyes were set too far apart. Her beaked face kept turning from one side to the other. Now and again she loosed that evil cackling while the rus circled about her. And between her hands she flapped his belt back and forth as one displays a battle trophy.

Aylinn—no—his thoughts instantly forbade any contact with their party. He had been caught, he knew now, by glamorie. None of the rest must fall victim to this. For those practiced in that art were able to summon up any sort of scene which could reach the innermost thoughts of their prey and draw them.

He could see a little of his surroundings, though from within this crack his sight was limited. There stood a veritable forest of these huge rough monoliths of rock, streaked by generations of droppings, and the smell was enough to turn his stomach.

The birds, having driven him into this prison, were alighting on some of the outcrops. But the eyes in their raw red heads were turned in his direction. Their mistress swung the belt again. It hurtled out through the air and was gone, beyond his range of sight. Then she squatted down, put her clawed hands within another crevice, and jerked out a blood-clotted hunk of meat. Some of the nearer birds stirred and she pinched off bits which she flung up so that they caught them neatly, as if this were a trick they had done many times before.

Having pecked the few remaining shreds from a section of broken bone, she stuck forth a long, narrow purplish tongue and licked her claws. Then once more she cocked her head to view him out of her right eye.

"Noooo—runnnnns—noooo follow—" The words were so garbled he could hardly make them out. But somehow his thoughts leaped to what he thought she meant.

He had been the prey because as a were he would pick up once more the trail of those out of Garth Howell. How much did this creature and those she had companied with understand about his party, anyway?

Kethan made no attempt to answer. His wounds, shallow as they were, smarted, and he wondered briefly what sort of filth the claws might have left in his broken skin.

His captor leaned back against the nearest outcrop. Her lidded eyes closed, but Kethan had no hope that she slept. Or, if she did, her rus guard were always awake.

To remain here without a struggle was not of his nature. Nor could he hope for any rescue. Therefore, he dropped his own bloodied head on the arms he had folded across his up-pulled knees and set up mind wards. But first he dared a probe and discovered, of course, that this place was well warded. Firdun knew the keys to such, but that talent was not one the weres owned. He suddenly had a vision—there out of what appeared to be a haze rode Aylinn astride Morna, barebacked as if she had mounted in a hurry, Trussant trotting to match her. Behind moved other figures he did not doubt were the rest of the party. He cut contact instantly, before he even tried to reach his foster sister, for fear that whatever glamorie lay here could pick some hint from his own mind which would bring her within reach of this monster.

He did not have farsight. It was too bad, he thought with a wry twist, that the talents could not be sorted out so one always had a supply of those most necessary. Not farsight—but something else!

Kethan's cramped body tensed. Then that call—that queer seeking which had brought him out of camp—was *not* connected with this trap after all! Dare he open to what he sensed now, or was it just another trick?

Instead, purposefully, and without the aid of his vanished belt, he strove to touch that level of him which was were. He could not make the change without the belt—no. But could he *think* were?

Like one edging along a very narrow path, on either side of which there was a threatening drop, Kethan proceeded to do what he had never done before. He had always fought to hold the pard under, keep his human part in control. Never when he was in man form had he tried to think were. But it seemed that now he must use any possible defense—and perhaps so find an actual weapon.

Thus he sought that other path. He fought to think of himself padding on four feet, his sight, hearing, and sense of smell far beyond anything his human form possessed. Almost . . . almost . . .

There! He had been alert enough to catch that fugitive other sense, the one which had drawn him. And it was certainly not of this place of horror. Even as he, it was imprisoned here. Feline . . . were? No, it did not respond to that suggestion he dared to send. Not were—but certainly not wholly animal, even though it went in four-footed form. He had a quick glimpse of shining black fur, a sniff of scent—female, in fear, and yet still a warrior.

At his tentative touch there was an instant withdrawal and he waited patiently, not seeking. Let her come to his summons, understand what he was and that he was no threat to her.

Suddenly he was seeing—with the same odd clarity as he did when the pard shape was upon him. But not through *his* eyes.

There was the forest of rocks, the birds soaring and settling now and again. And there was a crevice, even smaller than the one he had found. But this was not at ground level—rather, it was halfway up one of the rocks. Then he was somehow inside it and looking out, with red rage tearing at him because of the birds. There was blood on the rock and drifting feathers.

She had given a good accounting of herself. It was also plain that she saw no possible way of escape and had set herself grimly to die with as much trouble to the enemy as she could.

Now, even as he had looked through her eyes, his pard sense loosed her within his mind and made clear what lay about them.

*Fight!* That came as fiercely as if it were hissed in his ears.

Fight? *Weapon—belt—*he made the translation and hoped that she would catch it. Only with the belt did he have a chance against the birds and this Waste-born monster.

*Belt?* It came as a question, and he quickly strove to visualize it as it had been so long familiar to him.

There was a mind-silence—she had withdrawn. Perhaps she could see no value in his information. The bird woman opened both eyes, clicked her beak like jaws together, and arose. She was looking beyond him, plainly engrossed in whatever had aroused her.

Without a glance in his direction she left in her queer hopping gait, leaving the rus on sentinel duty behind.

*Others*— The mind-touch awakened again. *She calls the flock.*

*Not here,* he returned quickly, for none of the birds nearby had withdrawn.

*Here. Water, food—must find—*

The words instantly turned on his own thirst and hunger. Outside the sun was nearly gone. Though he lacked the night sight of the pard, he somehow felt encouraged by that withdrawal of full light. He kept his eyes on the birds. Several of them had taken wing and coasted off. Had the monster set some ward on him? Delicately he probed. None he could sense.

*Water—food—* Again those words reached him on pard-send.

*The birds watch,* he cautioned.

*Death time not yet—she has not said so. They allow water—food—*

He had been so cramped in the crevice that he had trouble working his way out of it. To his complete surprise he saw that the rus in sight were perched on the tops of the outcrops and none of them stirred.

Somehow Kethan made it to his feet. Water and food—yes— but more than that, he wanted to find the belt his captor had tossed away. He started to edge fully into the open and stood for a long moment, feeling queasy and ill from the stench of this place.

*Water*— It was a summons. But far more important was the hope of finding once more his belt.

The bird woman had stood so. The scene was sharply pictured in his mind and she had flung the belt in . . . that direction!

He fought the pain of his cramped legs and dared to lurch onto the next of the pillars, clutching tightly at the rough stone to keep from falling. To his continued amazement none of the birds now roosting above did more than stare down at him.

*Come—water!* That mind-urge was sharp. But Kethan's sight ranged slowly from the littered and dung-thick ground to the pillars about, paying no attention. The belt. . . .

It was fast growing darker. There seemed to be clouds rising to blot out the remains of the sunset, and the shadows linking pillar to pillar thickened until he nearly despaired that he could ever sight what he sought even though it might lay directly before him.

Surely it must have spun in this direction—he could not be wrong about that. Search the ground, then follow the line of each rough pillar to its crest where the rus sat watching. Nothing.

He had set his shoulders against one of those outcrops. The foul odors stirred up by his traveling over the dung-thick ground were enough to stifle a man. Then—

Was it his own binding with that artifact which set it slightly a-swing? He was certain, though he could not see it clearly, that the belt dangled well out of his reach halfway up one of the crags, looped over a jutting spur of rock.

Kethan, heartened, came with a swift lurch to stand beneath it. But it was far above his reach and, though he surveyed the ground around him in frustrated anger, he could see no rock he could drag into place which would help him catch that tantalizing strip of hide. To attempt to climb the rock itself was perhaps the only answer, but when he laid bruised and beak-torn hands on its surface he could find no irregularity which would give him either finger- or toehold. The rus above were growing restless. Several of them came at him, they would have him badly torn with no chance to defend himself.

He coughed and coughed with a force which seemed to tear at his lungs. Some of the offal above must have been dislodged. If he could drink—

Water. That did not come as a true call but rather a memory. To remain frozen here perhaps until his tormentor returned was the act of a fool. He had found the belt, and he would now find a way to claim it.

Now he loosed his own mind-send. *Water?*

It was like the thread spun by a spider, so delicate a tracing that even one of his sobbing breaths could break it. Ahead—to the east. If those obscene birds aloft had caught it also, it meant nothing to them, or else their will joined with the other to send him on.

But as Kethan went, he marked the way which would bring him back to the belt. Long days of wood-ranging, both as man and pard, had heightened senses to remember points of land, and these rocky points were so dissimilar he could sight easily those to be used on a return trail.

The cramps in his legs at least eased, though his thirst and hunger were there to weaken him. And as he came into an open space—like a glade in a true forest—he was wavering. Here were tightly bunched plants sprouting, tall stalks on which hung bell blossoms pallidly alight. And around those swung the foul insects attracted by the offal.

But tightly closed in upon itself as each plant was, there were wide spaces between each. One of his boots crushed down upon the empty remains of insects that had earlier fallen prey to these rooted hunters.

Beyond was a dark pool. And at its edge crouched a fur body, lean nearly to the point of starvation. A head lifted and wide, night-brightened eyes caught his.

He could see now that this other was indeed a cat—larger by a third than those he had seen in Arvon. One ear was raggedly torn and as it hunched around away from the water, he could also see that one leg moved stiffly. Yet its head came up with a small hiss of warning.

Oddly enough at that moment what flashed into Kethan's fore-mind was the traditional keep greeting of the Dalesfolk.

*I give traveler's thanks for the greeting. May good fortune hold this household.*

And then he was stopped by the thought which broke through his unconscious return to keep ways.

*Drink—eat—*

It would seem that this fellow captive had only two things on her mind. Drink, yes. He knelt by the pool and dipped in one hand. The liquid seemed turgid and faintly warm, and certainly as he held it closer to his lips the smell was such that one would not class it, he thought with irony, with the first squeezings of the harvest seasons.

But it was liquid and it soothed his dry mouth and went down his throat easily enough. He cupped both hands together and drank again. All right, here was water, unless it was poisoned by some chance of the Waste. He allowed himself two more gulps. But food . . .

The dim light provided by those ghostly flowers showed him that his companion had left the poolside and was limping toward a large rock oddly shaped with an overhang which formed a minia-ture cave. From that she emerged again, dragging a bundle which already showed signs of having been badly mauled.

He joined her to draw back a piece of hide covering which was scored again and again by what could only be the claws of the rus. What lay within was a very small portion of dried meat, beginning to smell, and with tooth marks set about its edges.

It was a very small portion and Kethan looked from it to the cat, who settled down again, seeming to find it difficult to arrange her damaged leg to her satisfaction. He was hungry enough, yes, even to snatch up that offered portion and eat it all himself. But another thought began to expand in his mind.

The cat obviously had no chance against either a flock attack by the rus or a swift pounce from the bird woman. But he had been tricked out of his belt—therefore the pard had meant the greater danger. This was only hopeful guessing, but he could prove it one way or another—with help.

He indicated the meat and the cat and tried to simply mind-send. *Let sister one eat. Then this one has something to show.*

The cat continued to stare at him. *No eat?* came at last so faint he could hardly catch the words.

Kethan nodded vigorously enough to set some of his scratches smarting again. *This one.* He dug his thumb into his chest vigorously. *Weapon—get free—if sister help.* He hoped that he was speaking the truth in that.

The cat looked at the meat and then attacked it ravenously. His own tongue swept over his lips and he fought against the ache in his middle.

Having finished the last scrap of the pitiful ration, the cat sat up and regarded him again.

*What do?*

*Come.* He could not even be sure the rus would let them go, but it was the first step to freedom for them both. Kethan stopped and caught up the cat, trying not to mishandle the injured leg. Under that matted fur the body was nearly a rack of bones. How long had this poor thing been here? he wondered.

He retraced his path until he came again to where the belt was looped out of reach. Holding the cat against his chest, he pointed up to the barely discernible strip of fur.

"Weapon." He looked deeply into the feline eyes now turned up to stare at him and allowed his mind to fill with the vision of the pard in all his hunting force, claws and fangs against the rus.

Somehow he knew she had captured that picture, understood. Now her head turned and she looked up at the belt. He could hold her as high as a rough series of small nicks or pocks in the rock.

She might have two body lengths more to climb, and then she would have to reach out a paw and push the belt (which he could only hope was not too well anchored) off and down, leaping so he might catch her.

Cats held certain mysteries of their own. He had heard enough of the old legends to know that in the past they had shown powers apart from mankind. Could she—would she?

She moved now in his arms, her head turned toward the pillar up which he would boost her. He shot a glance at the now practically invisible rus. None of the creatures had moved. Could he hope that they slept?

Standing on tiptoe, he held the cat to the farthest extent of his reach. In spite of her favoring that paw, she now used the seemingly disabled limb and planted it apparently against the rock, but he was sure she had found a hole. Then he drew a deep breath and was able to push her a fraction higher.

In a second of time she was totally out of his hold, a black blot against the yellow-red stone. She wriggled herself about and he caught his breath, sure she would fall, moving in as close as he could. Her paw went out and struck full on the heavily carved jargoon of the buckle, sending the belt swinging. Then the balance failed and the artifact fell within his reach. But he was waiting for the cat, tense for her and the coming attack of the birds.

Fortune favored him in that he caught her, holding her tightly to him, sure he could feel her small heart racing against his larger one. He placed her carefully on the ground between his feet and grabbed up the belt, locking it well around his waist.

The transition was swift—he was four-footed again and the cat straightened up to dab her nose briefly against the larger one he turned down in her direction. So far, so good.

Now to get out of this prison. If he took the cat on his back and the birds attacked, he could not defend her—she would be swept away and torn to pieces. Therefore gently he licked her head, and then gripped at the nape of her neck as easily as he could in the way a mother would carry a kitten.

They returned to that place where he had hidden in the crevice. But it would seem that now ill fortune took a part in the game.

There was a shriek and several rus took to the air, planing down at them. Kethan nosed the cat back into the crevice and stationed himself before it.

For all his lack of food and rest, he was able to summon the lithe agility of his kind. With a roar he arose, using his great forepaws, the cruelly curved claws, well in a wide sweep which caught and smashed several attackers against the rocks. He had chosen his position well; they could not come on him from behind.

Twice more they whirled down, but he had the pard's night eyes now and could see them coming. He was ready. One he caught in his fangs, spitting out in disgust the thing's musty-feathered body with the life crushed out of it. And with one paw and then the other he fended off and destroyed enough of the others so that they now held away, screeching aloud to the night.

Then came she for whom they called, with great hopping strides between the pillars of her stronghold, her beak mouth open as she hissed aloud her rage.

The birds stayed back now, seemingly willing to leave the battle to their mistress. Her head swung widely back and forth as she viewed Kethan first through one coal-red eye and then the other.

But he knew this was his final chance. Summoning all the energy left in his body, he sprang. Her beak scored the top of his head as he evaded her attack at one of his eyes. Both of his forepaws pounded home on her chest, sending her back by the fury of that blow against a pillar. He heard her scream of pain and anger and felt brittle bones snap. Then she slid down and folded together. Plainly, for now, she was finished. He did not know whether he had delivered a death blow or not.

Whirling, he seized the cat once more by the neck hold, leaping out and beyond the beginning circle of the pillars into the open Waste once again. Behind him the air fairly shook with the clamor of the rus, though oddly enough, none of them attempted to follow him away from their own stronghold.

## CHAPTER TWENTY-TWO

# The Fane of the Three, the Waste, West

The battle energy which had brought Kethan out of that foul nesting place began to fail. His head drooped and he realized that the cat's body, frail as it was, was dragging the ground.

However, he could see those waiting and he realized that they could not reach him because of some ward. This, he could only hope, was set to keep out invasion, not to keep prisoners in.

Aylinn's moonflower wand was the beacon to which Kethan held, though there were deeper glows on either side of her. One was a strange dark-piercing violet which he associated with Elysha and the other a pale gray as if Ibycus's ring was waking.

The clamor of the birds rose harsh and heavy behind him, but none of them had yet attacked. Were they so under the command of that Waste monster that they would not do so without orders?

At last he knew that he could not drag his companion any farther. He loosed his grip on the loose neck folds and crouched. For too long the heap of black fur lay where he had dropped it. He began to lick as he would the wounds of his own kind and he strove to reach with mind-touch.

*Climb—back—* he repeated the thought over and over until at last the cat did stir. Hoping he was understood, Kethan crouched as low as he could on the baked clay as the body uncurled very slowly and then crawled, as if to rise to its feet was more than it could hope now to do. It nudged against the pard's side, as he strove to flatten himself even further. Then he felt the sharp pain of claws catching through his fur, points rasping his skin as the other climbed. A weight settled on his back, but the punishment of the claws still held and Kethan hoped the cat was well anchored even though the experience was painful for him.

With care he arose from his crouch, trying to make sure that weight did not shift at any movement of his. Then once more he faced that cluster of lights which meant safety. But his pace was not in leaps now. He placed one paw before the other with great care.

It seemed to him that the whole of the night must waste away before he could reach his goal. The ward—it was there for him also. Almost he could have howled his frustration to the night sky.

But a figure he could hardly see in that limited light moved out a little ahead of the three sources holding so steady. There was movement, but Kethan could no longer, in spite of pard night sight, follow what that other did. Dimly he realized that the ward was being challenged. Firdun—wards were his talent and if any could break through this barrier, it would be him!

Kethan's head drooped almost to the ground now. He wondered, even if Firdun was successful, if he could manage the few more paces to get he and his companion out.

Then there came a howling cry from his companion and a feeling that somewhere, not quite in the time he knew, a door had opened, or a barrier fallen. So heartened, he stumbled on to feel the healing of the moonflowers, as well as an inpouring of energy. Only he was too spent now. He crumbled to the ground and felt faintly the scratching of claws. But as he went into a soothing darkness, nothing mattered anymore.

Aylinn was on her knees in an instant, pulling at the length of the pard. Her hands sought his middle. A moment later she had shot the bolt of the jargoon buckle and pulled away the belt so that now a very battered and bloodstained young man rested at their feet.

Elysha stood in the same instant and caught up the cat, cradling its starved body against her.

"Uta, what evil sucked you in to that?" There was a crooning note in her voice as she held the animal against her breast.

"Out of here!" Firdun's voice was an order which caught all their attention. "There may well be a backlash—that was a fourfold bespelling."

He had already bent over Kethan while Ibycus and Guret moved up on the other side. The were was limp in their combined hold; they could not arouse him enough to move even with their aid. So they carried him somewhat clumsily, well aware that he might well be wounded worse than the damage they could see. Then Obred and Lero arrived, that same hammocklike device stretched between two of the horses, which snorted and pawed the earth but were easily forced to obey, and Kethan was transported. So they moved through the night, Aylinn walking beside the swaying hammock in which her foster brother lay, impatient to be allowed to tend him, though Ibycus and Firdun, and even Elysha, appeared to be gripped by the same conviction that they must be on the move and as quickly as possible.

Kethan had not stirred since he had fallen except when the hands about him moved him by their will. But she could see that his face between the smeared filth and dried blood was that of one who slept at peace, had not fallen into deep unconsciousness.

They headed south for a space, Ibycus now and then bringing them to a pause while he studied the stars overhead. He also gazed often into the murky gem on his finger and once sharply changed their direction. Elysha carried the cat and sometimes Aylinn caught a fringe of mind-send between the two. The wisewoman had insisted that she be given a packet of meat and she also carried her saddle water bottle slung over her shoulder, offering its contents to her charge at intervals.

Dawn was once more visible enough that Firdun could see that the eternal pan of cracked yellow clay over which they had traveled through most of the night had again changed. This time there was no reddish moss to carpet the ground, nor were the small bushes beginning to show in any color except natural green. For a moment or two, remembering well that glamorie of the trap, he had eyed the landscape distrustfully.

Now they followed, he was sure, a directly western course. But they must also be well south of the trail those from Garth Howell had taken. They came to a stand of trees and Ibycus at last called a halt.

Kethan did not rouse even when Aylinn loosed her healer's bag and made measured choices. He did swallow water when his head was raised against her shoulder and a cup held to his lips. However, it was as if he moved in his sleep and his eyes remained closed. She had a frightening thought that the rough scratches might hold some poison.

Elysha joined her and together they stripped away his badly rent clothing so she might treat each and every one of those cuts. For the first time he moved on his own, his hands going to his waist, and he gave a slight moan until Aylinn put his wandering fingers on his belt, though she did not fasten it once more about him.

The trees marked a spring, and the grass a little beyond their circle drew whinnies from their mounts, who wanted freedom to graze. The two Kioga tribesmen rode out and came back very soon, carrying a creature not unlike a leaper but twice it in size, roughly butchered between them. Firdun, exploring around the spring, returned with a double handful of sweet root.

Among them the cat moved, apparently in better shape now than her rescuer. She had gone to sit beside him, her eyes on Aylinn, almost as if she needed to make sure he was under proper care. Now she hunkered down, her paws folded under her. Seeing the half-healed gashes on her bony body, Aylinn brought forth more salves and set about anointing them, paying extra attention to the torn ear, the animal permitting her touch as if it were expected.

*One—three—* Aylinn started at that sudden mind-touch. The cat had extended her injured leg as if to draw the girl's full attention to it.

The moonmaid knew little of tame cats. However, with snowcat and pard sharing her family, she certainly was aware of the proper mind-levels for communication at least within their species.

"Moon." she shaped the word with her lips as well as spoke it aloud.

*One—three—female Power.* The answer came promptly.

"True," she agreed. "Greetings, sister-in-fur."

*Uta.* The cat replied that same name with which Elysha had first greeted her. *One—three—waiting—*

Aylinn was putting a light binding of leaf cloth over the slashed leg.

"Waiting where, Uta?" To her knowledge there were very few moonmaids and she had heard of none who dared the Waste.

*See soon. Feel good. He will awake soon.* The cat nodded toward Kethan. *Brave fighter—cat lord—*

"He is man also," Aylinn found herself saying, "as you can see."

*Much not seen by eye. Man-pard—great warrior.*

Uta deliberately closed her eyes and it was apparent she considered their conversation over—leaving Aylinn a bit resentful, with a lot of questions she would like to ask. That this animal was not of the same breed as those cats who had joined households she was very sure. But neither was she a were! The Waste was certainly full of mysteries. Perhaps one could never come to the end of them.

She curled up by Kethan and followed the cat's example, finding sleep ready to seize upon her. But the same was not so for Ibycus, sitting not far away. The scowl line between his eyes had deepened greatly since they had left the Eyrie. Nor did he look up in greeting as Elysha came up to kneel beside him, though at no invitation of his.

"Our party grows." The ever-present scent which clung to her garments encompassed them both. Ibycus forced a cough and she laughed.

"Age never set heavy on you before, Lord Mage; do not invite its burdens now. I would like to hear Uta's tale, but you have more in mind."

Her bracelets flashed as she indicated the hand lying on his knee, the dull stone of the ring now without any signs of life.

Ibycus gave an exaggerated sigh. It was plain she was not going to leave him alone. But then, when had she ever? His memory flashed back over seasons too many to count now, to when he had seen her first, a child not yet into girlhood casting the snapped-off heads of grass flowers into a pool and watching intently as they swirled and were borne away by the current.

Had he only possessed the power of foresight . . . But he had not. Perhaps it was youth then also which betrayed him, so that he had thrown himself down beside her. Nor had she feared him for a stranger. When she turned to look at him she might have been welcoming one of her kin.

They had talked—and it had not been a child to whom he spoke that day. Wisdom already grew within her and her talent truly amazed him with its hints of Power to come. So he had lingered, not only by the pool, but in the hold of the Silvermantle lord who had taken her into fosterage after the death of his sister.

In spite of himself Ibycus had been drawn back season after season until she was maid-grown and demanded as her right that he take her as pupil. But as time passed she had wanted more, to be made free of the innermost of his thoughts as if she would sink herself wholly into him so they might become one. Then he had summoned up his full strength and held the last barrier, so she had left him in rage—rage rooted in hurt. He had sometimes wondered . . .

No, this was no time for memories, but for the here and now. However, if he did not offer her an explanation she would dig for it and so upset the delicate balances of the Powers with which he must play.

"I must speak with the Gryphon—with Alon if it is possible," he told her. "What are we? Less than two handfuls and we know not still what hides at Garth Howell which might feed those who have gone forth."

Now he stroked the dull gem with the forefinger of his other hand. Fingers touched lightly on his arm. "Draw from me, Lord Mage, if there be need," she said quietly, all the half mockery gone out of her voice.

Ibycus stared into the stone. At first there was no change and then tiny threads of color flickered across its surface. These drew together, thickened. But the effort to hold, and to enhance, what he had summoned was great. It might be that the baneful Waste itself would defeat him.

Alon! He did not repeat that name aloud, but it sounded through his mind. Now he felt that other strain finding its way like blood through a vein into his body. She was indeed feeding his Power as she had promised.

Alon! The colored threads were certainly brighter, thicker. It was like looking into a mirror surface, for the very stone of the ring seemed to swell, to provide him with a wider vision.

That was Alon, right enough—behind him a smudged expanse which might or might not be a poor showing of the Eyrie court-yard. However, Alon's head had turned, he was looking up and out-ward to meet Ibycus's compelling stare.

"How fares it with you?"

Ibycus knew he had little time to spare. "One gate found—it is sealed. You have news out of Lormt?"

"Little enough. Hilarion labors. So must Garth Howell. There is an incoming of darkness."

"It threatens you?"

"Not yet. It gathers there, it waits. You track those gone from the Garth?"

"We were forced from their trail. We seek it again—they head west still. How—" What more Ibycus meant to say vanished, for the face in the stone was gone. Instead there was a dark roiling cloud.

Instantly the mage was on guard. Into that spreading darkness shot a jagged bolt of lightning, and less than a heartbeat later the lightning was tinged with violet. Twice that crossed the stone, then darkness and lightning disappeared and only the dull gray oval lay under their gaze.

"Garth Howell?" Elysha's hand had fallen away from his arm. She was breathing faster.

Ibycus shrugged. "With what may wander hereabouts unchal-lenged, who may guess? We need a sanctuary for a space."

*One—three—waiting—* Uta had uncoiled and now limped over to Elysha.

"A moon shrine!" The woman was startled. "You can show the way?"

*Was going—bird demon caught me.*

Even as Uta had awakened, so now Kethan moved. He stared un-believing up at the trees over his head for a moment and then blinked. His stirring roused Aylinn and she sat up yawning, like a young girl who had missed her proper sleep. But she turned to her foster brother fast enough, her hand going to his bandaged forehead.

"How do you feel?"

He grinned. "Hungry, sister mine. Have you a roasting sheep well ready on the fire?"

She moved as if to aid him, but he managed quickly to sit up without her help. His clothing was now largely a matter of tatters and much of it Aylinn had cut away when she tended his wounds. But his first act was to buckle on the belt which had lain tightly beneath his hands during his sleep.

They gathered by the fire where a leaper had roasted and shared out the meat after Kethan had drawn a fresh shirt and jerkin from his saddlebags. Guret and the other Kioga seemed more than a little surprised when Ibycus announced that they had a new guide, the cat Kethan had brought out of the rus roost. Kethan himself scooped up the limping Uta and, mounted on his shadow horse, settled her as comfortably as possible.

The green country held as they rode. They had started at nooning, but Uta seemed certain they would reach their promised shelter before nightfall.

*Little sister.* Kethan struggled to find the proper level of mindsend. *How do you?*

*Well—moon power healing—belly full.*

Then he asked the question which had lain at the bottom of his mind since his awakening. Though the others had seen no signs of being followed, still he kept a wary eye now and then on the sky overhead and his ears were alert for the screeching cries of the rus. That they had managed to win free of that prison seemed more and more fantastic to him.

It was he whom the bird-thing had been told to capture—because of them all he was best at reading a trail. And he was far from sure that, in those last moments of frenzied attack, he had done more than perhaps temporarily cripple her. What did Uta know—as she, too, had been captive there?

*Sassfang little power,* came the message. *Only in her own place can she hold. There is no follow feel.*

Somehow he was able to accept that. He still held to the fore of their party, even though he rode as a man since Uta was in his charge. But he surveyed the country through which they passed with a scout's eye.

There were more and more copses of trees such as the one in which they had camped. And, while the green of the grass appeared overlaid with a dulling gray as if a rain of dust had fallen not too long ago, it *was* grass and had not the inherent menace of that yellow baked clay.

Now they could see a rise of what looked to be a rocky cliff face before them. However, this crag stood alone, unaccompanied by any other outcrops, and the closer they came toward it the more visible was a glitter, as if pockets of pure crystals studded its sides in no regular patterns.

It also was surrounded by trees, but such trees! They stood only a little taller than a mounted man, but their branches spread wide, meeting those of their neighbors to form a roof.

Also they looked to bear two kinds of leaves—one wide and fleshy thick, the other in a tight roll—unless those latter marked some buds or fruit not yet ready for the harvest.

"Laran!" Aylinn pushed Morna up beside Kethan. "Laran—oh, indeed this is blessed land!"

Though those trees had formed a roof of branches, there was room to move under them if they dismounted and led their horses and pack train. Luckily those matted branches grew only at the crowns of the trees and the trunks below were bare.

Firdun was aware, as he urged the pack train along, of a growing fragrance, even more potent than that which clung to Aylinn's moonflowers or to Elysha's garments. Also once he was under that roof of branches a feeling of utter peace such as he had never known before encased him. It was as if all the world, with its sorrows, fears, and alarms was so warded that nothing could penetrate here except that which was of goodwill.

The grove of encircling trees was not a large one. They came out into the open again to face flashes of light. What they had seen from afar was no crag alone in a level land. If it had been assembled by some purpose, those who had worked so had not followed the patterns known to mankind.

This was a mighty throne backed by the crystal-studded white rock. No human could ever have been accommodated by that seat, so high did it tower. But there was one seated there, and they came to an awed halt. Between them and the throne was a round pool or else a mirror of stain-free metal and the figure on the throne leaned forward a little as if staring down at its surface.

Uta squirmed in Kethan's arms until he set her down. Limping, certainly of them all showing no awe, she approached the throne.

The figure seated there was so muffled in a robe or veils, which were even drawn tightly over its head, that the travelers could not see its true nature. But the hands which lay uncovered on either arm of the throne were of human fashion yet twice the size, with long fingers, the nails of which were formed of crystals.

Aylinn sank to her knees, her moonflower wand outheld as a warrior might offer his sword to his lord.

"One of three, three in one." Her voice sounded as if she were on the verge of tears. "That thy servant is allowed this meeting is more . . ." She was truly weeping now, the tears wet on her sun-browned cheeks.

Kethan found himself on his knees also, and heard a stir about as the rest also paid homage. There were many great Old Ones of the legends. The earthly ties with such were said to exist throughout their world. That Uta had led them to one such sanctuary was plain.

That which the sitter represented might be long since withdrawn, but not to Aylinn and many others. Even if it were only a representation, there was that about it which made this, for those who walked in the Light, holy ground.

That peace Firdun had felt when he entered here was armor against all the Dark. But now there seemed to be a questioning, a desire to know why that peace was troubled by their coming.

He felt uneasy for a moment or so, as would any unbelieving intruder in a sacred place. But that unease was swept away. There was no harm in his coming. That which he had followed all his life, his talent, opened wider—like a flower under the sun. He had been judged and found worthy.

Elysha moved forward, almost equal with Aylinn, her head thrown back, her eyes searching that veiled face for what could not be seen.

"Gunnora in all glory! Earth Mother, Sky Mother, Dweller in the Deep Waters—all in one. What you have given is ever at your service."

Perhaps even more now, Firdun felt that searching and weighing. Perhaps they all learned more of themselves than their kind ever knew. But though they had been united in purpose from the start for this venture, now they were welded, melded, worked upon as a smith works sword steel to do what must be done.

Then—

They knew that presence which had been there, for the time of that weighing was gone. Nothing was left but the form which could hold Her as She willed, when She willed. However, She had made them free, given them guesting for this night within Her sanctuary, and they were honored more than any sitting in a High Seat of a hall.


# CHAPTER TWENTY-THREE

# The Meeting in the Waste, West

Guret and his two tribesmen approached Ibycus, though they made a wide circle past the throne and its silent occupant.

"Lord"—though there was a note of deference in Guret's voice, there was also a hint of defiance—"we would take the four-footed ones out to the open meadows where they may be staked to graze at their will. This High One"—he shot a glance over his shoulder at the throne—"is like our Mother of Mares and yet we are not truly Her children. That She has given us Her blessing is a wondrous thing, but we would not intrude upon that which is not of our heritage."

Ibycus nodded. "Do as you will, Horsemaster. But hold this to you—what abides here is friend to all of the Light, and Her power is both wide and everlasting."

Thus the Kioga led the mounts and the packhorses out of the shadow of the trees, but none of the others followed.

As dusk settled down, those podlike buds on the trees began to show wider cracks as if the night was meant for their blooming. And a perfume scented the air. Though the travelers got out supplies for a meal, none of them seemed to be inclined to do more than nibble at a bit of journey cake, take more than a sip now and then from their water bottles.

Hunger was banished, along with all distress and uneasiness. Aylinn went to stand just under the limb fringe of one of those trees. The buds had opened wide and flattened, loosing white petals which gave off a glow far deeper than the gleam of her own moonflowers. She dared to reach up and give the lightest of touches to the nearest one.

Then her hand jerked back in dismay, for the blossom floated free into the air, the petals wide as white wings. It did not fall, even though there was no breeze to bear it—none Aylinn could feel. Its flight was to the left and then it settled down onto the surface of that mirror pool at the foot of the throne.

Kethan and Firdun had both watched her near the tree and now each moved in, as might guards. But Aylinn had dropped to her knees, leaning out over the surface, which the landing blossom had not troubled into life.

Slowly her hand moved forward. Firdun stepped closer as if to prevent her, but Kethan's arm was out, a barrier to wall him away.

With infinite care the girl inserted her fingers under the edge of the nearest petal and, without touching it more than she must, she drew it toward her.

At last she stepped back, her moon wand lying unnoticed by her side, the splendid bloom resting on the palm of her hand. From her throat there arose a soft crooning, as if her wonder at what she held could not be kept silent.

Soft fur brushed against Kethan as he settled down beside his foster sister. It seemed at that moment there was nothing else in the world except that one perfect flower. Yet it was not for his taking—that he also knew.

Aylinn held the flower at the height of her breast. There her moon badge was a circle of glory. Not taking her eyes from what she held, she groped for her wand and held that to the same height. The flower which had topped it for so long was fading, its petals becoming gauze-thin. Then those fluttered loose and were gone. Slowly, as if at any moment she feared what she held might be taken from her, Aylinn advanced the wand toward the flower, slipped the tip of it under its petals.

So she held it. On Kethan's knee a paw moved, a black-furred head was raised high to watch. About them there was a stirring, a feeling that some potent Power wrought, not by their will, but another's.

Aylinn raised the wand. With it she saluted the throned one as a warrior would raise a sword in homage.

"Moonsworn I have always been by the beliefs of my people," she said. "Now—now, One in Three, I tread any path *you* open for my feet. That I have been chosen so—" Her voice broke and once more she was crying. "Mother, Sister, Ancient One, make of me now what you will!"

She bowed her head over the wand she had drawn back against her slender body. Kethan longed to put his arm about her, draw her close, for he had a feeling that in these moments she was going farther away, even though she had not moved.

Uta reared up on his lap, putting her paws against his chest and looking up into his face. He heard Firdun stir, get to his feet also, and swing away.

Slowly Kethan got up, keeping his hold on the cat, and left

Aylinn alone. Or was she so? Perhaps there were others now who would welcome her.

With a growing emptiness in him, Kethan turned his back upon the throned one and strode back into the trees. The blooms had mostly opened and he felt as heavy of body, as drained of energy as he had when he had escaped from the place of the rus. He tumbled on the bedroll he had spread out earlier and stretched out, dimly aware that those scratches and hurts he had felt were gone. There was only the peace.

Determined, he turned his head away so he could not see the crystal throne. Uta was still with him, a warm comforting armload of fur.

His eyes closed.

Something stirred, not only against his body, but in his mind, breaking the euphoria produced by the flowers. He was aware of, very far off, a kind of summoning which was not an alarm, merely a call—a call he must answer.

Perhaps that first light of the flowers had faded a fraction; he was sure when he opened his eyes that he could not see as clearly. There was a shadow of a shadow—yet it brought with it no feeling of alarm, rather awoke him further, determined to see what stood there, weaving a little as if it stood unsteadily.

Kethan's hand went to his belt. Pard eyes—let him have pard eyes the better for seeing—let him have them—now!

And certainly some fraction of that keenness came to him. For see he did. Not Aylinn, silver white as he had always known her; not Elysha, aflame with the emotions she held in control; not—not the Lady. No, he was a man and she would not come so to him.

But there *was* a woman there—and such a woman as he had never seen in either Arvon or the Dales. She was small, perhaps her head might come a little above his own shoulder if they stood together. (But he found that he could not get to his feet, rather was frozen where he was.) Her hair was short, showing none of the looping braids or locks which he was used to. Rather, it fit her head like a silken cap, with only a lock or two slightly longer, reaching to touch her shoulders.

Her face had some of the triangular shape known among the Old Ones, with a pointed chin and large eyes which were green or yellow—he could not be sure which.

She was fuller of body than Aylinn, but not statuesque as Elysha. And covering her, yet molding close to show breasts and hips, was a dark single garmet, seemingly made of one piece, with no skirt or overdress, covering her from throat to wrist to ankle.

Kethan's nostrils expanded. He had not only pard sight now but pard sense of scent. This was a female which awoke in him something which had been long asleep and now would move him to . . . But move he could not.

*Who are you?* He thought he had asked that aloud and then realized that he had used mind-send.

He saw her smile, showing sharp-pointed teeth. She raised both hands and smoothed herself down the length of her body as far as her hips, as if in some feminine reassurance that she was appealing as she wished to be.

Kethan made a supreme effort. He did not want to be wholly pard and so perhaps drive this wondrous apparition from him; he only wanted to touch, to make sure that he saw what he believed stood there.

Somehow he succeeded. His fingertips slipped down her thigh until he could hold no longer and his hand fell helplessly against his own body.

*You like . . . what you see?* Her mind-send was high-pitched and there was something of an effort in it.

*I like.* And his send was close to the pard's growl.

She laughed silently, making no sound. *Be patient, four-foot. If fate is kind we all gain what we strive the most to obtain. I have waited—long . . .* Her voice trailed away.

Kethan summoned the last of his strength and tried to catch her. But like the moonflower earlier, she faded and was gone. Now he sat alone and the peace of this place was broken for him.

That his visitor had been from the Dark Side he knew was impossible. Was she some servant of the throned one who had dared to make her presence so known to him? Or was she a sending?

He simply knew that he could no longer sleep. Uta, curled by his feet, uttered a sleepy protest. He half covered her with the edge of his sleeping mat and struck outward through the trees toward the outworld, certain that he must find something which was real enough for him to understand.

"Who goes?" That demand out of the dark argued that some other of their group had found this place an enigma which might not be wholly accepted as good.

"Firdun?" He recognized the voice.

There was movement in the darkness and a hand clasped his arm with a punishing grip. "The talents are many; we each have our own. That we know. But—has your sister this night found a path which will lead her totally away from the ways of our world?"

"I do not know," Kethan answered truthfully. He was shaken a little out of his preoccupation with his late visitor, to wonder at why this son of the Gryphon would be so moved by the ceremony they had watched.

"She is your kin—" Firdun was beginning, when Kethan interrupted him.

"We are not blood kin, but fosterling. I am were, as you well know. Aylinn was raised daughter to my mother, who is a Wise-woman and healer. Discovering she had great talent, she was sent to Linark—and there discovered she was Moon called."

"There are those women of Estcarp"—Kethan could not see Firdun's face, but Firdun's voice was bitter—"who raised the power to wrack mountains. But they look upon men as lesser beings. Oh"—there was a vigorous swish of air in the dark as if the speaker had flung his arms wide—"I do not know what I seek to say—but if Aylinn goes from us—"

"That will not happen while we quest." Kethan was guessing. Aylinn—the Gryphon son—men were drawn to women and women to men and had been since the days the world had begun. Sometimes it was ill done and ended in sorrow; sometimes it was as with Kethan's parents, Gillan and Herrel, such a bond as nothing could sever. But no one could speak for another in such matters. "She will be with us," he repeated, knowing at the same time it was chill comfort, "until we have finished what we would do. Time changes many matters, and talents can fit to talents in a fashion one might not believe."

His answer was first a sigh, and then Firdun said: "The Kioga camp nearby . . . we can share their watch." He spoke as if sleep was now beyond his hope.

Well away from the grove of the throne, Guret, armed and alert, was following such a trail as only an expert horsemaster could sight. For the most part the mounts they had carefully chosen from the Kioga herds for this venture were well trained—to the point of standing as if hitched when the reins were flipped over their heads to touch the ground until their riders remounted.

Heretofore only the packhorses, who were ever contrary beasts, had to be picketed when they camped. But for the past few days the young gelding Vasan had provided something of a problem. Guret blamed most of this restlessness on the presence of the were mounts, even though those were as perfectly behaved themselves as any war-trained horse and he could not find anything in their recent actions to fault them.

Tonight, perhaps because they were still bemused by what they had seen in that strange fane, the Kioga had moved out to camp in the familiar open without paying any special attention to the beasts they loosed to good forage. They had busied themselves as usual with the packhorses, but their own mounts they had left to their usual freedom.

However, it was customary for a sentry on duty—and they had posted their sentries here as they would in any unknown territory—to check the horses, moving among them with those soft words which had reassured them from colthood.

And Guret had discovered that Vasan was not beside his usual bond mate Vartin. Having widened his circle of search and discovering no sign of the horse at visual distance from the small herd, he had returned to camp, awakened Obred, and told him that he would trail the stray. It was not long since they had been loosed and he wondered how and why Vasan had taken himself off. He was one of Guret's own private string (each of the Kioga had brought three mounts so that they could change and not overweary the horses if the need arose), and Guret felt responsible for such unlikely behavior.

Guret was gone before Firdun and Kethan joined the Kioga camp and Obred had already vanished into the darkness to take up his sentry duties.

The land was at least level and there were within easy distance no more strands of trees. Also there was a moon overhead even though it was waning. Guret whistled and stood listening for any answering thud of hooves.

When he was not so answered, he went to hands and knees, locating where the taller grass was trampled. Oddly enough, Vasan was not moving like a grazing horse, but rather as if he had already been summoned.

Guret had shed mail and helm and left them in camp. The night was so warm, and that insidious promise of peace had been so all-prevailing, that he had not thought of the gear he had left piled by his bedroll until now. He wavered between returning to arm, to perhaps give some kind of an alarm, and then he made his decision. No. Vasan could not have strayed too far. There was another copse of trees not far ahead now and perhaps that proved a screen for the horse.

Guret had been well tutored in all the tricks of tracking horses. Since the life of the clan depended upon their trained mounts, the loss of even one could not be accepted. He now found a stream by nearly sliding down a slick clay bank to where there was a narrow runnel of water well below the surface of the plain.

There another searching of the ground revealed footprints—leading north, as if Vasan had chosen not to cross that shallow stream but rather moved beside it. Here and there bunches of grass had been snatched for the eating; the gelding had not lingered to graze.

Again Guret tried the calling whistle. Only the cry of a night bird sounded in answer. Now he began to question his choice. To go trailing on into the unknown dark was a risk that was folly to take.

He had just risen to his feet from tracing another hoof mark in the clay when a scream cut through the air. At least he had his sword, having taken that up as a matter of course when he had gone on sentry. That was out of his scabbard and ready in his hand as he pounded forward.

There were more of those screams. Some he was sure were of the pain and terror of a horse. Vasan, surely.

The stream took a curve to the left but still pointed north. Now there were other cries—human? He could not tell, but scout craft slowed his forward plunge. He must know the nature of the danger before he burst into some battle like an untrained boy.

He took to the side of the stream bank, though this was overgrown by a tough thicket of tall-standing reeds so he had to cut his way with the sword. Most of these towered above his head now so that he could see practically nothing of what lay ahead.

"Great Ones—Old Ones—the Dark rises!"

Certainly Vasan had never voiced that! But an instant later the battle scream of a horse in dire defense broke again.

Guret threw himself forward through the last curtain of the reeds. There reared a horse, striking out with forefeet against small-ish things which scuttled here and there across the ground. The willow screen had cut off some of the light but not enough to mask the fact that there was indeed a shadowy figure standing on hind feet, human in seeming, and it was striking down at the scuttling enemy with what looked to be a sword, or at least a part of one.

The Kioga had already chosen sides. He hurled himself on and, to his utter amazement, the scuttling things did not turn to attack him but rather scattered the closer he approached them.

He thrust and raised his sword. On the point of it was impaled something so alien even in this dim light that with a sharp twist of his wrist he hurled it away.

Then he expected them at last to turn on him. Vasan was proving his battle worth, bringing hooves down in a regular beat, now and then lowering his head to seize on one of the scrambling enemy and toss it away.

"By the One in Three—" Where those words had come from Guret could not tell, but they filled his mind, fell swiftly from his lips. "By the Maid, by the Lady, by the Old One who keeps the last gate of all, give us of your strength and Power."

That shadow by the bank lurched forward a fraction. It had dropped its sword. Now it fumbled at its breast and he wondered if the crawlers had managed to inflict some wound.

"Lady—" The voice was very low. "She who elects the death hour—be with us all."

Guret was gripped by a force he had felt only twice before, when he had faced some sneaker out of Garth Howell and made sure the evil-born did not return. He waded into the creepers that laid about him. Somehow the very blade of his sword gave forth light now so that he could see the things—spiders, frogs, things of no known species. They were dying without uttering a sound. Then, breathing heavily, Guret stood by a pile of the strange dead and there was no more stirring across the ground.

Vasan whinnied, then snorted, tramping over his late prey to push his head against Guret's shoulder, once more the perfect-mannered mount.

"You are wounded?" Guret pulled the horse's forelock gently as he asked of the stranger.

"No more than a bite or two." There was no quiver in that answer. "The urings will not be returning to *His* call!"

Booted foot shot out and lifted one of the bodies. "I have to thank you, but that She could send one of Hers to bring me aid— after—after—" The shadow form gasped and crumpled down. Guret went into action. He found that the body he lifted was not in war gear but rather wore a soft covering, which was both a thigh-length jerkin and breeches.

The breath which touched against his cheek was soft and came in a pattern as if the stranger wept. Vasan was already by Guret.

The horse without orders accomplished the most demanding of all its training, kneeling. Guret boosted the stranger up and was glad to see that hands came forth to tangle in Vasan's mane. Then he vaulted up behind and headed back toward the camp.

He found those awaiting him alert. Since it was faintly dawn, he supposed that his night search had taken longer than he thought. Lero was instantly by his side.

"Shield brother—what—"

Both Firdun and Kethan crowded in on the other side to free him of his burden. Only moments later they had the stranger stretched out on a bedroll. Over them still blew the perfume of the tree flowers which were again folding into their tight buds. And under that tent of trees Aylinn came on the run, her healer's bag bumping against her shoulder.

In better light Guret was able to see his prize for the first time. The stranger was very slender and slight of figure, and the pale face turned up to them, eyes closed, was that of a boy hardly into youth. Kethan had reached for one of the limp hands and now turned it over. Cut deep into the flesh were the bloody marks of bonds. There were bruises showing darkly on his face also, and as Firdun investigated further, pulling off boots, he uttered an exclamation of anger at the show of more bond marks between scratches, and even a bite which might have come from the things the boy had fought.

They aided Aylinn to strip him. Ribs stood out as if he had been nearly starved. She busied herself with her potions, tending each wound with swift speed and all her care.

"'Tis young Hardin of Hol, Silvermantle." Elysha stood over them now. "But he is of Garth Howell!"

For a second or two Aylinn paused and then shook her head firmly. "Not so—look and be sure." She took up her moonflower wand, which had been slipped through the side thong of her healer's sack.

Out the wand swung under her firm grip. The flower now topping it had not closed, as had those over them. Rather, it was brighter than the moonflowers she had always carried to center her Power.

Slowly she passed the flower above that young body, head to

foot and back again. When she had finished, he stirred and his eyes opened. His first sight must have been of Aylinn, for he cowered into the covering on which they had laid him.

"Unclean." Once more there were tears visible in his eyes. "I am no longer—"

"Look." Aylinn commanded sharply. "Look and believe!"

"The evil one broke the true bonds." His bandaged hand arose to half-hide his face. "He called upon one of the Great Dark Ones and I was given—"

"No one can be given without his will," Aylinn stated sternly. "Did you then surrender your will to this one of the Great Dark?"

His head turned from side to side. "No, no—not willingly. But then I was in another place and saw—and the will of that which looked upon me made me crawl at its feet."

"You wear marks of bondage," Aylinn said, "and those are freshly torn. Thus where you went was not willingly. Nor are you any hound of the dark to howl at his master's bidding." She turned to Kethan and Firdun, who stood behind her now. "Bring him—gently!"

Thus they carried him between them and he was very light of weight, until they came again before the throne and its silent occupant. He had closed his eyes as they arrived and there was a look upon him of one who had thrown away all the good life could offer.

"Lift him up!" again Aylinn ordered decisively. "Place him there." She pointed to the lap of the veiled one. The boy let out a weak cry, tried to struggle from their hold, but together they settled him where Aylinn indicated.

Then they stepped back almost as one while the healer, her moonflower blazing on the rod, again touched the forehead of the boy.

"*Lady—mother—life-giver*—this one has suffered from the evil which stands ready to assault us all. Look into his heart; know that he did not fail through any fault of his choosing. Cherish him as a newborn, cherish him as one growing—give him back his knowing of self."

The answer came as a victory cry to reach into all their minds:

"This is My son, born by My will. The Dark has wrought ill to bring him down. But that which was and is truly Hardin—is free."

The boy gasped and uttered a short cry and then went limp. Aylinn nodded and Kethan and Firdun lifted him down to settle him on one of the bedrolls.

"He will rest," the girl said, "and when he rouses again he will know that what he fears was only that—a fear to be swept away."

"You know him?" Ibycus had turned to Elysha.

"I saw him once—on the day that tangle-witted father of his dispatched him to Garth Howell. His mother had the Moon talent, you see, and Lord Prytan was without power. He tried to get his lady to promise not to seek out the Lady—but one does not tell the sea to stop washing upon the shore. Thus when she was on a mission to the Voices he had the boy taken.

"Knowing a little of Prytan I can guess that it was more of a bargain than a gift. Who knows what those of Garth Howell might have promised in return? To have a fresh young soul dedicated to the Lady and nurtured carefully in Her ways to offer to some Power who wished to batten on riven knowledge—yes, that would suit Garth Howell. They might even offer Prytan a few small tricks in return, but no true talent."

"His mother?" queried Aylinn.

"The last rumor was that she had not returned from the Voices. At least she was never seen in Silvermantle lands again."

"How did you find him?" Ibycus, still staring down at the sleeping boy, asked Guret. Guret told them his tale of the missing horse and the battle by the stream.

"So—can we not think now," Ibycus replied slowly, "that this Hardin accompanied the party into the east? Their present mage seems fond of sacrifices. And the urings—they can be commanded, though they are not too forceful in combat. So the boy escapes— or—" Now he paused and held up the ring. "Or seems to, so that he can join in some way with us and they can have eyes and ears in our camp." He gave a short bark of laughter.

"If they planned such, it will not hold now. The lad is cleansed of all touch of the Dark. They would have to recapture him and once more attempt ensorcellment. But that he can give *us* information is an unexpected boon."

## CHAPTER TWENTY-FOUR

# Gryphon's Eyrie, Arvon, Western Trail, the Waste

Alon hunched over the table, hands planted on either side of the glass hemisphere, its curved surface up. His face was gaunt and marked with the lines of hours of strain. Now he shook his head so violently Eydryth shivered. All his talent was summoned, but lacking focus.

He nodded toward her again and patiently, as she had for nearly all the morning, she played her harp and crooned wordlessly, striving this time to alter in the slightest the sounds, so that she might have the good fortune to hit on that which would be his aid.

They had discovered during the past days of labor that the full melding of Power did not reach what Alon needed. As a last resort Eydryth had suggested trying her own talent—the harp and song which had been her protection and weapon.

"No." Small feet thudded across the room and Trevor was pounding on her knee. "No so—so!" His child's voice was several notes higher than the scale which she had always considered the most powerful, likely to provide what she needed.

Eydryth swallowed. Her throat felt dry, as if she had been

singing half the night in some inn for a grudged ration of dry bread and stale cheese.

Alon leaned back a little. His attention had turned to Trevor, who was continuing to demand his sister's attention with a cry of "No—so."

Eydryth reached for the goblet of herb-infused water Joisan had set there earlier before the rest of them had withdrawn to ensure such silence as was possible for this experiment. She allowed the liquid to rinse about her mouth and then swallowed.

Trevor had stilled his protest but had planted himself firmly before her, his fists on his hips, looking up as if he were supervising labor. When his sister put down the goblet, he came a little closer. Reaching out one finger, he touched a harp string.

They were made of quan iron, finally spun as threads, those strings. Nearly everlasting and embedded with a force no living mage could explain.

Eydryth heard the note. It was like a faint echo from the slight touch. She prided herself on the fact that she could remember any note she had heard—just as any ballad listened to once was recorded in her memory.

Now she touched the string in turn, with the familiarity of one to whom this instrument was a part of life itself.

It rang forth. She listened and again summoned it. This time she strove to fit her own voice to it. Three times she tried, Trevor crowding ever closer, looking anxiously up into her face. Then note and murmured croon melded.

Alon's head jerked around to the hemisphere. It was no longer stubbornly clear. At the same time Trevor fashioned something which was not unlike a word—if "Ahhhhlaa" could be given that title. And it almost became one with the notes Eydryth added one to another, fluting still but in a different range.

The hemisphere before Alon was no longer vacant. A weaving of violet-blue swirled within it. As the harp continued and Eydryth and Trevor added their parts, Alon began an incantation.

At first his voice sounded hurried, as if he must reach some goal in a very limited time, and then the girl could sense that he was forcing himself to keep a measured beat. Beat—yes! The ancient words were also fitting themselves to that eerie music.

They were getting through—by the will of the Lady they were getting through! Not by the apparatus Alon had earlier used, which had so hopelessly failed them, but by this.

Her fingers felt sticky with sweat as they swept the strings. Her voice was once again drying her throat. Eydryth settled herself to endure. Trevor seemed to have no ill effects and his "Aaaaalaa" was clear and carrying.

Within the hemisphere the blue whirled vigorously and then was gone. They were looking at a face they had hardly dared hope to see again—Hilarion. There was excitement and exultation in his expression.

*The warding*— The words were mind-sent, not spoken. *The warding*— Symbols flashed in a wild pattern through Eydryth's head. Some she recognized as representing certain powers still known; others were strange.

Alon sat staring down at the small representation of Hilarion, his hands on the sides of his head as if to hold within all that was being fed him.

At last there was an ending. "We have warded." That was intelligible speech again. "Do you do likewise?"

However, the mist was upon Hilarion once again, sweeping across the hemisphere, and he was gone. Eydryth reached quickly for the herb drink and emptied two swift gulps down her aching throat. Then she offered it to Trevor, who drank more slowly as if he did not need refreshment so badly. She was watching Alon as he leaned back in his seat.

From the pile of parchments in a muddle not too far from his hand he drew one, and with his writing stick was setting down a mixture of lines, curves, triangles, and spheres. Did he remember it all? Certainly he must, for he had studied with Hilarion since boyhood and was adept-bred himself.

"So." He let the writing stick fall and roll from him, his attention only for the symbols he had outlined. He looked up at

Eydryth and Trevor then, and for a moment or so he was the youth she had met in Estcarp, all somberness gone from his face.

"Ibycus has destroyed one gate," she said hesitatingly.

"Yes, but it should be visited once again—the new warding full-set!" He flung out an arm and pulled Trevor to him in a hug. "How knew you the way, little brother?"

"I just did." All that temporary authority appeared to have deserted the boy. "We go to hunt gates now?"

Alon shook his head. "Not yet—we have others hunting them for us. Also we must keep an eye on Garth Howell." Some of the tension had again stiffened his features. "But we must tell Ibycus."

"Through that?" Trevor wanted to know, pointing to the hemisphere.

"No—that has done its duty, little one. It has held more power than we can control. See—" He tapped the crystal with a fingertip and it shattered, the broken bits in turn becoming dust. Now he turned to the girl. "Rest, heart's lady. We shall need the full meld to search out Ibycus, and that at moonrise."

She had laid aside her harp and now he had an arm about her shoulders, was drawing her up against him. She needed that steadying, for she felt that without it she could not keep her feet.

But that Alon had managed to do this—and those at Lormt . . . Hilarion, the others had found the answer. It was enough to make one feel dizzy with relief.

They might still have Garth Howell to reckon with, but who knew—Perhaps with study Alon could turn this same formula on that haunt of Darkness and seal it also. After this hour Eydryth could believe anything was possible.

Ibycus had taken a place close beside the boy, who now appeared in the depths of slumber. Now and again he regarded his ring, staring into its dull stone as if he would summon up answers to questions his mind proposed but could not solve. Though the day advanced, they made no move to travel onward. All of them could guess that locked in the sleeper was the information they needed the most now.

The Kioga kept out of the grove, their attention mainly for the mounts, since they wanted no more such wanderings as had drawn Guret away. He described several times to the tribesmen the nature of those ground-clinging creatures which had held horse and man at bay.

"Those of the Mantle Lands have mounts indeed," Obred remarked as he chewed his noon rations. "But they are not close kin to their herds as we, the People, have always been. How was it, then, that this young lordling has also the gift of calling? And why Vasan, who had not chosen him at the fall roundup?"

"I think"—Lero glanced around him as if to make sure there were no others than his own tribesmen about him—"that the Mother of Mares has some purpose in all this."

As one, the three of them made the touch to forehead and then heart which honored that sacred name. There were many stories of the way the Mother dealt with those in which She had some interest, and it could be that the strange wandering gelding indeed had a purpose—to bring Guret to the scene before the stranger was pulled down. He remembered now the odd fact that the urings (as the stranger named them) had fled him even before his sword started harvesting their lives. Her Hand over him? Perhaps; only a shaman could have borne witness to that.

"Where does the old mage think to lead us now?" Obred changed the subject.

"That is his choice and we have yet to hear it," returned Guret.

Ibycus held his ring-befingered hand out over the boy lying still within the sanctuary of the fane.

"Hardin of Hol?" he called softly as one might to awaken one from rest. "Hardin of Hol."

The boy's eyes did not open, but his head turned from one side to another and a faint frown line showed between his brows. Like all those of the Mantle Lands, he was plainly of the Old Race, pale of skin in spite of life in the open, dark of hair with the delicate, slanting brows of the same shade. Though he had not yet reached

313

his full man's growth, the firmness of his jaw and his well-formed features showed that he was indeed well to look upon.

"Hardin of Hol!" called Ibycus for the third time, and this time more loudly.

Aylinn sat cross-legged at the boy's head, her healer's eyes sharp to catch the difference in him. At her back was Kethan, the weight of Uta resting across his legs, a low purr to be heard now and then.

But Elysha was on the other side of Hardin's body and now she put out a hand warning off Ibycus. The mage looked up with a frown to which she paid no attention; rather, she leaned forward a fraction and spoke herself.

"Hardin, son of Ylassa. . . ."

There was a small choking cry from the boy in answer to that and his eyes opened, staring straight at her.

"Mother—" he began and then, so swiftly he caught them all by surprise, he drew in upon himself, one hand pawing at his side as if to palm a weapon. "You are—" It was clear that he was fully conscious now. But he paused, his eyes surveying her sharply.

"Last midsummer we shared a guesting cup," Elysha returned in an ordinary voice. "I was the Lady Ylassa's chamber guest."

He rubbed his hand across his eyes. "Yes. You brought her the message—you rode with her out of Hol." He was on his knees now and he grabbed at her shoulders, digging his fingers in as he gave her a vigorous shake. "Shadow creeper, her blood debt is mine." With the force of his attack he overbore her backward.

Kethan sprang to action with Firdun. Thin and wasted as the boy seemed to be, his rage was such that it took the two of them to hold him.

Elysha arose, smoothing some tatters from her shirt at the edge of her jerkin. But it was Aylinn who swung past her to where the three still struggled, and her wand blazed.

Hardin gave a choked cry and all the strength seemed instantly wiped out of him. He flung back his head and his eyes went wide. He stared now at the great seated figure as if nothing else existed now in his confused world.

"Hardin." Still smoothing her torn sleeve, Elysha deliberately moved so she stood between him and the throne, that he could see her fully. "The Lady Ylassa is safe. She was called by the Voices and serves them now."

"My lord—he said—" the boy choked on the words and was plainly struggling for control. "When he ordered me with him on a hunt . . ." Now there was another note in his voice, anger was returning. "We—he said we were to guest in Garth Howell. But— they gave me of the guesting cup and when I drank—" Again he sought for and found self control. "I was a prisoner and they said that he—he had given me freely to them and I was of value because I was her son!"

"Did they also tell you that she had agreed?" Elysha asked.

"Lies! They serve the father of lies there! They have a new leader—one Jakata—he is mighty in power and has made covenant with that which waits beyond—"

It was Ibycus who interrupted. "Waits beyond what?"

Firdun and Kethan had released their hold on Hardin and now he swung around to confront the mage. "Beyond a gate—the greatest of the gates. It spoke to them—the Garth has spell dreamers, three of them—and by those they know what happens elsewhere. Jakata says that the time wheel has spun and these are the old days come again. He is an adept—and from behind him the Dark will rule."

Ibycus was nodding. "And this gate, boy—does Jakata hunt it now, to the west?"

"Yes, he was summoned. It is said—I heard the guards speak— that there was a blood-drinking and a soul-darkening. . . . Oh"— his face lost years; it was now the desolate one which might be shown by a hopeless child—"I—I dreamed. They used pain and other ways I do not understand save that they were against all which was of the Light." He looked nearly as pale as the image behind him now. "I was a warrior. I have ridden against the hill demons when they come to ravage and I have slain in the name of the Light—but they overthrew me and I am . . .

"Stranger"—he grasped at Firdun now—"use your sword. I

know that you march against the Dark. Let my defiled blood be the first you shed! Give me that much armsman's grace!"

Aylinn moved to face him.

"Look upon me, Hardin. Have you seen my like before?"

He lifted his head. "You—you are one of the moon-called."

"As is your mother. Whose temporary dwelling is seated there?" She pointed to the throned one.

"The One in Three." He moved his hands and Firdun dropped his last hold on him, allowing him to make the gesture he wished. Trailing lines of blue followed his passing fingers. He gasped and staggered, save that Kethan was there to steady him.

Aylinn held out her wand until it nearly touched his breast. "Hardin of Hol. In Her eyes you are a worthy son of one who serves Her well. There is no spot in you, no rot through which the Dark can reach. Take and hold." She extended the wand until it brushed his hand.

Very slowly his fingers advanced to grasp it, and then hers withdrew, and hold it alone he did. The moonflower at its tip spent its scent on the air. Hardin fell to his knees. With both hands he gave the wand back to Aylinn.

"Reborn you are, Hardin. Chosen servant of One in Three. And as such—"

"As such"—his voice was now firm—"I shall live and ride, hold the sword of war, the open land of peace, for all my days. And"—there was an eagerness on his face as he arose once more and went unerringly to Ibycus—"mage, what I know is yours and perhaps it can make a difference."

Ibycus moved his ring finger and a line of light broke free. It did not quite touch Hardin, but it was evident that it was meant to indicate him.

"I think you have much which will be of aid to us," the mage said. "Now let us listen."

It was almost, Firdun thought to himself, like one of the storytelling sessions which were used in the Kioga camps for impressing upon children the history and hard-learned knowledge of those who had gone before.

Jakata plainly had many of the skills granted by history to the mage company of adepts—those mages who had once ruled and then brought close to complete death and ruin this world. He had sought out Garth Howell when it was merely a repository for half-forgotten and little-understood knowledge. Though he appeared a young man, it was said that he had not apparently aged a season since he had been there.

At first he had spent time listening courteously to those who had long studied there. But he had also gone seeking for himself in sections of the underground storage rooms which had not been entered for generations. He had always shown an aptitude for the solving of puzzles and began to bring out in the meetings of the scholars unusual matters hitherto unknown. At last it had become a custom for him once every so many tendays to conduct what was not quite a class or an exhibition, but a combination of both, and so drew to him most of the younger students.

From these he had chosen a devoted band to whom his word was the revelation of one of the Great Old Ones. Yet he had given no sign that he sought anything but knowledge for the sake of knowledge.

Slowly there had come a splitting of the company at Garth Howell. Those older mages, well-entrenched in their studies for the sake of learning alone, stood aside and Jakata made no attempt to influence them, in fact paid them great courtesy whenever the occasion demanded.

Of the others a handful had left—again no one gainsaying their withdrawal. So in the end the active members of the community were all his fervent followers.

The Mantle Lordships for the most part held to the ancient belief in the Voices—those revered as being the spirits of ancestors willing to remain in touch with the world that those of their blood might be aided by their advice. Here and there, however, a lord like Prytan was intrigued by the rumors of what might be going on and, if he was ambitious, started casting about for ways in which he might profit.

At length Jakata had said that he was commanded to provide a

Voice himself—one for the coming age of new rule. He ordered a pilgrimage to Dragon Crest to offer a blood sacrifice. But on the way they had been subjected to such a storm of magic as they had never believed existed, and Jakata had been aroused to a claim of Power beyond any mage since the Great Old Ones.

They made a capture, and a rich one: one of the fabled Gryphon line whom all knew were favored by the Light above most. And in spite of the rage of the magic, he had been readied for sacrifice, only to have his own talent somehow aided by the release of such potent Power, and he escaped.

However, Jakata had not been dismayed by this. Instead he was feverishly set on a new venture. A sacrifice at Dragon Crest was as nothing to the opening of the portal through which some great leader could come and, through his dream seekers, he learned where that portal was, with the promise that when they reached it all would be made plain to them.

Hardin had been chosen as sacrifice this time and was being transported with the company westward. When he came to that part of the story, he faltered, for he could not himself explain how he was freed.

Ibycus cut in. "It is more than you they want for the feasting of their Dark lord, Hardin. Therefore they loosed you, being sure that the bonds of spirit they had set upon you were well locked. So were you brought to us—though"—he smiled—"it was all a little clumsy. I think your Jakata perhaps left the details to someone of his company not so well schooled.

"However, they shall get what they want, for we shall seek out the gate even as they are doing. And though none can ever foresee the end, by the time we reach there we shall have our answer."

The next morning they moved out. Hardin joined Guret and showed himself nearly as good a horseman as the Kioga—they were soon talking horses together. Also he was able to play their guide northward for the space of two days, having scouted in the hills during the demon raids and learned some of the skills.

On the third day they found the remains of the camp from which he had escaped, or been allowed to escape, and then Kethan as pard tracker took over. The young Silvermantle lord watched the were go into action with amazement. His people knew the weres, of course. At intervals their nobles had hosted weres. But none had ever come into Hol, and to see the tawny pard slip into the tall grass where a man had ridden was a surprise.

However, Kethan's shadow horse still had a rider. Uta had fit herself in the saddle there and the mount accepted her easily. So they went, Kethan on trail and the Kioga and Firdun taking turns riding point.

## CHAPTER TWENTY-FIVE

# The Wellspring of Evil, the Waste, West

It was a good morning, and the land around was not yellow clay, though the growth on it was sparse and rough, with here and there a curiously twisted tree to stand sentinel. Also the scent was running well, though there began to be more about it than the natural odors left behind by men and horses. There seemed to be a whiff now and then of a faint stench—a taint such as might be given off by old death lying long unburied.

Kethan followed a hint of water which must have drawn those others before him. That brought him in sight of tumbled blocks of masonry: Such stones he had never seen before, for they were the dark green of fir needles mottled here and there by bands and trails of a lighter shade.

Cautiously he scouted the place. Here the grass had grown tall.

If he went belly deep in it and stalked as if following a pronghorn, he did not believe he could be sighted save from the air—or by the trembling of the grass he crept through.

There came a sharp hiss and he swerved to the right. A grass serpent nearly as thick around as one of his own furred limbs raised head, viewed him with unblinking eyes. The reptile bulged thickly in the middle, which meant it had recently fed and only wanted now to find a place to rest and digest its meal. Kethan backed away and the weaving head began to lower again. Such snakes were edible but not to the taste of any who could find more palatable food. Anyway, he was far more suspicious and curious than he was hungry at that moment.

He made a half circle of the broken wall, for a circular wall it was proving to be. Once more he picked up the scent trail. Only—

Kethan crouched low and pawed at his nose, though he knew that he had no way of shutting that stench out of his nostrils. This was not the faint hint of evil which he had sorted out of the tracks, but a blast of noisome smell.

While it came up from the trail true enough, it was stronger when he turned his head back toward the wall. That, he was sure, was its real source, and he was not going to leave some station of the Dark behind without learning its nature.

He sent out a fine mind-probe, then started so that he nearly arose to full height in his cover. Those he followed had plainly left this place, but what had they left behind?

Once more he drew himself forward, belly brushing the grass bent down by his weight. Now he could see a break in the wall which was not caused by age but had been intended. The trail led from that, and along it he now padded.

Kethan did not want to try the mind-probe again—it was too easily a way of alerting something on guard. Yet he had sensed in it more pain than anger. Now he was at that gate and able to see what lay beyond.

In the exact center of a circular pavement of the same green stone was the curbing of what could only be a well. But set up beside it, to cast an ominous shadow, was what Kethan first thought to be one of those dread knights who served Garth Howell.

Then he could smell the freshly spilled blood, and saw the pool of it about the boots of he who stood there. No, rather he was propped up by spears wedged into cracks of the pavement, his body lashed to them, even his neck and forehead in loops to keep them aloft, for his helm was missing.

His hands had been shorn of gauntlets and were lashed before him, and the fingers—

Kethan's nose wrinkled. They had been hacked away. Blood spotting on the curb of the well suggested where they might have disappeared.

Kethan did not approach the corpse directly; rather, he slunk along the wall, making a full circle of the space and surveying it from all sides.

There came suddenly, over the buzz of insects which were gathering in swarms, a faint moan. The eyelids in that uplifted head twitched. Kethan halted, paw raised.

So—it was true—this one still lived. That he was evil, Kethan did not in the least question. Though why his own must have treated him so was perhaps something to be discovered, might be useful for his own party. Ibycus—the picture of the mage grew strong in his mind. Toward it he aimed another sending and knew he was answered.

There were birds—the scavengers of the Waste gathering. He watched them with care waiting for the rus to appear. But if they hunted, they had not found this prey.

He had no wish to be caught within those sinister walls and found a way for himself across a broken section, retracing his own trail to meet the sooner with those who followed. That they might communicate the better, he assumed man's form just as the first of the Kioga outriders came into view, bow strung and ready, his trained mount following a weaving way.

Obred did not join Kethan. The were knew—and had become more or less indifferent to the fact—that the tribesmen found it hard to accept one of his kind, even once proven to be wholly of the Light. Now he waved and Obred flourished his bow.

It did not take long for the rest of the party to come into view—Lero urging the pack animals, in spite of their complaining, to a pace to keep him and them well in sight of the rest.

Ibycus was in the lead, but Elysha was close after—not entirely to the mage's wishes, Kethan was sure. Then came Kethan's sister, matching pace companionably with Trussant, on whom Uta still balanced, then Firdun and Guret, armed and flanking Hardin, though certainly they were not acting as guards.

Ibycus dismounted somewhat stiffly. The hand bearing the ring was against his breast and Kethan thought he saw a play of color there—but not the blue of true Power.

"So what have you found us this time, young Kethan?" he asked as he tramped forward.

"A puzzle," Kethan returned, "and a dying man."

"One hurt?" Aylinn was off Morna in an instant, swinging the strap of her bag across her shoulders. "Where is he?"

The Kioga took up watch, riding in circle around the green ruin as Kethan led the rest into the place of the well.

"Oh!" Aylinn would have run forward, but Elysha seized her by the arm.

"What you see may not be," she spoke sharply. "This one is of Garth Howell."

"But he is injured," Aylinn insisted angrily. "By Healer's Oath—"

"Even for Healer's Oath," Elysha admonished, "would you bring disaster and the Dark upon us all?"

The girl struggled, attempting to free herself, but Elysha held her back. It was Ibycus who approached the tethered man, the others giving him good room.

The mage upheld his hand and pointed the ring, not at the man's breast but at his loop-held head.

"By the Star, by the wave, by the earth which holds the grave," the mage said slowly. "Speak now, you who have been sent to give us what message your lord wishes."

The bluish lips in the gray face moved, but the eyes above re-

mained closed: "You—follow—death—" That voice came very faintly as if from far away.

"As all men do from the time of their begetting," the mage made answer. "Did Jakata think playing games fit to frighten children would hold us back?"

Now the finger he held up blazed like a black flame. "You have served your master—"

But the figure before him might not have heard anything he had to say. "The One who comes claims its day. Follow, fools, and die the sooner for it."

Then the mouth dropped open and a dark tongue protruded between a yellow straggle of teeth.

Ibycus wrote in the air with the ring, and the symbols which began as slashes of blood turned to spears of darkness. He spoke aloud. Those symbols moved sluggishly. It might have been they resented his command, but at length they wavered toward the dead man, fastened on him. The rest of the company pressed back as flame burst from the wracked body, eating with a raging intensity until there was nothing left but a scorched mark on the pavement.

"He—he was Salsazar, of Jakata's guard. He was on duty the night I got free." There was a shakiness in Hardin's voice.

"He was not of the living as we know them—perhaps for many years," Elysha answered.

"Out—out with you!" That cry came from Firdun. He grabbed for Aylinn, bringing Elysha also, as the woman still had grip upon the girl. "Out with you—a ward has broken—what comes?"

Kethan leaped forward and had an arm around the mage, jerking him backward, pushing Hardin as he reached him. Then they were outside the space. But not before Kethan, at least, caught sight of what was rising from the well. He had seen death newcome, he had seen the evidence of death long past left to crumble back to the earth. But these figures rising as if winged from that dark circle were death unnaturally alive—and they were many. Shadows at first, they lapped like water over the well curb and floated about the wall.

However, broken as that was, it seemed to prevent their coming

farther. The things were becoming more solid of body. Not all were of humankind. There were monsters among them which only the most blackened mind of a Dark mage could conceive. And about them was such a stench that the travelers reeled farther back.

Ibycus shook himself free from the hold Kethan still kept on him. His ring was still blazing. Now he shouted over his shoulder to Firdun: "The curse of Unwin in the Day of Last Desolation. Remember it, boy!"

His hand was on Firdun's shoulder now as they faced the battered walls. Through the holes they could see what gathered, growing stronger with every moment in the air.

Firdun's voice came as loud as Ibycus's in a measured range of words. Old words, words which, when they were uttered, seemed to make the ground under their feet move. And the mage matched him word for word, his flaming finger still at point.

The sun over them paled. Guret and his tribesmen could no longer control the horses; they reared, struggled loose of rein hold, and scattered. Kethan staggered as a warm and heavy-furred body leaped to his shoulder. And then he was standing, one arm around Aylinn and the other supporting Uta on his chest.

Above the circle of the broken wall the sky darkened, yet more gray-white became the things now rising above its edge, struggling. They might be throwing themselves against some barrier. Ibycus's hand, now raised high, became a torch, the flame bending toward the broken-edged circle.

The mage's voice rolled thunderwise and Firdun's words were like lightning bolts in accordance to this storm of Power. Yet it was plain that some manner of control was being exerted to keep those unholy emanations rooted still to the vile source from which they had sprung.

At last those two voices spoke as one, called upon a single name. Kethan reeled where he stood, steadying Aylinn, who was now shaking and uttering small moans. Uta's claws bit deeply into his shoulder. The cat's ears were flattened to her skull, her mouth open in a vast hiss of rage.

Did the land under them move? Kethan could never afterward

be sure. He only knew that this was like the storm of raw magic which had buffeted all the world at the beginning of this venture.

Down upon the whirling bone-white shapes swooped the clouds. A lid might be so placed on a seething pot. Ibycus was on his knees, Elysha behind him now offering firm support, while Firdun reeled back to crash against Hardin, sending them both to the ground.

On the ground where stood the circle of the wall swelled a vast black bubble. But only for a moment. Then it burst and they were all struck with the Power surge.

"Kethan!"

He lay looking up at a sky which was once more blue and peaceful. The only cloud in sight was one small white puffy fluff. Aylinn was still clinging to him, her face buried against him.

He drew a deep breath and then another. A rough tongue swung against his chin and he looked up into Uta's eyes. There was . . . an emptiness, as if something had been withdrawn from their world—hastily and with great force—and that which they knew was seeping only slowly back to fill the gap.

"Ibycus—dear master—"

Disturbing both Aylinn and Uta, Kethan levered himself up. Elysha sat on the ground, the mage's head held against her breast, and her face was drawn. Years might have descended upon her. But the man she held moved. His eyes moved.

Strangely enough, he smiled with some of the gentleness Kethan remembered from when the mage had made his few visits to the Green Tower as a guest and friend.

"Not yet, Elysha. I may be bendable at time, but the breaking has not come. Now let us see what the Ancient Ones have given their aid to accomplish." He twisted loose from her hold and sat up.

So directed, they all looked toward that stronghold of the Dark.

It was—not!

Where those tumbled stones had marked the wall, there was not a single pebble showing to mark a circle of ground. Clay pottery taken from the kiln after a long baking might have borne the same gleaming surface as that platter of green laid down flat-surfaced.

Ibycus laughed. There was something euphoric in that sound.

"An effective stopper, glory given to the Great Names! There lies that now which no Dark can break."

However, it was plain he had paid for his efforts. When he tried to get to his feet, he stumbled, and Kethan was quick to aid him up. Firdun still lay in the matted grass, Hardin beside him.

Aylinn hurried, wand forward, but Elysha was there first. "Power sister," she commanded.

So they knelt on either side of Firdun's body. On his breast, as they turned his face upward to the sky, Aylinn laid the moonflower wand, and then she clasped hands with Elysha over him.

Their eyes were closed and there was a distinct sign of strain in both their faces. Kethan looked to the mage.

"He is drained?" he asked, and shivered himself from the chill that thought brought to him. He had heard warnings enough in the past that the overuse of Power might even burn out the talent—leaving one weaponless indeed.

Ibycus joined the women and stood looking down at Firdun. "He is blood of the Gryphon; he himself does not know the extent of what he can do. No other could have called the Great Name except one of near-adept Power."

As if his judgment were one of Aylinn's cordials, Firdun opened his eyes, staring upward, and it must have been Ibycus whom he first saw for he asked: "It was done?"

"Done and well done!" Ibycus answered promptly. "Though now we know that those we follow have gone very far along the Dark road. Or else they are fools—and I do not believe Jakata to be such. What he searches for may give him the power of Grelias."

That name was nearly an oath. No man said it lightly, nor had for nearly a thousand years. For it was last borne by the one who nearly triumphed in the Great Battle which had left the world men then knew in ruins.

"It would seem, then," Firdun replied grimly, "that we use what speed we can to stop him."

But to reassemble their party was not an easy task. Those who had been near the well moved yet farther away.

The Kioga came trailing back to camp one at a time, each bringing some of the mounts. Packs had been lost, bucked off in spite of the lashings, and they had to sort out all their gear again and find what their losses in supplies might be.

Kethan, again in pard shape, went seeking and found two of the packs, broken open and the contents trampled. He dared not go near the horses and could only indicate the finds he made.

They had set up a rough camp by nighttime. Luckily most of their animals had been retaken. In addition, Guret had shot a small pronghorn and his two fellow tribesmen had knocked over some long-legged, gaunt-bodied birds they flushed out of the grass in their going.

Kethan had also located water—a spring some distance from the site of the well. But none of them dared to drink until Aylinn pronounced it clear of any taint.

They ate, if meagerly, and were prepared to settle for the night, the mounts this time securely picketed. Suddenly Ibycus, seated by the small fire they had made, interrupted—not with any word, but by holding his ring out into the light of the flames. To Kethan's relief it was burning blue.

"Message . . ." Ibycus bent his head forward. He was so placed that none of the others could see exactly what appeared in the oval stone when the blue light paled to white. A second later he spoke without looking up.

"Firdun!"

It took only an instant for the other to change places with Elysha and crowd forward to look into the seeing ring.

"You are ward-trained," the mage said. "Watch—remember!"

The he spoke to the ring itself as if it were a person.

"Alon, we are ready."

Without any suggestion, Elysha moved in behind the mage and placed her hands on his shoulders, and Aylinn, pushing past Kethan, did the same for Firdun, somewhat to her foster brother's surprise. Kethan himself was left to grasp with each hand one of the women's and then felt Uta leap into his lap.

Whatever Alon was relaying to Ibycus they could not hear. Kethan caught a glimpse of changes of light within the ring stone as if patterns formed and changed there. Then he felt the pull of Power being drawn upon, as if Elysha and his foster sister were already feeding Ibycus and Firdun nearly at the top of their strength. He nearly started with surprise when he felt warmth and energy rising in him. It could only be that Uta was linked in their endeavors.

Time no longer meant anything. They were caught up away from the world they knew for the purpose of the Power, and to that alone could they answer now.

At length the ring turned blue once again. And Ibycus's voice rang out hurriedly as if to reach someone already departing.

"Understood!"

The usual weakness and need to reorient themselves with their proper world followed, but they were still languid when the mage began to talk.

"They have labored well at Lormt. Hilarion and others, working with bits and hints from ancient words, found the formula for warding the gates—for all time. They are already putting that into use overseas, and the Gryphon's clan will do the same in Arvon and the Dales. But we face something more ominous—a wholly Dark gate to which Garth Howell is pledged. And for that we must produce the ward."

Now he looked at Firdun. "It is fully yours? Two at least of us must know it."

The other nodded. "What was shown I shall remember. There my talent holds."

"As you rightly proved this day, Gryphon's son," said the mage.

The Kioga this night divided the watches among themselves, leaving the others to rest. It would be his task, Kethan knew, to be up with the dawn, or even before, to seek out once more the trail of those from Garth Howell. Also he must go with double caution, as who knew what traps this Jakata might be able to set?

He rolled himself in his blankets but missed the warmth of Uta. She was usually tucked against his side with her slumber-inducing purr. Feeling oddly deserted, he allowed himself to sleep. The night was hunting time for the cat tribe and she was probably off on affairs she believed of more importance than companionship with humans—or weres.

Usually Kethan's dreams were disordered fragments, many of them to do with the chase, and never were they very clear or vivid. Not like this—if it was a dream.

He was certainly not lying on trampled grass and scratchy blankets under the open sky. Instead he was in pard form right enough, but with the human portion of him standing aside watching what was happening, what was to happen.

There were two great pillars carved from rock before him and to his pard sight they glowed, golden as his own eyes. Sitting on the crown of each was the figure of a cat facing what lay behind him: sentries, yet taking their ease, for they sat upright with their tails curled over their paws.

So cleverly had they been carved that they seemed to hold a spark of life and be all-knowing and all-hearing. Between them ran the shattered pavement of a road long since worn by time. Beyond the pillars there appeared to be only a gathering of dusky shadow, though he felt no warning of evil about it.

However, what was most important was that delicate scent which reached him. Once before he had been drawn to answer that message—and then had fallen prey to the bird woman. But this time it was overwhelming, appealing to instincts which made the human part of him uneasy.

Still, so compelling that was, he could not turn from the path but padded between the cat pillars and into the duskiness which he found did not in the least blind his night sight.

Moved by an impulse he could not understand, he held high his head and uttered a yowling cry—no challenge but rather in a way a plea that he must know what was happening and why.

She slipped from between two rocks and stood looking at him. As his coat was gold, so hers was black and she was not as large. But to his pard sight this was beauty such as his human eyes had never sighted.

He slackened pace as she hissed slightly, a warning that she was independent and gave her favors only when she pleased.

He prowled back and forth a few paces from her to display his muscular form, the fact that he was a warrior among pards, one worthy to be looked upon with favor.

Again she yowled—

## CHAPTER TWENTY-SIX

# The Web Lands, The Waste, West

**W**anton *changling!* The pard snarled and slewed around in the dust, earth. Behind him he heard a hiss become a growl.

*Female foolishness,* that voice inside his head continued. *Will this poor world never be free of female foolishness?*

Completely bemused, the pard looked to his black counterpart. It would seem these snappish words were not being aimed in his direction. Her ears were flattened to her skull and her fangs shone against her black fur.

*Try some foolishness yourself, oldster—time your blood ran a little faster. Just because you have turned your back on certain matters that does not mean that they have ceased to exist. Each of us have our rights—*

*Not,* her send was interrupted sharply, *when the desires of one challenges the purposes of all. Try this again and you will be the worse for it.*

Kethan blinked and blinked again. He lay on his back looking up at paling stars. And he was man, not pard. But some of that aroused in him made him restless and he sat up. A dream, of course, but such a one as seemed as real as a true sending. And that voice . . . Ibycus! Surely it had been Ibycus who had broken into that most interesting meeting.

He looked around. The mage was apparently asleep a distance away, his cloak pulled over him against the fall of dew. Then he himself was aware that Uta's warm body was no longer fit to his side. The cat was still missing. Night hunting—as he himself had gone many times for the sheer joy of running free under the moon.

Uta—the black cat—and she who had met him by the cat-crowned pillars? No, that other had been a match for his pard size—a dream weaving in all surety.

However, he was too fully awake now to try to sleep again. Kethan sat up, his knees against his chest, his arms about them. How much of any were was beast, how much man? He was only one-third were by blood, his father a halfling, his mother a Wise-woman from overseas. He had been raised as a man and would never perhaps have learned his heritage had not Ibycus, in his guise of trader, brought the pard belt to his supposed father's castle.

Without the belt he could not make the change as perhaps a true-bred were could do. And he could remember his first fears when the changes had come without his control, before he had learned to master his talent. Now he was well practiced in slipping in and out of the beast's role, and he took pride in what his animal senses could uncover while hidden to the denser humankind.

He avoided the other sleepers and went to the spring, where he shed shirt and jerkin and doused head and shoulders into water which was cold enough to bring a gasp out of him. Squinting up at the graying sky, he decided that they were in for a fair day—and perhaps a hot one. Best make sure all their water bottles were well filled.

As he stood up and stretched, he faced west. There appeared to be no break in this scrub-filled land. And he thought that the trail of those from Garth Howell ought to be easy to pick up—at least for a pard.

The rest of the camp were astir by the time he returned. Sleeping mats and blankets were rolled and there was already food laid out. Lately Kethan had taken to leaving his share, being well able as a hunter pard to supply his own needs on the march.

Uta had returned and seemed to be of the same mind. Her night's hunting must have been good, for she turned aside from what Aylinn offered her and went to sit by Trussant, plainly ready to once more be carried at her ease.

Before Kethan was ready for his own change, Elysha suddenly appeared beside him. Those strange, compelling violet eyes of hers caught and held him. She had the faintest quirk of a smile about her lips.

"Good trailing. However"—now the smile had vanished—"there are dreams and dreams. Make very sure, young were one, that you discover which is which. And take nothing which is different to be what it seems until it is proven so. "

Then she was gone again before he could answer. Dreams? Had that venture in the night been a dream of Elysha's spinning? He remembered Firdun's story of her cloud castle, which had seemed as real as the ground beneath it. For one who dealt deeply in glamorie, a dream-sending should be an easy task.

However, this was day not night and the trail awaited him. He made the change and took the lead with a long graceful bound.

Firdun elected to ride point today, taking the northern swing while Guret matched him to the south. Watching Kethan's departure, he felt a twinge of envy. How did it feel to run free in a body so unlike the one one was born into? Yet in camp Kethan seemed a quiet young man, like the son of any mantle lord. Firdun had heard tales of the ferocity of the weres in battle, but to hear and see were two different things. Kethan as a man, for all his fine armor—which rode mostly in a bundle on that strange mount of his—appeared a most amiable and peaceful sort.

The were's foster sister . . . Firdun always felt a little awkward in her presence, especially since he had watched her draw Hardin back from the Dark hold. His own sister was all vivid color, her dark hair usually threaded with golden chains, her skirt and breeches of gold or rich rust brown—like unto the legendary scales of the Gryphon. Her eyes were golden also, and she was such as enlivened any company she joined. But Aylinn was like her beloved moon, and as far from any man's touch. Firdun tried not to watch her so much when they were in company, for fear that others would note his regard.

Her talents ranged to a very high level and, though he had been brought in to company with Ibycus in reducing the things from that foul well, he felt like a untutored boy beside a mage mistress when they were together.

How much Power *had* the Great Ones seen fit to grant him? Alon had tested him several times and often surprised them both with the results of such measurement. He could not shape-change, but he could produce a certain amount of glamorie, though certainly nothing to rival that Elysha was able to summon. He could ward, and he could break wards. He had no healing ability, but that was mainly a talent which was female, not male.

On the other hand, he could hold his own against any arms master he had met at a mantle hold. Jervon and his father had seen to that. In open battle where powers were not evoked, he could give good account of himself, he was sure.

Yet at the Eyrie he was the one without because he could not meld. Perhaps, once this journey was behind them, he might go seeking a place of his own. The Sulcar captains were always ready to sign a good fighting man for their voyages. The Falconers served them so for years—and they traveled into places as unknown to the world at large as this Waste was unknown to men from the east.

He jerked his thoughts around to the business at hand, an intent study of the land through which he rode. There had been no sign of Kethan since he had taken off as they left; however, any alarm he would send could be picked up by most of them.

This was dreary countryside, though according to the old tales it had once been well settled, by a people who had knowledge long since forgotten. He knew that the furtive traders from the Dales who dared to venture here brought back many strange and even beautiful artifacts. But they were jealous of their hunting grounds. So far this party's contact with the past had been that place of the pyramids, the long-pillared pool, and the well enclosure. Surely there was more to be found.

At nooning the group drew together and shared rations and a very scant amount of water, most of which they gave to their beasts. The countryside was becoming more and more desert. Where they had been greeted on their first venturing into this country by the plains of cracked yellow clay, and then passed into the place of red earth and veined foliage, now the ground showed wavelike stretches of a gray-blue coarse sand.

There were fewer and fewer plants to be seen, and the gnarled trees were missing. However, from portions of the sand there protruded tall poles which did not appear to be a natural growth. They were the same hue as the shade and about the size of four boar spears bound together.

There was no tumbled masonry about to suggest ruins as there had been at the well. Guret and Firdun studied several of the poles near their temporary resting place and found them a puzzle. Though they were slightly rough in texture to the touch, they did not seem to be rock, and inquiring touches left the fingers tingling for a moment or two.

Ibycus tested them with his ring. There was a responsive color but very pale, and it matched the hue of the sand in which the poles were planted. They were not set up in any pattern, but scattered here and there, with a good distance between each of the poles.

The travelers tried when they started out again to angle well away from those standards, being cautious enough to avoid anything for which there was no practical explanation. Mind-send from Kethan assured them that they were still on the trail of the Garth Howell party.

Ibycus's head suddenly jerked skyward. The sun had been cloaked in part by a haze and now his ring color was deepening toward a murky red-blue.

"Watch aloft!" he shouted. "Get the horses moving—ride!"

As if his words were a spell, the haze thickened in places. And from it balls broke loose, while the sand in which the poles were footed began to run like water. Not only were the travelers being threatened from above, but below also. The Kioga, Hardin, and Firdun were trying to press the loose horses to a faster pace and yet keep them away from that rippling. Aylinn had bow in hand and arrows ready.

A round object thrust upward out of the disturbed sand and instantly she let fly at it. Her arrow struck true and rebounded, the thing paying no attention to the attack.

Something which resembled the forepart of a giant worm was pulling into the light and it was not alone. The rippling sand parted to let through others like it, while down from the sky dropped what might have been fishers' nets, each weighted with a black ball-shaped body. The nets caught on the poles, swung wide, back and forth.

One of the extra horses screamed horribly and reared. A web traveler clung to its neck to thrust fangs deep into its throat, and the worms nearest to the attack writhed toward the doomed animal at a surprising speed. The Kioga were urging on the animals, but Firdun turned and rode for the horse already kicking on the ground and thrust with his sword. There was a spurting of greenish ichor mixed with blood and the thing shivered like a punctured bag.

"Away—they are poisonous!" Ibycus shouted.

Firdun's mount leaped over the nearest worm and he drew back to help form a rearguard with the mage, Hardin (now equipped with a Kioga bow), and Aylinn. Ibycus threw out his arm to wave them all on. One of the web creatures struck at him, but Elysha's forearm swept up and there was a violet flash from her bracelet.

The web thing burst, spattering the ground with matter which steamed like acid. There was another horse down, and a Kioga trying to ride close enough for a shot at the attacker was nearly thrown as his horse reared to avoid one of the worms.

With their riding webs fast to the poles, the spider things could swing hard enough to whirl themselves a great distance. Their ground-bound allies whipped about, one sweeping a Kioga's mount from its feet. Luckily the rider sprawled out and away from his downed horse while the attacker fed upon the screaming animal. He charged toward the thing on foot in spite of Ibycus's shouts to keep his distance.

This time Firdun spurred between, knocking the Kioga back and slashing at the worm at mid-body. He barely avoided the whipping tail of the thing and then was nearly knocked from his saddle by one of the spiders. However, the frenzied fighting of his horse to be free and away prevented the creature from a true strike and a backswing of sword sent it spinning to smash against one of the poles from which dropped an empty web.

Luckily that line of poles did not extend forever. And it looked as if both the swinging spider things and the worms were unable to leave their close vicinity. The Kioga were again striving to bring the pack train and the spare mounts into line when there sounded a distant roaring.

Wind swept at them with a buffeting force, freeing some of the webs. Whether or not the creatures could actually control the flight of their carrying strands, those now in flight could not tell, but at least ten were riding the gusts of wind toward them.

It was several moments before Firdun grasped the fact that they were being herded. Their attempts to outride and outrun those wind riders sent them following a southern direction. Guret, Lero, and Hardin began to prove the Kioga expertise, and that of a Mantle hunter, with their bows.

But these were not easy targets. They appeared to ride currents of air which rose or dropped without any pattern. Those steady streams of air also gathered up puffs of grit from the gravel waves, sending it to sting flesh, threaten the eyes of the would-be fighters.

The travelers were away from the poles now and at least the worms appeared to have made no attempt to follow them. A lucky shot burst another of the web riders, and Obred uttered a war cry. Still the wind blew steadily and the web riders showed no signs of giving up pursuit.

Then lightning struck straight across the path of those web-borne horrors. Struck once, and again. Several webs were rent and the creatures in them burst and gone. It was then that Firdun's horse stumbled and he was thrown, crashing down on his shoulder so that his sword fell from a numbed hand. A web had touched ground not too far away. Its occupant, apparently uninjured, leaped for the man. His horse had recovered to plunge on. Firdun had stooped to try to recover his sword when sanity returned. Ward . . . what would ward such a creature as this?

He had never been forced to face the summoning of formulas so fast, but somehow his half-dazed mind was able to sort out words and he shouted them.

The lightning whips still struck back and forth through the spinning webs but did not approach him and he had a feeling that they in themselves might be as deadly to his kind as the creatures they sought to destroy.

That thing which had started its leap at him crashed in midair against what he had so quickly summoned—a shield. Still clinging to that materialization, it thudded to the ground, the shield flattened over it. Firdun shook his head slowly. Why had he not drawn on this talent when the web riders first appeared? He had been as open to attack as a Dalesman of no talent.

Now he flung up his right hand, still numb from his fall, and forced his fingers into patterns which should be as familiar and easy to him as drawing breath into his lungs. Only he struggled as might an apprentice of the least talent. It was as if he himself were somehow in ward, kept from exercising his powers except when he drew upon the very limits of his energy.

The lightning flashes were coming farther apart and weakening. At the very moment he became aware of that, Firdun was forced to his knees. A mighty hand might have reached out of the sky to flatten him for the puny powerless thing he was. Something was draining, gnawing at his memory. He could not recall the proper gestures, the words, as much of him as his own name.

Then followed fear, not that which was the natural result of their battle, but rather a fear which was an emptiness—in him! Warrior and warder as he was, Firdun uttered a cry, his whole body shuddering. He could not move any more than if he really were encased in one of the wind-driven nets.

To be so shaken by raw fear was worse than taking a wound in the flesh, for this reached far deeper, left him a quivering nothing. Nothing—no! He was Firdun of the Gryphon. He clung to the thought-picture of that Gryphon.

Landsil, one of the Great Old Ones, who had stood twice against the utmost power of the Dark and won. Landsil! Instead of the jumble of Power words he had tried to keep in sequence, Firdun now centered on that one name, held to it as the only security in his present world.

The hand which pressed—there was no hand! He heard now the beat of mighty wings. And the gale those raised banished that which had entrapped him. From Landsil's gift had come his talent, and once more the Gryphon returned to his breed that gift.

Firdun pulled to his feet. The web riders had not been swept from the sky even by those lightning bolts which had now vanished. But they were wavering, and that push of wind which had sent them in pursuit was dying—it was dead.

Drifting webs settled on the scrub land. Firdun held up his head. Just as Ibycus had drawn from him more than he thought he had had at the well, so now he brought up his full strength. The air between him and those webs glimmered oddly. He could sense more than feel the freezing cold which was gathering. There was surely a sheen of frost already on the withering grass.

No movement, no wind, no bodies emerging from the webs. The webs themselves were turning into crystals, glistening in a sun which now cut through the haze overhead. Firdun picked up his sword, rammed the blade twice in the soil to clean it of the noisome ichor of the slain, and sheathed it. Turning, he looked for the others.

Aylinn was kneeling on the ground beside a figure in purple clothing. Elysha—struck down by poisons? He was sure that the webs had not carried past where he had taken his involuntary stand. Ibycus knelt at her other side. The Kioga were urging the animals together in some semblance of order, but Hardin stood a little apart, eyeing Firdun as he came, as one might look upon an adept. One hand was covering his mouth.

As Firdun advanced, the young lord was shaken out of his trance.

"Jakata," he said. "He used his Power—and it did not hold." His hand arose in a warrior's salute. "Lord, they spoke of the Gryphon breed at Garth Howell and Jakata laughed. I think he does otherwise at this hour."

"The Lady." Firdun only nodded at the boy's speech and went on to where those other three were gathered.

He had never seen such an expression on Ibycus's face before. And beneath the one he could not read he sensed the other's rage.

"Heart-held"—that was Elysha, her voice thin but her words precise and confident—"this was another testing—be not so disturbed that it came. That one we follow will use every fraction of the Dark which lies in this dreary land to try us." She raised her hands a little and Firdun saw that the gems in her bracelets no longer held their rich gleam. He was sure then he knew from whence had come those lightning flashes.

Now Ibycus stood up. "Fool, I am a fool. He must know this land far more than any have believed possible—and he makes it serve him."

"But"—Elysha laughed and raised herself with Aylinn's help—"he does not know the mettle of those who move against him. Landsil's get, I salute you," she said to Firdun.

"Hardly an adept," Firdun returned, "or perhaps even a 'prentice of promise. But there was no warning from Kethan."

Aylinn looked up, her face very sober. "He is alive and free. Were that not so, I would know it. Perhaps his way, though still westward, did not follow this same route."

The pard was crouched in the best spot of cover he could sight in this country, which had changed again from the dry plains they had known. He had caught and eaten a fat waddling bird in the last of the long grasses and had feasted well. Now he was tonguing his paws but still keeping a watchful eye on what lay below this perch of his.

His trailing sense had not been taxed this day. It had been easy to pick up the scent. Earlier he had found only a deserted campsite. But the traces he nosed out angled now a little more to the north, and the land was beginning to rise. Not only were there hills here to break the monotony of the plain, but they were fast growing taller and there was a smudge on the horizon which promised greater heights.

However, below was what was of more interest now. For they had camped early and there had been quite an amount of stirring about even after they had halted. They had put up wards and he had no thought of testing those. His pard range of sight was enough to let him spy out what mischief they might be preparing without getting close enough to trigger such unseen defenses.

The major portion of the party had withdrawn to the farther end of the valley before him and were there setting up some shelters and had started a fire. But the one he knew to be Jakata, together with the two underlings, wearing sage's drab robes, were busily at work in another direction. The two sages had chopped down several small shrubs and dug out the remainder of their roots, pulled the coarse grass up by the roots, working with the haste of those who dared not even think of disobeying any order. Their leader had seated himself on a rock to one side and sat staring into space as if he were inducing a trance.

That they intended calling upon some Power, Kethan was well aware even before the sages began to draw lines on the bare earth with branches they had stripped and sharpened. They were busied for some time before their leader took part in the action.

Rising from his seat, he picked up a mage staff of some dark wood, rune-carven and crowned with a monstrous head. The others were setting out what looked to Kethan at this distance to be short, thick clubs, planting them end up here and there among their carefully formed designs.

Having finished, they hurried out of the maze of lines, and Kethan was certain that they would just as soon be elsewhere during the rest of the proceedings.

Jakata raised his staff and pointed it at one of those clubs, which immediately produced flame as might a candle. He methodically continued until he stood in a circle of fire.

Kethan growled deep in his throat. The stench of evil was growing stronger by the moment. He was well aware that Jakata knew exactly what he was doing, for the pressure of Power was rising. Kethan debated a withdrawal, but when the Power did not increase past a certain point he was sure his presence would not be revealed.

Jakata snapped his fingers and the two others moved reluctantly toward him. They did not come alone. From behind a rock they dragged a smaller figure, hands bound together, squealing and sobbing as they forced it forward.

To Kethan the captive was a new form of life. No bigger than a half-grown child, it was very slender of body, and, that being bare, he could see that the skin was very dark brown. What hair it had was clustered in tightly tied lumps on its head and it was plainly female and, in spite of its small size, mature.

The pard's lips drew back in a silent snarl. That Jakata intended to use this small female for some bloody summoning he was certain, and his whole nature, both man and beast, revolted against being a silent and not interfering witness of such an act.

The sages thrust their captive down on her knees before Jakata. One of them whipped out a thick cord which he looped around the prisoner, each of the guards thus holding an end taut to keep her firmly in place.

Kethan stirred; his muscles ached for him to leap down and deal with Jakata. But he well knew that this Dark lord must be close to an adept in Power and no prey for a were.

Now the man in Kethan began to take control. His talent was based on his own body, but he had a second heritage. Gillan of the Green Tower had borne him, and even the weres had come to know that she was beyond their Powers when they had tried to break the bond between her and her were mate.

Gillan's gifts were like her foster daughter's. She served the Lady as a healer, but she had other talents she could call upon. The Power building here was growing like the roaring of a furnace.

Jakata might feel that he held it well in leash, but if the Dark beckoned, so would the Light follow.

Kethan had no moonflowers beneath his paws; such magic was for women. But this was a woman captive and perhaps so some plea might well be made for her. He had never even thought of trying this before.

*Yes!* The mind-send was sharp and he knew it. He turned his head quickly, but there was no sign of that sleek, black-furred form. But she was with him now—in his mind.

*Yes!* Her encouragement came again and Kethan gave a leap of mind, not body, into paths he had never trod before.

## CHAPTER TWENTY-SEVEN

# The Wing Ways, the Waste, West

The candles . . . Kethan's pard sight concentrated on the two nearest ones. He noted that the sages who rope-imprisoned the captive stood well outside the designs which were centered by Jakata. And he sensed there were wards in place. As in all the old knowledge, when a mage would dare a summoning, he or she took such precautions as possible to keep under control the thing they called upon.

The light of thick clublike brands was a dark red and the smoke given off by their burning arose in straight lines into the air. That they provided the bedrock of safety was his guess.

Fire was no friend to beasts; only humans had tamed it partly to their will. He snarled silently again. How—

*Look!* came again that command out of nowhere. And as if that unknown other now had control of his body functions, see he did.

That mass of grass and brush which had been so ruthlessly grubbed away to clear Jakata's designing was not empty. Though its inhabitants had made no attempt to defend their protection against that clearance, they were beginning to move in now.

By himself he could never have touched such alien creatures with mind-send. Yet there was an answer as that Power out of nowhere directed him to touch and link, touch and link. He did not even know what they were. Insects? Reptiles? Grubs torn from the earth?

However, link with them he did, until he had a heaving weapon of sorts. That he directed, his concentration on his task so great that he lost his outer sight of what was below. There were more an-swers—even farther removed from any touch he had known. And he knew that not only the dwellers in that brush and earth but the ravaged plants themselves were awakening to a kind of life un-known to them before.

He aimed his silent and unbelievable army and sent them toward their goal, his body so tense that his very bones began to ache.

A ragged root—it was too stiff to be a snake—moved toward the nearest candle. There was a humping of the ground also, and even without sight Kethan knew that dwellers in the earth were tunnel-ing ahead.

The pressure of the gathering Power was intense. It seemed al-most that it would crush him where he crouched. But it was not complete—it could not be as long as *she* kept guard.

Jakata's rolling chant echoed back from the low hills and Kethan fought to shut his ears to it.

*Let me in!*

This time the voice was a sharp order, so swift and powerful he could not help but obey. He went against all nature, both human and were, and opened to that call.

It pulsed through him, that new energy. He watched, even if dimly, that root wreath itself about the thick candle. At the same

343

time the ground around it heaved. It tottered, fell inward, and its flame was quenched against one of those drawings in the earth.

Kethan lay nearly spent under the crushing anger of that which had sought this path. But he was allowed no time to fight for himself. Again he must do what was to be done by inner power alone.

The were's mind seemed to give a sharp lurch. He dropped his hold upon the things of the grass and the earth. Instead he centered his being on "seeing." Out of that mass of grass and grubbed-up soil there leaped what were his own. Pards no larger than the hand of the mage who was now waving furiously, pards raised to battle fury, able to spring above their own height into the air.

Kethan, shorn of strength, lay dim-eyed. But he saw Jakata stumble back, fling out his arm. One of those small brown forms had teeth, vise-set, in the mage's flesh. Two others hung and clawed nearly belt-high on his body.

He heard screams. The two sages had dropped their ropes and were running, one with a pard form clinging to his thigh. Jakata was using his wizard's staff, seeking to beat to death those who had attacked him.

But by that battle he was torn away from his own summoning. Now there was black anger in the air—Kethan thought he could almost see it as a cloud gathering about the mage.

Aroused now to his immediate danger, Jakata threw back his head and screamed—and the words which issued from his lips could be seen like coals of blazing fire.

She who had shown him the way had not deserted Kethan. Those small vicious balls of fur below thinned, disappeared. He could feel that substance from which they were born return to him. But there was still action below. That which had come at the summoning was not to be lightly dismissed. Kethan could feel in his own body the struggle being made by Jakata to save himself.

But he also saw something else. That small captive who had been constrained within the circle of the candles was on her feet and running, though her hands were still tied.

She threw herself in a frantic leap over the pile of brush, crashing down, to be buried within that mass by the very force of her landing. Kethan stood, shook himself.

He had no time now to try to realize what had happened to him; he could only go into battle as he was.

"Great Warrior!"

It echoed in his mind as he, too, leaped down to the edge of that brush. Judging from the continued screaming shouts of Jakata, the mage was still engaged in striving to send back to its own plane that which he had called. Of the two sages there was no sign.

But Kethan sighted the wild shaking of the brush mass and reached that point just as the bloody, well-scratched body won into the open. She stared at him for a wild-eyed moment and then with a whimper folded in upon herself, falling in a small huddle before him.

He had to make a quick choice, and perhaps it might be a fatal one. As pard he could not get her out of danger; as a man he and she might have a thin chance. He made the change, glad that the mass of cuttings walled him away from the patterned ground. Stooping, he caught up that bony little body, slinging her over his shoulder as he made the climb back up to where he had perched. At any moment he expected to feel some dart cut them both down, a demon fire from the mage staff to send him out of life forever.

But that extra spurt of strength which was were heritage carried him up and behind a sheltering spur of rock unharmed, to his utter surprise. Perhaps Jakata, in the midst of his own battle, had not seen them at all.

He still held the child-woman against him. Now she once more opened her eyes, staring up into his face. But this time she showed no terror.

"Fal-so-lee! Artez Manga?" Her voice was as thin as the chirp of a small bird.

He did not want to use mind-send. If her people did not use it, such a touch might once more overwhelm her. But she was not speaking trade talk, and he knew no way to answer her.

Setting her carefully on the ground, he half turned toward the rocks which were a barrier against what lay below. There were signs the traders used. He sorted them out now from memory. Then his hands moved in the simplest ones suggesting escape and freedom. Quickly then he broke the cord binding her wrists, leaving them braceleted with deep gouges.

He used the sign for "away." She nodded vehemently and scrambled up to her feet. A moment later her hand closed about his and she tugged him with her northward. The jangle of chant from Jakata still reached them; perhaps they *did* have time to make a good run for it.

Only he could not travel here in human form. A strange wanderer in the open with no horse or gear would catch instant attention from any scout. As a pard . . .

Gently Kethan released that small hand and took several strides away. She watched him first wonderingly and then with growing agitation. His sign language was so limited, and how could anyone explain thus his nature?

Three times he slowly signed "friend—safe," and on the third signal her own small hands echoed his gestures. Drawing a deep breath, he made the change.

A small muffled cry echoed in his ears as he went four-footed once again. She was backing away, both hands over her mouth now and her whole body trembling. He stood where he was and because he must somehow make contact he sent a mind-probe.

*Friend—no hurt—friend!*

She had halted her retreat, though her body was still shaking. Slowly then she began to move, and Kethan stood still. She made a complete circle about him some distance away. Then, as if she could no longer find the strength to move, she suddenly sat down.

Had his mind-send really reached her? He could not tell as yet, and to intrude upon her again might be harmful.

Then her shoulders straightened; she was very apparently bracing herself for some action. Slowly she got to her feet again and came toward him.

To his surprise and dismay, she sank to her knees before him and crouched until she could touch her forehead to the ground.

"Great Old One." The words she spoke she also thought, and he dared to catch the thought.

But he felt uncomfortable. If she saw in him one of the great ones of the past, that might lead to trouble.

*We go—your home*, he thought steadily. That much he could do; see her safely back to her own kind.

She raised her head and for a long moment stared at him. Then, very slowly, she nodded. Rising, she came close to him and put out a hand cautiously to touch his furred head.

Kethan was again aware of the danger below them. He could still hear a faint droning which might be Jakata's chant and he had no desire to linger near that scene of the mage's struggle with whatever he had called upon.

*Go,* he mind-sent.

She smoothed the fur on his head and then again nodded and set off in a northly direction. The land here grew increasingly rugged. After a while she was limping, her bared feet fretted by the rough stones and gravel. Yet she did not break pace.

Once or twice she paused and looked searchingly around as if in search of some landmark. It was during the second of these pauses that Kethan took time to mind-reach for his own companions. Aylinn was the easiest to touch, for they had long been able to exchange so.

But the Aylinn who answered him was not his usual tranquil sister. There had been trouble. What trap had he not found in time to warn them off?

She did not explain—only that they were free and on the move again. Quickly he sketched for her the activities of Jakata and urged that they keep their distance until Ibycus could decide what was to be done. It might be that the Dark Mage could lose his battle, and things only the Ancient Old Ones might have been able to cope with would be loosed.

Ibycus, Firdun—both had the ward talent, and he believed that Elysha also knew something of it, for glamorie was often part of warding. They would be on the watch now.

His small companion had started on a step or two while he had communicated with his foster sister. Now she looked back and beckoned and he loped along behind her.

The footing here was better, and he saw indications that the use of tools must have once, very long ago, smoothed a path which was steadily climbing into the heights.

At length they were on a ledge, with the rock wall to their left and a sharp drop on the right. But the way was nearly wide enough to give access to a wagon and they kept close to the wall.

The stone of the wall was of a startling bright ocher hue with veins of black. Nor was it a smooth surface. Cut deeply into the stone were patterns—some running like record runes, others in the form of people and animals. Though greatly weather-worn, they were still visible.

He recognized the image of a snowcat—the most formidable of felines—and birds, or at least winged creatures. However, the figures meant to represent people were sticklike drawings a child might make.

Again his guide came to a halt, facing a section of cliff which was incised with symbols he was sure made up an inscription.

Stretching out her arm, she used a fingertip to trace those cuttings line by line and her voice arose in a singsong he could not understand.

The inscription bordered a round of shining black stone, forming a frame for it, and some trick of polishing had left that inner section smooth like a mirror, though showing no reflection. As her voice died away, she leaned a little forward, standing on tiptoe to place both hands palm-flat on that empty surface, holding them so as she again spoke.

Finally she stepped back. *We go—guards meet—up!* Her send weaved in and out and she pointed toward the ledge road before them, which was slanting at far steeper angle now.

In spite of the fact that she limped and left small bloodstains on the stone from her bruised feet, she quickened pace until she was almost running and Kethan padded easily behind. The ledge emerged on what must be a plateau well above the country below.

Kethan swung around to gaze south. Did Darkness still hang

there or had Jakata's spell-casting been finished one way or another?

He thought he could see wisps of what could be smoke, but those were fast disappearing in the air. It was not too far from sunset now. But in this upper world of heights and rocks there might be any number of shelters.

A flapping sound from overhead brought him around, belly low, a snarl rising in him as a new scent reached his nostrils. He had never forgotten the rus and since they served the Dark they might also have come to Jakata's calling.

His small companion was standing some distance away, her arms folded about herself as if she felt the chill of the winds which were sweeping down from the peaks ahead. In the air, nearing her with great swoops, were three men surely of her own kind, yet equipped with wings apparently fashioned by stretching thin scraped hide over stout ribs.

That the wings were not a part of them, Kethan discovered as he watched them come to a gliding landing near the woman. Those pinions were fastened in place by a harness for shoulders and waist.

The first to touch ground struggled out of his wings and ran to the woman. A moment later she was tightly held against him. For him alone she existed at that second. But his two companions now moved swiftly between Kethan and the two embracing.

Along with the harness for the wings, each carried a rod with a vicious-looking hooked point and they separated to come at him from two different directions.

"Kaasha Vingue!"

The girl had caught a glimpse of what they would do and called out sharply. They halted, looking from the pard to her and back again. She wriggled free of that tight hold upon her and caught the hand of he who had greeted her so in a torrent of excited speech.

Kethan straightened from his crouch. *Friend,* he tried to mind-send.

The startled expressions of all three men proved they had not expected that.

The two with their strange spears were still very wary, moving one slow step and then another. But the girl brought the third directly to Kethan. Her mind-send was ragged and he had to strain to catch some of its meaning: *Great Old One—Man—four feet—show.*

To change would leave him defenseless. His sword and armor were still packed on Trussant—or at least he hoped they were. As a pard he could be a fighter strong enough to face even an armed man. Could he trust the woman to the point of making the change?

*Four—two—* Now she had dropped her companion's hand to sign the message.

Reluctantly Kethan decided to make the change. There was a concentrated murmur of awe from all of them as he stood there as a man. The girl was smiling and nodding and again addressed the newcomers with excited speech.

Once more she caught the hand of him who had greeted her first, drawing him forward. She transferred her grip to his wrist and pushed his hand, half curled in a fist, at Kethan, who held out his own right hand palm up, in the ancient peace sign.

The stranger's flesh touched his. Fingers ran over his skin as if seeking fur.

Then the man turned to the others.

"Kaasha Vingue!"

Their spears went point down to the ground and both of them knelt, raising their left hands high in salute.

*Friend,* Kethan signed. And all three vigorously nodded.

*Up,* the woman gestured. But now Kethan shook his head.

*Go—own—people,* he mind-sent.

The four gathered together at that and their high voices cheeped back and forth. At length the woman returned to him.

*Evil—moves,* she sent. *Black land.* She swung out her arm toward the west in a vigorous gesture and her expression was one of fear mixed with loathing. *Be—safe.*

*No safe when evil moves!* All of them must have picked up that mind-send, for they were nodding vigorously. *Power—Power of Light comes—I find path.*

She seemed to consider that and then turned to the man who had shed his wings. After something which sounded like a question, he went back to his discarded harness and opened a pocket-like pouch fastened to the waist strap.

He came back with what looked like a square of dull crystal, so dark in hue as to seem almost rock. The woman took it and faced Kethan.

With the small plaque flat on one palm, she covered it with her other.

*I—Poquen. He—*she pointed to the man beside her—*Yil.*

Kethan indicated himself and said his name. Which she repeated twice, seeking the right inflection.

*Bad country—easily lost—you come here.* She pointed directly to the plateau on which they stood. *Take hands so.* She held out her own, holding the crystal to explain. *Call Pequin—Yil—will come— show—right path.*

He could accept that somewhere to the west was whatever Jakata hunted—and it could only be a gate. If the Dark Mage was now willing to call upon such Powers as he had tried to raise, then he needed more power or else was pressed for time.

The sooner their own party caught up with those from Garth Howell, the better.

*I go.* He changed again and she came closer, holding out that flat crystal. Luckily it was of a size he could carry in his mouth.

They raised hands in a last salute and he turned away. The crystal was cool in his mouth, but he was thirsty and hungry. Somewhere on the way back to join with the others, he must eat and drink.

Ibycus sat on a hammock. He had a small stick in his hand and was thrusting it into the ground, only to pull it forth again, his eyes not on his busy hands but half closed as he went over in such detail as she could supply all Aylinn had just told him. There was a tingling in the air, and Jakata was responsible. Whether Kethan's interference had really defeated what the mage had tried, they could not be sure, but he was of the opinion that it had. How much of the evil he had tried to summon had rebounded on him?

Jakata: they knew so little of him. Though Ibycus had no dealings with Garth Howell—not since the day they stood for the Dark in the great battle—he could accept that they had records maybe as great as those of Lormt.

The mage sighed. Ever since the news of the discoveries at Lormt, the knowledge uncovered by the falling of tower and wall, he had been planning to go overseas. But he was oathed to this land, one of the last of the guardians.

And it was here and now the loathsome Darkness crawled. He had searched memory well both during the days and in dreams at night, trying to understand what drew Jakata. That it must be one of the major gates, he was sure—though he had thought that most of those were destroyed along with their makers.

"The gate of Ranchild."

Ibycus started and dropped his stock. Elysha stood there watching him, that small half smile she used so much when she looked at him curving her lips.

"But—"

"Yes, the records state that that vanished with a goodly section of the land, that the fire mountains and the sea met in battle, to leave nothing behind. You have held the Power for long, Lord Master. You have shared it—a little." Now her mouth quirked in what was not a smile.

"Ranchild—he muddled his own brewing."

"To end a world," she agreed. "But who knows what hidden roots can bring to a new sprouting?"

Ibycus thrust his twig with almost vicious power into the ground again. "We must have a sending—to the Eyrie. If they have touch again with Hilarion and Lormt, perhaps there is some news from overseas which can strengthen our stand."

"Not you," Elysha returned. "To launch a sending, and receive from it when Jakata is meddling with nastiness we cannot identify, is a risk—master that you are. You can remember much of the old

days—when it suits you to do so. Remember then how you dealt with it."

He was on his feet now, staring at her. "Always you want more than you can possess—" he was beginning with a hint of rising rage.

"Do I, Lord Master?" Her violet eyes seemed very large and they held his so he could not turn away—though he resented fiercely within him that she could still move him so.

"You cannot," she continued, "refuse to use any weapon which lies at your hand. This is no longer between us, but the fate of all we know lies upon our heads, hands, and talents. Therefore I call upon you to this venture, and by the Favor of the Three in One you cannot deny me! I have also such a shield as I had not before, even with all your preparation. The moonmaid is an anchorage you cannot fault. Therefore—this night let us see what we can see. Dare you refuse this?"

The twig snapped in his fingers. Old memories stirred, old emotions he had thought dead. She had the right of it. He could not refuse her offer—whatever weapon lay at hand must be used—and he felt that time raced on their heels and in this could be their last and greatest enemy.

## CHAPTER TWENTY-EIGHT

# The Seeking, the Waste

They had pushed on, well away from the valley of the web riders, and it was dusk before they made camp. Ibycus had ridden at the fore of their company and had not spoken, nor did anyone attempt

to contact him, such was the expression on his face, the very stance of his body in the saddle.

Aylinn, as was necessary with the were mounts, kept to one side. That there was a bout with Power brewing, she was aware. Kethan reached her, but even of his report she repeated only the bare facts to the mage as they started this steady ride westward.

She glanced now at Trussant, keeping perfect pace with her mare, and for a moment was startled. Had there been a shadow of a form in the saddle there? What if the Powers they had drawn and released were thinning some curtain of time or space? Then she shook her head at such folly. No shadow, just Uta, holding with a deep-clawed grip to her perch.

The cat's head was turned toward the girl now, those large eyes surveying her with a kind of measurement, a questioning Aylinn could not understand.

It seemed that the farther they rode, the more sere and ominous the land became. There was still vegetation—grass—a stunted tree or so. While now across the far horizon arose a banding which could only mean heights, and stark ones.

Out of the tall grass trotted a well-known shape and Aylinn sighed with relief. Then Kethan arose man tall and waited for her.

The coming of the were broke through that isolation which had held Ibycus all through the past hours. He wheeled his unwilling mount and rode up to them.

"Report!" His voice held no hint of friendliness. He might have been a war leader irritated by the late arrival of some scout.

Kethan's face was oddly stretched and now he raised hand to mouth and brought out a piece of dull crystal which, to Aylinn, looked much like the setting of the mage's ring. It flared like make-light and on the mage's hand that ring answered with as brief and bright a surge of light.

"You bring us what?" That sharpness was not gone from the mage's tone.

"Perhaps allies, perhaps only goodwill, perhaps a key to what lies before us," Kethan answered. "The winged people will welcome us if we follow their road—and they have no goodwill for Jakata."

Ibycus nodded. "Well enough. Is there proper camp land near, a place which can be warded well?"

"Beyond the second rise is a stream—though it is hardly more than a trickle."

Aylinn's head had swung in the direction of her brother's pointing finger. Her moonflower wand was extended to follow the line he indicated.

The sun was nearly down, hidden now behind that line of hills beyond, and only the brilliantly painted sky gave them light.

"It is clear," the girl said. "No ward, no shadows in wait."

"Ward?" Firdun had come up to join them. He had changed, Kethan thought, glancing up at him. When they had left the Eyrie, a youth had ridden with them. Now it was as if some of the great burden of what must be Ibycus's years had shifted to Firdun. Now, like Aylinn, he faced in the same direction.

"Barren land," he said a moment later.

"Let us to it, then." The mage, still frowning, waved Kethan into the saddle. Uta quickly shifted to clear space for him and they rode with the rest strung out behind him.

Elysha, as Ibycus, had been silent through that march. Letting her horse's reins fall, though the mount appeared willing to follow the right trail, she had turned her bracelets around and around her wrists, her eyes half hooded as she went. Firdun had felt an indrawing of Power even as he had sensed when those of the Eyrie were about to meld. He had seen her with Ibycus earlier in the day, and the ill temper of the mage had first shown then. It could well be that this mistress of glamorie was evoking her own talent for some reason.

They crossed one of the rounded hills and there was indeed the scent of water to set their beasts to a faster pace. However, at the mage's orders, their party broke in two as they dismounted. Guret and his fellow tribesmen offed the camp gear from the horses and then herded all the beasts downstream, leaving a clear space between them. Hardin had hesitated, glancing from the mage to the Kioga, but when Ibycus showed no sign of dismissal, he remained.

A beckoning finger brought Firdun to the mage's side.

"Warding we need, and you alone can hold it here, for another task will be mine. We know that Jakata already plays with Powers which may have escaped him—even though we have not yet been attacked. Therefore give me such a warding as could stand against the very Wary One of Uin."

Firdun swallowed before he answered. "Lord, what talent I have is at your command. Whether that is great or less can only be measured in action."

"And action we shall certainly have!" Ibycus said sourly, swinging away to approach Elysha. She had slipped her bracelets from her wrists, and Kethan was sure that he saw a line of smoky purple haze wreath them as she clicked them together end to end so now she held a circlet.

It was Hardin who seemed to know what was needed without being ordered. He pulled loose an arm's grasp of the grass about, then another, unrolling the cloak he had been lent and spreading it over the improvised bed.

Without a word, Elysha fastened the circlet of her bracelets over her head so that it banded across her forehead. She then held out her left hand to Aylinn.

"Our Lady's mount runs the sky this night, sister, in full glory. You are my anchorage. Her chosen."

Aylinn nodded. As Elysha settled herself on the grassy nest, Aylinn took that outstretched hand and wrapped it under hers about the wand. The mage moved slowly, reluctantly, Kethan thought. However, he at last seated himself at Elysha's head.

"Ward!" he again commanded. Firdun summoned in a rush his talent. He mind-built a wall of fire and it shone moon-bright about them. Perhaps it was even beyond just his own seeing now, for he heard a gasp which might have come from Hardin.

Kethan had knelt behind his foster sister, his hands cupping her shoulders lightly. Then he was aware of a weight against his own back, heard the soft purr of Uta in his ears. What powers the strange cat might have were apparently to be freely offered.

Ibycus's hands moved and the guide gem came to life, as did the moonflower of Aylinn's wand. His lips were shaping words, yet

silently so no sound except their own heightened breathing broke the silence of the dusk. Slowly, a sentry on duty, Firdun paced around the wall his eyes saw, if theirs did not. Always, with each step, he strengthened the section he passed with all the vigor he could summon.

It seemed to Kethan that time had stopped, or that they had stepped beyond the pull of its stream. Around Elysha's head the brilliance of the jewels increased until they spread to mask her features with violet light.

The movement of the mage's hands was continuous. He was leaning slightly forward as if that fire about Elysha's head was drawing him.

The woman's body lay motionless. Kethan could no longer see even the steady rise and fall of her breast, as if breath itself had left her.

He was more and more aware of Uta's warmth against him, for, from Elysha and the mage, there now spread a chill. Aylinn's flesh, too, was cold. He willed, with the strength of both man and pard, warmth into her. And always Firdun walked his sentry.

There was a faint cry from Elysha. Quickly Ibycus's right hand flashed downward to lie heart high on her breast and Kethan felt Aylinn tense, and strove to give her aid.

Firdun's pace quickened. Now Kethan could see Firdun had caught upon Hardin and drew him up and along with him. The boy might not have any talent, but he was moon-blessed and so had some strength of will and body to add to theirs.

The warmth Uta gave him, Kethan passed on as he could. It seemed almost as if that purr had become a chant, one never meant for human ears to hear.

"I am here." Not Elysha's voice, though her lips had opened upon the words. It was a man who spoke.

"What can you tell us of the Gate of Ranchild?" Ibycus asked.

First it would seem that the other had no answer, for there was a long pause. And then:

"Ranchild ruled in Garth Howell in his day. The Gryphon found him a dire danger. He was said to be on his way to escape through the gate when Landsil matched with him and won. If there is memory of the gate, it lies within Garth Howell."

"What does Garth Howell now?"

"They appear to bide their time. Since Jakata went forth, they have kept strictly within their own wards."

"And there is nothing more about the gate?" pressed Ibycus.

"Only that it is in the Land of the Dead to the west and none have sought it since Ranchild went. Some say that Landsil hurled him through and sealed it. But seals wear with time. What would you have us do?"

"There may be more to learn at Lormt."

"We shall ask as best we can. But those of Lormt did not gather much from Arvon—nothing after the Great War. If you need what we have to give if and when you reach the gate—ask. There are Dark forces abroad—they are easily sensed. This Jakata may be far more than he seems."

Elysha suddenly moaned. Her head swung from side to side. Kethan felt the strong pull through Aylinn. Yes, the Dark was moving and not only in Arvon, but also here!

Did or did not a shape pace now outside Firdun's ward? Was it only visible to sense and not to sight? The old adage that Power drew Power might well be proven here this night. Kethan dared to loose a fraction of beast's gifts of sight, sound, smell—

Smell! The scent was very faint, but it held all the vileness he had found at the place of the well. Neither sight nor sound served him and still he could see that Firdun and the boy from Silvermantle, hand-linked now, moved more slowly, Firdun half facing outward as if he matched pace with something which was slyly testing the strength of their defenses.

Ibycus arched over Elysha's head, still behazed by the color from her circlet. She quieted. Then suddenly she sat bolt upright, brushing against the mage. Her eyes were like brilliant holes to be seen through the haze.

Aylinn swung the moon wand between those eyes and the outer darkness as Elysha's head turned in that direction. And the pull of her need drained from Kethan almost more than he could give.

The haze about her head was fading and they could see the twist of her features. Fear, yes, but, more than that, loathing, as if she looked upon something grossly unnatural.

Ibycus had slewed around in the same direction and now his hands were grasping his own staff. From his forefinger shot the beam of the ring, brilliantly white.

"Not—so!" Those words came from Elysha. The full-throated masculine voice began to fade as if the speaker drew farther from them. Elysha tried to twist free the hand Aylinn had anchored to the wand—the other went to pluck at the circlet.

Both bracelets were now loose in her left hand, but she remained linked to Aylinn. She swung the length of glowing gems in the air and it was like lightning striking over Firdun's head—out into what now seemed the depth of dark beyond.

Ibycus's staff moved, raised, pointing in the same direction as those lightning flashes. They snapped against the length of age-hardened wood, seeming to use it as a guide outward.

Firdun leaped to one side, dragging Hardin with him. That spear point of flame, fashioned by its contact with the mage's staff, struck outward.

Rage—pain—denial—rage—

Like gusts of wind those emotions burst forth—but all beyond the barrier Firdun had set. Now the mage was shoulder to shoulder with him, still aiming the living fire outward. The backwash of raw hatred was like the blast of a tempest. They shivered under it, but none of them dropped hand, lost control.

"By the Stars of the Great Ones, by the will of That Beyond, by the oathed Power of the Light." It was Firdun who cast that incantation. "By Landsil, by Theorn, by Gailarian, and Thrius, by the Claws of the Gryphon, the fangs of the weres, the will of the Lady—we are no meat for your eating."

Was he actually growing taller with every word, Ibycus seeming in his shadow? Now he reached out and caught at the mage's staff. Nor did Ibycus attempt to deny him that touch.

"Get you into the Dark from which you crawled." There was the same force in Firdun's command as there might have been in the mage's earlier. "By _____ it is willed!"

The name he called upon then was like a blast of storm upon them all and Kethan knew that he had heard one of the Great Names which only the Power-possessed might use.

The fire wreathing the mage's staff drew from straight, spear-thin lines into a ball. It leaped forward. Kethan sensed what the wand controlled even as its Power burst all bonds. He had sight more of mind than body, when that fire broke upon a dark mass which swayed, and thrust forth limbs which were almost tentacles. He swayed and held his own position only by a great effort against waves of torment and rage which strove to tear them down even as the thing withdrew.

Ibycus had loosed his hold on the staff and Firdun was plainly leaning upon it to keep himself erect. Aylinn released Elysha's hold on the moon wand. It fell to her knees as if she could not hold it, light as it was. Kethan felt Uta's warmth vanish. The cat must have loosed her hold on him.

Though the strength was wrung out of them all, they knew also that they were free. But Firdun swung around to face Ibycus squarely.

"What have you done to me?" His voice scaled up as if he were back in boyhood again.

"Nothing." The mage seemed in no hurry to take back his staff, which Firdun was thrusting in his direction. "We must all make our choices for ourselves, Gryphon-born."

Firdun lifted the staff as if he would hurl it from him. Then, his eyes seeing afire, he threw it so the mage caught it easily before it touched the ground.

"I will choose as I wish," the young man said. "I am what I am— and none shall make me other."

Ibycus smiled wearily. "So say we all upon occasion. Yes, your choice is your own. But at this moment we are bound together and only failure of our mission will tear us apart."

Firdun's head went down. His empty hands clasped, opened,

and clasped again. Then he finally raised one and muttered some words, and Kethan knew their ward was down.

Aylinn leaned back against her foster brother's shoulder. "It is not well," she said, so softly that he hardly heard her.

"In what way?"

"Kethan, you know that I have sometimes—when the Lady empowers me—foresight. For Elysha—for him." She nodded toward Ibycus. "It is perhaps only my inner fear, but out of this we shall all come changed. We have taken up the weapons of the Great Old Ones and some of those are not for us."

As always they all felt the overpowering fatigue which followed the Power drain. And they were eager to join the Kioga, eat of roasting grass hens on improvised spits at the fire, drink, and find their bedrolls. Firdun had not spoken with any since they had left the place he had warded. He ate little and put his bedroll a little apart. There was a strange, set cast to his features, as if he were no longer the comrade they had known. Now and again he looked toward Ibycus, scowling, as if the mage had set him to some task he hated.

Even as Firdun watched the mage covertly, so Kethan saw Aylinn watch Firdun. Her face was nearly as sober as his. With the moon directly above them, she, too, drew apart, and Kethan knew that she communed in her own way with the Lady, this time with a troubled heart.

He made very sure the stone he had brought from the winged ones was safe. He put it, wrapped in a bit of cloth, under where his head would rest—having a ghost of an idea that perhaps it would foster dreams. And this night he wanted to escape—escape into that dream of the valley guarded by stone cats and the black-furred, beautiful one who had enticed him there.

Only this time he did not go four-footed. He recognized the pillars with their seated cats, but he was all man this night in spite of his strong-willed desire to change.

Then *she* stepped into the open from behind one of the pillars— not a cat now. Her head with its short-cut, thick black hair came to a little above his shoulder; her slender body revealed by the straight one-piece garment she wore was human, graceful, even as she had possessed feline grace before.

"Lady . . ." He hesitated, not knowing how to address her.

She smiled but did not answer. Instead she came to him, soft-footed, and raised both hands to draw down his head. He felt her soft lips nuzzle against his cheek.

"Great Warrior," she breathed rather than spoke. "It has been so long for this one."

Without being fully conscious of his action, Kethan's arms went about her, drawing her even closer.

"Beautiful one—who are you who comes to me so?"

He heard a soft chuckle. "Learn the answer to that, Great Warrior, and when I come I shall stay—as you wish. It has been so long." Now she sighed.

Even as she sighed, she faded to nothingness in his arms and was gone. And he cried out hopelessly even as he saw the cat pillars also spin into nothingness.

If he dreamed more that night he did not remember it. With the morning his frustration sent him out on scout even before the camp was dismantled.

He took the same trail he had followed before, save that he no longer tried to trace out the scent of Jakata's people. The winged ones had promised an easier way to what they called the Land of the Dead, and Ibycus believed that that was the direction in which Jakata was headed—if he had survived the evil he had called up.

"Though doubtless he did," the mage had commented as they decided on Kethan's direction, "or we would not have been tracked last night. Unless he loosed what cannot be controlled. But if that were so, this"—he held out his finger ring, the same dull stone now power empty—"would have given us warning."

The trail led them more to the north, and as the day advanced, the distant mountains raised a jagged barrier across the horizon. Once they skirted ruins of some size—a keep which might have been even greater than their Gryphon's Eyrie, Firdun thought. But they did not approach closely, and there was a feeling of desolation and despair which appeared to reach out to them from those tumbled walls.

Here, too, were the remains of walled fields where once crops had been sown. Even here and there a degenerate lone stalk of grain waved a tassle in the breeze. But the travelers did avail themselves of what was furnished by an ancient orchard. Most of the older trees had moldered away, but there had been fresh saplings arising from long-rotted fruit. And several of these bore a heavily ripe crop, so the travelers made that their nooning and relished the sweetness of fresh fruit again.

By afternoon they had reached the beginning of the heights. There was the remains of an old road, but they did not follow that. Rather, Kethan scouted a more difficult way up and down the reaches of some valleys, being careful to note if there were any signs of past habitation there. A large cellar hole suggested that there might once have been a hunting lodge. About it was a strong smell of bear and he mind-sent back a warning to avoid the possible den.

For two days they traveled so. At first their pace was slow, for they had all suffered from the draining of Power, but strength returned. Firdun had kept to himself. Nor did he sleep well at night, for the import of what had happened weighed upon him. He was no adept like Alon, no master of both the lesser and the great Powers. Yet he could not deny that in those moments when he had grasped Ibycus's staff it had seemed that a key turned deep within him.

He bit down upon sour fear. Many times he had wondered how Kethan could reconcile his two selves, pard and man. Now he wondered if he himself had, in some way, been splintered and now carried a second being within. Though he had always felt the loss of not being one of the melding Eyrie, yet that act of his had seemed to come as if he had planned it and knew that it would succeed.

"Firdun?" Startled, he looked up. They had dismounted to lead their horses up a rough grade. He realized that his horse had been snorting and sidling, and he saw that Aylinn with Morna had caught up with him.

"Moonlady?" he returned, soothing his horse. She wreathed her reins about Morna's saddle horn and the were horse dropped back, still following steadily.

"But I am Aylinn," she said now. "Trail companions follow no formal speech. Firdun, is all well with you?"

He wanted to turn her off with a quick denial. Somehow he could not.

"I wonder," he said slowly, finding it difficult to put his unease into words, "if I am still Firdun."

"The Power uses us hard sometimes. But one carries what one was born to hold. If you are more than warder, more than what your kin line has believed, is it not better to face that and accept? I . . . sometimes I can foresee . . . a little."

She was looking beyond him upslope now to where Elysha was walking beside her mare. Ibycus was in the lead well ahead; Aylinn had not seen them together since the night of bespelling.

"And you have foreseen?" Firdun demanded. Perhaps she *could* supply some answer to his disordered musings.

"Loss," she said quietly. "Just an emptiness where life should be."

"For all of us?" he asked again, entirely alert now.

"No. Nor can I tell you which in surety. But there will be gain also, Firdun. Do not shrink from what will come for you alone. It is as the Great Power designs. We are children and have our tasks to learn."

"Nor is that easy!" His voice was harsh. "Aylinn, you are a healer—how can one heal a fear of the unknown?"

"One accepts," she answered softly. "Firdun, you doubt yourself. Look upon what stands behind you. You are of the Gryphon line—Kerovan fathered you, Joison is your mother. They were far apart in talents and gifts yet they came together to form a stronger whole. I heard you call on Landsil in the night. Would one of little talent dare such an awakening of old forces?"

"Ibycus stands alone." He stared ahead to where the mage was just disappearing over the crest of the height up which they were making their way. "I—I do not want such a life."

"Nor need you choose so. Think of Alon, or Hilarion. Do they hold themselves apart from others, adepts though they be? Ibycus is the ancient warden of this land, but he is also a man and makes men's choices, and others can do also. Ah, look!"

She suddenly pointed to the sky. There was a dark speck there, growing ever larger as they watched. Somehow it did not have the right shape to be a bird.

"One of the flying people!" the girl cried as it sank behind the heights. "What freedom—to use the very sky as a path."

They quickened pace and then she dropped back to Morna and Trussant, where Uta rode with the air of one for whom that very mount had been trained. The last scramble up the slope was a slippery one and they had to take it with caution, though they longed to run.

Then at last they looked out on a plateau of red, black-veined rock and saw Kethan, in pard form, accompanied by a small figure who had discarded the wings and came forward to greet the newcomers.

## CHAPTER TWENTY-NINE

# The Road to the Land of the Dead, the Waste

There had once been a road through these brittle cliffs, but lava flow and violent earth-twisting had left only the faintest traces. The badly shattered surface was little trouble for those winged forms coasting above the party as they now crawled painfully along. But this was the only way to what they sought.

Now they rode at a walking pace and in armor, for the warning given them had been clear. This broken land had its own menaces, although Kethan could not guess what might lair in such a desolate place.

Then the brighter-colored lands over which they traveled were well behind them. Coarse black sand drifted and the winged ones warned of setting foot on the porous rock where domed bubbles could break under any weight and entrap man or beast in the hollow below.

They wound single file in the direction their winged scouts waved them, often having to dismount and lead their horses. Aylinn was kept busy at each pause tending cuts from the raw knife edges of the broken stones, and Kethan's pads would have been lamed within an hour, so he rode as a man.

It was on the second day's journey into this dire place that they came upon one of the reptilian mounts of a Garth Howell breed. It had been literally torn apart, most of its belly gone and the rest clawed and broken.

*Rock crawler.*

It was from Uta that send had come. Kethan could smell the fetor of the dead thing and now he sighted what seemed to be a narrow trail metallically bright under the sun. It looped down from the heights above and, even as he eyed it, Trussant gave one of the deep whinnies of his kind and sidled as far as he could from corpse and trail.

*What is this thing?* Kethan aimed at the cat, who spat as the horse whinnied, her ears flattening against her skull.

*Crawler—eater of all.*

She had no more sent that message than one of the high rocks moved, uncoiled, became something alive. The were's shout of warning carried along the trail as he urged his mount around to face the thing.

Its rough skin matched exactly the rocks over which it now traveled, so movement alone could reveal its presence. A huge mouth gaped, showing a double row of stained teeth.

He could see no legs as it slid down toward him, nor did it curve its passage as might a snake. Instead it appeared to slip with ease over the most jagged fringes of the rocks, leaving behind a metallic, gleaming trail, perhaps of slime.

Nor did it utter any sound. But the horses of the party were going wild and Kethan saw Ibycus bucked from his seat to land on the sharp fragments of the trail.

The thing reared its forepart now. Greenish liquid dripped from the corners of its huge mouth. Kethan could distinguish neither eyes nor ears, but plainly this creature had some sense which alerted it and drew it in his direction. He caught Uta by the back of her neck, dropped her behind him, and then drew sword.

Weres did not fight with fang and claw alone. The battle heat was rising fast in him, but he did not will the change this time. Plainly the creature was heavily defended with scales and he thought even a pard would have no chance with this.

"Together." Firdun forced his horse in beside Kethan. "The head."

Yes, the head. But there was no eye one could transfix, only that open cavern of a mouth. Both horses were wild with fear and Kethan knew that they could not force the animals closer. He lunged out of the saddle and ducked to avoid the metal battle shoes as Trussant reared.

There came the sharp whistle of Kioga arrows. But those which reached the thing clicked harmlessly to the ground.

"On the move," he half shouted over the din of the milling party behind. "I take right."

"So be it!" Firdun made answer. He was also afoot. But he was swinging something in one hand, one of the saddlebags.

And the monstrous head seemed to center on that. Kethan had scrambled up the short incline. The vile stench which arose from it set him gasping for air. That bag Firdun had hurled was caught, the great teeth clamped on it.

"The head."

Kethan had not needed that suggestion. In spite of the weight of his mail and sword, he leaped, not as surely as the pard might have done, but well enough to bring him tottering on the back of the thing. His boots slipped and then found purchase on the huge back scales which arose in ridged lines.

He fully expected the monster to hump its body, endeavoring so to throw him off. But that did not come. Instead he saw Firdun below moving from side to side, throwing rocks which left his hands cut and bleeding, so holding the attention of the monster.

Twice it lowered its head under that barrage of rocks. Firdun had been joined by Guret in the assault now. Apparently this rock-bred thing was slow of brain. Kethan leaned forward a fraction. Yes, when the head swung to his right he thought he could see a kind of dark crevice between the scales. They could not be entirely fast set or the thing could not move.

"To the right," he shouted.

He almost brought about his disaster, for his voice coming from above appeared to reach some hidden hearing organ of the crawler. It lifted its head with a jerk and Kethan fell to his knees, feeling the points of those ridge scales cut his flesh. But he did not lose his grip on his sword, nor did he slip to the ground. Now the rain of rocks were coming from his right and that head went down again.

His chance was a small one and he dared not wait any longer to take it. Holding the sword with both hands, he thrust down with all his strength and skill at that dark line which might be a seam between the scales.

The quan iron blade struck, was held for a moment, and then went deep, as Kethan pushed with all the might he could summon. But he could not hold that long. This time the thick body beneath him convulsed. The forepart arose with a twist which tore loose his hold on the sword hilt and he was tossed out and down, landing painfully with one hand impaled on a splinter of rock.

The massive body convulsed again and rolled toward Kethan, who was too dazed and wedged within the rocks to evade it. Down from the skies swooped the winged guides, their hooked spears ready. The spears caught and held in the rough ridges of that body, shifting it enough so that Kethan escaped the full impact of the dying creature. His legs were trapped beneath its weight, but that was all.

Firdun was already climbing to where the were lay, and behind him came Hardin and Guret. Their united strength shoved the still-quivering body from him and then he was pulled free and aided in descent to join the rest of the party.

They later learned from the winged folk that there were but a few of these rock crawlers and each jealously guarded its own hunting space, so there was little chance of a second attack.

Kethan, screwing his face from the potion Aylinn forced upon him, his hand bound with more of her healing salves, knew that for the present he could not change, and a part of him found the pain of that realization as sharp as a wound.

There were no streams or springs in this desolate barren country. But, as they climbed another peak to wedge through, the air which struck them carried a new scent.

"Sea winds!" Elysha said. "We come to the very end of the world, Master Mage."

Ibycus had been riding as one deep in thought, all his attention turned inward, so that Firdun had urged his mount closer and once or twice caught at the loose reins the mage seemed almost ready to let fall.

"The end of the world . . ." Kethan had seen the great sea of the east on a visit to the Dales seasons ago. But that there was another sea, no man had ever said. Certainly the Sulcars, who prided themselves on their mastery of the waves, never mentioned other waters to be plowed.

Ibycus's head jerked up as if he had been pulled awake from some dream or trance.

"Yes," he repeated somberly, "there awaits the end of the world."

However, they were not the first to find it, for one of their winged guides glided overhead and landed neatly on the outcrop of rock almost directly in the mage's path, so he had to pull up his horse.

*Those of evil—wait.* Firdun was close enough to the other two to pick up the send. *Their fighters stand ready for battle He who wears the cloak of the Dark goes ahead to call his master.*

*There are the black knights below,* came back Aylinn's send. *They stand ready and there is an open plain.*

They halted and Ibycus was again his alert self, as if he had made some decision and would stand by it.

"Guret," he called, and the Kioga, who had dismounted to inspect his horse's hooves, raised his head and came forward. "Remember the Take Song of Warren?"

The horsemaster blinked and then nodded. "It is a desperate trick, Lord." He glanced back at the huddled horse people. "And a deadly one." The tribesman's jaw was set and it seemed for a moment he might defy Ibycus's suggestions.

Kethan slipped his arm out of the sling. The weight of the sword was back; Hardin had worked it out of the body of that rocky nightmare. Firdun was drawing his own blade.

"Arrows," he said. "Kioga are good marksmen. But the beasts will have little protection."

Guret's face was bleak. "If it must be so, let it be."

He strode back to where his tribesmen were and at his orders they began to unload, dropping the packs without much caution. They were scowling and it was plain they were opposed to what was to be done. Kethan pushed ahead a little.

The remnants of the old road gave patches of good footing. But they were emerging on a plain of what looked to be coarse black sand, bad footing for any horseback maneuvers. Yes, there were those who waited. Six of them, so encased in black armor to match the footing under their snake-headed mounts as to seem fashioned completely of metal.

Each carried a tube, its butt against the rider's hip. And one could well believe that they held the secret of some old and powerful weapon. Of Jakata and his two attendants there was only a glimpse. They were urging their own horses through the slippery and hoof-engulfing surface of the plain, headed for a vast dome of black rock.

Aylinn had her bow, Kethan and Firdun had their swords, Hardin one of the Kioga boar spears. Who knew what forces the mage or Elysha could summon?

However, Ibycus was speaking again and even the three winged ones who had been the guides for this day had alighted within hearing.

"Those are deadly killers," the mage said slowly. "But they are a wall we must pass. Firdun, it may well take both of us to ward what Jakata would open. Thus . . ." He paused so long Kethan believed that he did not want to continue at all. The mage suddenly seemed changed. This haggared man was not the holder of Power that Kethan had known for so long, but rather one who for the first time was gnawed by doubt.

"Thus—" again it was Elysha who spoke aloud what must be his thoughts, "comrades, let Guret do what his kinsman of long ago did in battle. Loose the mounts which are free, ride with them, and open a way, for we are of little account, being only servants of the Light, and we use what weapons we must in that service!"

There was a murmur from the Kioga. Firdun well knew the bonds between rider and horse with those people; he had been a sworn brother in the tents since childhood.

"Cut us a path, servants of Light!" Ibycus's voice held his old decisiveness now.

The Kioga were passing among the animals. By each horse, one of the Kioga stopped, and, putting hands to either side of its head, touched his own forehead to that of the beast and held it so for a breath out of time.

They knew that they had been sighted. That grim black line below had come to a halt. The winged people took to the air and Kethan wondered if they were withdrawing. Claws caught at his shoulders for a firm hold. He was so used to Uta's presence now that he had not even known when she had taken her place with him.

Then Guret cried out something with the ring of a battle slogan. The free animals went forward at a trot and then a gallop. Behind them rode the three Kioga, Kethan, and Aylinn. The reins of Morna laid loosely as his foster sister set arrow to bow, her moon wand thrust to safety at her belt.

Behind them came Ibycus, flanked by Firdun and Elysha—who

had taken her place even though Ibycus had opened his mouth as if to refuse her.

They were down from the heights now. The beasts of their train were slipping and plunging, their race hindered by the sand which trapped their feet.

One of those black knights moved, reversed a tube he held, and pointed to the Kioga stallion who led that race. There was a flash of flame and the horse screamed in agony, but the pace of the others carried them on.

The Kioga were shooting and Kethan saw one knight jerk and fall from his saddle, but mainly the tribesmen had been aiming at the mounts of that grim company and three sank, bristling with arrows.

Then Trussant, aflame with battle rage, brought Kethan close enough to exchange blows with one of the knights. They were sending their flames and Kethan felt the sear of one flash which came too near. He ducked and cut not at the body of the knight but at those hands which grasped the deadly rod. The quan iron blazed almost as brightly as the flames and passed, cutting off both gauntleted hands, deep into the neck of the serpent horse, whose shriek below was lost in other screams and cries. The winged people were taking their own vengeance, swooping over the now-broken line of knights to hook with their spears and drag from their saddles men even as they took aim.

Kethan could sense no magic. This was a fight free from Power and he rejoiced in it even though the change was not on him.

The melee swung this way and that. There were bodies of both beasts and men trampled into the sand. The fire weapons appeared to be easily exhausted. Perhaps, Kethan thought fleetingly, they were the gift of Dark Power and could not be recharged.

He was dimly aware that Uta's weight was no longer against his back. Perhaps she had been swept from her hold. Then there was no one ahead of him and he urged Trussant around.

One of the armor-encased knights staggered by him on foot, both hands clawing at his own head. Uta's black form was pressed as tightly to his helm as when she rode with Kethan, but now her claws were locked in the visor as she spat and howled her anger.

The knight stumbled closer and Kethan swung his sword, taking the same care he would have under his father's eyes in the arms court of the Green Tower. A blow on the shoulder sent the staggering man to his knees and Trussant reared as trained, bringing down both quan-iron-shod hooves on the faltering man, driving him deep into the sand as Uta sprang free.

Kethan looked around for another enemy. But what he saw was only the wastage at the end of the battle. The knights and the monster mounts lay dead. But also there were the bodies of seared horses, and a limping Kioga was cutting the throats of some who still screamed.

Jakata's guard had failed, but somehow Kethan was sure that the Dark Mage had already forgotten these servants, that he was too intent upon reaching his goal.

Now the were raised his head and stared toward that black hump. He saw riders making the best speed they could in the sand and knew that Ibycus, Elysha, and Firdun had gotten through.

Still there was no end. Morna moved up beside him. Aylinn's bow was gone, her moonflower wand was in her hands, her eyes were wide.

"We must go on." She echoed his own thoughts.

They had lost Obred, and Guret rode chanting the death song of a warrior who had won his triumph. But they felt too much the pressure which was building around them now to remain.

For there was Power awakening. Would they be in time to stop Jakata from his spelling? They could not urge their horses now to more than a walk and the party ahead grew smaller and smaller, sometimes half covered by the sand which arose a little like dust to cloak them.

Of Jakata and those with him, Kethan could no longer catch sight. But he hoped that the other three were close enough behind Jakata to interfere with any sorcery he might intend.

The spells which summoned or controlled major Powers were never easily enacted and Jakata would need time.

There was a small black shape trotting by the side of his horse. Uta! He called to her, but she kept steadily on as if she were now on some quest of her own and must not be distracted from it.

She was even drawing ahead, for, though Trussant kept to the best pace Kethan could urge on him, the cat steadily left him behind. She was not running, yet the shifting sand did not appear to slow her.

However, the sensation of drawing Powers was increasing. And now it weighted them down, though they fought against it. Aylinn summoned Hardin, Guret, and Lero to join her. Each of them she touched in turn with the moonflower, holding it out to Kethan at the last.

The heaviness which had been weighing upon him was lessened. But something else was astir. At first he thought that the black sand might have been summoned up in dust devils such as plagued many who ventured into the Waste.

Only this was not black—the haze was more rust red in shade— and it did not whirl, it stood. He blinked twice. Uta was not walking in sand, she was pattering down a street—a wider, better-paved way than even one of the Dale seaports could boast. While on either hand arose, as plants might grow out of rich earth, walls, houses, mighty towers, and buildings. Glamorie he well knew, but even though he could tell what it was, he could no longer pierce through it.

Also he thought that he caught glimpses now and then of shadow figures moving among those buildings, even along the pavement on which he now appeared to ride. Before him, that hump of black rock which had become their goal was fast altering. It formed an arch with carven pillars on either side.

Yet there was also a menace in these shadows. Kethan felt the newcomers were far from welcome here, and he began to watch alertly on each side the doorways in those buildings, the alleys and street mouths which they passed.

The shadows took on no stronger outlines. All of his party were riding close together now. The winged people had not accompanied them and Kethan felt suddenly very wary and alone.

He longed to change, but dared not, knowing that in spite of Alyinn's treatment he could not go four-footed until better healed.

"Glamorie," he said aloud as if to reassure himself.

"True," his foster sister answered. "It is out of the past—we are seeing what once was. Time itself is being drawn to this place."

He had always heard that the Great Old Ones had cities and castles—which their descendants had not been able to match. This must have been one of them. The space before the arch cleared, seemed to tighten in an odd way as if more substance had been added to the ghostly frame. Elysha dealt in glamorie—was it she who was calling back what once was?

That flavor of sea wind in the air was strong. Once this must have been a lord among cities—until twisted Power brought it to bare rock.

The road widened as they neared the gate so that there was a large space. There stood those they sought, both friend and foe.

## CHAPTER THIRTY

# An End and a Beginning, the Waste

The blood-red robe of the one figure before the center portion of the gate identified Jakata. He was standing, but those two sages who had accompanied him were huddled to the ground, unmoving. Kethan wondered briefly if they had served as some sacrifices for their master.

He had to call upon his own reserves under the weaving, the

massing of Power centered here. Somehow he had slipped from the saddle and was afoot. A figure moved to his right—Aylinn, her moon wand held in both hands before her breast. The flower which topped it seemed wan—as if it, also, had been sucked dry of potency. On his left was Hardin, and behind him Guret and Lero. Then he was aware that he was indeed tramping on stone pavement, that the walls were solid.

They were also drawing in, those wisps of shadows which had the faint likeness to beings. Yet none of them had features he could distinguish, nor did any approach close enough to touch.

The three who had gone before stood as steady as Jakata. Ibycus was in the center, his staff held in both of his hands. Somehow he appeared to loom taller, as if what he called upon filled him past the confines of his body. To his left was Elysha, the blaze of her bracelets bands of fire. She was calm of face as one who waited, having marshaled all her strength and contained it ready.

Firdun's sword and helm lay slightly behind him. He might have tossed aside as useless those weapons of common humankind. The youth who had ridden out of the Eyrie was gone now. His gaunt face was strained, as if he also gathered and held that which must be used in this final meeting.

Forward trotted another, her black fur allowing her to be easily seen. She moved with purpose as if she had been summoned and must answer. So Uta came to Elysha and stood statue still.

Kethan moved on, Aylinn matching him step for step. He did not know what had become of the others. Perhaps this last battle was not for them. The pard in him wished for freedom, fought to take form, swelling with the waves of energy circling about them, but he held to his present form. Somehow he understood that, were he to release that other within, he might forever lose the man in the beast.

He could hear the faint crooning song Aylinn was voicing. Words so old that time had nearly erased them. The moon was not above to favor her now, but still she entered into the Maiden's ritual. And her moonflower appeared to revive.

Firdun stared straight ahead of him, not at the red-robed figure who postured and chanted before the gate. The man was but the key; it was what lay beyond him that must be faced.

Jakata was well aware of them—how else could it be with the currents of magic circling about? Yet he had not glanced in their direction, his attention all for what he would do.

His black staff pointed first to one of the prone sages and then to the other. It was not the bodies which arose at his bidding, but shadow things, more material than those Kethan had seen in the city. But all which was human and of the world of light lay still, now just husks discarded.

Those shadows flanked Jakata, one on either side. And they changed, growing taller, more visible. It was they who turned to face Ibycus and the others now.

The ring of the mage's finger was blazing. He gripped his staff almost as if it were an anchorage he must hold to.

"Neevor . . ." That thing out of the shadows which had arisen on Jakata's left at his bidding showed a discernible face now. It was no monster—there was almost a serene beauty in it. However, Firdun, seeing it, felt an icy chill.

"Neevor!" Those lips were shaping a small tight smile. "Well met, brother."

Ibycus's features were set. He looked beyond the thing which addressed him at Jakata.

"Brother." That greeting was repeated softly, almost caressingly. "We meet again."

"Not so," the mage returned. "Long ago our paths parted, if you are indeed some remnant of him whose liking you strive to wear. At Car Re Targen there was a parting, and Car Re Targen has been tumbled stone for countless seasons. You are not Mawlin—you are not!"

"Deny me as you please, I stand here, brother."

He was fully solid now—that shadow-born thing. And such a one as might loom well over Ibycus, only the mage raised his ring hand and the beam of light from that stone struck full into the face of the thing slowly advancing. It writhed, cried out.

"Ill done, brother. Death you have given, death you will have in return."

"Ill lived," Ibycus answered, "and even more ill in dying. You do not walk again."

There was agony twisting that fair face now and Firdun swayed, for a pain which was not his and yet seemed of his giving, struck through him. Then it was gone. He saw that Ibycus leaned now on his staff as if he needed its support.

Almost within the archway Jakata postured and moved as he might in some formal dance at a feasting.

"Ibycus . . ." the second of the shadow-born spoke. This was a woman. As her companion, she was fair of face, well endowed of body. Looking upon her, Firdun felt a drawing which almost brought him a half step forward.

"Beloved." Her voice was husky; it beckoned, promised. What man could stand against the lure she had become?

"Love does not last past betrayal, Athal who was."

"I am not *was*—beloved—I *am*!" She opened wide her arms.

Firdun almost could have rushed forward, but that call was not for him. He saw from the corner of his eyes the purple blaze which now seemed to half hide Elysha.

The woman-thing laughed and one wanted to join with her. A musky, languorous scent filled the air. Her eyes promised . . .

"Remember the morning in the great chamber—Ibycus? Then you swore many things, did you not? Among them an eternal bond for us. Remember the night upon the river when you said the very stars were mirrored in my eyes and you were in your might? Remember—"

"Remember," Ibycus interrupted her languorous voice, "how it was with you when we came to the last stand at Weyrnhold."

Tears came into those large eyes, spilled over on her ivory cheeks.

"I am your true love, Ibycus, come again. Weyrnhold was long ago—I was young—and afraid."

"Afraid?" That word uttered with scorn had not come from the mage but from Elysha. "Afraid of losing what mattered most to you—your power over men."

The languorous beckoning look was gone. The vision's smile became as near a snarl as any human lips could shape.

"Stupid nothingling! Have all your sighs and longings brought *you* what you wish—this man?"

"What any man would give a woman must come with truth and trust," Elysha's voice rang out. "I do not lay your traps."

Athal laughed, spitefully this time. "And where do you stand, nothingling?"

"Beside him you would bend to your own purposes. I take only what is given freely."

"Enough!" Ibycus raised his ring hand. "We lose time with this chitter-chatter. Be gone, Athal, to seek again what you chose at Weyrnhold. Such choices are made only once and forever hold."

"No!" Her voice rose to a shriek. "You cannot be lost to—"

The thrust of the ring light caught her in midstep as she would have flung herself at him. Her screams rang in Firdun's head until he half turned on the mage who would inflict such pain on anyone, man or woman.

Then she was gone and with her disappeared that spell which had begun to entangle him also. Ibycus leaned even heavier on his staff. Elysha advanced a hand but did not quite touch him.

Then he straightened and his voice rang out with all the old force and power.

"Shall we cease with games, Jakata? You have thrown the challenge. Now make good your threat."

The Dark Mage had ceased his strange pacing back and forth. His wand swung between two fingers and he smiled as had the woman.

"You have lived long, Warden. I think your day is done. I have unlocked the gate and—"

His words centered all their eyes upon that archway. There was a hum in the air, a feeling of compression about them which was partly anticipation. The inside of the arch was black, as hidden as a starless, moonless night—or the very depths in which the greatest of evil nested.

"Firdun!" Ibycus did not look at him, but he was instantly alert at that call. He must remember—it was now that that which had been given must be used.

He spoke the first of those words in unity with the mage. Even as Ibycus drew patterns in the air with his ring finger, so did Firdun echo them. He felt drawn out of himself, melded into something larger, stronger than he had ever known—he who could not meld.

And the chant continued. There was a roiling within the darkness of the gate. That which Jakata had summoned was at hand. Though Firdun could not see it, the stench filled his nostrils, the first wave of black power washed around him. But he held and the words came. As he spoke them, they issued from his lips not as speech but as points of light, and those points formed patterns.

Again came the surge of evil. Before them Jakata swelled, grew. His arms were flung out and then drawn to his breast as if he embraced the blackness, drew it toward him to be one with him or he the symbol of it.

A length of black lashed out as Jakata pointed now at Ibycus. The mage swayed, but his voice continued, and Firdun's with it. More of the star-words gathered, and from one side came stabs of purple lightning such as Elysha had summoned before.

The giant which was now Jakata threw back his head and laughed. While behind him the dark beyond the gate thickened, split, thickened again, as if some force gathered there to be launched at the outer world.

Jakata was now framed in a half circling of tentacles which issued out of the dark. The words which were stars had clustered into a form like the head of a spear. Jakata moved. His leap did not carry him to Ibycus; instead his giant form faltered as he stumbled. The mage pointed with his ring.

The tottering figure of the Dark Mage was caught, light spear at his breast. And the force of that pushed him back. Those tentacles about him writhed, fastened on the other parts of the gateway as if they would help to lever outward that which lurked hungrily within.

Some of the star-words had fallen on impact with the Dark Mage, but now Ibycus was beginning the formula for the second time and Firdun, feeling weaker by the moment, followed.

Then—the lashlike arms snapped closed, about Jakata. And within their hold he shrank once more to human size, his handsome face convulsed with pain and terror. Back into the archway he was drawn. Now the star-words were no longer a spear point. Rather they were shaping in the form of such an armed hatch as might defend a hold. Bars thickened, crossed, melted together.

A mighty blast of evil in its final struggle shook them all. Firdun was on his knees now, holding desperately as he could to the task he had been set. Warder he was—and this was the great warding.

He could see Ibycus weaving back and forth, keeping his feet only by his hold on the staff. Then from the mage's forefinger flashed a last and great starburst. It struck full center on that weaving of the light. There was a sound which sent them deaf. They all fell to the ground.

There was complete silence, Kethan, lying face down where that last great blast had thrown him, heard only his own breath coming raggedly. He made a great effort and forced his head around.

The gate . . . there was no gate, no arch, no city risen out of the past! Even the black lump which had stood there and which they had seen from afar was flattened—gone. Washing up about where it had been was a lacing of white wave. The clean smell of the sea came to clear the air and out of the sky wheeled birds, white of wing, swooping and soaring as if they played some game.

Between Kethan and that world's end lay the others. He had not been the first to stir. Aylinn was drawing herself inch by inch toward the two who lay so close together—Ibycus, his head half hidden by his crooked arm, and Elysha, whose hand rested on him as if she had made a final effort to aid.

There was Firdun also, his hands planted on the ground, visibly straining to raise his body. And beyond him another. Another . . .

Was Kethan caught once more in one of those dream visions?

No, the city was gone, the gate was gone, what remained now was only the truth. On his hands and knees Kethan pushed toward those who had defeated and survived—or had they?

Aylinn was on her knees now, pulling at Ibycus, striving to roll over his limp body. Elysha raised her head, struggled upward to aid the girl.

But for this moment there was another calling Kethan, calling him with something deeper than magic which could be learned, something which was bred into him and was now aroused.

He dared not try to rise higher than hands and knees, and, with each pull forward, his lungs labored and his head shook as he doggedly fought the terrible weakness of his body. He was dimly aware that Firdun was stirring now, but his attention was all for that other.

She lay curled as if she slept. Her face was toward him and she was all he remembered from that night vision—save that now on her forehead above and between her closed eyes was a point of light, star bright.

Kethan pulled himself along with a fierce need to know. Had life itself been drawn from her? He collapsed at last beside her body and put out a hand which shook to touch her cheek. His lady of fur, his lady of—

Her eyes opened slowly and at first it was as if she did not understand what she saw. Her hand moved slowly over the soft black suit as if hunting for something gone.

"Uta!" He had cupped his own hand under her head, drew it to rest against his shoulder. "Uta!" And he knew that that was the name she bore.

There was surprise on her face, and then a surge of light like happiness.

"It is served—my time of exile. . . ." Her voice was hardly above the softest of murmurs, but he heard it easily. Now she looked straight at Kethan. "No, great warrior, I am not of the kin—no were. But shapechanging was set upon me long ago. How . . ." Her hand went to her forehead, where that spark gleamed ever brighter. "The promise is fulfilled at last."

Tears gathered in her eyes and spilled onto her cheeks. "Yes, it was promised, but so long . . . so long . . ."

"The past is gone." Kethan drew her even closer. He wanted this treasure he had found to be a second part of him. Now his lips touched the salt of the tears on her cheeks. Then found her own lips waiting for him. What did the past matter for either of them now?

"Uta." He wanted to sing her name, but he had no bard's voice. Her arms were about him now, her lips as eager as his. They were lost in that magic which had nothing to do with sorcery until a cry startled them.

Aylinn held her flower staff across Ibycus's body. The mage's eyes were open. He looked at her, then to Firdun on his knees by him, and, lastly, up to her who cradled his head.

Somehow Kethan gained his feet and drew Uta up beside him. Together they stumbled toward the others. Ibycus's eyes steadied now upon them.

"Well done, huntress and far wanderer. Serving the Light has broken the burden you have carried so long." His voice was the faintest trace of sound. "Neatly did you trip that Dark one."

"Lord . . ." Uta dropped from Kethan's hold once more to her knees. "The time of exile—"

The mage smiled. "Is past. You bear your pardon and will hold it all your days. Also you have chosen and are chosen, and that is as it should be." Now his gaze passed to Aylinn. "Do not fret yourself, Moon Daughter. To every living thing there comes an ending. For every Power there is a price. Payment is now demanded of me."

"Be not so sure!" they heard Elysha say. "You have always been so quick, so sure, dear lord, of the needs of duty, of everything but that which lies deep-buried within you. It is time for the seed to open, and let the plant grow and flower."

Swiftly, before he could protest, she shifted his head and shoulders to Aylinn's hold. Then she walked some space away as they watched her wonderingly.

Up went her arms and around each wrist blazed fierce purple

fire. "I summon—let me be answered!" she cried—demanding, not pleading.

They saw it take form in the air even as had the vanished city, but far brighter, like a rainbow, glittering with scattered bursts of colors. Steadily it grew more visible as it descended, more solid, until, as it met the ground, Firdun felt a tremor, heard sound.

Then Elysha beckoned to them. "Bring my lord."

Kethan and Firdun between them took him up. His weight seemed no more than a fraction, like that of a child, his body shrunken, his face shadowed as if age were fast creeping upon him. They carried him as easily as they could and Elysha pointed to a place within the palace's wide-open gate. She stood there as if for anchorage until they left him, and then returned running.

"Glamorie, then, dear heart?" he asked.

She laughed. "To each his own. It has always served me well."

He had held to his staff during their transport. Now he lifted his other hand to keep them where they were and they saw that the ring stone was cracked, shifting away in ash like bits.

"Firdun"—there was more strength in the mage's voice now—"well have you served and even better will you serve. He who is a warder passes ward to the proper one when his time has come. Take you this."

He held out the staff. Firdun wanted nothing so much as to refuse. But there was that in him now which made him accept it.

"Gryphon's get," Ibycus continued. "You are not less than your kin, only called to walk another path. And I hold no doubt that you will tread it well. Now my time is past and I think my lady grows impatient." He smiled at Elysha, who now took his head up against her shoulder once more. "Return you to the Eyrie, that your story will be known there and at Lormt. There still lie pools of the Dark, but if the gates are closed as they will be, there will be nothing to feed them from afar. May the grace of the Power watch over you."

His eyes closed and he sank deeper into Elysha's hold as the castle arose from the black sand. It was bright enough to make them close their eyes and when they opened them again it was gone.

Aylinn rubbed her hand across tear-wet cheeks. Firdun stood with the staff in both hands now. There was a grim, shut look about him as if he was no longer one of them but faced a duty which was drawing all light and laughter out of his life forever. Aylinn studied him for a long moment, then she came to him, holding out her moon wand so that it matched in straight uprightness the staff. The flower was fully open, though they stood in the light of late afternoon.

"No path must be walked alone," she said. And the light in the flower appeared to pulse as she spoke. "There are many different ways of warding and watching, Firdun. Shut no doors until you are sure."

Frowning, he looked at her, his lower lip caught between his teeth. His shoulders had slumped as if the staff had become a burden to pull him down.

"Ibycus rode alone."

"Ibycus was one man; you are another. Make your own choices, Firdun. Do not accept past ones as duties which must be followed. Look you."

She held her moon wand closer until one of the outstretched petals of the flower touched the staff only a finger's-breadth away from his own hold.

It was as if some of the stars which had been words sprung to life again, running along the length of the age-darkened shaft. Firdun gave a small broken cry.

"Aylinn!" Just as her wand had come to him freely, so did she now.

"With you—with you I can."

"Of course you can," she answered triumphantly. "Ibycus knew it or he would not have passed his Power to you. You will come to be even as he was—the hope of many, a sure shield against the Dark."

"Lord . . ."

They turned their heads.

It was Hardin and Guret with Lero, standing together. And Hardin pointed to the lace of waves. Those caught together in new understanding, felt the wash of water now about their feet, splashing upward.

"The sea comes."

Kethan laughed. "A time for all felines to withdraw! And we have a long road before us."

"Let it be so," Firdun said. It seemed to the others that there was a new note in his voice. Almost, Aylinn thought fleetingly, that if she closed her eyes she might have believed that had been spoken by Ibycus himself. A long road, but not alone—no, never alone.

And, as they drew back, the sea washed up over where the gate had been.

## Interlude: Es Port, Es City, Estcarp

It was a fair enough day, and the sea wind which poked intrusively into the tower lookout was fresh rather than chilling. But the Lady Loyse drew her double woolen scarf more tightly around her shoulders, even though she was well aware that the chill she felt lay within her and was not an assault from without.

She tried not to count the days she had stood here, looking out over the great harbor, past the evil black blot that was Gorm, the cursed. There were ships aplenty. It was a good summer for traders, and the Sulcars were making the best of brisk winds and stormless seas. She could count five ships at anchor now—but not the one which meant the most.

The sea she knew—the worst of it. Verlaine, where she had been born, had been one of the old menaces. They had not been pirates, those of that hold—but equally as evil, for they had thrived on wrecks, and nature aided them in the worst storms by driving ships full on the fang teeth which lay beneath the water not far offshore. Verlaine could not have been the only one of its kind. What wrecker lords ruled in the north, in Alizon, overseas in the lands unknown?

There were there pirates also. However, a nest of them had been efficiently cleaned out near Seakeep in the northernmost Dales.

The Dark was abroad and where it might manifest itself next, or in what fashion, who could say? They had some communication with the Eyrie in Arvon, but that was far from the coast and those laboring there knew nothing of the perils of the sea.

"What spell would you set upon the waters, dear heart?"

Though he wore heavy boots with his half armor, he had not made enough sound to distract her from her concentration, so she was startled as he moved up beside her, his strong arm, well muscled from axe-swinging, closing about her waist. She turned her head and looked directly into his eyes.

Koris, now Defender and War Marshal, virtual ruler of Estcarp, was no taller than she, but she had seen him deal so well in battle that no foe dared come at last to face his wide-shouldered frame.

Loyse forced a laugh. "I am like a green maid waiting for . . ." She hesitated and was lost, but she would not let him see tears—never that.

"You are a very great lady"—he was speaking directly against her cheek now, his breath warm—"and you have a son gone from your hearth."

"News?" she asked that, even though she knew that if there had been and, he would have told her at once.

"The *Tall Sails* is in from Seakeep. Their master took barge before they came to direct anchorage. He has only rumors and some knowledge—that the bergs are unusually numerous and faring farther south this season.

"Also"—and now he had drawn a little away from her—"Vixen has asked for a meeting." Lightness was gone from both his voice and his face. Loyse pursed her mouth as if he had offered her something sour to taste.

"Let us go, then." She turned toward the winding stair. "Koris, you dealt so many years with those of Vixen's kind. How did you keep your tongue ever civil? I had thought that the new gathering of witches were of a more calm and peaceful nature—until she was wished upon us for our contact."

"Dear heart, Vixen is as nothing to some of the High Ones in the old days. They armored me well. Nor is she like her sisters now—except there may be one or two lingering on. But the strongest died or were burned out with the Turning and the new ones are more tolerant of us."

They came down to the barge which would take them upriver to the city, and the rowers set their oars to a sharpened drumbeat which not only kept their swing of arms to a rapid pull but warned any craft ahead of them to give right of way.

Loyse did not settle back into the cushions at the stern but sat bolt upright. Could there have been news from one of the gate-seeking parties which was important enough to force Vixen to call them? Had there come some discovery from Lormt? She had a small regretful thought at how little Lormt had yet aided them. The Sulcar records uncovered there were all of a later date when the sea people had made strong contact with Estcarp and the Dales. So little as a guide—a legend! But then, legends sometimes yielded up their cores of truth. At least Estcarp and Escore were cleansed of any of the unfortunate and threatening openings into other times and places. And they had been well able to follow the southern seekers.

With Arvon . . . who knew unless Hilarion had once more opened his spellway with the Gryphon's stock?

"They have only a limited season." She spoke one of her fears aloud. "These in the south, in Arvon, need not fear an early winter."

"True." Koris did not try to belittle her word-concealed fear. "But Captain Stymir has traded north and gone farther than any of his people for generations. He knows well what is to be feared."

She knew that as well as he, and she was ashamed to be so on edge. Their son Simond was battle-tested. And he had Trusla by his side. No one yet knew just what powers she had—she refused to be tested by the witches—but that she possessed such was very visible to anyone also talented.

At least Vixen had not been foisted on Simond and Trusla. Frost, their selected witch, was of the new blood: very well trained and yet amiable with those outside her own small calling.

Ancient Es loomed over them and then the citadel engulfed them. Loyse, though Verlaine had been old and had much of a dark history, had never felt at ease in these halls. All was too old—seeming to reach back before people were people and other presences dwelt here.

Koris kept his office in the lower room of one tower and it was there that the most private business was conducted. They had no sooner entered than Vixen was upon them. Loyse resented bitterly—for Koris's sake—that this witch, chosen to be their contact with her kind and Lormt, loomed well above both of them. Nor was she beanpole-thin as might have seemed in keeping with their austerity, but as broad-shouldered and hulking as a man at arms.

As usual all her face except for her eyes was impassive. Those two points of light half hidden by the puff of her cheeks were never pleasant to face. Loyse had her share of highborn pride and she had nothing to be ashamed of in her past, yet when Vixen cast one of her cutting glances in her direction she felt as if she were still back under her father's cruel rule.

Koris had seated his lady with all the formal courtesy of the court (that, too, was a small reminder of his rule here) and had waved Vixen to a seat across the small table piled high with maps and reports.

"You have news, Lady?" He came directly to the point.

"Of a kind." Her thick tongue swept across her lips as if she savored what she had to say. Which meant, Loyse knew, it was trouble. "Our watch sister near Korinth has sent a warning."

"Korinth." Koris was already reaching for a map. "Yes, the secondary new settlement of the Sulcar, north of the Alizon Border."

Loyse wanted to smile but kept any signs of levity under strict control. Did Vixen think that she could for a moment know more of his duties than Koris?

If she was irritated by the fact that a meant barb had not gone home, the witch did not show it.

"They have given refuse to strangers," she continued. "People not of their kind, nor Alizonderns, nor of the Old Race. These are fleeing from the north and their shaman"—she used the word with a tone of disgust—"babbles of trouble building. They dream, do these strangers, and take a nightmare born of lack of food—or too much of it—for some revelation from the Great Power."

Koris's attention seemed fully for the map. "If the winds continued fair, the *Wave Cleaver* should be at anchorage there. Stymir has kin in Korinth and so access to the latest rumors out of the Great Cold. Their wisewoman accepts these refugees as such in truth?"

Vixen gave a curt nod. Loyse thought it was plain she would like to express an opposite opinion.

"Well enough. With the storm of the Magestone's passing, raw power doubtless passed around the world. Who knows what balance it may have upset in these lands we know nothing of?"

Loyse's fingers tightened in a hard clasp where her hands lay on her lap.

"What is the news from Lormt?" Koris asked with the same tone in which he would have required a report from one of his menie.

"They dig and they delve, and that adept urges them on. But as yet he has no answers and he has no touch with Arvon."

"And it is southward these refugees flee." Koris was busy with the map again. "Of your favor, Lady, call upon this outland sister of yours and ask for all she can tell us—even to the smallest detail. It may even be necessary for her to leave her post and go to Korinth to learn all we should know."

Now there was a shadow of expression on Vixen's face—a none too pleasant one. "The sisters are assigned by the Council in the Place of Wisdom. Only those selected to protect these expeditions move about."

"I do not think that the council will refuse any request which has a bearing on the safety of this world," Koris returned. "Now—what news has come from the Lady Frost?"

"None, save that which was beamed last night. The captain comments on the unusual number of icebergs. Frost is to speak with the shaman in Korinth today."

"Then"—Koris leaned back a little in his chair—"we should have a good reporting, so your watcher will not have to fare north from her post to give us one."

Loyse saw how hard Vixen's hands were gripping her jewel. There was not always a smooth joining of the generations of witches. And those chosen to go with the searchers were of the younger. Luckily Frost had impressed all of those at the choosing with her quiet strength and goodwill.

Vixen arose with a swirl of her gray robe. "What is sent you will have in good time, Lord Marshal." Without any further adieu she strode out of the room.

"Trouble in the north." Loyse allowed herself enough relaxation to repeat that. "My heart, when have we not faced trouble in one quarter of the world or another?" A weariness had settled on Koris.

"True. But it is easier to fight in person than to wait on this shuttling back and forth of news!"

Now he reached out and put his hand on that map, and impulsively she laid hers on it.

"He is of your blood and mine, Loyse. And neither of us ever accepted defeat, nor were we disappointed by having it forced upon us. He is also man grown. He has taken a mate of his choice—one we can respect. And the jewel selected the two of them. It is always the harder for the watcher than the doer. I send to Simon tonight—he prowls the north Border, since we still are not sure what boils in Alizon. Though it seems by rumor that that young lordling Lady Mereth tamed is very busy. If his actions can keep his countrymen within their own Borders, baying for each other's throats, he serves us well. Loyse"—his grip on her hand was tight now—"it seems our destiny to be ever on the alert. I think that peace is not to be our portion, so let us bear that as we can. This much have I gained from war—my dear lady, without whom my life would be a barren thing."

"As I have gained you, my dearest of lords. In the end good comes out of evil—or else of what value is life itself? I made my choice long ago," Loyse said slowly. "Never have I regretted it. Now I shall teach myself not to regret that Simond has made his also—or else it has been made for him—as perhaps it was for me. We have been blessed, my heart."

"As we shall be again." Koris took her into his arms and they were one—as it had been for so long and would continue always to be.

## CHAPTER THIRTY-ONE

# Korinth, North of Alizon

So new . . . Trusla moved closer to Simond. The canal which ran through the center of this town was not strange to one who had been born and raised in Tor Marsh, where all clan houses existed on islands divided by bogs and channels. But there she had always been aware of a feeling of kin-age—of timelessness where things remained always the same from season to season.

And when Simond had taken her to Es City, that was a place of awesome age—as was even the keep where they had later made their home together.

Here were no stone walls—only barked log houses, many of them still roofless, all the center of activity. The mud from the last rain was thick enough between these crude shelters to be ankle deep if one were forced off one of the planked walks. Always one could hear the pound of hammers, the shouts of those raising beams, warnings to get out of the way of this or that train of burden bearers.

The ship from which they had embarked only a short time since had come heavily laden with supplies to keep those hammers busy. And after Sulcar custom the women were busy as the men, poling laden craft along the canal, even steadying materials for the builders and wielding axes themselves.

Trusla had never before heard of creating a whole new town, but there were many things in this strange world outside Tor Marsh of which she had been unaware.

"Ware!"

Simond's arms about her waist swung her back, with himself, to avoid a team of sweating men linked together by a log slung in a series of rope loops.

All those so busy around her were so very big. They towered above her, even above Simond, who partly shared her Tor blood. She had found it difficult to adjust to life on board the ship, not that she allowed anyone to guess that.

"In here." Simond was now urging her along one of the muddy plank walks toward a large house which looked finished, even though the scent of freshly cut wood met them at the wide-open door. As they entered, Trusla hoped they were not breaking any custom.

"Ha, welcome. Come in, come in! Bertel, the guesting horns for our friends!"

To Trusla's ears that came as a roar. She had to bend her head well back to see the grinning face of her host. Even among his own kind Mangus Shieldarm was reckoned tall.

She found herself installed in a chair which was certainly older than the walls about her, its hide-cushioned seat well worn, and her feet did not quite touch the floor over which were scattered rugs of fur as well as the woven kind she was used to.

A tall girl with long blond braids was at her side before she was securely seated, a drinking horn in one hand and the guesting plate of bread and salt in the other. Trusla accepted the horn and a piece of the bread dipped in salt and spoke in as easy a voice as she could summon.

"Fair fortune to this house and all who shelter here. May your hunters be skilled, your crops ripen well, and your ships return safely to port."

She did not dare glance at Simond to see if she had learned that correctly from his coaching. The girl was handing another horn and the bread dish to him now.

"And may your voyage, my Lady, my Lord, be easy and your search trail open and free." Mangus drank deeply from the horn he himself held.

"Now . . ." He waved and Bertel disappeared. "There is news! All-Knowing One"—he raised his voice to a near shout again—"they have arrived and wait."

A curtain woven in strange and colorful patterns was swept to one side at his hail and a woman entered, a little ahead of her companions. Perhaps she had once stood nearly as tall as Mangus, but now she walked slowly, her back rounded so she had to peer up to see them. Most of her thin white hair was covered with a blue-green hood—the color of the sea at its calmest—and a large part of her body was concealed by a cloak matching it.

A step or so behind her was another woman, much younger, wearing the usual jerkin, shirt, and breeches of the Sulcars but with a scarf of the green-blue crossing from right shoulder to left hip. She carried (as if it were something most precious) a small drum, a hint of great age about its scuffed surface.

Just behind these two came Frost, the witch out of Estcarp assigned to their mission. She was young and though Trusla had been wary of her at first (the witches of Estcarp having had an awesome reputation in the past), Trusla had come to like listening to her explanations of things strange to the Tor girl.

The fourth and last of the party was strange enough to center all their attention once they sighted her. Beside the somber gray robe of the witch she was a blaze of color. Trusla could not guess her age or even her race—she was certainly not Sulcar, nor like any of Estcarp.

From her shoulders drooped a cape of feathers which she did not wear closely held as did the old woman. They were brilliantly black and white, set in patterns, and the cloak was loose enough to show that under it she wore a thigh-length garment of shining white fur, sleek and edged at the throat with fluffy down. Her feet and legs were covered with boots up to the thigh, seeming to offer the advantage of both shoes and trousers. As far up as her knees these were closely bound to the leg with narrow ribbonlike strings on which were strung large beads in a multitude of brilliant crystallike colors.

Her black hair was looped up and clubbed at the nape of her neck with more of the beaded strings. Against the white of the jerkin her skin looked dark and her eyes had a curious upward slant at the corners. She walked as one with authority, but what Trusla noted, with an odd feeling of kinship, was that she, too, was short, towered over by both Frost and the Sulcars.

"Here be those out of Estcarp, All-Knowing One." Mangus himself placed a chair for the oldest woman, and her attendant took her place behind her, while Mangus seated Frost and the stranger.

"This is the Lady Trusla out of Tor," Mangus was continuing, "and Lord Simond, son to Marshal Koris."

The woman in green favored each of them with a measuring stare, which Trusla met firmly. Of old she had dealings with priestesses and gave formal honor to their calling, whether they would be friends or not.

"The Lady is known to you all." The witch inclined her head in a short nod. "And this is the Winged One of the Latts." Trusla thought he looked a little uncertainly toward the woman in fur and feathers.

She did not nod, but she eyed Trusla and Simond and then smiled, remaining silent.

"Your mission is well known," Mangus began, reaching for his drinking horn as if to sustain himself, and then pushing it away. "All we know about the sea lanes to the north, and the legends thereof, has already been given you.

"As you know, we are establishing Korinth as a meeting port for our ships in the north trade. A moon ago we became hosts for others. Winged One, these have been sent by the Great Powers of the south to deal with what may be the very root of your own trouble. Let them hear what has befallen your people."

There was a long pause. She might either have been assembling her words or still be weighing the purposes of those about to hear them, but at last she spoke, using the trade language, but so accented Trusla and Simond had to listen very carefully and could not be sure they always understood. There had been no attempt at mind-send and it was not for them to initiate it.

"We live . . . north." She made a small sweeping gesture with one hand. "Hunt—the wasbear fears our spears and arrows as do the shadow hounds and the furred mountains."

There was pride in her voice and when she spoke of the bears she had stroked the fur of her jerkin.

"Always there is fear." She was picking her words slowly. "But most fears we have always lived with and they are a part of us— they are like the great snows, the bitter winters—our life. Now comes something else."

She stirred in her seat, edging forward on the cushion which was nearly too wide for her. "All peoples have their powers. You of Estcarp"—she nodded to Frost—"can summon that which is greater than any living being. You"—now she spoke to the woman in green—"can drum up or lay a storm, speak over great distances, doubtless do other things to make one marvel.

"We Latts . . . dream." She seemed a little uncomfortable, as if she doubted their belief. "Dreams find us game to be hunted, those who have lost their trail, foretell the worst of the storms. They can tell us how to heal the sick, the wounded, how to deal with others—others save the Dark!" Now her voice rose sharply and Trusla saw Simond tense, even as she was doing.

"This Dark is not known to us before, nor have we any kin song about it save one—and that allies an ancient evil with the north. By this legend we know that we have been driven once before— southward.

"Now it whispers in our dreams, it taints the flow of truth—our hunters are sent on the wrong trails. There have been deaths which should not have come. So we gather what we have and we come south, hoping to reach beyond the hand of the Dark. This land is fairer, but it is not ours. Also if the dream goes deep, as it should for the Power to rise, the shadow lurks and we must withdraw."

"You feel such interference even now?" Frost was fingering her jewel.

"Twice. I do not enter the deep dream, for I have not the Power to hold walls when my need is only to seek."

"Perhaps we may have an aid for that," the witch said crisply. "But that this thing stirs in the north, of that you are sure?"

The woman of the Latts was frowning a little. "Are you sure when your crystal clouds against your will, Woman of Power? All which is of the Light is aware when the Dark prowls. This began when there was a great beating of the Wide Wings—such as none have known before. A storm it was, and yet it was not. For the thing which struck upon us we have no words. And it was as if that summoned the Dark—which was eager to come.

"These good traders who had known our people for many seasons tell us to settle near—that together we shall fight evil. We are strong, we are ready. Yet how does one fight when one knows not the nature of the enemy? Now you from the south come and say that the Dark is moving upon our whole world and that you hunt the source to deal with it. You know not even the touch of the Great Cold. Even the strongest of our hunters do not venture into the ice palaces. Though there are those among us who have seen them from afar.

"The Dark can use the land itself to bring you death."

"Yet still shall we search," Simond's voice came clearly. "Not only do some of us deal with Power, but there are those behind us who can work through us. This world has faced an ending drawn by Power before—and the Dark went down to defeat. If we die, it shall be still fighting."

She measured him eye to eye. "Boasting I know—it is the way of hunters. But you are not boasting, young chieftain. What you say you truly believe. Well enough—if you would carry war to the enemy, go with the best of dreams."

"Do more than dream for us." Trusla sat straighter. "You say your hunters know of the lands beyond. Can ships go there?"

Mangus was already shaking his head when the woman answered. "Not so, for the ice ever covered the sea. A ship seeking a hunting trail there would be crushed by the great mountains of floating ice."

"Then if we must take to land"—Simond again took a part as if he knew what was in Trusla's mind—"we shall need guides. Can we find such among your people?"

There had been no formality in his request, it was a straight question and she answered it as straightly. "It shall be put before our Speaking Fire. It will be by choice if any such go."

He nodded. "As it should be."

Frost fingered her jewel. "Messages have come from the south. I have told our sister"—she bowed her head slightly toward the Latt woman—"of Lormt and what we hope to find there. There is much to be shifted and considered, tested. Hilarion is the last of the adepts and his chosen knowledge was along a special path, but now he has turned to that which did not interest him before. He has managed to contact those of the Gryphon in Arvon with a warning—and they, too, report trouble already on the march there. Their party ventures westward into lands unknown. However, our tie with them was broken and we know not how matters go now with them."

There was a small sound from Mangus as if he cleared his throat. He had set down his horn on a small side table and now produced a roll of map parchment.

"We are seafarers, as all know, though the records of Lormt have little for us. This"—he was unrolling the square he held—"is a combination of reports from those captains who in the past have ventured north to the farthest extent—which can only be done at the height of the warm season. Added . . ." he hesitated and glanced at the woman in green, "is what is remembered from very ancient times. We have only this that we are sure of: that our people are not of this world—a condition we share with other races here—and that we entered on board ships through a far northern gate.

"Since it may be that any gateway may be a danger, now it would seem we must return to our beginnings—if we can—and there see how it fares."

"The moon hangs full tonight." The woman in green reached out her hand and her attendant held up the small drum so that she could tap lightly on it with her fingers.

The sound might be slight, but Simond's hand went to sword hilt, and Trusla caught breath in a small gasp. For it seemed that tapping somehow echoed oddly through their bodies.

"The drum will speak." The woman withdrew her hand. Then Trusla blinked, seeing the witch jewel on Frost's breast gleam with life for only an instant, while the shaman of the Latts held out both brown hands and drew patterns in the air.

"Old bones need rest." The woman in green hauled herself up from her chair. "Do you," she said, turning her full attention now on Trusla and Simond, "answer when the drum calls. What the sea accepts will be made plain."

She shuffled off with her attendant, with no more of a farewell. But it seemed that neither Frost nor the woman of the Latts was prepared to break up their conference.

It was the witch who spoke first. "Those who have come from the south, sister, have been selected by the Power. The star light has touched Captain Stymir, and these two out of Estcarp. If any of your blood wish to try our trail, will they agree to such testing?"

Toward woman of the Latts she held out her hand and on its palm lay her jewel, dull gray and seeming without life. But, perhaps even to her own amazement, as she turned slightly toward the stranger, it broke forth with light as rainbowed as the strings of beads which made up part of the other's clothing.

The slanted eyes narrowed. "I serve my people," she said slowly. "It is laid upon me and my kind. Why does this Power thing of yours call *me*?"

"I cannot tell," Frost returned, "save it is not mine to command in this matter any more than it was when we stood in the great hall of Es Citadel and it chose from all the company there. Power calls to Power, and there is always the greater purpose."

The woman's hand twitched as if she would raise them to ward off some unwelcome thing. She raised her head higher and her lips pointed now, not toward the others, but to the fresh-set beams above them. From those lips poured sounds, as body-filling in their way as the tapping of the drum had been. Trusla saw not the room about her, but a stretch of sand, and the sand moved, arose, became—and then was not, though the single instant of sight had left a residue of new energy within her.

What Simond felt, she did not know; Mangus seemed only puzzled. But the witch jewel in Frost's hold flashed again.

There had been a question asked, that much Trusla was as certain of as if she had heard the words. Now there was silence.

But only for a breath or two. Then from nowhere she could discern, came an ear-torturing roar such as might burst from the jaws of some beast mightier than they had ever seen.

The shaman seemed to huddle down into her chair, draw in upon herself. Yet she showed no sign of fear, only of one facing a burden which must be carried with care.

There followed a clatter of someone entering the room, armed and ready, an axe in hand as if some attack had already begun. Like the shaman, he was dressed in furred garments, but he wore no feathered cloak, instead three long black feathers pointed at an angle backward from a beaded band about his forehead and hair.

A thong of hide supported on his chest a rounded ball half black as the feathers, half gold. And the face he turned toward the southerners was grim as he bowed his head quickly to the shaman and asked something in his own tongue. He could not be much older than Simond, but he walked with the assurance of a well-tested armsman.

"It is well," the shaman spoke in the trade tongue. "This one is Odanki, of my own kin blood. He is a rover, one who has seen ice palaces."

He was staring suspiciously at all of them now. "What would you do, south people?" His trade speech was curt.

"Sister," the shaman spoke now to Frost, "try this one with your testing. We have no Speaking Fire, but already your Power and mine have melded enough that I will be bound by the Voice of Arska. Even as we have all heard, that Great One seems to wish to take part in this."

Frost's hand shifted to confront the Latt. Instantly the jewel flared to life.

The Latt stepped back, frowning, his upper lip lifting a little as some beast might threaten a snarl. But now the shaman slid off her too-high seat and came to him swiftly, laying a hand on his axe arm. She spoke with a solemn intonation like an oath, and he listened to her, his snarl fading, a look of wonderment on his face.

Then suddenly he dropped to one knee and, catching hold of the nearest edge of the other's feather cloak, raised it to his lips.

"Arska," continued the shaman, "has brought you one of our best. But now since I am also chosen for this searching I must speak with my people, assure them that Arska will raise up those to help them in time of danger."

She passed their circle of chairs, the hunter falling in behind her, and was out of the door and gone before any one of them could summon words.

"Lady"—Mangus broke the silence left by that swift exit—"this all who know them can tell you of the Latts: they are a proud people, rovers with no settled home. If they give their word, so it is kept. If they cannot for some reason keep it, then the next of kin will pick up their duty. Their hunters are fine fighting men and know much of their frozen world. Of the powers of their shaman . . ." he shrugged. "I am not talented; I cannot vouch for what they can do."

"She is a true sister," Frost answered, "her power runs deep and full, though it comes from another source. There is nothing of the Dark."

"But," Simond cut in, "did she not say that any guide who

would volunteer to go with us must do so of free will? Was this one not summoned?"

Frost smiled. "As you, Simond? We are but the tools of Greater Forces and a workman chooses his tools to suit the work which must be done. Also, I do not think the shaman chose this Odanki; I believe he was summoned by something greater than she. And by this"—she patted her once more dead gray pendant—"that was certainly proven.

"Now"—she looked to Mangus—"this map you and your knowable captains have put together—where will it lead us?"

"In truth, Lady, across the world as we know it. Look you."

They all crowded around the table from which he had lifted his drinking horn and looked down at the maze of lines, some drawn in sturdy black and some in less steady red.

"See—this far up coast . . ." he was running a thick forefinger along one of the black lines, "you can go without too much danger—though the icebergs are much larger in number this season. Here"—he stabbed down—"you will swing westward, clear to Arvon's land, though I do not think any of them have ever ventured to explore it.

"This is Dargh. Of that you keep clear. It is surely of the Dark and they say that men there eat their own kind in times when the waller fish do not run well. Beyond Dargh, on the continent itself, there is a Sulcar trading post. We call it End of the World—I cannot twist my tongue to give you its native name."

"There are natives there?" Simond asked.

"Yes, their land is free in places from the ever-steady ice because of hot springs. There is even feed for their load beasts. Horses, mind you"—he held out a hand about four feet from the floor—"no larger. And yet there are grodeer nearly as tall as this house and they say other strange beasts. I have seen great tusks of ivory once in a while which have come from End of the World and men tell strange tales of furred walking mountains. But then why should we laugh at such tales? For the farther a man travels, the more marvels he chances to see.

"You will learn what you can there. These Latts speak of ice palaces on this side of the ocean. Perhaps such lie farther north there also, for our legends speak of such."

"These red lines . . ." Simond pointed to the closest on the map, "what do they signify?"

"Tracks of ships which have never returned," Mangus answered shortly. "These northern seas hold as many traps as a land where the Dark abides. Yet the legends tie in with some of these voyages and so we record them."

He rolled the map up as if he did not want to think of some of those records, and handed the roll to Simond.

"Stymir still has provisions to load. Give this to him as I promised. He has made two trips north and knows well some of the dangers. In fact he fought off a raid of the Dargh man-eaters three seasons ago. And he added two new islands to our records—one of which had some strangeness about it that he would never talk about."

"A place of the Dark?" Trusla was only too aware of strange places and usually there was good reason for keeping away from them.

"Perhaps."

A workman was waiting impatiently at the open door and they guessed that Mangus had taken time from pressing duties for this meeting. Frost said that she wished to consult with the Sulcar wise-woman again, so once more Trusla and Simond were left to return alone to that newly constructed warehouse-to-be where the passengers and the crew of the *Wave Cleaver* were temporarily housed.

"Ice palaces," Trusla spoke. "Real palaces?"

"More likely just the edges of great glaciers," Simond returned. "Such at a distance might well seem to be as great as Es and perhaps wind-carved into towers and walls."

"These Latts . . ." she began again, Simond seeming very far away suddenly, as if he were caught up in some tight weaving of thoughts. "They have beautiful furs. And their shaman—she is not as strange and apart as some of the wisewomen even in the south."

"We shall certainly learn more," Simond agreed. "They will have us to Lormt when we return and shake out of us every bit of memory our minds hold—all to add to their store." He laughed. "Perhaps before we come to the end of this venture we shall be able to even astound Morfew himself."

*This venture*, Trusla thought. Yet the Latts said that some master thing of the Dark had driven them from their homelands. What kind of monster must they face, perhaps among those ice palaces?

## CHAPTER THIRTY-TWO

# *Korinth, the Northern Sea*

The constant sounds of activity had died away with the coming of sundown. But the growing town was still alive when Trusla went to the impromptu market down on the wharf. Another ship had made port at nooning and samples of its cargo were already being placed to catch the eye—and gather a crowd.

This had been a risky project on the part of the captain, for he had not carried building materials or needful supplies, but rather what those in the bare-wall town might consider at this point to be luxuries. There were fabrics which could make curtains and wall hangings, dishes both for display and daily use, even such things as spices and those dried flower petals which would fight the heavy scent of woodsmoke in the rooms.

To Trusla's surprise there were buyers enough gathering to bargain with those the captain had designated to be merchants for the day. And she saw change hands lengths of ivory tusks, and bundles of furs at a brisk pace, the buyer going away with this ornamentation for houses perhaps still roofless.

It was when she was shouldered aside by one of the brawny

women who wore a heavy hammer in her belt that Trusla stopped short, refusing to move again in spite of another shove.

What had drawn her eyes was an earthenware bottle. It was wide-mouthed and its cover had been removed to show its contents. How such an object had turned up in this cargo, and moreover, how the present owner had obtained it, she could not guess. Somehow she could not believe that the seller knew what she was offering, for it was a woman tending this trestle table. The contents of that jar were a door into the past—though to the eye the jar was filled with sand—red-gold sand—seemingly as fine ground as dust. Such sand she knew—such sand had changed her life and opened a door upon the world for her.

"Xactol!" she whispered. Did or did not that sand stir a little? Or was it only her wish that made it seem so? "Sand sister."

She jerked at a silver bangle on her thin wrist. It was all she could think of now for exchange. The woman looming over her had put down a full gold piece out of Estcarp for a length of dull blue and rust red weaving and a set of carven wooden bowls. Now the stall keeper was looking to her.

"Your jar." Trusla pointed so there would be no mistake.

The stall keeper picked it up, turning it this way and that. "Out of Estcarp—well fired, can be used at the hearthside if you wish. The sand . . ." She must have caught Trusla's glance; the girl feared spillage due to the other's quick movements. "That is nothing. The dealers there pack them so against breakage. Two silver twists, Lady."

She was studying Trusla closely now, seeming to have noted for the first time that Trusla was a stranger, not a townswoman.

"I give this." The fen girl held out her bangle. It was surely worth more than two twists of that silver wire which the traders used for small transactions. Then she thought that the woman was eyeing her almost with suspicion and she added hastily, "Such are made in my village." She was improvising. "I find it here to be a lucky matter."

Now the woman grinned. "Ah, don't we need all the luck we can draw to us, Lady? It is yours." But she was quick enough to drop the bracelet into her money pouch. "Here"—she reached down into a box beneath the table—"you need the rest of your luck, or what you hope to hold can run out with the first dip." She slapped down on the table a round of smoothed wood which was plainly meant to cork the jar and Trusla speedily put it into place.

Holding her prize tightly, she made her way through the crowd and back to the warehouse-inn. Simond was off with the captain and their map, but for the moment she was very glad she was alone.

Settling down on one of the two stools their small alcove held, she loosed the hide curtain and let it fall into place to give privacy. The jar she placed with care on the other stool, as she had no table. Her hand went to loosen that cover and then she let it fall instead to the top of the stool. For the moment she did not want to prove herself right or wrong, she just called on memory.

There had been a shelving floor of such sand under the moon and that sand had moved, given birth to one whom Trusla sometimes saw fleetingly in dreams and had always longed to see again. Xactol—sand sister—that one had named herself, and in Trusla she had awakened knowledge that there was indeed a need for one who was unlike her companions. Since then Trusla had made small experiments on her own—very carefully.

When she had returned with Simond, each saving the other from certain death, the witches had wished to test her, for being Tor and apart, they thirsted to know what powers or talents those of her race might have. But the witches were no longer all-powerful and already she had mated with Simond, thus destroying most of her value to them. But inside she was sure that her sand sister had awakened more than Trusla could understand.

She remembered one day when she and Simond had gone fishing (or he had fished and she had explored the small island they had chosen) and she had discovered a stretch of silver-gray sand. It had not held the same feeling for her, yet it drew her to it.

On its surface she had drawn—designs she had not remembered she knew, though she was a weaver. And the designs had sent her into a sort of dream in which she had done something which had great meaning. But when she had roused again at Simond's call, the sand was bare of any marking and of the dream she remembered only that feeling of accomplishment.

Now—if it were true that she held in this jar sand out of Tor, what might she do?

"Trusla!" Simond's voice drew her back into the here and now. She saw the curtain sway at his touch, but she knew he would not enter without her bidding. Swiftly she transferred the jar into her own pack. Why she must keep this secret she could not say—only that for now it was hers alone.

She swept aside the curtain and Simond stood smiling widely. He kissed her cheek and then threw himself on the bunk, his legs stretched out, one arm reaching for Trusla to draw her to his side.

"No more hammers, no more mud, no more sawing." He made a kind of chant out of it. "The *Wave Cleaver* is loaded and ship-shape, as the captain says. With the dawn we can be off again away from this mud pie and off to do what we are meant to do."

Trusla could understand his excitement and she was careful to try to equal it. But she feared she would never make a good sea rover. The cramped cabin was so small that this alcove seemed a lord's hall when she stole a look around. Luckily only yesterday she had washed and freshened with dried herbs almost all of the cloth-ing except what they now wore. And Simond had spent hours bur-nishing their mail coats and making sure their weapons were keen of edge.

His smile had faded a little and there was an anxious note in his voice as he continued, "There is this, heart holder. Because of the addition of the Latts to our party, our quarters will be changed. I shall have a hammock with this Odanki in the mate's quarters and the shaman will come with you."

She should have expected something like this. Frost, by reason of her rank, had a hastily constructed cubby off the captain's main cabin and the rest of them would have to make what room they could.

"The Latt woman seems one of goodwill." Simond had sat up

again now and was watching her. "Were it instead that wisewoman whom Mangus gives ear to now."

Trusla laughed. "Were it so, I think I should choose to walk— there is the shore and later maybe ice thick enough to bear one up. Yes, I think that the Latt will be a good cabin mate. Only . . ." Now she threw her arms around him tightly. "It will not be Simond to keep me warm at night!"

"My loss also, dear one. Now—let us see to the packing." But his return embrace and the hoarseness of his voice was a small comfort she could cherish.

Their sailing out of Korinth was certainly not a quiet and unnoted one. The green-robed drummer led a procession of women who whistled and moaned, and made sounds so close to enraged waves that Trusla could close her eyes and believe the sea already washed about them.

Not to be outdone by the invoking of Sulcar powers and good fortune, the Latt party was nearly as great. But here it was the men who chanted, waving spears and axes as if challenging to battle. Their chosen champion had added a sword to one of the packs he shouldered. From the second one fluttered feathers and Trusla guessed that that held the possessions of the shaman. Cuddled in the left arm of the woman was a small furry shape which moved, turning a round head constantly as if it would see everything as quickly as possible.

The Latts knelt and raised a keening cry—one which could touch even those not of their race. Then they deliberately arose and turned their backs, though still they stood in ordered ranks, as if they must not look upon the withdrawal of the shaman and her champion.

Nor did she turn her head to look at them, but marched steadily up the gangplank, Odanki a step or so behind, the creature still held in her arm. Trusla eyed that warily. Sharing a cabin with another woman was one thing, but that the shaman had brought a pet with her. . . .

However, they stood a little away from her as the ship cast off moorings and they began their journey to the open sea—luck cheers from those thronging the walk rising even above the cries of their wisewoman and her followers.

Trusla hesitated for a moment and then made her way to the shaman. "Wise One, our cabin lies this way."

Those dark, oblique eyes fastened on her and the woman nodded. Now that she was close enough, the girl could better see the creature in the wisewoman's arms. At first she thought it a child bundled so heavily in furs that only a section of its reddish face and two large eyes were visible.

Then the shaman set it carefully down. Though it stood on its hind feet, this was no child. It was entirely covered, except for the palms of its quite humanlike hands and face, with thick dark hair over which lay an outer sheen of silver as if every tip bore frost. With one of those hands it held tightly to the shaman's bead-twisted legging-boots; the other was at its mouth as it stared over its fists at Trusla.

"The little one?" she ventured. No child, nor pet—she had heard at Lormt and Estcarp of some workers of Power who augmented their strength by energies drawn from nonhuman beings. Was this one such?

The Latt woman was smiling, her hand dropping to the round furred head which she smoothed soothingly.

"This be Kankil, who has chosen my tent as her home. Such seldom trust our kind, but when they do, then those so chosen are greatly blessed. Yes, she serves in the Power."

Trusla had not been aware of any mind-reading touch, but perhaps this reading of her question had only been a guess on the other's part.

"Now." The Latt came forward a step or so and held out her other hand, Kankil coming with her. "The naming of names is given only among friends—do you also have that custom?"

"Some of us." Trusla nodded, her attention divided between the shaman and her small companion. "I am Trusla, as the Lord Mangus named me—my true name. So also is it with Simond, who is my dear lord."

"And in our tents I am Inquit. For between us there lies no shadow of the Dark. But you are not of these sea people, these Sulcars, blessed as they are for the helping hands they reached to us."

"No, I come from a southern land—Tor Marsh. And my lord also bears a portion of such blood, for he is son to Koris of Gorm, also of Tor Marsh breed and now Lord Marshal of Estcarp."

Kankil suddenly loosed her hold of Inquit's legging and skipped to Trusla. No one could see in this mite any danger. The girl dared greatly and smoothed the small head turned up toward her, feeling fur softer than spider silk beneath her fingers.

"It is well. Now we share tent." Inquit laughed. "Though I do not think it will be as large as those within my tribe's holding."

Trusla felt soft furred fingers steal into her hand and she grasped them gently, turning to lead the way to their cabin. She felt a queer touch of shame as if she regretted she had no better to offer. Some of Simond's gear was still piled in a corner, for they had no other place to put it and the interior was in Trusla's eye woefully crowded. Inquit's tribesman had dropped her pack by the door and she pulled it in while Kankil leaped out of the way onto the bunk.

"One always learns from journeying," Inquit observed. "The Sulcars live mainly on their ships—it is good that they are so large, for then their quarters can better serve such as we are."

Trusla had pulled open one of the cupboards below the bunk, and then indicated the pegs on the wall, on one of which already swung her fishskin storm coat. She must get another for Inquit also.

The Latt shaman was already busy with her pack and Trusla edged past her beyond the door to give her full room to arrange her belongings as best she could.

Already she herself felt a little unsteady at the rise and fall of the ship; they must be nearing where the canal gave upon the sea. She hoped she would not disgrace herself as she had the first three days of this voyage when her stomach had rebelled against her.

The boat rocked perilously and chunks of ice sometimes nudged against the sides. A skin boat, not even honest wood, and how long would it be before the sea had her?

Audha huddled in upon herself. Rogar had stopped moaning long ago in this piece of the Netherworld which had caught them fast. She hoped dully his torment was over now, as the end had come to Lothar Longsword and Tortain Staymir earlier. If she were a true battleman of Skilter's line, as she had always believed she was—false, false pride—she would rock this miserable excuse for a boat and bring an end to torment.

Sooner or later the sea would have them all, dead and alive, but some small core within her kept her from bringing it all to a quick finish. A Sulcar endured to the end, unless, like the great Osberic, he could die taking with him the enemy in force.

What she had seen in the past few days made her believe that the Light had indeed forsaken this world. Could icebergs sail with a direct purpose, herd a ship? She would have said that that was a story to frighten a boastful child. Yet—by the Ruler of Storms, this she had seen, had suffered with all others of the *Flying Crossbeak*.

They had been bound farther north than usual, Captain Harsson having had good trade the previous season with End of the World, that post which clung to the very edge of the unknown. She was a wavereader and this had been only her second voyage as such without a mistress waver to oversee her reports.

Audha bit down savagely on the ice-rusted edge of her frozen sea cloak. She would take blood oath before the very inner altar that she had not erred. Their voyage had been easy—in the beginning.

It seemed then the bergs had been spewed forth out of the night itself like harpoons of the flipper hunters. By morning's light there had been a shifting wall of giant drifting ice before them. One no prudent captain would dare to think of threading.

And it centered on *them*! By the Ruler of Storms—the stuff had centered. Though they changed course, so did the bergs. Men who had spent nearly all their lives in the northern trade had watched unbelievingly. And the waves—she had watched until her eyes had nearly frozen solid, but the patterns made no sense.

Instead, out of nowhere, had come a current, seeming to spread from the bergs to catch upon them. They fought to come about, to retreat before what they could not understand—using every trick of seamanship countless generations had passed along.

But always the ship had been driven westward, though they fought fiercely to gain the open sea they could sight in the east. There had been no wind; the frosted sails gave them no aid. At length the captain had ordered the longboat to be put over with rowers to see whether, as a last resort, they could break free of the path of the bergs.

Audha shuddered—her mind kept going back always over the past. If they had done this, or tried that . . . But there had been no real choice. For then, out of nowhere, had come the fog, and the boat was swallowed up by it. It almost seemed that they had a chance in spite of veering blindly.

Until . . . until—oh, Blessed Mother in the Deeps—they had heard those shrieks and cries, and moments later, before they could stand to arms, the demons had been upon them, clambering over the sides of the *Flying Crossbeak* in a filthy wave.

The fog had served those well, covering their attack from their small skin boats which crowded around the ship like maggots on a poor dying thing.

A shadow had loomed out of the fog to where she sat in the bow seat of the wavereader and a blow had sent her into darkness before she really knew what had come upon them.

She did not remember their coming to Dargh the accursed; they must have dragged her still-unconscious body. The screaming had aroused her to life—pleas and cries which sent her near to madness. Among them she was sure she detected Varga's voice—and young Kertha. . . . There were other screams and an insane howling and she had somehow managed to shut herself back into the darkness.

But her body would not let her spirit escape and she awoke again. As she tried to move, she found she was trussed like a swimmer intended for the market. It was very dim, but she could see enough to understand that she lay in a stinking hole and that she was not alone in her captivity. Someone was moaning in a monotonous cry, and she nearly gagged on the stench of blood, human waste, and general filth around her.

"Audha?"

Her own name had roused her further. She was at least able to turn her head and see a second prisoner almost within touching distance.

"Rogar?" she ventured. Rogar Farkerson was kin, her mother's cousin, and he had been one of her teachers in Sulcar lore over the years. She had been proud that he had spoken up for her when the captain was choosing a wavereader.

"You are wounded?" he asked quickly.

His question made her aware of her aching head. But she could not detect any other hurts.

"No." She refused the aching. "We—we are on Dargh?"

For a moment he did not answer and then when he spoke his voice was harsh.

"We are. That slime out of the fog took us! But—we have a chance, maybe—those left of us. Lothar is speared, but they do not know our stock, these demons. They believed him sore hurt and did not take care in his binding, being very eager for their—their feasting."

Audha swallowed convulsively. She forced from her mind the memory of those cries.

"Now they lie like drunk. Dargh needs fear no attack—the ice has closed in. We—we they are keeping for further sport and eating. Better we died cleanly in the sea. Lothar now works to free Tortain. For Hugin we can do nothing, he is near sped—may the Great Gate open for him soon. Now—can you move closer to me, girl? They use hide for their ties and hide can be chewed—and I, thank the Wind Ruler, still have a full set of teeth well used to tough chewing."

So they had won free, the four of them. Once he could crawl again, Rogar had made to the other side of that place and bent over a shape lying there. A moment or two later the moaning stopped.

"I think his kin will claim no blood debt," came Lothar's voice out of the shadows. "You have served a comrade well and we shall send a lantern a-voyage for him and the others."

Audha had been listening to any sound from outside. The walling about her seemed to be made of skins laced together, though under them, mostly hidden by refuse, was a pavement of stones. Also this cage appeared to be half sunken below the surface of the ground.

Roger and Tortain went to work on the hides on their upper walls. One could not possibly use teeth there, Audha thought, and nearly laughed hysterically, but it seemed they had found tools of a sort—cracked and sharp-edged bones. She moved up beside Lothar. Though she was no wisewoman healer, she knew something of wound tending, as did all the seafarers, among whom many skills had to be used.

She had not even light enough to see how badly he was hurt. At her questioning he admitted that a spear had cut him in the shoulder. She had no supplies, but she helped improvise a sling to give him what ease she could and he assured her that the wound had stopped bleeding and perhaps was hardly more than a graze.

The hide split at last. There was more light beyond, but they were facing away from it. Probably fires of some size still burned before the straggle of huts. Audha gagged again at the newest of foul odors—burned flesh.

Indeed their gruesome feast must have reacted on the demons like drink, for the prisoners could see nor hear no stirring at all. It might be that the raiders had so seldom such a large supply of food at hand that they had eaten themselves into a stupor.

The four worked their way out of that noisome prison and kept the firelight at their backs. Audha touched Lothar and whispered: "Wave wash."

With her ears as their guide now, they made a wide detour around the rest of the huts they could sight and came to a beach. Not only a beach, but a good choice of the skin boats drawn up out of the water's touch.

Even together they might not have been able to launch a ship's boat, but the skin one slid along and they gingerly took their places in it. Rogar stumbled on two paddles laid in safekeeping at the bottom and, armed with one of these, Tortain with the other, they had forced a passageway.

Once out from land, they could see better the fires on the shore—and worse. There was the *Flying Crossbeak*, crushed between a rocky cliff and a giant berg, smashed past all hope. Ice floated here also, but it was in smaller pieces and, though Audha feared for a space that it might follow the strange and uncanny action of the bergs and herd them back toward the hellish island, these seemed to follow no pattern.

So they had won free from Dargh, but to what purpose? Lothar's hurt showed in the morning to be much worse, and later he raved in delirium. Audha had held his head on her knee, but she had no water to give him when he called for it.

They had to stop paddling after a while, for their hands were blue with cold. So now they floated under the morning sun—but not back to Dargh.

There were no supplies on board. Oddly enough, Tortain, a bear of a man, was the first to fail. His heart, Audha thought, gnawed out of him. And then Lothar. Now it was another day, another night, another day since they had won free. Why did she live? She was sure Rogar was close to death. The sun that first morning had showed a fearsome bruise down his jaw and neck, though he had made no complaint.

Sulcar courage, Sulcar skill—all for nothing. She could watch the wave patterns now and they were drifting southward away from that monstrous trap of the bergs. But why, her mind worried dimly with the idea, had those bergs seemed to act with purpose against their ship? She knew of no power strong enough to command the flow of ice.

# CHAPTER THIRTY-THREE

# The North Sea

Drums were beating somewhere and it was icy cold. There was death in that cold. Trusla opened her eyes. Dream—no, someone was pounding on the door of their cabin. Inquit was already astir in the dark and she felt Kankil against her, whimpering.

There was lantern light outside as the Latt shaman slid open the door. And people in the passageway. Berg—somehow that struck into Trusla's mind—one of the bergs about which they told such legends must threaten the *Wave Cleaver* now.

She struggled into her clothing, an act which should have been easy after all the weeks she had practiced it. Inquit was back pulling on her own furred gear. The Latt shaman was muttering to herself what sounded to Trusla like some kind of an invocation, and she hesitated to break into that with a question.

But she was behind the shaman, Kankil having made a leap from the bunk to hold to her mistress; when they went out.

It was Captain Stymir and with him the old seamaster Joul, no longer a ship's ruler but given all respect and welcome aboard any ship he chose to honor with his presence because of his vast lore of knowledge.

"She—she is like one mindless!" The captain broke into speech as soon as he again sighted the shaman. "If you have the healing touch, wisewoman, do you aid her. Two voyages has she made under my flag and a better wavereader no ship could wish for. Now—in the night she runs screaming across the deck and would have thrown herself overboard had Hansa not caught her. He still holds her fast, she fighting and screaming."

Indeed Trusla could now hear the shrill cries of a woman who might be utterly demented.

"I have some healer's knowledge, yes, Captain. But it is for the hurts such as my people suffer. There are wounds of the mind and spirit which require greater knowledge than mine. Have up the witch; her kind is said to be able to face demons and deal them death."

"She has been called. Hansa has taken our Undia into the great cabin. But it took all his strength and he is a powerful man, whereas she is but a maid."

The screams came hoarsely now, if louder, as they found their way to the great cabin. It seemed to Trusla that the chill she had felt upon awakening was also growing stronger.

They had lit a number of lanterns so that there was light enough to see the girl struggling madly in the hold of the Sulcar seaman who towered above her. His face was streaming blood from the raking of her nails, and spatters of foam flew from the corners of her mouth every time she voiced one of those screeches.

Undia had always seemed a shy and retiring person. And Trusla had learned enough since the voyage started to know that she had her own Power talent—one esteemed and carefully fostered when discovered. For some reason it was possessed mainly by females and those of certain kin lines so that each girl child was carefully watched from infanthood for any signs of such gifts. Wavereaders they were called, and it appeared that some unknown sense allowed them to gauge currents, to find guide paths through the sea. As with the witches, they kept apart except for their own kind, and Trusla had often wondered if they were not lonely; a ship at the most carried two, one being an apprentice. But only Undia had sailed with them and Trusla would have sworn that she was as levelheaded and free from any demon possession as Inquit or Frost. Yet her mad struggles now were certainly born of the Dark.

Frost stood within touching distance, though those struggling bodies did not touch her. On her breast the jewel was alive—with a shade of green light which had something forbidding about it. Trusla herself suddenly saw a frightening change in the fighting girl. The signs of fear-born rage were gone—her face smoothed, and for an instant out of time it was not Undia who now slumped slackly against Hansa, but another girl.

The stranger's face was there clearly. Trusla could hear the gasps of those around her, a kind of whistling noise from Kankil. Then it was Undia, but limp and unconscious.

"Possessed!"

Trusla heard that fateful exclamation from some one of them, but Frost spoke suddenly and sparingly in answer.

"This is not fully a sending from the Dark but a cry for help. Lay her there. She will not struggle again." She indicated the lone bench to one side. Then she turned to Inquit, a measuring look in her eyes.

417

The shaman faced her as silently, but some unheard question must have been asked and answered as both of them moved to stand over the unconscious girl. Inquit motioned to Trusla and pointed to a small brass bowl on the wide table which apparently served the captain as a desk.

Trusla luckily found it empty and stood holding it at the shaman's gesture. From some hidden pocket in her fur tunic Inquit produced a small packet which she opened with great care, dropping but a pinch of its contents into the bowl.

She had given no open order to Kankil, but the small furry creature climbed up beside the unconscious girl and deliberately spread its own body face down across hers so that their hearts must have been close together. Now the shaman took the bowl and snapped her fingers at it. A small thread of mist arose and she paced slowly about the bench, the bowl outheld and the mist, seemingly inexhaustible, weaving a pattern in the air back and forth across Undia.

Having done so, she stepped aside and Frost took her place at the girl's head. She slipped the chain of her jewel from around her neck and with it touched Undia's sweat-beaded forehead.

"What lies within be told without," she commanded.

Undia's eyes did not open, nor did she seem in any way aware of the listeners. But speak she did now—in a broken series of small phrases as if the effort of bringing forth the message she had to give was almost too much for her strength.

"The ice herds—fog—demons—" Undia's face twisted as if even to bring forth that name caused her pain now. "Dargh—feast—Rogar, Lothar, Tortain—left—me—left—only ones. Creep—get skin boat—take to sea. Cold, oh, cold that eats the bones. Death comes as friend. Lothar dies—Tortain—Rogar—better a quick death in the sea—rock the boat over—no, Sulcar dies not except at the Call. Cold—read the waves—I can read the waves again—too late—south—but only ice—always the ice floating about. Wind Ruler, hear me! Mother of the Deeps, hear me! I am Audha of the *Flying Crossbeak*, wavereader—let the cold take me quickly—oh, quickly."

Frost looked across the girl's body to the captain. "This maid is a wavereader of great talent—I have heard that from several of you. Can she be led by this other so that we can find her still alive?"

Captain Stymir looked amazed. "How know you that such can be done? It is one of the hidden talents. But then, Lady Frost, I take it that all talents are open to your reading. Ask her pattern. No—wait a moment."

He near leaped to the table desk and brought out a white square of wood and one of the black sticks kept for short reckonings. "Now!" he commanded.

"Audha," Frost addressed the unknown as if she stood there before them, "tell us of the patterns you see." The jewel in her hand was now flashing white, straight at the closed eyes of Undia.

Again she spoke—this time the words made no sense as far as Trusla was concerned. But the captain's writing fingers flew as he put down a series of symbols.

"Will we find her alive?" he asked as he handed the square of wood to his mate.

"If my sister here can keep her living," Frost said in a low voice.

Inquit's dark eyes gleamed through the mist cover she had woven. "There is still a living spark. The little one feeds that through this one. What can be done we shall do."

Trusla felt her helplessness. This was no usual healing matter, though even there her skills were limited. Then she felt arms about her, strong support. Simond was always there when she needed him most. She sighed with a small feeling of relief.

"Best to go!" Inquit waved her hand, and, except for Frost, those gathered there left her to her own use of Power, hearing her strong voice raised in a chant as they left.

Trusla still stood within the circle of Simond's arm as they stood together in the growing light of dawn. By all the signs it would be a fair day. But she was haunted by the thought of that skin boat with its sad cargo adrift somewhere ahead.

Joul took the wavereader's position at the bow, the captain at his shoulder. Now and then he called out some direction, which was passed to those working the ship. They had taken an easterly course and could see afar the rise of cliffs like an open jar ready to engulf the sea.

Rations in the forms of bowls of mutton stew were passed and they ate as they stood to their posts, dipping the hard ship biscuit into the liquid to make it chewable.

Now the sun sent both light and warmth down upon them. Here and there it appeared to be reflected from the waves in strange flashes—or, Trusla thought, she was too eager by far to find something amiss.

"She—that Audha—spoke of ships being herded by bergs," she commented after she had drunk the last few drops from her bowl. "How can that be? I do not know this north. What out of the Dark could so threaten?"

"We shall doubtless discover that in our own time," Simond returned bleakly. "This is a part of the world where our kind live only on sufferance; sea, ice, and rock hold the real rule."

There was a cry from the lookout on the masthead. And it brought them all to the side of the deck. Then a sharp spate of orders sent the trained Sulcars to launch one of the smaller ship's boats. Men swung down on ropes to man it and it pushed away from the *Wave Cleaver.*

Even Trusla could see their goal, a dark, strangely shaped thing which rode low in the waves, and toward that the ship's boat flew with a flashing of oars.

It was too far away for those on the ship to see more than vague movements, but some of those suggested that bodies were being transferred from the derelict to their own craft. And the native boat was left behind as the ship's boat came swiftly across the waves.

Those on board were ready and dropped slinglike nets, each of which was brought up with care to be swung over the rail. The stiff, contorted bodies—surely all were dead. But then a hand moved out to catch at the netting that held it and Trusla heard a small cheer from those ready to receive the lost.

They did not even unroll the net from about that one and Hansa gathered up the slender body and carried it as he might a child back to the great cabin. Trusla saw Inquit stand at the door, waving vigorously. But when the captain and some others of the crew would have followed, she slid the door shut in their faces with a determined shove.

The three others who had been lifted aboard were indeed dead. Under the captain's tight-lipped orders they were straightened to lie on wide strips of sailcloth. Their frozen hands were somehow loosened enough to be brought to lay on their breasts, and into the loose hold of those hands was fitted the shaft of a boarding axe—the warrior's key to the Last Gate.

Trusla turned away. These were not kin who lay here—but in final things all were kin. However, she felt as if she were intruding on something not meant for her eyes and sensed that Simond agreed. Together they went to the fore of the ship, where old Joul still sat in the wavereader's perch.

"May the Fire Fangs of the Bosken avenge them." He nearly made a song of the words, weaving back and forth in his narrow seat. "May I live to see Dargh be wiped from the living world. Lothar Longsword, Tortain Staymir, who stood at the last ingathering with pride of victory over the greatest varse any man had ever harpooned before. Rogar—now, there was a man. Many a well-spun tale he had for shipmates when we drank together. He was at the fall of Sulcarkeep—one of the few who took to the message boats by the order of Osberic himself. The maid—she I do not know—but she has carved herself a part in the next bard-singing—and she shall have it, by the Breath of the Wave Driver Himself!"

He glanced around at the two who had ventured to come up behind him.

"We remember our kin gone before," he said fiercely. "Though we cannot give these good shipmates land burial, the sea welcomes always the Sulcars. For we have made it our own. We build towns now—but once there was only the sea and it kept us for the time given us. It is only just that it receives us at the last."

Receive the three it did. Sewn into their shrouds, and with Joul himself summoned to chant their deeds and kin names, and the captain to empty into the waves the farewell cup for their going. Wreathed with thick lengths of chain, they went down into waves, which seemed higher, stronger, as if eager to receive them.

But Audha was not among them. It seemed that whatever power

the Latt shaman and the Estcarp witch could summon kept her back from that last journey.

In spite of Audha's broken warning of what might lie ahead, the *Wave Cleaver* kept on course once they had picked up those in the skin boat. During the day Trusla made a visit to her cabin searching for that jar of sand she had found in the wharfside market. She did not try to free the wooden stopper but sat with it in her hands. As she turned it around and around in her fingers, the sorrow and some of the ever-present uneasiness was drawn out of her. Closing her eyes, she sought to summon every scrap of memory from a past that for a while she had struggled hard to forget.

Life in Tor Marsh was no easier for those who followed its boggy ways than it was for these Sulcars who depended upon what seemed to her an element which could become treacherous at any moment—the sea. But it was what one was bred to which seemed the lesser evil—if one could deem it so.

Among her kin she had been the lesser—the near outcast one. Only because Blind Mafra had spoken for her was she now here. She had never felt the rich warmth of kin approval. Among her kind there were no individual mothers, and she had no idea who had fathered her at the Moon Dancing. But this—once more she turned the jar and thought of what had freed her—this was as much a part of her as her lifeblood.

Now she did loosen the cap and very slowly put a finger within. Yes, it felt the same, she could not deny that. The soft powder enclosed her finger and clung. Trusla had no understanding of why she now did as she did, but she raised that coated finger to her lips and licked her flesh clean. There was a very faint taste—like that of Tor water—and a whiff of fragrance.

"Little sister . . ."

She heard that—or only hoped?

"You are more than you think. And you shall learn, ah, how you shall learn!"

"Xatol?" she said wonderingly, without opening her eyes. For she was seeing not the cramped cabin in which she sat, but rather the small strip of beach flowing with sand like this, and that sand rising to dance in the moonlight, to become one she yearned to join—to be one part of.

"Go to the one who is near the Great Sleep." Yes, she was hearing that clearly. "Give her of your strength. Two Powers hold her in this world; let the third bind her safe herein."

Trusla put the jar into hiding once again and then went directly to the great cabin. The door was slid shut, but she put out her hand as if she had been summoned from within and opened it far enough to slide through.

Undia no longer lay on the bench but was now on a mat of blankets on the floor, Audha so close beside her that they touched at shoulder, arm, and hip. Both of them had been stripped of clothing and that mist which Inquit had summoned still hung in the air. Kankil sat by their heads, a soft furred paw on each forehead. Her eyes were closed and there was a faint sound like a hum or a purr sounding from her.

Frost had settled cross-legged by their feet and her jewel flared and dimmed, flared to dim again as she pointed it to them.

Neither woman seemed to notice Trusla, but she went confidently forward to kneel beside the stranger out of the sea—Audha. She reached forward and placed her hand on the girl's breast, chill as death under her touch.

Then she closed her eyes. Sand—a long stretch of sand—sand which arose about her, for this time *she* danced there, whirled and dipped, felt the caress of the powdery stuff against her skin. Now she deliberately did what she had never dared to do before. She called—not to summon but to demand—to raise Power which none of her kind had ever had, or so she believed.

The sand about her as she danced was warm, grew warmer, nearly flame-hot, and now she took command of it with all her strength, channeled it, sent that heat of life where it must go.

This was like no struggle she had known since the time she had fought to keep life in her when Simond broke the barrier that let them both through into the outer world. Somehow she held, and fed that heat of life—fed it with all the strength in her—to fight the chill, to banish the grasping fingers of death.

At last she sagged, crumpling backward to the floor. Dimly she heard a low moan and knew that she had won. Then there were arms about her settling her against a pillow. And mistily, as if she viewed it all still through a fall of sand, she saw Frost and Inquit busy wrapping the two girls with blankets. Making signs above them—the witch with her jewel and the shaman with her hands.

Something soft and warm nestled against her, reached up short arms to clasp hands about her neck. Kankil was with her now, purring steadily, and somehow she felt strengthened by the rhythm of that sound.

"Trusla! What have they done to you?" Through that relaxing hum she heard Simond's cry. He was on his knees beside her, holding her, his arms enfolding her along with Kankil, who still clung to her as might a child to its parent.

There was a flashing light. She tried to close her eyes against it but could not. Ice—ice come out of the sea—no, she was still warm, she had not been swallowed up by the freezing water.

Then she could see that it was Frost's jewel burning bright, not to harm or threaten but to awaken her fully to the here and now.

Undia first came into sight beyond the brilliance of that gem. She held a blanket close about her and under the sea tan her face was greenish pale. But there was no longer any madness in her eyes and she was drinking thirstily from a cup Inquit held to her lips.

*Audha?* Trusla shaped the name with her lips rather than said it aloud.

"She sleeps, sister," Frost answered gently. For the first time she used the form of address which welcomed Trusla among those with the Power. Power—sand—she had danced with sand and commanded it to be obeyed. Abruptly she straightened in Simond's hold.

"Xactol!" Never before had she said that name aloud within the hearing of another, even Simond.

Frost's head was a little inclined to one side, as if she were weighing the word she had heard. Then she smiled and all the stiffness Trusla instinctively associated with the witches was gone.

"We serve many different aspects, perhaps, but they are all of the same Power, whether you name the Flame, Gunnora, or—"

"Arska," Inquit broke in. She had settled Undia and now was pulling a furred covering over Audha. "This one lives—perhaps because there is a need for her yet to walk this world. We have proved that the Light has reached out to her. But she will sleep. Kankil. . . ."

Trusla's arms tightened for an instant, reluctant to let the little one go. But she had Simond now. The shaman's small creature ran to where her mistress bent over Audha and then she delightedly slid her small body under that cloaking fur and disappeared. Trusla had good reason to believe that once again she was lending the comfort which she radiated to one who needed her the most.

"Trusla." Simond's voice was soft, like a caress—when he said her name in that fashion it was as if they were an indivisible part of one another. "You must rest."

Before she could move or protest, he had her fully in his arms and was carrying her back to her cabin—how she wished now it was theirs. But he settled beside her as if that thought also was in his mind and he smoothed her hair and then kissed her, not with passion, but with joy that they were together.

She did sleep and she had no dreams. She did not dance with the sand, she did not cower away from the ravings of Undia, she went only into velvet darkness which opened and closed about her, holding her safe and soft.

But others dreamed. Twice Frost had to use the witch jewel to drive Audha into deeper unconsciousness and Kankil whimpered and cried out as the raging memories cut across the sleeper's mind.

All that Undia had reported when they had been in such strange contact across the sea leagues was indeed the truth. Twice over Frost had to fight away Audha reliving all which lay just behind her.

At length she seemed to sink into such a depth of exhaustion that the healing of the jewel was no longer needed. Then Inquit and Frost faced each other across her now-quiet body and the face of each woman was grim with foreboding.

"I know not the north," Frost said hardly above a whisper. "What evil walks there? Tell me legends, sister, even if you do not know the truth."

"We had only the dreams to plague us," the shaman answered. "But in the last days before we trailed south those were strong enough to kill—and they did!" Her fingers moved on her knee as if she sketched patterns there. "The Power runs in kin lines with us, sister. I am the daughter of a daughter of a daughter who was dreamer for a much greater tribe. For we are now a remnant of a people. And always, in each generation, there were evil dreams—but they were not so strong. The Power could destroy them and none died or went mad. Then . . ." she took a deep breath, "I know not of my own accord what happened. But from you I learned of the wild magic which struck when the gate stone was gone. And I can understand the fears your people have of the Dark arising outworld and perhaps coming to us. This poor child speaks of icebergs which herd ships to their doom. Only of the Dark could such things come."

Frost nodded and once more slipped the chain of her jewel over her head so it lay again gray and lusterless on her breast.

"Always the Dark." She gave a weary sigh.

But Inquit was smiling wryly. "Always the Dark, sister, but we can marshal good fighters on our side, and we shall."

## CHAPTER THIRTY-FOUR

# West Coast Voyage, North

The *Wave Cleaver* had altered course soon after they had picked up the drifting boat. As yet there had been no signs of any floating bergs, but Captain Stymir was willing to take the longer route, that he might not encounter whatever had brought the *Flying Crossbeak* and its crew to their end.

Dargh was well marked on the map used by any ship bearing north, but it lay closer east than west. Their new course would add extra days of sailing onto their voyage, as on the west there were treacherous shoals and reefs among which few ever wished to hunt a path.

Undia had recovered by the second day after the ordeal she had partly shared with Audha and insisted on returning to her post at the prow—though for the first day Joul remained at hand.

Audha still remained in deep slumber in Undia's bunk. Frost and Inquit took turns visiting her, though Kankil was always cuddled close to her unmoving body. Trusla felt she had little to offer now, but concern pulled her in the same direction several times each day.

She sensed that the Sulcars of the crew were tense and apprehensive. Axes and swords had been loosened of the oiled covering which kept them from rust at sea. And it seemed that all day long the screech of metal against an edging whetstone could be heard. They kept a lookout on the midmast, though those had to be changed hourly because of the nip of the wind.

From time to time Undia raised the horn which hung at her belt and blew patterns of notes which set the crew to various tasks, most of which Trusla could only guess at. Simond had been summoned twice by the captain and she guessed that his own knowledge of possible attacks from the Dark were examined. After all, though his service had been only on land, for the past months he had been heading one of Koris's Estcarp search parties and twice they made finds which had sent a witch riding in a hurry to lay some trouble to rest.

On the fourth day they sighted the first warning of the rough way ahead. Sometime in the past an unknown who had feared the traps the sea laid had erected, on a wave-washed cone of rough rock sometimes completely hidden by the water, a cairn which appeared to be fused together. At least the wrath of the sea about it had not beaten it away.

At the tip of that rugged pile was set a round of metal. And the sea had not had its way with that, either, for it was not dimmed. Undia swung up a rod with a similar disk at its end. There was flash from the cairn-set plate.

"Hothrot's light." The tall Hansa came up beside Trusla as he spoke. "'Tis said that he gave one of his own eyes to win that beacon for us all. It is true that some Power holds it steady."

The ship veered again slightly. Undia leaned forward in her seat, her attention fast-fixed on the waves into which their prow plowed. Another blast from her horn caused a flurry of activity.

Now Trusla could see the dark rise of the western coast. Unknown land. That which was known of Arvon, where the four Mantle overlords held reign, was to the south. She had seen some furs on the wharf market tables—some of a dull gray—which most of the buyers had avoided and she had overheard named stinkwolf. Indeed they had smelled strong, and Trusla had heard from one complaining customer that they came from some beast unknown in the east and a peril to be avoided in the west.

For the rest of the day and through the dusk, which came very late in these northern reaches at this time of year, the *Wave Cleaver* followed the pattern set by Undia's horn.

At last the captain himself ordered her from her perch and Joul took her place so that she could eat and drink. However, she refused to go to her cabin but lay on a wad of sail and blanket they spread for her.

Trusla made a final trip to see Audha before she herself sought sleep. Frost sat cross-legged on the deck planking, her body swinging to the motion of the boat. Her head had fallen forward on her breast and she plainly dozed.

Inquit slid open the door behind Trusla and edged in. Their vigil was beginning to affect both women. By the limited light of the lantern swinging from its hook above, they looked gaunt and strained.

Just as Inquit closed the door, Audha moved. She had lain every time Trusla had seen her in that same stiff, unnatural position as when they had arranged her so on the bunk. But now her head turned from side to side and she sighed and then gave a small cough and her blue eyes opened.

She stared at Trusla in bewilderment and then turned her head weakly to survey what she could of the cabin.

Kankil raised her soft head from the girl's shoulder and patted her cheek gently. Both Frost and Inquit half pushed Trusla aside to go to their charge.

"What watch?" Her voice was thin. "My watch—I must keep my watch." She sat up suddenly and collapsed as quickly. "My head spins . . . but the watch."

"The watch is kept, little one." Frost's voice held its most gentle note. "You are safe—this is the *Wave Cleaver*."

Audha's eyes seemed to open farther. She raised a hand and pushed aside Kankil as if she desired no comfort, no tending.

"Then—then I dreamed true." Her face twisted as if some pain wrenched at her lean middle. "We—we were taken—but how— how did I come here, Lady?" She reached up now and grasped the sleeve of Frost's robe, nearly jerking the witch down upon her with a sudden show of strength. "The captain—tell the captain—the Dargh—"

"We are well away from that plague spot," Inquit said, drawing Audha's attention to her.

"You—you are Latt." The girl spoke as one now dazed. "And you . . ." She looked to Frost, and then shrank down into the bunk, loosing her hold on the other quickly. "You are a witch—out of Estcarp. Witchery—it was dire witchery as caught us. What do you weave now?"

She was shaking, and, without thinking, Trusla pushed past Frost, though her smaller form could not hide the taller witch. As Kankil had done, she patted the other gently.

"We seek woven witchery to break its web, wavereader. It was the Power of these"—she indicated Inquit and Frost—"who, with the aid of our own wavereader, found you."

The girl bit her lip. "It must be by some favor of Power I live. Rogar—Lothar—Tortain?"

Trusla shook her head. "They walk the Road of Heroes' Grace. But you remain."

Now the girl clutched Trusla's hand, holding it tightly. "Perhaps I lived to warn. There is that which moves. Something drove the bergs so that our ship was herded like one of the wasan to the fall slaughtering. Dargh . . ." She shuddered, and Trusla settled herself precariously on the side of the bunk and somehow brought Audha up into her own arms.

"All is well," she crooned, as she would have to one of the little ones in the children's room in the great house where she had been born. "We are far from Dargh. Our captain has chosen a western way."

The girl in her hold stiffened. "That is the way of peril also—though only by rocks and the whims of the sea and not the beastliness of maneaters. To voyage so is a great danger, though it has been done."

"As we shall do again. Captain Stymir has made other northern voyages. Many of the perils are already known to him." But she saw the shadow of uneasiness still on Audha's face.

Inquit had moved up beside Trusla. "We are of the north, though we do not take to the sea except for the hunt. Yes, there grows danger, but it is that which we are sworn to seek and face—Power to Power. Now you must eat and grow strong and perhaps in a few days you can aid Undia with the watching, for she has no 'prentice on this voyage."

The feeling of calmness and good sense which Inquit projected now was such that Trusla could also feel. After a last lingering look at Audha, Frost slipped out of the cabin and the other two proceeded to tend their charge. At length she slept again and this time it seemed that she rested naturally.

However, there was a meeting in the great cabin at dusk. The *Wave Cleaver* had again altered course several degrees east, since the strain of trying to read the wave run in this dull northern light was too much for either Undia or Joul, though both stayed stubbornly at the bow post.

Captain Stymir had out his map and was regarding it closely.

"We are beginning to sight ice—not real bergs but still visible. And the western reefs devour ships as a hungry man clears his dinner plate. From what can be guessed, the *Flying Crossbeak* was taking the way of most caution—eastward—before swinging toward the western shore. A peninsula that is well armored with reefs and tricky currents. Yet we must round it to reach End of the World." He looked to Frost.

"Lady, you have your own way of foreseeing, is that not true?"

"No one can truly foresee, Captain," she replied. "For life is made up of choices. We can sometimes tell what lies ahead for this choice or that. I do have the Power"—and her hand instinctively cupped her jewel—"to know whether any menace of the Dark lurks ahead—but that range is limited."

"You have tried it." He made that more statement than question.

"I have. There is a shadowing in the north. Also a blot of evil which I believe to be this Dargh. The Dark draws energy from pain, fear, violent death. See for yourself." She slipped off the chain and now her jewel dangled over the map. It began to swing and yet somehow they were sure that she did not urge it so. Then it settled in the air as if an invisible pocket held it, aslant on the chain and to the east on the map.

"Is this your Dargh?" she asked.

"It is Dargh right enough, but certainly not mine, nor that of any true man. Those who den there have no right to the name of humankind."

The color of the jewel was changing now. There was a dull red glow—it might be an ember scraped from some hearth, so dark a red that it was nearly black. Simond's sword hand curled, to grip a weapon he did not draw. He had seen such a message given once before, when he had ridden the outer reaches of Estcarp seeking any entrance for the Dark. Then the witch in their company had been close enough to be sisterhood to alert them and draw Power. And a thing which might have once been a circle of slimed green rock had died in flame focused through her jewel—erased before it could once more be used.

"Can it be destroyed? I saw what happened in the Glade of Bone Trees," he blurted out.

"Only a great summoning can cleanse such a Dargh," the witch replied. "You witnessed the erasure of something very old—that which set it was long gone. This lives and gathers. But it is only a servant, or so it would seem."

The captain made a dry sound which was far from a laugh, if that was what he had intended.

"You give us faint encouragement, Lady Frost."

"If what we are now seeking is indeed the gate through which your people came, Captain, why did they chance such a journey into the unknown? The Sulcars are spoken of as lovers of trade and gain and they have served not only themselves but also our world well by those very matters. But above all else, as a goad, there hangs fear.

"The best recorded entrance of a whole people uncovered so far at Lormt is that of the Dalefolk. Their wisefolk deliberately opened that door to escape some disaster so great that, lest some longing for a part of the past would move them to eventual return, they closed and sealed it behind them with the strongest Powers they could against any reopening. The Kioga—they fled a war and found a land they could make their own. And those others who through the years have come singly—such as Simon Tregarth— have been hunted by their kind and took a final chance for escape.

"Your legend of a northern gate through which you passed on ships—tell me, Captain, you have known it from childhood. Is it not deliberately obtuse? If those who come thus into our seas fled, then what did they flee? The wild Power loosed when the Mage-stone went from us was enough to arouse many sleeping things— and it has. The shadows that have driven the Latts from their home ranges with evil and deadly dreams—this affair of the *Flying Cross-beak*—does that not suggest that perhaps some lock *your* people put upon a gate is weakening, that something beyond is drawing to it, or perhaps experimenting with that of the Dark it can summon and control?"

Stymir had shifted a little in his chair. "And if we follow the hints of legend to this gate, Lady, and it opens—how do we battle?"

"They search now at Lormt, as you know, for the ultimate sealing of all gates. Hilarion remains and he is an adept such as could gather power into his hands and hurl it like lightning. Even we of the jewel"—she held hers close again—"who have been favored above most by the talent, cannot command such forces as an adept summons. But if his Powers, plus all we can feed him—and there are many talents, each with their own strength and virtue—fails, then there will be a sequel battle such as this world has not often seen.

"I cannot chart a sea path for you, Captain. That is the talent which is of your blood. What I can do is foretell any blight of the Dark which lies across our path. And at this time I see nothing which threatens save the weapons of nature herself."

The captain reached within a coffer on the table which served him as a desk. He brought out a plaque of what looked to Simond like clear ice, yet in the warmth of the cabin it showed no signs of melting.

"Three years ago"—Stymir seemed reluctant to say anything, turning to plaque about in his callused hands—"I made the voyage to End of the World. It is never one popular with my people, but if a man succeeds, the return is great. Not only are there precious furs such as can be found in no other land, but when the ice streams run from beneath the glaciers still farther north, men seeking in their gravel beds find gold nuggets, as well as gems, held prisoner by the ice for seasons and released only by the chance of a melt.

"This is such a thing." He laid the plaque on the table. "It is something not even our Storm Talkers can understand. Though it seems ice, it is not, nor is it glass, which would not have existed for a fraction of an hour candle in such a rough cradle. But from the north it came, and now . . . look into it, Lady, and tell us what can be seen."

Simond had already noted a dark spot in the middle of the plaque, though all the rest of it was crystal clear. It appeared to him that as the witch leaned closer to view the find, that spot not only grew darker but larger. Also suddenly small sparks of light glittered at one end, coming alive as might stars in the southern nights.

"It is . . ." She had held her jewel pointed toward it and there was a flicker from those star points. "It is a ship—ice-trapped, yet not destroyed. And those stars . . ."

"If they are stars," said the Captain, "then they are ones we do not know, we who use such light as part of our guiding. Nor is the ship like the one on which we now travel."

Frost had taken a step away and now those others there drew closer to study the find in turn. Among them Odanki was the first to speak. As a rule he was silent in most company; Simond thought that he deliberately listened to gain knowledge of these strangers around him, jealously in turn guarding his own inner self as best he could.

"That is the Foot of Arska." He did not quite touch finger to the plaque, but he indicated plainly the stars. "Not always is it so—for Arska walks the skies of the world and sometimes His tracks are different—but there is a long time between such differences."

"Yet you call the constellation by name, and we who travel the northern waters do not see them so." The captain was frowning.

"To Arska there is no time as we know it," the young Latt hunter responded calmly. "We, too, have our guide maps, and they are of the sky. Twice has Arska's trail changed since our Rememberers kept records."

Simond caught his breath. He had listened and read enough of the records at Lormt to know that mankind's time was swallowed up when the stars appeared to move and that seasons beyond counting lay between such shiftings. How long must these Latt records run? It would seem that his unspoken question was already one to be voiced from Frost herself.

"Your shaman, hunter, has told us that you have no tradition of any gate—any offworld beginnings."

He smiled with a flash of white teeth clear against his dark skin. "That is certainly the truth. Do *you* have a gate memory, Powerful One?"

She was frowning a little. "No," she returned. "Nor do any of the true Old Race. It is our belief that we have been here always—and that there were no gates until the adepts created them as doors for learning or amusement."

"So . . ." he faced her straightly. "Perhaps we are 'Old Ones' also, but of a different breed. Our Rememberers tell of the coming of these shipmen, and also of a war to the southward, when a people who were one with animals they called hounds strove to drive us north and out of the land which was once ours."

Alizon, thought Simond. But by all they had learned from Kasarian in Lormt, it had been a good thousand years or more since the hounds had entered this world. So if the Latts had ever had such a gate, it lay so far back in time that it was truly lost.

"We were never a people great in numbers," Odanki was continuing, "but we found a place we could make our own and Arska signed His judgment of us then in the skies. So"—he came back to the matter immediately at hand—"there are Arska prints and they shine upon a ship which you say, Captain, is not one of your kind."

Simond could catch only a shortened sidewise view of that shadow at the heart of the plaque. Even he who was no seaman could make an outline of another type of vessel. This one had no masts; instead, in the center section of its deck, there was an erection like a tower standing to a goodly height.

Captain Stymir's eyes had been fastened intently upon it as if the thing had more meaning than any of the questions and answers about him. Simond saw the captain's features stiffen, his thin-lipped mouth straighten into a line. Did he indeed begin to recognize it?

"It is a thing of evil," he said. "It . . ." He reached for the plaque as if he would dash it to the decking, destroy it utterly.

Simond swung out his hand to intercept the other's. "It is a key." He did not know why those words had come to him, but he knew they must be said.

"You are right, southerner." Surprising them all, Odanki spoke again. "This was found, you tell us, Captain, in one of the summer glacier streams. Thus it is out of the upper ice—from the great

halls we have seen from afar. It is a track such as a hunter will follow to find his prey."

Captain Stymir looked up at the young Latt. "Your track," he
said almost jeeringly, "has lain long. The quarry must have far since
vanished."

"Not so." Odanki seemed unshaken by the captain's tone. "The
ice holds what it takes far past generations of any kinline. Last
warm season Savfak took a hunting party northeast. There are
sometimes the great horned ones to be found there—thin though
the forage is. Into that land the moving ice has flung a wide arm. It
was a warmer season than any but the oldest could remember and
the weather was good.

"Savfak found trail and we took it. It was lost at last at the foot
of the ice wall. But in that wall . . ." he paused, "by the honor of
the past kin I swear that we saw what was encased there—such a
beast as never any hunter had faced before. Three men standing on
each other's shoulders could perhaps have reached its back, and its
mouth was open, showing such fangs as were out of natural
growth.

"It was of the ice and we left it to that hold. But things can be
indeed kept very long in such storage. Who knows, Captain, how
long the ice held this picture thing of yours?"

"Your legend speaks of a gate through which your ships came,"
Frost said. "We know that this quest of ours is overseen and ap-
pointed by Powers we do not question. Perhaps you do have now a
guide of sorts. In End of the World can you not seek out the one
who traded this to you and discover all he knows?"

"That much can be done. But—look—it fades!" said the captain. The flicks of stars were gone, and the ship was again a black
blot growing ever less.

Frost had once more put on her jewel. "Power summons Power,"
she commented. "When it is needed, we can raise it again."

"Things washed from the ice barriers—great beasts caught
within." Trusla marveled at Simond's report of the meeting in the

captain's cabin. "Could such beasts come alive again?" she wondered.

"This land," Simond returned with a grin, "has seen even stranger things in its time. Lady Frost has gone to report to Es and to gather any news which may have been passed from Lormt."

Trusla knew the deep trances which were part of any such communication. It might be some time before the witch would rejoin them to share what she had learned. The sun was warm here. She had been able to discard her cloak. She knew that this strange country did have its summer, though it was very short. But it was long enough to start runnels of water in streams from under the tall glacier walls.

People would have spread out from End of the World preparing for the threat of next season's cold. She had listened to the talk of the seamen enough to know of the fishing which went on long into the night dusk, the cargoes brought back to be spread on racks and dried.

Then there were the herds of horses—somehow Trusla found it difficult to think of horses not much larger than wolfhounds—shaggy, except where the marks of packs had worn away some of the strands of hair. These were no Torgians, not even equal to the mountain ponies—certainly very far removed from the proud Keplians she had seen in Es, who considered themselves the equal if not superior to her own species.

There would be pack trains of these miniature beasts gone out of the trading post—each with some prospector or hunter. At the same time there might be another ship in harbor, since this was the open season. . . .

Another ship! She thought of Audha. The Sulcar girl seemed to be nearly recovered. At least she no longer was plagued by the nightmares which Frost and Inquit apparently had driven out of her memory.

In fact she seemed uneasy in her idleness and had offered her services to relieve Undia, though the latter appeared not to wish that.

A small brown furred figure bounded across the deck now, uttering a small squeaky cry Trusla now recognized as her own name as Kankil believed it to be. She held out her arms and the little one threw herself in a tight hug. Kankil was firmly bonded with Inquit, but somehow with all that had been going on, Trusla had never been able to satisfy her curiosity concerning the shaman's companion. Were those of Kankil's kind common among the Latts? Where did they come from otherwise? Certainly they were far from being pet animals. Holding this loving warmth close to her, she wished— when all this trail was safely over—she might find a Kankil also to companion her.

Inquit had followed her small companion and now sat down cross-legged on the deck beside Trusla. She no longer wore her feather cloak and the lacings of her white fur tunic were undone so that the sun reached the thin skin undergarments she wore and part of her own skin.

She sniffed deeply and then nodded. "Not far now, Trusla. The land breezes already seek us. See . . ." She pointed to a dark line across the sea, which they were veering east again to avoid. "That is the snout of the traders' land. It shall not be long before we come to anchorage there."

## CHAPTER THIRTY-FIVE

# End of the World, North

It was not a good day as they maneuvered into the pocket harbor of the farthest known northern Sulcar port. But in spite of the drizzle of rain soaking her cloak, Trusla had kept to the deck. On either side there were cliffs, tall and black, save for here and there where streamers of some kind of sea growth oozed down the forbidding stone. Before them was the single entrance to the open land beyond.

But there were no buildings that Trusla could distinguish. There were no age-old towers and walls, nor the bustling newness of Korinth. There was one long wharf, wet with overslapping waves, and beyond that, what seemed to be a wild-handed scattering of rounded humps.

The trade flag snapped from the *Wave Cleaver*'s main mast and a similar streamer of faded cloth had half wrapped itself around a pole ashore. Also there were those waiting on the wharf, beginning to shout greetings and questions even before any on the ship were within hearing distance.

The welcomers were an oddly mixed lot. Sulcars towered over others who were not too far from the Latts in size and coloring, though their clothing was less of fur, seeming to be hides far more closely fitted to their bodies. Their hair was long and drawn up in stiff, thick knots held so by carven circlets. As far as Trusla could see, there was no distinction between man and woman in the style of clothing. However, the colors, in contrast to the somberness of the lands about them, were vivid—for those hide shirts and breeches were dyed in brilliant shades and wide whirls of patterns.

"First ship!" One of the Sulcars had made a funnel of his hands and shouted up to them as they eased into anchorage at the wharf. "First ship luck!"

Behind him two more Sulcars were carrying out a barrel, balancing it between them and now knocking into one end of it a spigot while two laughing women dropped by it a basket of drinking horns.

That the first ship of the season was a great occasion the passengers on the *Wave Cleaver* were quick to understand. A drummer and two flutists appeared farther down the wharf and started to underlay the shouting with music of a sort, and it was like a feast day in the south.

Some time later, Trusla was coughing from a sip of a cup one of the women had offered her, clinging to Simond lest they be separated and whirled away into an impromptu dance which had begun down wharf. They were joined by Frost and Inquit, Odanki like a bodyguard behind her, Kankil clinging, slightly wild-eyed, to the shaman.

So Trusla was introduced to a third kind of city and one which was so different that at first she was secretly a little dubious about entering the door a grinning Sulcar had pulled open for her. It was before this mound that the trade flag had been raised and manifestly it must be the main building of End of the World.

It was necessary to go down a short flight of steps, each consisting of a worn rock set in the earth in order to reach the doorway which their host kept waving them toward. This was more a burrow than a house. Set well down in the earth, more than a Sulcar's-height deep, the floor was a patchwork of stones fit together with skill. More stones paneled the wall of the first room into which they had come. But covering those for the most part were hides, painted as brightly as the clothing the owners wore.

Across one end of the room, farthest from the main door, was a raised ledge. This was heaped with cushions which looked as plump as if no weight had ever rested on them.

Above their heads were great curved pieces of bone, which must have been carefully matched for length, as they met in the center. Between these stretched tightly more hide, probably several thicknesses of it. Trusla, remembering what she had seen outside, believed the builders covered this foundation with layers of earth and sod, perhaps with some packing from the sticky seaweed.

There were, she was to discover, four rooms in all. The one in which they were now received was in the nature of the official hall. Behind it were two other chambers divided by high curtains, and, beyond them, a cooking place which extended out with a lower roof from the main dwelling.

The exuberant heartiness of the man who had welcomed them vanished when he waved them to seats among the cushions, which Trusla discovered were remarkably soft. He made them known to two women already waiting there. One was his wife and the other, whose strictest attention had been for Frost and Inquit, was a contrast to the other women they had seen. Her garment reached nearly to her ankles and was patterned only in white. A wide buckle of strips of bone was bound around her waist and she also had a kind of frontlet running from the neckline of her garment down to that girdle. This was patterned with a mixture of bone heads and stones of green and blue. A band of the same type of work drew her long hair into a fastening behind her neck.

Different from the aged wisewoman they had seen at Korinth, this woman was young, or at least wore an appearance of youth to match Frost's. She had no drum, nor any attendant drummer, but she did hold a staff also of bone yellowed by time and carved with both runes and suggestions of weird creatures which might have been seaborn.

"This be our Watcher—the Lady Svan." Lady Svan inclined her head but still held her gaze on the other two women of Power in the room, Frost and Inquit. "And my House Lady, Gagna." Again a bowed head but there was lively curiosity to be read on the features of his wife.

It was Frost who made first answer. "To this house good fortune such as the Light sends. I am called Frost and am of the Sisterhood of Estcarp of the south." She looked to Inquit, and the Latt shaman, brave in her feathered robe, holding and stroking Kankil, said in turn:

"For the blood kin of the Latts I have been Power-chosen to deliver the great Call when that is needed. My public name is Inquit, and this little one be my dream anchor."

"These be the Lady Trusla and Lord Simond out of Es," Captain Stymir said with proper courtesy.

"Out of Es," repeated the Lady Svan. "Far have you come, yet not for trading. Captain"—she spoke sharply now, as if she found this company not greatly to her liking—"twice have the runes been read and the answer always lies on the Dark side. What danger follows on your heels? If you run hither for shelter, then know that that we cannot grant."

"Cannot"—Frost's voice was very soft and yet it held a core of ice—"or will not, Watcher? We do not flee, we seek, and that seeking may mean life or death for all which lies upon this earth."

"As already evil has struck," the captain interjected when Svan did not reply at once. "The *Flying Crossbeak* has fallen to the Dark." Swiftly he told the main points of Audha's story.

"Bergs that herd ships!" the trade master burst out. "That is against all nature."

"Nature can be commanded by Power," returned Frost.

"Truth," agreed Svan. It was plain that her distrust of them was growing. "Did not your sisters cause the mountains to dance at your bidding not so long ago? What danger do you hunt here? This is a near barren land; we cling to the edge of it because we have learned how to make our compromises with nature. Let that balance be overset and indeed our lives shall cease to be."

"How do you know that already the Dark does not lumber toward you like a wounded great boar who will have its vengeance?" Inquit was eyeing the Watcher almost as coldly as the other was viewing the whole of their party. "You have cast runes, you say, and what led you to that, Watcher?" She leaned forward a little. "Did you also dream?"

Svan flushed. "You speak boldly of hidden things," she snapped.

"I speak so because it is a time for boldness, Woman of Power. We do not deal now with the fate of a single town, or even that of a single kin tribe. It is forbidden by Arska for His Voice to leave His people, yet I stand here under His orders. And this witch out of Es travels not for any pleasure. Listen to what may come upon us. Something perhaps worse than icebergs which herd ships into the waiting caldrons of maneaters."

Oddly enough, it was not to Captain Stymir she gestured, but to Simond.

And he told of their quest starkly with no such embellishments as a bard would use. First of the loss of the Magestone and the wide rip of wild Power which answered that, and then of their concern about other gates which might be so unlocked—ready to open to the demand perhaps of new horrors from without.

He spoke of those who searched in Estcarp and Escore, and the party which was heading even farther south to lands unknown. Of the message alert sent to Arvon and what those who received it also decided upon. He told of the falling of Lormt's fourth tower, of the strange storerooms that collapse had uncovered and of how all the sages of learning struggled there to find answers to what those of action might meet.

A serving lad came with ship's lanterns to set around as the light began to fail, and twice the Trade Master pushed a drink horn into Simond's hand as his voice grew hoarse.

Trusla could see that he had truly won to their side the Lady Gagna and the Trade Master. She tried to read behind the impassive mask that the Watcher continued to wear. At least the woman had at last turned her gaze from Frost and Inquit and was, she was sure, listening intently.

When at last Simond was done, his voice was harsh from use, for Trusla knew that he had put into his account all the force he could summon. Simond was not a man of many words, preferring mainly to listen and not to address any company in form. Now the Trade Master turned to the Watcher.

"Lady, by the right of office given me in this town, I ask you now, once more the runes!"

She did not move or answer him at once, her attention still on Simond. Trusla longed to voice aloud her own irritation that this Sulcar witch could not see at once it was the truth he was speaking.

Then at last Svan raised her chin almost defiantly as she replied, "There is no moon this night, Trade Master."

Frost moved so the cushions about her rustled. She held her gem a little away from her breast so that it dangled from its chain. "There is Power and Power," she said crisply. "We must come to a decision, for I am under pledge to report to my sisterhood and learn from them in return." In the heart of the jewel there was a spark of white fire.

"Well enough," the Trade Master's heavier voice responded. "But first we eat and restore ourselves."

There was no answer from the Watcher. Trusla noted that Inquit's gaze followed the Sulcar wisewoman steadily and she had a suspicion that the Latt shaman was not pleased by the Svan's attitude.

It seemed that by unspoken consent among the whole party no more reference was made to the quest. But as several others, both men and women who apparently had some say in the affairs of the town, came in and small blocks of tables were strung together to support dishes of steaming stew and hard ships' crackers in place of bread, there was excited talk of the fate of the *Flying Crossbeak*. Audha's story had apparently sped through this company.

"Such should be wiped from the earth!" declared one young man, not wholly Sulcar by birth, for his hair was dark and he had slightly obliquely set eyes.

The Sulcar seated beside him brought his fist down on his portion of the shared table with almost enough strength to send the dishes spinning, filled though they were.

"Dargh was talked of at the last All Gather," he burst out. "And what was said then? That we could not spare fighters or ships enough to take the island. It is pitted with caves to which those demons flee whenever they are threatened. We can destroy their foul dens and kill maybe a hand's worth"—he held up his hand now and wriggled the fingers—"that are too old or stupid to take to hiding in time. If we stay for a period, they creep out at night and pick off any sentry and are gone where even our best trackers cannot follow. They are of the Dark and the Dark favors them. But this matter of icebergs which drive a ship to them—Dunamon himself, who knows the northern seas as a wasbear knows the hunting flows, swears that this maid is sure of what she saw.

"I tell you, shipmates and kin blood, if some Power has turned the very force of nature against us—then what comes of our outpost here? The demons of Dargh twice raided our holdings here when we were building. We drove them off at cost and then have sat well pleased our battle honors because they came not again. But what if they have now a force which turns aside axe and sword?"

"There is this, Trade Master"—Inquit had popped a round of vegetables from her stew into Kankil's mouth—"when there is a gather of Dark forces, drawing in to its core all such as can be influenced by it, then when it falls, so does its followers. For Power unleashed does not halt until all which threatens it is gone—and the Light is very sure."

The Sulcar man grimaced. "Wisewoman, we who have no talents and are drawn into the affairs of Great Ones also may be wiped away. Tell us the truth—what do you seek here? Save for Dargh, we suffer no threat."

"You have a path," Captain Stymir put in. He pushed aside his dish and from a belt pouch produced the plaque he had shown those on board the *Wave Cleaver*. "What story have you about the coming of the Sulcars?" He asked that with force enough to rivet their full attention.

The man who had been speaking was quick enough to answer. "That our far kin came on ships through an ice gate into this land."

"And why did they come?" For the first time Simond spoke again after his long spell of reporting news.

"The saying is that they fled some danger," the Sulcar growled. "Many people on this world have such tales of their own. But the seasons between that time and this have been past the counting even for the Rememberers."

"How far north has any ship gone in—say in the past fifty seasons, Trade Master?" Simond persisted.

The Trade Master answered with authority. "Evan Longnose took the *Raven* past the ice wall that season when there was more heat."

"Only his longboat returned, crewed by four dead men," answered the other Sulcar flatly. "We do not go beyond the high wall unless some hunter is a witless fool."

"But," Captain Stymir now cut in, "this is the season for the running of the under-ice streams. More than half your people here are already on the trek to mine them as well as set their traps. This, as the Trade Master knows, was found two seasons ago by Jan Hessar in one such stream."

He laid the plaque on the board before him and those who had not already viewed it on shipboard crowded closer to see it.

"This is a thing of Power—the Lady Frost has tested it." He bowed his head a fraction in the witch's direction. "But Dark Power. Like the gold and gems you pick from the gravel of the ice streams, this was borne slowly into light—probably by the ice itself and then freed through the seasonal melting. Therefore it has a source beyond our explorations."

"To go by ship is folly!" burst out the Sulcar. "And over the ice mountains? What fool would try to set a trail? And . . ." he paused to scowl at the plaque, "who knows what awaits at the other end?"

"We shall see," Stymir said quietly. "This is perhaps a key. We know of gates; which one will this one open?"

"Enough!" The Trade Master ended the discussion. "All this talk of evil is enough to unsettle any stomach. Tell us of how things go in Korinth, what trade has come in from the Dales." And he gazed at them from under bristling brows.

Captain Stymir was the first to grin in answer. "Well enough. You have heard the worst; now let us turn to the best. The Dale lords squabble as usual among themselves. Though since the Falconers have established an Eyrie in the north there are no more sea raiders thinking to fill their chests with the products of honest traders' labor.

"Lord Imry works to bring all the forces under him, but the southern holders who suffered the most in the Alizon invasion are not so ready to relinquish any authority. The three major ports have been largely rebuilt and there is a steady stream of traders—especially in wool and artifacts from the Waste."

Lady Gagna shivered. "Such are unchancy," she commented.

The captain agreed. "True, but none are taken aboard until they have been examined by a sage or one of the Dames of the Flame abbeys. And they have their own way of dealing with that which is cursed. Estcarp is quiet now—Koris is a good lord and justly esteemed, and Simon Tregarth sits at his right hand.

"Escore boils now and then and perhaps always will, but the Tregarth sons and those of the Green Valley are good guardians. In the far south several seasons ago the Port of Dead Ships was destroyed, and there is much talk now of an exploring expedition to head farther than Var in that direction, after the search for the gates is behind us.

"So far, outwardly, all follows the usual pattern."

*But,* Trusla though, *why?* At least the Trade Master knew what occupied the minds of most thoughtful people now, talented or untalented.

She and Simond had been offered quarters in one of the empty houses, the owner of which had gone off for the summer harvesting of whatever this land had to offer. The misty rain had stopped and they did not need a lantern to guide them, for the strange light which held in this north during the summer season was still giving the impression of day.

Trusla gave a sigh which was partially of happiness when she shed again her cloak and left it to dry, draped over two wall hooks.

"You are tired." Simond, having shed his own cape, came to her.

"I am very proud," she said, and linked her arms about his neck, drawing him as close as she could. "For my lord presented our cause as no one else might have. You do not deal in power and thus you see matters as most of these people do. Their Watcher . . ." She ended that with a long kiss and savored the good feeling of his touch along her small body.

"Their Watcher . . ." he said, having marked her chin line and down to her throat with his lips, "you do not like her."

"I do not know her. But, my lord, this night let us forget all guests and Powers, witches, shamans, and Watchers, and keep some hours for us alone."

He laughed softly. "Always you are the wise one, my lady. So be it. The Lady's moon lamp may not shine upon us, but Her grace will fill us."

In this odd light Trusla did not know how long she slept—for it had certainly been late when, with her head on Simond's shoulder, she had sunk into the deepest and sweetest sleep she had known for what seemed a very long time.

At first she was puzzled when she opened her eyes. She lay alone on the wide bed and this was certainly not the cabin of the ship with its cramped space. No—she rubbed her eyes—this was a house, or so the people here deemed it—and they had reached port. But this would be only the beginning, and perhaps the easiest portion of their traveling was behind her.

There was a soft rap at the door and, when she answered, one of the women who appeared to fuse Sulcar and alien features came in carrying a pitcher of water from which steam arose.

"Your lord said you were greatly wearied, but now it is the noon time for eating." She was pouring a portion of the water into a basin, laying out a coarse strip of weaving as a towel.

"I am indeed a lazy slugabed." Trusla laughed and hurried to wash. Then she hunted out clean underclothing, even if it was sadly wrinkled, and she felt at ease as she came to join the others at the Trade Master's hall.

For the first time she saw Audha among that company. Youth seemed to have been drawn out of the wavereader's face. Her jaw was set and she gazed ahead as if she saw nothing of what was about her. Kankil sat close to her, paw hand on her knee, and Inquit was just beyond, keeping a close eye on the girl.

## CHAPTER THIRTY-SIX

# The Reading of the Runes

There was no talk of their mission or the immediate past among those gathered there. Most of the conversation concerned a promising run of flat fish which could be harvested with ease as the predators which followed such schools drove them into the shallows.

Once pulled out of the sea, they were quickly prepared and put on smoking frames—a harvest which would help the trading station survive during the winter to come. In addition there was some excitement over a report brought in by a young hunter that some of the great horns had been sighted not too far away.

There were also comments on the possible luck of the back-country trackers, those who mined the ice streams, and those driving the horses to summer pasturage. Trusla had already seen those small beasts which seemed to be the only domesticated animals those of this Border settlement had.

In general appearance they were horses right enough, but far removed from even the hill ponies of the south, being hardly larger then the great hounds some of the Dales lords and noblemen of Karstan kept for boar hunting or to beat off attacks from the vicious Gray Ones. Their coats were shaggy in rough patches, as they were shedding the thick hair which covered them in winter, and they were gaunt. No one larger than Kankil could hope to mount one, and they were used for packing alone.

A woman near Trusla, as she sat to accept a ship biscuit coated with a tart-sweet jam, was discussing with a friend the fact that several of the small beasts had been returned lately with injured hooves, needing special attention, and that she hoped there would not be an epidemic of such to curtail the summer work.

However, Trusla's attention kept returning to Audha. Though Trusla had tended the girl on shipboard, the wavereader's eyes had passed over her with no sign of recognition and the Estcarpian sensed that Inquit, too, was disturbed by her aloofness.

Those gathered here—mainly, Trusla believed, to give reports of one or another of the town's activities—began to drift out again. There was no sign of Captain Stymir, but Frost was settled among the cushions a little away from the others. She had smiled and nodded to Trusla, yet about her was an aura of waiting—though if she were truly impatient she kept the signs of that hidden.

Simond appeared in the doorway, gave lordship hand greeting to the Trade Master, and bowed to the others. He was quickly followed by Odanki, the Latt taking a place against the wall, leaning a little on his harpoonlike spear.

The Trade Master clapped his hands. At that signal three more of the people gathered there got to their feet and left. The master of the Sulcar town now held between his knees a small drum, not unlike, Trusla thought, that which she had seen carried for the wisewoman in Korinth.

With the very tips of his big fingers he tapped out a series of small raps and there followed silence. Only Audha turned her head, as if aroused for the first time out of some deep well of thought, to look at him searchingly.

Three times the Trade Master used that signal and as the sound of the last beat died away, the Watcher came. At first Trusla thought she was wearing a mask and then realized that those splashes of color were paint, so arranged as to make the woman's features no longer human in appearance but rather like some dream thing.

The Trade Master placed the drum on the floor now, and Svan went to her knees before it.

"The moon is not lit." There was ice in that.

"Neither is your Power hidden by day," he answered her levelly. "Do you say that you control less in the way of forces than this lady witch or this shaman and dreamer of the Latts?"

There was conflict here; Trusla could feel the tension. No one questioned the abilities of a talented one unless it was in the form of a challenge. Yet this Sulcar was goading his own Watcher.

"So be it." Svan shrugged slightly. Her head swung slowly so that she eyed each gathered there. "The reading will be of your demanding. Now . . ." she had slipped out of her sleeve a short, slender knife and held it to the Trade Master.

He applied the needle tip of that to his forefinger and a drop of blood answered. Then he shook his hand so that it spattered down upon the surface of the drum.

"Let those who search now pay," she said stiffly.

Inquit reached for the knife and followed the Trade Master's example, squatting forward so her blood drop also landed on the drum top. She passed the blade to Simond.

He shucked off the gauntlets he had been wearing and prepared to draw blood. Trusla half raised her hand. She knew nothing of the nature of the Watcher's power. Would this act lock them to the will of the Sulcar wisewoman? Simond had no talent shield to stand between him and such usage.

Svan looked beyond Simond to her, and the heavily painted face seemed to express something which was beyond the girl to understand.

"You are already bound to this mission; for the runes all blood must be read," she said.

Trusla caught a glimpse of Frost and the witch was nodding encouragingly, so she did not protest Simond's contribution to the drum and made her own. However, the Watcher did not look to Frost. Perhaps this was a matter of Power so alien that one could cancel out the other—of such she had heard.

But another moved, and before Trusla could return the knife, it was snatched from her hold and Audha stood beside the drum.

"I claim blood debt!" Her voice was high and thick with challenge. "By all the Laws of the Wave, Wind, and Sea, I am now a part of any hunt which will bring down that which has slain kin and shipmates. By the Deep Mother do I swear this."

And her drop of blood fell to the taut top of the drum. Trusla could almost believe that there had been the faint whisper of sound as it struck and spattered.

The Watcher nodded. "Such is your right, since you alone have come from a life-shedding. May the Lord of Storms use you as you wish."

Audha subsided once more among the cushions. There was now life in her face, and her eyes were on the Watcher as if she must not miss anything Svan might do.

The Watcher pulled the drum to her. She was sitting cross-legged, the drum midway between her knees. From the front of her robe she brought out a pouch stained a dull black but with a fringe of scarlet feather tips around it.

Loosening its string, she shook out into her hand what Trusla thought were a palmful of rounded pebbles. Four she inspected and dropped back into the pouch, the rest she closed her fist upon, but before she moved again she looked first at Inquit as if she considered her the lesser danger, and then to Frost.

"Still what you hold, Shaman and Witch, this is not a stew in which you have the stirring."

Having sent each of them a final fierce glance from her paint-rimmed eyes, she tossed the pebbles onto the bloodstained cover of the drum.

There was a loud roll as if the fall of those stones had been instead a heavy beat. And the sound echoed. Trusla felt a tingle of the skin—Power was awake, and here.

Though the drum remained stationary, the pebbles continued to roll. They appeared drawn (in an unpleasant way, Trusla thought) to the blood drops and each moved like a sentient thing until it had touched each of those splotches.

They gathered—like hunters in conference. Then that tight cycle broke and they began each to spin, the whirl taking it away from its fellows. At last they were quiet and Trusla thought she could distinguish something which might be a pattern not unlike the wildly laid-on paint which masked the Watcher.

They waited in silence. Svan displayed no wish to continue to the next part of the ceremony. Almost, Trusla thought, like a sulky child forced to show off some art before strangers.

She herself could see now the pebbles were deeply slashed with markings in most of which blood now drew thin lines. Svan's hand came up and she waved it with an odd motion as if she mimicked the passing of sea waves over the stones.

One or two pebbles seemed to tremble but did not leave their chosen place. However, something else—something beyond sight and hearing—had awakened.

Svan's mouth was now near a snarl. She mouthed words. But that feeling of being looked upon continued. It was Frost and Inquit who answered. The shaman swung about on her pillows, Kankil giving a muted cry, plastering herself against the broad breast of the Latt woman. The shaman's hands raised and moved. One did not need too much imagination to guess that her gestures were those of a tried and trained hunter throwing darts.

Frost cupped her jewel so that no gleam of light moved in the Watcher's direction, but Trusla could see it was alive and bright as the full midsummer moon.

That which had come unbidden flinched. Trusla could feel it even as if her own body had responded so. Then it was gone.

"North," Frost said. Inquit nodded. The Watcher's shoulders seemed to draw together as if she would avoid some blow. She leaned further over the rune stones.

"The Dark awaits," she said. "It will take such knowledge as all the talent here cannot raise to lay it. But we are left no choice, for that which has been awakened seeks prey—it hungers and would feed. You will go to it, because you are oathed and chosen, but you are but blades of summer grass before the first frost. Death—death and ending—"

"Not so!" Frost's voice rang with authority. "We are but the point of the spear and behind us stands an army. Do not forget that there is greater knowledge now being hunted, hunted by those who know how to use what they can find. By this"—Frost's fingers caressed her jewel—"can I speak with my sisters, and they in turn have very ancient and powerful knowledge to draw upon. There are many talents, each having its own force. As a smith forges a sword, sometimes choosing pieces of very old and famous weapons of the past to unite with all his skill to the new, so shall we in the end face this blight. It lies to the north. . . ."

That was more statement than question but the Watcher answered, "It lies north in the land where no tracker can go."

"Yet," pressed the witch, "you can give us more information than that, Rune Reader."

"Already the knowledge of the trail is yours. Hunt out Hessar and ask of his ice river. Your captain flourishes that which he names a key for the unlocking of mysteries. Very well, follow that lead and come upon the rightful gate—if you can."

She was on her feet and stooped to sweep up the pebbles, returning them, still bloodstained, to their pouch. Then she caught up the drum itself before the Trade Master could move—if it were his to reclaim.

"I have read the runes—you will go and there is no turning back. Nor do I believe any return!" Settling the drum on her hip, she swept out of the room.

Simond's hand closed on Trusla's arm. "Let us be out of here," he said in a voice so low as to be hidden under the broken sentences of the other. "It does no good to see the Dark before it comes upon one. I have been at arms practice with the shipmen this morning. Come and let me show you what this land can be with summer upon it."

She was pleased enough to go. There was no drizzle of rain, but a fair day under the sun. There was the ever-present scent of the sea in short breezes which ruffled her hair and plucked at the collar of her jerkin. But there were other scents also, and she drew a deep breath of wonder and delight.

For the world around them, including the rounded tops of the burrowlike houses, was a vivid green, and that green was broken by patches of flowers like jewels on the feast dress of some Dales lady. The green and flowers reached as far as she could see, broken only here and there by workers.

She saw ground which had certainly been put to the plow, and looked to Simond questioningly, for surely the growing season was too short for any grain.

"It is a kind of root thing they grow," he explained. "And it serves them well, for it is best eaten when it has been frozen and needs to be dug out. There are berries, too." He pointed to a number of children, more than she had seen before in the town, who were out in one section of the green land, basket in hand, hunting under the low-growing leaves for the fruit. Most of them, she noted with a smile, already had a chin streaked with juice.

Down a beaten trail of a road came a train of the small horses. They had pack racks on their backs, but the bags were not full, rather looped up. Three drovers accompanied them: a Sulcar, a young woman of the native people, and a half-grown girl who combined features from them both.

One of the pickers arose and came running. "Helgy?" She greeted the girl. "But it is not time for return—is there something wrong?"

Unconsciously Simond and Trusla had drawn closer. The woman glanced at them and then gave a longer look, but the Sulcar snapped his fingers at the fruit picker. "Off with you, Ragan, or you will get the rough side of your aunt's tongue for a half-full basket."

He spoke in a pleasant, bantering tone, but there was a shadowed expression on his face which suggested darker thoughts.

Somehow the day no longer seemed so bright. And the child who had come running to greet her friend did not return to her picking at once but stood looking after the small train as it entered the town.

"Trouble." Trusla did not need that warning from Simond. She half expected to see clouds gathering in the sky overhead. They were there right enough, but they were small and as fleece-white as the Dales sheep.

However, it was enough to send them both back themselves, though they kept a slower pace, letting the distance between them and the travelers widen. There were other surprised calls as those three came into the town. By the time they had reached the Trade Master's headquarters, a number of people, some who had so abruptly left their jobs that they still carried tools in their hands, began to mass there.

Odanki appeared silently out of nowhere and with his bulk and the natural air of a guardsman opened a passage for Trusla and Simond. They found the room already crowded with townspeople— though only the Sulcar drover had come to face the Trade Master.

Neither Inquit nor Frost were there, but the Watcher had a prominent place on the long lounge.

"Alward, his mate, their sons, dead." The Sulcar newcomer held out his hands in a wide sweep as if to suggest the complete disaster he was mentioning. "Their beasts torn apart as well—and no wasbear alone could kill so. Also this is the season when those seek the heights, not the tundra. And this I swear, by the Ruler of Storms, there was no weapon mark on them that we could find—but their bodies were so ill used . . ." his face was gray now and he swallowed convulsively twice before he continued, "that we could not be sure. Godard came for me after he found them and we dealt with them as best we could. Their supplies were not looted, but rather bestially defiled. Then, since I had my hearthwoman and my daughter with me, we came back here, for all must know. Perhaps other prospectors such as Alward have also been so slain.

"Trade Master, I was mate on the *Thunderer* and served at three raidings along the Alizon coast. Yet never have I seen such bloody work as this. Nor were there any true trails."

"Alward . . ." the Trade Master repeated as if he could not believe what he heard. His gaze swept for a moment beyond the speaker and lit on Simond.

"Lord Simond, what news had you out of Arvon? Could evil fester up from there?"

"Not at last reporting," Simond replied. "There are the Mantlelands as far north as we have recorded and no great trouble reported newly there."

"From the north." The Watcher's dry voice nearly covered his last words. "This comes from the north. Alward spoke of traveling toward the Fangs of Gar this season, did he not? And you, Othor, did you not head in that general direction also?"

"It is so, Watcher," he agreed. "We left together with our trains, Alward and his sons and my close kin, and did not separate until the third day out. He had some thought of trying the stream before the Fangs, for Hessar has done well there and this year turned to the west where no one else had gone."

"You say there were no trails," the Trade Master said. "Yet I know your hunting eye, Othor, and surely you sighted something."

The man loosened a small bundle fastened to his belt. "Only this, Trade Master."

The bundle seemed to consist of a great many folds. When finally he lay it open, those about him shrank back as far as they could, for there arose from a small twist of grayish hair he showed a violent stench. Trusla recognized it at once. Once smelled, it could never be forgotten—stinkwolf!

"Not in the tundra," one of the men near them said in quick denial. "They are of the southern broken lands and do not venture far from their foul dens. 'Tis said that they cannot live apart from close to where they are whelped and that the land itself rises to kill them if they try to do so."

"Enough!" The Trade Master was waving a hand and Othor quickly rewrapped his bundle, though the smell seemed to linger on.

"It calls." The Watcher's face was twisted in an expression of deep distaste. "Dark summons Dark. If trouble moves from the north, then it may well be drawing to it now anything which will aid it—even as a cruising captain may summon other ships to join him in a raid upon wreckers."

"Trade Master," Othor demanded, "news must be sent to all the trappers, the prospectors. Our camps are never large and they can be easily picked off, one by one, by whatever creeps upon us now."

"True." The Trade Master looked to the Watcher. "Can the Recall be given?"

"If it is not already too late." There seemed to be no wish in her to be reassuring, and those listening now had dour expressions. There was a murmuring and a stirring.

Trusla slipped out with Simond, determined to find Frost, while Simond himself headed to contact the captain. As she went, she speculated unhappily about what this new threat would mean to them. They had decided to hire a guide and a pack train within a day or two and head out in the direction Hessar had chosen for his season's labors, for the captain was certain, and both Frost and Inquit appeared willing to back him, that the location of the stream in which the plaque had been found would be the point from which they would start their search.

More than ever she wished that she had talent—to be like the woman in some bard's song who could summon up from the earth itself dead heroes buried centuries since in order to form an army

of the Light. As it was, she was sure that, even with all the inhabitants of End of the World armed and ready, they could not hope to
put a full troop in the field. Nor could they mount any of those
fighters. She was a passable archer only; her art was but newly
learned under Simond's direction. Sword work was beyond her, she
had not the strength to swing a battle blade. But her knife was
skilled and she had what Simond called a natural talent for throwing the perfectly balanced blade that was always with her.

She had nothing more—no spells. The sand—the jar of sand?
She had used it in Audha's aid, yes, but as a restorative, not a
weapon. Anyway, when and if she ventured forth from this earth-
bound town, she intended to take it with her.

There was Frost's gem and Trusla was duly aware that the witch
jewel had such powers as one could hardly speculate upon. What
Inquit could summon up she could not guess.

But somehow of this she was sure: their real search had not yet
begun and it would not be stopped here by a skirmish with the unknown.

She called her name before the door of the house which had
been turned over to Frost and Inquit. A small chirp answered her
and the door was edged back, with some effort, by Kankil, who
reached up to grab Trusla's hand and draw her in.

Like any hearthwife, Inquit was busy turning the contents of a
skillet at the fire so that the fresh-caught fish on it would be evenly
browned. And Frost, her long sleeves well rolled up, was tasting
critically the contents of a pot she had just swung away from the
greater heat of the inner fire.

To see the two of them busied at homely tasks was oddly reassuring, perhaps more so than if she had come in upon some summoning of Power. They seemed in good accord with each other
and secretly she was glad that the sourish Watcher was not here to
put them all upon their dignity.

But Frost let the spoon drip most of its contents into the fire,
which blazed up in answer.

"There is trouble," she said. Trusla almost believed she heard the faintest of sighs as if the witch gathered up again, for bearing an ever-present burden.

She waved Trusla to a seat on one of the cushions. Though Inquit did not lay aside her long-handled fork and her fish did not suffer from lack of tending, she, too, was watching the girl.

"There is trouble," Trusla confirmed. Swiftly she outlined the events of the morning, the return of Othor and his family and the ill news he brought.

Inquit shrugged. "How else could it be?" she asked apparently of the room itself. "The Watcher is right. If evil stirs, it becomes needful that it draws strength from somewhere—and how better than from summoning those it can command to do its will? These poor folk died hard deaths and that also is the way of evil, for blood is its feasting drink and never can it get enough of it. No, we have been too easy with ourselves. Now we call together those who must venture and lay what plans we can."

## CHAPTER THIRTY-SEVEN

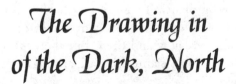

# The Drawing in of the Dark, North

For a number of the nearly endless days, with summer dusk banishing the dark, people returned to End of the World: families— kin clans—single trappers, and prospectors. But there were others who would never come again. There were grisly finds of at least three devastated camps with dead.

One of the last to arrive, a brawny giant of a man oddly

matched by a teammate who was a native, dragged at a distance behind the last pack animal in his party the tattered remnants of a grizzled gray thing broken and torn and exuding such a stench that he cut it free before he came to the circle of earth houses.

It was viewed at a distance by those with hardy stomachs, who agreed that what Hessar had snared in a rope trap was truly a stinkwolf. But that these had been the only attackers, many of the returning hunters denied—even though none of them had seen any human opponents.

There were conferences held in the Trade Master's hall, and on the fourth day of the indrawing a second ship made harbor. The *Spindrift* had come up along the coast from the Dales and their news was eagerly listened to.

"There is trouble aplenty," Captain Varmir declared. "Not in the Dales themselves, though they are restless—there have been two blood feuds between kin clans since the Year Turning, and Imry has his hands full with these hot-tempered swordsters.

"But ill news has spread from Arvon of danger in the Waste. That pest hole could hide any danger until it grows strong enough to engulf half a ship's crew. There is a place named Garth Howell."

Frost started and her hand went up as if to hide her jewel from menace.

"The traders are getting out," Captain Varmir continued, "and they have stories in plenty. Those of Garth Howell never troubled the land much—stay out of their claimed territory and you need only watch your back now and then. But those who carry rumors now say that it has been claimed by a Dark master and that those within it do his will.

"All the mantlelords have warded and will not stir from within those wards. But it is also said that some with the true Power are now daring the Waste itself, to bring Light into the Dark. May the Storm Ruler give them His axe and spear!"

"What say the shoreliners of the broken lands?" the Trade Master demanded.

"Little enough. That has always been outlaw territory and if the Dark eats up what hides there, the better for all concerned."

"Not eats," Frost said, and though she spoke quietly there was a sudden silence and all murmurs of talk in the hall stopped. "Not eats, but calls—or drives. Garth Howell . . ." There was such a look of revulsion now on her face that Trusla was amazed. She had never thought one of the nearly impassive witches could show such emotion. "Garth Howell is no fortress, no boundary holding. It is a place of storage of ancient knowledge. What if they have uncovered there, even as the mountains fall uncovered such at Lormt, things hidden and forgotten? Do any of these rumors, Captain, speak of travel northward?"

"No, lady, only that those of the Light travel west, and one who spoke with me in Quayth said that they were possessors of Power and on the trail of the Dark."

"As we should be also," Frost said slowly.

The Trade Master answered her quickly: "Lady, you have heard all our people have to say of the tundra. Where is any army you can summon to back you?"

Her lips curved into the faintest of smiles. "Trade Master, each of us has our purpose in life. What I and those with me have been sent to do must be accomplished." Suddenly she opened her hand and for an instant the jewel blazed.

"I will speak with my sisters now, and then there is much to be done."

She rose and left them. Something small and soft tumbled from the seat cushions and pattered after her, and then Inquit moved. Trusla felt the pull on her. Though she was not of their sisterhood, yet she was now compelled to follow.

With the return of the many summer-scattered parties, the newcomers no longer had the use of their homes. No one, though, had appeared to claim that which the shaman and the witch shared, and it was toward that that Frost now led the way.

Once within the larger foreroom, Inquit went straight to the fire and threw into the small core still living there something she had drawn from within her fur tunic—which must, Trusla had long since decided, have a number of pockets.

The red coals on the hearth flared green and she smelled a

strong puff such as came from the burning of the needlelike leaves of some northern trees.

Frost bent her head a little forward and drew that fragrance deep into her lungs, then settled herself on the cushioned ledge at the side of the room. Kankil curled up above her head, round eyes on the witch's face.

Trusla found a quiet shadow as far away from the witch as she could manage lest she disturb the other, and Inquit sat cross-legged by the fire, swaying slowly back and forth, her eyes closed. At length that swaying stopped and Trusla had the thought that the Latt had entered her own form of trance.

The girl closed her eyes, not for need of sleep, but because she felt she must shut out the world about her. And opened the doors of memory once more to the night of her awakening, her oneness for a space with another.

She was once more dancing on the carpet of red sand, yet there was a purpose in this. Like any maiden being trained for the ways of Volt, there were steps which were right and those which destroyed the weaving. One went so—and so—then one turned a fraction in another direction and this time took three steps, the next time nine.

Trusla set herself to embed in memory for all time the pattern of that dancing—for there would be a need in days to come. Twice through she danced that measure. The Sand Sister did not appear. This venture was her own to carry out. Yet she could feel the warmth of the other's care about her like a cloak.

"So be it."

Trusla opened her eyes. Her feet had trod the last of that measure—it was finished. She had learned what that which was in her desired her to learn. Frost sat up, though she leaned against one of the pillows, and the girl guessed that the witch had suffered from the usual energy drain laid upon those who used Power.

Inquit turned her head slowly, and her eyelids looked heavy as if she strove now to awaken from a dream. "So be it," she echoed he witch. "And it must be soon. That we hold Power it must sense, but so far it has had the besting of our kind. A ship and its people destroyed, camps turned into sinkholes of corruption at its will. The longer we sit, the stronger it grows. Captain Stymir was right—that which Hessar found in the ice river is the key."

"They labor at Lormt," Frost said. "Hilarion is the last of the early adepts. His searching must bring the answers we need. Those on the south trail have overcome some traps, but they head to even greater."

Neither of them looked to Trusla, nor seemed to be interested in what she had to report. For now she was satisfied that was so, for she could not have explained what she had done—or what she was meant to do.

They went together to Captain Stymir and discovered that he had somewhat anticipated them by meeting with Hessar. The plaque the latter had found lay between them on the small table in the captain's cabin of the ship. Simond was there and again he must have been at arms practice, for, though he had put aside his face-masking helm and thrown back the underhood of chain mail, he was still in full field gear. Matching him was Odanki, and they were both intent on the piece of skin scrawled with markings which the captain anchored in place with one thumb.

"No, Captain, I have not returned," Hessar was saying as the three women entered. "Nor would I take up the like of that again. It is an unchancy thing. Also"—a glare as if he were issuing some challenge struck them all from under his bushy brows—"believe me or not, but that water—it seemed ice-born even as are all such streams. But by Blood Oath, I tell you, it was warm!"

He appeared to be waiting for scoffing dismissal of his story. But Captain Stymir looked thoughtful.

It was the shaman who broke that short silence. "There is a strange place in our own lands," she said. "Ice lies around it—but within those walls there are springs which are hot enough to scald the hair from a leaper. And from them run—until they disappear underground—streams which are warm. Healing, too, though the smell is not pleasant. Those with an aching of the bones could lie in such streams where the heat was less and come out feeling limber once again. I have seen this place. When I was in my appren-

ticeship to Narvana I went with her. She harvested some of the
water, and some of the ill-smelling encrustations about the hottest
of the pools—which she kept and used for the good of the skin. If
such a place is in one part of the world, why can its like not exist
elsewhere? Hessar's stream may be the guide to it."

The Sulcar prospector nodded. But his scowl did not lighten.
"Unnatural things are best left alone," he commented gruffly.

However, he did agree to mark his trail to the ice stream, though
he utterly refused to be the guide there, even when Captain Stymir
offered him what Simond knew would be a well-filled purse even
in Es.

It would appear that no one in End of the World wanted to be a
part of what they would do. When Simond and Odanki went to
buy packhorses they were refused, except for four with hanging
heads which looked as if they were of small use to their present
owners. Nor would any of the townspeople volunteer as guides.

They gained but one more for their party and she came to them
in battle dress, a hard scowl on her face.

"I am blood-sworn to gather toll for my shipmates," Audha declared defiantly as she faced them. The girl had changed. She was
still lean of body, but Trusla, during her own bow practice each
day, had seen the wavereader in training combat with any who
would give her an opponent. And during the final days before they
planned to leave, that trainer was most always Odanki—nor did he
ever spare her, as far as Trusla could judge.

They had their supplies, but it was the Trade Master who at the
end ordered them a selection of better beasts chosen from those
owned by his own kin. However, these small creatures could not
carry packs even as full as a hill pony of the south. So the party
pared and pared again all they had brought with them.

They were assured there was game to be found clear up to the
very verge of the ice wall. In fact, along the foot of that even
greathorns were to be found. And such plants as could nourish a
traveler were carefully displayed and the virtues of each explained.

However, Trusla was well aware that those who helped never expected to see the party again. In fact, a few were hinting that their

very presence in the port perhaps could bring down the Dark on bystanders.

Stymir formally turned the captaincy of his ship over to his mate. Oddly enough, at the last moment he gained them another recruit—old Joul, who actually appeared where they were assembling the pack train with an animal of his own, a seaman's well-corded chest on its pack frame.

Since there was no real dawn in this land that was nearly always light, Trusla was not sure what time their small party moved out. But early as it was, there were those gathered to watch them. The attitude of those watchers, however, was somber, and there was none of the bright joking and friendly calls which had marked their embarcation from Korinth.

The Trade Master marched with them to the end of the scattered burrows of the village, but the Watcher, though appearing bedabbled in her ceremonial paint, made no such concession to ceremony. In fact, it was plain that she was glad to see the last of them.

Odanki, Simond, Stymir, old Joul, and even Audha strode along with full complements of weapons and armor, helms covering their heads. As usual Frost was well to the fore with her swift smooth stride. She carried no visible weapons, but she had accepted from the Trade Master a seasoned staff with the admonition that it was sometimes wiser to test patches of footing ahead. Matching her, the bulk of her feather cloak and furred cloth making her look almost square from behind, was Inquit, who led one of the horses, on the back of which, above the rolled belongings of the shaman, perched Kankil, who alone of their present company appeared to treat this faring forth as a good and exciting adventure.

There were no roads to follow here, only the traces of trails made by those who had gone out earlier this season and returned during the past few days. But they did have a guide, as they need only lift their heads to view it.

The glaciers in their slow march had covered the land, but even with their weight they had not completely defeated some show of the rock crowns of a cluster of northern mountains. It was toward one of these that Hessar had pointed them and somewhere along its cloaking glacier—if it *did* exist at present—they would find the seasonal drainage stream.

The land about them was so fair under the clear sky that Trusla found it hard to believe that evil had already marked it. However, long before nooning they were to have proof of what had occurred before and could be done to the unsuspecting travelers.

They saw the smoke first—tendrils befouling the air—before the odor of the burning reached them. Stymir and Simond split off from the party, but not until Inquit had joined them, moving as swiftly, in spite of her heavy clothing, as the men.

Frost took up position between the rest of the party and those going to investigate. She was holding her jewel and it was beginning to glow. But she made no attempt to stop them.

They did not go far. Those waiting could still see them as they stood together on a slight rise staring ahead—and then they returned at a swifter pace than they had gone.

"A death camp," the captain explained curtly. "We must not be caught in the open so."

"Nor shall we," replied Frost. "We have warning." She had slipped off the chain of the jewel and now held it lying flat on her palm before her. It glowed, not with the clear light of day, but rather with a dull and blackish color. Yet when Frost swung her hand toward the points of the half-buried mountains, it cleared.

"There be caves along the ice wall," Joul rasped. "Better a wall to the back, even if it be ice, than have to face four ways at once and perhaps find ourselves a fifth one and them in it we don't want to meet."

They no longer kept to the even pace of their morning's start. And when they halted to rest the animals and take some food for themselves, they ate with weapons close at hand. As they continued to travel steadily far into the dusky night with only a few such rests, the third day brought them to the ice wall.

Joul had been right. The edge of the glacier was pitted and jagged with falls of ice, some of it carrying great embedded boulders. It was among such that they set up a camp as a midpoint for their searching.

That night Frost again communicated with her sisterhood while entranced. But this time Inquit kept guard, sitting image-still at the witch's feet while Kankil guarded her head. Trusla, on impulse, brought out her sand jar and sat with it between her hands, but she did not allow herself any entrance into dreaming.

"There is a find," Frost reported at the loosening of her trance state. "Hilarion works against time to unravel some ancient puzzles. And"—now she was very sober—"this much fortune allows us. For some reason, that which awaits has for a space withdrawn. Whether this is a ruse on its part so that we shall enter its nets without sensing them, or whether it has exhausted more Power than it can now summon, who knows? For this space we are free, though how long that freedom will last I do not know."

"The more reason we find our stream, and speedily!" the captain said.

Simond stirred. "We have already marked streams," he said slowly. "One at least seems to agree with Hessar's description. Lady," he addressed Frost directly, "is there any way that something found can be again attracted to the place of its finding?"

Inquit clapped her hand over her mouth. Kankil, who had been in her usual resting position against the shaman, sent out a series of loud chirps and made almost wild gestures with her small paw-hands.

"Give me the find," the shaman commanded the captain.

He hesitated, watching the now extremely excited Kankil dubiously. Then he did produce the plaque. In the glow of the day that black center dot was this time fully visible. Kankil made a quick dart forward and wrested it out of his hands before he could stop her.

"Here—" He made a grab for the small creature, only to have Odanki suddenly between them.

Kankil brushed the mosslike tundra growth smooth and set the plaque at a precise angle on it, making several small adjustments, until she seemed sure that she was correct in what she would do.

Having so placed the plaque, she dropped cross-legged beside it. Holding out her hand with the stubby index finger pointing, she moved her hand as if it were fastened by a cord to the plaque. The plaque had, Trusla was sure, taken on a glow of its own, and certainly the blot which was its core was growing larger and darker.

It was clear to all of them that Kankil in no way touched the plaque where it lay. Yet suddenly the block lifted far enough so that space could be seen between it and the tundra on which it had rested.

Now Kankil, still holding her finger in position, scrambled to her feet. She moved as if she led one of the pack animals forward, while the plaque slid through the air definitely to some purpose.

The rest hastened to join her. Frost's jewel was again agleam, but once more with the white light of acceptance. They pushed on, silently, for they were all intent on what they were watching. There came the soft sound of running water and Kankil now stood on the bank of one of the lesser streams they had charted, not one they had considered a major find.

Slowly Kankil lowered her finger and the plaque sank to earth at the very edge of the stream. She looked over her shoulder to Inquit and shrilled those thrilling notes which Trusla had come to know signified pride and accomplishment.

Leaving the plaque lying now inert, she flung herself into the shaman's outstretched arms and hugged the woman.

"There are many talents, Captain. No one, even the ancient adepts, could count nor command them all. This little one is a talented searcher. She has found your stream."

The captain stopped to pick up the plaque. It slipped out of his fingers into the water and he grabbed frantically to get it back. Now he stared up at them all in utter amazement.

"It *must* be Hessar's stream in truth—the water is warm."

Which set them all to testing it. Compared to the icy, biting cold of the other streams, this was indeed warm and yet it flowed, as they could well see, out of a fractured crack in the ice wall, the chilling breath of which reached them.

They moved camp after Stymir was at last able to reclaim his trophy from the water, though the horses were unruly and could not be brought to drink of the stream or graze near it.

There was an odor to the water true enough. Yet the shaman's testing could produce no sign of anything poisonous. Now it remained for them to strike into the country of the ice itself.

Regarding those treacherous walls of the glacier which they had been warned to keep at a distance from, they could see no way of climbing to move inland. Odanki, the only one among them who knew the ice lands, declared at once that such a feat was impossible.

Nor could they take the pack beasts on any such climb, and to cut their supplies to less than half at near the very beginning of their journey would be utter folly. There remained then only one road for them—the bed of the stream itself. Stymir and Odanki tested it with staff and the poles of spears. Here it was not deep, though the bottom was dangerous, being strewn with stones released and washed down into the open. There were no fish or other life to be seen.

However, the fissure through which it came was nearly as tall as a ship's foremast and venturing in by degrees the men reported that that ceiling did not lower. However, the unpleasant smell of the water seemed caught under the ice roof to strike anyone daring to travel so.

That night they held a full conference, each giving an opinion. As Simond pointed out, Frost smiling and nodding as he spoke, they had never really believed that what they were sent to do would be an easy task. They had Frost's jewel for a warning and, though the shaman did not advance any details, she let it be known that she, also, had her ways of Power for protection and practical foreseeing. It was Audha who had the last word. As she was usually silent and aloof, her voice brought silence when she spoke:

"If there is but a single path, then that is the way I take with the morning. I cannot rest until my kin's blood is cleansed from me. I know little of your Light and Dark battles—to me this is a life debt and only I can pay it. Therefore I shall go."

And they accepted that she spoke the truth. Her ordeal in Dargh had left her with only one purpose—to repay death with death, and as all Sulcars she would hold to it.

## CHAPTER THIRTY-EIGHT

# Into the Land of Ice, North

It was impossible to force the packhorses to follow the road provided by the stream—not only because of their complete refusal to be dragged into the lapping water, but also because the rough bottom of the cut threatened broken legs for the small beasts.

Yet the party was reluctant not only to leave a larger part of their supplies behind, but to let the animals themselves drift free on the tundra, where it was very plain that something was eager to slay all invaders.

Inquit and Kankil of them all were able to round up the small beasts and hold them quiet while Frost went from one to the next, touching each with her jewel and so setting upon them some warding—though how strong that would be against what had already struck here, the travelers had no way of telling.

Their gear was then broken down into individual packs, and they assumed layers of spare clothing over that which they already wore, in protection against the freezing cold which they were certain awaited them ahead. Into a larger pouch she could swing from her belt, Trusla managed to stuff the jar of sand.

They had a last very hearty meal, consuming supplies which could not be taken. The horses had already wandered off, grazing as they went. They did not scatter apart far but kept close enough that they might be in a recognized herd.

The horses were finally gone, small black dots to be seen only in the distance but certainly heading on the back trail, when, after a rest period Stymir urged on them all, the travelers gathered together for their own departure. Each was equipped with a staff of sorts—mainly a stout spear—from the spare supplies. Because of the rough footing, they had to proceed at a slow pace and make sure that every step was as stable as possible. Still there were falls, plunging the unfortunate forward into the water—which luckily never reached more than thigh high.

The crevice—though it offered only the narrowest strip of footing on either side of the stream—did not narrow as they went. But it did close overhead so that they moved through a strange dusky world, transparent in places and elsewhere containing dark blots that were perhaps rocks carried forward by the eternal invisible movement of the ice.

"It is warmer!" They had halted for a breathing space and Captain Stymir drew off his heavy glove to plunge his hand into the water. He was right, as the others' experiments quickly confirmed. The stream, which had been only faintly warm when they had first found it, was distinctly heated to a higher degree.

One good result of this appeared to be its effect on the size of the fissure, as that continued to widen until they could splash along at its sides in lower water.

"Aaaagha." Odanki, who had been in the lead, suddenly halted, with so little warning that Frost had to catch at his pack to keep herself on her feet. There seemed to be a jog here in the way they were following. The ice wall which projected, forcing the stream to one side, was opaque and dark. Trusla, expecting to see a rock of some monstrous size, pushed a little on until Simond caught her in a nearly bruising grip.

This was no rock! What it might be she could not, for a moment, understand. In some places the encasing ice had thinned enough so she could see what seemed to be a cluster of snakes, each of them larger than a man's leg in girth, frozen together in a contorted knot.

Above those rose a dome which ended in a great beaklike projection, and there were two saucer-sized pits which might once have sheltered eyes.

The ice had melted back a little in one place so that the tip end of one of those snakelike appendages was freed to trail down to the water. But from the position in which the creature had been frozen it seemed that it was about to launch itself straight at them if they tried to pass, if it could at its will break its prison.

"Sethgar!" The Sulcar captain stood looking up at the thing which towered well over him. "But—but demons do not lie in ice!" He looked to Frost. "Lady, we have a very ancient tale of such as this—that they acted as do the Hounds of Alizon but the masters they obeyed were beyond the power of men to battle." He suddenly caught at his fur overgarment and brought forth the plaque.

There was a glow about it and he spat out an oath, nearly dropping it into the water, as if it had burned or cut his fingers. At the same time Frost's jewel flared red.

"It is dead, long dead." Inquit used the tip of her spear to poke at that dangled bit the ice had released. It quivered under her prodding, but that was all.

"This Sethgar," Simond demanded. "It was a thing of the sea, was it not?"

Certainly they could not see any form of legs—only those lengthy snakelike appendages.

"Yes. But . . ." the captain was staring down at the plaque he held. Once more it resembled a small window through which they could see into . . . where? Another world? Trusla wondered.

The strange black ship was far clearer in every detail now. And, plainly clinging to the deck near the bow, was a dark mass which could be just such a creature as they faced now.

"It seems"—Frost cradled her jewel against her—"that if your legend of coming through some ice gate in the north is correct, then we are finding proof of what hunted your people here, and we follow the proper trail."

Stymir visibly shuddered. "Lady, some tales are told for the pleasure of listeners who, sitting by a comfortable fire, enjoy to shudder at what does not exist. To see a demon come to life is no light thing."

"It is no demon." Odanki had advanced, spear in hand. Now he struck the ice wall which covered the monster. A chip or two broke off, but there was no other change. "This is old, old, and long since dead—the ice will release it in time and it will rot into nothingness like any dead thing."

Joul uttered a cackle of laughter. "The Latt has the right of it, Captain. It is true that even men have been lost in ice crevices only to be spouted forth years later looking as they did when they went in."

In Stymir's hold the plaque appeared to dull and he looked down at it and then shrugged. "So be it. But the Lady is right— what we search for must lie ahead."

There was no way here to establish any resting place. Though their pace from the start had been a slow one, bodies began to ache from the constant care one must take to avoid the perils of the footing. They ate sparingly as they went and Trusla began to wonder if she could keep up—the ice crevice appeared to have no end.

Odanki had scooped up Kankil and the little one rode on his shoulders, chirping now and then, perhaps to herself, for no one answered her.

The mist came first, Trusla suddenly realized that the water had been growing ever warmer as they went and now there was a thin cloud rising from it ahead.

Luckily the passage widened ever larger and there was a stretch of mixed earth and gravel on either side of the stream which was fast becoming truly hot. But, in spite of their efforts, they were lagging, though advancing doggedly.

Now there was a smell also, one which irritated throat and nose and set them coughing. It was perhaps borne by that stream.

Trusla dug her spear butt into the ground and pulled herself on. Simond had tried to take her pack beside his own some time back, but she refused. Each must give all one could to this venture.

Then they came out of the hold of the ice, into a world they could not believe at first look existed. They must have been struck down by some glamorie during that march.

There was a sharp slope to the ground ahead. The stream developed rapidly high banks and from it the strong odor arose, thick enough to drive them back from the water.

At a space beyond, the ground was free of any hint of ice, and green with a growth not unlike that of the summer-freed tundra. There were clumps of color which could only be flowers, and the air above them was so humid and sultry that their bodies, under all their layers of clothing, were as wet as if they had just climbed from baths.

Then, as if to announce their coming, straight out of a patch of mud of many colors there arose with a roar a plume of spray. Audha cried out and jumped back, catching a heel in the thick vegetation and sprawling on her back, nursing one hand with the other as if some droplets of the spray had reached her.

They were cautious in their venturing farther into this strange place of heat amid the cold. They saw the rise of the mountains beyond, and more glaciers there, but here the heat was almost that of midsummer in the south and they were panting, striving to move farther away from that muddy space which made up about half of the open earth. This was spotted with holes which fountained up at startling intervals to add to the heat and the smell.

At length they retreated to a grouping of rocks behind which the glaciers showed not too far away. Waterlogged clothing had to be shed, though whether any of this would dry they could not guess.

The grassland had inhabitants. Odanki dug out from a shallow den a fat little creature which both the Latts seemed to recognize, and one of Simond's arrows gave them a beast not unlike one of the leapers of their homeland, save that it was thicker of body.

So they ate and then their bodies demanded rest from the trials of the day. It was, Trusla thought, early morning when she settled on a still-damp bank cushioned by the moss beneath.

For the shaman there appeared to be no rest. The Estcarpian girl was too spent to do more than watch, but when Frost and the Latt woman drew a little away, she realized that Inquit intended a use of

Power, though Frost did not seem ready to rouse her talent. Perhaps she was anchorage for the shaman.

Trusla expected to dance once more in her dreams—to follow the pattern laid in her mind upon the sand. Instead . . .

Like one of the house pests of the ancient holds it came nibbling—seeking. Though it exerted no great Power, Trusla was well aware that it held such in abeyance. Curious—*she* presented some puzzle to what came spying.

Then there was a very clear picture. She was not a part of this but only a watcher—though there was a part of her which fought to aid.

They were fleeing, those white-sailed ships. Sulcar ships, she knew, even if their main sails were painted with strange patterns. Behind them all the sea and sky was dark—not with the honest dusk of night, but rather as if something like a great sword blade swept across the sky and sea.

There were lights on each ship, the strongest coming from their bows. Not from lanterns, she was certain, but rather as if each vessel had a life force of its own.

Out of the sea, near a lagging rearguard ship, arose huge snake arms—even greater than she had seen as part of the ice-bound creature. Those strove to seize upon the ship. But the light at the prow suddenly blazed high, and the sea thing fell away as if blinded.

So they came—with the Dark ever behind them. Now she could see that the waters boiled with a multitude of the monsters. But she sensed that on one of those ships rode a great will, one who had honed talent and Power into a weapon, wasting nothing of what he could control until this hour when it was needed most.

Out of the curtain of the Dark burst another ship and this one she also knew—for she had seen its likeness in the plaque which had drawn them here. It flashed forward though it carried no sails, like a thing with sentient life.

The Sulcar ships drew into line, sailing as close to each other as they dared. They were like a thread forced through the eye of a needle, and the black ship was fast upon their wakes.

There was a burst of light, so eye searing that Trusla cried out and all was darkness. She was in Simond's arms and he was calling her name with concern. There were others around, but all she could do for the present was to cling to him and wait for her dimmed eyes to clear.

One of them came to kneel beside where Simond held her, eyeing her searchingly.

"You have dreamed!"

Through even Simond's calling her name those three words sounded clearly. And Trusla answered:

"I have—seen—" For certainly that had been no dream, such as one small talent wove.

Then there was another beside the Latt shaman, and with her coming was a glint of light which made the world about Trusla fully real again. She told them—of that flight of ships before the curtain of the everlasting Dark, of the black ship which had come to cut the waves of their wakes, and then of the light which had left her blinded so she had not seen any more of that flight.

"The gate," Frost said. In her hold her jewel lost that spark of light which had fully aroused the girl. "And those who fled—surely they had Power of their own. What kind, Captain? What did your ancient kin use to defeat the Dark which would have followed?"

He shook his head. "Lady, some Power we have over storms and freaks of the sea. But none else which any of our blood could tell you. Could it not be that this destroying light came from that which pursued?"

"Yet you stand, Sulcar man, in a world you swear was never yours to begin with. No, I think that your far kin won free. Free and able to leave the warning which you carry now—the likeness of their enemy."

"In the ice . . ." the Latt shaman was no longer looking at Trusla; rather, it was as if she stared inward. "I dreamed also—not of the past as did this one, but of what happens now and—"

She got no further, for out in that mud and steam there whipped up into the air a great lash and the heat of it reached them even as far as they were from the fount.

There was a second such and a third, driving them back against the wall of stone and ice. And each was closer. So they moved toward the north for the boiling spray which now seared the green growth in the direction from which they had come. At last they appeared trapped in a shallow break of the wall while back and forth across what had been a richly green land beat whips of steaming mud and water, the fumes of which set them coughing and fighting for good air to breathe.

Trusla saw a swing of light. Frost's jewel, flaming like an earth-tied star, swung back and forth. Beside her the shaman was—in spite of coughing—chanting. The girl saw Inquit's hand raise, in it one of the long feathers she must have pulled from the edging of her cloak. Three times she waved it and then let fly, and fly it did—out into that streaming mush of what had once been land.

It was not a bird—no, as it went it became more like a long-shafted dart, flung straight as a small hunting spear. Into a rain of blistering mud it winged.

The column, fed from some inferno below, broke as if the shaman had sliced it with a great sword. The light from Frost's jewel caught another threading pillar, setting it awhirl inside a narrow space.

They knew this upheaval for what it was: no act of nature. Rather, the attack of something which was alien—alien enough perhaps not to realize that they had such protection or strengths. If it had not realized that, it accepted such knowledge quickly. No more geysers arose from the mud, though long streaks of stinking, steaming earth had withered the green which had first welcomed them.

Trusla choked rackingly and still held to Simond. But that oppressive feeling that they were being confronted by something entirely alien to all they knew had withdrawn now.

"Qwayster." Joul had drawn his sword as if to use that in defense. "The breath of Qwayster!" Beside him Captain Stymir stood, a gray cast under the sea tan on his face. He was coughing, tears streaming from his blue eyes, a small red patch on one arm showing under a smoking hole burned in his tunic.

"Have you given us a true name, seaman?" Frost asked, her jewel still at ready, though no more fountains were rising. "Do we now face some adept known and named?"

It was the captain who was shaking his head. "Demon, Lady. Another out of ancient tales: a force which could be commanded by one of great Power—to use the earth itself as a weapon. Was it not so with you of Estcarp when you made the southern mountains turn to your will?"

"That took the Power of all the sisterhood," she said slowly. "Do you tell us now, Captain, that our enemies may be legion?"

Inquit stopped smoothing the edge of her cloak as if she had been soothing it for the loss of the feather. "Not many but one. But very old. It has slept long and now it wakes. Did I not dream also? Yes, we are on the proper road, but that one has been astir for only a short time. It was the wild magic doubtless that called her forth."

"*Her?*" Simond's surprise was plain.

The shaman smiled. "One woman does not mistake the magic of another, young lordling. To touch talent to talent is to learn. Yes, what we are to face is no adept, but one as wily and perhaps as Dark-filled as any who fought in the Great War to blast our world long since. Only this one is not of our universe. She thinks, she seeks, she feels her way—she is wily as an old wasbear with cubs to defend, and as greedy as a direwolf pinched by winter hunger. She will watch—and I think perhaps continue to test us. But she is not going to waste any great Power until we face her in her own place, where she feels that she is strongest."

"And where is that place?" demanded the captain.

"It shall call us as she wishes. Nor must we fight such a call, for only face-to-face can we make the final testing. Your talk of gates, southern-born, is true. This one was caught on our side of one, entrapped in the Power which closed it upon her kin. She took the way of long sleep, waiting for that which would aid her. Then the wild magic broke the web she herself had woven."

A woman—if such could be counted a woman, Trusla thought. But then the witches had wrought great things and there were tales that there had been women also among the ancient adepts. Only—

the girl shivered—the thought that it was female made it somehow more monstrous.

They spent what was left of the night in the small patch of green which had survived the attack of the mud. The choking steam subsided. Odanki and Simond went on scout when the camp roused and they had eaten, edging along the wall of the valley. Trusla was not aware until she was repacking her shoulder bag that Audha had disappeared. The Sulcar girl was always so quiet and retiring that half the time one forgot that she was one of them.

If Audha had not followed Simond and the Latt hunter, then she could have only gone in one direction—backtrailing. And Trusla was still dubious about those attacks of mud.

She spoke to Inquit, and by the shaman's sober face she apparently shared Trusla's concern. It was then that Kankil caught at the edge of Trusla's tunic and urged her along, chirping as usual but not as if she went in any fear.

"We go—the little one knows," Inquit said. At her agreement, which Kankil seemed to understand, the small one loosed her hold on Trusla and bounded ahead.

They still kept to the edge of the cliff's foot. None of the masses of mud had reached this far and there was a green fringe. Kankil gave a sudden squeal and threw herself on her knees, clawing aside the thick mass of leaves to reveal bright berries. She gathered a pawful of these and brought them back to the shaman and then went to harvest some for Trusla. The fresh taste of the fruit seemed to banish some of the stale remains of yesterday's memories.

Though they were tempted to stop and harvest more, they went on, coming to a place where a great wedge of rock extended out into the valley. It had been well scoured by the ice which had carried it here, but now, Trusla noted, as she had not when they had passed it before, there was an opening of sorts between it and the cliff and it was into that Kankil pattered.

Once more they strode over uneven gravel, but there was no stream to wade this time. Instead Inquit pointed to a scraped place on the wall as if someone had left a sign on purpose.

It was beyond that, under the overhang of the rock, that they found a new road. Trusla eyed it in wonder before turning to Inquit for confirmation.

"It—it is a stair!" But who had it served? There was none in this country to have built such a range of wide steps. Yet it was plain that that had been done.

But they had not yet tried that trail when they sighted something else—a sight which halted even the agile Kankil.

Set to one side of this way was a ledge, chiseled into the rock with the same precision and craft which had built the stairway. And on it . . .

Trusla gasped. A row of skulls had been set with care, but what made them so hideous was the fact that each bony dome of the bodiless head had been covered with a luxuriant growth of the same moss as that which grew over the ground below, so that it would seem the weathered bones were fully haired.

Inquit's first astonishment seemed quickly past. She had approached the line and was studying them carefully, though she did not touch any.

"Not man as we know," she said. "Look at the size of the eye holes, and this ridge of bone above those. Also they are wider in the jaw. No, not men."

Trusla was willing to accept that verdict without any examination of her own. There were races in Escore which certainly bore little resemblance to humankind and yet held intelligence as great or greater than her species. It could well have been that some such had once lived here.

Now the shaman seemed to have lost interest in the line of skulls. Instead she brought out the long-bladed knife which served her for so many purposes. With the point of this she was digging along a space between the skulls and the edge of the ledge. Soil, roots of plants, and small stones scattered under her assault. But what she had uncovered was not the natural roughness of the rock but deeply incised lines which had the appearance of runes.

Beginning on the left Inquit touched each of those symbols with knifepoint again, and repeated some click-click of her native speech. However, she was shaking her head decidedly. "Not a spell of my knowledge. Best leave it alone. And best of all move to find Audha. She may be bound where it is dangerous to go."

## CHAPTER THIRTY-NINE

# The Lair of the Ice Worms, North

With a cautious eye at frequent intervals for the mud lake, Simond and the Latt hunter kept as close to the ice and rock wall of the valley as possible. Simond half expected some advice from Frost—even that the witch might accompany them—but she had not come. In fact, Frost had seated herself by the rocks where they had camped, and Simond had a strong belief that she had withdrawn into herself in some form of trance.

They could not follow a straight line, but luckily the margin between the wall and the mud continued and they kept to this. There were still the spouting of geysers to be seen, but they were small and few. Perhaps whatever force had sent them in action against the invaders slept again.

Odanki grunted and pointed with his spear. Arching up from the meager green of the ground growth here were bones, curved like ribs but certainly larger than those serving any animal Simond had ever seen.

The Latt squatted on his heels and tugged at the remnants of the skeleton. At his touch the bones flaked and two broke, and he uttered an exclamation of disgust. His disturbance of the remains had moved them enough so that Simond could now see great branching horns, far more weighty he would have believed possible for any beast to wear comfortably.

Odanki turned his attention to these, prodding forcibly with the butt of his spear. They seemed to have outlasted the bones, for they did not crack. He grunted and then got to his feet and dragged at the best handholds he could find, freeing both the horns and the skull wearing them from the hold of the ground.

"Greathorn," he commented. "Good!"

Strong as the young Latt was, he apparently could not drag his trophy far and Simond helped him pull it closer to the cliff. It was plain that Odanki had found what was treasure as far as he was concerned.

Yet he was willing enough to leave it when Simond suggested that they move ahead. Those cliffs of glacier they could see in the distance arose so quickly they almost appeared to race before them as they tramped on. Simond wondered if the fumes they had inhaled had in some way affected their sight.

On they went, though they made no more discoveries. Then suddenly there was a change and the ground beneath them began to slope slowly downward. Simond readied himself to face perhaps another set of mud pools and spouts.

However, not only were those now behind them, but they felt a chill which struck with doubled force, since they had been in the unexpected warmth of the valley for so long. The ground growth became a ragged fringe and there were not only rocks but the tips of ice formations showing, some to catch the light and reflect it.

This broken land led to what Simond could only think of as a lake. Yet one which no waves moved but rather which held the glitter of glass—a smooth stretch on which there were no cracks or crevices.

Odanki pushed with spear point. There was a *ping* and a splinter flashed upward.

"Solid ice," he commented. To Simond's surprise the Latt sat down on the edge of this threat of dangerous footing and burrowed into the pack he carried slung over one shoulder.

What he brought out might have been chipped from the same great horns as the ones they had discovered. And he fit curved frames, one over each trail boot, testing several times each fastening. When he stood again he rocked awkwardly from foot to foot and then deliberately stepped down upon that glassy surface, using his spear to steady himself.

He moved out a space and then curved back, nodding to Simond as he came.

"I go across." He indicated the far side of that ice lake. "Have no runners for you."

Before Simond could protest, Odanki did head out from the shore, slipping along on the ice, apparently well satisfied with his method of progress, leaving the Estcarpian fuming behind.

But there was nothing Simond could do. The Latt was plainly used in his own land to such odds and was ready for them. However, Simond had no intention of returning alone to camp, his part of their scout having ended so abruptly. Why had the Latt not shared from the beginning these aids? Or else they were so common to his people that he had thought Simond already knew of them.

The Estcarpain watched carefully the Latt's progress until suddenly he became aware of something else. Though the ice seemed clear when looked down upon, it was opaque beneath the surface and seemed solid. Only Odanki's shadow, pale in this thin sunlight, stretched in the opposite direction. However, now there *was* a vague trace of movement beneath him under that ice.

Since here certainly the unknown was to be feared, Simond shouted. When Odanki turned his head to look back toward him, the Estcarpain waved vigorously, first to that half-hidden movement in the ice and then for the other to return.

Only his warning was a fraction too late. Suddenly the Latt floundered. Around him spread a patch of fast-melting ice. He was fighting for footing as might one who had been caught in quicksand. He cried out in a shout which held both pain and fear.

Simond measured the distance between the shore and where the hunter struggled. Though Odanki floundered and fought, that space of melting ice had slowed in enlarging. Simond threw a twist of rope about a rock and pushed off away from the shore.

By great effort the Latt had reached the edge of that melting ice, wedging his spear across that point from side to side. But he shrieked—not fear now, but pain.

Simond teetered forward on the ice, hoping that the sand and gravel frozen into the soles of his thick boots would give him some steadiness. Small and slight though he might seem, his Tor blood gave him a strength of arm and shoulder which might equal, if not better, Odanki's.

Somehow the Estcarpian was able to fight his way toward the Latt, though what had attacked the latter remained well hidden under the ice shield. Simond knotted the other end of the rope into a loop. The Latt cried out and raised an arm to wave him back, but Simond was able to throw that circle over the upheld arm.

Then he dropped to his hands and knees and turned his back on the hunter, beginning to crawl for the shore, taking the strain of the other's weight on his shoulders. Always he looked beneath him for any shadow moving under the ice.

There was a sudden loosening of the strain, and, holding fiercely to the rope, he dared to look back. The Latt had somehow clambered out of the ice mush and was using both arms to propel himself in a frantic slide toward Simond.

After breathless moments they crawled out on the shore, Simond jerking Odanki with him. For the larger man had suddenly gone limp. Simond looked down the length of the Latt's body.

There was torn hide clothing, there was blood—and a trio of things which brought bile up into Simond's throat. He beat at them as they still held to their prey, for Odanki could only feebly raise his hands now, smashing them against the firm ground.

One had dug itself so deeply into its intended feast that Simond had to grab it with one hand and slash with a knife he held in the other—only to cry out himself as the body he stubbornly held until it was free of the Latt's leg was like a branding iron laid across his own flesh. The things were soft and pink, with wedge-shaped heads which flamed into fire-red and were nearly the length of an arrow. Luckily their removal into the outer air apparently seemed to weaken them, and Simond was able to kill the last and let the burning body fall.

That things of such heat could lair in the ice was like another form of Power and certainly one he could not understand. He worked over Odanki quickly, stanching the bleeding bites, while the other lay his arm flung across his eyes as if he could not bring himself to look upon Simond's work.

There were bites, and torn flesh, but the Estcarpian applied the powders and pads each of them carried for emergencies. Then he urged Odanki to chew a twist of root which he knew was a painkiller.

That there might be vemon in those bites worried Simond. And he was not sure he could get Odanki back to camp on his own. At length he dragged the Latt as far from the edge of the ice lake as he could and covered him with handfuls of earth to keep him warm.

Before Simond left to summon help, he went back to view the inhabitants of the lake. Their brilliant color was fading fast now as their broken bodies cooled. But they were still repulsive—like great worms. They carried the fringes of many small legs on either side, and the open mouths of those horny wedge-shaped heads were well equipped with double rows of teeth.

When Simond returned with Stymir and Joul to aid the Latt, Odanki insisted that he would walk with help, and he did. Simond supposed it was the Latt's horror of the very nature of his enemies which had added earlier to the loss of blood to weaken him.

Both the Sulcars had inspected the bodies with open astonishment, being forced to believe that Simond and Odanki were right: the creatures could generate such heat in their bodies that they could melt the ice and so trap prey they could probably see as shadows on the surface above them. Even after lying dead in the cool air, those flame-hot wedge heads still held a good degree of heat.

"Do they live in the mud?" Simond wondered. "But then why hunt prey in the ice?"

Stymir laughed grimly. "You can ask many *whys* for things one comes across traveling, Lord Simond. This is another freak of nature."

"Not something sent?" Simond wondered.

"I think not. Come, let us get our comrade back to those who have healing Power."

As they passed the horned skull, Odanki made them promise that that also would be retrieved. Stymir tested the strength of the horns and then agreed. "Such are good tools upon occasion," he told Simond. "It will do no harm for us to see what can be done with this pair, especially since he may be in camp for some time." He gave a meaningful glance toward the hunter.

When Simond returned to camp for the second time, he looked around for Trusla, surprised that she was not in sight. Joul mentioned that with the shaman and her familiar his wife had gone to hunt Audha, who had disappeared. He would immediately have set out on their trail—perhaps ice worms were not the only strange perils to be met with—but Frost stopped him.

She looked very gaunt and drawn, and he was sure that she had been using some Powers, so that a thrust of fear went through him.

"Listen." She kept him both silent and pinned with her eyes, so that he could not leave her. "They have broken the secret lockings—Hilarion and those of Lormt. I have it here." She touched not her jewel but her forehead. "But lest something happen to me, the secret must now be shared. The shaman is gone, as is Trusla—both having talents. The Sulcars—they had never been able to use any Power unless it deals directly with the sea. Therefore . . ."

He took a step backward. "Lady, I am no lore master—nor even of the Old Blood."

"No, not of *our* Old Ones, but of others. You come from those who once sheltered under the wings of Volt, who was mighty as any adept. You say you have no talents, and perhaps by the measuring of others you do not. But you can remember—though the passages of long memory have never been opened for you. Therefore—you *must* remember. And if I cannot reach the end of this quest, you will share this memory and those with Power shall put it to use. Come."

He had been slowly retreating, she following him step by step, and now they were behind a shelter of rocks, out of sight of the rest of the company. He tried to dodge, be free of what she would lay upon him, but he could not move.

Up came her hand holding her jewel. It did not blaze, but rather issued forth a soft, golden light. In him the fears which had stirred settled and were gone. Simond felt the touch of the jewel to his forehead between his eyes.

There was a strange sensation—as if he walked down a hall lined on either hand with doors, all closed. On them glimmered symbols which he felt, as he noted each, he should know, that they were a part of a past he could not quite understand.

Then he came to the final door, the one which ended the hallway. It did not open, but simply disappeared. Now he faced a great wall of the same soft gleaming color as had accompanied him on this journey. There was a sighing—like the soft slow beat of great wings.

On the wall a great clawed hand began to write. Each symbol it formed was in the precious blue which meant refuge from all which was of the Dark. Though Simond did not understand, he also knew that he would not forget those symbols. They would be a part of him until this life's end.

Softness, like the tips of great feathers brushed against his cheek. He knew it for a blessing and a farewell. Simond blinked and Frost stood before him holding a gem once more turning gray.

"You remember?" Frost asked.

Immediately there flashed into his mind those symbols. He also knew, without being told, that though he did not know their meaning, he could, when there was need, voice each of them in turn.

Frost smiled. "Yes," she said, "always when there is a need the Light will answer. Now—you would find your lady, and . . ." she hesitated, a slight frown now drawing her brows together, "there is need there, also. I cannot understand." Now she was speaking more to herself than to him, and he was eager to be gone. "There is something calling—but if it is born of the Dark, it is of no evil we know."

Simond was already on his way, Stymir behind him, and they followed the same trail which had been laid out for the women that morning. There was no sign of any troubling of the mud pool except for a stray geyser now and then well away from them. However, the stinking mud and seared ground growth remained as a warning.

The Estcarpain had served on scouting expeditions enough to pick up the signs of passing left by those they hunted—the more so since the women had taken no trouble to conceal their going. So he and the captain came to the stairway and started up.

They halted by the row of skulls, and Simond saw quickly the runes Inquit had uncovered.

"What is the meaning?" he demanded. There were too many mysteries in this place, and, even if this was a very old one, that did not render any message it held harmless.

The captain had gone down on one knee, the better to inspect the near-invisible lines, and then set to picking with his own knife-point at those still hidden.

"This"—he used the knifepoint to indicate one of the runes— "is the old form used in the master scrolls for the Ruler of Storms. This"—he had selected another—"is a plea. It is Sulcar—but so old . . . I can give you no meaning for the rest."

"Those are not Sulcar skulls." Simond had been studying the row with their green gloss of what might be hair.

"No," Stymir agreed at once. "And my people were never ones to take heads as battle trophies as some of the Dark-ruled barbarians do. But that my kin came this way I will swear."

Simond had already placed his foot on the next step. "They went on—see, there is a scrape of boot edge. What brought Audha in this way?"

"What has brought all of us? We seek for the lost. What? An enemy, a gate, something which threatens us? Can it not be that that which we seek can use one of *us* to its own purposes?"

"She swore blood oath against that threat." Simond tried to keep his voice level. "Do you mean that in doing so this wavereader opened herself to the very purpose of that which she hates?"

Once in the past he himself had been insidiously taken over, to be used for another's bloodlust in sacrifice. It had been Trusla who had broken the bond he did not even realize held him, and brought him to freedom. So he well knew that such things could be.

"Who knows?" the captain replied.

They had reached the top of that very ancient stairway and were looking out now over the rough surface of the glacier toward those distant mountains. Simond's frustration became anger. Trusla knew nothing of such lands, but Inquit was of the north and surely must be well aware of the perils of the way ahead.

However, a moment later he sighted dark dots moving steadily toward the mountains, though they went slowly and with caution. But the thought of a break in a snow arch, a fall into a tomb crevice, caught at Simond until he found it hard to breathe.

Three dots: two larger, one small. So they had not yet caught up with Audha. There were signs of a trail right enough, but that could have been left by those they themselves followed.

"It is the little one who leads," Stymir pointed out. "Perhaps some talent of hers is what they depend upon as guide."

Simond wanted nothing more at that moment than to seize upon Kankil and jerk her back, bring them all to camp once again. But the captain was right. There was a space between the shaman and her familiar and Trusla brought up the rear.

They had heard plenty of stories in Korinth and again in End of the World about the perils of the glaciers. Not only was the footing highly treacherous, but oftentimes glaciers provided lairs for the great wasbears, and to approach any such while its owner was in residence was to call upon death foolishly.

"How much farther?" Trusla brushed a string of hair back under the fur which framed her face within her hood. The bite of the cold after the warmth of the valley seemed doubly severe. She had tucked her hands into her armpits to warm them a fraction every time she and her companions halted. For their progress was not steady, since Kankil cast back and forth for the trail continually.

Where could Audha be bound? There was nothing but this ever-lasting ice, cold, and those stark mountains in the distance. Was she being called?

Knowing how her own Tor people could apply that compulsion on occasion, the thought had come to her much earlier in the day that that was what might have happened. She suggested it, and, to vanquish her one small hope, Inquit had agreed. Wisdom suggested that they turn back, yet Kankil chirped and clicked and the shaman followed. Glancing behind several times, Trusla was not sure she *could* find once more that stairway into this dreary country.

They came to the end as Kankil huddled on the edge of a great crevice which appeared to descend to the very depths of the earth. And there the trail ended.

Trusla looked down with a shudder and turned swiftly away. She could well envision what had happened. Audha, reaching this cut-off, yet still compelled to go forward, could have blindly marched over the lip of that break and lie so far below that no one would ever see her again.

Inquit prowled back and forth along the crevice. Oddly enough, she never looked down, but rather stared across the width of the break. There was certainly no sign that a bridge of any kind had ever existed here.

"She fell. She is dead," Trusla said at last. As the wind whipped around her, she felt as if she, too, would soon be gone, lapped forever in ice as had been the monster they had seen.

"No." Inquit's denial was flat. "There is still life essence to be sensed—the little one knows. But it is true that from where we stand we cannot now follow."

"Where we stand we shall be frozen stiff," Trusla returned. "What do you mean that Kankil knows? Knows what? Did Audha grow wings and is she off to the mountains?"

Inquit gave her a hard stare. "There is more than one kind of wings, Tor woman. I seek mine in sleep, and dreams can carry one afar."

Trusla stamped her foot and a small ridge of ice cracked. "You cannot sleep and dream here! I do not believe that any Power would hold you so."

"Exactly right. But dream I shall. Now we return; there are those already searching for us and we must not scatter our forces too widely. I do not know. . . ." For another long moment she stood, gazing ahead across the crevice. "I would speak with the witch. We do not hold the same talents, but together . . . Well enough. Come child, before, as you threaten, you turn into a pillar of ice."

So they turned their backs upon the crevice and started their retreat, again Kankil bouncing ahead as if she knew that they still needed a guide.

Suddenly, as they went, Trusla sighted two figures headed toward them. That was Simond! The cold which ate at her no longer bound her to shuffling, halting steps. She passed Kankil, taking only caution that she not make a misstep. Then Simond's arms were around her. He was shaking her until her head bobbed on her shoulders and then he enveloped her in a hug which drove all that ice from her veins.

## CHAPTER FORTY

# The Ice Palace, North

Audha floated in and out of the world through which she slipped and slid. Around her, she was dimly aware, were walls of dark ice within which shadowy things loomed now and then. Yet she was not conscious of cold. That drawing was fast upon her, and nothing mattered but that she finish this journey.

All which had been her earlier life faded and no longer had any meaning. She could not even remember now the faces of her ship-mates, nor of those with whom she had recently traveled, even though now and then she had a moment or two when she glanced from one ice wall to the other expecting faintly to see forms she knew.

One thing she had not lost in this journey, and that was the avid need to see what waited at the end of it. She fell over bad footing, rose again to keep on.

Now she began to sense that she was not alone after all—yet who or what accompanied her was beyond her range of sight. She felt fear once or twice, and then that was wiped from her as a cloth might soothe her sweating face.

She hungered and thirsted, and now and then she absently picked at the ice of the wall and sucked at it. Still whatever drew her kept her going. She had brought no pack or supplies with her, only the spear which served her as a support and a staff, and the knife at her belt.

How long she walked in that daze within the crevice she did not know. The dusky light always appeared the same, as if it clung about her to give her sight, after a fashion.

Then the crevice began to narrow, until at last her shoulders were brushing walls and the footing was slanting more and more sharply upward. At length she drew her knife and dug in as best she could to draw herself forward, and at last floundered weakly into the open once again.

Vaguely she knew that to remain where her exertions had brought her was to fall prey to the cold, but she wanted nothing more than to remain where she was, to let the dullness close down upon her mind and forget all which lay behind, or might wait on her ahead.

Yet that compulsion would not release her. With the spear as a steadying staff, somehow Audha got to her knees and then hauled herself to her feet. Then she looked around.

The plain of the glacier stretched about, but, not too far ahead, a rocky rise split the ice flow. And to Audha's blinking eyes there appeared a strange glow at one side—almost the reflection of a fire. Though how could such be here?

It must be more of this eerie weaving of thought patterns which suggested such a thing. However, because she had no other real goal, she started for that, taking one shaky step at a time, unable to keep going without digging in the spear.

The glow did not disappear. In fact, it was growing brighter. The girl almost believed she could feel a gentle warmth in the air.

Audha pulled herself around the edge of a rock pile and was met by warmth but not by any flames. She slumped rather than seated herself so she could hold out her mittened hands toward what stood there.

Her thoughts began to move again, as if they also had been frozen, and she was curious. Sitting on a flat base was a cone perhaps as high as her waist were she standing. The light from it did not flicker as would flame, but it appeared to Audha to be of some kind of metal, and iridescent lines crawled around its bulk.

She felt that this was no thing of Power on the level that the talented knew Power. Rather, like a ship, it was something built for a purpose. Yet she had never heard of any such form of light and heat before.

Who had set it here to succor her? Those she traveled with spoke always of the Dark in hiding ahead. And—memory was beginning to return with more force—the icebergs had herded her ship to the foul destruction of Dargh.

"You are a she. . . ."

Audha started; her knife was out. Those words seemed to issue from the cone.

"I am Audha, wavereader." She held on to what she could of her control. "Yes"—she was guessing at the meaning of what she had heard—"I am a woman."

"She—woman," the voice repeated as if learning new words. "You come to kill." There was almost a disdainful note in that. "Kill—kill."

The anger which filled Audha and had brought her on this mission might have been released by the heat. Once more her mind

was swarming with broken memories of Dargh and their escape—
and the death of those others, shipmates all.

"I am oathed by blood." What was she doing, sitting here in the
ice talking to a cone of metal? Perhaps it was only a death vision, as
were sometimes said to be seen by those dying, and she really lay
back in the crevice near the last Great Gate with no friend-hand to
hold at her going.

"Kill—always—kill. Long—so long—to wait, and now kill—
kill again!"

There was a strangeness to the voice. Audha's awakened rage
seemed too much to expend upon a voice and a bit of metal.

"Who are you?" she demanded now. She was sure that the cone
was only a device for some Power and she must face the thing behind it for the sake of her own sanity.

A word was spoken in reply, but so tangled did it sound that
Audha could neither have spoken it nor understood. It could be a
name—or a rank—or an office. She hesitated and then tried again.

"I am a woman—what are you?"

There was no swift reply. Perhaps the other was either measuring
Audha in some way or else did not quite understand.

"I am female," the answer came at last. "Once I was ____ !"

Again a gabble the girl could not translate. Though somehow
she received a strong impression of the sea—almost as if for a moment she had stood on board with a fair wind filling sails over her
head. Sea . . . her memory made a small jump. That—that thing
frozen in the ice—it was, the Power had told them, of the sea. "Female? Frozen there?"

"Not xagoth-slog!" The voice now echoed anger of an insult. "I
am . . ."

This time the answer came one word at a time. The cone voice
might be attempting to pick out of Audha's own mind the proper
words.

"Ship—wind power—all obey."

"Officer—or perhaps even a shaman," the Sulcar girl guessed.
But what they hunted was evil. Was she now confronted by some
creature of the full Dark who could strike with blasting energy?

"Lost—ship caught—in ice. I will Power to hold me safe until they come—my mates and young—to set me free. Ice holds—I sleep—long and long and long. Then comes a great wave of power—not Stiffli power"—Audha thought she got that word right this time—"but it broke apart all bonds laid to protect. I rise—still there is ice. And when I use the sight there is a ship—a ship of the killers. I have nothing—only the ice—and here the ice obeys my power. I send it to kill—"

"To kill my ship, my shipmates!" Audha's knife was free in her hand. But her arm would no longer obey her; it would not rise from her side. And how she could have slain the cone, she had no idea.

"Now others come. They hold Power known to this world." The voice was continuing in spite of Audha's rage, and she found herself forced to listen. "They will be drawn even as you were drawn, slog female, and I shall use their power to win free and back to the world which is mine."

The girl was breaking through that which held her quiescent, usable to this thing.

"Be not so sure." She found she was able to control her knife hand now, but still saw no way she could turn its point against this alien thing. "There are those in this world who can make mountains walk and can close such gates to other places with ease." She built upon her bluff as speedily as she could.

"Yes." To her astonishment the thing readily agreed to that. "But then I have . . . you!"

Against every fraction of will Audha could summon, the compulsion snapped down upon her again. She stood up, not by a willing of her own. The cone whirled so that its color flow gave her vertigo, and she closed her eyes.

"Come!"

Her body, her eyes, were no longer under her own command. She looked and saw that the whirling cone had somehow collapsed into a ball. It did not quite rest upon the rock, but rather floated purposefully forward. Then Audha discovered that she could do nothing but follow it.

Her body ached with fatigue and she was so hungry her stomach seemed shrunken into a tight knot, but still she followed, chained by that other's will.

It wove a way among more and more of the rocky outcrops. At least it continued to project some of its saving warmth to keep her stumbling feet moving. Dark rocks.

Then—

Once more the ball was whirling. From its substance there spun a strip of near-invisible stuff—glass or clear ice—or some substance Audha had no knowledge of. It grew wider, and slanted upward, clearly visible among the rocks because of its continued play of color.

"Come!"

The order brought her forward in spite of all the force of her own will she raised to fight it. The girl felt her foot set on that half-seen way, her body tense with strain and the bite of fear.

It was lifting her up as easily as a leaf caught in a wind gust. She ached to hold still, afraid of losing her balance and falling to those rocks steadily growing smaller below her. Then she began to realize that she was encased in something as stiff as the ice from which she had come, as much a prisoner as any chains could bind her.

Dizzy, she closed her eyes—then opened them quickly again, fearing that she might miss some important change in this unbelievable transport.

Though she was well above the ground now, the rocks still loomed about her. And it seemed to her that they turned ugly, wind-worn faces to leer at her as she swung by them. She summoned what strength she had for a question.

"Where—?" but she got no further. Now that commanding force had even seized upon her tongue. She could see snow shifting from the breath of wind in the heights, yet that lash of cold did not reach her, even when they passed through what seemed a small blizzard.

This was indeed Power, and such as she had never heard described before. The length of light on which she was anchored swept around another tall spire of rock. They were heading straight for the mountainside, she thought sickly, foreseeing her helpless body dashed against that unyielding wall.

But no, there was an opening and the ball which provided her passage headed straight for that. They came under an arch of a snow bridge to voyage across a plateau, and on that stood . . .

Audha was so weakened by her ordeal that now she saw what she could not possibly believe. Yet, though she blinked and blinked again, and firmly told herself not to be captured by any glamorie, that continued to stand foresquare and the ball was starting an easy curve of descent to bring her to it.

The Sulcar girl had seen Es City, the oldest and greatest of the works of humankind (plus perhaps the talents of the adepts) on the eastern continent. She had walked the streets of all the major Dales ports. This . . . was far beyond the labors which had brought such into being.

It seemed to be fashioned of the same strange material as produced the cone ball, and the colors which played across it were even richer in hue. Yet there were towers which were not opaque but like glass or the clearest of ice. And, strangest of all, in spite of where it stood—in the midst of this most desolate and barren land—there was a space beyond its outer walls which was carpeted with green. She caught a glimpse of flowers among the low-growing plants.

The ball which had brought her was at ground level now, approaching the castle which towered over her. And the closer Audha was carried, the more differences she noted in its building compared with what she knew. The edges of roofs curled outward and slightly upward and here and there along them were what she first took to be the heads of sentries, small though they seemed to be.

Then she knew them for carvings of creatures which certainly looked humanoid, not monstrous, but who wore expressions of sadness and despair.

Only a very large carving placed over the main entrance lacked that doleful touch. It was the head of what could only be a woman, her hair free and loosed about as if the wind itself were caught in it. Human—and yet was it so?

The forehead was high and wide, with unusually thick brows over eyes. Then the head narrowed to a very pointed chin beneath a small mouth. The nose was low-bridged, nearly flat, and wide of nostril. As Audha stared up at that face there appeared sparks of orange, almost like the tips of flames, in those eyes only for an instant, and then her captor swept her on under the archway.

She was instantly aware of the warmth which closed about her, stronger than that given off even by the cone. They did not cross any courtyard but were instantly in a great hall.

But an empty one. Here was none of the coming and going of servants one saw even in a Dales hold. No guards stood by the four curtained doorways—two on either side—past which she was swept.

Nor was there any dais to lift above the general servants and guests the ruler of this place. Instead, as the hall came to a halt, she was left firm-footed on the floor by the disappearance of that trail which had carried her, to discover she was facing something with the appearance of a broad but clouded mirror. She could see something of her own body reflected there, but also there appeared, farther in, dark in which she could not even distinguish any true shape.

"You have a choice, female of this world," the voice which had been in the cone again rang out. "I can set you—so—"

Instantly Audha was encased in a pillar of ice. And with that about her, her mind seemed to dull; that which she truly was shrank smaller and smaller.

"Or"—so she could still hear the voice—"you can serve me."

Audha shivered. She had heard all her life of bargains with the Dark and that no one ever won such. The end was always worse than even the stupid fool who fell to the wiles of evil could imagine.

"Serve you how?" She tried to play for time, to learn just how deeply she was now enmeshed with the black power.

"You will give me the use of your body. I do not know what you mean by the 'Dark' your kind seem to fear so much. Who judges what is wrong and what is right? I have been caught in a trap and held away from all my kind. To return to them I use what I can of the Powers I know.

"I would learn more of those with you who have Powers of your own. If they are greater than I—then so be it. But if I can summon more and achieve what I would—then who can judge that I am 'evil'?"

Logical enough, but Audha remembered Dargh.

After a moment of silence the voice continued. "So you have ties with others of your kind and you would avenge them. Do you not understand even yet it was because of your hate and anger you opened the door to me? Yes, I loosed the ice upon your ship. That was an enemy—the kind I followed across the Vors Sea before I was trapped. My blood died also in that battle. Your anger I have known, and have learned the folly of it. But it was those of your own kind who brought death to your shipmates. No order from me set it so. My Power moved as I tested it after many years. I saw a ship like unto those which had driven me here to linger alone— and so I shall send them off and away from me."

"There were other killings," Audha said hotly. "The camps of the trappers overrun."

"Power calls and there was something here which was ready to answer my call, though I did not know the nature of it. But enough of this balancing of good and evil. What will you? Remain sealed in the ice for all time, or give me the use of your body that I may safely contact those of Power with whom you travel?"

"So that you can slay them, having learned enough?" demanded the girl.

"Quick thinking, female—but inclined to be stupid. Trust is hard to come by. I have none for those of your kind who manned the ships that drew me here. But . . ." There was a long silence, and then she spoke again, "Who is the greatest of Power among you?"

Audha wanted nothing more than to deny any answer to that, but suddenly she found that the truth could be pulled out of her whether she wished or not.

"Frost is a witch of Estcarp. No one truly knows the extent of their Power."

"Then it is she with whom you and I will deal. I wait no longer. If you refuse me entrance, I can force it. Then you shall become as the slogs, a thing to be used only as tool."

She was right: in her innermost thought the girl knew it. And she also realized that the choice between the pillar and being a slave had been only a choice. One she no longer had time to make even if she chose.

Out of that mirror expanse before her came a thrust of light which struck her full in the face. Before she could even cry out she was whirled into a darkness so deep it was like being smoothed in the very depths of the earth.

## CHAPTER FORTY-ONE

# A Meeting of Powers, North

After such a fall . . ." Odanki shook his head. "No, you must give up hope, Lady Trusla. Such crevices descend very far into the ice and the cold is such that any so caught are frozen soon. Also— to attempt to climb down in rescue, no and no."

He was seated with his bandaged leg out before him on the ground while his hands were busy at work all the time he flattened her faint hope of reaching Audha. The great horns Simond and he had discovered had been dragged back to their improvised camp and he was busy chopping and cutting, but what he was working on she had no idea.

"Not so." Inquit had come up behind them. "She lives." There was such flat certainty in the shaman's voice that Trusla was on her feet, eager to move to prove that statement the truth.

Frost was behind the Latt woman. Her usually impassive face wore the suggestion of a frown.

"There is a ward," she said slowly, "but not such as are known to those of my talent."

"She has been taken by the Dark!" Trusla was quick to interpret that. Though she had no strong ties with the Sulcar girl, who had always held aloof even in their small company, she felt a need for haste to free her from whatever dire force held rule in the high rocks and snow above the warm mud pocket.

However, Frost was holding her jewel out, pointing in the general direction which they guessed lay between them and the vanished girl.

That gem which was her guide to the difference between the Dark and the Light had not flared crimson or, the worst of all, smoky black. Nor was it blue, as it would have been had Audha sought a place of the Light. Instead the grayish stone held within its depths a flickering which was greenish in hue, and that pulsed as if to warn them that the talent it revealed was putting some force to work.

They had gathered around, drawn by the sight of the strange color. And now Frost spoke again. "Neither of the Light nor the Dark—something in between."

"Such a something," Simond was emboldened to say, "could turn either way." He did not know why he was so sure of that, but he was. "But that which drove the ship to Dargh certainly was evil. That which brought death to the camps, that which we seek—it is of the Dark."

Frost still cupped the jewel in her hand. "If we judge by the acts you mention—yes, the Dark waits. But never has the talisman been wrong—and this shows something new." She extended her hand a short distance toward Inquit. "What say you, sister?"

They were startled by the small creature leaping for the Latt's shoulder. Kankil's round head was very close to Inquit's and she was chirping loudly, certainly in excitement—or warning?

"How strong is that ward, sister?" the shaman asked Frost. "Is it held by some method which you know?"

The witch closed her eyes and raised her gem until it touched her forehead above and between her eyes. She stood, holding all their attention now. Even Kankil had ceased her chittering.

"It is strong," she said at last. "But it is not of any setting which I know."

Simond was surprised. Having known the Powers of the witches from his birth, he could not imagine they lacked any such knowledge of what was a relatively simple use of the talent.

"What of yours?" Frost asked, almost sharply, of the shaman.

Kankil slid down the Latt woman's bulky form but kept tight hold of her at thigh level. Inquit reached out for the edge of her feather cloak and selected, after careful inspection, one of the large quills which fringed it. Twisting that free, she lifted it and sent it gliding, as she might loose a bird. It did not swoop again to earth as they had expected, but rather rose higher and higher, until it was equal in height to the top of the cliff beside them.

There, as they watched, it started off in the direction of the glacier surface, steady in flight, though it used no wings.

It disappeared from sight and yet they were somehow all still watching the sky. Now Inquit was chanting and, with her, the cheeping of Kankil kept an echoing pattern. They continued to watch.

Then Inquit jerked as if, out of somewhere, she had been struck a sharp blow. For the first time Trusla heard Kankil's soft voice rise to a shriek. But the shaman kept her feet. She only looked to Frost, shaking her head.

"Sister, the ward holds also against that Power which is mine. Yet behind it—there is no challenge of the Dark building."

Now the witch spoke to the others. "If a gate awaits above, it holds no threat for now. But we must move with caution."

The captain laughed. "Lady, we have no wish to sail within arrow length of the enemy. Yet it would seem that Audha's disappearance is the first true trail mark that what we seek lies in that direction."

Inquit turned to her hunter. "We go as one or we do not go. When can you trail again?"

Odanki pushed out his leg and ran his hands cautiously down over the stockinglike bandages Inquit had provided. "Another day—that will also give me time to finish these." He still had his lap full of scraps of the stone-hard horn. "And if we go into the heart of the great ice, we shall need them."

Simond dubiously eyed the curved bits the other was fitting together. He had seen those foot pieces which had taken Odanki out on the frozen lake, but he had no idea what the Latt now labored on. Certainly no one would try the lake passage again. The glacier way above was trouble enough.

Joul came back to camp later in the day with a brace of white birds, thick of feathers but unfortunately lean of flesh. At least the party had a few mouthfuls of meat to flavor their stew. Frost had gone off by herself again, and Trusla was sure that the witch was trying either to pick up Audha's trail in spite of the warding or to communicate with her own sisterhood. She came back at last very pale, and dropped rather than sat beside the shaman.

The Latt woman reached out and, as if Frost were Kankil, patted her shoulder. "Eh, sister, do not waste strength; you may need for later. There is a rough way before us and we do not know how long a one."

That night Trusla did not sleep steadily, though she was tired from her exertions of the day. Instead she crept out of the doubled sleeping roll, taking care not to rouse Simond, and went to her gear. The party had decided early that they must again cut the size of their packs since much of the way would mean more climbing. And there was that she was sure she must not forget.

She felt rather than saw the jar of red sand. It was a slightly awkward shape, but she was sure she could fit it into the front of her long fur tunic.

What Odanki worked upon steadily the previous day, he showed to them early the next morning. Like those odd things which had allowed him to cross the slickness of the ice lake, these were also meant for aids—not only for feet, but hands as well. And he measured carefully, using his supply of thongs with care, until each of the party had, to swing from belt for future use, two sets of what really resembled, Trusla thought, claws. She could understand the value of such in crossing the rough ice above.

Frost did not attempt any more visions, nor did the shaman. Rather, with Trusla's help, they put together packets of herb salves, what was left of the bandages, and anything they might need for a possible injury.

Odanki went through a series of exercises, putting some strain on his legs. However, they had healed somewhat, and the last evening they remained in the area of mud, Frost had him uncover his hurts, inspected them carefully, and then held her jewel a finger's breadth above the wounds, passing it slowly back and forth. It did not flash fire, but Trusla was sure she had seen a spark in its depth.

Once more they took the pathway of the stair, Trusla with Simond close on her heels, then the shaman and the others. The Estcarpian girl turned her head when they passed the grim warning of that line of skulls. Were these the remains of sentient beings, or the being as they now faced? Yet they gave off nothing—there were no remnants of any slaying Power here.

When they reached the head of that stair and looked out upon the plateau of the glacier, Trusla shivered. That huge crevice which had swallowed Audha was not the only one, she suspected. Though they had divided the coils of ship ropes among them, to be looped over shoulders, and they had Odanki's strange claws for an aid, still this was a threatening world.

They moved slowly, taking care with their footing, in some places traveling roped together. But it did not take them long to reach that crevice down which Audha had disappeared. As they approached it, a figure moved out to meet them.

"Audha!" Trusla cried out, and the voices of the others joined hers.

The Sulcar girl was calm-faced. She might have left them only seconds earlier and suffered no ills during that short absence. Kankil chirped and made one of her leaps toward Audha, seeming almost as willing to warmly welcome the wavereader as she would have her mistress.

However, she did not complete that leap. With a complicated twist of her body, she landed on the ice, still some distance from Audha, to simply stand, her paw-hand to her lips, her eyes wide.

A strangeness touched them all now. Their greetings cut off and they kept their distance. There was no change in Audha's expression. She was eyeing them calmly in an aloof way, as if she met with strangers. So she surveyed each in turn—her gaze sliding quickly over the men, though Simond believed there had been an awareness close to anger in those searching eyes when she sighted the captain.

However, it was the women who received her main attention. Trusla she appeared to dismiss quickly, the Latt shaman held her a little longer, but then her full gaze centered on Frost.

"Audha!" Frost's thankful cry was repeated, only now it had a questioning note. It seemed for the space of a breath or two the other did not hear her. That steady and measuring gaze had fallen from Frost's face to the jewel at the witch's breast.

No longer dull and gray, the stone appeared as if set in a gemmed frame of colored brilliance. Those colors rippled so one could not swear that this stone was red or yellow, green or blue, but took on each hue in turn.

Frost showed no surprise at the change in her jewel. When she spoke, it was a level question: "For whom do you speak?"

A slight flush arose on Audha's pale face. "I am again your comrade in search."

But even her words were delivered in the monotone of one repeating a learned ritual.

The shaman's hands were moving. Perhaps one of those gestures was an order, for Kankil went slowly, step by step, to stand before the Sulcar girl. She held up her paw at a stiff angle so they were all able to see it. One of her stubby fingers arose to point to Audha and then a second was beside it.

Possession! Trusla tensed and shivered. That was a forbidden use of the talent unless the one so possessed agreed. With what had Audha made a pact? Surely such was intended for all their undoing.

"You see." Frost was not speaking to the girl, Simond knew. He had hand to sword hilt, yet this struggle was not meant for steel, but rather to be waged on another plane. "You see—now what comes of that seeing?"

"You are?" Audha's voice had taken on a different timber—an arrogance which was certainly no part of the companion they had known.

To the surprise of the others, Frost laughed, and Inquit smiled broadly.

Trusla thought she understood. Did this other they now dealt with believe they would surrender their *names* so foolishly?

But Frost was answering: "It would seem we face a trade, Audha-who-is-not. You have gauged us for what we are. Therefore let us not act as children at a fair, gawking at what we do not understand. Name for name—but we shall accept the one by which you face the world, even as we also wear such."

The jewel's glittering edge did not dim and although it seemed unnaturally still, and none of them could feel a hint of draft, the wide feathers fringing Inquit's cloak stirred slightly even as a bird might move wings before taking flight.

It would seem to be now a battle of wills. Then the other spoke through her new servant.

"You company with Sulcars—with the slayers—and yet you expect anything save *this* from me!"

Audha's voice arose to a shriek. Trusla gasped. The group had not been spread out, but rather gathered close to the girl they had discovered; thus the bubble which arose around them, though it crowded them even closer together, was not too large.

Both the captain and Simond cried out, and steel met that barely visible barrier. To no purpose. It might seem that they were contained in a vast cage of Var glass but one which did not yield to any assault from metal.

It was cold, suddenly far colder. That bubble could be of clear ice and now they would freeze.

Frost simply pointed her jewel at the half-visible expanse before her. The glittering encirclement of the gem gathered together and formed a rainbow-hued ray. It touched their temporary prison and that shattered, great pieces of the ice falling away. Odanki swung out his spear at one still-standing fragment and sent it after the rest.

"So you command the ice," commented Frost. "Yes, that must be so, or we would not come upon you here. What else can you call upon, stranger?"

They came as if they had arisen out of the many crevices in the glaciers—such beasts as Trusla had never seen save for furs on a trader's counter. There was a pack of short-legged but fast-moving, grizzle-coated things from which arose a stench to sicken one, at last one of the huge white wasbears, and some dark slinking forms which, though furred, seemed to writhe across the ice like serpents.

The shaman loosened one of her fringe feathers. Stymir had already shot an arrow, which went neatly home in the shoulder of the nearest wasbear but did not in any manner slow that creature in its steady advance.

Now Inquit shouldered past the captain and deliberately leaned over so that her feather was touching the ice under their feet. With the briskness of a hearthwife busy about her daily tasks, she swept that feather forward, eluding the hand with which the captain tried to stop her. So she swept, pacing forward. And on her fifth stride . . .

The pack of ravening animals was gone!

"It does little good," she said complacently, straightening up and carefully inserting her feather back into whatever knot had held it previously, "to dream against dreamers."

No emotion showed on Audha's face. She was like one of those near-human-sized figures the landsmen put in their fields to keep birds from the early crops.

"Do we play games, stranger, or do we act as sisters in Power? What do you summon next—a glacier to sweep us away?" Once more Frost laughed.

"I summon . . . you!"

From around them now whirled small chunks of ice, streamers of snow. Trusla caught at Simond, only to find him as unsteady as she. Yet they held together. The others they could see only as forms which appeared and disappeared as the very stuff on which they stood rose to gather them in.

There was no clear sight of what was happening. Trusla only knew that there was no longer any solid surface under her boots. Yet she was not falling, nor was Simond. At least, caught up in this maelstrom, they were still together. There was a terrifying sense of being in a place where there was nothing stable except the man she clung to. Then, with force enough to bring a cry out of her, she did strike a level surface which held steady and she heard Simond swear and kick out, fighting to get to his feet and take her with him.

The storm of snow and ice particles was settling and they could see again the rest of the party. Odanki was spitting strange words with as much force as Simond. He had to lean heavily on his spear to get to his feet. The venture had done little good for his healing wounds.

The rest looked wonderingly around. Perhaps the shaman and the witch and Kankil had been prepared in some way for this wild journey. However, to the rest it had been a use of Power and therefore as awful as it was effective.

Audha was certainly still with them—whether she remained possessed by their opponent or not. In fact, she was close to Frost, who was shaking herself as if to banish the gathered snow and ice from her furred garments.

This was certainly not the brink of the crevice where they had found the Sulcar girl. What faced them now was enough to keep them statue still, just looking for a moment or so.

For here was a mountain fortress, such as the Sulcars and Simond knew represented a bastion nearly untakeable by any mortal means. Flashes of colored light which matched the encirclement of Frost's jewel played along the walls and appeared to leap from tower to tower. It was, Simond was certain, the hold of a ruler with unlimited means and perhaps unlimited manpower.

Still, because it did not resemble the stone he knew, he had a feeling, that it, too, was an exertion of Power alone.

There was an open doorway facing them in obvious invitation—too obvious. They did not stir from where the ice storm had deposited them. *They* did not—but Audha did.

She had been shoulder to shoulder with Frost when the storm had cleared. Now her hand shot forward, so swiftly they did not mark her action until too late.

Her fist grabbed about the jewel and she gave it such a vicious jerk as brought the witch forward and nearly to her knees. Then the chain must have snapped, for the jewel was free in Audha's hold—blazing.

The Sulcar girl cried out, shook her hand, tried to rid herself of what she held. Apparently the jewel was also at battle now. However, she herself was snatched up bodily and taken from them, to be dropped, now wailing, at that open doorway. Yet—she still held the gem.

Frost started forward. She slipped and slid in a tangle to the feet of the shaman, who was quick to come to her aid. Now they were aware that between them and the castle was a stretch of glass-smooth ice.

Odanki pushed to the edge of that. Sitting down, he fastened the thongs with claws over his boots, while Trusla and Simond fought to bring Frost and Inquit back to stable footing. It would seem a nearly impossible task. The ice might have been coated in turn with wax or grease; it possessed just the right consistency to send them sprawling. They were panting when they finally pulled back to the small stretch where the storm had deposited them.

Audha had not moved from her place in the doorway. Why she had not gone on within, Trusla could not guess. But then Frost might have picked that thought out of the girl's mind, for she said, "She will not take it within her sanctuary."

"Just so, sister." Inquit was soothing Kankil, who had found her slide on the ice somehow unusually unnerving. "It might well serve you as a key were it taken within. She will—"

"Hold it for ransom, perhaps." Captain Stymir stood, hands on hips, his eyes narrowed as he studied the castle.

Odanki had tightened the last strap over his boot. With a look of confidence, he raised his unwounded leg and brought it down with a distinct stamp on the edge of that spread of ice—only to lose his balance and spin out, the claw strapped to his mittens and his boots making no impression on the slick surface, a cry of complete amazement bursting out of him. All his wriggling only took him farther from the shore until he was marooned near halfway between the party and the castle.

Trusla had never seen a witch without her jewel and it was very well known that that was the focus of her Power. If the dweller in the castle did summon Audha to her and take the gem, could it wrest control of Frost's energies for her own use? The jewels were a secret and no one outside of the sisterhood knew just how great a weapon they were or what a witch deprived of one could do.

Trusla caught her lower lip between her teeth as she thought. Perhaps this was the time that her dream was brought into being. Simond was busy with the captain and Joul trying to throw a rope to the Latt hunter and draw him back. There was no one to stop her.

From her inner pocket she brought the jar. Somehow the very feel of it gave her confidence. In her mind was set exactly what was to be done, just as she had dreamed it nights ago.

She loosened the cork and shook into her hand a small palm full of the sand. With care she set the jar on the ice between her feet to keep it upright and hurled the sand she held out over the ice.

There was no wind she could feel to make it drift, but move it did, though in no straight path but rather wavering and in patches, with the ice showing in between.

She had shed her pack, even her belt. Now she picked up the jar and closed her eyes. There was no ice, nothing but the sand for her feet, and that other presence was not too far away, watching with approval.

Trusla began to dance.

# CHAPTER FORTY-TWO

# *Into the Halls of Ice, North*

Trusla was caught in that dream which she would never forget. She swayed and turned, only the bulk of her heavy trail clothing disguising her graceful surrender to what lay in her mind. Twice she halted and once more shook sand into her hand and sent it flying. But she did not open her eyes—for she was not there. No, she danced in the moonlight beside a pool, weaving her steps to match those of the being who had summoned her and now sustained her past any fear or misgiving.

The others watched her in awe, though Simond had dropped his hold on the rope by which they were towing Odanki back to security and would have tried to follow her had not the shaman stepped in between.

"Young lord, to each her own magic. She dances now with a Power which is hers alone, and no harm to her comes of obeying such a command."

"Possessed?" he flared, and glanced beyond Trusla to Audha. The girl still crouched in the door of that unbelievable castle, her hands held, very apparently against her will, about Frost's jewel.

"Not so! She has opened a door to that which was given her as a birth gift—to be held against just such a time as this." Inquit's cape fluttered a little, though no wind had touched it. The edge of it

511

arose before him and he had a sudden idea that, fragile as that feathered weaving looked, it might be a formidable barrier.

Right—now left—and two steps right again. She touched no slippery ice spread as she went. For the last time Trusla paused to toss out once again what the jar contained. That carrier seemed much lighter.

She opened her eyes. There were the three steps leading up to that gaping door. But there was light above the entrance. She felt a touch of warmth—no more than a spring breeze might carry—as she looked up at that carven head which spanned the top of the portal.

Though the face remained a mask, the eyes were fully open. They held the blue-green of far seas—and intelligence—as well as anger and perhaps some dismay. Audha moaned and Trusla took the last three steps which brought her under the head and to the side of the Sulcar girl.

As Trusla looked down at Audha, she saw no longer that mask-like serenity but rather a twisted grimace of pain, and with that the awakening. Perhaps that which waited had released her hold on her prisoner.

Placing the sand jar back in the inner sling of her fur overgarment, Trusla went to her knees, for only so could she face Audha squarely. She held out her hands and said simply: "Give it to me!"

The painful grimace on the Sulcar girl's face contracted even more. She was swinging her cupped hands back and forth, striving to push them apart and release the jewel.

Trusla straightened a little. Her fingers still felt slightly gritty from the sand. That and the Power it held for her had defeated one Power; could it another?

Reaching forward, she cupped her sandy fingers around Audha's, jerking, shaking hands. "Loose!" she commanded. But she knew that truly it was not to the girl she spoke now but to the Power behind her. "By the will of Xactol of the sand—be this lock broken!"

Audha's hands went rigid in her grasp and the girl screamed, a thin plaint, like that of a child in deep despair.

But loosen her grasp did, though the fingers remained crooked as if they still would hold fast what she had taken.

The jewel felt cold with the sting of ice-borne mountain water. It seemed to twist of itself as if to be free of Trusla's grasp, but she did not give way. So—

So—it would seem that perhaps Trusla had won, only to lose. There arose a harsh, grinding sound. The surface on which they now both crouched shifted under them. Trusla ducked as a large fragment fell from above.

There were cracks opening in those solid walls. The colors which ran across them flamed even more fiercely. She saw two of the carven heads crash and splinter into bits. The castle was shattering around them.

A pointed shaft, looking as viciously perilous as a spear, skimmed by Audha so close that it slit the edge of her outer fur tunic.

Trusla looked for the pattern of sand on the ice. Save for a red stain here and there, it was gone. Yet they would be safer out on that slippery surface than here. She folded the jewel into what she hoped would be safety. Then, catching the much larger Sulcar girl by the shoulders, she gave her the most vigorous pull she could, stumbling herself as she went backward, but getting them both into a sprawl in the open.

The continued destruction of the castle made her push and pull Audha—who seemed utterly helpless—as far as she could from the rain of splinters coming from those walls. The slickness of the ice lake was an aid now instead of a hindrance and they whirled together out of reach just as one of the towers which was part of the entrance came crashing where they had been only moments earlier.

Then they were not alone. Simond had her—though he did not urge her to her feet, but rather wrapped her hands around the rope which girdled him, and they both skidded away from the rain of sharp-edged ice fragments.

However, even as the castle ceased to be, so now the slick ice vanished and they were crawling over the rough surface of the mountain ways again.

There was a final ponderous sound from behind and then Trusla found herself, her grip on Simond iron-hard, and beside her Frost. The thought uppermost in her now was what had sent her into the maelstrom of falling ice. She loosed one hand from her anchorage with Simond and fumbled in her tunic—to bring out the jewel.

It was dull and gray again. The lights which had played about it were gone. She wanted to be rid of it as soon as possible and when Frost took it, she sighed and relaxed against Simond's broad shoulder at her back.

"To each her own talent," said the witch. There seemed to be moisture in her eyes and certainly at that moment she looked more like one who lived apart from Powers than at any time Trusla had seen her. "Yours has served us well, little sister."

"Audha." Trusla could see the shaman a little distance away kneeling beside the limp figure of the Sulcar. "She—"

That comforting shadow of humanness was gone from Frost's face and Trusla shivered. What would be the wrath of a witch whose very source of power had been stolen?

"Audha is . . . gone," Frost answered. "What moved her like a leashed hound withdrew when you took the gem. That one wanted it and yet feared to bring the unknown within her own stronghold. She has no use for a tool which has failed her. And it is the Sulcars who drew her worst hatred."

"Dead . . ." Trusla turned her head, unable for that moment to look upon the other girl. Ill fortune had been with her, and always at the bidding of this thing they still faced.

"Perhaps it would be better so. Not dead, but spirit-drained. Our sister of the Latts is a dreamer. Perhaps a dream—when there is time—can reach into the depths and call forth again that which is Audha. Now she is a child—or less than a child."

"The castle?" Trusla did not want to think more of Audha. To be a body without an innermost dwelling was to attract the worst of the Dark, though she knew that both Frost and Inquit would do what they could to protect Audha from that last outrage.

"Is gone. Look," Simond said in her ear. He shifted around, drawing her with him so they stared across that expanse which had been glass smooth. It was broken and creviced now, fragments of ice forming barriers. Where those towers had stood, the colors racing over them, there stood now rock, black crags. Yet just at the point where that open gate had beckoned them in, there was a deep and dark hole, some passage or cave cut out of that rocky core.

"Glamorie?" She would not have been surprised if Frost had answered her yes. Trusla knew well that a master or mistress of the Power could create a whole city by choice, though such creations never lasted for any length of time.

"In its way. Except . . ." Frost was twisting the links of her broken chain apart, striving to rejoin them to hold the jewel once more. There was a raw red line on the small portion of her neck Trusla could see within the thick fur framing her face and edging her hood. "Except," she repeated, having completed her task to her satisfaction, "that which held the castle still sits in waiting there."

Captain Stymir came up behind them. "No place to strive to twist someone out as one pries a mussel from its shell, unless we know more."

"No," Frost agreed. "We do not enter that web. But I think that she who shelters there now has something to consider."

"To fight on enemy territory when one knows nothing of the odds," Simond commented, "has never availed any attacker much in the end."

"To fight . . ." Now it was the shaman who joined them. Audha lay on a padding of cloaks. Curled very close beside her, Kankil stroked the girl's blank face gently with one hand. "To fight is not always the answer."

"You have shown that one how foolish it is to stand against your Power." Odanki limped up. He was gazing proudly at the shaman. "Set the dream demons on her—they will twist her!" His hands moved as if he held a length of hide between them and were indeed twisting it.

"None of us knows the extent of the other's Powers," Frost returned. "Also, there is this. By the virtue of the talent I cannot truly read this one is of the Dark as we know it. Perhaps it is entrapped."

"Entrapped?" the captain nearly exploded.

"Captain," Frost asked, "what is that dim legend that your people entered into this world through a gate? What do we now hunt but that same gate? Perhaps something else has also been caught so—an alien to this world, a world which she has found barren and forbidding. Your people were free when your ships plowed into our sea—as dangerous as that is in this north. For someone who had no ship—no—"

"The ship in the plaque!" Stymir interrupted, and jerked that out of hiding. When he held it out into the wan light of day, they could see the change.

The black blot in the center was indeed in outline something akin to a ship, but far different than those the Sulcars sailed. It was long and narrow, and, where a midmast should be, there was a single tall and wide wedge, too solid-looking to be classed a sail. There was only one figure on the deck and that, as far as they could see, was a lump which had some of the attributes of the thing they had seen frozen in the ice.

"That thing—that *thing* could do this?" The captain's arm swung out in the direction of the shattered castle.

"No—it was a servant of some kind," Frost said slowly, "and that ship was close on the Sulcars as they fled. They gained freedom—perhaps this ship did not."

"If we only knew more . . ." Trusla did not mean that as a complaint.

"But we do not!" the captain returned savagely, swinging the plaque wide in his hand as if he would hurl it from him.

"It is as one weaves a feather robe," Inquit commented. "One studies the pattern and one places a quill there and quill here to make the proper pattern. But she who abides within there"—the shaman nodded toward the cave entrance—"is the only one who perhaps knows that pattern. And if our efforts continue to counter her, what may she send against us? She has tried us three times—three failures—and such as she does not take kindly to that."

"Therefore"—Frost's hand was again upon her jewel—"we seek her out. And we may still have a guide." Abruptly she left their company and went to where Audha lay, Kankil still curled beside her, crooning in her ear softly and patting her cheek.

Trusla would have thought the girl asleep or unconscious, but her eyes were open, staring up into the sky where already the night was clouding in.

Frost knelt and touched the Sulcar girl with the same gentleness that Kankil used. She sat so, linked by her fingers on the other's forehead, pushing back the heavily furred edge of Audha's hood. Her own face smoothed, her eyes closed. She was seeking, the Estcarpian girl was sure, for some spark of life or thought upon which she could seize as a bond to draw the other back to them.

"We wait, we eat," Inquit announced. "We ready ourselves. For it is not to stand upon ice and await the will of another that we have come here."

Eat they did, very sparingly of their provisions. Trusla sucked a long splinter of ice Simond handed her, gaining from its melting the water her body must have. Yet as they made what preparations they could, all their eyes kept returning to that waiting cavern which grew ever darker.

It was Kankil who managed to get some food into Audha, pressing tiny bits of journey cake into the girl's mouth and then smoothing her throat as if to urge her to swallow.

"She is not mindless." Frost held her share of cake in one hand while the other hovered over her jewel. "It is as if she has fled into a very deep part within her, and there locked in that which she has always been. When we move—she will come. The little one"—she indicated Kankil—"will be her guide."

Frost and Inquit stepped out with a confidence Trusla was certainly far from feeling. However, she matched strides with Simond and that was easeful in itself. Behind them Audha moved, her right hand tightly held by Kankil, whose chirping rose and fell as if she were singing some ritual to keep her charge on her feet.

Then came the Sulcars and Odanki, all ready with weapons, even though it was in their minds that battle steel had no power here.

The dark of the cave mouth closed about them. But if their

enemy meant to keep them so blinded, that ploy failed from the first, for Frost's jewel gave forth a thin gray light.

That did not reach far, but it was enough to show sure footage ahead. However, they were not far into the opening before they were fronted by something new. Even as the towers and walls of the ice palace had failed to hold, now they could see the broken remains of another barrier, the sharp points left in what might be a frame, warning them away.

It gave steel its chance, for the men came to the fore to break and beat to shards all which threatened them. Now Audha first showed signs of true life.

"She—the shadow one—this was her abiding place." The words came loudly and the Sulcar girl balked when Kankil attempted to urge her on. At last it was the shaman who took strong hold of Audha's upper arm, drawing her along with due care to keep away from the splinters.

That they were indeed in a place which was of a different nature they realized as they gathered in a group on the other side of that broken barrier. For the cold which had struck at them so long was gone.

It was not only warmer, but there was a strong scent.

"The sea!" Captain Stymir exclaimed.

Perhaps, but something more also, Trusla was sure. The ocean scent was cut by a whiff now and then of a spicy odor—certainly not unpleasant. Frost's limited jewel light showed them something else as well—squarely across their path, yet leaving them room on either side for their passage, was a length of dull-colored metal. When the light of the jewel touched it, there developed flickers of colored light, wan and hardly visible, just enough to show that the object was oval, pointed at each end, yet wide in the middle section and deep.

As Frost held their improvised lamp closer, they could see that the interior was oddly shaped, as if a body had been half sunk in some protective lining. The outline remaining was the source of that spicy fragrance. A bed of some sort, Trusla believed, and a far more comfortable one than she herself had known for many days.

"She is gone!" That cry came from Audha. Pulling hard against the grip the shaman kept on her, she reached the side of that resting place and flailed out with both hands into the empty space as if her touch would supply what her sight did not.

The passage plainly led beyond that bed, if bed it was, and when they had drawn Audha away from it, they ventured on. The smell of the sea lingered with them and the warmth continued. They threw back their furred hoods, loosened the throat ties of their coats.

"There is a slope. We are going down!" Odanki suddenly exclaimed.

It was true. But the descent was a gradual one. Around them the way remained dark and smooth. Their footing appeared to be rock; they could be traversing now the heart of some mountain.

The interruption to their journey struck without any warning. There was a growling as if rock scraped rock heavily, then that gradual slope became a slide as slick as if it had been greased. They lost their footing; body thudded against body as they tried vainly to somehow control that furious descent.

Trusla heard the exclamations of the men, and rising above them, she heard chanting: two bespelling runes though not quite fusing, showing that both the shaman and the witch were calling upon Power.

This time, however, that which they needed did not answer. Instead, in what was a tangle of bodies and wildly flailing limbs, they left the hold of the tube and came out into light which held not only the colors but the heat of flames.

Here was another cavern or space—so wide that one could not see the far end of it. Only a short distance from them was a pit. It gave off the same stench as the mud pool. And across its molten surface (for it seemed to be not true mud but rather a flowing of fire) were fountains of flame and sparks arose. The heat hit at them with almost the same intensity as torches held close to their bodies, and Trusla was sure that the fur of her clothing was singed by it.

Mostly on hands and knees, they crawled back as far as they could get from that flame pool. There was no possible chance of their retracing their wild journey through the tube. If they were to find a way out, they must venture either right or left as close to the wall as they could.

But before they came to any decision, one of the flame fountains very close to the edge of that pool leaped higher, grew thicker, firmer, as they watched wide-eyed.

This was no flame pillar, for rather a woman stood there, her white body untouched by any sign of burn. Even her hair, which did not lie upon her shoulders but waved about her as if wind-driven, was not singed.

She was humanoid—but she was not human. Simond, who knew the strange breeds which flourished in Escore, was sure of that. And Trusla, seeing the flash of those sea-green eyes, knew that it had been a representation of this face which had been over the door of that vanished castle.

Reaching out, the woman caught a tendril of flame. It hardened in her hold into a shaft not unlike a spear. Deliberately she drew back her arm and threw the fiery point striking straight for Captain Stymir.

"Sulcar." Her voice was a hiss and her mouth seemed to twist into a grimace of pure hatred.

On the breast of the captain's fur tunic a patch of hair seared and smoked.

But at the same time there was another weapon in the air. Inquit might have been expecting just such an attack. One of her feathers penetrated the outer flame fence of that pool. It struck down and there was a puff of heavy smoke, and the fire died around the woman.

"Yaaahhh!" Sheer fury was the base of that cry as the other flung her arms high. Fire burst into being in the air itself, to swirl toward them like rain wind-driven.

"By the Will which is ever—the Power which dies not, the Light which never yields to Dark . . ." Almost as loud as the fire woman's screams of rage arose that chant, sounding somehow cool, calm, and confident. Frost faced the other squarely, and now she took one deliberate step and then another toward her.

What Power the witch was able to call upon, Trusla could never afterward guess, but that rain of fire winked out and the flames from which it had bubbled sank back.

"Hate—why do you carry this burden of hate?" Still as calm and clear as the words of the ritual came Frost's voice now.

The woman stood very still amid the lowered flames, her eyes fixed solely on the witch. "To all is allowed blood price—is that not also a belief of this barren land of yours?" she sneered.

"Greater yet is one who asks no price. Long ago was the act for which you seek vengeance—exile from your world—"

"My world," the other cut in. "Not so—maybe now the death mounds for my kind. We hunted only for a refuge. And those"— she flung out a pointing hand toward the Sulcars—"would see us dead—because we differed from them. Our poor beasts they killed as monsters—our talents made us demons. Some of us died in their fires. But we were strong, and when we learned the secrets of their world, we turned the very earth they would hold against them. Yes, drove them from land to land, island to island, for we had secrets their pitiful excuses for Power holders could not understand.

"We drove them! I, Urseta Vat Yan, led the fleet which hunted them down. But they had among them someone different, someone who had come through space, or time, or followed some path we did not know. And that one opened the way for them, so they escaped. But for me and mine—the gate locked itself upon us and there was no key for its opening."

"Hate can be a powerful lock on any gate," Frost said, still calm against the heat of the other's tongue. "Hate, cherished and fed, brings madness. I call upon you now, Urseta Vat Yan—you are a sister in Power. Use that Power as it should be used—unlock the gate within you."

The woman's face was still a scowl of anger. It seemed to those watching that rage itself now fueled the flames among which she stood. Then, without any answer, she vanished and straightaway the fire in the pit failed. So darkness drew in from all sides.

# CHAPTER FORTY-THREE

# Through the Mists of Time, North

Again it was Audha who provided them with a guide. Uttering a desolate cry, she rushed about the edge of the almost extinct fire pit, heading now for the darkness beyond, her arms outstretched, her hands grasping the air as if she would seize upon some greatly desired thing held just beyond her reach.

"She seeks that of herself the other still holds." Though she was running, the shaman's voice was steady. "Thus she will lead us to whatever place that one seeks now for refuge—or else lies in wait." And her last words were grim.

The light of the jewel was now so frail, all Trusla could see were the shadows of the two before her half cloaking it. The smell of the sea was stronger now and she wondered if some trick of the path they now followed would dump them down another swift descent into the cruelly cold waters of the north. Yet about them the passage still seemed warm.

Trusla was panting now—the steady speed of the running Sulcar girl was such that she could not equal it, bundled as she was in sweat-sticky furs and hides which imprisoned her body. Still Audha showed no sign of slacking.

Somehow they had found their way back—or Audha had led them—out of that mountain-hidden hall into another passage.

The sea scent was there also, but it was tempered by other odors.

Trusla called on failing strength to draw a deep breath. Not spice, no—it had been long seasons since the perfume had wrapped her under the moonlight in Tor Marsh. She kept glancing down at the darkness about her boots, half expecting to see the wide-open blooms of the march-moon, then long, wide petals curling upward about her feet. But this was not Tor, she thought confusedly. There could not be any such sweetness spread for them to tread on.

Light again—pale at first. Trusla raised her hand to run across the slick skin of her forehead. She felt a queer reaching—as if something sorted their thoughts and memories for a purpose of its own.

There was in this black hole a blaze of light to her right. Oddly enough, those running with her did not even turn their heads in that direction. But Trusla had somehow drawn apart from Simond and there was distance between her and the rest now. She turned her head, looked, and stopped.

Tor Marsh had never been a happy place for her. But now here was a wide door open into all its familiar islands, bogs, and ways. She could hear the drums and her childhood training responded to their beat. There—there just a step or so away was the house which had been her own home. A shadowy figure moved in the doorway—Mafra leaning on her staff, waiting for Trusla to lead her out into a mist-veiled road.

But the girl was jerked back by a grasp, fingers dug so deeply that she could feel the bruising that they set upon her skin.

"No—"

"Come!" The voice was harsh and carried the weight of a command in it. She was dragged along at a queer, almost shuffling pace as if the one who had taken her captive could not walk with a straight stride.

"Shadow—dream—" the voice continued in her ears.

But Mafra was coming out of the hall door, her head up, her head turning, as if her blind eyes were following Trusla as she was so dragged away from her. The girl tried to shift against that compelling hold—to beat and kick for her freedom. But the one who held her was not to be so easily escaped, though she heard a gasp or two of pain as if she had managed to do her captor a hurt.

Her beating hands, when they could find a surface, brushed fur and hide. Certainly it was not chance alone which brought a smear of something else across her fist. She did not know why she raised her knuckles to her lips and licked them, why she had halted in her fight for freedom.

She licked, and the few small grains of powdery sand were on her tongue. As if a curtain were snatched away, Trusla no longer saw Tor Marsh. Mafra did not wait there for her tending. It was only dark, very dark, for the only light, that shallow beam of Frost's jewel, was well ahead.

"Glamorie." She knew now who had kept her out of that trap, for trap it must have been. Perhaps since Audha had proved not useful for their enemy, she had been second choice. But she remembered now how the Latt hunter had sprawled across that spread of ice where the sand had given her footing. In his floundering he must have struck one of those patches, leaving spread grains clinging to his clothing as her safeguard now.

He was limping, and though he kept doggedly onward, her vigorous struggle with him might well have opened his hurts.

"All is well!" she said in a breathless voice. "The glamorie vision is gone."

His answer was a grunt, and she heard the thud of his spear butt against the rock as he pulled himself along.

"Trusla!" One of those shadows ahead turned back and was running in their direction. "Trusla?"

"We are here. There was a glamorie, but Odanki held me from it!" Should she blurt out her half-suspicion that the enemy now sought another tool and had made a try for her?

The light ahead had stopped. She could see some kind of a struggle going on and then one of those shadows flopped to the ground, the witch light held above the prone figure.

Simond, without a word, gave a shoulder as crutch to the Latt hunter. Making the best time they possibly could, they joined the others.

It was Audha who lay, again tended by Kankil. The shaman, her feather cape spreading wide across the rock, bent over her. Now Frost knelt to once more touch the girl's forehead.

"No one can slay shadows!" Odanki's denial sprang, Simond was sure, from the fact that thus far all the battles had been between the women, and he given no chance to aid in any skirmish.

Frost looked across Audha's body to Trusla.

"You were sought." That was no question but a statement. Her features, even seen by the slim light of the jewel, held a new austerity.

"There was a glamorie—a picture of Tor Marsh—like a door— and one to whom I owe a debt waiting there. It was Odanki who knew it for what it was. He held me back."

"So, having nearly broken one weapon, she seeks for another," commented Inquit.

"The dead do not war!" Stymir snarled.

"Always steel for the men—but certain things cannot truly die, Captain. Nor can you, I think, use that sword of yours on this menace, even if she were to stand with empty hands before you. When the snowcat is pursued hotly, she heads for her den, as every wall of that she knows well and she will use all she knows. This one's hate is still hot and perhaps it will never cool." There was a tinge of feeling in those last words.

"How does she?" The captain moved closer to look at Audha.

"Life force is drowned—perhaps to set the glamorie. But she lives and it is certain that she will obey."

Kankil chittered and reached out a hand to touch the shaman's cloak. Inquit nodded. "You have done your best, sister. Let us now see what else can be done. But we need time." She raised her head and looked about her. "Stark though this be, we must camp, rest, eat, for we cannot go on if our bodies fail us, no matter how our spirits urge us."

It was a strange camp indeed. They had left most of their supplies behind except for all the food they could carry. So there were no sleeping mats, only their cloaks, and the men lay harshly in their prisoning armor.

Having shared out meager portions, Inquit produced another bag from beneath her cloak and took out a packet. When she loosed the string of that, Frost frowned, but the shaman spoke directly to the witch.

"Sister, we eat scraps now and we do not know if we can find more food. To deal in this"—she held the bag open—"is, as I well know, a chancy thing and one which must be well considered. But if we are to drop for faintness in these paths, how will that benefit us? I say to you all that what I hold is a precious thing for a Latt hunter, for a traveler caught in a long storm. It grows sparsely and its harvesting is left only to those of the great knowledge.

"Place a pinch of this upon your tongue and then take what rest you can. I will swear by Arska that whatever virtue has been grown into it will serve you well."

The Sulcars seemed a fraction reluctant, but Odanki took his pinch at once and Simond followed, with Trusla eager to join him. She had heard many tales of strange herbs, and legends said that some could keep one awake and hearty for even days with no other nourishment.

After Frost and Inquit had dipped into the contents of the bag, and they watched the shaman put a pinch of it into Audha's mouth as Kankil held that open, the Sulcar captain and Joul took their share.

The four men insisted on dividing up watches while the women stretched out to sleep. Inquit took again one of her long quills and drew a warding circle about their whole group, and they placed Audha between Frost and the shaman, Kankil as usual curled up beside the girl.

Trusla was crouched on the deck of a ship, the wind slapping at the sail over her head. There were screams and cries filling the air and she realized that she was on the very edge of a battle.

Sulcars, their faces convulsed with rage, were fighting Sulcars. Then there rang a shout—words she did not understand, though which had meaning for the men before her. Their individual engagements broke off and they formed an irregular circle around two of their number.

She knew those faces. Her memory moved sluggishly at her bidding. The smaller man? His name—Joul. Who was Joul?

There was shouting again from the watching men. Some apparently were cheering on Joul. The others' cries held jeering notes, and the tall man they drew in to back—that was . . . Captain Stymir!

One could feel hate in the air, as heavy and blistering as the wind. The men circled slowly, eyes fast on each other, deadly purpose in every line of their tense bodies.

"Kill—kill—this is your deadly enemy who has been delivered into your hands. Kill, if you wish to bear the name of 'man.'"

Trusla whimpered, her hands to her head. That order had not come out of the air as any honest sound, but seemed to vibrate within her. She knew little of swordplay—only what she had learned watching Simond and his squad at exercises. The Tor men knew no niceties of dueling. And to Trusla these two were most ill-matched, Stymir towering over Joul. Yet, such was the precision with which the smaller man moved, she could not believe that any combat would be one-sided.

Joul hunkered low and gave a hop forward not unlike that of a fen frog, his double-bladed axe swinging up and back, barely missing Stymir's legs—While only a scrambling scuttle kept the captain's sword from striking home.

The cries from the watching men grew louder. Still louder yet was that screamed order which must strike within their heads also, for Trusla saw both duelists retreat a pace, as if momentarily bereft of self-control.

"Kill—this be your enemy—kill!"

It was no one of the watchers who was shouting that. The girl arose from her crouch. She might still be somewhat in a mind-maze from what she saw, but the truth was beginning to break within her now. What she witnessed was not the full truth.

At that moment of recognition suggesting they were again within the Power hold of another, she saw a shadowy figure rise behind Joul, stepping through the line of watching, shouting sailors as if they were but sea mist. Arms wrapped around the small man's shoulders and he was jerked backward, falling with his captor to the decking.

However, there had been one also who had moved upon Stymir at the same time, as tall, as broad-shouldered and threatening as the captain was at that moment. There was a flash of hand and Stymir's sword clattered down. He cried out and caught his wrist. Now there were arms around about him also and he was captive, fighting fiercely for freedom. That struggle grew less—even as had the movements where Joul had gone down.

Yet none of the watching sailors seemed to see what was going on. They still watched the center of their irregular circle and their voices rang as if they cheered on a deadly engagement.

Just as the doorway into Tor Marsh had vanished, so did the ship, the sailors. There was only left in the very dim light Simond kneeling on Joul, the older man's arms outspread and pinned now to the rock of the passageway—while Odanki, in spite of favoring his leg, held the captain in a hug like that of a wasbear which had closed for the final crushing of some prey.

For a moment all Trusla could hear was the heavy breathing of the men, though their struggles had come to an end. Now there was more light as Frost came to stand between them. The Estcarpain girl saw the wicked masks of rage fade from the faces of the two Sulcars. In their place appeared bewilderment with an overshadowing of shame.

"What—what did we do?" There was such uncertainty in the captain's voice. It sounded close to the high note uttered by a boy on the edge of some great fear. "Joul—kin-friend—blood brother. I—I was fighting again Rajar, the ship slayer."

"And I"—Joul had been released by Simond and was sitting

up—"was on the *Pearl Queen* off Kaynur when we were raided by the demon craft—their captain being my meat."

"You are Sulcar, and in your past," Frost said quietly, "there lies much violence and death. The one who matches talents with us sent you back in time—"

"Thinking we would kill each other," broke in the Captain, "and so save her the trouble."

"Undoubtedly one of her thoughts," agreed Frost. "She does not understand that in this we all stand together. Simond, Odanki, she could not bring into *your* past." She looked now to the two who had loosed their captives and were stepping back. "No. But each of you are also men of war. Simond has ridden with the forces of Estcarp and Escore against worse dangers than shadows, and you, Odanki, have known the terrors of the wilderness. Each man holds in his past some time when death brushed him by as one of the shaman's feathers can brush. We were warded well, but not against our own memories and emotions."

"Therefore," Simond said stolidly as one accepting a task he could not relish or dare refuse, "we must be watched also until we can win to the end and see her face-to-face."

He looked now straight at Trusla. "My lady, it is against all which lies within my heart, but this I desire you now to promise. That if I come close to you, you will be on your guard, that you will stay with Inquit or Lady Frost—no matter how much I may urge you not to do so."

"No!" She would have gone to him then, but he stepped back, raising his hand to ward her off.

"Yes!" There was the same ring of iron in his voice which she had heard Koris and Simon Tregarth use upon occasion, and inwardly, much as she wished to refuse, she knew he was right.

"He speaks straight-tongued." Odanki centered his attention on the shaman. "Greatly was I honored that you chose me above all others to be your champion, Dreamer and Voice of Arska. Yet if this evil one could bring you down by my hand, then only the Outer Dark will be mine."

Frost turned her jewel around in her hands. "There is this—

all of us have fought the Dark in one manner or another. Yet this one is truly not of the Dark as we envision it in our world. Think on what she said: that a gate was opened for the Sulcar escape—not by one of their blood with great talent, but by a stranger. Can we not then believe that one of the adepts who played their gate games in the past was responsible for both the flight of the Sulcar ships and accidentally for the capture of her own vessel?

"She spoke of wars and evils—the Dark adepts took delight in such meddling. It might well be that one such was careless enough to begin what could not be finished on that other world. If so, that the Sulcars were saved was perhaps the only victory."

"You would speak for her?" the captain asked.

"I would that we speak *with* her. And until that time we must be on guard. She has not entirely released Audha—perhaps she cannot. Thus we still have a tie which will sooner or later bring us face-to-face. Only when talent stands against talent can we convince her that this world is not hers to play with."

"You would return her to her own?" Trusla asked softly.

"If such can be done before the gate is sealed, and that is her own wish—why not? The darkness she awoke here is that which is centered in her alone, and perhaps in her own world it is not born of evil but of fear and despair. Therefore let us hunt this to the end."

As they had been awakened so abruptly from their rest, they took a longer space before they began the march again. Then shaman and Frost worked over Audha. Though Trusla had no knowledge of the Powers they used, each in her own way, she believed that they entered the near-comatose girl's mind, seeking now to stimulate that factor which sent her ever seeking the one who had taken from her the part which made her more than body.

Mindful of what Simond had said, Trusla did not sit beside him as she wished. The fear his suggestion had planted in her was ever to the fore of her mind. What great danger had he faced in the past that could come upon him again? She knew of the horrors of Escore, of the Border war with Alizon, with many chances for such to be summoned again.

But he seemed to be sleeping calmly. Now she took note that both Captain Stymir and Joul had arranged themselves on either side of the Latt hunter and on his breast lay one of the feathers from the shaman's cloak. At least that was Power of his own people, and she believed its influence was as strong as Inquit could make it.

She herself, now that the storm of that awaking to battle was past, felt strong and eager, ready to march. Let them find what they sought and face this Urseta Vat Yan. That they were bound for the gate, Trusla was somehow sure. And she wanted, with all the force within her, to find it.

Simond slept on. Nor was there any change for the hunter. Might it be that the Power could reach only the Sulcars because they were the enemies of old? That she had been nearly trapped—she could well accept that the menace could not work through a male, but needed her who had the least talent of all to take Audha's place.

At that conclusion, Trusla deliberately closed her eyes to visualize the sand of the dancing. She had used the last of that precious powder, the only alien weapon she had. Now she still held to her vision.

There was no dancer to stir the sand slightly. Instead, in the midst of its carpet a man slept, his face turned up to be fully revealed in the moonlight. Greatly daring, Trusla reached. A tendril of sand no thicker than her thumb arose at his head. It whirled and yet it seemed full-rooted there.

Again the sand moved, this time inches away from his worn boots—arose and stayed. The girl gave a deep sigh of gratitude. Odanki had his feather guard; now Trusla was sure she had made Simond as safe as her small Power would let her. Her confidence in that was followed by something else—a mixture of curiosity and belief. So her talent was not exhausted, as she had thought. When this journey was over, maybe she could learn more, enough to encompass Simond and herself and bring them safety and fortune for a lifetime.

## CHAPTER FORTY-FOUR

# The Ship out of Time, North

Simond was locked into his thoughts as he swung along beside Odanki. Before them went Trusla and he was sure that she was purposely lagging behind, hoping for him to join her. But that fear which had been born of the attack on the two Sulcar warriors strode beside him, step by step.

What monster out of his own past could this alien woman of Power summon to blank out all of him except the need to slay? Resolutely he tried not to think of the past—of his long scouts through his homeland, of the sharp attacks along the Alizon Borders, of the things he had helped to hunt down in Escore. He found memory along those paths almost too strong. So he deliberately called up those words of power which Frost had locked into his mind, those which would ward any gate for all time.

He could almost see them etched in the blue fire on the air before him as he went—assuring him that none had been lost.

Trusla and Inquit were supporting Audha between them, Frost a step or so in advance with her jewel giving them still light enough to see the rock under and about them. The girl was blank of face, and yet, whenever they paused for a short rest, she tugged at those who partnered her and had to be pulled down to be seated.

Kankil still showed attachment to the Sulcar girl, climbing at once into her lap when she was down, patting her set face gently, and crooning. It was as if the shaman's familiar was laboring like a healer to return Audha to them fully herself again.

Night and day no longer had any meaning here, though they kept to a pattern of rest periods and eating the last few crumbs of their supplies. Whatever Inquit had given them appeared to stretch those very meager mouthfuls so they arose again refreshed and with the energy of one who had feasted well.

It was not Frost's jewel which was preceding them now, but rather a thin, grayish light from ahead, far ahead. As they walked forward that grew stronger, while the odd warmth which had wrapped around them diminished. So they paused to pull on and latch hoods, seek out the mittens ready to be worn.

They came out into day. Small blasts of stinging snow struck at them and they could feel the ice of the air they reluctantly were forced to draw into their lungs.

Deep as the passage through the mountain and glacier had been, they faced again a world lying below them. Ice-circled hummocks and the broken footing of glaciers again awaited them.

However, across that plain stood such a wall as bore little resemblance to the glaciers—though such must have added to it through the centuries. It was more like a mighty barrier set up by man's purpose, not nature's, and there were the faint markings of something which had once been ice-free and was not choked. From the foot of that—

Water! Surely they could see the flash of dull sunlight on open water! It was filled with small floating islands of ice. It led to the right.

"East." The Captain and Odanki spoke almost together.

East? Did the ancient sea so long hidden lie in that direction? And was this the gate they had come so far to find?

The claws Odanki had fashioned out of the horns gave them the ability to descend—with ropes to provide additional safety—the wall on whose crest they had emerged.

Then it was that Odanki cried out, held spear with his right hand and long belt knife with the other. For one of those humps which they had taken for outcrops of the ice moved.

To Trusla it was like a white-frosted tree rising well above her head. A red mouth opened and there was a roar, echoed menacingly back from the cliff behind them. She had seen only the hides of wasbears, and the creature of vision their foe had set upon them, but she had heard enough hunters' tales here in the north to know that they were the monarchs of the frozen world, intent on holding their hunting rights and instinctive enemies of any men. Only was this real—or was Odanki being tested in his own way of life?

Then she saw Audha jerk free the hold Inquit had resumed on her arm once they had made the descent. In her mittened hand the girl grabbed up a chunk of ice two fists thick and, before they could move, hurtled it through the air, to strike full on the furred shoulder of the animal.

The strangely elongated head of the creature swept in her direction and it went to four feet from its first threatening upright stance. Inquit tried to catch the girl again, but now she had pulled loose from Frost as well, her strength such that she brought the witch off balance and to her knees.

Again the wasbear roared. Its small eyes gleamed as red as its open, well-fanged mouth. Then it charged. Trusla would not have believed that such a bulk could have sprung so swiftly from its position.

Audha made no attempt to even pick up another ice ball in a vain attempt to stop it, Rather, she also sped. Not toward any of her companions but out over the rough ice, and the wasbear followed her.

There was a flash through the air. The spear Odanki had thrown thumped home in that thick body, to be dragged along, its butt catching in the ice furrows. The wasbear turned its head and snapped at the weapon. Its fangs cut through the shaft as if it were no more than a twig, though blood continued to run from a hole in its upper shoulder.

Audha was screaming now—not, Trusla realized, in fear or for aid, but rather as if she fronted some invader of a ship on which she sailed. Luck had been with her so far and she had not stumbled.

Now there came the *whang* of a bowstring and the wasbear shrieked as an arrow bit deep into its outstretched neck.

"No!" Audha's voice cut through the cries of the animal. "She has me in part—let her take me in whole!"

The strong, clear light of Frost's gem cut through the air. In spite of its swift movements, the beam struck the animal between those red eyes. It reared once more to its hind feet, teetering back and forth as might a man who had taken a death stroke. Then it crumpled in upon itself and collapsed, the ice splintering under the weight of its body.

"No—" There was a sound in the voice of the Sulcar girl which hurt as much as if they had watched her being cut down without any defense.

She rounded on Frost as the men approached the wasbear warily. Such were notoriously hard to kill and had often risen seemingly from death to account direfully with their would-be hunters.

"Why? You have had your will of me." Audha nearly spat the words at Frost. "You have used her tie with me to seek her out. Now let me go free. By steel or the fangs of such as that—it does not matter. I cannot be myself again."

"What is held can be returned," the witch answered her. "We have not yet come to the end of the road set us."

But Audha once more was lost to them, sunk back into the prison deep inside herself.

Trusla ventured to question Frost. "Can she be saved from this?"

Frost nodded. "Power may have many sources, but it answers also to certain defined rules. One who is ensorcelled can be released—if the will is there. However, she said she had brought us to our goal. Now we must wait to discover all we can. For in knowledge itself is Power."

Odanki and Simond were butchering the wasbear. It certainly was not any trap out of glamorie. Trusla felt queasy as she watched their busy knives and the red fountaining over the snow.

She moved away from that gory spot, closer to the icy river. She was surprised that the bear chase had carried them so far—now the mysterious cliff rose close at hand. But her companions were just now more interested in food.

She knew well that the northerners, the Latts, and the people of End of the World could and did eat raw meat, for there was often no chance of making a fire. She had seen Latt children chewing happily on such strips while watching their elders preparing food to be frozen or dried against the fasting of winter. But surely . . .

Inquit left her in no suspense as to what use they were going to make of the kill. Odanki, with some ceremony, had brought the shaman a gory offering and she gave him gracious thanks for his courtesy.

Thus they ate again—after a fashion—though Trusla, in spite of all the willpower she could summon, went aside and lost vigorously the few mouthfuls she had been able to choke down.

When they finished what they could, they went to that scrap of open water. It was like a nearly choked river and it flowed out of sight of those standing at this level. But Frost's attention was mainly for the ghost of a gate they all believed they could see, from which that river issued.

She waved to the Latt hunter and, when he joined her, asked, "Can that wall be climbed? We need to know how wide this may be."

He nodded and rounded the outspring of the river from the cleft under the choked remains of an opening. Once more resorting to his climbing claws, with the other men behind him, he began to climb. The ice was rough enough to give them good holds and the Sulcars, used to climbing into shrouds in ill weather, seemed to find this as easy as did Odanti. Simond came last. He was still holding away from the others, unable to forget that some trick might be played to entrap him.

Audha stood still, as if pillar-frozen in the cold, her eyes straining unseeingly before her as if her attempt to die at the claws of the wasbear had exhausted what was left of her energy. Trusla's attention was all for Simond. Within her mittens her hands clenched, wanting to believe that he had only a climb before him and no rise of old danger.

The Latt reached the top and disappeared from sight, apparently to do just what Frost had asked of him—measure the width of that barrier. His shout carried down and Trusla cringed. Then she realized that as no warning, but rather surprise.

Simond had safely scrambled over the edge and disappeared after the others and then Odanki returned, waving an arm vigorously, the Sulcars and Simond busy dropping the ropes. It was plain they wanted the women to join them.

Bringing Audha up was a problem. At last they looped part of a hide rope under her arms while Inquit, her feather cloak billowing wide, climbed beside the seemingly helpless girl, giving a hand now and then to aid that limp body to avoid some outcrop of the ice.

The top when they reached it seemed reasonably flat, nor was it any thick glacier field but limited in size. However, the Sulcars hurried the women forward and pointed down.

There was a thick mist hanging close to ground level below, hiding whatever might be there—solid ice or berg-filled water. However, it was what projected into that mist which centered their attention. This was no ledge of rock—nor any freak of nature. Even land-bred Trusla could guess she was looking down at the stern of some kind of ship, nearly as large as the *Wave Cleaver*. But it glistened as if covered against the wearing of time with a transparent coating of ice.

"The ship . . ." Captain Stymir had brought out his plaque and was staring first at it and then what lay beneath them. Though their find was halfway covered by the heavy ice, they could see the stern plainly, as well as part of that rise of the strange hump which appeared to take the place of sails.

Now the captain turned to Frost. "We have found the gate, Lady. Let your Powers now destroy it—and the thing which survived."

"The gate, yes, but I have not yet the Power." She took a step from them and held out her arms. On her breast her jewel was flashing fire which was answered from a pinnacle of ice nearby—or was it ice? Those rainbows of rippling color. . . .

"Kin in Power," Frost called into the chill air. "We have found what we have sought—yet I do not believe you guard it against us."

Rainbow tendrils moved like living roots along the ground, encircling them. Yet neither Frost nor the shaman appeared ready to counter what might be an attack of Power.

Frost had shed her mittens, so they hung by strings, to bare her inner, gloved hands. She did not touch her jewel; rather, her fingers moved in the air. And slightly behind her Inquit spread wide that feather cloak so that Trusla almost could hear the whisper of great wings about them.

"By my Power"—Frost's twisting fingers left trails of blue light in the air—"I swear truce. For you are not of the Dark we know."

Those lines forming the circle about them began to whirl, until the colors became such a streak of mingled light as to hurt the eyes if one tried to watch them. And that ground-held halo of light drew in toward them before it halted. Around and around it spun, ever faster, rising a little from surface level to form a low wall. There was a low moaning wail and Audha sank to her knees, her hands before her face.

"By my Power"—Frost's voice now held a note of command—"I swear truce." Her busy hands were stilled and fell to her sides.

The wall still whirled and Trusla was sure somehow that none of them would be able to cross it—perhaps even Frost's Powers might be tried to the uppermost.

How long did they wait there? First there came the warmth they had known in the underways. Winds might sweep snow, as they saw around them, but they did not feel the bite of those drafts.

Then, as if she walked out of some unseen door in the air before them, she appeared. Across her body played the many ribbons of color, granting her clothing of a kind. In her hands she balanced a globe so large even her two palms and fingers could not encompass it. That held raging fire, such fire as had fed the mountain pit.

Her long hair, which seemed to change in shade constantly if one tried to look at it, crackled about her, and sparks were thrown off from its coils. In her triangular face her large green eyes showed no pupils—they could have been pieces of lantern glass behind which flames held steady.

"Why?" The single word rang in all their heads but they knew it was meant for Frost.

"Because, even as this gate was used, it was not done so by the will of your breed. We move now to close forever all such openings into other worlds, thus pledging that there shall never more be any entrapment of the innocent, nor invasion of evil, nor meddling in what is not for us."

The woman continued to stare at Frost.

"You are one of great Power in this world." In her hands that globe swung a little. "Can Power stand against Power?"

"Why should it?" Frost asked. "The Dark is always with us—even as it must be in the world you know. If you were of the Dark we would have long since discovered it. What you have done you can undo. . . ." She turned her head a little to look to Audha.

"Sulcar slut," spat the other.

"The stars move." For the first time Inquit spoke. "They have moved—the time wheel turns. Here the Sulcars live in peace. Perhaps in your world they no longer exist."

The woman laughed, and that laugh was sword-edged. "How well you have read us, feather flapper. Yes, knowing my kin, I think that world is now wholly ours."

Trusla was aware of a growling throat sound from the captain, yet not loud enough perhaps to be heard by the others.

"So we make a truce—then you do as you came to do: destroy this trap which was sprung by some Power from your own brewing. What then of me?"

Frost deliberately looked to Captain Stymir now. "Captain, ships and things of the sea are known to you. This gate is half open, for it holds something which exists now in two worlds. Can this ship be freed into its own place once more?"

Trusla saw the woman clutch the ball of fire even closer to her. She was watching the captain as a huntress watches prey.

"Lady, of Power such as yours I know nothing. The ship looks to be fully sheathed in ice. To free it might be a task beyond your strength."

Again the woman laughed. "A Sulcar who speaks the truth as he knows it—this is indeed a change in the way things be. Worry not about my sweet *Storm Flitter*. What you see is the time-dispelling casing I set upon her, even as I went myself into the deep sleep. Those who were my guard . . ." Her head bent as she looked at the ball she held. "When I awoke through the roar of that great wild Power of yours, the spells had faded and they were . . . gone. Happily so, for perhaps they returned, in spirit, home. I wove too well—though perhaps there was a reason for that also. Witch Woman"—she twirled the ball in her hands—"you have opened your mind to me. It is true as you think, we need no more gates, and perhaps it is also true that this one exists still because my ship is half-bottled in it. Can you swear to release it and me with your spelling?"

"Who can swear certainly to anything of the Power?" Frost returned. "The gate I can close, once your ship is freed. But consider this, Sister in Power. You will be in your own world; however, as the shaman says, it has been long—the stars have changed."

The woman was smiling. "Let my future be my own. It is no concern of yours, Witch Woman. What I return to, if I can, will be mine to face. Perhaps I have even become a legend for the telling."

With one hand she slapped the side of the ball she held and that encirclement of color disappeared.

"What of the Sulcar girl? What you have taken from her—is it gone forever, then?" Frost demanded.

The woman shrugged. "They are a Powerless lot, save when they have weapons to hand. Who cares?"

As one the captain and Joul moved forward and they were followed closely by the Latt and Simond.

"But we do have weapons." The captain's voice was low, almost caressing, as if he held in his hand not a drawn sword but some well-loved thing.

The woman seemed to consider him, her head a little to one side. "Fire and steel, yes. But I have this." She had posed the fire ball on the palm of her hand as if she steadied it for tossing. Then she smiled. "And I would be quickly answered, would I not, you who deign to call me Sister in Power, with such fates as you could hope to bring upon me. This much I will promise. I do not know the full strength I have taken from this slut. But I know what can be returned, if and when matters go to my satisfaction."

As swiftly as she had appeared she was gone, and her going brought them to the edge of the gate to look down again at the ship in its clear ice envelope.

"Can it be done?" the captain demanded of Frost.

"We can only tell when we try. But note you cannot see the place in which that ship now rests. That is not any mist given off by the substances of this world."

It was true, the ship was plain enough to be seen half-caught in the ancient trap of the gate. But behind and around it was not really a mist but a fog, which, even as they watched, appeared to thicken and hide. What it covered, they could not see. If anything moved in it, they could not tell. It was . . . just as it had been for countless generations now. And no one suggested a climb down into that rolling grayness.

Instead, left rather at a loss since their proposed partner in labor had chosen to disappear, they climbed down once more and Frost went to study the gate, Simond with her.

"Hilarion did not foresee such as this," she said. "I can strive to reach Es or Arvon. Still, the otherworld Power alive here may interfere with that." She sighed. "It is difficult to depend upon another, and one who cannot be trusted."

"She may yet spring some trap?" Simond demanded, well aware that he might be the target. "Lady, let me be put under watch, for she may still think that I will serve her purpose. I ask of you, should I fail in such a testing, will you look to Trusla? Her people will have none of her because she saved my life, as you well know. She will need someone to stand beside her."

Frost had been bending her head a little forward, studying the jewel now resting on her palm. "I think this stranger will not trouble us so again, Simond. There was truth in what she said: if she believes we can offer her a return to her own world, then she will link Powers."

"But it has been so long." Without them realizing it, Trusla had joined them. She could not bear now to have Simond too far away. "To return to a world one does not know, that has moved apart . . ."

"There is this," Frost said. "Simon Tregarth, when he sought the Port of Dead Ships and found the floating derelict which was from his own world, discovered that time was different between us. There was evidence on the ship that he had spent more years apart than he had reckoned. This Urseta Vat Yan could even possibly discover that such transition works in an opposite fashion. For no two Powers are alike—just as no world copies another to the last blade of grass."

"I hope"—Trusla had captured Simond's hand and held it close—"that that is so for her."

# CHAPTER FORTY-FIVE

# Gate Fall and New Day's Dawning, North

They had seen no more of the woman who called herself Urseta Vat Yan. Frost spent much time pacing out a line which spanned those very ancient outlines of the now-ice-choked passage. She could not approach it too closely; the sluggish stream issued from its foot. Finally she appeared to have made up her mind on some point and summoned them to a meeting.

Once they were so assembled, she singled out Audha, touched

the girl's forehead, and repeated, as she might a ritual, the name they had heard days earlier:

"Urseta Vat Yan!"

Names had Power. Perhaps the alien from the otherworld had held Frost's talent so low that she had not believed the witch could so compel her.

But now that shimmer of rainbow across the ice spread upward. Once more they saw the stranger as she wished them to behold her, whether it was in her natural body or not.

She did not hold her ball of fire this time. It hung above her head, and the warmth from it even they could feel. But her green eyes were hard, and as the warmth of the ball, so could her anger be sensed by all of them.

"What would you, Witch Woman?" she demanded.

"What we have spoken of, Urseta Vat Yan—the end of what we have come to do."

Trusla saw a forked point of tongue show and sweep over the other's lower lip.

"You would bring down your gate—and crush my ship. So much for all your brave words of mutual understanding."

"No." Frost showed a patience Trusla had not expected. "We shall force the gate to close, yes. But can you loose your ship on the same signal? This is an act which, to my knowledge, has never been tried before. And this also will I tell you—those who lock the gate may not survive."

She was facing the woman very straightly, gray eyes locked to the pupilless green. The ball of flame spun suddenly, and short tongues of flame fringed it around. Once more Trusla saw that double point of tongue show for an instant.

Then Frost's words struck home to Trusla herself. The witch had chosen Simond to share her task—that might mean she was about to kill him! No—and no!

She discovered that she could not utter that scream of denial aloud, nor could she move to wind arms about him, hold him safe. Power held them fast to the will of those other two. Even Inquit stood silent, her cloak tightly about her as if it were a shield against forces they could feel rising now.

The green eyes appeared to flicker rather than blink. Now the woman reached upward and caught the ball, holding it to her even as Frost held her jewel.

"Such payment . . ." she said slowly.

Frost's face was still serene. "Such payment—if it is asked of us—we shall give willingly. However, this, too, I must make clear to you if you choose your own path. Time has sped—you may be returning to a far different world than you left."

"A different world, a kin-gone world," the woman repeated slowly. "Yet if that means years will drop upon me even as the snow whirls in this barren place, still I will be . . . home."

She tossed the ball from one hand to the other and the colors in it flamed so high she might have been holding a portion of sun far warmer than this country had ever seen. Then she turned partially away.

"My Power is not of your world. If you loose what you can command at the same moment, perhaps neither of us shall profit."

"Agreed." Frost's voice was still calm and untroubled. "You uncase your ship first and then we shall tackle the gate."

Still the woman hesitated—and then gave a toss of her head which sent her spark-laden hair streaming into the air.

"So be it—and how better a time than now, Witch Woman?"

Frost looked to Simond. Quietly, as they had been speaking, he had been unbuckling, unlacing, dropping to the ground the mail, the weapons of which he had always been so proud. Those who dealt with the greater Power did not bring steel to such a meeting. He stood at that moment in his fur underjerkin, even his belt knife out of its sheath.

Trusla swayed. In spite of all her efforts, she could not go to him. But he turned to face her.

"Heart's core for me"—he spoke as if the two of them stood alone and there were none else to hear—"much have you given me. Now give me the last gift of all—your courage."

She saw him only through a glaze of tears. Without Simond,

what would she be? But what she saw in his face brought a whisper of answer which it seemed the restraining Power would allow her now:

"You have all of me—forever."

She had to crouch there, for her legs refused to support her any longer, and she watched him go, shoulder to shoulder with Frost, who had also shed the bulk of her outergarments. They had fit Odanki's claws and were once more climbing. There was a brilliant flash of flame and the alien was already above them, perched on the middle of the faintly defined archway.

Trusla, pain binding her as with chains, had to watch Simond, now but a small dark figure, cross that arch—move out on the other side away from her and beyond the gate boundaries. If she could only stand with him there!

Urseta Vat Yan, tossing her ball from hand to hand as one about to play some childish game, disappeared toward the far end of the archway. They could no longer see her—only the sparks of her constantly turbulent hair.

Then a hand fell on Trusla's shoulder, and she smelled that spicy scent which clung ever to the feather cloak of the shaman.

A quill the other held swept the ice and snow before where she huddled and the girl saw, as through a window—or into a mirror. There was the thick curtain of cloud, with only visible the protruding stern of the alien ship. But that was brightly lit now, for standing on the deck was Urseta, and she hurled the ball into the air. Faint and far away Trusla caught her call. Along one side of the ship rolled the ball, and then along the other, and the ice was gone as if it were mist puffed away.

Then once more the instrument of Power returned to Urseta and she stood looking upward, even though Trusla doubted she could see the other two at the gate—certainly not any of them waiting below.

However, her voice came clearly enough, ringing in their heads.

"I cannot leave any anchorage here now. Take what is of your world and time!" The ball broke into halves, each of which became a small ball in turn. One she threw into the air with all her might, and the other she hurled with even greater force straight before her to where the other half of her ship was still imprisoned.

There was a bursting apart—sight, sound, feeling were all a part of it. Trusla heard the roll of those other two voices speaking words which had not been voiced for centuries. Through suddenly dimmed eyes she tried to see Simond, but there was descending on them something else. Faded as if its journey through the air had nearly dimmed its Power came the fireball. It struck full upon the head of Audha, who had stood forgotten among them, gripped in the dazed state which mainly held her.

Trusla had just time to see the rainbow fire compass the Sulcar girl before she heard that other sound: the roar of rock and ice, shattering under the hammer of true Power, the cliffs shuddering and scaling off great chunks.

"Simond!" She covered her face with her hands. Maybe if fortune favored her one of those great slabs would find her.

It would seem that the roaring of the broken gate would never stop. Snow half buried them, and Trusla dimly felt pain as a razor-edged splinter cut along her arm, slitting the fur and hide as if it were a knife.

The silence in the end was as overpowering in its way as had been the noise of the destruction. Somehow Trusla forced herself to look up—

Up at what? Where there had stood a wall barrier was a jumble of broken slabs, some seeming as great in size as a Sulcar ship.

Ship? Half-dazedly she tried to center her eyes on where that ship had once been caught. Did it lay crushed under this pounding, or had the woman indeed made her return?

"Lady Trusla!" Someone was tugging at her, striving to pull her free of the ice which half covered her. Bleared of eye, she looked up into the face of Audha.

There was spirit behind those eyes again, concern in the Sulcar girl's expression. Truly what Urseta had taken she had, at that last moment, returned. Faintly Trusla was happy—faintly—for nothing mattered now that Simond was not here.

There came the sound of rushing water and she could hear calling in the distance, though that meant nothing to her now. That stream which had edged from under the gate was now a river, shearing off pieces of ice which bumped along in what seemed a strong current whirling eastward.

"Aaaaheee, ahhheee!" That cry broke through the confusion in her head. She was dimly aware of Audha digging swiftly about her, dragging her out of the mass of snow which half covered her. Not too far away Kankil was also digging, throwing a storm of snow and bits of ice into the air as she screamed over and over again that ear-piercing cry.

Odanki suddenly towered over the shaman's small familiar and his big hands added to the welter of snow they were throwing into the air. Then the hunter stopped and, using both hands, pulled the shaman out.

However, even before she was raised to more than her knees, she was pointing to one side, crying in her own tongue nearly as loud as Kankil. The captain, staggering a little, came up. One arm hung limp and Joul was close to give him a hand.

But at the shaman's insistence not only did the Sulcar man leave the captain, but Audha also moved to aid. Trusla remained dully where she was, watching them, as might a detached dreamer, work to bring out Frost.

At first she thought that the witch was dead, struck down by the very Power she had summoned. Then the girl was aware that the jewel on the other's breast was showing a spark of fire.

Only . . . Trusla tried to get to her feet, and when she discovered she could not make it, she started on hands and knees to the river. If Simond's side of the gate had collapsed even as Frost's—and it looked as if it had—then he lay buried across that barrier of rushing water. The longer he remained below any heap of snow and splintered ice, the sooner the last flickers of life would be frozen out of him. That he was not yet dead Trusla could believe. Surely that shutting off of warmth and good, of her very heart hold, would be sensed by her.

She paid no attention to those behind her, pausing for a breath or so now and then to watch that other shore, see some small splotch of hide clothing perhaps among the everlasting blue-white of the snow. Then she was at the water's edge and that was a perilous perch, but the danger meant nothing to her now.

The ice was still breaking off in pieces, to be rolled over in the water, carried away. And she knew this much of this land: to throw herself into that frantic stream and hope to reach the other shore was merely to reach out for death. Though in the end that is what she might well do.

She was dimly aware of someone who was standing now beside where she crouched in despair. The softness of a feather brushed against her and then a small warm body, almost like a brazier of coals, hurled itself upon her.

Inquit—Kankil. Of what matter their coming? There was nothing which would bridge that waterway—and no sign beyond of where to hunt.

"Little sister." The Latt woman's hand rested softly on her head. "He is not dead."

Trusla shrugged. What matter? He would soon be so. She looked into nothingness and knew its bite.

Kankil was patting her face with soft paw-hands, crooning with a rumbling purr which reached into Trusla's own body but did not soften the growing bleakness there.

"What can be done?" It took a moment or so for Trusla to realize that the shaman was not speaking to her but to Odanki, who had come up on her other side.

"To cross in this flood—Voice of Arska, that is impossible for anyone, for we cannot grow wings and fly."

Trusla started up, dislodging Kankil from her lap with a sharp shove. She was on her feet, teetering on the very edge of the water, only half aware that a firm hold had fastened on the back of her belt.

But she had not been mistaken! Surely, by the Greatest of Powers, her eyes had not played her false now. That dark arm seemingly grown out of the very earth was showing clear against the snow. A moment or so later there was a cascade of chunks, then head, another arm, shoulders appeared!

"Simond!" Trusla screamed with all the power her lungs could summon.

He tried to rise and sprawled forward on his face. She would have thrown herself into that flood now if the hold on her had not remained so very strong.

No, he was not stirring now. They must reach him! Cover him with the garments he had discarded, somehow get him warm— bring life back to him!

Trusla tried to turn and fight that hold, but she was as entrapped as if the ice had risen to wall her in. She screamed at Inquit.

"He must have help!"

"There is no way to cross the river in such a flood." Captain Stymir, his left arm now lashed across his breast, came up to them. "Unless . . ." He looked to the shaman. "Many times Power has done what force of arm and heart cannot. The witch seems to sleep; we cannot rouse her. Thus what she might be able to control we cannot call upon. And you, Shaman?"

"Animals I may command in the name of Arska, winds I can summon and sometimes lighten storms, and there are other things. But here I stand as you, Captain."

Trusla's breath was coming in dry sobs. "Simond, Simond"—she made of his name a plea, like some ritual which could not escape answer.

He moved. Somehow he had levered himself up on his hands, though his head still hung as if any effort was too great for him.

"Simond, Simond." Perhaps it was her calling which reached him, kept him from lying waiting for death.

"Hunter!"

That one word was so imperative that it broke all their attention centered on the struggling man.

It was Audha who had come to them. Yet—it was not the Audha Trusla had known, beaten by adversity, robbed of her birthright. Now the Sulcar girl put out a hand to lay fingertips on Odanki's bulky arm. He jerked and his mouth opened, but what he might have wished to say was swallowed up in the question she asked:

"You are one who knows the ice. If there be an air bridge, would you risk a crossing? You alone, for I do not know . . ." She hesitated. "I have yet much to learn."

"A bridge?" he repeated almost stupidly, as if he could not believe that she had asked that. "To bridge that . . ." he pointed to the ever-flowing flood.

Trusla saw Inquit's eyes narrow and then the shaman herself spoke.

"You have followed the flippered ones out on the floating bergs. You stand as my man and shield. If there be a bridge, dare you cross it?"

He shook his head as if he could not believe what she was saying. "I am the Lord Simond's bondsman for my very life! Did he not bring me out of the very jaws of the worms? Show me your bridge!"

Audha moved a little apart from them, even as Frost did when she would deal with Power. She flung wide her arms and in the wide space between her hands danced color, ribbons of color such as had run across the walls of the ice palace.

The fingers of her left hand slacked apart and those ribbons of color shot out over the river even as Trusla had seen a fisherman of the marshes throw a baited line. The tip of the rainbow touched a floating cake of extra width and drew it toward them. It nudged a second and then a third. In spite of the battering of the water—perhaps that now flowed *beneath* what Audha wrought and did not try full strength against it—there was a bridge.

"Go with speed," she ordered. "I do not know how long . . ."

Odanki had already thrown aside his long outer tunic and his bow and quiver. But he still had spear in hand and was using that in a way odd to Trusla, to give himself a running start to jump for the nearest bobbing cake of ice. Trusla wanted to close her eyes; she was sure that what the hunter attempted now was beyond the ability of any man.

Yet, though the strangely hooked-together cakes bobbed, they did not spill him into that current. With his spear hooked well into the ice of the opposite bank, he pulled himself up and over. Though he was limping more, he was still moving at nearly running speed.

He reached that dark blot which was Simond and with a struggle somehow got the limp body over his shoulders, almost as he might carry a kill to camp. Beside her Trusla heard Inquit making sharp rasping cries even as might some great bird working itself up to its highest point of energy.

Audha's expression was not unlike the one Frost wore when she called upon her Power. Also—somehow her Sulcar features appeared to alter a little—she was not quite Audha anymore. But the ribbons of light continued to flow from her.

Inquit took two steps coming up behind her. The shaman's glove and mitten had been loosed and her hand was free in the cold. But those fingers went forth and closed on Audha's neck where the hood had slipped from her head. Inquit's eyes were closed and her expression was one of deep concentration.

Odanki's pace, for all his efforts, was slowing. He had Simond and was approaching the edge of the river once more with uneven strides. Reaching the bank, he paused and shifted his burden a little and then leaped. Under the combined weight of both men, the ice dipped and water washed, but Odanki was already taking off for the next portion of that bridge.

What moved her Trusla could not have told, for pure fear had kept her held in place, but now she felt Kankil's hand close on her and when the small creature drew her, she was able to take the steps to Inquit's side. Kankil reached up with her other stubby fingers to catch at the shaman's dangling hand.

A drawing such as she had never known gripped Trusla. Still she chanted, as her own private ritual, Simond's name. But she realized that even as the shaman was feeding Power to Audha, so she was now a part of that chain. Her will arose fiercely, trying to feed all she could into that linkage.

The hunter was past the middle of the river. Only it seemed to Trusla that those colored bands which built his path were not holding steady; rather, they faded and then pulsed anew at intervals as if they were near the end of their Power to hold.

Joul and the captain had been working frenziedly at a section of rope, the captain's one-handed efforts sometimes more of a hindrance than a help. Joul took over their labor, fashioned a loop, and then cast with a seaman's eye.

Odanki was caught and held by Joul's coil and the captain held the shore end. The ribbons flickered—but the Sulcars were ready and gave a great forward pull. Odanki slammed against the bank. Audha's hand fell to her side. The lights were gone, but the shaman had moved with speed and Trusla was with her.

Scrambling, pulling, seizing on whatever part of the two came to hand, they worked together and brought both the hunter and his burden ashore.

Trusla caught at Simond, his head falling back against her shoulder. Was she still chanting his name? Perhaps—for his eyes opened and he was looking up at her, a slow smile curving his lips as if the flesh were too frozen to answer his will.

"Not—this—time, Heart . . ." Those eyes fluttered, shut again.

The party had no means of building a fire—and they needed the heat to live. Inquit went to Audha. The girl stood nearly as blank of face as when she had moved to Urseta's will, but when the shaman laid hand upon her shoulder, she shuddered and came alive again.

"Who are you?" the shaman asked.

Audha laughed. "I am *Audha*, wavereader. But that one, when she would take me for her servant, entered into me. And when she left . . . she took what she claimed as hers, but she could not take all. For something of it had rooted. Just"—she laughed again—"as some of the hated Sulcar had rooted in her. Perhaps that will mean a new beginning for her also."

The shaman nodded. "That is possible—as none can deny. She had control over warmth, that one. What can you do with that?"

Audha's smile was gone. "Wisewoman, I am not Urseta, only one to whom some small shreds of Power have come. It may be that I have lost all that I had, for now I know I am empty and it is useless for me to try."

"Rightly so." They were startled by Frost. There was the weary look upon her which she always wore when she had been entranced. But her jewel was ablaze.

"I have spoken to Korinth and the Watcher there was already

warned from Lormt that aid was needed. Now . . ." Her hands cupped the jewel and she knelt beside Simond, passing the blaze of its light down from the crown of his head to his feet. He sighed as he turned his head a fraction closer to Trusla's breasts.

"Be not afraid, child," Frost said. "He will lie unknowing and unharmed now until they come for us. Now let us see to this champion of yours, Inquit. He was well chosen and deserves high honor."

Odanki also lay on the ice, but his eyes were wide open, first in apprehension and then softening with awe as Frost's gleaming symbol of Power passed over him. As with Simond, he seemed to fall asleep, and Inquit, unfastening her feather robe, drew it over him.

"Lady, you spoke of help," Stymir said. "In this land such must come soon."

"As it will. Be sure, Captain, every drum calls for wind launching."

She stood for a moment looking back at the ruins of the gate. That strange fog which had blanked out what lay on the other side was no longer to be seen—only rough foothills which arose in the distance to mountain height.

"I hope," she said, "that she will be served as well in her own world and time as we shall be in ours. For there was nothing of true evil in her, only strangeness, and despair and the burden of terrible loneliness. Let us wish her all good fortune, as perhaps such thoughts will carry past all barriers, seen and unseen."

And looking around that half circle of faces, Trusla knew that Frost's appeal was truly answered. Might Urset Vat Yan find at least a portion of what she had lost. For them . . . it was done, all the struggle and peril. They had only to wait, for none of them could doubt that what the witch had promised was the truth; their own needed help was on the way.

# EPILOGUE

❧

# Es City, Estcarp

$The$ seasons had turned and once more it was spring, even though few signs of a renewing world showed within the age-old capital of Estcarp.

But the outer harbor was crowded with ships, and the streets were decked in festival array as they had never been in memory.

Not only was every inn packed to the point that sleeping room at night was allotted to guests on the floors of already crowded rooms, but every household had opened doors to distant kin, or strangers recommended by such.

There was constant traffic on the streets, even to the meanest of alleys. So much so that the guard had been ordered out early to patrol ways for provision wagons to bring in needed stores.

Crowds gathered day and night to watch the passing of notables they had heard of sometimes all their lives but had never thought to actually look upon.

The center of this busy and confused web was again the great hall of the citadel itself, though sometimes there was an overflow into the courtyard when newcomers must be received with full ceremony.

Flags of noble houses signified the presence of every family of note—even some from troubled Karsten, where there was still a bitter struggle in process for the ducal throne. And strangest of all were two banners those of Estcarp had in their lives faced only in battle—bearing variations of the hounds of Alizon.

All those gathered knew that once more their world had changed—not this time by the awesome Power which pulled down mountains and moved rivers, but because it was the beginning of a new age.

Just as it had taken those shaken by disaster in the mountains to welcome life again in strange places, so was it now that all faced change to which many came warily, but from which there was no escape.

In the great hall once more there was the gathering of those of Power: those who ruled, those in whose grasp now the future of their world rested. They might peer warily at one another, but they listened and understood—even if some did only dimly.

One representative of each of the ruling houses occupied a chair on the dais, for there was limited room, and the chairs themselves were crowded so tightly together that no one occupant could move without disturbing a fellow.

Here showed a gray robe of the witches—she who was presently Knowledge Holder. They recognized her in their company as Diamond, since all witches' true names were forgotten when they came to the Place of Wisdom. Her chair needed no banner above it—there was no mistaking a witch. Her serene face showed no sign of aging and it was true she was one of the younger sisters lately come to her office.

There was Simon Tregarth, outlander, founder with his witch wife Jaelithe of a house which had served Estcarp and Escore mightily over the years. Then came Jaelithe herself, and beyond her Hilarion, the last of the great adepts, and Dahaun of the Green Valley, high in the holding of Power. Next to her, those from overseas: Alon and Eydryth of the Gryphon line; Firdun, who was now protector of the Waste; and from the Dales, Lord Imry, whose constant struggle to bring peace to the holdings there was at last near completion.

Beside him was Kerovan, Lord of the Eyrie, preserving distance between the Dales lord and he who represented the enemy the Dales had brought to bitter defeat: Lord Kasarian out of Alizon. Strangest of all were the two who were plainly close comrades but of different species altogether. One was the Lady Eleeri, another outlander who had come to right, through her own efforts, an ancient wrong. Close across her shoulder was the head of a Keplian mare, her blue eyes shrewdly aware of all about them.

Last of all two women, their furred and much-beaded dress strange in this company. The one wore, like a ruler's mantle, a cloak of feathers, and the other, her gold hair in Sulcar braids, sat with her eyes downcast as if she felt she had no place there.

It was given to Koris as commander in this place to speak first, and as he did so the murmur of voices in the throng below quieted.

"What honor can we give those who have faced the Dark and come forth victors? The deeds of such are meat for bards, and their names will last into the far future when all the rest here shall be forgot. But once more shall they be told in this company, gathered from all our known world, so that their honor can be made manifest in all countries, in every hall, by the hearth of every holding."

He paused. There was a hum of voices as those massed to listen agreed.

"We rode in Estcarp and Escore to good purpose—though it will be long before the last roots of the Dark can be dragged from growth in our earth.

"To the south, crossing lands unknown before, we hail these." He spoke slowly, pausing for a fraction after each name:

"The Lady Eleeri, her Lord Romar, the Keplian kind who are our true comrades. With them as watch, guard, and guide, the Lady Mouse of the sisterhood, two Falconers and armsmen of courage, as well as the Lady Liara out of Alizon and chosen armsmen."

At that name Kasarian stirred and sought the face of one near the fore of the listeners.

"Also they were joined by another outlander, a mighty warrior for the Light—Gruck—and she who is the chosen Voice of Gunnora, and her friend the cat, Chief. There went also one of the house which had ever been a strong support for us—Keris Tregarth. All have heard the tale of how he went into the Dark to serve and that the Light called him forth as a true son.

"The Voice and Gruck do not stand here today. It is by their choice that they remain in the south, where more of our people of knowledge will join them later.

"In Arvon there were also those who came at the call of need. The House of the Gryphon held fast, and those they sent forth are of the same strength of mind and body. Firdun, of their own blood, and the were Kethan and his foster sister, the healer Aylinn. With them the Kioga, Guret and their warriors—one of whom went to the last reward of Heroes—may Obred be ever honored so. Also one saved from the Dark—as well as the Lady Uta, who joined to be their guide. And lastly Ibycus, he who was protector of the land from the ancient days, and the Lady Elysha.

"They fought the Dark in many ways and in the end lost both Ibycus and the Lady Elysha, whose work for the Light was deemed finished. Now Firdun will ride the Waste and the trails and perhaps in time there will be others to join him.

"But those who went north also gained. The Lady Frost and the Shaman Inquit united in strength—though their Powers differed greatly. And the Lord Simond and his Lady Trusla were not far behind them. Nor was Captain Stymir and his mate Joul. The Latt champion Odanki, whose great strength was their safety many times, served better than any other might have. And last of all there is the Lady Audha, who brought back to us, through sore troubling of spirit, new knowledge." He glanced at the Sulcar girl, who still looked down and did not meet the eyes of any there.

"Now since these, no matter what their heritage, won for us the safety of our world, have again been named in full honor, we do not forget those of Lormt: the adept Hilarion, the Lady Mereth, the sage scholars who sought the final knowledge. To say thanks for such services is a too small thing. We can only give them our heart gratitude.

"So we have once more changed our world. And now we call

upon those who have asked that they be allowed to speak about certain things at this meeting that there be no thought of any secret and misunderstanding in the future. Lady Diamond . . ."

There was a stir as the witch arose. Her hand covered her jewel as if that touch provided her with some strength as she spoke.

"In the past there has been bitterness and denial—we have believed that the Power was only truly ours. But such useless pride was first swept away at the Turning. And now we have also had much to learn, we who thought ourselves above schooling. Our domain is still this land—or any other which needs what we have to offer. But we do not rule in Es any longer. Those who have talent and wish to come to us we shall welcome gladly. However, it will be by their choice, not ours. The Place of Wisdom is now our citadel and therein shall our order abide."

Koris bowed his head. "Lady, none will deny your gifts and those of your daughters. That we labor toward a common end is truly a way of life we shall welcome."

She had seated herself when Koris swung to Kasarian.

"Lord, we have been blood enemies for all our lives and the lives of our fathers before us. Still, since you found your door to Lormt, surely there is hope that we, also, can have peace along our Borders."

When the young Alizondern arose to answer, it was almost as if his white hair shown silver. His hands moved in the traditional formal gestures of his kind even as he answered.

"To the ignorant belongs fear, Lord Marshal. I have learned what one of my blood might never have known had not chance and my curiosity transported me into your Lormt. We are a country of treachery, hatred, and spying. There are those among us who will never accept even a truce with you. But those are the elder lords for the most part, and they are ever at each other's throats. There is an easier way to gain rulership than by steel and poison, and it is one I am trying to learn.

"There is one here to whom I owe an honor debt." He looked down into the company below. "My sister Liara has taught me that the fabled line of the great mage does run true in us. If she wishes—chooses—I offer her great danger but also a part in change."

Slowly the girl arose from where she had been seated.

"You are Hound Master of the House," she said clearly. "If I be in truth Hearthmistress at present under that roof . . ." she hesitated. "I am Alizondern, knowing the tricks and terrors which assault all our houses. Somehow I believe that I am indeed the one to stand behind you."

"No." He shook his head. "Beside me, as the first Lady of our line stood beside her Lord when all others would pull him down. Though I trust it will not come to that end for us."

"What of the Dales, Lord Imry?" Koris asked.

The dark-haired man who appeared to wear a permanent line of frown—or anxiety—between his eyes replied slowly.

"The Dales have suffered in the past by ever bickering. We fell to Alizon at first because each lord would fight only for his own holding. This is a lesson now held ever before us. By the end of this season we shall hold a conference to decide some matters. Commander Terlach"—he inclined his head toward a Falconer in the crowd—"has already cleared outlaws from the north hills as far as Quayth. We shall listen to him, a master of the trade of leading men."

"Thus be it," Koris said slowly, each word carrying with it nearly the force of an oath. "Always the Dark will rise—for it cannot be entirely driven from any world of man—and then the Light must arm for battle. But no longer need we fear that any outlander evil can burst or creep upon us unaware, perhaps summoned by some perverted talent. For we have Powers of our own, more and stronger than we may now know, just as we have discovered parts of our world before unknown. Perhaps it is now our duty to further that knowledge of both land and sea beyond the maps and charts. We must ever strive to learn more and put what is so learned to proper use.

"This I say, and all here will agree: once more there has been a Turning. Mountains may not have walked, but rather Powers. And from this time forward we shall search and stand sentinel. The old gives way to new, and it is in my reckoning good will come of this and we shall prosper."

He was silent for a long moment and then said—as one who makes a solemn promise:

"The gates are closed."